ROBERT GODDARD

Debt *of* Dishonour

POSEIDON PRESS

New York London Toronto Sydney Tokyo Singapore

POSEIDON PRESS

Simon & Schuster Building
Rockefeller Center
1230 Avenue of the Americas
New York, New York 10020

Originally published in England by Bantam Press, a division of Transworld Publishers Ltd., as *Take No Farewell.*

POSEIDON PRESS is a registered trademark of Simon & Schuster Inc.

POSEIDON PRESS colophon is a trademark of Simon & Schuster Inc.

Manufactured in the United States of America

3   5   7   9   10   8   6   4   2

Library of Congress Cataloging-in-Publication Data

Goddard, Robert.
[Take no farewell]
Debt of dishonour/Robert Goddard.
p.   cm.
"Originally published in England by Bantam Press . . . as Take no farewell"—T.p.
verso.
I. Title.
PR6057.O33D4   1992
823'.914—dc20   91-27506
CIP

ACKNOWLEDGEMENT

I am grateful to Christopher Bennett for advice and information about the architectural profession past and present.

LEGAL NOTE

Since the period in which this book is set, the laws of England and Wales relating to capital punishment, criminal appeals, intestacy, inheritance and the revocation of wills have all been revised. In particular, significant reforms have arisen from the Administration of Estates Act 1925, the Law of Property Act 1925, the Inheritance (Family Provision) Act 1938 and the Murder (Abolition of Death Penalty) Act 1965.

PROLOGUE

It snowed in the night. I sat where now I stand, watching the wind scatter the flakes in the haloes of the street-lamps, listening as its high, moaning voice strained among the chimneypots. All night, and all last evening from the earliest tinge of dusk, I sat where now I stand – and waited.

And now the waiting is nearly over. The sun is up, low in a clear, cold sky and, thrown up from the snow-covered pavement, a strange, reflected half-light creeps across the ceiling of the room. An hour, it signals, to the moment I have long known this day would hold. An hour – or less – to the sombre end of my flight from self.

What is she thinking, across the city in her crowded, brick-bound solitude? What farewell is she bidding, what leave is she taking, of that meagre portion of this world? When the hour is up, when the time is come, what will I seem to her? What will I seem to myself?

A taxi-cab has turned in at the end of the mews. It has come to collect me, come to bear me away in answer to a summons I once believed I could evade for ever. Once, but no longer. Not since that day last autumn when I heard her name again after twelve years' silence and knew – for all my efforts to stifle the knowledge – that an old deceit was about to claim its due. Not since that day, which now, as the cab glides to a halt, black and burnished against the bare white carpet of snow, I relive in my memory. That day, and all the days since.

9

CHAPTER

ONE

'The Caswells of Hereford. Weren't they clients of yours, Geoffrey?'

I may have flushed at Angela's words, or started. More likely my practised features betrayed no reaction whatsoever, eagerly though she would have scanned them for sign of one. Between my wife and me there existed then, as there had for some years past, a curiously unjustified hostility, a mutual disappointment forever in search of trivial slights that could elevate it to the status of a major grievance. Assuming therefore that she was, as usual, trying to catch me out, I merely raised my eyebrows, as if I had not heard her distinctly.

'The Caswells of Hereford, Geoffrey. More precisely, Victor Caswell and his wife, Consuela. Didn't you design a house for them?'

I frowned and set down my cup carefully in its saucer, with only the faintest of clinks. I made to brush a toast-crumb from my sleeve and gazed past Angela towards the window. Tuesday 25 September 1923, according to the very newspaper she had folded open before her. A quarter past eight, by the unreliable clock on the mantelpiece – a gift from one of her aunts. Weather forecast: rainy with bright intervals, one such interval being currently responsible for a flood of sunlight that sparkled on the surface of the marmalade and cast a dazzling aura round my wife's barely inclined head. It restored the gold to her hair – but could not drain the acid from her voice.

11

'Clouds Frome, near Hereford. Surely I've heard you speak of it. Wasn't it your first big commission?'

Clouds Frome. Yes, she was right. First and therefore dearest, first and also bleakest, through no fault of its design or construction, for the fault lay elsewhere. I had not seen its walls – whose every stone and crevice had once been as familiar as the lines of my own palm – for twelve years. I had not even looked at its photograph in that back copy of *The Builder* whose place in my study I knew so well. I had not wanted so much as to glimpse it. I had not dared to. Because of the name my wife had just dredged from a drowned but unforgotten past. The Caswells of Hereford. Victor and Consuela. Especially Consuela.

I cleared my throat and looked at Angela and found, as expected, her blue-green eyes trained upon me, her plucked eyebrows raised, one more than the other in a gesture of doubt, her mouth compressed, sharp lines forming – as surely they once did not – about the junction of chin and cheek.

'Yes,' I said. 'I built Clouds Frome for the Caswells. A long time ago. Before we met. What of it?'

'You didn't read this article, then?' She tapped the folded newspaper with the glazed nail of her forefinger as the sunlight vanished from the room and a sudden chill succeeded it.

'No. I hardly glanced at the paper this morning.'

I could almost have suspected Angela was about to smile. There was a tremor at the edges of her lips, a glint of something in her eyes. Then that false, blank, unrevealing openness which had become the face she most often turned upon me. 'It's as well I spotted this, then. Otherwise you might not have known.'

'Known what, my dear?'

'Which could have been embarrassing,' she disingenuously proceeded, 'if somebody had asked you whether you thought she was capable of such a thing.'

'Capable of what?'

Angela looked down at the newspaper, intent, it seemed, on infuriating me, and devoted several seconds to a brow-furrowed pretence of re-reading. Then she retrieved her cigarette from the china ashtray beside her plate, drew deeply on it, and blandly announced: 'Murder.' A plume of exhaled smoke climbed towards the ceiling-rose. 'There doesn't seem much room for doubt.'

It is hard now to recall the emotions with which I read that terse, unyielding paragraph, harder still to recall with what few words I dismissed the subject before claiming that I had quite forgotten the time, had an early appointment at the office and must, yes really must, be on my way at once. I do not for a moment suppose that Angela was deceived by my performance. She would have seen – as she had hoped to see – that I was not merely surprised by what I read, but trouble in the depth of my soul. She would have known that leaving the newspaper discarded on the table meant nothing, that five minutes away, out of sight of the house, I could and would buy another copy from a street-vendor and lean for support against some railings whilst I read again those brief, charged, tolling sentences.

HEREFORD POISONING CASE

There was a sensational development yesterday in police investigations of the murder of Rosemary Caswell, niece of wealthy Herefordshire business-man Victor Caswell. Consuela Caswell, Mr Caswell's Brazilian-born wife, appeared before Hereford magistrates charged with the murder of Miss Caswell, and the attempted murder of Mr Caswell, by the administration of poison at the family home, Clouds Frome, near Hereford, on Sunday the ninth of September. She was arrested on Friday, following a police search of Clouds Frome, during which a quantity of arsenic and several incriminating letters were found and removed. Mrs Caswell pleaded not guilty to the charges and was remanded in custody for a week.

The Underground that morning was even more crowded than usual, but I was grateful for the press of strap-hangers round my seat, grateful for the privacy they unintentionally gave me in which to re-read incessantly and tease for meaning one small, obscure block of print. HEREFORD POISONING CASE, wedged without ceremony amidst the sweepings of a dozen courts. Drunken brawls. Domestic incidents. Break-ins. Burglaries. And murder. In Hereford. In a family I knew and a house I built. By a woman I . . . How could this be?

'I beg your pardon?' The man in the seat to my left was peering at me through pebble-lensed glasses. His face wore an irritated frown. Evidently I had spoken my thoughts aloud and, equally evidently, he was fearful lest his completion of the *Daily Telegraph* crossword was to be interrupted by a fellow-traveller of dubious sanity. Already I could seem to hear his petulant voice

13

complaining to a long-suffering wife in Ruislip that such incidents were becoming distressingly common.

'Nothing.' I tried to smile. 'Nothing at all. I'm sorry.'

'Quite all right.' He slapped the newspaper against his knee and began to ink in a clue.

Quite all right? No, it was not that. All was wrong, if the truth be told. All was very wrong.

I had once loved Consuela Caswell. I had once loved her and she had once loved me. There had seemed for a brief space nothing that could mean more to me than what we felt for each other. But that was twelve years in the past, that was all forgotten, if not forgiven, and so there was no reason – no reason founded on logic or good sense – why this turn of events should have moved me as it did. And yet, and yet . . . Life grows sadder as we grow older, peppered with wrong-turnings and regrets, weighed down by a creeping awareness of our own worthlessness. When ambition is thwarted and hope blunted, what is there left but to mourn our mistakes? And in Consuela's case, worse than a mistake: a betrayal.

My precipitate departure from Suffolk Terrace had left me with time to spare, which was time I badly needed. Accordingly, I broke my journey at Charing Cross and went the rest of the way on foot, along the Embankment as far as Blackfriars Bridge, then through a maze of narrow streets to St Paul's, there to pause and gaze in wonderment, as I so often have, at Wren's majestic dome. Thirty-four years in the building and Wren already older than I am now when he began. Where did he find the energy, where the inspiration, where the courage to embark upon such a project? Twelve years ago it was a comfort to me to know that such things were possible, for still then, in my imagination, I could aspire to such achievements myself. But no longer. Daring had failed where originality had faltered. A country house I no longer visited. The ashes of a burnt-out hotel. A rag-bag of mock Tudor villas and utilitarian office-blocks. A failed marriage and a debased profession: all there was to show for a decade of trimming before the wind.

The crowds swept along Cheapside, jostling and shouting to be heard above the traffic. Car horns and squealing brakes, the news-vendors' cries and rain beginning to fall. I moved as in a dream, a dream of what might have been if my nerve had been stronger, my resolution greater, my love for Consuela proof

14

against the snares of self-interest. Why did I betray her? It is swiftly explained. For my career. For the sake of prosperity and respectability. Which amounted, it seemed to me that morning, to little more than the grey weeping blankness above my head.

5A Frederick's Place has been the hub of my professional life since Imry and I set up there together in 1907. Whenever I climb its rickety stairs, whenever I smell again its aroma of old paper and older wood, I think of Imry and me as we were then: short of work and scarcely able to summon the rent, but young, energetic, richer than now in every way save one, determined to make a show in the world, intent upon building well and being known for what we built. Such are the painful ephemera of youth, for Imry will never bound up those stairs again, nor will I sketch grand designs on discarded envelopes. Life is what we make it and middle age the time when what we have made can no longer be ignored. That morning last September, I eyed the brass plate – Renshaw & Staddon, A.R.I.B.A. – with a curious distaste and ascended the stairs preparing stratagems in my mind to cope with the hours that lay ahead.

'Morning, Mr Staddon,' said Reg Vimpany, when he saw me enter.

'Good morning, Reg. Where is everybody?'

'Doris will be late. Her teeth, you remember?'

'Oh yes,' I lied.

'Kevin's gone for some milk.'

'Aha.'

'And Mr Newsom,' he added with heavy emphasis, 'is not yet with us.'

'Never mind. Remind me. What's on?'

'Well, I need to go through the Mannerdown tenders with you. You've Pargeter to see this afternoon. And you told Mr Harrison you'd slip out to the Amberglade site at some point.'

'Ah yes. Mr Harrison may have to wait. As for the tenders, shall we say eleven o'clock?'

'Very well, sir.'

'Thanks, Reg.'

I retreated to my office, well aware that poor Reg would be shaking his head in disapproval of my slackness. He was fifteen years older than me and the only chief assistant we had ever had: dependable, unflappable and content, it seemed, to preserve a certain level of efficiency in our affairs however scant our gratitude.

15

Once I had closed my office door, a sense of refuge closed about me. There was time and peace in which to think, an opportunity to apply reason to what little I knew. Consuela had been charged with Rosemary Caswell's murder. And Rosemary Caswell was her husband's niece. I could not even remember the girl. There was a nephew, certainly, an unpleasant little boy of eight or nine who must be twenty-odd by now. But a niece? The boy's sister, presumably. What was she to Consuela? And why the additional charge of attempted murder? Flinging my coat and hat onto their hooks and gazing through the window at the red-bricked flank of Dauntsey House, I realized how much worse than a terrible truth was the hint of half a story.

'Watch'er, Mr Staddon!' With a theatrical rattle of the door handle, Kevin Loader, our irrepressibly disrespectful office boy, had entered the room. Sometimes I welcomed his jaunty, cocksure breath of vitality, but this was not such a time. He made a spring-heeled progress to my desk, deposited a bundle of mail in the in-tray and treated me to a lop-sided grin. 'One o' yer 'ouses in the news, I see, Mr Staddon.'

'What?'

'Clahds Frome. Read abaht it in me *Sketch* on the bus this very mornin'. Murder most foul, seemingly. Ain't you 'eard?'

'Oh, yes. I believe I did . . . read something.'

'What's the truth of it, then?'

'I've really no idea, Kevin.'

'Come on. You must know the family.'

'It was a long time ago. Before the war. I hardly remember.'

He moved closer, the grin still plastered to his gossip-hungry face. 'This Conshuler. Bit of a looker, is she?' I shook my head, hoping he would desist. 'They always are, aren't they?'

'Who are?'

'Murderesses,' he hissed gleefully. 'Specially the poisonin' kind.'

After throwing Kevin out, I sat down and forced myself to smoke a calming cigarette. As matters stood, I was under no obligation to intervene in whatever had befallen the Caswells. No obligation, that is, that the world would recognize. Far less did I have any right to interfere. Such rights as I might have had I had forfeited, long ago. Yet I had to know more. That much was certain. To pretend nothing had happened, to keep a weather eye open for a further report of court proceedings but otherwise

16

remain sublimely indifferent, was beyond me. So, remembering the name of the local newspaper from my many visits to Hereford all those years ago, I telephoned their offices and prevailed upon them to send me copies of their last two weekly editions. I did not tell them why I wanted them and they did not ask. Only my guilty conscience suggested they might guess.

Where do the lines begin to be traced that lead two people together in this life? How far back lies the origin of their convergent destinies? Some time between disposing of the Mannerdown tenders and tolerating a peroration by the tireless Pargeter on a new range of emulsion paints, I dug out my earliest office diaries and computed, as I had never before, the date and time of my first meeting with Consuela Caswell. It was on my second visit to Hereford, in November 1908, after the commission for Clouds Frome had been settled and the site selected. Tuesday 17 November, as I now learned, around four o'clock in the afternoon. That, at all events, was when I had recorded that I was expected to take tea with Mr and Mrs Caswell, wealthy client and wife. But such precision did not for an instant deceive me. Our meeting was not the rushed contrivance of a diary jotting, but the inevitable product of the innumerable conjunctions and connections that govern all our lives.

It would be possible, for instance, to settle the responsibility on Ernest Gillow, the charming and tolerant man to whose architectural practice of music halls and taverns I was articled upon leaving Oxford in 1903. Gillow was himself a Cambridge man and took me on as a favour to my father, whose stockbroking services he had often employed. It was to transpire that a contemporary of his at King's, Cambridge, was none other than Mortimer Caswell, eldest son of the founder of G. P. Caswell & Co., cider-makers of Hereford. When, in due course of time, Mortimer Caswell's younger brother, Victor, returned from ten or more years in South America with a fortune in rubber behind him and a Brazilian wife on his arm, it was only to be expected that he would deem the construction of an impressive country residence an appropriate mark of his success. Mortimer suggested Gillow as the obvious man to recommend a young and enthusiastic architect, and it was only a year since I had left his practice, so Gillow no doubt thought he was doing me a considerable favour by putting my name forward. As indeed he was, in every sense that he could be expected to understand.

It was on 21 October 1908 – so my diary records – that I travelled to Hereford to view the site of Clouds Frome with my prospective client. London was fog-bound, but in the west all was sun-bathed contentment. As the train neared Hereford in the early afternoon, I gazed through the window with growing enchantment at the golden woods, the busy orchards, the deep green pastures and rolling hills of a landscape I hardly knew. My hopes rose as high as the clear blue sky, for this, surely, was the opportunity any young architect dreams of, the chance to match style and place in a form for which he will always be remembered.

I had by this time exchanged several letters with Victor Caswell and had spoken to him once by telephone. There was therefore no doubt in my mind that he was one of the two tall, slim, well-dressed figures waiting near the ticket-barrier at Hereford station, but which one was not clear. Facially there was little to tell them apart. Both were lean-faced and moustachioed, one adorned in morning suit and top hat, the other in flecked green tweed and a rakish cloth cap. It was the latter, in fact, who identified himself as Victor.

'My brother Mortimer,' he explained over handshakes. 'He's come along to give us the benefit of his opinion.'

There was much fraternal good humour on Victor's part but little sign of reciprocation by Mortimer. Their close physical similarity seemed designed to compensate, in fact, for otherwise contrasting character. Victor was eager to set off, and even a brief detour to my hotel frustrated him. He owned a gleaming green and gold Mercedes tourer, quite the most splendid motor-car I had ever travelled in, and attracted many admiring glances as he drove through Hereford, where horse-drawn traffic was still the norm. Out along the dusty by-roads west of the city, he worked up what seemed a furious pace whilst shooting questions back at me over his shoulder about architects I respected, styles I liked and materials I favoured. His face and voice were animated by something midway between pride and pleasure, an impatient, consuming urge to celebrate all that he had achieved.

As for Mortimer, who sat beside me in the rear, hunched down amidst the polished leather and clasping the brim of his hat, he seemed all that his brother was not: glum, silent and deeply pessimistic. When I ventured a platitudinous enquiry about the cider trade, he countered with the humourless observation: 'It's just a business, young man, like any other.'

18

We crossed a river which I took to be the Wye (and later learned was the Lugg), then began to climb into wooded hill country, acre upon acre of somnolent Herefordshire stretching away behind us. Before long, Victor pulled off the road by a field gate and there we left the car, striking out across sloping pastureland fringed by wood till we reached a hedgerow stile and halted to admire the gentle fall of the land west towards the flood plain of the Lugg and Hereford beyond.

'That's the site below us,' Victor announced, as soon as Mortimer and I had caught up with him. 'These three fields, the orchard further down and the farm between. You can see the farmhouse roof there.' His arm pointed towards a distant wedge of thatch half-hidden in a fold of the land. It was the first I had heard of an existing building and, anticipating the questions I might ask, he added: 'The tenant has notice to quit next Lady Day, Staddon, so have no fear on that score. I shall have a demolition gang in the yard the very next day.'

'The Doaks,' said Mortimer in a matter-of-fact tone, 'have farmed Clouds Frome for six generations.'

'Time for a change, then,' said Victor with a grin. 'Except for the name. Clouds Frome. Yes, I like it. What do you think, Staddon?'

'Perfect, I should have thought.'

'And the site, the prospect, the lie of the land. What do you make of them?'

'They're all perfect.' And I was not lying. I was not even exaggerating. What I saw before me, taking shape amidst the autumnal fields, was a house to crown Victor's success and launch mine. 'I can build you a fine home here, Mr Caswell.'

'I don't want an artless pile, Staddon. I don't want a mausoleum.' He slapped the stile with his gloves for emphasis. 'I want a house to breathe in, a house to glory in. I want the best.'

'Then you shall have it, Mr Caswell.' Suddenly, his greed was mine too, my ambition as boundless as his.

'You're paying Paston over the odds for this land, aren't you?' put in Mortimer, but already I sensed that nothing could restrain his brother's enthusiasm.

'What if I am?' Victor countered with another grin. 'I can afford to.'

'It's no way to do business.'

'I daresay not, but this isn't a question of business. It's a question of vision.'

19

And that, it seemed, settled the matter. Mortimer fell silent, Victor lit a cigar and I climbed up onto the stile to gain a wider view. Clouds Frome Farm stood in a hollow, open to the south and west but backed to the north and east by the hill we had climbed. There was a stream audible in the hanger of trees to our right, descending towards the farm, and a breathtaking panorama beyond it of rolling pastures, with the Black Mountains forming a distant western horizon. A grand house, reached by a winding drive from the high road below, with water nearby and a sheltered yet open setting: it was scarcely possible to imagine anything better. My brain raced to embrace the opportunity.

'Well, Staddon?' said Victor when I had climbed down.

'I'd be proud to build a house for you here, sir.' It was the simple truth and all, for the moment, that I could think of to say.

'And would it be a house I could be proud of as well?'

'Oh yes.' I glanced back at the view. 'I'm sure of it.'

'Then set to work.' He shook my hand firmly. 'Set to work with a will.'

I meant what I said that day when I stood with the Caswell brothers on the breezy heights above Clouds Frome in the thin October sunlight. That house became and still remains the best I was capable of and the best, I believe, any architect, whatever his fee, could have achieved in the circumstances. I returned to London the following day with most of the outline already formed in my head and half of it sketched out on a sheaf of hotel notepaper. Something elegant yet rural, restrained yet wholly original. That was my intention and that, as the plans took shape, was what seemed to lie within my grasp. A happy blend of manorial and domestic, rooted in the landscape and formed of local materials, serving the practical needs of its occupants yet assuring, by deft touches, its own self-confident novelty.

Victor Caswell was not, I already knew, a man to quibble over money. Once my drafts of what he might have had commended themselves to him, he was prepared to pay whatever it cost to implement them. With five months at our disposal before the tenant quit Clouds Frome Farm, there was moreover time in which to tailor every detail to his satisfaction. It was with this in mind that he invited me down to Hereford a few weeks later, mentioning in his letter that he wished me to meet his wife in order to explain my ideas to her and to take note of any decorative preferences she might wish to express. So it was that on 17 November I travelled to Hereford once more, bubbling over with enthusiasm for what I proposed and little knowing that I would encounter there something very different from anything I could imagine. For I was to encounter Consuela.

I had asked the *Hereford Times* to send their back copies to Frederick's Place rather than Suffolk Terrace, having no wish to remind Angela of a subject which she seemed to have forgotten by the evening of the same day. They arrived on Thursday, anonymously parcelled, and I immediately found an excuse for immuring myself in my office in order to study them.

The story they told was disjointed and unsatisfactory. The names of people and places I knew came to me as from a realm of dreams, with no fixed point to guide my thoughts. The issue of 13 September reported with neither prominence nor embellishment the death three days before, following a sudden illness, of Miss Rosemary Caswell, eighteen-year-old daughter of Mortimer Caswell, respected proprietor of the local cider-making firm. An inquest had been opened and adjourned pending a *post mortem*. By 20 September, however, sensational developments had intruded. Sir Bernard Spilsbury, the celebrated Home Office forensic expert, had conducted the *post mortem* and had concluded that death was due to poisoning by arsenic. At the re-convened inquest it was revealed that Miss Caswell's mother and her uncle, Victor, had both been ill with symptoms similar to though less acute than Rosemary's following a tea attended by all three at Clouds Frome on Sunday 9 September. A verdict of wilful murder by unknown persons had been returned by the inquest jury and a police investigation set in motion. Officers from Scotland Yard were believed to be assisting the local constabulary and an early arrest was confidently anticipated.

As I already knew, an arrest had indeed followed. But why Consuela? What were the incriminating letters referred to in the report of her court appearance? And what, if any, was the evidence against her? As to that, I still had no clue. Yet one inconsistency at least had emerged for my thoughts to chafe on. If both Victor and his sister-in-law had been ill at the same time as Rosemary, why did the charge of attempted murder refer only to Victor? I cast my mind back to the day of my first meeting with Consuela, scanning all that I recalled of it in the frail hope that her guilt or innocence might even then have been apparent.

*

21

Between their return from South America and the completion of Clouds Frome, Victor and Consuela lived with Mortimer and his family in a large, gloomy Victorian house called Fern Lodge, a stuccoed pile of few architectural merits set amidst an excess of fir trees on a windy summit towards the northern edge of the city. It was there, on a day of raw greyness contrasting sharply with my previous visit to Hereford, that I made my way for tea at the appointed time, clutching a valiseful of perspective views and floor plans for the new house. I was pitifully eager to please, painfully proud of my proposals and horribly nervous lest any aspect of them should fail to win approval.

So much has changed since 1908 in the mood and fashion of society that my introduction to the Caswell family seems now to date from a far more distant era than fifteen years ago. Perhaps fifty would be nearer the metaphorical mark, so remote does the atmosphere seem that enveloped me in the drawing-room of Fern Lodge that Tuesday afternoon. Victor was the only person present whom I had met before; Mortimer, it was explained, was attending to his business. Awaiting me meanwhile in a semi-circle of brocaded armchairs heavily shaded by thick curtains and large-leafed pot plants was a quartet of Caswell womenfolk: Mrs Susan Caswell, mother of Mortimer and Victor and widow of the founder of Caswell & Co. – frail and fussy in voluminous grey; Mrs Marjorie Caswell, wife of Mortimer – sharp-faced and clearly the mistress of the occasion in severe but expensive purple; Miss Hermione Caswell, elder sister of Mortimer and Victor – less rigidly inclined than the others to judge by her mischievous expression and carelessly flounced dress; and Mrs Peto, wife of Marjorie's brother, who now in my memory is no more than a cipher in washed-out turquoise.

Victor, whose heavy-lidded look suggested that afternoon tea with his female relatives was not a favourite pastime, explained that his wife would join us shortly. Then he perched himself glumly on a hard-backed chair and abandoned me to my fate, which was to unfold more plans than was wise amidst the teacups and cake-stands and to attempt the impossible feat of answering all the ladies' questions accurately and politely. Old Mrs Caswell had the decency to smile more than she spoke, but Marjorie and Hermione were unrestrained in their competing curiosity and led me a merry dance through what they knew or thought they knew of aspect and proportion. I made the elementary mistake of treating their observations seriously, not realizing that they were actually more interested in putting each other down than interrogating me. What with this and the slice of seed cake I had foolishly embarked upon, I was in a fine state of confusion when the door opened and Consuela entered.

I heard the rustle of her dress from behind me and saw Victor rise. I rose too and turned towards the door, which clicked shut as I did so. Then she was before me. Consuela Evelina Manchaca de Pombalho, for so she was born, abundantly more than any Caswell could ever be. Clad in a clinging, shimmering tea-gown of maroon and gold satin, trimmed with lace and gauze, she wore the most delicate of flowered hats far back on her head, a single long string of pearls, a lozenge-shaped brooch by her left breast and a plain gold wedding-ring. Otherwise there was no adornment, no distraction from her perfect figure, her slender neck and her finely featured face. In all of this she might have been no more than an unusually beautiful Englishwoman, but her complexion was darker than any Englishwoman's, her hair thicker, her lips fuller, her eyes more intense.

'My wife, Staddon,' said Victor, standing to one side as she approached. As he spoke, I thought I caught an unnecessary emphasis on the word *my* and, as I stooped to kiss her hand and drew back to look at her again, I could understand why. He had found this wild and troubling creature, he had tamed and married her, and now he had brought her home to parade on a satin chain.

I had muttered something about being her servant. Consuela looked at me directly for the first time and said, 'My husband tells me you are to build a home for us, Mr Staddon.' There was no more than the faintest hint of an accent in her voice. Her English was perfect, though more slowly spoken than a native's, lightly pitched and reserved in stark contrast to the gabbling of her in-laws.

'Yes, Mrs Caswell, I am. It will be my honour.'

'An honour too for us, I feel sure.'

'As to that . . .'

'Come and see Mr Staddon's plans, Consuela,' put in Marjorie from behind me.

'Yes, do,' said Hermione. 'They're really most promising, aren't they, Victor?'

'It's shaping well, certainly.' But Victor sounded positively indifferent. It was a baffling change from the enthusiasm he had displayed during our visit to the site and only the first of many such changes of mood I was to grow used to during our

23

association. He wanted a grand house to live in, a beautiful wife to live with and the respect of all who knew him, but sometimes I suspected that they were all only commodities to him, symbols of a success whose substance remained elusive.

Consuela sat down, accepted some tea and paid close attention to my explanations. Interruptions from Marjorie and Hermione were as frequent and banal as before, but Consuela's presence had an unexpectedly calming effect on me. She seemed instinctively to understand what I proposed and displayed more insight by her few searching questions than did all of the others' enquiries put together.

Hermione, when not competing with Marjorie for the conversational helm, revealed enough to suggest that a perceptive mind was being carefully veiled. During one of the brief liftings of that veil, she engaged me across the plan-strewn table and said, 'As you can see, Mr Staddon, Consuela has more of an eye for artistry than the rest of us.'

Marjorie looked affronted, Mrs Peto giggled, old Mrs Caswell grinned and Consuela lowered her gaze, but the point was well made. More palpably than any words could render it, I detected a sympathy towards me in this cautious, perceptive young woman. At the time, I attributed it to nothing more than a highly developed artistic sensibility and, for the moment, that was enough.

'Of course,' I stumbled, 'all of this can much more readily be appreciated when inspecting the site.'

'Victor has not yet taken me to Clouds Frome,' said Consuela.

'Time enough for that,' he put in, 'when we have vacant possession.'

'When you do,' I said, 'I'd be delighted to act as your guide, Mrs Caswell.'

'That's most kind, Mr Staddon. You must make a point of it.'

'I will. Most certainly I will.'

Then, for the first time since joining us, Consuela smiled. And with that smile my heart took flight.

It was near the end of the first week following Consuela's arrest when Giles Newsom, our senior assistant and aspiring partner, revealed that Kevin was not the only member of staff to have noticed the name of Clouds Frome in the papers. A good-looking young man noted for his elegance of dress and popularity with the fairer sex, Newsom was also a talented architect in the making. Imry had advocated taking him on when it became apparent that

24

he would never be able to resume a full-time share of the business and, though there had always been something too damnably self-assured about the fellow for my liking, he had justified Imry's confidence in the four years since.

Laziness, not incapacity, was Newsom's besetting fault and it was in such a mood that I found him, alone in the office, when I returned there late on Friday afternoon, feet on desk, cigarette in mouth, a copy of *The Architect's Journal* open before him. At other times I might have ventured a mild rebuke, but I felt too despondent on this occasion to make the effort.

'Still here, Giles?'

'Catching up with some reading, Mr Staddon.' He smiled and lowered his feet to the floor, but seemed otherwise unabashed. 'It always pays to keep abreast of developments, don't you find? New styles. New designs. New ideas.'

'I'm sure you're right.'

'Not that we can't learn as much from old ideas at times.'

'No?' I was beginning to suspect there was some purpose to his remarks that might make me regret this conversation.

'Definitely not. As a matter of fact, I was admiring one of your earliest designs only the other day.'

'Really? Which one?' As if I needed to ask.

'Clouds Frome. Reg showed me the article in that old copy of *The Builder*. It was the first time I'd ever seen it. I didn't even know we had it on file.'

'What of it?'

'*What of it?*' He looked at me in amused puzzlement. 'Why, it's just so good, of course. So simple, yet so effective. Function and style. For once, perfectly combined. I never knew—'

'I was capable of it?'

'Of course not.' He laughed. 'I'm trying to pay you a compliment, for goodness' sake. The blending of baronial hall and drawing-room really does come off. The pentagonal bay reinforcing the four gables at the rear. And that flagstoned causeway reaching out across the orchard. What did they call it? "A pier in a sea of blossom"? It's brilliant. Honestly, it is.'

'Kind of you to say so.'

'It's nothing less than the truth. It's just a pity . . .'

'Yes?'

'A pity commissions like that are so thin on the ground. I suppose before the war there were more clients to be found at the higher end of the market.'

'Perhaps.' I thought of Victor Caswell and reflected that clients like him had never been plentiful, which was probably just as well. 'But you only need one.'

'Do you mind if I ask you something about Clouds Frome, Mr Staddon?'

'Not at all.'

'Without wishing to cast aspersions on your other work, do you think it was the best building you ever designed?'

I sighed. 'Yes, Giles. I rather think it was.'

I decided, the day after taking tea with the Caswells at Fern Lodge, to delay my return to London until the evening, so that I might inspect the Clouds Frome site without my client for company. Accordingly, straight after breakfast, I engaged a fly at my hotel and had it take me to the high road side of the farm, intending to walk the few miles back to Hereford after satisfying my curiosity on a number of points.

It was a brighter day than Tuesday and I found the keen edge to the wind invigorating as I started up across a sloping field towards the orchard Victor had pointed out to me from above. Already, I had begun to refine my ideas to appeal to Consuela's sensitivity, to speculate how her comfort and convenience might at all stages be served. Already, I suppose, her approval had come to seem more important than the approval of any client's wife really should.

There was a narrow wicket-gate leading through the hedge into the orchard, which looked to be quite empty now the harvest was over. Beyond it, I knew, lay the farm, but for the moment the trees screened the buildings from my view.

As I unlooped the string that held the gate shut and stepped through, I was startled by the sudden appearance of a figure only a few yards away, materializing, it seemed, from amidst the trees. A short, wiry man of middle years dressed in threadbare tweeds and a flat cap, cradling over his left arm a broken shot-gun, he must, I suppose, have been obscured by one of the trunks until we were very nearly face to face.

I was too surprised at first to speak. He was unshaven, with narrow, suspicious eyes set in a gaunt, prominently boned face. He had been chewing something and spat it out now without ceremony, then said, 'Who might you be?' His tone suggested that, whatever my answer, I would not be welcome.

'My name's . . . Staddon. I'm an architect.'

'An architec'?' He stared at me in silence, as if assessing the merits of the breed. 'An' who might you be an architec' for, Mr Staddon?'

There seemed no point in prevarication. 'Mr Victor Caswell,' I said boldly.

'Ar. I reckoned as much.'

'I was just taking a look. I hope you don't mind.'

'Be all the same if I did, wouldn't it?'

'Well, no. Strictly speaking, I do need your permission, Mr . . . Mr, ah, Doak, is it?'

''E told you me name, did 'e?'

'Mr Caswell mentioned it, yes.'

'Surprised 'e remembered.'

'Do you have any objection to my . . . looking around?'

'Objection?' He spat again. 'Come over 'ere aways, boy.'

I followed him across the orchard and caught my first sight of the farm. It was a low-roofed house of cob and thatch with a walled yard and tumble-down barns to one side. About it and the orchard hung an air of neglect, a suggestion of prolonged struggle recently abandoned. 'Do you live here alone, Mr Doak?'

He nodded. 'Since me wife died two year ago.'

'No children?'

'We 'ad a son, but 'e died afore 'is mother, so alone is what I am now. Mebbe that makes this business rest easier on your conscience. Or mebbe you don't 'ave a conscience. Your employer don't 'ave one, so why should you?'

'Well, I—'

'Will you keep any of it?'

'Any of what?'

'The farm, boy, the farm.' He pointed towards the house through the trees. The barns needed re-thatching, I could clearly see, the yard gate re-hanging. There was a broken window on the upper floor of the house and another window, further along, sagging from its hinges.

'No. I don't think so. Except . . .'

''Cep' what?' He glared round at me.

'The name. Mr Caswell likes the name. It'll still be called Clouds Frome.'

'Will it now?'

We had come to the farther edge of the orchard. Doak stopped and leaned against the wicket-fence. He pulled a drinking flask from his pocket, took a swig from it and offered it to me. I shook my head.

'Caswell's got 'is brother to take me on at the cider works in 'Ereford come next Lady Day. Did 'e tell you?'

'No.'

'It's only for the sake o' that I didn' run you out of 'ere on a pole. For the sake of a job labourin' for a family who'd 've laboured for us once. For the sake of—' He spat over the fence. 'Me family owned this land once. All of it.'

'What happened?'

''Ard times, boy, 'ard times.' He snorted. ''Cep' for the Caswells o' this world.'

'It'll be a wrench to leave, I imagine.'

He looked at me scornfully, as if I could not begin to understand what leaving Clouds Frome would mean to him. 'Doaks owned and farmed this land when Caswells were scrabblin' in the mud for pig-apples. So 'ow d'you think that makes me feel when one of 'em buys it from under me?'

I could give no answer, no answer that would not seem either trite or impertinent. I looked away in my embarrassment.

'I can't stop Caswell buyin' Clouds Frome,' Doak went on. ''E 'as the money an' 'e thinks 'e 'as the right. But this I'll tell you, boy, this I'll tell you for nought. 'E can own this place, but 'e can't be 'appy 'ere. 'E can live 'ere, but 'e can't prosper 'ere. The time 'll come when Victor Caswell will rue the day he ever thought of buildin' an 'ouse for 'imself 'ere – at Clouds Frome.'

I thought little enough of Doak's remarks at the time. I dismissed them as the empty product of envy and disappointment. And so they probably were, though, strangely, none could subsequently have denied that Ivor Doak had been proved correct. Abundantly correct.

CHAPTER

TWO

Knowing Angela's curiosity would be revived as soon as Consuela's next court appearance was reported in the press, I took care to ensure that I had to leave the house uncommonly early the following Tuesday. I had secured a ten o'clock appointment in Whitstable with the secretary of a golf club aspiring to grander accommodation, so was obliged to set off for Victoria station whilst Angela was still in bed.

I had slept poorly since first hearing of Consuela's plight, unable to rid my mind of the contrast between all that I remembered of her and the privations of a police cell in Hereford. Greater knowledge of the charges against her seemed likely to afford some kind of relief, so it was with eager haste that I bought a copy of *The Times* in Kensington High Street and sat on a bench to study the legal page.

A full hearing, it transpired, had now commenced in Hereford magistrates' court. It was reported in detail and with a prominence which suggested that public interest in the case was heightening. Prosecuting counsel had addressed the bench at length, setting out the basis of the charge. It would be shown, he had said, by reference to certain letters found in the accused's possession, that she had reason to harbour malice against her husband. It would be further shown that a quantity of arsenious oxide had been found in her possession along with the letters. On Sunday 9 September she had been due to take tea as usual with her husband and their daughter—

29

I broke off. They had a child. I had never supposed, never guessed, that they might have. It was an unremarkable discovery, yet a devastating one. It seemed suddenly to make everything far worse. Consuela and Victor had a child, whereas Angela and I . . . I forced my attention back to the newspaper.

Consuela, Victor and their daughter (whom the report did not name) had been about to commence tea in the drawing-room at Clouds Frome when unexpected visitors had arrived: Marjorie and her daughter Rosemary, who had called by on a whim whilst returning from a luncheon engagement with Marjorie's brother and his family in Ross-on-Wye. The tea party had lasted about an hour, then Marjorie and Rosemary had pressed on home to Hereford. Several hours later, both Marjorie and Rosemary had been taken ill at Fern Lodge with symptoms of acute food poisoning, whilst Victor had fallen ill with identical symptoms at Clouds Frome. Rosemary's was much the most serious case of the three, vomiting and diarrhoea giving place to paralysis, unconsciousness and death late the following evening.

The Crown's contention was that the accused had placed sufficient arsenic in the sugar-bowl to kill her husband, who, unlike his wife and daughter, regularly took sugar in tea, but that Marjorie and Rosemary, who also took sugar, had inadvertently shared the dose and that Rosemary had somehow consumed the major part.

The prosecution's first witness was Dr Stringfellow, who had attended all three patients. No impurity or tainting of food or drink could have accounted, in his judgement, for the severity of Rosemary Caswell's illness. He had therefore felt obliged to withhold a death certificate until a specialist in the detection of poisons could carry out a *post mortem*. He had also taken specimens of the other two patients' urine for the specialist's examination. The subsequent discovery of arsenic in these samples and in the body of the deceased had not surprised him; he had feared from the start that it would be so.

With Dr Stringfellow's testimony the first day of the hearing had ended.

Poison has always seemed to me the most sinister of threats to life, lurking unsuspected in food or drink, masked by other tastes, then striking hours later when the meal is half-forgotten. Perhaps that is what Ivor Doak meant about Victor's acquisition of Clouds Frome: that something in the land and place was bound to resist him and, in the end, do its best to destroy him.

Yet was it possible to see Consuela as the agent of that destruction? Surely not. She was no poisoner. The cold, scheming intelligence required for such a crime was alien to her nature. Clearly, however, the police believed otherwise and had evidence to support them in that belief. And what did I have? Nothing, except my distant memories of Consuela to stumble after in vain.

It was a few days after Easter, 1909, when I welcomed Consuela on her first visit to Clouds Frome. The builders had only been on the site for a fortnight and there was consequently little to see but mud and trenchwork. The last load of rubble from the farm had, however, been removed and I, at least, could begin to envisage the splendour of the finished house. The question was whether I could persuade others to do so, though even this can hardly explain the anxiety I felt about Consuela's reaction.

She arrived in mid-afternoon, accompanied by her sister-in-law Hermione, in Mortimer Caswell's chauffeur-driven motor-car, a high-roofed limousine with closed seats at the rear lacking the *joie de vivre* of Victor's Mercedes. I had been talking to the foreman, George Smith, when I heard the sound of it approaching up the rutted track from the road and suddenly felt conscious of my shabby, mud-spattered appearance as I hurried down to meet them.

It was a perfect spring day and Consuela, as she stepped lightly down from the car, was in every sense its perfect complement. The simplicity of her dress was remarkable in that era of opulence: cream skirt and coat with the faintest of stripes, pale yellow blouse fastened by a brooch, straw hat delicately trimmed with feathers, white gloves and fringed parasol; but no boa, no veil, no conspicuous jewellery or unnecessary ornament. She smiled as if it was a genuine pleasure to see me and I could not help hoping it was.

'Good afternoon, Mr Staddon.'

'Good afternoon, Mrs Caswell.' I held her hand briefly in mine. 'I can't tell you how delighted I am that you came.'

She looked at me intently for a moment and said softly, 'I promised I would.'

At that instant Hermione completed her descent from the car. She was costumed in tweed, with a scarf fastened round hat and throat, taking no risks, it seemed, with fickle April warmth. She tolerated my courtesies with good-humoured impatience, then demanded to know when the tour would begin.

The tour comprised my attempts to explain where and to what effect the different rooms of the house would be located and how the gardens would be laid out. I had planned the house to face north, with the drive curving up past the orchard to reach the front. To the rear were to be ponds and ornamental gardens, with a pergola of wisteria or clematis leading out along a flagstoned causeway into the orchard, which fell away below with the slope of the land. Wilder, wooded gardens would lie north of the house on climbing ground, walled kitchen garden, glasshouses and gardener's cottage to the sheltered east. The house itself was to be a compressed H, with two gables to the front and four to the rear supplemented by a pentagonal bay, kitchens, stables and garage adjoining to one side. By loading corridor space to the front, I ensured that all the principal rooms and most of the bedrooms had good southern views. The bay, moreover, gave light and grandeur to the drawing-room as well as the master bedroom. The materials were to be local sandstone and slate, the overall effect one of solidity and grace.

How much of this was apparent to Hermione I could not tell. She evidently preferred the method of things to their meaning. To my surprise, she found a soul-mate in Smith and was content to ply him with questions whilst I escorted Consuela up to the fringes of the wood north of the site, from where the best panorama was to be obtained. We stopped beneath the spreading branches of a horse chestnut and looked back down at the strew of cart-tracks and board-walks, at the builders' muddy gougings and the sea of apple blossom beyond – Doak's last crop, which he would never harvest.

'I thought,' I ventured cautiously, 'that a summer-house on this spot might—'

'It would be perfect,' she interrupted, glancing round at me. Sunlight and shade were dappled across her face, blurring her expression. But of her beauty there could be no blurring.

'I'm glad you like the idea.'

'It seems to me, Mr Staddon, that I like all your ideas. Victor was very lucky to find such a talented architect.'

'You're too generous. I'm only doing the best I can.'

'I should like roses in the gardens,' she said, her mood seeming to change suddenly. And, equally suddenly, I felt that nothing could be allowed to stand in the way of any request she might choose to make.

'An arbour, perhaps,' I said, thinking rapidly. 'Or a rose-seat.'

'They would remind me of home.' Her voice was wistful and nostalgic. 'Of the warmth and sweetness of the Brazilian sun.'

'Where was your home, Mrs Caswell?'

'*A Casa das Rosas*.' She smiled. 'The House of Roses. Rua São Clemente, Rio de Janeiro. The house where I was born. The house my father built when he had made his fortune.'

'Is it as delightful as it sounds?'

She made no reply and I sensed that the subject of her distant home was one best not preyed upon. Yet I could not let the opportunity to learn more about her slip from my grasp. I felt a sudden need to trespass upon her secret thoughts.

'Do you miss it very much?'

She looked away and her gloved fingers tightened round the handle of the parasol. 'How long will it take to build this house, Mr Staddon?' she asked in a murmur.

'Two years will see you and Mr Caswell in residence.'

'Two years?'

'No doubt that seems a long time, but I can assure you—'

She raised her hand to silence me. 'It does not seem a long time.' Her gaze drifted up into the woods behind us. 'In some ways . . .' She stopped and I knew she would not continue. In that instant there seemed more sadnesses and longings locked within her than one person could bear, far less one as beautiful as she.

'Your sister-in-law is waving to us, Mrs Caswell. Perhaps we should rejoin her.'

Consuela flashed a glance at me that seemed to convey an immense impatience with the proprieties she was expected to observe. Then, as quickly, it was gone, replaced by lowered eyes and the faintest of smiles. 'Yes,' she said. 'Of course we should.' And with that she set off down the slope.

One of Angela's most infuriating characteristics is her facility for unexpected changes of mood and tactic. She can summon anger from placidity at a moment's notice and revert just as quickly. When one confidently anticipates a terrier-like pursuit of an unwelcome topic, she displays only a consuming indifference. So it was with the newspaper reports of Consuela's hearing. For all Angela said about them one might have supposed she had not even noticed them. Though, somehow, I did not believe that was the case.

33

The second day of the hearing had been devoted to the testimony of the two people who had survived the alleged poisoning: Marjorie and Victor. Marjorie described returning from Ross-on-Wye with her daughter on the afternoon in question. They had decided to call at Clouds Frome on their way. Victor – not Consuela, she stressed – had invited them to stay for tea. Marjorie had noticed nothing unusual in anything that was said or done. Consuela was subdued, but not abnormally so. Marjorie had consumed two cups of tea with milk and sugar and a slice of fruit cake. Rosemary had consumed about the same. Tea had already been laid when they arrived and Consuela had waited upon them. She had poured the tea and sliced the cake, leaving her guests to help themselves to milk, lemon or sugar. Rosemary had, to the best of Marjorie's recollection, been the first to spoon sugar from the bowl. They had left after about an hour. Later that evening, they had both begun to feel unwell. Neither had eaten any dinner. By ten o'clock Rosemary was being violently and repeatedly sick, Marjorie scarcely less so. Dr Stringfellow had been summoned. He had expressed concern about Rosemary's condition in particular and had spoken of food poisoning as the likeliest explanation. A telephone call to Clouds Frome had established that Victor was also ill, but neither Consuela nor Jacinta—

So Jacinta was their daughter's name. It sounded as beautiful as I might have expected. It also sounded more Portuguese than English, which surprised me. I would have expected Victor to insist upon an English name for any child of his.

Neither Consuela nor Jacinta had been ill. That was the point which prosecuting counsel had been at pains to stress. And, what was more, Consuela had summoned no assistance for her sick husband until Dr Stringfellow had volunteered to proceed to Clouds Frome straight from Fern Lodge.

Marjorie's testimony had concluded with a harrowing account of Rosemary's last hours and a tribute to 'the sweetest and most loyal of daughters a mother could ask for', by which, evidently, the court had been much moved. Whether I would have been as well I could not tell. It was doubly odd to read the statements of people I knew and yet not to know how they appeared as they made them, what expression they wore, what tone they adopted. Marjorie Caswell had always seemed stiff-necked and unyielding to me, but that was no justification for denying her the sentiments natural to a grieving mother. The fact that I did not want to believe Consuela capable of murder was no reason to think all her accusers were liars.

Nevertheless, Victor's testimony would have struck a false note with me whether or not I had a personal interest in the case. Encouraged by the prosecuting counsel, he had emphasized that he would have preferred not to give evidence against his wife. (The right of spouses not to bear witness against each other evidently did not apply where one of them was accused of violence against the other. This, I began to suspect, was what lay behind the additional charge of attempted murder. Without it, Victor would not have been able to parade his misgivings on the point.)

Victor had confirmed the essentials of Marjorie's account. As to events prior to her arrival at Clouds Frome, he said tea had already been laid when he joined his wife in the drawing-room. Shortly afterwards, Jacinta had been brought down by her governess. And shortly after that Marjorie and Rosemary had presented themselves at the door. He saw no significance in the fact that he rather than Consuela had invited them to stay, but he did agree that, if they had not arrived, he alone would have taken sugar from the bowl because his wife and daughter habitually took nothing but lemon with tea.

At the tail-end of the proceedings, a vital issue had been touched upon by prosecuting counsel.

'We will hear later that the police found certain letters in your wife's possession – anonymous letters, that is, of the poison-pen variety – which could have caused her to suspect you of infidelity. Was there, in fact, any justification for such suggestions being made to her?'

'None whatever.'

'You are and have always been a faithful husband?'

'Yes.'

'And have thought of your marriage as a happy one?'

'I have.'

His protestations had doubtless created a good impression on the court, as they were intended to. And who was there, after all, to contradict him – beyond Consuela, silent in the dock, and I? For I knew he was lying. Not about the letters, not yet at any rate. But about his marriage. Faithful? No. Happy? A thousand times no. About recent events at Clouds Frome I was as ignorant as any other newspaper-reader. But about the marriage of Victor and Consuela Caswell I knew as much as they did themselves.

During the months following Consuela's first visit to Clouds Frome, my conscious mind devoted itself to the solution of practical problems. Grand conceptions and artful designs are ever at the mercy of wind, weather and human error. Success as an architect, I learned then and never forgot, involves scurrying between quarries and woodyards, clambering up scaffolding and stabbling through mud, usually at ungodly hours, and always in the pursuit of an elusive excellence. I was never again as meticulous, never as tireless, as I was when Clouds Frome began to rise, and my dreams with it, from its peerless site between the woods and river on the hills above Hereford.

It must have been a year or more before I was aware of how inextricably my ambitions for the house had become wound up with my emotions concerning those who were to live in it. If anything, I saw more of Consuela than of Victor. She would visit the site every couple of weeks in the company of Hermione, Marjorie or Victor himself, or on rare occasions with Mortimer. Invariably, it was with Consuela rather than her companion that I found myself discussing progress and, also invariably, other subjects would rapidly intrude: why I had become an architect, what she thought of England and the English. She told me once that she was more forthcoming with me than with any of Victor's family, that it was refreshing to be able to spend time with somebody whose horizons extended beyond Hereford and the economics of cider-making.

I had supposed Victor would share such a broader view. After all, he had made his mark in another continent, had seen and experienced more of the world than any of his relatives. Strangely, however, Consuela implied that this was not the case and I too noted the grudging, secretive side to his nature. He was, in many ways, the perfect client – prompt to pay and slow to interfere – but he was also the most forbidding of men: unpredictable and uncommunicative, with no warmth of character, no humanity of spirit. The more I knew him, the less I understood him. The more time I spent with him, the less I wanted to. Superficially, or at a distance, he might seem the most handsome and accommodating of men. But beneath the veneer, apparent at close quarters, there was a personality in which scorn and malice churned away to some purpose of its own. According to Hermione, the gossip of the family, he had been sent to South America by his father to prove himself after failing to make the grade in the cider trade, initially to work in the Brazilian branch of a London bank. Quite how he had moved so successfully into the rubber business she seemed not to know, but certain it was that he had returned to England with the air – and the money – of a man who had proved a point and did not intend to let anyone forget it, a point which included being able to acquire and to keep a wife like Consuela.

My feelings for Consuela passed through several stages. They began with an undeniable attraction. Then, as she revealed more of herself to me, I came to pity her for the dull and empty life Victor obliged her to lead. Next, my disapproval of his treatment of her turned into an active resentment. There was envy there too, of course, and frustrated desire, but it was his dominion over her personality rather than her body that truly sickened me. By the spring of 1910, I had begun to suspect that the house I was building was to be little more than a decorative prison in which he could confine and control her more effectively than ever.

I recall a particular occasion from that time which brought to the surface many strands of the dislike I felt for Victor Caswell. The slaters had just begun work on the roof and Victor had warned me that he would be bringing a friend to see the progress they had made. It was the sort of interruption I was well used to, but the sort I found easy to bear only when Consuela was its cause. As it was, when the Mercedes growled up the track and I went down to meet it, all I felt was a vast unwillingness to be as pleasant and informative as I knew I should.

Victor's friend was introduced to me as Major Royston Turnbull, though when he had last seen a parade-ground was anybody's guess. He was tall – well over six feet – and running to fat, clad in a generously cut mushroom-coloured suit, with a paisley-patterned waistcoat beneath, and a huge-brimmed fedora. He was smoking a cigar in a holder and this, combined with the quantity of gold glittering about him in watch-chain, tie-pin and signet ring, created in my mind more the impression of a dubious Latin business-man than any officer in even the slackest of regiments. Not that there was anything Latin about his features. His hair was fair, his face firm and ruddy-cheeked, his eyes grey-blue and sparkling. They were old acquaintances, Victor explained, from South America; Major Turnbull was now domiciled in the South of France and had insisted on visiting Clouds Frome during a fleeting return to England. I can say without hesitation that I have never felt a more instinctive aversion to any man than I felt to Major Royston Turnbull.

They had brought with them Mortimer Caswell's son, Spencer, presently on holiday from prep school. He was a slightly built lad of nine or ten who had inherited much of his father's taciturnity and had added to it a brooding, narrow-eyed expression that made one suspect he was plotting where he was probably merely sulking.

It will be apparent from my description that no set of visitors could have been more calculated to oppress my already flagging spirits. Victor, perhaps for his friend's benefit, was in one of his expansive, glad-handed moods, striding around the site and chatting to the workmen with a warmth that must have made them think they were dreaming. He even tried to jolly young Spencer out of his glumness, insisting that the lad accompany him on an ascent to the slaters' platform.

This left Major Turnbull and me to sit on a couple of camp-stools in the sunny lee of the site office, discussing not architecture but, to my surprise, the Caswells. To a man he had only just met he seemed willing to volunteer the most intimate observations of his friend's family, a willingness which at first I found quite baffling.

'You're highly spoken of at Fern Lodge, Staddon.'

'I'm delighted to hear it.'

'Not that I envy you. Working for Victor can't be a bed of roses.'

'I've no complaints.'

'You wouldn't have though, would you?' He glanced round at me. 'Tell me, what do you make of him?'

'What do you make of him, Major? He's your friend, not mine.'

Turnbull laughed. 'Neatly evaded. Very neatly.' Then he looked up at the scaffolded house, where we could see Victor bouncing along a lofty platform of planks with Spencer beside him. 'I think Victor's made a mistake by settling here. An understandable mistake, but a mistake nonetheless.'

'What makes you say that?'

'I know him, Staddon, better than he knows himself. Met him first more than ten years ago, in Santiago. We found ourselves in a few tight spots together, I don't mind admitting, but they were the sort of spots to test a man's mettle, so I think I can claim to know the stuff Victor's made of. Travel. Risk. Variety. They're what he needs, and they're what he can't find here. He should have grubbed up his roots, not returned to them.'

'You think so?'

'I do. Above all, he shouldn't have brought Consuela here to be buried in *his* past.' Another glance in my direction. 'She has a high regard for your talents, I'm told.'

Deliberately, I did not meet his eyes. 'Told? By whom?'

'Not by the lady herself. She's too cautious for that. But by Victor. He resents her ease in your company. It seems you're able to find a response in her which he never has.'

'I don't know what you—'

'An intellectual response, that is. Consuela has a fine brain as well as a fine body. Not that I need to—'

'I don't think we should be discussing Mrs Caswell like this.' I was making a show of my own anger now to mask any hint of an admission.

'You're probably right,' said Turnbull, undaunted, 'but I hold that no topic should be taboo between two men of the world. Victor does not require or expect imagination in women, only compliance. He married Consuela for two reasons: to possess her and to be seen to possess her. Making her happy did not figure in the list.'

'Perhaps it should have.' Instantly, I regretted saying as much.

'It wouldn't be difficult of course, would it?' Suddenly his voice was softer and more confidential, as if he were whispering in my ear, though in fact he had not moved.

'What wouldn't?'

'Making her happy, Staddon. What else? Haven't you dreamed of doing so? I have, I freely confess. Not just for the infinite pleasure of increasing her knowledge of the sexual arts, but—'

'I won't listen to any more of this!' I leapt to my feet and glared down at Turnbull, who puffed on his cigar and smiled benignly. 'How dare you speak of Mrs Caswell in such a way?'

'Don't be so touchy, Staddon. I've only said what you've thought often enough, I'll be bound.'

'You most certainly—'

'Besides, if lust were all there was to it, there'd be no problem, would there?'

'What the devil do you mean?'

He rose slowly to his full height, which was a full six inches above mine. Looking up into his eyes, I realized for the first time that everything he had said had been carefully judged, every implication delicately gauged – and my reaction with it. 'I mean,' he said softly, 'that it may have crossed your mind – or may yet cross it – that you would be a worthier companion in life for Consuela than Victor could ever be. You would be correct, of course, but you would also be immensely unwise. You would be courting great danger as well as great beauty, you see, and I should not like to think of your doing so merely for the want of a warning from me.' And with that, to my astonishment, he winked at me.

'You should have come too, Royston!' It was Victor's voice, from only a few yards away. I swung round and saw him striding towards us, with Spencer trailing dejectedly in the rear.

'No head for heights,' Turnbull responded.

'I trust Staddon's been entertaining you?'

'Why, yes. Mr Staddon and I have had a most diverting discussion, haven't we?'

'Er . . . yes,' I mumbled.

'It transpires that we have a great deal in common.'

'Can't think what,' said Victor with a frown.

'It's a question of philosophy, my friend.'

'Don't know what you're talking about, Royston. Only hope Staddon does.'

But Victor's protestations, then as on a subsequent occasion, did not deceive me. He had become jealous of my standing in his wife's eyes and had recruited Turnbull to warn me off. The warning was premature and all the more offensive because of it, but I knew in my own mind that it was not entirely undeserved. And I also knew that, for a host of common-sense reasons, it was a warning I would do well to heed.

'Case 'ottin' up nicely I see, Mr Staddon.' It was the Thursday morning of Consuela's hearing in Hereford and, in London, Kevin Loader was insisting that I should have the benefit of the *Daily Sketch*'s perspective on events. 'They got a photo of the party today, y'know. Seems I was right.'

'About what, Kevin?'

''Er looks, o' course. See what I mean?'

He thrust the newspaper towards me and there, blurred but instantly recognizable, was Consuela's face. She was being bustled into court by two policewomen and appeared scarcely to be aware of the camera lens, staring dreamily ahead as if her thoughts were on anything but the proceedings that awaited her. She was wearing a long fur-trimmed overcoat and a wide-brimmed hat with a feather in the band. She looked thinner than I remembered, but otherwise little altered by the years.

'Stirrin' up an 'ornet's nest in 'Ereford, by all accounts,' Kevin went on. 'Crowds bayin' for 'er blood. That sort o' thing. Shockin', ain't it?'

But the vicious moods of a mob were no shock to me. Whether in Hereford or the Place de la Concorde, they could always be relied upon to shame humanity. And, according to Kevin's *Sketch*, those drawn to Consuela's hearing were performing to type.

The small number of them admitted to the court on Wednesday had heard a day of medical and police evidence. Sir Bernard Spilsbury, the famous Home Office forensic expert, had explained the findings of his *post mortem* examination of Rosemary Caswell. Analysis of the samples he had taken from her vital organs had shown enough arsenic to have killed everybody present at the Clouds Frome tea party of 9 September. There was no doubt whatever that she was the victim of acute arsenical poisoning. As to the samples of urine Dr Stringfellow had supplied from his other two patients, these had also been found to contain arsenic, although the quantity was trivial compared with that present in the deceased. He had notified Scotland Yard and the Herefordshire constabulary of his findings on 17 September, four days after carrying out the *post mortem*.

Chief Inspector Wright of Scotland Yard had then taken up the story. He had proceeded to Hereford on 18 September and assumed control of the local constabulary's investigation. It was clear from the first that the tea party at Clouds Frome was the only occasion on which poison could have been administered to all three of those afflicted. The house had therefore become the focus of his enquiries. By a process of elimination, he had established that the only item of food or drink consumed by Rosemary, Marjorie and Victor but not by Consuela or Jacinta was sugar. Since this was white and granulated, it was an ideal medium in which to conceal arsenic. And since Rosemary and Marjorie had arrived unexpectedly *after* the presumed conceal- ment of arsenic, it followed that Victor – the only other habitual consumer of sugar – was the intended victim. Rosemary had been the first to spoon some from the bowl. According to her mother, she generally took three spoonfuls per cup of tea. It could therefore be assumed that she had unluckily helped herself to the bulk of the arsenic, leaving only traces for her mother and uncle.

Since Wright believed Victor to be the object of a murder attempt, urgency had attached itself to finding the murderer, who might theoretically strike again at any time. He had questioned the kitchenmaid who had laid the tea tray and the footman who had taken it to the drawing-room. Neither had aroused his suspicion. What had, however, was the fact that Consuela had been alone in the drawing-room when tea arrived. He had thereupon applied for a search warrant in the hope that discovery of a cache of arsenic would lead him to the murderer.

The search of Clouds Frome had taken place on 21 September. In one of the outhouses they had found an opened tin of powdered weed-killer called *Weed Out*, which the gardener, Banyard, had confirmed to be arsenic-based. He had been unable to say whether the tin contained less than he would have expected, but he freely admitted that anybody could have had access to it; the outhouses were never locked. Later, at the back of a drawer in Consuela's bedroom, a policewoman had found a blue-paper twist containing white powder which analysis showed to be arsenious oxide and three letters still in their envelopes held together by a rubber band. The letters were addressed to Consuela and had been posted in Hereford on 20 August, 27 August and 3 September, at intervals therefore of exactly one week. They were anonymous, written, according to a graphologist, in a disguised hand and contained one reiterated allegation: that Victor Caswell was pursuing an affair with another woman. When questioned, Consuela had denied all knowledge of the items; she had never received any of the letters. Wright had pointed out to her that since the letters were correctly addressed and stamped, her denial of receipt was unsustainable, but she had insisted that no such letters had ever reached her. In the face of this and the discovery of arsenious oxide, Wright had arrested her and later charged her on two counts – murder and attempted murder.

'Looks bad, dunnit, Mr Staddon?'

'Bad for whom, Kevin?'

'Conshuler Caswell, o' course. The letters and the arsenic. The motive and the method. 'Ow's she gonna get outa' that?'

How indeed? As Kevin said, it looked bad. Very bad.

'Tell you what I think, Mr Staddon. I think she's for the rope.'

And that, I suppose, was the first moment when I became aware of what was really at stake in this affair. Consuela's life. Or her death.

*

42

I did not heed Major Turnbull's warning. More accurately, I bore it in mind but to no effect. What is rational and well-advised can often seem insignificant compared with the other compulsions that rule our lives. I continued to see Consuela and to become more and more infatuated with her as the spring of 1910 gave way to summer. A fine summer it was too, with few interruptions to work at Clouds Frome and fewer still to the progress of my acquaintance with its future mistress, a progress towards the brink of love.

There were occasions, as there were bound to be, when we met by chance during my visits to Hereford. Consuela would happen to be emerging from a milliner's shop as I was crossing the road from my hotel. Or I would happen to find myself on Castle Green at the time of her regular afternoon stroll. Such coincidences were part of our silent conspiracy: to meet as often as possible because we craved each other's company, yet never to admit what the source of that craving might be.

We both knew though, well enough, and I suspect the real reason why we never expressed in words what was happening to us was that we feared – for excellent reasons – that it could not continue. Consuela had been taught by her religion and her upbringing to believe that marriage was irrevocable save by death. She would be ostracized by her church and her family if she ever acted contrary to such a principle. As for me, I did not find it hard to imagine what difficulties in finding future work an architect who had stolen his client's wife might have.

Victor himself made it easy for me to excuse my conduct. Towards Consuela he was never better than inattentive. Generally, he displayed a presumptuousness bordering on contempt. No doubt he considered that the right and proper way for a husband to behave towards a wife, but I did not. Nor did Hermione's various hints that he was disappointed by Consuela's failure to produce a son and heir seem to me to justify his behaviour. I knew from Consuela that their marriage had been agreed behind the closed door of her father's study long before her own view of the matter had been sought. The price of coffee on the international market had been falling for some years and the fortunes of the Manchaca de Pombalho family ebbing as a result. What Victor Caswell had offered the old man in exchange for his daughter's hand was financial salvation: a share in his rubber empire. Accordingly, it had been made clear to Consuela that the match was not one she could refuse. Abandoned by her family to a loveless marriage in a country she did not know, was it any wonder that she was drawn to the only man who showed her anything besides scorn and indifference?

Consuela did have one confidante besides me: her maid, Lizzie Thaxter. A Herefordshire girl of quick wits and bright demeanour, she would probably have guessed what we were about if her mistress had not told her and, besides, there had never been any secrets between them. I suspect, indeed, that a shared sense of subjugation made them natural allies. Before long, Lizzie had become our go-between, pressing a note suggesting time and place into my hand as I left Fern Lodge or delivering a message to my hotel and waiting for the reply. It was clear Lizzie had no liking for the Caswells and equally clear that she enjoyed her secret role in our rebellion against them. Her father and two of her brothers worked for the paper mill in Ross-on-Wye owned by Marjorie's brother, Grenville Peto, and he was evidently noted for his harshness as an employer; perhaps this was the origin of her resentment. Whatever her real motive, it was certain that without Lizzie's help Consuela and I could not have seen as much of each other as we did.

And so the months passed. The snatched and plotted time we spent together came to matter more and more. And the completion of Clouds Frome, looming ever closer, came to seem less and less desirable. For once the house was finished I would have no reason to visit Hereford or call at Fern Lodge; no pretext for meeting or speaking to the wife of my client. What we would do then – how we would resolve the crisis our emotions were leading us towards – I could not imagine.

Around the end of November, 1910, word reached Consuela from Rio de Janeiro that her father was dying. With Victor's consent, she decided to return home at once in the hope of arriving before it was all over. Her departure was hastily arranged and I only learned of it the day before she set off. A message via Lizzie had implored me to be on the riverside path in Bishop's Meadow within the hour. I was not late – indeed I was early – but Consuela was there before me, pacing up and down by a bench and staring pensively across the river at the cathedral. When she told me the news from Rio, I took it that this explained her distracted state and did my best to console her. But there was more to it than that, as I swiftly learned.

'These tidings of my father have woken me from a dream,' she announced, avoiding my gaze as she did so.

'A dream of what?'

'Of you and me. Of our future.'

'Is it a dream?'

'Oh yes. You know that as well as I do.'

'Consuela—'

'Listen to me Geoffrey! This is very important. I am married to Victor, not you, however dearly I wish it were otherwise. And you are an architect with a career to consider, however much you might like to forget it. We cannot ignore what we are. We cannot afford to.'

'As far as I'm concerned, we can't ignore what we mean to each other.'

'We may have to.'

'Harsh words, Consuela. Do you really mean them?'

There were tears in her eyes now. She had worn a veil, no doubt in the hope of disguising them, but it had not succeeded. The selfish hope came to me that she was weeping for us rather than her father. 'I leave tomorrow,' she said with a sigh. 'Only because of that have I found the courage to end this, before it is too late.'

'When will you return?'

'I don't know. Six weeks. Two months. I cannot say.'

'Then why end anything? I'll still be here.'

'Don't you understand?' Her lips were trembling as she spoke. I understood all too well and my pretence of not being able to rose to rebuke me in the face of her determination. 'If we cannot acknowledge our love to the world, I would rather stifle it. If we cannot be man and wife, we must be nothing.'

'Not even friends?'

She smiled. 'Friendship between us means love. And love we cannot have.'

'Therefore?'

'Therefore I shall go home to Rio, mourn my father and comfort my mother. And you will finish Clouds Frome and go on to your next commission.'

'Surely—'

In a gesture that took me aback, she raised her gloved hand and pressed it against my lips. 'Say no more, Geoffrey, in case my courage deserts me. Believe me, this is for the best.'

I shook my head dumbly. Her hand fell away. Then she moved past me, a last sweep of her eyes engaging mine. I heard the rustle of her skirt fading into the distance and knew I might never see her again. I longed to turn round and call her back to me with declarations of love and promises for the future. But I did not move, I did not speak. There were no promises I could make and be sure of keeping, no vows I could utter and be sure of honouring. We both knew that and it sufficed to hold us apart. For the moment.

The fourth day of Consuela's hearing had been given over to the testimony of various servants at Clouds Frome. A kitchenmaid called Mabel Glynn had described laying the tray and filling the urn for tea on the afternoon of 9 September. A freshly baked fruit cake, sliced and buttered bread, raspberry jam, tea, milk – and sugar. Such were the ingredients of the tragedy that had followed. The sugar had been spooned into the bowl from a jar and was neither the first nor the last taken from that jar. She had been horrified to learn that it was probably used to administer poison, but by then sugar from the same jar had been consumed at several meals, so she was at least relieved to know that the fault could not lie in the kitchen.

A footman called Frederick Noyce had recounted delivering tea to the drawing-room, where he had found Consuela alone. She had thanked him and asked him to inform her husband that it was ready; she would herself speak to Miss Roebuck, the governess, on the internal telephone and have her daughter sent down to join them. Consuela had seemed, Noyce thought, entirely normal. He had found his master in his study and given him her message. He had been on his way back to the kitchen when the doorbell had rung, heralding the arrival of Marjorie and Rosemary. He had shown them in and been despatched to fetch extra crockery and cutlery. Upon delivering these he had noticed only a genial family gathering in progress. He, like Mabel Glynn, had been horrified to learn of the poisoning, but he had been adamant that the sugar-bowl had not left his sight between its collection from the kitchen and its delivery to the drawing-room.

Next came a servant whose name I recognized: John Gleasure. A footman at Fern Lodge who had moved with Victor to Clouds Frome, Gleasure had since become his valet. Concerned to hear from the butler, Danby, that his master had not felt well enough for dinner, he had gone up to Victor's room to see if there was anything he required. Finding him sick and in considerable pain, he had reported his concern to Consuela, but she had not thought it necessary to call for a doctor so late. Thanks to Marjorie's telephone call, of course, Dr Stringfellow had shortly arrived. A tentative enquiry from the prosecuting counsel had elicited a firm denial from Gleasure that Victor had been having an affair. 'Inconceivable, sir. I should have been sure to know of it. And I did not.'

So much for the loyal valet. Banyard, the gardener, was clearly a less respectful character. Responding to a suggestion from the bench that the storage of arsenic on unsecured premises was irresponsible, he had contested that that was for his employer to decide – and he never had. As for who might know that he used *Weed Out*, he had agreed that Consuela took more of an interest in the garden than did Victor. It was even possible that he had mentioned it to her during one of their regular discussions. 'I couldn't say as I did and I couldn't say as I didn't.'

The last witness of the day had been Consuela's maid, Cathel Simpson. (What, I wondered, had become of Lizzie?) She was the person best placed to judge Consuela's reaction to the anonymous letters, but she had resolutely refused to admit any knowledge of them, insisting that they and the twist of arsenic had almost certainly not been in the drawer where they were found when she had last opened it for the purposes of removing or replacing items of her mistress's underclothing, which she thought she had done the previous day. As to Consuela's state of mind, this had been entirely normal before, during and after the tea party of 9 September.

There was small comfort in any of this for Consuela. None of the servants had maligned her. Indeed, the impression created by the report was that they all liked her. But that did not matter. What mattered was the weight of evidence being piled up against her. Alone when tea was served. In receipt of letters questioning her husband's fidelity. Aware of *Weed Out*'s poisonous contents. Aware also of how easy it was to remove some. And found in possession of the letters as well as a quantity of arsenic. I did not believe she had tried to murder Victor, but clearly most of the citizens of Hereford did. A Brazilian-born wife seeking to poison her Hereford-born husband and killing his innocent niece by mistake: it was enough to excite their worst prejudices. And according to *The Times* those prejudices were now apparent in the unruly scenes being witnessed daily outside the court. The odds against Consuela were lengthening. Wherever her thoughts turned in the lonely darkness of her cell, she can have found no hope.

*

In the immediate wake of Consuela's departure for Brazil, I gave way to self-pity. I was still too young then to understand that the path to happiness cannot always be trodden and too self-centred to realize that others could suffer more grievously than I. In my more rational moments, I accepted the necessity of what Consuela had done, but such moments were outweighed by the memories of her that I cherished: the sight of her approaching along a path, the sound of her voice close to my ear, the cautious intimacies exchanged, the tremulous hopes embraced.

Some of this I poured out in a long letter to her. I wondered how it would find her, in what mood, on what occasion, at the House of Roses in distant Rio. I did not expect a reply, for she was likely to return as quickly as any letter could reach me, but still I found myself sifting through my mail every morning in search of her handwriting beneath a Brazilian stamp.

I could hardly ask Victor when Consuela was expected back and it was, in fact, Hermione who told me that they had received a telegram reporting her father's death on 22 January; it was thought she would stay for a week or so after the funeral, then return to England. By now, I was finding it ever more difficult to know how I should react when she was within reach once more: whether to obey her parting instruction or seek to recover what we had once enjoyed.

Perhaps it was as well, in the circumstances, that I had other matters to occupy my mind. In early February, 1911, one of the carpenters at Clouds Frome, Tom Malahide, was arrested for complicity in a robbery at Peto's Paper Mill in Ross. To my astonishment, I learned that his confederate was none other than Lizzie Thaxter's brother, Peter. He had been stealing bank-note printing plates for some months from the mill, where he worked on the maintenance of the plate-making machinery, and passing them to Malahide, who then conveyed them to a corrupt engraver in Birmingham to complete a potentially highly lucrative counterfeiting racket. Random stock-taking at the mill had revealed the discrepancy and the police had soon identified Thaxter as the thief. He and Malahide had been arrested during a hand-over of plates and the engraver shortly afterwards.

Lizzie had accompanied Consuela to Brazil, which was as well, for Victor would probably have dismissed her simply for being related to one of the gang had she been in Hereford at the time. As it was, he assuaged his feelings by criticizing me and the builder for employing suspect characters and so dragging his name and that of his new house through the mud. No matter that Malahide had come to us with an exemplary character. Nor that Peto's should have taken better precautions. I was still required to do penance over an agonizing luncheon at Fern Lodge attended by Marjorie's brother – the outraged mill-owner himself, Grenville Peto. I can remember with awful clarity stumbling out an apology I did not owe to this dreadful, inflated bullfrog of a man, whilst Marjorie and Mortimer looked on censoriously and Victor squirmed with an embarrassment I knew he would make me suffer for later.

That episode made me glad to think how soon the house would be finished. There was, indeed, no reason why it should not be ready for occupation by Easter. I could feel well pleased with what I had achieved. Its final appearance really did match its promise, the stolid gables and elegant chimneys couched perfectly between orchard and wooded hilltop. All had been done to the highest of standards and even Victor had grudgingly to admit that it was a job well done.

The first weekend of March found me at my flat in Pimlico, contemplating the lonely existence I had led in London since my commitments in Hereford – both professional and emotional – had come to bulk so large. It was Saturday night and Imry had urged me to accompany him and his decorative cousin Mona to the latest Somerset Maugham play at The Duke of York's. But I had declined the invitation, preferring to check and re-check the plans and schedules of Clouds Frome. I had commissioned some photographs at Victor's request and now, sifting through the prints, I reassured myself that the house was all I had envisaged that day, two and a half years before, when I had seen the site for the first time. And so it was, all and more; there was no doubt of that. I should have felt proud and exhilarated. I should have been out celebrating my success. Instead, I sat absorbed in dimension and proportion, poring over measurements and lists of materials, peering at every photograph in the brightest of lamplight, seeking the flaw in the design that my heart told me was there. And knowing I would not find it. For the flaw was in me, not Clouds Frome at all.

I recall now every detail of that night, every facet of its colour and shade: the purple barrel of the pen I wrote with, the amber hue of the whisky in my glass, the grey whorls of cigarette smoke climbing towards the ceiling – and the blackness of the London night, pressing against the windows.

A few minutes after eleven o'clock. I can remember checking how late it was by my watch, stubbing out a cigarette, massaging my forehead, then rising from the couch and walking to the window. The panes were misty: it was growing cold outside. But coldness, in that moment, was what I most desired. I pulled up the sash and leaned out into the chill darkness, breathed in deeply and glanced down into the street.

She was standing beneath a lamp-post on the opposite pavement, a slight and motionless figure staring straight up at me as I felt sure she had been staring up at the window before I had even reached it, a figure in mourning black whom I knew well. What had brought her there I could only guess, what she was thinking I did not dare to. There was something of doubt as well as scrutiny in her gaze – and something also of hope. Half a minute of silent appraisal passed that seemed to compress within it all the weeks of her absence. Then I signalled that I would come down and raced to the door.

She was standing on my side of the road by the time I reached the front steps of the block. At closer range, her anguish was unmistakable. Her dark eyes scoured my face, her lips quivered uncertainly. As I descended towards her, she moved back a pace. There must be space between us, her expression conveyed: there must be a frontier across which the first tokens could be exchanged.

'I didn't know you were in England,' I said after another silent interval.

'Nobody knows I am.' Her voice was breathless and strained. 'Except Lizzie.'

'Has Lizzie heard—'

'About her brother? Oh yes. We had a telegram from Victor just before sailing. I've sent her to see her family in Ross.'

'Then you're alone?'

'Yes. We docked this afternoon. Five days earlier than I told Victor to expect us.'

'You . . . over-estimated the passage?'

'No, Geoffrey. I did not over-estimate the passage.'

The implications of her remark assailed me. What had happened? What did she mean? 'Won't you come in?' I stumbled.

'I'm not sure. To be honest, I think I hoped you wouldn't be at home.'

'Why?'

'Because then I'd have to return to Hereford straightaway.'

'And you don't want to?'

In her eyes I had my answer. She walked up the steps and halted beside me. Now her gaze was averted, her voice scarcely rising above a whisper. 'I told my mother, and my father before he died, that life with Victor is a torment to me, that I can never love him, that he can never make me happy. I pleaded with them for help, for advice, for refuge at the very least.'

'What did they say?'

'They spoke of duty. They spoke of *their* honour and *my* obligations.'

'As *you* did, when last we met.'

'Yes.' Now she looked at me, some dart of lamplight catching her eyes beneath the brim of her hat. 'But that was before I watched my father die and saw what his code amounted to: a dutiful death and an honourable grave. They're not enough, Geoffrey, not enough for me.'

'Consuela—'

'Tell me to go away if you like. Tell me to go back to my hotel and take the first train to Hereford tomorrow. You'd only be following the advice I gave you. And it was good advice, it really was.'

'Was it? I'm not sure. And neither are you.'

'But we must be sure, mustn't we? One way or the other.'

The truth was that certainty lay beyond our grasp. But neither of us wanted to admit as much, dallying as we were with more unpredictable futures than there were stars in the sky above our heads. 'Come inside, Consuela,' I urged. 'We can—'

As on that last occasion, three months before in Hereford, she silenced me with one hand laid softly against my mouth. But this time she said nothing and, this time, she had removed her glove. I felt the touch of her bare fingers on my lips more intensely, it seemed, than I would have felt even a kiss. Then I reached up, took her hand in mine and led her up the remaining steps towards the door.

HEREFORD POISONING CASE

Mrs Consuela Caswell was yesterday committed for trial on charges of murder and attempted murder at the conclusion of a five-day hearing at Hereford magistrates' court. Mr Hebthorpe, prosecuting counsel, summed up the Crown's case in a two-hour speech in which he reviewed all the evidence and contended that it represented the very strongest *prima facie* case against Mrs Caswell. Her jealousy had been aroused, he said, by malicious suggestions that her husband had been unfaithful to her. She had then set out to poison him in a ruthless and calculating manner, only to see her husband's young and totally innocent niece consume the poison in his place. She had made no attempt to intervene and had allowed Miss Caswell to proceed to an agonizing death. She had then continued to hoard arsenic against the day when she might make another attempt on her husband's life.

After a brief retirement, the magistrates announced that they were minded to commit Mrs Caswell for trial at the next assizes. Mr Windrush, her solicitor, indicated that she wished to reserve her defence.

Unruly scenes followed outside the court when Mrs Caswell was taken to a police van in order to be driven to Gloucester Prison. There was much shouting and jostling by the crowd. Objects were thrown and an egg struck Mrs Caswell on the arm. Three people were arrested. Mrs Caswell's foreign origins and the wide respect in which her husband's family are held in Hereford, compounded by the distressing circumstances of the case, are thought to explain the animosity felt towards her.

'Are you going in to the office today, Geoffrey?'

It was Saturday morning in Suffolk Terrace, dull and grey with a fine drizzle falling beyond the windows. Angela, whose silence on the subject of Consuela's hearing was still unbroken, eyed me in a way that was peculiarly hers: satirical, superior, playful as it might seem to others and had once to me. 'No,' I replied, turning the page of the newspaper.

'I told Maudie Davenport I'd go with her to Harrods. The autumn fashions are in, you know.'

'Really?'

'And Maudie's a great one for beating the crush. So I must dash.'

'Of course.'

'What will you be up to?' Already she was halfway across the room, oblivious to whatever answer I might give.

'This and that.'

'Well, don't overdo it, will you?'

'I'll be sure not to.' My gaze, and with it my thoughts, reverted to the newspaper in my hands. I turned back to the page I had just been studying. *Mrs Consuela Caswell was yesterday committed for trial on charges of murder and attempted murder.* It had been inevitable, of course. So much evidence, so damning and incontrovertible – no other outcome had been possible. Yet the reality was worse than the expectation. A hostile crowd baying for 'the foreign bitch's neck'. An acrid splatter of rotten egg on her sleeve, worn like a badge of shame. Then the sullen company of two stern-faced wardresses on the jolting van-ride back to prison. The squalor and the horror of it all washed over my imagination. And there, at the centre, fixed by my memory, was the contrast that made it so hard to bear.

'*Querido Geoffrey.*' It was the phrase Consuela used that March night thirteen years ago, when she surrendered herself to me for the first time, her private, whispered endearment, the one fragment of Portuguese she permitted herself to employ. '*Querido Geoffrey.*'

I had banked up the fire and it flung in answer a golden swathe of light across the room, falling on the hills and valleys of the rumpled sheets, the mounds of the pillows, the columns of the bed-posts. And on Consuela. She was mine completely, to have and to hold, for one night only, for the immensity of time and the eternity of intent that it seemed to represent.

'You're beautiful, Consuela. I can't believe how beautiful.'

'For you, Geoffrey. Only for you. All for you.'

Her dark eyes, nervous and questing. Her still darker hair, falling and sliding through my fingers. Her lips, moving against my cheek as she murmured what I wanted to hear. Her hands, clutching and caressing. And her flesh, burning to my touch, golden to my sight. Our limbs entwined. Our bodies joined. Too much passion. Too much ecstasy. Too much trust for time to preserve.

'I love you, Consuela.'

'And I love you. Don't desert me now, Geoffrey. Not after this.'

'Never.' I kissed her. 'I will never desert you.'

'I couldn't bear it if you did.'

'I won't.'

'You promise?'

'As God is my witness.' I kissed her again and smiled. 'I am yours for ever.'

CHAPTER

THREE

When the doctors told Imry he could hope for no improvement in his condition so long as he inflicted the smogs of London on his lungs, he bought a cottage out at Wendover, on the scarp of the Chilterns, where he led a quiet fresh-air existence, doing a modest amount of work for the partnership whilst endeavouring to recover his health. We spoke every few days by telephone and saw each other at least once a month, so he was by no means out of touch. And besides, even if he had made no contribution to the work at all, I would still have sought his advice on other matters.

For Imry Renshaw is the best and firmest of friends, that rarest of gems in the seams of humanity: a genuinely good man. Never down-hearted, never reproachful, never less than those who know him hope to find him. He realizes that the effects of the mustard gas he inhaled in 1916 will never leave him, that his condition, in all probability, will slowly worsen, but he will not admit as much, to himself or to others. He faces all the missiles of life with cheerful defiance.

There were two reasons why I felt the need of Imry's company that Saturday last October, when my wife and Maudie Davenport went to select their fifteen guinea gowns at Harrods. I needed to speak to somebody about Consuela's plight. I needed to convince myself – or be persuaded – that there was nothing I could do to help her. Imry was the only person I could turn to, the nearest I knew to a disinterested observer. And he had one other recommendation. He alone knew how I had betrayed Consuela in the past.

54

I reached Wendover a little after midday and followed the familiar route from the station up a winding lane to Imry's half-timbered cottage, Sunnylea. His housekeeper was on the premises and offered to include me in the meal she was preparing. As for my friend, he was to be found in an outhouse, planting bulbs in pots and puffing on the pipe he had been advised to give up. He had discovered the joys of gardening since leaving London and would regularly discourse, given half a chance, on the miraculous qualities of home-grown vegetables. But the role of carefree countryman did not fool me for an instant. He still looked thinner and hollower-chested than he should, he still seemed perpetually short of breath and any digging or lifting, when it came to it, would be done by another.

'Hello, Geoff. Good to see you.' In the warmth of his voice and his smile was the assurance that his words were sincere.

'Hello, Imry. How are you?'

'Not at all bad. Has Mrs Lewis offered you lunch?'

'Yes.'

'Splendid.' He dibbled in the last bulb and turned to face me. 'To what do I owe the pleasure, Geoff? This isn't a scheduled visit.'

I grinned. 'Spur of the moment.'

'Really? Not the spur of something else?'

I shrugged. 'Such as?'

He stepped across to the other side of the shed and pulled a newspaper from a pile of old copies wedged under a broken sieve. Then he folded it open at a particular page and handed it to me. It was Wednesday's *Daily Telegraph* and carried a prominent report of the second day of Consuela's hearing.

'Ah,' I said weakly.

'Want to talk about it?'

'Yes. I rather think I do.'

It was after lunch, by a sizzling log fire, over jugs of some local ale he favoured, that Imry and I discussed the case. At first, the relief of simply being able to speak of it was enough for me, but once that barrier was surmounted another lay in wait. Was she guilty or not?

'It was only a hearing,' Imry pointed out. 'No defence evidence was heard.'

'But if there'd been a convincing answer to the allegations, surely her solicitor would have given it.'

'Obviously he didn't think he could prevent committal, so there was no point showing his hand.'

'That sounds like clutching at straws.'

'You mean you think she's guilty?'

'What else can I think? You read the evidence as well as I did. Anybody who didn't know her would take it for granted she was guilty.'

'You're right, of course. The patrons of the White Swan have already convicted her. Even Mrs Lewis has contributed her two penn'orth of condemnation.'

'Well then?'

'The verdict of the ill-informed is hardly the point, is it? I don't want to trample on past confidences, Geoff, but you do know the lady, don't you? And her husband. What's your opinion – your *real* opinion?'

I thought for a moment, then said, 'It's conceivable Consuela might murder Victor. If any man could goad his wife into murdering him, it's probably Victor Caswell. But poison is out of the question. She isn't cruel or calculating enough for that. And there's another objection. Those anonymous letters they found suggesting he was having an affair.'

'What about them?'

'She wouldn't have cared, Imry. She wouldn't have given a damn.'

'No jealousy? No resentment?'

'None. You can't be jealous of somebody you loathe.'

'But you haven't seen either of them for more than ten years. Isn't it possible—'

'That they've changed? No. As a matter of fact, I don't believe it is.'

'So how do you explain the circumstances?'

'I don't. I can't. That's just the point. I don't know enough to explain anything.'

'But you're wondering if you should try to find out?'

'Yes.'

'How could you?'

'Speak to some of the witnesses, I suppose.'

'Or to Consuela?'

'It had crossed my mind.'

Imry leaned forward to stoke the fire. 'Do you think she'd want to see you?'

'After what I did, you mean? No, she probably wouldn't. It

56

might salve my conscience, but it could just as easily increase her agony of mind. Besides, no doubt her solicitor is competent enough. He'll assemble a defence with no need of help from me.'

'And if Angela came to hear you were trying to help her?'

'There'd be hell to pay.'

'So there's everything to be said for leaving well alone?'

'Yes, there is. It's the wisest course. It's the easiest course. But is it the right one?'

'I don't know, Geoff, I really don't. If I did, I'd tell you.'

'I suppose I hoped . . .'

'That I'd have an instant answer? Sorry, old chap. This is one dilemma only you can resolve.'

I grinned ruefully. 'Perhaps I should have resolved it a long time ago.'

Imry nodded. 'Perhaps you should at that.'

What did I know of Consuela? What did I know of the woman to whom I had once sworn love and loyalty? Only what she had told me herself, of course. Only what she had allowed me to understand.

She was born in Rio de Janeiro on 3 August 1888, the youngest of the seven children of Luís Antônio Manchaca de Pombalho, wealthy coffee merchant and ship-owner. She had three sisters, but none of them, apparently, could rival the startling beauty of young Consuela Evelina. At eight she was sent to the Collège de Sion in Petropolis, to be educated and refined by French nuns. Piety, decorum, application, delicacy and politeness. These were ingrained along with the language and literature of France and England, held to be incomparably superior to those of her native land. It was a regime intended to fit her for early matrimony and obedient motherhood.

In 1905, when Consuela was seventeen, her mother and one of her brothers took her to Paris for six months for a final polishing in the ways of cultured society. When she returned, she found that a new figure had appeared in her father's business life, an Englishman named Victor Caswell, who was reputed to have made a fortune in the rubber plantations of Acre, vast tracts of which he owned. From that point on, Victor's involvement in her family's financial affairs and his courtship of Consuela proceeded in tandem. And Consuela, offered such a suitable and convenient match, felt she could not put forward mere dislike as an objection. They were married in Rio in October 1907.

Within a matter of weeks, Consuela made three horrifying discoveries. Firstly that she was unable to satisfy her husband sexually. Secondly that he was prepared to resort to the high-class prostitutes who abounded in Rio to obtain such satisfaction. And thirdly that he proposed to retire to England as soon as possible, taking her with him and thus away from the friends and relatives who were her one consolation.

I can only imagine the desolation of spirit Consuela must have experienced on being ushered into Fern Lodge, Hereford, in the late winter of 1908, and introduced for the first time to the family of which she had become an unwitting member. Hereford and the Caswells must have seemed unbearably grey and grudging after the colour and vitality of Rio. Small wonder that she abandoned herself to a secret misery and responded with total indifference to Victor's announcement a few months later that he was to build a country house for them to live in.

Then, one November afternoon, I walked into her life, the humble young London architect her husband had hired. What happened from that point on was inevitable once the spark of mutual attraction had been ignited, for, though no paragon, I had enough decency and sensitivity to make marriage to Victor seem an even worse torment than it had before. For my part, Consuela's beauty – her fragile nobility, her yearning for love and freedom – was irresistible. And so, through the course of more than two years, we contended with – and defeated – caution, diffidence, doubt, propriety, even better judgement, and found ourselves lovers in the end.

It was as lovers that Consuela and I awoke in the bedroom of my Pimlico flat on Sunday morning, 5 March 1911. To find her in my arms seemed even more of a miracle then than it had the night before. I left her dozing and walked to the window, pulled back the curtains and gazed out at the sky-line of the city. How happy I felt, how proud, how deliriously in love. I could have flung the window open and shouted to the prim and proper house-tops in triumph. I could have proclaimed to the world that Consuela was mine and would never be another's. But I did not. Instead, it was triumph enough to look back at the bed where she lay, her dark hair spread across the pale pillow, the perfection of her shoulder and flank displayed where I had thrown back the sheet.

She stirred and reached out for me, then finding me gone,

opened her eyes, raised herself on one elbow and smiled at the sight of me standing by the window.

'You are here after all.'

'Of course.'

'I thought – for an instant – that you might have—'

'Left?' I walked back to the bed and sat down beside her. 'Silly. Such a silly thought.'

'Was it? One of us must leave, sooner or later. If not you, then I.'

'To go where?'

'Hereford. You know I must return there.'

'Must you? Must you really?' I leaned forward and kissed her.

'If I am to escape him it must be planned. It must be arranged so he cannot prevent it.'

'I'll do anything you ask. Anything – to make you mine.' My hand slipped down to her breast.

'Oh Geoffrey, if only it could always be like this.'

'It can be. It will be.'

So it seemed to me then. In that dawn hour as we embraced and joined once more across the rumpled bed, our bodies bathed in pallid morning sunlight, there seemed no pleasure we could not give each other, no joy we could not share, no hope we could not fulfil.

'What are we to do, Geoffrey?'

Her head lay on my shoulder, her hair stirring against my cheek. The morning light had strengthened across the ceiling above us and beyond the window church bells could be heard on the still sabbath air. When I turned to kiss her, I saw a thoughtfulness in her eyes, an earnestness that had not been there before.

'Everything I said last time we met is still true, you know.'

'But we're committed to each other now, Consuela. Body and soul.'

'Yes. And that is why I asked: what are we to do?'

'You must leave him. Divorce him. I'll take all the blame.'

'You cannot. I am a married woman. And my religion does not recognize divorce. So you see, Geoffrey: the blame will all be mine.'

'Can you bear it?'

'With your help, I think I can. But it won't be easy. There's no point pretending it will. My family will disown me. I shall be penniless.'

59

'We can live from my work.'

'Can we? How much work will you have left once Victor has dragged your name and character through the courts?'

'Enough.'

'Do you really believe that?'

'We could go abroad. There are openings for architects all over the Empire. Canada. Australia. South Africa. India. Places where nobody would care about our past or hold a divorce against us.'

'Yes.' Her eyes drifted out of focus. 'That is what we would have to do, of course.'

'It's what we *will* do, Consuela.'

Her gaze moved back to meet mine. 'When?'

'As soon as possible.'

'But when? Every moment will be an ordeal once I am back with him. His eyes watching me, his hands—'

I pressed my fingers against her lips. 'Don't speak of it. It's too awful.'

'But it's what I must endure.'

I took a deep breath, stared up at the ceiling and struggled to address the realities of our predicament. 'We must go abroad. There's no alternative. Then he can do his worst and it can't touch us. But it won't be easy for me to establish myself in another country. I have a few contacts – not many – and a little money. But not enough. Victor owes me the greater portion of two years' fees, but I can't ask for them until Clouds Frome is finished.'

'You mean we must wait for Victor to pay you?'

'Yes. I'm sorry, truly sorry. I don't want you to return to him for a single night. But our whole future is at stake. We must follow our heads as well as our hearts.'

'How long?'

'I can push the builder to hand the house over within a month. But there'll be a host of minor problems, there always are, and the builder's own account to wrangle over. It would look suspicious if I asked for my fee before all that's settled. Say another month. And Victor may not pay promptly. But by the end of May, God willing . . .'

'The end of May? It sounds like forever.'

'No, Consuela. Forever is what we'll have afterwards. Are three months too heavy a price to pay for the rest of our lives together?'

60

She kissed me. '*Querido Geoffrey*. I can be brave for three months – for longer if necessary. But when the waiting is over, you will come for me?'

'Yes, my love. Never doubt it.'

When Consuela and I parted that afternoon at Paddington station, our plans were laid, our future mapped out. Only the thought that it was part of our grand strategy made the separation bearable and, even then, only just. Until Clouds Frome was finished and my fee paid, Consuela would impersonate as best she could the uncomplaining wife whilst I continued to pose as the dutiful architect. Months of agony and suspense loomed ahead, but both of us were confident we could survive them for the sake of what promised to follow.

Not that we were destined to be denied each other's company during this period. I was a frequent visitor to Hereford over the ensuing weeks, calling frequently on my client to report on the completion of his new house and cajoling the painters and electricians into finishing their work ahead of time. In some ways I would have preferred not to see Consuela at all. To meet her in the drawing-room of Fern Lodge and swap comments about the weather, whilst the memory of all we had done was so fresh and clear in my mind, was unmitigated torture. And I at least had Clouds Frome to distract me. For Consuela the pretence was remorseless, the suspense endless.

We continued to communicate through Lizzie Thaxter, whose brother was now in prison, awaiting trial. She never mentioned him to me, but it was obvious that she was under considerable strain. Victor had insisted, I was told, that if she was to remain in their service she must disown her brother and have no contact of any kind with him. They were harsh terms, but terms she had felt bound to accept, since Grenville Peto had dismissed her father and other brother in the aftermath of Peter Thaxter's arrest and contributions from Lizzie were therefore vital to the family's survival. She posted letters to me from Consuela and undertook the delivery of replies. Thus we were able to meet from time to time without Victor or any of the Caswells in attendance, to exchange reassurances of our love and to discuss how the future stood.

Victor and Consuela took up residence at Clouds Frome on 12 April. The care I had taken and the expense I had persuaded Victor to incur were rewarded by fewer problems than I might

61

have feared. But there was a garage still to be finished, a drive to be laid and a kitchen-garden wall to be erected. Victor therefore felt in no hurry to settle with me or the builder, and I could not risk arousing his suspicions by pressing for settlement. There were times when I imagined I could detect an inkling of the truth in the way he spoke or looked at me and I knew that our only hope lay in governing our impatience.

My estimate that the end of May would see an end to our waiting and hoping proved optimistic. Thanks to the appearance of damp in the dining-room chimney-breast, a delay of several weeks was inevitable. At first Consuela seemed close to distraction at the news, pouring out her disappointment to me in a long and emotional letter. But, by the time I was able to contrive a meeting with her, she had become resigned to the situation, summoning from her reserves of inner strength a self-control which was, in the circumstances, extraordinary. Our only consolation was that the remedial work meant I had to pay several visits to Clouds Frome. During these it always proved possible to snatch a few minutes alone with her.

Snatched minutes were mere tantalizing glimpses, however, of the intimacy we looked forward to. By the middle of June, I was at last able to submit a final statement of account. I could see no reason for Victor to quibble with any of the details and it was hard to imagine him failing to settle within a few weeks. Suddenly, the end was in sight, the end that would also be the beginning of my future with Consuela.

The world, of course, careers on its way heedless of individual ordeals and crises. June 1911 found most Londoners in the grip of coronation fever and, as the great day approached, it seemed to become the all-consuming topic of conversation and attention. I could summon no interest in pomp and pageantry at such a time and was surprised to receive a letter from Consuela a few days beforehand saying that she intended to make up a party with Marjorie, Hermione and the Petos and visit London for the occasion. A client of Caswell & Co. had apparently invited them to view the Royal Progress from the top floor of his premises in Regent Street. As I read on, her enthusiasm for the trip became understandable. She intended to become lost in the crowd as they made their way to Regent Street, spend the day with me in Pimlico, then reappear at their hotel later. The prospect was a delicious one, for we had not been able to relax in each other's company since early March. As for my work, it had already become clear that nothing could be accomplished on such a day. Imry for one would be brandishing a miniature Union flag in the crowd somewhere along The Mall. Perhaps we should not have taken such a risk when we were so close to our goal and caution was essential, but we had been denied the closeness we craved for too long. Neither of us had the heart to let such an opportunity slip.

'*Querido Geoffrey*. Hold me close. So close I may forget what the past three months have been like.'

'I'm sorry it's taken so long. So very sorry.'

'Tell me it's nearly over.'

'It is.'

'When will we be together without the need for plotting and planning?'

'A few weeks. No more. As soon as he pays. We'll go to France till the dust settles. We'll honeymoon in Paris.'

'And then?'

'Then, my love, we'll go wherever we want to.'

'You spoke of contacts.'

'Don't worry. We won't starve.' (What I did not tell Consuela was that those few acquaintances to whom I had mentioned the idea of setting up abroad had advised me strongly against it. Why go, had been the consensus, when my career seemed so promising in England? As for Imry, I still had not told him what was in my mind.)

'I wouldn't care if we did starve. It would be better than this lie my life has become. Every day, every minute I spend with him. Concealing. Pretending. Deceiving. He is not a good man, but sometimes I think he is not so bad that he deserves this. If only . . .'

'If only what?'

'We did not need his money.'

'It's money I've worked for, Consuela. It's money he owes me.'

'I know. And yet . . . He will come after us. I know he will. What if he finds us?'

'He won't.'

'But if he does?'

'There's nothing he can do to stop us, Consuela. He can sue, of course, but that's all. The law is his only remedy. And it's one we can bear.'

'You're right, I know, but sometimes I think—'

'Try not to. Just hold on for a little longer yet.'

There was a difference in her that day, a nervousness, a presentiment that even at the last we could be cheated. She trembled as I caressed her, a trembling I could not still. There seemed no way of calming her, no way of reaching the part of her that was troubled. She had given herself willingly to me before, but now something seemed to hold her back and taint our love-making. Afterwards she wept, but she would not tell me why. Then, earlier than seemed necessary, she dressed and set off for her hotel.

The first week of July brought a cheque from Victor settling my fee in full. It was accompanied by a letter from him, inviting me to attend a house-warming party at Clouds Frome, which he was staging on Friday the fourteenth, and to stay on for the weekend. By the next post came a letter from Consuela, telling me that she knew of Victor's intention to invite me and urging me to accept. During the ensuing weekend, she suggested, we would have an opportunity to plan our escape. She also implored me to forgive any awkwardness in her manner when last we had met, which she attributed to the strain of prolonged dissembling.

Who, I wondered, was really the dissembler – Consuela or me? I had not, in truth, looked beyond the rapturous prospect of carrying her off to Paris for the rest of the summer. My vaunted plans for a new life in another continent were no farther advanced than when I had first proclaimed them.

Nor had I told Imry, as I would shortly have to, that he was about to lose his partner. The longer I postponed doing so, the less warning he would have and the less reasonable my action would seem. But postponement was all I felt equal to. When I thought of Consuela – her beauty, her simplicity, her faith in me – the way ahead seemed clear. But when I thought of all we would bring down around our heads – disgrace, penury, exile and condemnation – my resolution faltered.

It was on Wednesday 12 July, only two days before the Clouds Frome house-warming, that I kept an appointment with Ashley Thornton, the hotelier, at his offices in Piccadilly. I had assumed that extension or refurbishment of one of his hotels was what he wished to discuss, although my preoccupied state ensured that I had given little thought to the matter. In view of my intentions, I ought to have passed such a commitment over to Imry, but that would have forced me to tell him just what my intentions were. So it was that I found myself, distracted and struggling to concentrate, in Thornton's office overlooking Green Park on a morning of broiling heat.

Thornton was a dapper little man with prematurely white hair and an apparent immunity to the temperature. He had a knowing, ironical twist to the mouth and a patient watchfulness about the eyes. Later I would come to know these characteristics and what they betokened, but for the moment all I detected was polite and measured scrutiny. These were the days before his knighthood – before, come to that, the bulk of his fame – but he was nonetheless a client I should have been eager to cultivate. As I would have been, but for all the uncertainties by which I felt beset.

'They tell me you're a rising star in the architectural firmament, young man,' Thornton announced as soon as we were alone.

'I wouldn't say that, sir.'

'No false modesty, please. It doesn't pay in my business and I don't suppose it does in yours either. The piece about you in this month's *Builder* has been brought to my attention.'

'You mean about Clouds Frome?'

'Yes. The house is your creation, isn't it?'

'Well . . . yes.'

'I like it. It's impressively original. My congratulations.'

'Thank you.'

'But I didn't ask you here simply to congratulate you.'

'No, sir. I didn't imagine you had.' By now I had begun to anticipate what was coming. Thornton wanted a Clouds Frome of his own: a Home Counties residence for a successful hotelier. An abiding curse of the architect is the client who merely wants him to duplicate his previous work, the more so since they are usually the clients with enough money to overcome his reluctance.

'Hitherto, I've prospered by buying and modernizing old hotels. Recently, I've come to feel – and my board agrees – that an hotel built specifically for us, here in London, would be a timely and profitable extension to our enterprise.'

'I'm sure you're right, sir.' Not a house, then, and not a copy of an old design. A hotel, and a big one at that. My name associated with a London landmark. It sounded almost too good to be true.

'It's my belief that we need something individual, something stamped with our identity. I don't want another Carlton or

Waldorf. I don't want mile after mile of cast plaster mouldings or half the African jungle transplated in the lounge.' By now he had left his desk and was standing by the open windows gazing out across Green Park. 'Luxury, of course, in the highest degree. Every modern convenience. Everything, indeed, that the discerning traveller could possibly require. Elegance rather than grandeur. Comfort rather than opulence. You follow my drift?'

'Indeed I do, sir. It's just the objective with which I could most readily sympathize.'

'Good.' Thornton smiled. 'We have an option on a site in Russell Square. How would you like to design something for us in such a location?'

'Very much. It goes without saying. I'd be honoured.'

'I should tell you that you're not the only architect we've approached. We've also asked Mewès & Davis to submit a design.'

With the Ritz to their credit, Mewès & Davis were the obvious choice. It hardly seemed possible that I could be considered as an alternative. 'An excellent firm,' I stumbled, 'with the highest credentials.'

'Who appeal to some more conservative members of the board,' said Thornton. 'But as I told you, young man, I favour an element of novelty. That is what took my eye about Clouds Frome. *Your* work. Nobody else's.'

It can happen sometimes that one architect's style and his alone will satisfy a client. Then matters of reputation became irrelevant. For me to be such an architect and Ashley Thornton such a client was a stroke of the most amazing good fortune. No matter what his board thought, his expression implied, he would make the final decision. He was giving me a chance I would have been a fool to ignore. 'I believe I'm equal to the task, sir. It's a challenge I'd be proud to accept.' I found myself on my feet, shaking him by the hand.

'I'd like to have preliminary sketches by the end of the month. Do you think you can manage that?'

'I'm sure I can.'

'Splendid. Our head of planning can give you all the necessary details. I'll have him see you now.'

We moved towards the door, delectable possibilities multiplying in my head. A large hotel in the middle of Bloomsbury. A client requiring only the best who was also an admirer of my work. Space in which to express myself and the money with which to do it. The Hotel Thornton: its entrance, its façade, its proportions already forming in my imagination. For its architect, celebrity, wealth, even glory. The potential was limitless, the attraction irresistible.

Half an hour later, I was striding east along Piccadilly, rehearsing the pleasures of telling Imry what a prize had just fallen into our lap. Suddenly, I pulled up sharply, so sharply that somebody behind collided with me. I should have apologized, but all I did was stare dumbly as they grumbled and glowered. I felt, for the moment, incapable of speech. It was as if a cloud had blotted out the sun. A realization had come to me with ghastly force, more ghastly still because I had forgotten it till then, forgotten what could not possibly be accomplished if Thornton's proposal were to become a reality.

I sought refuge in one of the arcades leading to Jermyn Street and there, leaning against an art dealer's window, I struggled to collect my thoughts. Even if Thornton was the most broad-minded of men, his fellow-directors were unlikely to be. And, besides, I could not design a London hotel from a bolt-hole in Paris, far less the other side of the world. It was completely out of the question. I was a few days away from transforming my life and Consuela's with it. I had no business accepting Thornton's offer or dreaming of the fame and fortune it might lead to, for they could not be mine if my vows to Consuela were to be honoured. The only course open to me was to return at once to Thornton's office and to withdraw from the affair as swiftly and gracefully as possible.

I walked slowly down the arcade and reached its end. Right lay the direction I should have taken, but I turned left and quickened my pace. Jermyn Street was empty in the oven-hot air and I was walking fast, though not fast enough for my peace of mind. I was not sweating. I did not even feel warm. Something cold and hard and ruthless had formed within me, something I could neither admit nor defeat. And I hurried on, surrendering to its grip.

Imry opened a bottle of champagne when he heard the news. He knew, as did I, that a hotel such as Thornton envisaged would be the making of our partnership. We took a cab to Russell Square and sat on a bench in the gardens forming its centre, smoking celebratory cigars and surveying the block of buildings which our client had acquired.

'How did you pull this off, Geoff?' said Imry with a grin. 'It's the chance of a lifetime.'

'He'd seen the piece in *The Builder* about Clouds Frome.'

'But an hotel? I'd have expected him to look no further than Mewès & Davis. Or Fitzroy Doll.'

'He wants something different. Something original.'

'Then let him have it, I say. Any idea what you'll suggest?'

The afternoon sun was dazzling, the pigeons on the grass about us torpid in the heat. Shafts of brilliance seemed to invade the square from all angles and it was this perhaps – this scorching purity of light – that planted the concept in my mind.

'Simplicity, Imry, that's the key. Steel frame, I think, to maximize daylight. Stone-faced to give it weight and authority. A Classical frontage, blending happily with its surroundings. Inside, all the richness of detail the patrons would expect, but no baroque gloom or palm court undergrowth. Light and space. The apogee of luxury – with room to breathe.' I turned to look at him. 'What do you think?'

He was still grinning. 'I think it sounds wonderful.'

'I'll need your help, of course. Elevations, projections, floor plans, artist's impressions. We need to present Thornton with a complete set of proposals by the end of the month.'

'Then I suggest we knuckle down. Some midnight oil needs to be burned. You'll cancel your weekend at Clouds Frome, I take it? We can work through—'

'No!' I interrupted. 'I have to go to Clouds Frome.'

'But surely—'

'Don't try to dissuade me, Imry. You'll be wasting your breath. I must be there, take it from me.'

'Some problem I don't know about, old chap?'

'You could say that.'

'If I can offer any advice – help in any way—'

'Thanks, but nobody can help me with this. It's something I have to deal with alone. When I get back, I'll be able to give the Thornton project my undivided attention. Until then . . .'

'Yes?'

'Until then, Imry, wish me luck.'

My shame deepens as my tale progresses. How could I have done it? How could I have turned my back on all the hopes and dreams I had shared with Consuela? She had offered to give up everything for me and this was her reward. To be thrown over.

Abandoned. Betrayed. And for what? Not for the sake of duty or moral scruple, but because of greed, because of my selfish desire to be thought and acclaimed a famous architect. A pile of stones in a London square. A cairn to spurious immortality. That was all. Something the younger version of myself I hardly recognize craved more than the love and loyalty of a beautiful woman. And what he craved he was to have, measured in rubble, brick-dust and hollow applause. He did not pause to count the cost. He did not consider for one moment the repercussions his treachery would have. He was young, vain, cruel and foolish. And he was something else as well. He was a man I despise. He was what I once was, the one thing I can never escape. And his are the debts I am still paying. To this very day. Out of self-loathing comes candour. I shall not spare myself. I shall not try to soften the shameful record of my conduct from that moment on. I tried to convince myself I was only doing what was right and sensible, ending an impossible dalliance, extricating Consuela from an unsustainable future. But that was a lie and I knew it. The truth was that I had decided to disregard her needs, her ambitions and her hopes in order to pursue my own. The truth was that I had decided to betray her.

'Do you know the worst of it, Imry?' I said, as we stood in the doorway of Sunnylea that Saturday afternoon last October.

'You think she may be guilty after all.'

'Yes.'

'And you think that makes you guilty too.'

'Well it does, doesn't it? If I'd not treated her so despicably. If I'd not thrown her over for the sake of a juicy commission. If I'd not soured her whole life just to advance my paltry career.'

'Then twelve years on she might not have tried to murder her husband?'

'That's it, isn't it? That's the whole point. That's what I can't put out of my mind.' I looked at him directly. 'You remember that summer's day we sat in Russell Square, puffing on our cigars, gazing avariciously at the spot where the Thornton was to be built?'

'Of course.'

'If I'd told you then why I was going to Clouds Frome that weekend – what I meant to do there – what would you have said?'

'It's an easy question to answer now, old chap. Now we know what became of the Thornton and of the lady you abandoned in order to build it.'

'And of my marriage,' I countered. 'And of *your* health.'

'Yes. All of those things, waiting to ambush a pair of swell-headed young men. But we didn't know any of it then, did we? We didn't know what was lying in wait for us.'

'So what would you have said, without the benefit of hindsight?'

Imry gazed past me into the middle distance. 'I don't know, Geoff.' Then he looked back at me and smiled. 'And we'll never know, will we? It's too late to find out.'

CHAPTER

FOUR

Friday 14 July 1911 was, like so many days that summer, one of unremitting heat. London was a furnace and to quit it for the weekend was in some ways a relief. But the four-and-a-half-hour train journey to Hereford also gave me unwanted leisure in which to consider what awaited me there. In my pocket I carried the gold-edged invitation to Victor's house-warming, copperplate sepia on a cream ground with a pen-and-ink study of the Clouds Frome frontage at its head. *Mr and Mrs Victor Caswell request the pleasure* . . . It was as much as I could do not to tear the card into shreds and cast them from the window. Clouds Frome was my creation and this was the first time I was to pass a night beneath its roof. But it was also likely to be the last time. Whatever the outcome of my visit, it was hard to imagine that I could ever return.

I reached Stoke Edith, the little country station a few miles short of Hereford which was the nearest stop to Clouds Frome, around two o'clock, and set off to walk the rest of the way along the lanes. The locality seemed stunned and breathless, the orchards and fields sapped of colour. I found myself wishing it could have been dark or cold or wet, anything rather than this azure-skied perfection which only deepened the shame I felt at my intentions.

A half-hour tramp took me into the wooded hills and fields above the flood-plain of the Lugg. Even with the height I had gained, however, there was no relief from the heat; Hereford and

71

the distant horizon waved like wheat in the stupefying haze. Then, as I rounded Backbury Hill and began to descend towards the village of Mordiford, Clouds Frome itself came into view.

To see a house that is elegant in its own right as well as appropriate to its surroundings is always a pleasure. To see it and know one owns it adds pride to that pleasure. But to see it and know one built it – designed it, crafted it, shaped it in every particular – is a unique joy, a deep and abiding source of satisfaction. So it was for me that day, when I saw Clouds Frome, newly finished and not yet mellowed by time and weather, but already sure of itself and its setting, already displaying the qualities I had striven to bestow upon it.

I set my bag down by the hedge, leaned against a field-gate and lit a cigarette. As I lingered there, smoking it through, I let the shape of the house – its sun-etched image of roofs and gables – imprint itself on my mind. The curving drive; the orchard awash with blossom; the wooded hilltop behind: these were the frame, these were the context, of the house I had brought into being. And the walls; the windows; the high chimneys; the sunlight flashing on the tall panes of the swelling bay: these were my own, these were the products of my hand and brain.

Fifty yards down the road, I came to the entrance and turned in. The pillars on either side were raw and white, the paint on the name-board so fresh it might only just have dried, the tar macadam on the drive black and unblemished. But all that, I knew, would change. Lichen would mottle the pillars, the paint would fade and peel, pot-holes and weeds would invade the drive. Where would I be, I wondered, and what would I be doing when age and decay made their first inroads in all this proud immaturity?

I started up the drive slowly, savouring the leisurely pace of my approach. The beech trees that would one day make a leafy avenue of the route were mere staked saplings now, offering no obstruction to my view of the house, and the pillars and beams of the pergola stretching out on its flagstoned causeway above the orchard were bare of the wisteria that would one day swathe them. Workmen were active amongst them, however, fixing flower-baskets and what looked like fairy-lights to the undersides of the beams. Preparations for the house-warming were evidently well advanced.

I rounded the curve in the drive and gained my first view of the front of the house. How strange it was to have no mundane business to conduct there, no problem so simple as plumbing or damp-coursing to solve. Would that I had, I could not help thinking. Would that I had a dozen recalcitrant stonemasons to face rather than the one person I was bound now to betray.

I must have been seen from the house, for as I moved across the courtyard towards the arched porchway, the oaken door opened and Danby, the butler, smiled out at me in greeting.

'Good afternoon, Mr Staddon. It's a pleasure to see you.'

'Hello, Danby. How are you?'

'Very well, thank you, sir. Let me take your bag. Gleasure will deliver it to your room.' A footman appeared behind him: tall and well built with sleeked-down black hair, a squarish jaw and strangely mournful eyes. When he took my bag from Danby, it was obvious that it seemed much lighter to him than it had to us. 'We've put you in the orchard suite, sir,' Danby continued. 'I do hope that meets with your approval.'

'Couldn't be better. Have you many guests staying?'

'Other than Mr Caswell's family, just you and Major Turnbull, sir.'

My heart sank. The odious but perceptive Turnbull was somebody I had no wish to meet again.

'Mrs Caswell is in the drawing-room at present, sir. I'm sure she'd be delighted to see you. Some tea, perhaps?'

'Er . . . no thank you.' Suddenly, my mind was alive with unfounded suspicions. Even the attentive Danby could seem guilty of sarcasm if his every word was analysed. 'I think I'll go up to my room first.' I fanned myself with my hat. 'Hot, isn't it?'

'Yes, sir. Uncommonly.'

Consuela must have known I had arrived and must have thought it odd I did not immediately join her in the drawing-room, but she could hardly have guessed the reason. I needed time to gather my wits and prepare what I would say to her. I washed the grime of the journey from my face, unpacked and changed into blazer and flannels. In the mirror, as I struggled to arrange my cravat with suddenly disobedient fingers, I could see reflected a furtive cast to my features that I had never seen there before. Would Consuela see it as well? I could only pray she would not.

I left the orchard suite with a curious sense of remoteness, following my steps along the landing as if they were those of another man. To my left, internal windows gave me glimpses of the hall below, sunlight flooding across the polished wood and dragon-patterned rugs. Everything I had planned had come to pass in this house – solidity, comfort, novelty, the satisfying fall of golden light on well-pointed stonework – yet much more I had not planned meant I could take no pleasure from my success.

I descended the stairs – feeling the waxed smoothness of the banister rail beneath my palm, noting how my view of the hall expanded with each of the quarter-landings – then turned towards the drawing-room. The double doors were open. For coolness, I wondered, or for warning of approach?

She was sitting on a sofa near the windows that gave on to the ornamental garden. The windows were open, but no breath of air entered, only the low hum of a bee from a trailing loop of honeysuckle; only stillness and a dust-moted wedge of sunlight that seemed to stand like a barrier between us, blurring and confusing the image of her that reached me. Her dress was of cream and gold, elegant yet insubstantial. Her hair was drawn up and no string of pearls compromised the slender perfection of her neck, but the lozenge-shaped brooch was in its normal place; I saw it glint in the sun as she leaned forward and slipped the book she had been reading beneath a cushion.

'Is all well, Geoffrey?'

'Of course. What makes you ask?'

'The way you stand there. So stern and silent.'

I hurried across the room and took her hand. Now would have been the moment. Now, before resolution could falter or delay compound the offence, I should have told her what I had decided. But her delicate fingers were trembling, her dark eyes were roving my face in search of reassurance. And she was so very, very beautiful. I sat down on the edge of the sofa and kissed her, knowing as I did so that once I had told her I would never again feel her full lips yielding against my own, never again enjoy all that was still mine for the asking.

'*Querido Geoffrey*. This is the beginning of the end.'

'What?' I flushed, then saw in her open, trusting face that I had misunderstood.

'We can escape now,' she said with a smile. 'There is nothing left to wait for.'

'No. There isn't.'

'So, when shall we leave?'

'As soon . . . Well . . .'

'I have an idea how to manage it.'

'You do?'

74

'It must be when Victor is occupied, when he is unable to interfere, when he has no way of knowing where I am or what I am doing.'

'Yes, of course.'

'Next Tuesday there will be such an opportunity. Victor is—' She broke off and drew away from me. 'We will speak later.' Then she nodded towards the door.

I had heard nothing, but, as I looked round, there was a laugh from the direction of the hall that sounded horribly familiar and, a second later, Victor entered alongside Major Royston Turnbull. The sight of them made me flinch: Victor in tweeds, his broad grin and bristling moustache composing a gash across his face; Turnbull in a loose-fitting linen suit, cigar distorting his mouth into a leer.

'Staddon!' Victor exclaimed. 'You got here, then.'

I rose and shook his hand. 'It was kind of you to invite me.'

'Not at all, not at all.'

Turnbull inclined his head in greeting. 'Pleasure to meet you again, Staddon.'

'And you, Major.'

'Already monopolizing the ravishing Consuela's company, I see.'

'I wouldn't say that.'

'Pay Royston no heed,' said Victor. 'His style of humour's not to everyone's taste.' He laughed, but nobody joined in. Victor seemed in an unusually good mood; perhaps the prospect of a party was bringing out the best in him, though I could not help doubting it. 'You must take a look at the ornamental garden, Staddon. It's a picture, isn't it, Royston?'

'Indeed. One might say that the external charms of Clouds Frome are almost the equal of those within it.' Turnbull's eyes met mine with a mirthless sparkle.

'I didn't think it could look so good in its first year,' said Victor, 'but Banyard's excelled himself. Come and admire his handiwork, Staddon.'

'Er . . . I'd be delighted to.'

'Consuela will excuse us. Won't you, my dear?'

'Yes,' came her voice, seemingly from a distance far beyond the bounds of the room. 'Of course.'

'I'm very pleased with the house, Staddon, really I am. It has everything you promised. Character. Elegance. Comfort. And

75

something else. Panache, you might say. Yes, that's it. If a house can have panache, then Clouds Frome has it in abundance. My neighbours admire it. My friends covet it. You've done a fine job, a damned fine job.'

We were walking the length of the pergola, glancing back at the ornamental garden and the house as we went. Victor was in a declamatory frame of mind, waving his boater at arm's length as he spoke, smiling and patting my shoulder at intervals. On my other side walked Turnbull, thumbs wedged in waistcoat pockets, head back and breathing deeply, as if sampling what little fresh air could penetrate the haze of smoke from his cigar.

'And my wife likes it. That's probably your most remarkable achievement, Staddon. Consuela can be pretty damned cool about a lot of things, I don't mind admitting. Found Hereford stuffy and boring after Rio, I dare say. But where Clouds Frome is concerned, it's a different matter. Becomes quite, well, quite animated. Isn't that right, Royston?'

'Indeed it is.'

Was it the house that had stirred Consuela – or its architect? Was Victor paying me a compliment – or giving notice that he had my measure? I did not know and all I could do, as we strolled on, each affecting amiability, was nod dumbly and grin appreciatively.

'I shall be happy here, Staddon, not a doubt of it. *We* shall be happy, if it comes to it – Consuela and I. Being mistress of Clouds Frome will bring her out of herself. You just see if it doesn't. And don't think you won't have the chance to, because I hope you'll always feel able to call and see us. As Clouds Frome's creator, you'll be assured of a permanent welcome.'

We reached the end of the pergola and slowly circled the statue of a wood-nymph set up on the flagstoned platform above the orchard. Still nothing could stem the flow of Victor's words, or rid me of the conviction that Turnbull's eyes, shaded by the brim of his panama, were trained upon me.

'It should be a splendid evening. Should be damned splendid, considering what it's cost me.' He laughed. 'But what does money matter at a time like this, eh? A beautiful wife and a beautiful house. I'll see them both in all their glory tonight.'

Dusk was beginning to settle upon Clouds Frome when I saw from the window of my room the first guests' motor-cars moving up the drive. The evening was destined to be magnificent, to judge by the pink hue already tinging the sky. Down in the ornamental garden, a swarm of gnats hovered over the surface of the lily pond and water pattered soothingly round the stone cherubim of the fountain. The air was sweet and sultry, afloat with the mingled scent of a dozen flowers and shrubs. It should have been – for some perhaps it was – an hour snatched from paradise. It should have been unblemished, the rose for once without a thorn. Instead, my soul rebelled at what it sensed. This was wrong, this was false in every way. Amidst all the finery, all the gaiety, all the perfection of what would follow, I would carry my own midwinter secret.

I crossed to the mirror and checked the straightness of my tie, then lifted the carnation from its bowl of water and secured it in my button-hole. It was time to answer the call of the music I could hear from the hall, time to plaster a smile to my face and join the grinning throng.

The hall was bedecked with flowers; red and white roses, chrysanthemums, dahlias, lilies and magnolias, all crystal-vased and swathed in fern. The French windows stood open to the aromas of the terrace and, in the corner of the room, a string quartet had embarked on a tuneful programme. About half the expected fifty guests had arrived and were separating into eagerly conversant knots by windows and side-tables. I noticed Gleasure among those circulating with tray-loads of champagne and canapes; most of the other waiters I took to be hired specially for the occasion. Danby stood by the door, announcing new arrivals, whilst Victor was holding court by the fireplace, with Consuela at his elbow.

Of her beauty nobody present could have been unaware. Her gown was of shot-silk blue, minimally decorated with lace and tulle. She wore a circlet of pearls in her hair and a diamond necklace about her throat. Her foreign blood seemed exaggerated, her exoticism accentuated, by her costume and its setting. And she was nervous. I could see the rapid rise and fall of her bosom, the writhings of her gloved fingers round the stem of her fan, the dartings of her dark eyes about the room. When her gaze met mine, there was the faintest of smiles, the briefest of yearning looks, then she turned back dutifully to her husband's friends.

The Caswell family had turned out in strength. Old Mrs Caswell was installed on a curved sofa in the bay window, beaming contentedly around the room. Mortimer was beside her, sour-faced and evidently out of sympathy with this and every other form of merry-making. Hermione, meanwhile, was laughing uproariously at the centre of a particularly noisy group near the dining-room doors. Marjorie was with the Petos, smiling and bobbing diplomatically; so far as I could judge, Grenville Peto's grudge against Victor had evaporated with the champagne bubbles. Of Major Turnbull there was no sign and, strangely, I found this more disturbing than the sight of him at centre stage.

It was whilst I was looking around for Turnbull that a portly little man with a bald head, wire-framed spectacles and a puffy look of perpetual affability tapped me on the elbow. 'You must be young Mr Staddon,' he said, grinning broadly.

'Why, yes. I don't believe—'

'Quarton. Arthur Quarton. Mr Caswell's solicitor.'

'Of course.' We had corresponded several times regarding Clouds Frome and had spoken at least once by telephone. 'Delighted to meet you, Mr Quarton.' We shook hands.

'A splendid occasion, don't you think?'

'Er . . . yes. Yes, indeed.'

'So good at last to see Victor come into his own, so to speak.'

'I'm not sure I . . .'

'Excuse me. What I mean is that, as the late Mr George Caswell's adviser, I know how pleased he would have been to see his son installed here with the fruits of his success.'

'I suppose he would, Mr Quarton. But wasn't it he who sent Victor to South America in the first place?'

'Yes.'

'Why was that exactly?'

The smile did not leave Quarton's face, but a cautious frown arrived to crumple it still further. 'Boys will be boys,' he said. 'The important thing is to reflect how well it's turned out. This house, for instance. You must be proud of what you've achieved here.'

'Yes, I am.'

'And Mrs Caswell, of course. Victor's finest acquisition on his travels.' My spirit rebelled at his description. He might have been speaking of the centre-piece of an ethnographic collection. Perhaps, for that matter, he was. 'A bewitching creature, don't you think?'

Quarton nodded towards Consuela and I felt myself turn to follow his gaze. There she still stood by her husband's side, eyes lowered, the rays of the setting sun glinting on her necklace and

78

shimmering about the folds of her dress. Bewitching? Yes. Truly she was, too bewitching altogether, for her own good and for mine.

The hall filled, with Major Turnbull among the late-comers. The champagne flowed. The gaiety proceeded. Faces grew red and voices hoarse. The candles were lit. Victor made a brief speech. Mr Tuder Hereford of Sufton, his most distinguished neighbour, replied on behalf of the guests. Supper was served: pigeon pie, ox tongues, poached salmon and lobster. Happy to find myself at a table where I knew nobody, I could only marvel at my fellow-guests' appetites – for gossip as well as food. There was a bleak undercurrent of envy which I could have foreseen but which surprised me nonetheless. What right, some tones of voice and gists of remark implied, had the black sheep of the Caswell family to return so wealthy from his exile, so sure of himself, so accommodating – and so well married?

It was from one such outspoken source that I learned of a forthcoming event in Hereford: the visit of the German Automobile Club, their party led by Prince Henry of Prussia, brother of the Kaiser. They were to lunch at the Mitre Hotel and among those joining them would be Victor. The date of their visit: Tuesday 18 July. This was surely the opportunity for escape to which Consuela had referred, though what she had in mind I could not guess.

Nor did I seem likely to find out that evening. Try as I might, it had proved impossible to exchange more with her than the odd highly public word. In the end, I slipped away and went out on to the terrace to smoke a cigarette in the hope that it would calm my nerves.

The night was as perfect as the day: stars scattered like dusted silver across the sky; the heady scent of jasmine wafting up from the garden; and an owl hooting somewhere beyond the orchard. I stood near the brightly lit windows and gazed in at the banquet. Consuela's table was closer to me now than when I had been in the same room. Victor was beside her, conversing intently with Mr Tuder Hereford. Consuela herself was exchanging pleasantries with a lady I took to be Mrs Tuder Hereford. It was clear to me from Consuela's strained and absent expression that she wished devoutly to be elsewhere, that her role as Victor's obedient and courteous wife was one she could not sustain much longer. She looked unbearably beautiful, irresistibly desirable.

And she was relying on me. She was trusting me absolutely. In that instant – but only for that instant – I determined that she should not trust in vain.

'What are you going to do, Staddon?'

It was Turnbull's voice, raised hardly above a whisper. When I swung round, I found he was standing disconcertingly close to me, grinning in that cocksure way of his that defied one to accuse him of sneering. 'I . . . beg your pardon?'

'Confoundedly stuffy in there, wasn't it? Don't blame you for seeking a breath of air. Sorry if I startled you.'

'You didn't.'

'I was simply wondering. With Clouds Frome finished, what will you do next?'

'Accept another commission, Major. I am offered them from time to time, you know.'

'I'm sure you are. Still, it's an uncertain occupation, isn't it? Architecture.'

'No less certain than most.'

'Reliant on reputation, I should have thought. Word of mouth. What gets round about a fellow. That sort of thing.'

'You're probably right.'

'Still, with all you've done here, I don't suppose you'll go short of work. Grape?' He held out his hand, from which dangled a small bunch of red grapes.

'No thank you.'

He picked one for himself, popped it into his mouth and nodded towards the window. 'Been enjoying yourself this evening?'

'How could I not? The hospitality's been lavish.'

'Victor hasn't stinted us, certainly. And even Consuela seems in a generous mood.' He spat some pips into the shrubbery and grinned more broadly still. 'At least as far as *décolletage* is concerned.'

Turnbull was trying to goad me. That much was clear. But on whose behalf? His own – or Victor's? Until I knew, it was vital I should not let myself be riled. 'Your remark seems in poor taste to me, Major.'

'Really? You ought to loosen your stays, Staddon. Or perhaps you'd like to loosen somebody else's.'

I took a deep breath. 'At the moment, I think I'd just like to go indoors.'

'Dark skin. Yielding flesh.' His eyes had not left mine for an instant. In them all the warmth of his tone was absent, all the breadth of his smile squeezed to nothing. 'Damn fine, these grapes. Are you sure you won't have one?'

He held out his hand, stretching it deliberately across my route to the French windows. He was daring me to brush past him, tempting me to give way to petulance and so reveal that his darts had found their mark. 'Quite sure,' I said, as levelly as I could. 'Keep them for yourself. And mind you don't choke on the pips.'

The grin vanished. The arm withdrew. He said nothing, but I was sure he watched me, all the way, as I walked back into the house.

Saturday, I had been informed, was to witness a cricket match in Mordiford between the village side and the Caswell & Co. works team. The match had been arranged at Victor's instigation as part of the Clouds Frome celebrations. As the only sportsman of the family, he was to captain Caswell & Co. Mortimer and the ladies would watch safely from the boundary's edge. Victor had also supplied a trophy for the winners – a silver cider-costrel – which he hoped would be annually contested. All in all, he seemed to be doing his level best to transform himself into the most traditional and generous of rural landowners.

The heat wave was unbroken and the match was due to start at eleven o'clock. I breakfasted late, with Turnbull, Hermione and Marjorie. Victor was already at the ground, whilst Consuela was reported to be keeping to her bed with a headache. In the circumstances, I could offer no plausible objection to accompanying them all into the village straight afterwards. As we were leaving, Lizzie managed to pass me a note from her mistress, which I buried deep in a pocket pending an opportunity to study it without interruption.

Such an opportunity did not arise until the match had started. It was played on a pleasantly situated ground fringed by elms, with a pink and white marquee hired by Victor serving as a pavilion. Victor won the toss and elected to bat. The Mordiford team looked as muscular and inexpert as might have been expected, but the Caswells appeared to find the contest enthralling, with Hermione shrieking out advice and encouragement to the batsmen. Turnbull slumped into a deck-chair, pulled his hat over his face and lapsed into a torpor for which I was grateful. It left me free to find a chair on the least populated side of the ground and open Consuela's note.

Querido Geoffrey, it read. *I have pleaded a headache to avoid attending the cricket match. Everyone else will be there, as well as most of the staff. Victor has recruited nearly all of them to play, cheer or serve lunch. I am sure nobody would notice if you slipped away. We must talk and make our plans. Do not fail me. Your loving Consuela.*

She was right, of course. We had to talk and the cricket match gave us the best chance of doing so we were likely to have. Strangely, however, I felt reluctant to do as she suggested. It was not that I dreaded telling her why her hopes of escape were to be dashed. Rather I suspected that, when it came to the point, I simply would not be able to tell her. This, more than anything, made me cling to delay like a drowning man to a raft.

Caswell & Co. lost a wicket, which brought Victor to the crease. For a man who had allegedly not held a bat in years he made a remarkably fluent start, playing a succession of flourishing drives. He cut an irritatingly handsome figure in his sparkling whites and striped cap and I found myself resenting the applause he attracted. I had just begun to hope that the fastest of the Mordiford bowlers might dig one in short at him when I caught sight of young Spencer Caswell shuffling towards me round the boundary. He was smartly turned out in knickerbocker suit and straw boater, but wore an expression of studied moroseness.

When he saw me, he stopped and stared for an instant, then said, 'Hello,' in a tone that seemed to blend equal measures of suspicion and indifference.

'Hello, young fellow. Are you enjoying the cricket?'

He glanced round at the game, watched Victor call his partner for a sharp single, then said, 'No.'

'But why not? Your uncle's doing so well.'

'They're letting him. Anyway, cricket's just a waste of time.' As I absorbed the lack of boyishness in these remarks, it occurred to me that I had never seen Spencer larking about or laughing, never behaving as children were supposed to. There was something disturbingly mature, almost cynical, about his character. That and his blank, set face, from which a pair of small piercing eyes stared out, seeming hardly ever to blink, created an impression of cold, hard aloofness.

'They tell me you're going to Harrow next year.'

'Yes. I am.'

'Well, they'll expect you to play cricket there. And Lord knows what other sports besides.'

'I don't care.'

'Tell me that when you're lying under a scrum on the rugger pitch one freezing winter's afternoon.'

But my light-heartedness was wasted on him. A smile did not even flicker about his pinched little mouth. 'I shan't care whatever they do to me. If anybody hurts me, I'll pay them back.'

'Will you, though?'

'Oh, yes. When I'm a man, I'll pay back everybody who ever hurt me.'

With that, he walked behind my chair and headed on round the boundary. I felt no inclination to call him back, was glad indeed to have to say no more to him. As I looked back at the cricket, a mighty shout went up against Victor for lbw. It was rejected. And the umpire who rejected it was none other, I realized, than Banyard, the Clouds Frome gardener. Perhaps Spencer was right after all.

I showed myself briefly in the marquee for lunch – cold chicken and yet more champagne, Victor toasting his undefeated half-century – then slipped away, hoping to discover on the solitary walk back to Clouds Frome enough resolution to show Consuela the honesty that was the least she deserved of me.

The house was enveloped in a silence that the heat seemed to render absolute. Almost everybody was engaged in some capacity at the match and I was confident of finding Consuela alone. There would never be, I knew, a better time to tell her what I had decided.

She was not in any of the reception rooms and there was no sign of her in the garden. Nor was there anybody to ask where she was. Danby, Gleasure and the maids were all catering for the lunching cricketers. Cook was probably on the premises, but I had no wish to disturb her. As for Lizzie, she seemed to have vanished.

When I tapped on the door of the master bedroom, it occurred to me that I had never been inside since it had been furnished. It enjoyed the finest prospect of any room in the house, with its broad bay-window looking out over garden and orchard. The ceiling was high and the fireplace vast. My intention had been for the design to combine privacy with pride, the intimacy of the bedchamber with the grandeur of possession. Many times since I had regretted devising the effect, regretted and resented all that it implied about Victor's ownership of his wife as well as his house.

'Who's there?' Consuela answered the knock softly, as if from a great distance.

'It's me.'

'Come in.'

The bedroom itself was empty, a vacant arena of granular, suspended sunlight. The door to Consuela's dressing-room stood open and I could see her beyond it, sitting by a mirror, brushing her long dark hair. She had just dried it, I thought, for it glistened damply as the brush swept through its strands. She wore a silk *peignoir* of some shade between pink and peach. It shimmered faintly as she turned to look at me.

'I'd hoped you would come sooner.'

'It wasn't easy to leave unobserved.' I moved into the centre of the room, feeling the hint of a breeze from the open windows to my right, letting my vision absorb the details of the furnishings: the wedding photograph on the mantelpiece, the jaguar-skin hearth-rug, the wide and canopied double bed. 'Are we alone?'

'Quite.' She set down the brush, rose from her seat and stepped into the room. 'I sent Lizzie to see her family. They have much to discuss.'

'Of course.'

'As do we.' She walked straight up to me and we embraced. It seemed so natural, so obvious, to find her in my arms, her lips brushing against mine, her body soft and inviting beneath the *peignoir*. 'You have heard Victor is to lunch with the Kaiser's brother on Tuesday?'

'Yes.'

'That is my opportunity to escape.' She kissed me and drew still closer. The sun was hot on my back, Consuela's flesh cool to my touch. In her the anticipation of liberty had stoked a reckless passion. In me something I would like to pretend was not mere lust unveiled its temptation. 'We shall be free, Geoffrey, free to live as we please.'

I should not have done it, should not have enacted that worst of all lies, there and then, in the bedroom I had designed for her husband. But I did. It was too easy, too potent, too delicious not to. Her pliant limbs wrapped about me. Her fluttering, clutching excitement. Her every secret mine. And the sheer carnal pleasure of violation. Her body, her trust and her marriage. All were abused, all deceived, by our frantic coupling across the canopied bed at Clouds Frome that breathless afternoon thirteen long years ago.

*

'In three days' time,' Consuela murmured as we lay together in a languor of physical contentment, 'we will not have to steal moments like this. We will be together – and at peace.'

It was too late to tell her now, far too late to do anything other than sustain the pretence. 'How do you propose to leave here?' I asked.

'By train. You should return to London on Monday, as Victor expects. On Tuesday he has his luncheon party with Prince Henry at the Mitre Hotel. I shall wait until he sets off for Hereford in the car, then I shall ask Danby to call a cab. I shall say I have suddenly remembered an appointment in Hereford. But I shall ask the driver to take me straight to the station, where I shall board the one o'clock train to London. It's due at Paddington just before six. Will you be there to meet me?'

'Yes.' I inclined my head to look at her, smiled and kissed her lightly on the nose. 'I'll be there.' The lie burned within me as I spoke it, but my talent for deception was intact. In Consuela's eyes as she gazed at me there was not the least shadow of a doubt.

Some minutes passed. I think we may have slept a little. At all events, I closed my eyes. When I opened them, Consuela had slipped from the bed and was walking across the room towards the half-curtained windows. More beautiful naked than in the most flattering finery, she seemed to me then sublimely desirable. I could still, I knew, honour the promises I had made to her. I could still elect to stand by her. And so long as she was near me, as long as I could feast my eyes upon her, I could still pretend that I would.

She shook her head and the black tresses of her hair slid across her shoulders. A shaft of sunlight caught the curve of her breast and stomach, caught and crystallized every pleasure I had ever taken from her.

She glanced back at me and, seeing that I was looking at her, smiled. 'The English are famed for their sense of irony. *Ironia*. I never understood it till now.'

'What do you mean?'

'This house, Geoffrey. Clouds Frome. You built it. And I live in it. But after Tuesday neither of us will ever be able to come here again.'

'Will you miss it?'

'I don't think so. Will you?'

'I can build other houses, Consuela. Dozens of others.'

'Will you build one for us?'

'If you want me to.'

'I think I do. Very much.'

The appeal in her voice seemed to summon me. I rose at its bidding, crossed to where she stood and wrapped her in my arms. She closed her eyes as I kissed her, then let her head fall onto my shoulder. Her hair was warm and fragrant against my cheek, her body smooth and golden where the sunlight fell upon it. A sudden realization of her loveliness swept over me and, with it, renewed desire, a desire so powerful that the future – and what I meant to do in it – dissolved into nothing. Every compartment of my mind, every recess of my imagination, was filled with the need to possess her once more.

Consuela looked up at me and whispered, 'You want me again?'

'I want you always.'

'Then you shall have me. Always.'

Desire and deceit surged within me. I was laughing as I carried her back to the bed and, seconds later, thrust triumphantly into her; laughing with a sound that in my memory resembles nothing but the baying of my own conscience.

There were ten to dinner at Clouds Frome that night: Victor and Consuela; Mortimer and Marjorie; Hermione and old Mrs Caswell; Mr and Mrs Peto; Major Turnbull and I. Naturally, the success of the house-warming and Caswell & Co.'s victory in the cricket match dominated conversation. The two events had filled Victor with an exultant sense of belonging, of restoration to his rightful domain, and his guests responded in kind.

I was seated between Hermione and Mrs Peto. Victor was at our end of the table, with Consuela at the other. There was scant need for me to converse in view of the garrulousness of others, for which I was grateful. The events of the day had left me confused, my resolution gone, my nerves in tatters. If I so much as glanced down the table at Consuela, my mind filled with the images of what we had done in Victor's marriage-bed that very afternoon. And I knew, as Consuela did not, just how wrong it had been. There was nothing for it but to drown my self-reproach in Victor's claret and pray for the end to come swiftly.

But it did not. And, during dessert, I found myself involved in an argument with the Caswell brothers that I should have avoided. Hermione, devouring strawberries with an undiminished appetite, took Mortimer to task for dismissing a member of his workforce. When I caught the man's name – Ivor Doak – I expressed an interest, sorry as I was to think that Doak of all people had fallen on hard times.

'Yes,' Mortimer starkly confirmed. 'I had to get rid of him. Fonder of emptying cider bottles than of filling them.'

'It's appalling,' put in Hermione. 'We owe that man a job if we owe him nothing else.'

'As far as I'm concerned,' said Mortimer, 'we owe him nothing.'

'The Doaks are an ancient Herefordshire family. If Ivor drinks, it's to forget what they've been reduced to.'

'My sister,' said Mortimer, smiling tartly at me, 'is a great believer in charity – usually at my expense.'

'I can't help agreeing with her,' I said. 'Surely it wouldn't hurt to be lenient on poor old Doak. As a former owner of this land—'

'A former *tenant*,' Victor interrupted. 'And a neglectful one at that. You're well rid of him, Mortimer. We're all well rid of him.'

'But what will he do for work now?' I protested.

'Starve or go hang,' snapped Victor. 'Who cares what a man like Ivor Doak does?' His vehemence seemed unnecessary, his scorn disproportionate. I could not understand why he should be so vengeful towards somebody who – so far as I knew – had never done him any harm.

'He needs to leave Hereford,' said Hermione, 'and all the memories it holds for him.'

'To go where?' asked Victor with a sarcastic curl to his mouth.

'Australia. He has a cousin who farms sheep there.'

'What my sister means, Staddon,' said Victor, 'is that Doak's uncle was transported to Western Australia fifty years ago for shooting a gamekeeper and that his progeny are still out there, allegedly eager to welcome and support their kinsman.'

'It happens to be true,' said Hermione. 'And you of all people, Victor, should appreciate the value of making a fresh start in life.'

Victor's face reddened. His voice dropped to a growl. 'If you think an addle-headed comparison like that is going to persuade me to put up Doak's passage-money to Perth—'

'I don't think any such thing! I know you and Mortimer too well to expect any gestures of decency towards somebody who's down on his luck.'

'His *luck*? Is that what you call running his farm into the ground? Is that what you call leaving Mortimer no alternative but to sack him? It's not bad luck that's got Ivor Doak where he is, woman. It's bad blood!'

'What perfect nonsense! All he needs—'

'Excuse me,' I said, leaning forward across the table, sorrow and regret for all I had lately done fastening themselves on the memory of my one encounter with the evicted tenant of Clouds Frome Farm. 'How much would it cost to pay Doak's passage?'

'More than even he could spend on drink,' said Victor.

Hermione ignored the remark. 'About forty pounds. More than he is able to raise. And more, I regret to say, than I can afford to lend him.'

Victor snorted. 'Forty pounds! I ask you.'

Hermione pressed on. 'Three months' wages for Ivor Doak, Mr Staddon, and loose change to my brothers. Yet still they begrudge it.'

'Prudent investment is the essence of good business,' said Mortimer. 'Investment in Ivor Doak would be the height of folly.'

But Hermione was undaunted. 'I'm confident he would repay us as soon as he found his feet.'

There was a dismissive grunt from Victor. Mortimer shook his head and returned to his pineapple. But Hermione glared defiantly round the table, where all other conversation had now ceased. Clumsy, tactless and aimlessly energetic, she had long been the one Caswell I had any regard for, but this, I knew, was not the reason why I warmed to her proposal. Sickened by my own conduct, I needed to prove that I was not as mean and selfish as Hermione's brothers; to prove it to myself and to demonstrate it to others. And so, with Consuela's admiring eyes upon me, I spoke.

'I'll lend Doak forty pounds.'

Victor's spoon clattered into its dish, but I refused to look at him. Instead, I merely smiled across the table at his sister. 'That's exceedingly generous of you, Mr Staddon,' she said. 'As it happens, I can supply half the amount myself.'

'Then I'll supply the balance.'

'You will?'

'Gladly.'

'Splendid! Together then, you and I will do out best to salvage poor Ivor.' She grinned round at her brothers. 'It is such a rare pleasure to find oneself dealing with a true gentleman.'

'You're a fool if you follow my sister's lead in this, Staddon.' The force of Victor's tone obliged me to look at him. To my surprise, he appeared genuinely angry that I should have made such an offer.

'I presume I can be a fool with my own money if I wish.'

'You mean the money I've just paid you.'

'I do have other resources besides the fee for this house.'

'Do you? Do you really?' He eyed me malevolently. 'You'll regret loaning money to Ivor Doak, Staddon. Take it from me, you'll regret it.' He meant what he said. That was clear from the thunderous expression on his face. But whether he meant it as a prediction or a threat was altogether less clear.

As the dispute dissolved and other conversations sprang up round the table, the doubt that Victor's remarks had sown in my mind ran and wriggled about my thoughts. Why did he care whether I gave Doak a helping hand? Why did he resent it so keenly? And why was he so sure, so very sure, that one day I would regret it?

Sunday was for me an ordeal of prolonged inactivity. A late breakfast. A more or less obligatory attendance at Mordiford Church. Luncheon. Then a torpid afternoon of croquet and tennis. Tea on the terrace. And the sun blazing down from a cloudless sky. Any neutral observer of the scene would have concluded that the Caswell family and their guests were passing the sabbath in contented ease.

How my thoughts ranged to and fro as the heavy hours plodded by. Both courses that I was bound to choose between seemed impossible to face. To lose Consuela or to sacrifice fame. Each chalice was poisoned, each decision foredoomed. I watched her serving tea, smiling at Turnbull's witticisms, deferring to her husband, strolling beneath the pergola. I watched her and she, I felt sure, watched me. And still certainty eluded me.

The afternoon gave way to evening. The hour for dinner approached. The party had been reduced to eight by now and its mood had become weary and circumspective. There was no mention of Ivor Doak, no enthusiastic recollection of the cricket match or the house-warming. We were all, I suppose, a little bored with each other's company. But boredom, though it may have appeared to be, was not the explanation for my distracted condition. Whenever I caught Consuela's eye between the epergnes and the candelabra, whenever I heard her soft voice amidst the murmur of conversation, I knew that the moment of decision was drawing ever closer, the moment to which I still felt unequal.

Dinner ended and the ladies made to withdraw. It was then, amidst the exchange of courteous wishes for a restful night, that I saw and spoke to her for the last time. How strange the stilted remarks we uttered seem now, how banal the guarded smiles and cautious glances with which we took our leave of each other.

'I catch an early train tomorrow, Mrs Caswell. Perhaps therefore I can thank you now for your hospitality this weekend.'

'Thank you for coming, Mr Staddon.' Her hand rested briefly in mine. 'I hope we will see you again soon.'

'I hope so too.'

'Goodnight, then.'

'Goodnight, Mrs Caswell.' She moved towards the door. 'And goodbye.'

Just one fleeting look back – the merest glimmer of her eyes that seemed to convey and bestow all her trust in me – and then she was gone.

The gentlemen did not linger long over their port. After one glass, Mortimer took himself off to bed, whereupon Victor proposed a few frames of billiards and Turnbull agreed. I was grateful to leave them to it and walk out into the sultry night.

Clouds Frome had fulfilled my every hope for it. That much was clear as I circled its elegant exterior, outlined against the star-shot sky. And Clouds Frome, with Thornton's commission mine for the taking, might only be the start. But a light burned in the window of the master bedroom, a light to remind me of Consuela's love. For her sake I should have been prepared to endure all and to sacrifice everything. But I could not force myself to feel more deeply than I did. I could not prevent myself longing for the opportunities loyalty to her might deny me. The truth was simple and the less palatable because of it. I did not love her enough.

I returned to the house. All was quiet, save for the crack of cue on ball from the billiards-room. I poured myself a tumblerful of scotch and carried it up to my bedroom. And there I took out a sheet of Victor's headed notepaper, sat at the desk and began to write.

16 July 1911

My dearest Consuela—

90

I began again. How dare I proclaim her as my dearest – or mine at all?

16 July 1911

Consuela,
It is as painful for me to write this as it will be painful for you
to read it. We cannot – we must not – proceed with your
plan. It would not be fair of me to let you sacrifice your good
name—

Once more I abandoned the draft. It was poor and spineless stuff. The least Consuela deserved of me now was the honesty I should have shown her earlier. I swallowed some whisky and nerved myself to tell her the truth. But how could I explain valuing my career more highly than her love? In the end, this brand of truth was worse than any deception. And so, with sincerity vanquished, I committed my weasel-words to the page.

16 July 1911

Consuela,
We cannot proceed with your plan. I have thought about this
very carefully and I have concluded that you were right last
November when you said the sacrifices we would have to
make in order to be together were too great. We have been
foolish and impetuous. I cannot let you destroy your position
in society for my sake. I cannot let you leave Victor to be
with me.
     Do not leave Clouds Frome on Tuesday. Do not come to
London. I know it will be hard at first to carry on with your
life here, but, as time passes, I am sure you will come to
appreciate that it is the best course of action for both of us. I
am sorry, truly sorry, for any disappointment this causes you,
but I am convinced that I am making the right decision.
Geoffrey.

And so it was done. I sealed the letter and finished the whisky, then lay down in search of the rest I did not deserve.

I was awake with the dawn, washing and dressing in haste, consumed with an appalling eagerness to be on my way. The Oxford and London Express was not due at Stoke Edith until just before half past seven, but I intended to be out of the house as early as possible. An hour or more of hungry solitude at the station was preferable to a single unnecessary minute at Clouds Frome once my message had been despatched.

It was five o'clock when I left the orchard suite and ascended to the second floor. I was making for the servants' wing and the room Consuelá had told me was Lizzie's. As lady's maid, she enjoyed a room to herself and I therefore felt safe in slipping the letter beneath her door, together with a note asking her to deliver it to Consuela as soon as possible.

As I neared my destination, however, the universal silence was broken by the faint but unmistakable sound of weeping. I stopped to listen and there was no doubt of it. Lizzie Thaxter – or somebody in her room – was crying. To leave the letter as I had planned seemed inadequate now, in some way insufficient. I knocked as softly as I could on the door. The weeping was abruptly cut off. I knocked again.

'Who's there?' It was Lizzie's voice, faltering and congested.

'Staddon,' I whispered.

There was a rustling beyond the door. Then it opened a few inches and Lizzie peered out at me. She was in her nightdress. Her hair was tousled and her eyes were red, with dark shadows beneath them. She had dried her tears, but could hardly have thought I had failed to hear her sobbing.

'What's wrong?' I said.

'Nothing.'

'I thought—'

'What do you want, Mr Staddon?'

'This letter—' I held out the envelope. 'It's for Consuela.'

She stared at it with an expression that I could have believed for an instant was one of horror. 'For Consuela?'

'Yes. It's very important. And urgent.'

'I'll see she gets it.' She reached out numbly and took it from me.

'Lizzie, are you sure you're all right?'

'Yes, Mr Staddon. Quite sure.' And, so saying, she closed the door.

I stood there in the silent corridor for a minute or so, puzzling over what had occurred. Lizzie was normally cheerful and ebullient. Even her brother's imprisonment had not seemed to depress her unduly. Why she should be sobbing her heart out in secret was beyond me. Clearly, however, she did not wish me to know the reason. And my business with her was concluded. She would deliver the letter to Consuela. I knew I could rely upon her for that. There was not another sound from beyond the door. To remain where I was would soon become dangerously conspicuous. So I turned and crept away.

92

*

Who was he, that selfish, conceited young man who strode down
the drive of Clouds Frome and out along the Stoke Edith road
one brilliant July morning thirteen years ago? What right did he
think he had to trample the dreams of others underfoot in pursuit
of his own? Even now, the answers sear my conscience. If only I
could halt him in his tracks and shake him till he understood the
consequences – every one of them, the great and the small – of
what he had done.

But I cannot. I cannot change or modify a single aspect of the
past I have bequeathed to myself. It is mine and nobody else's.
And so is the guilt that goes with it.

It was warm in the sun as I sat on the deserted platform at
Stoke Edith station, waiting for the train that would bear me back
to London. Another scorching day seemed guaranteed. I was
impatient to set off, but much of my recent anxiety had fallen
away. My course was set now, my boats were burned. I had left a
message for Consuela. I had posted a cheque to Hermione. I had
taken my leave. And now, albeit with an effort, I would set aside
all that Clouds Frome had meant to me. In time, with Thornton's
commission to fill my thoughts, I would forget it altogether.
Consuela's name would never pass my lips, her face never stray
across my memory. For a bad conscience is the best of all
amnesics, proof against every kind of reminder. Except the one
kind fate had reserved for me.

CHAPTER

FIVE

Architectural historians of the years immediately before the Great War will probably dwell, when they consider the landmarks of London, on Webb's east frontage for Buckingham Palace or Burnet's King Edward VII Galleries for the British Museum; Selfridge's department store, perhaps, or Blomfield's elevations for the western side of Piccadilly Circus. These soar obediently above the streets of the capital, waiting and deserving to be admired. Somewhere, in an obscure footnote, it may be mentioned that Ashley Thornton, the hotelier, commissioned the relatively unknown Geoffrey Staddon to build a grand hotel on Russell Square, which, in conception and execution, won many plaudits. On the other hand, it may not. For the Hotel Thornton labours under the profound disadvantage of no longer existing.

How strange it is – and yet how fitting – that the two buildings of which I was most proud were to be denied me: Clouds Frome, because I did not dare to return to it, and the Hotel Thornton, because there was nothing to return to. Exile and nullity seem now to share and shred between them all the hopes and achievements of my youth. And I have no right to complain.

It was all so vastly different when, in the autumn of 1911, I commenced work on the Thornton project and saw, in my mind's eye, no limit to the wealth and renown it might lead to. Consuela – and what I had done to her – was consigned to a locked cellar of my memory. I never heard from her after leaving Clouds Frome. There was no reproachful letter, no anguished telephone call, no outraged visit. I did not hear from Victor either or any member of his family. I was invited to no more weekends, enlisted in no more celebratory events. I was not even sent a Christmas card. And for all of this I was grateful.

The Hotel Thornton consumed my thoughts and energies. It became a forcing-house for my ambition, a vaulting steel-and-stone statement of what I could achieve. And in the process it altered me. The treachery I had shown towards Consuela was the first budding of a shameful ruthlessness. Nothing and nobody, I secretly believed, should be allowed to stand in my way or share the credit for my work. Thus Imry's contributions to my designs were to be suppressed and the builder's suggestions for improvements ignored. The project was to be mine and mine alone. When it was finished, the praise was to be for me and nobody else.

In Ashley Thornton I had found a patron ideally suited to my purposes. Too busy presiding over his existing hotels to interfere much in the construction of a new one, he was nonetheless an enthusiastic advocate of my ideas before his fellow-directors. At first, I was suspicious of him. Later, I came to like and admire him. Later still, I understood him. But understanding, as in most cases, did not come soon enough.

It was at a reception in one of Thornton's other London hotels – the Palatine – that I first met his daughter, Angela, later to become my wife. We argued, as I recall, about the coal miners' strike that was then on, which places the encounter in March 1912. She seemed to me then a woman of firmly feudal opinions, handsome rather than beautiful, but undeniably attractive in her combination of clear-eyed Englishness and feline sensuality. She was twenty-seven years old, vivacious, self-confident and altogether a challenging proposition. I began to cultivate her in the full knowledge of how useful such a connection might be. Before long, however, I realized that a genuine affection was developing between us. Was it ever love? I am not sure. We dignify too many dalliances and unions with that word. Perhaps it is fairer to say that she saw in me an appealing alternative to the empty-headed young men she was generally introduced to and that I saw in her the intelligent and socially accomplished wife I had convinced myself I needed. By the autumn of 1912 we had become engaged, much to Thornton's professed satisfaction. We were married at the village church near his Surrey home on 21 June 1913, with Imry as my best man and a vast gathering of

Thornton's friends, relatives and business associates in attendance.

When I recall the day now, it is as an event I witnessed but did not participate in. The sun shone obligingly. Angela looked more delicately entrancing than I have ever known her to, before or since. Thornton turned the reception into a gaudy and extravagant celebration of his own success. And I? I smiled and spoke my lines and conformed to the image most of the guests had of me: the talented architect whose artistic laxities would soon vanish under the supervision of his wife and the benign influence of his father-in-law.

We honeymooned on the Italian Lakes and returned to 27 Suffolk Terrace, the house Thornton had bought us as a wedding present. There Angela devoted herself to the life of an expensively maintained metropolitan wife: collecting fine furniture and fashionable clothes; cultivating an awesome number of similarly placed wives in Kensington, Knightsbridge and Bayswater; entertaining them and their husbands to dinner at least once a week; organizing bridge parties with equal frequency; and riding every few days in Hyde Park. It did not take me long to understand that in this new life she had acquired for herself I was merely one ingredient, important but not indispensable.

I should never have expected anything else, for Angela's attitude was, after all, only a mirror image of mine. We both had what we wanted: the sort of spouse the world seemed to require of us, one conferring status, companionship, respectability and a sparing allowance of conjugal passion. Almost as if it were part of a pre-determined timetable, Angela became pregnant within three months of our marriage, delivering the grandson her father earnestly desired a few days before our first wedding anniversary in June 1914.

By then the Hotel Thornton was complete. With impeccable timing, my father-in-law was able to announce the birth at the grand opening ceremony. The Princess Royal cut a tape and all present toasted hotel and baby in the same breath. The architectural press had commented favourably on my work and prestigious new commissions could now be expected. I had a son to dandle on my knee and a professional reputation verging on celebrity. I had nothing to complain of and everything to look forward to. All seemed right with the world.

But all, as we now know, was far from right with the world in the summer of 1914. The war, when it came in August, was not the brief and glorious adventure we had been led to expect. And the lives of everyone, even those far from the mud of Flanders, became bogged down in the grinding conflict that followed.

Imry insisted on volunteering for front-line service at the earliest possible opportunity. He also insisted that, as a husband and father, I should stay behind and manage the business. And so I did, faithfully believing the myth that it would all be over by Christmas. It was not, of course, and the start of 1915 saw the first Zeppelin raids over the south coast. I thought little of them. They were mere flea-bites by comparison with the hardships our troops – Imry among them – were enduring in France. By Easter London had come within their range, but still I failed to see what they portended.

On the night of 23 October 1915 a German bomb scored a direct hit on the Hotel Thornton. The structural damage would probably have been reparable but for the fire that immediately followed the explosion. The building was gutted and it is a miracle that no more than seventeen people lost their lives in the conflagration. When I visited Russell Square the following morning, it was to confront the crumbling, smoking shell of what I had spent nearly three years creating. I would not wish the experience on any architect. The months of toil; the drafts and re-drafts; the measurements and projections; the trials and revisions; the disputes and difficulties; the vision and its accomplishment: all laid waste in a night by fire, smoke and water. The sense of futility such a disaster imposes can never be shaken off. The fear that it may happen again corrodes the creative impulse and saps the determination to succeed. Why aim for perfection when it can so easily be snatched away? Why assume that what you build will endure or be remembered?

Worse was to follow, in my case, than the shock of destruction. At the inquest into the seventeen deaths, the coroner uttered some ill-informed remarks about the design of the hotel encouraging the spread of fire, remarks which the press chose to amplify. Suddenly, my name was associated not with a fine hotel but with a scandalous fire-trap. And there was nothing, given the vague nature of the accusations, that I could do to refute them. Thornton boldly promised to re-build after the war and to employ me as architect, but I detected a calculating insincerity in his assurances. The hotel would never be re-built and, even if it were, I would not be its architect. Thornton would be respected for standing by his son-in-law, but everybody would know what he really thought. The good name of Thornton Hotels would be preserved, but that of Geoffrey Staddon, A.R.I.B.A., would be irredeemably sullied.

I suppose it was frustrated rage at the injustice of press reaction to the fire that prompted me to enlist in the Army. Certainly it was not a late flowering of patriotism, given what Imry had told me about the imbecilic conduct of the war. He was invalided out early in 1916, suffering from the cumulative effects of mustard-gas poisoning, and this allowed me to pass what little business we had left into his hands. I obtained a commission in the Royal Engineers and found myself, by the autumn of 1916, not in France as I had anticipated, but in Egypt, applying my architectural training to bridge-building and barrack construction. And there I was to remain for the duration of hostilities, fulfilling a minor and unhazardous role in Allenby's strategy for the defeat of the Turks. I never fired a shot in anger, never took my place in a suicidal advance and never saw an enemy soldier who was not already a prisoner.

I did reach France in the end, but only after the Armistice, as a member of the forces assigned to reconstructing roads and railways and repairing buildings damaged during the long years of bombardment. It was vital work, of course, but irksome. All any of us wanted, once the war was over, was to go home.

My chance to do so came sooner than I had expected and in circumstances more dreadful than any I could have envisaged. Letters from Angela had told me that a virulent strain of influenza was sweeping London, but I thought little of it, even when she reported that Nora, our maid, had fallen ill. Then, early in March, came a letter informing me that our son had caught it and, within hours, a telegram summoning me home urgently. He had developed pneumonia and his life was feared for.

Edward Matthew Staddon. Born 18 June 1914. Died 10 March 1919. 'Suffer the little children to come unto me, and forbid them not: for of such is the kingdom of God.'

Scarcely a week has passed since his death when I have not found my homeward steps leading me to Brompton Cemetery and the sorrowful stone cherub standing above the plaintive inscription. Angela stopped going within a year and excised his name from our conversation at the same time. She removed his photograph from the drawing-room, threw away the last of his toys and took down the framed certificate of his baptism from the

98

nursery wall. I do not blame her. There is no reason why she should wish to join me beside his tiny grave on winter afternoons when the light of all the days, not just one, seems to be failing about me.

I have spoken to him more in death than in life, adjusting my tone and vocabulary as the years have passed to the age he would have attained, telling him secrets I can entrust to nobody else, seeking his advice on problems only he must know I have. Little Edward, so young and blameless, whose large blue eyes seem even now to rest upon me. Did you die for me? I sometimes wonder. Did you suffer on my account?

The expression on Angela's face and the inflexion of her voice, when I reached Suffolk Terrace and she told me he was dead, have never quite been shed with the passage of time. She grew some hard, protective shell that day which I could not hope to penetrate. We never speak of him. We never refer to anything, however obliquely, in which he played a part. And so the grief remains, unassuaged because unexpressed, something each feels deeply and blames the other for without good cause.

I resumed the senior partner's role at Renshaw & Staddon and Imry went into semi-retirement. Angela picked up the threads of her pre-war existence. The idea of re-building the Hotel Thornton was discreetly extinguished. And Edward's memory was left to wither. A brittle form of normality was re-cast about us, offering safety but little comfort in the years that lay ahead.

Then, last September, one unremarkable workaday morning, Angela saw the name of Consuela Caswell in the newspaper and chose to taunt me with it, unaware of what it meant to me. The first crack appeared at that moment, I suppose, the very first hair-line fracture in the life I had been content to lead. Initially it seemed nothing, the faintest of scratches, easily ignored, swiftly forgotten. Then it lengthened and widened and reached out, splitting and dividing, towards the farthest boundaries of my thoughts. And still I sought to disregard it. I read the reports. I examined my conscience. I consulted Imry. I told Edward the whole truth for the first time, standing by his leaf-drifted grave one grey and sombre afternoon. And the answer was always the same. *There is nothing you can do.* It was only what I wanted to hear, of course, only what I needed to believe. But it did not endure. And now I think it could never have sustained me through what was to follow. Now I think that, even if I had not been driven to act as I was, some other prompting would have achieved the same result in the end.

It was the afternoon of Friday 12 October 1923. A week had passed since Consuela's committal for trial. I was in my office, studying Newsom's sketch plans and perspective views for the Whitstable club-house commission, reflecting as I did so how felicitous his touch was becoming in such matters. I could not help resenting his talent, notwithstanding the credit I could claim for bringing him on. Renshaw & Staddon was beginning to rely on Newsom's skill and Vimpany's thoroughness too heavily for my peace of mind. It was high time I shouldered more of the burden, given that Imry's contribution was bound to decline and Newsom might move on to better things within a few years. Perhaps, it occurred to me, an immersion in work would help me shake off my present malaise.

I had just resolved to institute a change of regime along these lines when there was a knock at the door and Reg Vimpany looked into the room.

'There's a young lady to see you, Mr Staddon.'

'A young lady? I've no appointments, Reg. Who is she?'

'A *very* young lady, I should say. Gives her name as Miss Caswell.'

He cannot have missed the startled look on my face. 'Miss Caswell?' I murmured.

'Yes. The strange thing is, she can't be older than my Shirley, yet she's out on her own in the middle of London.'

Shirley Vimpany was twelve, so now there could be no doubt who my visitor was. 'And you say she wants to see me?'

'Insists, Mr Staddon. Positively insists.'

'Then show her in.'

She was smaller than even Reg's description had prepared me to expect. Clad in black laced shoes, grey stockings, navy blue mackintosh and grey cloche hat, she stared up at me with immense and avid seriousness. Her face was round and pale, her mouth compressed, but in her teak-brown eyes I saw at once the flash of her mother's gaze.

'Miss Caswell?'

She waited till Reg had closed the door behind her, then said: 'Are you Mr Geoffrey Staddon?' Her voice was soft but unfaltering, her pronunciation correct in every syllable. If I had

100

heard but not seen her, I am not sure I would have known she was a child at all.

'Yes. I'm Geoffrey Staddon.' I emerged from behind my desk.

'Good afternoon, Mr Staddon.' She pulled off her right glove and extended her hand towards me. 'I am Miss Jacinta Caswell.'

'Pleased to meet you, Miss Caswell.' I smiled and shook her hand. It was ice-cold and minute, engulfed in my own. Suddenly I remembered just how young she must be. 'Does your . . . your father know you're here?'

'No.'

'Well, I—'

'But my mother does.'

'Your mother?'

'Yes. She sent me, Mr Staddon.'

I leaned back against the desk for support and breathed out slowly. Jacinta's expression had not altered. She had followed my every movement with her stern, unflinching gaze. 'I think perhaps you should explain yourself, Miss Caswell.'

'May I sit down?'

'Why, yes, of course.' I pulled a chair round for her.

'May I also have a glass of milk and a biscuit? I have come rather a long way.'

'Milk . . . and a biscuit?'

'Yes please. If . . . if I may.'

Shaking my head in bemusement, I walked past her to the door and opened it. In the outer office, only Reg was maintaining a pretence of occupation. Doris was bent low over her typewriter, whispering animatedly to Kevin, who had craned back in his chair to listen. She looked up at me and flushed instantly. 'A glass of milk, Doris, if you please.' I snapped. 'And some biscuits.'

'Milk, Mr Staddon?'

'For my visitor.'

'Oh . . . I see. Right. Straightaway, Mr Staddon.'

'Thank you.'

I closed the door again and turned back to Jacinta. Only her eyes had moved, following me to and from the door; the sensation of being perpetually observed by her was becoming unnerving.

'How do you come to be in London?' I said, in as matter-of-fact a tone as I could command.

'I am going with my father to stay with his friend, Major Turnbull, in France. We arrived in London yesterday and will be

101

catching the boat-train tomorrow morning. My governess, Miss Roebuck, is coming with us. She took me out for a walk in St James's Park this afternoon and I ran away while she wasn't looking.'

'You ran away?'

'Don't worry, Mr Staddon. She didn't see me. I will say I got lost and wandered about until somebody showed me the way back to the hotel. Nobody will know I came here. That will be our secret.'

She had slipped away from her governess and somehow navigated a path to my office through the labyrinth of central London. That alone was a considerable achievement for a child, but she had also decided how to cover her tracks; she was cunning as well as resourceful. 'Your mother gave you this address?'

'No. I found it in the telephone directory at the hotel last night.'

'But you said your mother told you to come here.'

'She told me to come to you, Mr Staddon, but she didn't tell me how to. She didn't have time to.'

'Why not?'

'They had . . . They were taking her away. It was the last thing she said to me. I haven't seen her since. They haven't allowed me to.'

'Who haven't allowed you to?'

'My father. And Miss Roebuck.' There was a hint in the way she paired the names that it had been as much Miss Roebuck's decision as Victor's. I could not imagine him consulting a mere governess on such a point, but the painstaking precision with which Jacinta spoke seemed to command me to do so.

'When did you last see your mother?'

'Three weeks ago. The day the police searched Clouds Frome and . . . arrested her. Is it right, Mr Staddon, that you built Clouds Frome for my mother?'

'I built it, yes, but not—' I broke off as the door opened and Doris brought in the milk and biscuits. Jacinta took delivery of them solemnly, waited until Doris had gone again, then drank some of the milk and munched her way slowly through one of the biscuits. I looked at her in silence as she ate, wondering just how much anguish and uncertainty she had had to withstand during the three weeks of Consuela's absence. There was nothing to pity in her – none of the childish tearfulness I might have expected – yet a wave of sympathy swept over me as I watched her set down the glass carefully on the edge of my desk and brush the crumbs from her lips with a handkerchief. Then she tilted her head towards me, as if to signal that our conversation might resume.

'What did your mother say about me, Miss Caswell?'

'You may call me Jacinta if you wish.'

'All right. Jacinta. It's a beautiful name.'

'It's Portuguese for hyacinth. My mother speaks Portuguese. She was born in Brazil.'

'I know. Now, what did she say?'

'They only let her speak to me for a few minutes before they took her away. She kissed me and told me to be brave. She said that if she didn't come back I was to run away from Clouds Frome. She said that I was to find you and ask you to help me. Then we had to say goodbye. The police took her away in a motor-car. And I haven't seen her since. But I'm keeping my promise.'

'What promise?'

'I'm being brave. And I've found you. So now you will be able to help me, won't you?'

I looked away. Poor Jacinta, so young and trusting. She had been brave, it was true, but what help could I give her? What did Consuela expect of me? What did she think I would do? I swallowed hard.

'They say she murdered my cousin Rosemary, Mr Staddon. They say she put poison in her tea. But she didn't. It's not true.'

'No. I'm sure it isn't.'

'Of course it isn't. She told me it wasn't. And my mother never tells lies, never.'

I looked back at her and tried to shape a reassuring smile. 'The court will find that out, Jacinta. Your mother will soon be free. Perhaps you should just wait for her to be released.'

'Oh no, Mr Staddon, I can't do that.'

'Why not?'

'Because she won't be released unless we find out who really put poison in Rosemary's tea.'

So that was it. This little girl had resolved to prove her mother innocent. She had bided her time and guarded her tongue. She had calculated that she would need the assistance of an adult to make progress and had awaited her opportunity to contact the only adult her mother had indicated she might trust. And now she sat before me, solemn and expectant, whilst one half of my mind told me her idea was absurd and the other forbade me to disappoint her.

'I have a plan, Mr Staddon. I think it's rather a good plan. Would you like me to tell you what it is?'

'I'm not . . . All right. Tell me.'

'We will be in France for several weeks. I thought, while we were away, that you could go to Hereford and try to find out what really happened. My father wouldn't like you doing that. He would stop you. But if he wasn't there, he couldn't stop you, could he?'

'No. I suppose he couldn't. But what makes you think he'd want to?'

'He doesn't like you, Mr Staddon. I asked him about you and I could tell from what he said that he's frightened of you.'

Jacinta's gaze would not release me. She spoke with such simplicity, such conviction, that none of the reasons for thinking she was confused or mistaken seemed to matter. Naturally, a young girl would believe her mother was innocent, no matter how manifest her guilt. But was that all her determination signified? And why, if she was correct on the point, should Victor be frightened of me?

'I was sure you would agree with my plan, Mr Staddon. Otherwise, my mother would not have sent me to you.'

'I haven't agreed.'

'But you will, won't you?' For the first time, a shadow of uncertainty crossed her features. 'There isn't very much I can do on my own.'

'There isn't very much I can do either.'

'Oh, but there is. You can question Banyard about the weed-killer and Cathel about the letters and Noyce about serving tea. They won't tell me anything. They think I'm just a child. Whenever I ask them about the case, they pat me on the head and tell me to go away and play. But they wouldn't be able to do that to you, would they?'

I smiled. 'No. They wouldn't.'

'My mother didn't receive those letters, Mr Staddon, the letters they say prove she wanted to murder my father. If she had, she would have destroyed them, wouldn't she? It would only have been sensible.'

'Well, yes, I suppose—'

'So that means somebody put them there, hoping the police would find them.'

'Perhaps, but—'

'Which means whoever did that is the murderer.'

'I'm not sure.'

'I've worked it out carefully, Mr Staddon. It has to be the answer. All we need is the evidence. That is what I want you to find. You will try, won't you?'

I looked across at the window and watched the fast-moving clouds beyond the glass. Jacinta's idea was preposterously impractical. If evidence existed of the kind she envisaged, the police and Consuela's lawyers were better equipped to find it than I was. Besides, how could I explain to Angela that I suddenly had to visit Hereford? And what would I say to anybody there who knew me?

'You must speak to Aunt Hermione, Mr Staddon. She will tell you everything you need to know about my family. She has tea at three o'clock most afternoons at the Copper Kettle in King Street. You should look for her there rather than call at Fern Lodge, because Aunt Marjorie—'

'I haven't said I'll do any of this, Jacinta.' I nerved myself to resist the appeal in her large, sorrowful eyes. 'As a matter of fact . . .' My voice trailed into silence. How was I to frame my refusal, how excuse my rejection of her? She was pinning all her hopes on me, just as her mother had once done, her mother who now, after twelve years' silence, had sent her to plead for my help. Why, in the light of all the duplicity she knew I had been guilty of? Why me and nobody else? Then, later than it should have, the answer came to me. 'How old are you, Jacinta?'

'Eleven and a half.'

'So you were born – when, exactly?'

'The twenty-first of April, nineteen hundred and twelve.'

That was it, of course. It had to be. Now that she had said it, I realized I had known it from the moment she had entered the room. It was the only possible reason why Consuela should have encouraged her to find me. The consequences of what I had done at Clouds Frome in July 1911 reached out across the years to touch me and, instantly, I remembered the words Consuela had used that very day. *Ironia. I never understood it till now.*

'Why do you want to know when I was born, Mr Staddon?'

'No reason,' I murmured.

'You think I am too young to know what I am talking about, don't you?' There was a flush of anger in her face. She jumped up from her chair and glared at me, her mouth tightening.

105

'Everybody treats me as a stupid little girl. I didn't think you would as well. I thought you were different. I thought that was why my mother told me to ask for your help. Well, it would be easier if you helped me, but I shall do it on my own if I have to.'

'Sit down, Jacinta.'

'I would prefer to leave. If you are not going to help me, there is no—'

'But I am.'

'I beg your pardon?'

'I am going to help you. You and your mother. To the best of my ability. In every way that I can.' I would not have believed the relief that swept over me when I heard my own voice announcing my decision. I felt light-headed, almost intoxicated.

'You mean it?'

'Yes. I mean it.'

Then at last Jacinta smiled. It was her mother's smile, warm, instinctive and hauntingly familiar. Time – and all I thought I had learned from life – was unravelling before me. We might have been in the drawing-room at Fern Lodge fifteen years in the past, with everything that had happened since held in eerie suspension. My reaction was the same, my confidence intact, my hope bewilderingly recaptured. This time, I would not desert her.

'Sit down, Jacinta. We have plans to make, you and I.'

CHAPTER

SIX

When I set off for Hereford, trailing lies and excuses in my wake, I felt no regret for the deceptions I had practised. I had given Angela and the office staff to understand that a Midlands business-man had asked me to view with him possible sites for a country residence in the Malvern area and that the task might occupy me for several days. I am not sure they believed me. Angela for one seemed sceptical when I explained the purpose of my journey. But I did not care. Whatever she may have imagined, it was bound to be a long way from the truth.

And what was the truth? It seems to me now that I was filled with a secret joy, a joy that had its root in the hour I had spent with Jacinta. There seemed no reason why Consuela should have urged her to contact me other than what I would once have been horrified to discover but now yearned to believe. She was our daughter. I felt sure it was so and equally sure Consuela would confirm as much when I spoke to her, which I was determined to do as soon as possible. I did not blame her for concealing Jacinta's existence from me. She had no cause to think I would wish to acknowledge her. In the circumstances, it was only sensible to let Victor believe he had sired her. But for the perilous position in which she found herself, she would have told Jacinta nothing about me. But the fear of losing her had compelled her to act. If the girl was to be denied her mother, she must not be denied her real father.

I had mourned Edward for four years and Angela had made it

clear throughout those years that she wished for no more children to cause her grief. Now, out of the wilderness of the lonely middle age that loomed ahead of me, Jacinta had come, small, brave and fair, to seek my aid and warm me with her trust. I could have reasoned and temporized till domesday and probably would have done, but Jacinta's plea cut through my carefully assembled defences.

Perhaps the most bizarre aspect of my journey was that I was doing Jacinta's bidding, following not my own directions but those of an eleven-year-old girl. Whilst she kept her father under observation in France, I was to gather as much information in Hereford as I could, using the authority of adulthood which she did not enjoy. She would write to me at Renshaw & Staddon, I to her *poste restante* at St-Jean-Cap-Ferrat. We were to confide in nobody but each other. Of her family, including – indeed, especially – Victor, she spoke distantly and doubtfully. She loved only her mother and would trust only me – because her mother had said she could. What had forged her solemn, secretive nature I could not guess. Perhaps she felt herself no more a Caswell than Consuela did. Perhaps, all along, some instinct for the truth of her origins had embedded itself in her. The only certainty was her love for her mother, her absolute determination to help her in every way that she could.

I never once mentioned to Jacinta the gravity of Consuela's plight. I never hinted at what might ultimately be at stake. But she knew well enough. What she could not alter she did not discuss. What she might yet alter she gave her undivided attention. Three weeks before, I might have found in her a playful, carefree little girl. But I doubt it. I doubt, indeed, if she was ever as other children are. And if I am right, I am also to blame.

Jacinta's single-mindedness was contagious. It bred in me a superficial optimism that all would be well. But the delusion was brief. When I reached Hereford on the Tuesday evening following our meeting, it was already waning. I booked into the Green Dragon, where I had stayed so often before, and considered, over a solitary dinner, the task that lay before me. The interrogation of witnesses who had every reason to distrust me; enquiries which the Caswell family might well resent; intrusions into matters which were no concern of mine: I could expect neither aid nor welcome. But for the promises I had made Jacinta, I might have abandoned the attempt there and then.

The following morning was bright and mild. This, and a stroll round the cathedral after breakfast, as schoolchildren in their neat uniforms bustled about me, repaired my confidence. Normally, I would have been cut to the heart by the sight of so many young, excited faces. I would have remembered Edward and surrendered to melancholy. But not now. Not now Jacinta had entered my life and revived a dream of fatherhood.

As soon as nine o'clock had struck, I made my way to the offices of James Windrush, whom the newspapers had named as Consuela's solicitor. They comprised two first-floor rooms above an ironmonger's shop in Bridge Street, in the second of which I found a young man seated at a disordered desk, writing with an intensity that suggested he had already been there for some time.

'Mr Windrush?' I ventured.

He started violently and looked up at me. 'Yes. Can I help you?' His face was gaunt and unhealthily sallow. There was a look of slowly diminishing self-control about him which his snappish tone exacerbated.

'You're handling Mrs Caswell's defence, I believe.'

'Er . . . yes.' He half-rose and proffered a hand in greeting, but withdrew it before I could respond. 'What can I do for you, Mr . . .'

'Staddon. Geoffrey Staddon.'

He frowned, signalling that the name meant nothing to him. He was extremely tall, I now saw, and spectacularly thin. His black suit was becoming shiny from wear. All in all, the last thing he seemed likely to inspire was confidence.

'I'm an old friend of Mrs Caswell's. I'd like to help if I can.'

'Really?' He sounded incredulous.

'Yes. Is that so very strange?'

'No. Unique. Do you live in Hereford, Mr Staddon?'

'London.'

'Hm. Well, hereabouts, my client is regarded as a cross between Lucrezia Borgia and Morgan le Fay. You'll scour this city in vain looking for another friend of hers. But open my window and ask the first passer-by what they think and they'll tell you hanging's too good for her.'

'Surely it can't be as bad as that.'

'Take it from me, it is.'

'You don't sound optimistic.'

'I'm not.'

'Why did you take the case, then?'

He slumped back into his seat and flapped a hand at the only other chair in the room. I removed a pile of papers from it and sat down gingerly. Windrush rubbed his forehead vigorously, then smiled. 'To be honest, Mr Staddon, I need all the business I can get, but I'm likely to lose clients by accepting Mrs Caswell. According to my wife, it was an act of lunacy. Somebody had to do it, of course, though God knows who would have done if I'd refused. None of Hereford's other solicitors, I'd venture to suggest. It's not as if I was even Mrs Caswell's own choice. The police gave her my name as somebody unlikely to turn work down. It's not the highest of recommendations, is it?'

'Do you believe she's innocent, Mr Windrush?' I was becoming impatient with his self-pitying tone.

'For what it's worth, yes.'

'I should have thought it was worth everything.'

'Hardly. The prosecution have a considerable fund of evidence, you see. The letters, which my client denies receiving. The arsenic, which she denies possessing. And the servants, who between them refute the proposition that anybody other than my client could have poisoned the sugar. To outweigh all of that, I need to do more than protest her innocence. I need to prove that somebody else could have committed the murder *and* falsified the evidence against her. Any suggestions?'

'Well, no, but—'

'Nor has Mrs Caswell. You see my difficulty? Denial will not suffice. If she is innocent, she must be the victim of a conspiracy. But who are the conspirators? The servants are patently honest and, besides, they don't have the nerve or the intelligence to plan and carry out such a plot. Nor, as far as I can see, do they have anything to gain by it. That leaves the Caswell family. Good, solid, local stock who happen to employ a substantial proportion of Hereford's adult male population. And three of them were poisoned, not just the deceased. It is unbelievable that they poisoned themselves. So who are we to accuse?'

'I don't know. But if I can help in any way . . .'

Windrush held up a placatory hand. 'I'm sorry, Mr Staddon. I don't mean to be rude. This case is the very devil, but that's no fault of yours. Cigarette?' After lighting one for me as well as himself, he resumed in calmer vein. 'You say you're an old friend of Mrs Caswell's?'

'Yes.'

'Then perhaps there is a way you can help. I've tried to

persuade her to tell me everything that could conceivably be relevant. Who might bear her a grudge. Exact details of the days and weeks preceding Sunday the ninth of September. What everybody did that afternoon. Who came, who went, who left the room, however fleetingly. Who, in short, could have had the chance, never mind the motive, to commit the crime and fasten it on her.'

'And?'

'And very little. She seems unable to accept the seriousness of her position. She denies everything and accuses nobody. She left the drawing-room between the delivery of the tea-tray and the arrival of her husband and daughter and supposes that somebody could have slipped into the room and poisoned the sugar during that time. The same person presumably planted the arsenic and the letters in her room. But she has no proof of her absence from the drawing-room and no suggestion to make concerning the identity of the poisoner. We need more, Mr Staddon, much more.'

The time had come to reveal a little of my strategy. 'I'd thought of questioning some of the witnesses myself.'

'The police take a dim view of that kind of thing. It could be construed as interference. You'd have to be extremely careful. And there's another difficulty.'

'What?'

'Mr Caswell's gone to France pending the trial, taking his daughter and her governess with him, as well as Gleasure, his valet, who testified at the hearing. He's also dispensed with the services of Mrs Caswell's maid, Cathel Simpson, who's now working in Birmingham. The police know where she is, but they've not yet told me. So, as far as obtaining statements for the defence from these people is concerned, I'm hamstrung.'

'But you *did* say I could help, didn't you?'

'If you're an old friend of Mrs Caswell's, I suggest you urge her to be more . . . forthcoming. This is no time for reticence. She must tell me everything, every secret of her marriage, every significant incident of her life. If you can persuade her to do that, we may yet turn up the evidence we need.'

'I'll gladly try. When can I see her?'

'As a remand prisoner, she's allowed daily visits. I'm due to visit her this afternoon.'

'Then . . . tomorrow?'

'Very well. I'll tell her to expect you, Mr Staddon. And I'll

111

hope your efforts meet with more success than mine.'

It was as I was leaving shortly afterwards that I remembered to ask Windrush what he knew of Cathel Simpson's predecessor. Jacinta had never heard of Lizzie Thaxter and I was beginning to wonder what had become of her. But Windrush was no help. To him also the name meant nothing. My messenger of former times seemed to have vanished.

'You've not seen Mrs Caswell since before the war?' Windrush asked as he showed me to the door.

'No. We rather lost touch.'

'She's a beautiful woman and they say she was exquisite in her youth. I suppose that explains it.'

'Explains what?'

'How she can still command a friendship like yours. All this way, after all this time, to lend a helping hand. It's commendable, Mr Staddon, truly commendable.'

There was a slant to Windrush's words I did not care for. Declining to comment further, I bade him a cool good morning.

A cab would doubtless have been the quickest way to reach Clouds Frome, but I preferred the ten o'clock train to Stoke Edith. From there, through a landscape changed only by the season, I wound my way back up the lanes and years towards a place and time I had believed I would never re-visit. At the field-gate beyond Backbury Hill where I had smoked a cigarette and savoured my first view of the newly finished house twelve years before, I halted once more and turned to survey it.

Better even than fond memory had predicted, Clouds Frome met my gaze with calm, mellow assurance. For just this effect – just this firmly rooted sense of domain and purpose – I had planned and laboured. And my reward lay before me. Clouds Frome was a finer achievement than any I was now capable of. It stood upon a crest from which I had long since begun to descend. It mocked me with its perfection.

I did not linger. I could not bear to. Instead, I hurried on to the entrance and started up the drive. I had still not decided how to announce myself when I saw a group of men at work in the orchard, bagging up newly harvested apples and loading them on to a cart. Confident that none of them would recognize me, I called across to the nearest one.

'Excuse me. I'm looking for Albert Banyard, the head gardener. Do you know where I might find him?'

'Best try the kitchen garden, sir.' He pointed towards it. 'That's where I last saw 'im.'

I marched on up the drive, deliberately refraining from looking towards the house as I passed. The kitchen garden lay beyond it, in a slight hollow, sheltered by a ten-foot-high perimeter wall and screened from the house by a yew hedge. Along the back of the northern wall of the garden was a range of low-roofed brick buildings. In one of these I found a crock boy who directed me to the fruit house. This was a small thatched structure set in the lee of the hedge. As I approached, I could see a figure at work inside who looked very like the man I remembered: squat, powerfully built and perpetually flat-capped. He did not look up when I entered, but went on peering and prodding at the apples and pears laid out on shelves around the walls. It was indeed Banyard, his hair white where it had formerly been grey, but otherwise unaltered by the years. My dealings with him had been few, but they had left me with the impression of a cheerless, solitary individual unlikely to welcome any interruption, far less the questioning I had in mind.

'Mr Banyard?'

He glanced at me and nodded. 'What can I do for you, sir?'

'Perhaps you don't recognize me. I'm Geoffrey—'

'Staddon. Architec'. 'Course I reco'nize you.'

'Ah, splendid. Well—'

'What brings you 'ere, though? That's what I'm wonderin'.'

'It's a little difficult to explain. Could we . . . talk somewhere?'

'What about?'

'Er . . .' There seemed no point in prevarication. 'Mrs Caswell's trial.'

'Ar. Thought it might be.' He scratched his stubbly chin. 'These days, no party wants to talk to me 'bout anythin' else.' He deliberated for a few moments, then said: 'All right, Mr Staddon. Come through to my office.'

Banyard's office was one of the buildings set against the kitchen-garden wall. It contained little beyond a counter top scattered with scribbled notes, flowerpots and fragments of earth. Beneath this was a stool which Banyard pulled out and sat on before lighting his pipe and giving me his attention. As I stumbled through my explanation, his expression revealed not the slightest hint of his reaction.

'The reports I've read seem so extraordinary that I felt

113

compelled to verify them. I find it hard to believe Mrs Caswell could be a poisoner. Perhaps you do as well.'

'Can't say as I've considered it.'

'Not considered it?'

'Bain't my place to.'

'But surely. . . Don't you feel in any way responsible for what's happened?'

'Why should I?'

'Because your weed-killer was the source of the poison.'

'So they tell me.'

'Don't you believe them?'

'Can't say as I do. Mind, I can't say as I disbelieve 'em neither.'

I took a deep breath. There was nothing to be gained by becoming exasperated. 'Where did you store the weed-killer, Mr Banyard?'

'Same place as I store it now.'

'And that is?'

'You might as well see for yourself.' He led me out through the door and into the next shed. This was a more crowded replica of his office, with old sacking and broken flowerpots stacked on and beneath the counter top and hoes, rakes, shovels, brooms and spades propped around the walls. A wheelbarrow took up most of the floor space and standing in it were four large tins, one of which was labelled *Weed Out*. 'That's a new 'un,' he said. 'The police took t'other one away.'

'What do you use it for?'

'Weed-killin', sir. What do you think I use it for? Mr Caswell's very particular 'bout weeds. 'E don't like 'em. 'Cordingly, neither does I. Take the flagstones 'neath the pergoly. Your pergoly, I should say. Well' – he touched the tin with the toe of his boot – 'this shifts the weeds from 'tween 'em good 'an proper.'

'I see. At the hearing, you said Mrs Caswell took more of an interest in the garden than Mr Caswell.'

'So she does.'

'But the weed-killer was Mr Caswell's suggestion?'

'It weren't nobody's suggestion. It were my solution to a problem.'

'A problem identified by Mr Caswell.'

'*Mentioned* by Mr Caswell, ar.'

'And when did he first . . . mention it?'

'I don't rightly recall. Last spring, maybe. Last winter, p'raps.'

'Comparatively recently at all events.'

'Well, I don't—'

'Excuse me!' Somebody had spoken from close behind. When we turned round, it was to find Danby the butler staring at us. As soon as he recognized me, his face relaxed into a smile. 'Mr Staddon. It's you, sir, of all people.'

'What brings you down 'ere, Mr Danby?' asked Baynard suspiciously. 'This is a long way from your pantry. You'll be pickin' up somethin' nasty on the soles o' your fine shoes if you're not careful.'

Danby ignored him. 'You were seen arriving, Mr Staddon, but nobody knew who you were. Perhaps you'll come with me. I'm sure Mr Banyard won't mind.'

Whatever view Banyard took of the matter was not about to be disclosed, since Danby turned decisively on his heel and I felt obliged to follow him. The weakness of my position was at once apparent to me, for how was I to explain my presence at Clouds Frome without revealing intentions of which Danby's master would most certainly disapprove? As we passed through the gate in the yew-hedge and started along the path towards the house, I said, 'Perhaps I should have let you know I was here,' and instantly regretted my words.

'Perhaps you should, sir. Mr Caswell is away from home at present. As for Mrs Caswell, I take it you are aware of the recent sad turn of events affecting the household?'

'Yes. As a matter of fact—'

'I am under strict instruction to discourage visitors. We have been pestered by the yellow press, as you may imagine, and others of a morbidly curious frame of mind.'

'You thought I was one of those?'

'What else was I to think, sir? I could not help overhearing your conversation with Banyard. You seemed to be questioning him about matters pertaining to the murder.'

'I can't deny I was.' We halted at the courtyard entrance and faced each other. He did not seem about to invite me in. 'The fact is, Danby, that I was so horrified by what the newspapers reported that I decided to see what I could learn for myself. The accusations against Mrs Caswell are quite monstrous, as I'm sure you'll agree.'

'They are acutely distressing, sir. But, as I'm sure *you* will agree, such enquiries are best left to the appropriate authorities. If there's any message you wish to leave, I'll happily communicate it to Mr Caswell upon his return. Or, should you wish to write to him, I can furnish you with his address in France. Otherwise, there's really nothing—'

'There's no need. I'm well aware of his address. Major Turnbull's villa at Cap Ferrat, isn't it?'

Danby frowned. 'Do I take it, sir, that you knew Mr Caswell was away when you came here? If so—'

'When's he due back?'

At this, Danby permitted himself a sniff of affronted dignity. 'I really am not at liberty to discuss Mr Caswell's plans, sir. How, may I ask, did you—'

'He's taken Gleasure with him, I know. And Cathel Simpson's been dismissed, I believe.'

'Since Mrs Caswell is no longer in residence, a lady's maid is surplus to the household's requirements.'

'For the moment.'

'As you say, sir.'

'It's convenient, though, isn't it?'

'In what way, sir?'

'Never mind.' I was becoming impatient and sensed I would betray myself if I prolonged the discussion. 'I'll say good morning, Danby. There's no message. And I shan't be writing.' With that, I turned and set off down the drive.

Before I had even reached the high road, shame had taken the place of anger. I should not have gone straight to Banyard. I should not have antagonized Danby. I should not have allowed petulance to distort my judgement. As matters stood, I was now extremely unlikely to be able to talk to either Noyce, the footman, or Mabel Glynn, the kitchenmaid. All hope of gleaning anything useful from them had been dashed. Banyard might be willing to talk to me again, but to what end? Nothing he seemed disposed to reveal promised to add anything to his testimony.

At the end of the drive, I turned towards Mordiford rather than Stoke Edith, concluding that a long walk back to Hereford was a fitting treatment for my dissatisfaction. I had made a poor start to my efforts on Jacinta's behalf and the knowledge burned within me. Perhaps, I thought, if this was the best I was capable of, I should abandon my endeavours altogether.

Why I halted at Mordiford Church I do not know, but, on an impulse, I went in through the lych-gate and embarked on a circuit of the graveyard, recalling as I went the summer Sunday when the Caswells had assembled there, with me amongst them as an honoured guest. By the farthest wall, beyond which a sheep-grazed field sloped down towards the river, I paused to light a cigarette. As I struck the match, my attention was taken by a headstone erected a yard or so the wrong side of the graveyard wall and fenced off from the sheep with barbed wire. It occupied a small, triangular patch of land at the corner of the field, nearly hallowed, as it were, but not quite. I walked along until I was exactly opposite it and leaned across the wall to read the inscription. In it I found the answer to a question that had been troubling me. And found still more troubling questions to take its place.

ELIZABETH MARIGOLD THAXTER
DIED 20TH JULY 1911,
AGED TWENTY-TWO YEARS.
'FAREWELL LIZZIE'

The address of a sidesman was recorded in the church porch. It was one of a terrace of small cottages just beyond the Full Moon Inn. There, hoeing his vegetable patch, I found the obliging old fellow, who was happy to indulge my curiosity.

'She's buried in unsanctified ground, sir. As I recall, kinsfolk bought that patch o' land from Farmer Apperley so she'd be as near the church as the law could permit.'

'Why couldn't she be buried in the churchyard?' Already, I had guessed the answer, but I needed it to be confirmed.

'She were a suicide, sir. 'Anged 'erself, in the orchard up at Clouds Frome.'

So it was true. Three days after I had found her crying in her room and left my cowardly message in her keeping, Lizzie Thaxter had hanged herself.

'Lady's maid to Mrs Caswell, were Lizzie Thaxter,' the sidesman continued. 'Pretty little thing. Odd 'ow things turn out, ain't it?'

'In what sense?'

'Well, as things stand, the mistress is like to go the same way as 'er maid.' He shook his head dolefully. 'She's for the rope, they do say. And that means an unsanctified grave. Just like Lizzie.'

I left Mordiford in a daze, walking slowly westwards along the low, flat road across the flood plain towards Hereford. More than ever, now I had learned of Lizzie's fate, my actions of twelve years before rose to denounce me. How could I have been so selfish, so reckless of the consequences of what I did?

117

Absorbed in such gloomy reflections, I scarcely noticed the traffic that passed me on the road. To either side lay flat, featureless pastureland and behind, I well knew, the gables and high chimneys of Clouds Frome could be distinguished beneath the wooded slopes of Backbury Hill. But I chose not to look back. I kept my eyes trained firmly on the road ahead, as if by this one paltry device I could hold my conscience at arm's length.

I came to the next village, Hampton Bishop, and noted from a finger-post that it was another three miles to Hereford. On the western outskirts of the village lay a quaintly named inn, the Bunch of Carrots. The sight of it reminded me how welcome a drink would be and I was about to halt and enter the bar when the door was opened from the inside and a raggedly dressed customer, clearly inebriated for all that it was only just past noon, was pushed out into the yard by the landlord. I did not catch what was said. Various oaths and insults were exchanged before the door closed again and the drunkard turned away, looking towards me as he did so. Then he stopped in his tracks and gaped at me. As did I at him.

He was wearing a very old and frayed tweed suit, boots laced with coarse string and a collarless shirt that might once have been white. He had the beard and hair of a true tramp, grey, matted and threaded with strands of the haystack where he had evidently passed the previous night. His skin was dark and lined, stretched thinly over prominent brow, jaw and cheekbones. His eyes were close-set and wary, his shoulders hunched beneath a patched and bulging knapsack. It took me, I suppose, ten seconds to recognize him and convince myself that I was not mistaken. By the twitches and shifts of his own expression, I would judge that it took him about the same. He was Ivor Doak.

Neither of us spoke. I was dumbstruck. Doak had not gone to Australia. If he had, he would surely never have returned. As for the passage-money I had paid, had he drunk it away, or been cheated of it? It was scarcely credible that Hermione had not given it to him, for if so—

Suddenly, with a swift snatch of breath, Doak whirled round and sprinted away. On the far side of the yard was a wire fence and, beyond it, the grassy bank of a dyke protecting the village from the nearby river. As Doak reached the fence and made to climb over it, I found my voice and called after him, but he did not so much as glance back. He jumped down on the other side and ran up the slope, then turned away from the road and made off along the top of the dyke. Only then, and far too late, did I follow.

By the time I reached the top of the dyke, Doak was fifty yards ahead and running hard. Pursuit was useless. I retraced my steps to the yard and entered the inn, where the customers were few and the landlord, once I had complimented him on his ale, was happy to answer my questions.

'Yes, sir, that was Ivor Doak. Once a landowner in 'is own right, they do say, though nought but a vagabond now. 'E sometimes 'as drinkin' money, though the Lord knows where he gets it from, but 'e 'as this nasty 'abit o' spendin' it all, then orderin' one more drink and guzzlin' it 'afore 'e lets on as 'is pockets are empty. That's when I generally 'as to show 'im the door. As for travellin', I'd be surprised if 'e's ever bin as far as Glo'ster, let 'lone Austra'ia. I've kep' the Bunch since the year afore the war an' 'e's always bin roun' an' about in that time, more's the pity. I can't rightly give you an address, 'cos 'e don't 'ave one, less you count the 'edgerows in summer and the doorsteps of 'Ereford in winter. A gen'leman, 'e'd 'ave you believe, but def'nitely a gen'leman o' the road. That's our Ivor.'

Lizzie dead. Doak in Hereford. And small hope of enlightenment at Clouds Frome. These were the thoughts that filled my head as I paced my room at the Green Dragon, waiting for three o'clock, the hour when Hermione usually took tea at the Copper Kettle. I knew her well enough to believe that she at least would be open and frank, but now I had more questions to put to her than I could ever have anticipated. The possibility that she might absent herself this one afternoon had become unbearable.

But I need not have worried. Hermione was where Jacinta had said she would be, devouring tea and fancies at a pillar table in the midst of the crowded café. Thinner about the face and greyer about the head than I recalled, she had passed since our last encounter from a plain and spinsterish middle age to a spry and captivating venerability, as if her character and features had always known youth was not their forte and could only now assert themselves. Her smile, when she saw me threading my way through the close-packed tables towards her, was one of genuine welcome, so much so that I could almost have believed she was expecting me.

'Mr Staddon!' she trilled. 'What a pleasant surprise.' Several heads turned to inspect me and lulls descended on nearby conversations. The Copper Kettle suddenly seemed the last place to share a confidence unless it was to be shared with the whole of Hereford. Hermione invited me to join her and introduced me to her two companions, whose names I could not remember the second after I had been told them. An extra cup was summoned. My hat and coat were removed. Tea and cakes were pressed upon me. I stumbled out something about a commission in the locality. Hermione explained my profession to her two friends. As soon as my connection with Clouds Frome was borne in upon them, they enquired, wide-eyed, whether I had heard of 'the distressing case'. I admitted I had in tones designed to imply no more than a passing interest. Then, to my astonishment, Hermione kicked my shin so firmly under the table that I nearly spilt my tea. There was a stern look of warning on her face. Obediently, I changed the subject.

The Japanese earthquake (one of Hermione's companions was organizing charitable collections for its victims) and the phenomenon of the wireless (her other companion's husband had recently purchased a set) occupied us for twenty excruciating minutes. Then Hermione announced that she must be on her way just when they had both embarked on a second scone and were bound to remain. So it was that I found myself walking slowly back towards the Green Dragon with her, knowing I had only a few minutes in which to explain the true purpose of my visit to Hereford.

'It's a remarkable coincidence that your work should bring you back to this part of the world,' she said. 'Especially in the present circumstances. Who, may I ask, is your client?'

'I don't have one. And it's no coincidence.'

'Really?' She seemed monumentally unsurprised. 'Then why are you here?'

'Will you allow me to explain why in more discreet surroundings than the Copper Kettle?'

'I think I must, don't you?'

We chose a bench by Castle Pool, safely distant from prying ears, and pleasant enough in the autumn sunshine to make our presence there seem natural. I needed information from Hermione and knew I would have to reveal some part of my true intentions in return, so I told her I had always admired Consuela and found it impossible to believe she was a murderer. I had come to Hereford in order to visit her and to ask those closely involved in the case how matters really stood. Of Jacinta I said – and affected

120

to know – nothing. I described my reception at Clouds Frome, my discovery of Lizzie Thaxter's grave and my encounter with Ivor Doak. And only the last of these descriptions seemed to surprise her.

'I really ought to have written to you about poor Ivor, Mr Staddon. I'm sorry I didn't. To be honest, I felt so ashamed about encouraging you to lend him money, in view of what became of it, that I hadn't the heart to. He bought his ticket, you see, and I saw him on the train to London myself, the day before the ship was due to sail. Alas, he went out drinking in London that very night and fell among thieves. His ticket, passport and remaining cash were all stolen while he was in a stupor in some East End alehouse. It was weeks before he returned to Hereford and told me what had happened. He was remorseful, of course, but, since losing Clouds Frome, he's had this terrible weakness to his character that means, I suppose, Mortimer and Victor were right to advise you against helping him. He's gone from bad to worse over the years and now even I'd admit he's past helping. I don't wonder he took to his heels when he saw you, because his memory and conscience are intact, even if he is a drunken vagrant.'

'And Lizzie?'

'There's very little I can tell you. Nobody knows why she took her life, for she left no note and seemed to have no particular cause to be depressed. Her brother was still awaiting trial for his part in the robbery at Grenville Peto's mill, so that can hardly have been the reason. Consuela bought that patch of land for her to be buried in and paid for the stone. She insisted on doing so, as I recall, despite Victor's opposition. She seemed as baffled as everybody else by the girl's suicide, though sometimes I had the curious impression that she knew more of it than she was prepared to disclose.'

'Do you think there could be some connection between Lizzie's death and more recent events?'

'Good heavens, no. Whatever put that idea in your head?'

'I don't know. It's just that . . .' Suddenly I could bear the preliminaries no longer. 'Tell me, do you believe Consuela is guilty?'

Hermione studied me closely for a moment, then asked, 'Do you, Mr Staddon?'

'No. I've already said that—'

'But why not? Isn't the evidence damning?'

'Yes. So the newspapers suggest, anyway. But that isn't the point.'

'Then what is?'

'Instinct, I suppose. My instinct tells me that your sister-in-law is not a murderess. Not a poisoner, at all events.'

Hermione smiled. 'I agree.'

'You do?'

'Certainly. And I can't tell you what a relief it is to find an ally in the cause. Any suggestion of my views to my family inspires accusations of disloyalty. And I am sufficiently considerate of Mortimer and Marjorie's bereavement not to press my views upon them. Rosemary's death was a terrible event and I won't pretend otherwise, but why it obliges us all to assume Consuela was responsible for it I am at a loss to comprehend.'

'But you said yourself the evidence was damning.'

'Altogether too damning. If Consuela had wished to murder Victor – which I for one could well understand – I do not think she would fiddle-faddle around with weed-killer. The one advantage of poison over the shotgun I've often thought he deserves is that it can be administered without detection, slowly and surreptitiously. A single fatal dose entirely misses the point. Besides, Consuela is too merciful towards defenceless creatures – winged birds, wounded foxes, tearful serving-girls – to risk innocent lives. If she had known there was arsenic in the sugar, I am sure she would have prevented Marjorie and Rosemary eating it. And, if she had been responsible, she wouldn't have left the evidence lying about in a bedroom drawer waiting to be found. She had twelve days in which to dispose of it, Mr Staddon. Is it credible that she would not have done so, especially when the police gave notice of their intention to search the house?'

'Perhaps not, but the letters—'

'The letters! They are the most transparently falsified part of the case against her. If she had received them, she would have destroyed them. And murder prompted by accusations of infidelity against a husband is the act of a jealous, possessive woman. Consuela is neither jealous nor possessive. In fact—' She broke off.

'Yes?'

She deliberated for a moment, then said, 'Consuela's daughter means infinitely more to her than her husband. News that Victor had taken a mistress would be more a relief, I should have thought, than—'

'A *relief*?'

She arched her eyebrows at me. 'Spinsterhood should not always be taken to imply naïvety in such matters, Mr Staddon. I am ten years older than Victor. I have observed and studied his personality from the cradle. Consequently I am well placed to know that he is incapable of the finer sentiments. He equates love with greed and loyalty with obedience. And he has always displayed a capacity for physical cruelty which would have obliged me to advise any prospective bride to look elsewhere. Regrettably, I had no opportunity to offer such advice to Consuela. The idea that his fidelity should matter a jot to her is quite preposterous.'

Competing thoughts assailed me. Consuela had never complained of maltreatment at Victor's hands. But, if Hermione was right, the hope of escape I held out to her might have mattered even more than I had supposed.

'Have I shocked you, Mr Staddon? I do hope not. These young flappers think only they can be outspoken, but here's one Victorian relic who proposes to beat them at their own game.'

'I'm not shocked, except by your suggestion that Victor could have been violent towards Consuela. Can it really be true?'

'I'd be surprised if it weren't. He was a notorious bully at school and there was a frightful incident at Cambridge concerning the horse-whipping of a fellow-student that nearly led to his being sent down. Then, after he'd graduated and joined the family firm, there was a complaint from a parlourmaid at Fern Lodge that he'd . . . Well, I was never permitted to hear exactly what he was alleged to have done. The girl was dismissed and sent packing. But Papa's attitude suggested he believed most of what she had said.'

'Is that why Victor was sent to Brazil?'

'No. At least, not as far as I was ever told. He was consistently neglectful of his work, preferring the racecourse to the office any day. There was a number of increasingly bitter rows about his contribution. Mortimer resented the latitude he was allowed, of course. He was always the tortoise to Victor's hare. And Papa indulged Victor more than he ever had Mortimer. It all came to a head when the full and ghastly extent of Victor's gambling debts became known. Papa only agreed to settle them on condition that he go abroad. He was found a position with the London and River Plate Bank as a trainee manager at their branch office in Pernambuco and was shipped off there, urged by one and all to knuckle down and make something of himself.'

'And did he?'

'Not in the manner intended. He seldom wrote to us and what news we had of him was through Papa's acquaintance at the bank's London office. Three years passed, during which he was said to be doing tolerably well, then, out of the blue, came disaster. Financial irregularities had been discovered at the Pernambuco branch. Victor had apparently been using bank money to speculate on the Brazilian stock market and had lost it all in the process. He was dismissed at once and the bank only refrained from prosecuting him in order to avoid a scandal. We expected him to come home in disgrace, but, instead, he vanished. Papa received a letter from him declaring that he would remain in South America to seek his fortune and that he was the victim of bad luck and jealousy. No word of an apology, of course, nor hint of contrition. That was the last we heard of him for five years. Papa went to his grave thinking Victor was dead. But he was very far from dead. As far as I understand his account of those years, he went to Chile and met Major Turnbull, a man with a past far shadier even than his own. They formed a business partnership and within a few years had made their fortunes.'

'How?'

'He has told me much of the South American rubber trade, Mr Staddon, but I have remembered little. The essence of it, I believe, is this. He and Major Turnbull purchased various tracts of land suitable for rubber cultivation – called concessions – from the Brazilian government in a district called Acre, which actually belonged not to Brazil but to Bolivia. The concessions were cheap because, whilst Acre remained Bolivian territory, they were worthless. But the area was being rapidly settled by Brazilians and Victor and Major Turnbull calculated that Brazil would eventually annexe it. They were right and, as soon as it happened, they became rich men. It was an outrageous gamble, of course, by no means Victor's first. But this one came off. He retired to Rio de Janeiro to live off the proceeds and wrote to us announcing that he had come into his own at last. Mortimer was not best pleased, I may tell you. I fancy he would have preferred Victor to skulk back to England with his tail between his legs – or never come back at all. As it was, in hardly any time it seemed, he had married the daughter of a wealthy coffee merchant and was proclaiming his determination to return to Hereford and set himself up as a country gentleman.'

Silence fell. A woman with a baby in a pram walked slowly by. 'You've been very candid about your brother,' I said.

'The situation demands candour. Consuela's life is at stake.'

'Is it? Is it really?'

'Oh yes. Don't trouble to doubt it. A show of hands at the Copper Kettle any afternoon would see her condemned unanimously.'

'Why?'

'Because they look no further than the facts. And because they do not wish to look further. Consuela is foreign and Roman Catholic and beautiful. The ladies of the Copper Kettle hate her for all those reasons.'

'Then, what's to be done?'

'I don't know. Minds have already been made up, you see. Neither Mortimer nor Marjorie will discuss the matter with me. Victor has taken himself off to France and does not propose to return until the trial is imminent. Meanwhile, aside from that young booby Windrush, nobody is lifting a finger to help Consuela. That's why I was so delighted to see you here.'

'Have you spoken to Consuela since the hearing?'

'I haven't spoken to her since the day of Rosemary's funeral, more than a month ago. That, of course, was before we received confirmation that the poor girl had been poisoned. As soon as Consuela was arrested, Mortimer made it clear that none of us was to visit her or make any statements in support of her. Victor echoed this wish. I've never known my brothers so united before in anything. That alone should have made me suspicious, but Victor's display of grief for a niece he had always ignored was what really decided me. A lifetime's experience of my brothers' behaviour enables me to see through them at a glance. Whilst Mortimer's response to Rosemary's death is perfectly understandable, Victor's seems altogether more contrived. Amidst all the mourning and wringing of hands, he has failed to exhibit the one emotion such a dreadful experience might be expected to inspire: surprise. He has been everything he has needed to be, *except* taken unawares by events.'

'What are you implying – that he knew this was going to happen?'

Her eyes narrowed. 'I have sometimes thought so, Mr Staddon. But that can't be true, can it?'

Evensong in Hereford Cathedral that day was sparsely attended.

Leaning back in one of the stalls, listening to the choristers' voices rising and fading into the darkness above my head, I was grateful for the tranquillity their rituals imposed. Amidst the candle-light and priestly vestments, lulled by plainsong and prayer, I found it possible to believe there really was order and meaning in life. Surely the chaos of Consuela's arrest and pending trial was capable of resolution. It was only a mistake, after all, only a colossal misunderstanding to which her accusers would eventually awake.

Or was it? When the choristers filed away at the end of the service, I could not help wondering if Consuela had glimpsed any of their angelic faces in the jostling throng that had bayed for her neck outside the court every day of her hearing.

Consuela was now more than ever the centre of my thoughts. How would she receive me? How would I explain myself to her? In less than twenty-four hours, I would have to meet her gaze across a bare room in Gloucester Gaol, stern wardresses hanging on our every word, bleak recriminations tugging at my conscience. I yearned to see her again and make my peace with her. And yet I dreaded it also. Barely kept at arm's length there still remained my craven instinct for flight and hiding. Had it not been for the severity of Consuela's plight, a second desertion might have followed the first.

But it was too late to turn back now. Indeed, the information she might give me was about all there was left to sustain my hopes of helping her. I walked slowly back to the Green Dragon reviewing the harvest of my first day's endeavours on her account and admitting to myself that it was dismally meagre.

At the desk, the clerk told me a gentleman was waiting for me in the bar. It was Windrush. He had pulled his chair close to the fire, for all that it was a mild night, and was smoking frantically. He looked even more harassed and dejected than when I had seen him in the morning. He was chewing at his fingernails between each drag on the cigarette and looked up at me anxiously as I approached.

'I've just got back from Gloucester,' he said, without waiting for me to sit down. 'She won't see you, Staddon.'

'What?'

'She's quite adamant. Perhaps you know just how adamant she can be when she wishes. That's the worst of representing her. Either she's hardly concentrating at all or she's telling you exactly what to do.'

I took the chair beside him and pulled it close to the table, clinging to the frail hope that I had misunderstood him. 'What are you saying?' I whispered urgently.

'It's quite simple. I visited her this afternoon, as I told you I would, and warned her that you would do so tomorrow. The news seemed to take her aback. I'm bound to say it had a greater impact on her than anything I can recall. I've never seen her so ruffled before. Normally there's this monumental calm resting on her, as if she's unaware of what's happening. But not when I mentioned your name. She said that on no account were you to visit her. If you attempt to do so, she'll refuse to see you. And she will. Of that I'm certain.'

'But . . . why?'

'I don't know. I did ask, but all she would say was that you'd understand her reason.' He turned his head to look at me. 'Do you?'

In that instant I understood all too well. Why should she see me at a time of my choosing? It was I, after all, who had broken our last engagement – and had shrunk from seeing her ever since. 'No,' I heard myself say with heavy emphasis.

'Really? She seemed sure you would.'

'Well I don't!' I turned away and summoned the barman. Windrush's arched eyebrows suggested, however, that the distraction was useless. I had lied and he knew it. But he did not pursue the point. Instead, when our drinks had arrived and I had accepted his offer of a cigarette, he expressed regret at his client's behaviour.

'I'd hoped you might persuade her to be more reasonable, but clearly it's not to be. As matters stand, the preparation of a defence is virtually impossible.'

'Why?'

He lowered his voice. 'Mrs Caswell has negligible financial resources and, in the circumstances, can scarcely look to her husband for assistance. She's also refused to alert her family in Brazil, who might help her, to what is happening. I think she'd do well to apply for the trial to be transferred to London, where her chances of an impartial jury would be greatly enhanced, but such a transfer would be very expensive and pointless unless we could secure the services of a top London barrister, whose fee would match his reputation. You see my problem?'

What I saw was what Windrush wanted me to see: an opportunity to render Consuela a practical service. She would have forbidden him to tell me of his difficulties if he had asked her permission to do so, but clearly he had not. What he had in mind was a private agreement between us of which she need know nothing, an agreement to help her in spite of herself. 'Let me pay,' I said quietly.

'I can give you no definite idea of the scale of such expenditure. You must realize that. The cost of a transfer to London will be considerable.'

'But you think such a transfer would be advantageous?'

'It's essential. Hereford's already tried the case and found her guilty. Mrs Caswell would be happy to stand trial in London, but I haven't told her of the expense involved.'

'Then don't.'

He nodded. 'Very well.'

'Who will you ask to defend her?'

'If money were no object, I would approach Sir Henry Curtis-Bennett. He's soft-hearted enough to take the case and hard-headed enough to make something of it in court. But his basic fee is five hundred guineas. Then there are the—'

'Ask Sir Henry and leave his fee to me.'

He nodded again. 'Very well.'

'But Mrs Caswell must be kept in ignorance of my contributions.'

'Of course. That shouldn't be difficult to arrange.'

'It's agreed, then?'

He eyed me curiously, realizing, I suspect, that in me he had stumbled on some secret from his client's past, and realizing also that neither of us would ever tell him what the secret was. 'Yes,' he said. 'It's agreed.'

Windrush's meaning had been clear. Consuela would not see me. And I had no intention of trying to see her against her will. Yet still the following morning found me walking slowly past the gate of Gloucester Prison and back again, staring up at the high brick walls and the barred windows of the cell-blocks. What was she doing? I wondered. How was she passing this one day among the many she had already spent there? What thoughts – what hopes and doubts and fears – were revolving in her head? And could she see – if she cared to look – the solitary figure pacing to and fro in the street? Could she guess – and would she welcome – the little he was trying to do to help her?

I returned to Hereford feeling more despondent than at any

128

time since leaving London and convinced that acting as Windrush's paymaster was the limit of what I could accomplish on Jacinta's behalf. At the Green Dragon, however, a surprise awaited me. Mr Mortimer Caswell had telephoned and asked me to call on him at the premises of Caswell & Co. as soon as possible. It was a strange summons, from an unexpected source, but not one I was about to ignore.

The cider-works comprised a vast low-roofed warehouse with a tall smoking chimney at one end and piles of recently harvested apples covering most of the yard. An army of men was busy loading the apples into carts and transferring them to a conveyor-belt that led up to the first floor of the warehouse. When I eventually persuaded one of the men to spare me a moment, he directed me to the office entrance in the corner of the yard.

Mortimer received me in the board-room. An oil-painting of his founding father and a host of framed cider-making certificates adorned the wood-panelled walls, sunlight glinted warmly on the directors' table and three high windows looked out on the scene of industry below. Mortimer sat behind his desk at the far end of the room, looking small and hunched, more like a put-upon clerk than master of all he surveyed. He wore black, though whether from habit or mourning I could not decide, and he rose to greet me wearily, as if troubled in body and soul. His handshake was cold and fleeting, his face lined and doleful. In his eyes there was something unfathomable, something as scornful as it was cautious, as censorious as it was despairing.

'I'm obliged to you for coming, Mr Staddon,' he said. 'I won't keep you long. Take a seat.'

'Please accept my condolences on your recent loss,' I said as I sat down.

He stared at me for a moment, one eyebrow raised, before lowering himself into his chair. Then he leaned forward across the desk, fingertips joined, as if about to explain a disappointing set of accounts to his board. 'Danby telephoned me yesterday and told me of your visit to Clouds Frome. I gather you were questioning Banyard about the evidence he gave at the hearing. In Victor's absence, Danby felt he ought to advise me of such a curious turn of events.'

'Is it so curious?'

'I should have said so. What prompted it, Mr Staddon? I'm unaware that you've had anything to do with my family since you finished Clouds Frome.'

129

'That's true, but—'

'I also gather you met my sister yesterday afternoon and spent some time with her.'

'Did she tell you that?'

'She admitted it when challenged. You were seen at Castle Pool. It's not a good place for secret rendezvous.'

'It wasn't secret.'

'No? Then what was its purpose? Hermione was reticent on the point, which is unlike her – as you probably know.'

I sat back in my chair and tried to appear unconcerned. 'I had business in these parts. I met your sister by chance at the Copper Kettle. We took a stroll to Castle Pool. Among other things, we discussed Mrs Caswell's trial. I think you'd agree it would have been strange if we hadn't. Your sister has doubts about Mrs Caswell's guilt. So have I. We simply shared some thoughts on the matter.'

'Hmm.' Mortimer pushed out his lower lip and stared at me in silence for a moment, then said: 'Is your . . . business in these parts . . . complete?'

'No. Not yet.'

'A pity.'

'For whom?'

Again the silent stare, then: 'Danby had the impression that you knew Victor was away from home. Is that true?'

I countered with a question of my own. 'Why has he gone to France?'

'I hardly think my brother's movements – or the reasons for them – need concern you.'

'I could say the same of you about *my* movements.'

His eyes narrowed. For a moment, I thought his self-control might be about to snap. But it did not. Instead, he rose from his chair, moved to the nearest window and turned to look at me. 'My daughter is dead, Mr Staddon. It was a ghastly and shocking experience for those of us who witnessed it. My wife and my brother were also seriously ill. They too might have died. When the medical experts announced that they had been poisoned, do you suppose any of us wanted to believe that my brother's wife was responsible?'

'I don't know.'

'In that case, I suggest you leave those who do know in peace. Victor has gone to France to escape speculation and tittle-tattle of the kind my sister should know better than to encourage. If it were not for my commitments here, I believe I would join him.'

'Do you think Mrs Caswell is guilty?'

'The evidence uncovered by the police is irrefutable. But I am content to leave a final judgement to the court appointed to try her. And I strongly suggest—'

'That I do the same?'

'Yes. Exactly so, Mr Staddon. Leave it to those whose business it properly is.'

A few minutes later I was making my way out across Caswell & Co.'s yard, wondering if I had intruded too far on Mortimer's grief, when I noticed a figure ahead of me, leaning against one of the pillars of the main gate. He was a slightly built young man, wearing a chalk-stripe suit and rakishly angled fedora. He was smoking a cigarette and gazing about him with a languid, disdainful air. I felt at once that I knew him, but, before I could put a name to the face, he flashed a smile at me and said: 'It's Staddon, isn't it?'

'I'm sorry?'

'You probably don't recognize me in long trousers. I'm Spencer Caswell.'

As soon as he said it, I realized that he could be nobody else. For all the well-cut clothes and worldy mannerisms, his small, hard little eyes still conveyed the inarticulate resentments of the child he had been. He would have been counted handsome by some and that only intensified the aversion I felt for him. Something in the lofty pitch of his voice, in the arch of his brow and the coldness of his gaze, conveyed a presumption of superiority that instantly antagonized me – and was all the more galling because I sensed it was meant to.

'Been to see the old man?'

'If you mean your father—'

'Saw you going in. Felt sure it was a command appearance. Bit of a brouhaha at home last night. Your name was mentioned. But then I expect you know that, don't you?'

'I'm not sure I—'

'Walk back to your hotel with you?' He did not wait for me to reply, but pushed himself away from the gate-pillar and moved to my shoulder. 'Shouldn't mind a bit of a chin-wag, actually. I'm in no hurry to get back to Fern Lodge. You wouldn't call the domestic atmosphere congenial at present.'

'Would you not?'

He sniggered and offered me a cigarette. I shook my head. We walked on in silence for a few yards, then he said: 'Gather Aunt Hermione's been speaking out of turn. Always was inclined to. What brings you to sleepy Hereford, by the way?'

'Business.'

'Not Consuela's trial?' The way he used her first name without preface seemed calculated to sound disrespectful.

'I've read about it, like most people. And I spoke to your aunt about it. Our opinions happen to coincide.'

'So you think Consuela's innocent?'

'I think it's possible, yes.'

'The old man won't have thanked you for saying that.'

'I didn't expect him to.'

'Must be twelve years since we met. That ghastly cricket match at Mordiford. Remember?'

'Yes. I remember.'

'Who'd have thought then that my little sister would end up being poisoned – or that Consuela would be accused of murdering her?' He spoke almost light-heartedly, as if reflecting on the mild ironies of life. 'Fancy a drink before you go back to your hotel?' He glanced at his watch and smiled. 'They've just opened.'

'I'll press on, thanks all the same.'

'As you please. Only . . .'

'Yes?'

'If you've pumped Aunt Hermione, why not pump me as well?' He flicked his cigarette into the gutter and grinned. 'I've been known to be indiscreet in my cups.'

The more time I spent with Spencer Caswell, the more baffling his motives became. At first, I thought he was just short of a drinking companion. But in the nearby pub he led me to there were half a dozen bored young men who seemed to know him and would have been glad to stand him a round; even the barmaid looked disappointed when he ushered me away to a corner table. So, clearly, there was more to it than that.

With his long legs stretched out in front of him, a glass cradled on his chest and a cigarette casting smoke-patterns in time to his gestures, he seemed to require nothing more than an audience for his jaundiced assessment of Hereford in general and his own family in particular. Twenty-three years old and just too young to have enlisted before the end of the war, he had come down from Cambridge in 1922, destined to join Caswell & Co. for sheer lack

132

of a practical alternative. He did not trouble to disguise his scorn for business, or 'trade' as he called it. His talents, he claimed, lay elsewhere, though his besetting tragedy was that he did not know where. Shallow, self-centred and arrogant, he appeared to possess all the worst characteristics of pampered youth. In ordinary circumstances, I would have cut our meeting as short as possible and spared Mortimer a grain of sympathy for fathering such a son. But these were not ordinary circumstances. Spencer's egotistical maunderings offered me a badly needed insight into the realities of Caswell family life and therefore he found in me the eager listener he seemed to desire.

'Fact is, Staddon, I'm finding this whole business a bit of a bore. I mean, sister walks under a bus, we all say what a pity. Much weeping into handkerchieves, long faces at the funeral, then we get over it. Life goes on. But sister swallows arsenic in her tea and dies, aunt-in-law's arrested and facing trial, then there's just no end to it. Reporters thick as flies, gossip circulating round Hereford faster than the plague, ordinary activities suspended. Mother sits in a darkened room the livelong day and Father forbids light conversation, for God's sake. It's all very well for Uncle Victor – he can hide himself away in France – but what am I supposed to do? I don't even know how long it's going to go on. There's no date fixed for the trial yet. We could be talking about *months*.'

'When the trial does open,' I put in mildly, 'how do you think it will turn out?'

'Badly for Consuela. As far as I understand it, she has no answer to the charge. Motive, means, opportunity. She had them all, we're told.'

'You believe the evidence against her, then?'

'I didn't say that. They haven't shown *me* the letters. And I wasn't at the tea party. I'm no better informed than you are, if it comes to the point. But this I will say . . . .' He crouched forward and lowered his voice. 'Consuela's never struck me as a fool. So why leave the letters and a packet of arsenic lying around amongst her silk pretties waiting to be found?'

'You're suggesting somebody else put them there?'

'Not me. But you are, aren't you? How else are you going to argue her innocence? Your problem is: who would do such a thing?'

'I don't know.'

'Haven't you wondered, though?' His face was animated, his

133

eyes aglow with enthusiasm for the mental game he had embarked upon. 'If my much-lamented sister wasn't the intended victim, Uncle Victor must have been. And if Consuela wasn't the murderer, somebody else – for some other reason – must have wanted him dead. But he's still alive, which means their attempt to kill him failed. Yet there's been no second attempt. That could be because Consuela really is guilty, of course. Or it could be because fastening the crime on her was the real object of the exercise. It gets her out of the way, you see – most effectively.'

'Out of the way of what?'

Spencer grinned and leaned back in his chair, as if arousing my interest in his theory was a cause of deep satisfaction. He blew a cone of smoke towards the ceiling. 'I haven't taken the idea any further yet, but I turn it over in my mind quite regularly. It's more challenging than your average crossword-puzzle, after all.'

'And a great deal more serious,' I snapped. 'We're discussing a woman's life.'

'I ought to care, I know, but I'm not going to pretend I feel things when I don't. The beautiful bride Uncle Victor brought back from South America, aloof, exotic and unapproachable. That's all she ever was to me. I take as much interest in her fate as she would in mine: none at all. But perhaps you know her better than I do. Perhaps that's what's brought you all this way. Some dalliance during the building of Clouds Frome, was there?'

'That's an unwarranted and offensive suggestion.'

But my words could not touch him. His grin remained, as infuriating as he meant it to be. 'An entirely logical suggestion, I should have thought, but I'll not press it if you object so strongly.'

'I do.' I rose from my chair, suddenly eager to be out of his company. 'And I'll bid you good evening.'

'Cheerio, then.' He glanced up at me but otherwise moved not a muscle. 'Bear in mind what I said. Could be that somebody somewhere is rubbing their hands in glee at what's happened to Consuela. All you have to find out is: who?'

I left him then, still grinning, reclining in his chair and enveloped in smoke. By the time I had reached the Green Dragon, much of my anger had dissipated, leaving in its wake regret that I had allowed myself to be riled by him and a growing suspicion that, for all his cynicism and sarcasm, he might have chanced upon the truth. Maybe it had not mattered to the murderer who their victim was so long as Consuela was blamed for the death. Maybe her incarceration and possible execution were what they had really desired all along.

Then, as I rounded a bend in the corridor leading to my room, the obvious conclusion came to me, so suddenly and climactically that I cried aloud, 'Of course!' and startled a maid who was pushing a basket of laundry. I blundered out an apology to her and, as she went on her way, leaned back against the wall and remembered what Hermione had said about Victor's reaction to Rosemary's death. He had not seemed surprised. She could almost have believed he had expected it to happen. *'But that can't be true, can it?'* Her words and Spencer's blended in my mind. *'It gets her out of the way – most effectively.'* And with the recollection of their words came a perverse sense of relief, breaking over me like a wave. Now, at last, I felt I knew the name and purpose of the enemy and what I must do to save Consuela from him.

CHAPTER

SEVEN

'A holiday, Geoffrey? This is a most unexpected suggestion, I must say.'

'Timely, I'd have thought. Winter's drawing in. I feel in need of a tonic. And I haven't much work on at present. So why not?'

'Why not indeed? The French Riviera in November is vastly preferable to London, I won't deny.' Angela's eyes drifted out of focus. She was looking past me at something that existed only in the pretence I was staging for her benefit. Suddenly, I cursed myself for letting her choose from all the obvious and flattering reasons why I might have proposed such a jaunt. 'I don't believe we've been abroad together since . . . well, since our honeymoon.'

'High time we did, then. Base ourselves in Nice, I thought. Hire a car and explore the coast either side. Cannes. Monte Carlo. Cap Ferrat. Take two or three weeks about it. Relax. Enjoy ourselves.'

The smile on Angela's face was genuine and radiant, testimony to the success of my ploy. 'Yes,' she said. 'It really is an excellent idea. I can't think why we haven't done something like it before.'

'It'll take me a little while to make all the arrangements, of course.'

'Never mind. It'll be something to look forward to.'

'Good. That's settled, then.' I returned to my newspaper and Angela to the latest of her mother's multi-page letters. It was the Sunday following my return from Hereford and the moment I had judged most propitious for unveiling my plan. All I had to show for my visit was an assortment of stray hints that Victor knew more about his niece's death than he had cared to reveal. Evidently, his were the complaints that had prompted Banyard to obtain an arsenic-based weed-killer. If he wanted to be rid of Consuela – and admittedly I had no evidence that he did – matters could not have turned out better for him. Seen in that light, his sojourn in Cap Ferrat looked like an attempt to avoid unwelcome questions. There was one glaring objection to my theory, of course. Rosemary's death proved that the sugar at the tea party contained a fatal dose of arsenic. If she had not arrived unexpectedly to consume it, how could Victor have avoided doing so? Rehearse the events in my mind as often as I liked, I could find no answer. All I could cling to was the notion that, when I saw him and spoke to him, the truth would become clear.

Truth of another kind had begun to trouble me around this time. Who, I wondered, was I really trying to help? Consuela, whom I had not seen for twelve years? Jacinta, whose father I could not resist hoping and believing I was? Or myself? My conscience was in need of shriving, my life in need of direction. Now, in Consuela's plight, I had found both a puzzle and a mission.

That afternoon, I walked to Brompton Cemetery, put some fresh flowers on Edward's grave and told him what I was trying to do. Death had become my foe – little Edward's, which I had failed to foresee or prevent, and Consuela's, which loomed ahead at the far end of the law's long and winding road. Edward said nothing, of course. He listened patiently, then watched as I walked away. He neither reproached nor approved. Yet he served faithfully as my confessor.

That night, I wrote to Jacinta, warning her of my plans and asking how we might arrange to meet by chance at Cap Ferrat and so bring Victor and me together. She would devise some cunning stratagem; of that I was certain. I made no reference to my suspicions about Victor. For all her precocity, even Jacinta was surely not ready to hear it suggested that her own father had brought about her mother's downfall.

A few days later, Windrush visited me at Frederick's Place. He had come straight from an audience with the eminent barrister, Sir Henry Curtis-Bennett, and was happy to report that Sir Henry had agreed to lead Consuela's defence. The dignity of her bearing and the firmness of her testimony at the hearing had evidently impressed him, although he was unable to express much optimism at this stage. He would meet his client as soon as possible and assess her prospects thereafter. At all events, he would do his best, which according to Windrush was the very best the English bar had to offer.

The following Saturday, I journeyed to Wendover and paid a call on Imry. To him at least I could risk revealing what was in my mind and there was, besides, much to tell him: Jacinta's sudden appearance in my life; the details of my visit to Hereford; the frail theory I had formed to vindicate Consuela. To my surprise and disappointment, he seemed worried by what I had to say.

'You really think this girl's your daughter, Geoff?'

'Why else would Consuela have sent her to see me?'

'And you propose to let Angela meet her?'

'There's no reason why she should suspect anything. I could hardly go to Nice alone, could I?'

'I'm not sure you should be going at all.'

'What do you suggest I do? Give it up? Let justice take its course, even if that course is hopelessly misdirected?'

'You've no real reason to think it is misdirected. If Victor Caswell administered poison to himself, how could he be sure he wasn't going to swallow a fatal dose? And why should he be willing to take such an appalling risk?'

'That's what I intend to find out.'

Imry stared at me in silence for a moment, then said: 'I wish you luck, Geoff. I hope you're proved right, really I do, because if you're not . . .'

'Yes?'

'Then I fear this business will end badly – for you as well as Consuela.'

Our departure was eventually fixed for 5 November. Angela's enthusiasm for the trip heightened progressively as the day approached and, as it did so, grew harder for me to bear. She was more open and affectionate with me than at any time since Edward's death, having convinced herself that I was making a genuine effort to bridge the gap that had grown between us. If I had known she would react in such a way, I believe I would have told her the truth at the outset, but now it was too late. My deception had succeeded – all too well.

On 1 November – just when I had begun to fear it would not reach me before we left – a letter came from Jacinta. I had been arriving deliberately early at the office all week, in order to intercept the mail before Kevin or Doris could cast an inquisitive eye over it, and it is hard to describe my relief at the sight of the

138

French-stamped envelope nestling amongst the bills and the circulars in the cage that morning.

Jacinta's handwriting was neat and precise, her prose style as measured and adult as her speech. As I read her letter, standing in my office with my hat and coat still on, it was as if she was once more sitting opposite me, her large eyes trained upon me, her small face set and serious.

Villa d'Abricot
Saint-Jean-Cap-Ferrat
Alpes-Maritime
FRANCE
28th October 1923

Dear Mr Staddon,
Your letter of the 21st was waiting for me at the post office when I called there yesterday. Tonight is the first opportunity I have had to reply to it. This is because my governess, Miss Roebuck, constantly interrupts me. But she has gone out this evening with my father and Major Turnbull.

I was sorry you did not find out more in Hereford. Time is short, you know. Really it is *very* short.

If you are sure coming here will help, then, of course, you must. Every morning at ten o'clock, Miss Roebuck takes me for a walk along Promenade Maurice Rouvier. This is a footpath which runs past the end of the garden, leading to Beaulieu-sur-Mer. Sometimes my father accompanies us. Sometimes we have to take Major Turnbull's poodle, Bolivar. He is large, old, fat and disagreeable, like his owner. We normally take coffee at the Hotel Bristol in Beaulieu at about eleven o'clock. Then we walk back. We reach the villa a little after noon. This will give you a good idea of how easy it would be to meet. It will seem like a coincidence to the others. We will know differently, of course.

I do not like it here. The villa is very comfortable, but I want to be back in England, near my mother. I must not say too much about my mother, because it upsets me to think about her. I do think about her, of course, all the time. Have you seen her? How is she? Do tell me if you can.

Major Turnbull believes he is popular with children. He is not popular with me. I may as well tell you that I think he is completely obnoxious. He makes lots of *jokes*. My father hoots at them, but they are not at all funny. How can he *laugh*, I ask you, at a time like this? I do not like the effect

Major Turnbull has on him. It is not nice. Since we arrived here, Miss Roebuck has behaved more and more like a fine lady than a governess. I do not like that either. It is not right.

I must stop now. One of Major Turnbull's servants will be along soon to check that I have gone to bed. I will look forward to our meeting. Please, please have a safe journey.
Yours truly,
Jacinta Caswell.

When I had read the letter once, I sat down at my desk and read it a second time. The formal words, so carefully composed, conveyed to me a picture of a lonely and secretive girl, confined in a place of her father's choosing, wanting only to be elsewhere, rebelling against every trivial element in the existence imposed upon her. She was even obliged to take morning constitutionals by the shores of the Mediterranean whilst her mother . . .

It occurred to me then, more bitterly than before, how different and vastly happier Jacinta's life might have been, and Consuela's, and mine as well, if I had not scuttled away from Clouds Frome one fugitive dawn twelve years before. The Hotel Thornton not built and not burned down, Angela not married to me but to another, Edward not born to die so young, Consuela not abandoned, Victor's hold upon her not permitted to endure. All of it, every moment and every event, every failure and every tragedy, was in one sense my responsibility.

Poor Jacinta. I did not blame her for the annoyance she obviously felt at the paucity of my discoveries in Hereford. How was she to know, fretting through the days in the Villa d'Abricot, what I had come to suspect?

I thought of Victor Caswell, smiling, assured and relaxed. What was going through his mind as the days elapsed and Consuela's trial drew closer? Was he pleased with himself? I wondered. Was he confident that he had achieved his purpose? If so, his confidence was about to receive a dent, for only a week separated us, he and I, only a week at the end of which I would confront him and know at last whether my suspicions were correct.

I reached out and seized the brass paper-weight that lay beside the blotter on my desk, tightening my grip upon it until I could tighten it no more. Only a week and then I would know.

Angela and I arrived in Nice just before midday on 6 November. We had left London the previous morning in cold, damp weather, but dawn had shown us the coast of Marseilles bathed in clear, pellucid sunlight. We had sat in the saloon-car of the train, sipping coffee and watching the Mediterranean roll its sparkling breakers up the beach between Cannes and Nice. An exhilaration born of being somewhere we had never been before seemed almost tangible. Angela smiled and chattered without prompting. The warmth and the brightness made her happy, happy for once to be with me. How I wished we had made such a journey before, free of ulterior motive. Then Angela's mood could have been mine as well. As it was . . .

The taxi from the station bore us down through Nice's crowded streets. High, shuttered buildings raised their façades to either side. Old men with weather-lined faces lounged in pavement cafés, pigeons pecking at their feet. Housewives bustled in and out of shops, arms laden with *baguettes*. An overloaded tram rattled past us at an angle. Then we reached the sea-front and, turning on to it, saw all the charm of the Riviera in an instant. Palm trees swayed above the idle and wealthy as they took their ease on the broad promenade, the Mediterranean glinted in sapphire welcome, and, ahead, a pink-hued dome marked our destination: the Hotel Negresco.

Within minutes, it seemed, we were standing on the balcony of our room, looking out across the Baie des Anges, the sun warm on our faces but the air cold and dry. Behind us lay an opulently furnished suite, beneath a city of leisure.

'It's wonderful,' said Angela, as she leaned out over the railings. 'I think I'm going to like it here.' She threw back her head, closed her eyes and breathed in deeply. Her hair, falling over her shoulders, was golden in the sunlight. She had done the same, I remembered, at our hotel on Lake Maggiore, when we had arrived for our honeymoon one mellow afternoon in June, 1913, the year before the war, the year before the completion of the Thornton and the birth of Edward. I had slid my hand down her back and kissed her on the neck, and she had laughed, and we had walked back into the room and slowly undressed, and now . . . I kept my hand in my pocket and said nothing, for still at my elbow that other motive hovered, biding its time.

It was not until our third day in Nice that I hired a motor-car. Schooling myself not to rush such preliminaries – in order that they should not later appear contrived – I let Angela lead me round an assortment of furriers, jewellers, perfumiers and confectioners. She never tired of such expeditions, nor of promenading by the bay and socializing with other English guests at the hotel.

Mobility suited her equally well, however. I obtained a splendid maroon Lancia with detachable hood and Angela was swiftly in her element, being driven along the Corniche road to Menton, wind tossing back her hair, or inland along switchback byways beneath snow-capped peaks. Every day we grew more contented with each other's company. If I had hoped the trip would encourage a *rapprochement*, it could not have made a more promising start. For this reason – as much as nervousness about its outcome – I delayed the staged meeting with Jacinta beyond the date I had planned. We visited Beaulieu once, but took tea at the Metropole rather than coffee at the Bristol, and we did not stray along the footpath to Cap Ferrat. We drove out to the far end of the peninsula and back, passing many fine villas on the way. But none was the Villa d'Abricot.

In the end, it was Angela who made the choice. 'Shall we stop here and stretch our legs?' she said, as we neared Beaulieu on a morning excursion to Monte Carlo. It was the Monday following our arrival, 12 November, clear and bright after a Sunday of heavy rain. My watch showed half past ten. The time was right, the opportunity perfect. I could not refuse. I could not delay.

We halted the car by the casino and climbed out. The wooded flank of the Cap Ferrat peninsula looked green and inviting in the sunlight, the terracotta roofs of secluded residences peeking out from the trees. 'I believe there's a footpath that runs from near here to the village of Saint-Jean-Cap-Ferrat,' I remarked casually.

'Let's follow it, then,' Angela replied. She was wearing a wide-brimmed hat and a light cream coat over a yellow dress. She strode out purposefully in the direction I had pointed, rushing almost, it seemed to me, towards the encounter I had planned. I lit a cigarette to calm my nerves and caught her up.

The footpath left the road at the eastern end of the Baie des Fourmis. We started along it, with the blue waters of the bay beyond a low stone wall to our left and sloping, wooded gardens to our right. My heart jumped at the sight of a group of people walking towards us, but they were strangers. I rebuked myself silently. This had to appear accidental. This had to seem unexpected.

We paused by a bench set in a bulge of the wall and looked back at the elegant palm-fringed hotels of Beaulieu. Angela joined me in a cigarette and gazed out across the bay. 'What made you suggest Nice, Geoffrey?' she asked, leaning out over

142

the wall as she had leaned out over the balcony of the Negresco.

'We've never been here before.'

'No other reason?'

'Should there have been?'

'No. Except . . . It was inspired. That's all I meant.'

'Oh, I—'

I heard footsteps behind me and saw Angela glance at something over my shoulder. It could have been just another passer-by we did not know, yet I sensed it was not. I turned round slowly, ordering my voice and face to obey me, forbidding them to betray me.

Jacinta was standing a few feet away. She was wearing a pink dress and a dark topcoat. Her face was shaded by a broad-brimmed felt hat. In her left hand she held a long chain, at the other end of which strained a large and dishevelled poodle. Its fur was a mottled grey and it was panting heavily, dribbling as it did so.

'Good morning,' said Jacinta demurely.

'Good morning,' Angela replied. 'Are you English, young lady?'

'Yes.'

'Here on holiday?'

'Not really.' She looked at me for a fleeting moment, then back over her shoulder. 'Here comes my father.'

Two figures were approaching along the path. One was Victor, clad in a tweed suit and jag-patterned sweater, Cheshire hat thrown back on his head. Beside him was a woman I took to be Miss Roebuck. She was almost as tall as Victor and was wearing a woollen suit and cloche hat, the uniform, it might be thought, of the dowdy governess. But there was nothing dowdy about Miss Roebuck. Her nose and jaw were too prominent for conventional beauty, but there was a pride about her features and a self-confidence about her carriage that instantly seized the attention.

'Staddon!' said Victor, pulling up as he recognized me. 'What the devil—'

'Hello, Caswell.' I nodded at him and assessed, for an instant, the changes that twelve years had wrought in him. My immediate impression was that there had not been many. His moustache was flecked with grey, his face had grown leaner, edging towards his brother's gauntness. He was in his mid-fifties, I knew, but could have been taken for forty-five, so proof against time was the arrogance that turned his steps to swaggers and his smiles to sneers.

143

'Do you know this gentleman, Geoffrey?' said Angela from behind me.

'Well, yes, as a matter of fact I do. Mr Victor Caswell . . . My wife, Angela.' I stood between them as they shook hands. 'What a remarkable coincidence,' I continued. 'Are you staying near here?'

'Royston Turnbull lives at Cap Ferrat,' said Victor. 'Didn't you know?'

'I'm not sure. If so, I'd forgotten.'

Angela shot a piercing glare at me. The name of Caswell was familiar to her and the inconceivability that this meeting had been the coincidence I claimed was already racing across her mind.

'This is my daughter, Mrs Staddon – Jacinta. And Jacinta's governess – Miss Roebuck.'

Reprieved for the moment, I found myself looking at Miss Roebuck and she at me. At closer quarters, the modesty of her costume was exposed as a sham. There was a directness to her gaze and a tilt to her chin that denied all the servility of her office.

'How do you do, Mr Staddon.' Her voice was soft and low, yet here too sham was implicit. The tone was practised, the pitch prepared. 'The architect of Clouds Frome, if I'm not mistaken.'

'That's correct.'

'It's a beautiful house. You're to be congratulated.'

'Thank you.' Some instinct told me to say as little as possible to this woman. Already, I detected in her something I had never detected in anybody before. Her attention, however briefly bestowed, was total, her concentration absolute. For as long as we looked at each other, nothing about me escaped her. It was a deeply uncomfortable experience. I felt as if my eyes were windows and through them she could see and read every secret thought. I turned hurriedly away to face Victor. 'I was sorry to read of your recent family difficulties,' I said falteringly. 'It must—'

'*Difficulties*! You understate the case, Staddon. My wife tried to murder me.'

'It must have been an acutely distressing experience, Mr Caswell,' said Angela in conciliatory vain. 'I believe you suffered a bereavement at the same time. I'm sure my husband would wish to join me in extending our deepest sympathy.'

'Thank you, Mrs Staddon. That's kind of you. What brings you to Cap Ferrat, might I ask?'

144

'A holiday.' She glanced ominously at me. 'Nothing more.'

'Then I hope it will prove congenial. Now, if you'll excuse us—'

'Aren't you going to ask them back to the villa, Father?' put in Jacinta. 'Major Turnbull wouldn't want to miss them, would he? And I've never met Mr Staddon before. I'd like to hear how he built Clouds Frome.'

'He built it the way I told him to.'

'I'm sure you're very busy,' said Angela. 'We wouldn't want to intrude, would we, Geoffrey?'

'Intrude? No. Certainly not.'

Victor was about to speak, but the words, whatever they were to have been, froze on his lips. I had the briefest possible impression that he had looked at Miss Roebuck and she had signalled to him, with hand or eyes, to be cautious in his response. Whether that was the case or not, he smiled, shifted his balance and said: 'Perhaps my daughter has a point. Why don't you return with us to the Villa d'Abricot, since that's the direction you're heading in? Royston would never forgive us for letting the opportunity slip.'

'Have we time, Geoffrey?' countered Angela. 'Shouldn't we be on our way?'

I avoided her eyes as I replied. 'There's no hurry. We'd be delighted, Caswell, delighted.'

'That's settled then.' As Victor spoke, I glanced at Miss Roebuck and sensed once more her overwhelming perceptiveness. Every significant feature of the exchanges had revealed itself to her. She knew that Victor and I disliked each other, that Angela distrusted me, that Jacinta was anxious our encounter should be prolonged. And what did I know? Only that she, not Victor, had made the final decision as to whether it should be.

We covered the half mile to the Villa d'Abricot in varying states of awkwardness, Angela and Miss Roebuck debating the rejuvenating effects of the Mediterranean air whilst Victor strode ahead in silence, hands clasped behind his back. Jacinta brought up the rear with the slobbering Bolivar. I risked a couple of glances back at her and each time she smiled at me in encouragement.

At length we came to an arched wooden door set in a high stone wall to our right. Victor wrenched at the handle, but it would not yield. Then Miss Roebuck passed him the key. With a glower of irritation, he took it, unlocked the door and led us through.

145

We ascended a steep flight of steps, with a pair of grinning stone monkeys watching us from creeper-clad plinths at the top. We were in a large, east-sloping garden, where a rich and riotous design was teetering on the brink of wildness. Gravel paths led off in several directions towards dark over-hangs of pine and fir. Behind us, in the lee of the wall, enormous cacti reached towards the sky. Ahead, palm trees soared above thickets of bamboo and rhododendron. And everywhere the bare tendrils of some determined parasite were to be seen, choking shrubs and swathing masonry.

Jacinta slipped Bolivar from his chain and he loped off up the garden. As he vanished from our view, I turned to Victor and casually enquired: 'How long has Major Turnbull lived here?'

Victor made no answer. After a moment, Miss Roebuck said: 'I believe he settled here on his retirement from South America fifteen years ago.' She smiled at me. 'Isn't that correct, Mr Caswell?'

'Mm? Yes. About that.'

Emerging from a particularly overgrown patch, we suddenly came in sight of the house. It stood at the top of the slope on which the garden had been constructed, beyond a palm-fringed lily-pond and a steep grass bank. It was of conventional Mediterranean design, virtually square, with a long conservatory appended at one side. A loggia occupied the central third of the upper floor, marked by a row of arched pillars. Otherwise, the windows were classically regular, framed simply in white against the apricot wash of the walls.

'The doctors recommended rest and recuperation after the poisoning,' growled Victor, as if he had suddenly decided his presence at the villa required justification. 'My health's still not entirely recovered, you know.'

It was, I think, Angela's little frown and nod of understanding that provoked me into saying: 'Nothing to do with all the gossip and publicity, I suppose?'

'That too,' snapped Victor, glaring back at me. 'It wasn't fair to expose Jacinta to the clacking tongues of the ill-informed.'

'Of course it wasn't,' said Angela. 'We quite understand, don't we, Geoffrey?'

Once again I avoided her glance. 'Yes. I rather think I do.'

We rounded the pond, mounted the bank by a flight of steps and followed a gravel path along the back of the house towards the conservatory, traversing as we went a row of lichen-patched statues of mythical beasts – wyvern, griffin, merman and cockatrice – all of whom wore the same inane grins as the monkeys at the end of the garden. The conservatory itself was an extravagantly arched composition of glass and cast-iron, its interior obscured by streams of condensation and barriers of frondage. We entered by a narrow side-door and were met by sweet, humid air. Songbirds in a cage I could not see were in full voice against a tinkling melody of fountain-water. The huge leaves of exotic plants seemed to over-arch and receive us, disclosing at their centre a semi-circle of wicker chairs, in one of which Major Turnbull was taking his ease according to his nature.

He was at least a stone heavier than when last we had met and his fair hair had faded towards white. Yet he was still disarmingly handsome, his bulk offset by his height and the cut of his loose cream suit. His legs were propped up on a footstool, in his lap lay a newspaper and on a low table before him were a crumb-scattered plate and an empty coffee-cup with a cigar-butt in its saucer. Between his chair and the next stood a life-size plaster statue of a naked woman, voluptuously formed and possessed, her expression and pose suggested, by a disabling ecstasy. Major Turnbull was at that moment engaged in running his hand down her back. It came to rest on her right buttock and there remained as he smiled across at us.

'Well, well,' he said. 'Your stroll has proved unusually rewarding, Victor.'

I stepped forward. 'Remember me, Major?'

'There was no danger of my forgetting you, Staddon. None at all.' He gave the statue a farewell pat, swung his feet to the floor and rose to meet us. I noticed a limp that he had not exhibited before, but his upright bearing was otherwise intact. 'Your wife, I presume?' He flashed a smile at Angela by which I sensed she would be instantly charmed. As I completed the introductions, I glanced at her and saw that I was right.

'Mr and Mrs Staddon are here on holiday,' said Victor. 'We met them on the path. By chance.'

'A happy chance indeed. Welcome to the Villa d'Abricot, my humble home-from-home. Can I offer you some refreshment?'

'That would be very pleasant,' said Angela. Suddenly, her eagerness to be away had evaporated.

'Why not show them round first, Major?' put in Miss Roebuck. 'You know how proud you are of the villa.' She smiled at Angela. 'Major Turnbull has an exquisite collection of furniture and *objets*

147

d'art, Mrs Staddon. You should see them, you really should.'

'A capital notion, Miss Roebuck,' said Turnbull. 'It would be my pleasure.'

'Take Mrs Staddon by all means,' said Victor. 'But I'd appreciate a word with Staddon in private.' He looked across at me. 'Do you mind?'

'Not in the least.'

'In that case,' said Miss Roebuck, 'you and I should take ourselves off, Jacinta. Come along.'

Miss Roebuck led Jacinta back into the garden whilst Turnbull escorted Angela towards the open French windows that linked the conservatory with the rest of the house. In a matter of moments, Victor and I were alone, confronting each other across Turnbull's richly patterned rug and the remnants of his *petit déjeuner*. Victor's face was like a thunder-cloud. Anticipation of what he would say, as much as the humidity, prickled against my neck.

'I've had a full account of your visit to Hereford, Staddon, so we can drop the charade about holidays straightaway. What the devil do you mean by prying into my affairs?'

'I wouldn't call it prying.'

'Questioning Banyard. Plotting with my sister. Coming here uninvited. What would—'

'You didn't have to ask us in.'

'By God—' He broke off, aware, it seemed, that his voice might carry. He moved to the French windows, closed them and turned round, with his back against them. His voice was calmer now, his anger under control. 'I'd be obliged for an explanation of your conduct. I think you'll agree one's due.'

'Very well. I don't believe Consuela is capable of murder.'

'You don't, eh?'

'That's why I went to Hereford. And nothing I learned there lessened my certainty on the point.'

'So you decided to make a nuisance of yourself here as well?'

'You left me little choice. Most of the witnesses have conveniently left Hereford. And I gather you don't intend to return there until the trial begins.'

'What business is that of yours?'

'None. Except for this. You may have fooled everybody else, but you haven't fooled me.'

He strode slowly towards me and halted by the statue that Turnbull had fondled. He took a deep breath, then said: 'I'll have it plainly, if you don't mind. What exactly are you accusing me of?'

'Nothing – yet. But since I don't believe Consuela murdered your niece, I have to believe somebody else did, somebody who was also at the tea party and who may have covered his tracks by administering part of the poison to himself.'

'To what end, may I ask?'

'I thought you might tell me that.'

He slipped his hand round the statue's neck. 'What makes you so sure my wife is incapable of murder?'

'Everything I remember about her.'

'Everything? You were barely acquainted as I recall. Are you about to tell me you knew my wife better than I thought? Better than a jobbing architect had any right to?' His grip on the statue's neck tightened. His eyes engaged mine. How much he knew, or how little, was indecipherable. I could make no answer, merely stare dumbly back at him. 'If not, your interest in this matter is common effrontery.'

'Call it what you like. I'm not prepared to let her be hanged for want of action on my part that you may find objectionable.'

'She may have changed since you last met. Have you considered that?'

'Nobody as good and gentle as your wife—'

'Good and gentle? You don't know what you're talking about. Consuela's never been either of those things unless she wanted somebody as gullible as you to think she was. Quiet and still I'll grant you, so quiet and still you can hear her scheming little mind ticking away like a time-bomb. She'd have happily watched me swallow that arsenic and stood idly by whilst I retched out my last hours, and if that's what you call good and gentle you're an even bigger fool than I thought. As for the idea that I might have poisoned myself, I'd laugh in your face if it weren't so absurd. Have you any idea of the sheer damned agony arsenic inflicts? Of course not. Nor did I, until I'd spent six hours gagging on my own blood. I nearly died, Staddon, and it's not a death I'd wish on any man. The doctors told me that if I'd had a weaker constitution I'd have been done for. Do you seriously think I'd have taken a risk like that? And for what? What would I have gained by it?'

His vehemence confounded me. Now, like a creeping paralysis, doubt assailed me. Perhaps he was right. Perhaps Consuela was a murderess after all. 'You'd be rid of her,' I stumbled. 'Free to . . . to . . .' I clutched at a straw. 'Hermione remarked on how unsurprised you were. As if you were expecting it to happen.'

'And so I was.' His hand fell away from the statue. 'I'd been expecting her to do something for months. I don't know what. Run away. Lash out. Something drastic, at any rate. I never thought she'd go as far as murder, but, when she did, Hermione's right: it didn't surprise me.'

'But . . . but the letters. She hadn't been receiving them for months.'

'The final provocation as she saw it, I suppose.'

'Was there any truth in them?'

'No.'

'You have no plans to marry somebody else?'

'If I did, divorce would be easier to arrange than murder.'

'But Consuela's religion would preclude divorce.'

'Not if I took the blame. For God's sake, Staddon, face up to what's happened. Consuela tried to murder me because she hates me. Rosemary got in the way. And now Consuela has to answer for what she did. It's as simple as that. I don't know why you've chosen to involve yourself in this – and I don't want to know – but take my advice: give it up. If you don't—' He broke off and looked past me. 'What is it?'

When I turned round, it was to see John Gleasure standing a few feet away. I had not heard him come in and nor, presumably, had Victor. His hair was thinner than I remembered, but still jet-black and oiled down. He wore dark trousers, a white shirt and tie and a striped waistcoat. His expression was studiously blank and he had evidently managed with aplomb the transition from obliging footman to deferential valet. 'I was unaware that you had returned until Major Turnbull alerted me, sir. I thought I should ascertain whether you required anything.'

'Nothing.'

'Remember me, Gleasure?' I put in.

'Of course, Mr Staddon. What a pleasant surprise to see you again after all these years.' But his face betrayed neither pleasure nor surprise.

'Staddon here doesn't believe my wife's a murderer, Gleasure,' said Victor abruptly. 'He'll probably ask your opinion before he's done, so we may as well hear it now.'

'I wouldn't venture to express an opinion, sir.'

'Force yourself.'

Victor's heavy-handedness would have disconcerted many a

servant, but not Gleasure. 'Mr Staddon's disbelief is understand-able, but the facts permit of no alternative. Will that be all, sir?'

'Will it, Staddon?'

I nodded. 'Yes.'

Gleasure turned and left, closing the French windows behind him. As soon as they had clicked shut, Victor said: 'I hope you really mean that will be all, Staddon. I don't expect to hear anything of this kind from you again.'

'I can't give you any undertakings.'

'Can't you indeed?' He stepped closer. 'I haven't heard of any new buildings lately that you've designed. Retired from architec-ture, have you?'

'No.'

'Or just finding commissions hard to come by after the scandal over the Thornton fire? They made you the scapegoat, didn't they? And your wife is old Thornton's daughter, isn't she? That must have made it all particularly difficult for you. I should guess your marriage has never been the same since.' I glared at him and instantly knew it was the response he had wanted. He smiled broadly. 'Bad form to poke your nose into another fellow's private affairs, isn't it?' The smile vanished. 'Now you know how it feels.'

Before I could reply, the garden-door opened and Angela came in, flushed about the cheeks and wreathed in smiles. Turnbull limped in behind her, grinning like one of his own statues. 'Major Turnbull has a simply lovely house, Geoffrey,' Angela announced.

'Regrettably, I shan't have the opportunity to admire it.'

'Nonsense,' said Turnbull. 'I've invited you both to dinner on Wednesday night. And your wife has graciously accepted. I trust there's no difficulty.'

'No.' I glanced triumphantly at Victor. 'None at all.'

We took our leave via the garden. Angela said nothing as we walked down past the pond and already I could sense an iciness between us with which I was all too familiar. The discovery of my real reason for coming to Nice had hurt her deeply and had shamed me too, if the truth be told. But she would not admit as much. She had acknowledged our rifts over the years with silence rather than words and this latest was no exception.

Jacinta was waiting on the path ahead of us. She smiled as we approached and bade us both goodbye, insisting on the formality

151

of a handshake. Only when her tiny hand was enclosed in mine did I understand why, for it was then that she pressed a tightly folded piece of paper into my palm and signalled, by a slight compression of her lips, that I should keep its transmission a secret.

This was not difficult, given Angela's refusal to look at me. I tucked it into my pocket and walked on. When I glanced back from the top of the steps that led to the gate, Jacinta had vanished.

After a stilted lunch in Beaulieu, we motored back to Nice. By now, Angela was as I had too often known her before: cold, distant, uncommunicative and faintly scornful. I thought – as I have sometimes thought since – that if she had permitted herself to be angry, if she had allowed herself to rage or strike out at me, our marriage would not have descended into a slough of suppressed resentment. But we cannot change our natures. And so, helplessly, we wallowed where we were.

As soon as we reached the hotel, Angela announced that she had a headache and was in need of sleep. Leaving her to it, I went down to the bar, ordered a stiff whisky and retired to a window table. Filtered November sunlight on rich wood panelling had a soothing effect and the whisky burned away some of the humiliation Victor had inflicted on me. I took out Jacinta's note. It was written on a sheet of the thinnest paper in a minute hand.

> Dear Mr Staddon,
> I am glad you came. Now you have seen it all for yourself. She does not behave like a governess, does she? I sometimes think she behaves more like a *wife*. That is a terrible thought, I know. It makes me want my mother back, safe and well. It makes me want to cry. But I *will not*.
> I have thought of a way to check up on Miss Imogen Roebuck. But I cannot do it. You will have to. I have found out who she worked for before coming to us. She came in March this year, when Miss Sillifant left. It seems so long ago, but it is only eight months.
> Colonel and Mrs Browning of Jorum House, Blake Street, York. That was the name on the letter. If you could speak to them, they might tell you why she left. They might also tell you what she is really like. I do not know, you see. I do not think any of us knows. I do not think she lets us.

Do not try to speak to me about this when you next come
to the villa. It is too dangerous. Notes are better. You can
read them in secret, then burn them!
Yours truly,
Jacinta Caswell.

Obediently, I tore up the note and threw it on the fire. Then I
ordered another whisky and thought over what she had written.
Faithful, indefatigable Jacinta had reminded me of what I should
have concentrated on all along. However convincingly Victor had
answered my accusations, there was undoubtedly something
amiss in his relationship with Miss Roebuck. At times, it had
seemed that he was taking instructions from her, awaiting and
following her prompting. In such an arrogant man, this deference
to an employee was incredible, unless, as Jacinta had implied, her
status as governess had become a lie.

Jacinta was right. Miss Roebuck's character and career should
be probed in search of the truth. But how? I could hardly depart
abruptly for York without explanations and, even if I did, the
journey might be wasted.

Suddenly, the answer came to me. I hurried out to the
concierge and booked a telephone call to England, to be taken in
the reception kiosk rather than my room. Ten minutes later, I
found myself talking to Imry Renshaw on a crackling line.

'Imry?'

'That really you, Geoff?'

'Yes. I'm in Nice.'

'You should give it up, you know, and come home.'

'I have a favour to ask.'

'What is it?'

'You won't like it.'

'But I'll do it anyway. Isn't that what you mean?'

'I suppose it is.'

'Fire away, then. What do you want your old crock of a friend
to do that you can't?'

Angela chose to break her silence over dinner that evening in the
Negresco's restaurant, where hovering waiters and the proximity
of other diners precluded any raising of voices. She was at her
most elegant and remote, clad in her finest evening-gown,
smoking a cigarette in a holder and looking everywhere but at
me.

153

'You have often done things I found difficult to forgive, Geoffrey, but with this latest deception you have surpassed yourself. What amazes me is that you can ever have thought it would go undiscovered.'

'Perhaps I didn't.'

'Your client in Malvern was as fictitious as your wish for a holiday. That is perfectly clear to me now. You are determined to hound poor Mr Caswell in the misguided belief that, by so doing, you will help his wife. Your loyalty to this murderous creature is, of course, no great mystery to me. It stems, I presume, from an adulterous *liaison* during your building of Clouds Frome. Major Turnbull let slip that—'

'He let nothing slip! Anything Turnbull said was deliberate.'

'Major Turnbull is a gallant and courteous gentleman. It is, indeed, only to spare his feelings that I am prepared to honour our acceptance of his dinner invitation. What I wish to say to you is this. Your affair with Mrs Caswell is of no interest to me. It occurred before we even met. But I do not care to have it brought to my attention in such a way. Your behaviour has been outrageous and I must ask for your assurance that it will not continue. You must abandon this absurd and tasteless crusade.'

'Angela—'

'I do not wish to discuss it. What I have said is what must be.'

'I can't abandon it. You don't understand. Consuela Caswell—'

'Is a name I do not wish to hear mentioned.'

'You may have to hear it.'

'No, Geoffrey. If you are not prepared to comply with my request, I shall move to a single room. And when we return to England . . .'

'Yes?'

There was colour in her cheeks now. The mask of self-control had slipped. She stooped slightly and lowered her voice. 'I will not let you shame me by leading a tawdry and vulgar campaign on behalf of a former lover turned murderess. Is that clear?'

'Perfectly.'

'You agree to drop it, then?'

In my mind's eye I saw Jacinta's trusting, fretful face. I saw the high stone walls of Gloucester Gaol and imagined Imry packing a bag for the morning train to York. 'No,' I heard myself say. 'You must do what you think best, Angela. You must act according to your conscience. That's what I'm doing, you see. At long last. For the first time. And I won't stop.'

154

CHAPTER

EIGHT

Of the dinner party at the Villa d'Abricot I retain only a jumble of competing recollections: glimpses, snatches, passing images behind which the truth hovered, close at hand but out of sight. Turnbull had invited an American couple who were neighbours of his and they, in their innocence, no doubt think of it to this day as an unremarkable and civilized gathering. To the rest of us, however, bearing our burdens of secrecy and suspicion, it was an arena of unresolved conflict.

The boundaries of this arena were set by our outwardly genial host, Major Royston Turnbull. He took me on a tour of the house before dinner, his chest puffing out with pride as he revealed room after room filled with antique tapestries, oriental rugs, marquetry furniture, exotic statuary and fine porcelain. I began to understand then that there was more to him than the cynicism and bombast I had so far detected. He was an unapologetic sensualist, glorying in the tactile richness of his possessions: the smoothness of a table-top, the curve of a chair-leg, the delicacy of a glaze, the binding of a book. He would happily describe in detail how he had acquired such articles and always, I noticed, he claimed to have had the better of the bargain; he had never been cheated, never even outmanoeuvred. His vanity required him to believe this, of course, yet, strangely, I found myself believing it as well.

To Turnbull, human relations were no different from his hoard of *objets d'art*. They too were designed for his sensual gratification. He of all those who sat at the candle-lit dinner table was

155

most at ease, most in his element, because to him nothing could seem more agreeable than to watch and listen as his friends and acquaintances fenced and parried behind a screen of polite conversation.

Faces, expressions, casts of eye and twitches of mouth, are what remain now uppermost in my memory: Angela responding to Turnbull's blatant attentions with equally blatant encouragement – her moues and nods and purrs of pleasure; Victor saying little, but clenching his jaw and darting venomous looks at me; Miss Roebuck's cautious, indirect glances leavened by an imminent but never present smile; and Turnbull himself, grinning broadly, eyes half-closed, absorbed in his enjoyment of the occasion he had created.

For Imogen Roebuck to be among the dinner guests was, in its way, the most significant event of the evening. Turnbull had explained her attendance casually – 'I don't know enough decorative and intelligent females to let one go to waste just because she's a governess' – but I noticed that her status was not specified when she was introduced to his American neighbours. Here then was further evidence to support Jacinta's suspicions.

Miss Roebuck sat to my left, with Turnbull to my right at the head of the table. Angela sat opposite me, with Victor to her right. Thus I had little opportunity to look directly at Miss Roebuck, whilst her tone of voice, as she moved adroitly from one topic to another, betrayed only studied neutrality. She questioned me about my career. She sought my views on Cubist art and German inflation. She even asked my opinion of the poetry of T. S. Eliot. Always she led and I followed. The disquieting impression crept upon me that I was dealing with somebody who possessed far greater mental agility than me, somebody who could anticipate and pre-empt every attempt of mine to learn what she did not wish me to. And before us, paraded where it could not be ignored, was my wife's hostility, transmuted into a grinning, gulping enthusiasm for every word or glance that Turnbull spared her.

Angela wore a black velvet dress that she normally reserved for the opera, dramatically low-cut. She had drawn her hair back and encircled her slender neck with a pearl choker. She looked magnificent. But her half-turned face, her sparkling smile, her parted, playful lips, her pale, inviting breasts, quivering as she laughed, were not, I knew, displayed for my benefit. Turnbull's greedy, heavy-lidded gaze never left her. That for her was

156

success. I saw it and understood it. And so, I sensed, did Miss Roebuck.

At some point, Angela insisted that Turnbull should dine with us at the Negresco before we left Nice. He accepted. Then, upon hearing that we had not yet sampled the delights of the Casino at Monte Carlo, he insisted that we should accompany him there one evening. Angela accepted on my behalf. And so, with bewildering speed, a sequence of social occasions had been arranged at which they could proceed with their flirtation, a flirtation with which Angela clearly hoped to torment me.

But in this regard she had misjudged my mood. More shocking to me than any aspect of her behaviour was how indifferent I felt to it. I was in the grip of an obsession that left me no energy to invest in jealousy. This too, I suspect, Imogen Roebuck realized. This too she coolly stored away in her mental armoury, to be turned against me when the moment was right.

For the present, however, Miss Roebuck showed me only what she wanted me to see: deference, modesty, intelligence and a percipience amounting almost to telepathy. She made it apparent that she could guess my thoughts and, by so doing, issued a warning that she knew exactly what had brought me to the Villa d'Abricot. It was, after all, what had brought her there as well. It was why we were gathered at Turnbull's laden table. It was the real substance of our every exchange. And yet it was never mentioned.

As for Victor Caswell, he became strangely insubstantial in Miss Roebuck's presence, stricken into glum and glowering silence. It was as if he were embarrassed by her mental superiority. At times, I felt almost sorry for him, absurd though I knew the sentiment to be.

For this – and for much else that the evening held – let one last image stand. We were leaving and Turnbull had stepped out with us onto the drive, ostensibly to sample the air but actually to whisper some parting endearment into Angela's ear as he opened the car door for her. I looked away, quite deliberately, towards the villa. The front door was open and in the brightly lit hallway stood Victor and Miss Roebuck. She was plainly dressed in some costume of coral pink. Her hair was fashionably short. Her features were handsome rather than beautiful. But on her lips was a smile of regal detachment. And Victor was gaping at her, his jaw sagging, his shoulders hunched, his face squirming with some illegible emotion. Then I was sure – if I had not been before

157

– that whatever had happened at Clouds Frome, she, not Victor, had been its instigator.

I did not see Angela during the day following our dinner at the villa. She had carried out her threat to move to a single room and now we communicated only when practical necessity required us to. Assuming that the *couturiers* of Nice would occupy her happily, I drove to Beaulieu and sat in a bar, wondering if I should try to surprise Miss Roebuck by appearing at the Hotel Bristol when she customarily took morning coffee there with Jacinta.

I was still debating the point when, through the window, I saw John Gleasure entering a chemist's shop on the other side of the road. Our brief exchange in Victor's presence three days before had achieved nothing and I had been at a loss to know how I might go about questioning him further. Now, suddenly, the perfect opportunity had presented itself. When he emerged from the chemist's shop, I was waiting.

To say that he was a changed man when his employer was not watching and listening to him would be an exaggeration. Certainly, however, he was a more relaxed and accommodating version of himself than I had previously encountered. He readily accepted my offer of a drink and needed no prompting to explain that he had been collecting medicine for Victor, whose digestion had yet to make a full recovery from the poisoning. With scarcely more prompting, he recounted finding Victor in agony in his room at Clouds Frome.

'At one point I thought we were going to lose him, sir, I really did. It's a great relief to see him looking as well as he does now. The climate here has done him good. And Miss Roebuck's been a tower of strength.'

'Miss Roebuck?'

'She nursed him through the worst of his illness.'

'Did she indeed? I didn't know she was a nurse as well as a governess.'

He frowned at me for a moment, then said: 'We all did what we could, sir.'

'Naturally.' I attempted a reassuring smile. 'How long have you been Mr Caswell's valet, Gleasure? I remember you as a footman.'

'Since I came back from the war, sir, five years ago. Mr Danby valeted for Mr Caswell till then.'

158

'You spoke up loyally at the hearing, I believe. About the anonymous letters, I mean.'

'It wasn't loyalty, sir. It was the truth.'

'Of course.'

He leaned forward across the table. 'Mr Caswell might well regard my talking to you now as disloyal.'

'He might, at that. What you said when he asked you if you thought Mrs Caswell was guilty struck me as odd, you know.'

'Did it, sir? Why was that?'

'"The facts permit of no alternative." Those were your exact words, as I recall. Hardly unequivocal, were they? What precisely *is* your opinion?'

'I don't have one, sir.'

'You must have.'

'Not one I wish to share.'

His expression was unyielding. And yet his reluctance was eloquent in itself. I tried a different tack. 'Do you get on well with Miss Roebuck?'

'Neither well nor badly, sir. We merely share an employer.'

'I wondered if you thought she was perhaps, well, harbouring ideas above her station.'

Gleasure said nothing, but by his silence gave me a kind of answer. Then he swallowed the last of his beer and rose from the table. 'I must be on my way, sir. Thank you for the drink.'

'Do you think I'm wasting my time here?'

'That's not for me to say, sir.'

'Does that mean yes or no?'

He hesitated, seemed for an instant about to smile, then said: 'It means you must judge for yourself, Mr Staddon. It means that and nothing else.'

The following evening was set aside for our excursion to Monte Carlo. Turnbull had said he would collect us at eight o'clock. I waited for Angela in the salon of the hotel and watched as she emerged from the lift. She was as sumptuously dressed as I had anticipated, but in a gown I had not seen before. Its clinging, peach-hued silk showed off her figure to maximum effect. She must have bought it in Nice, I realized, with this occasion in mind. As she walked slowly towards me, she smiled, knowing what I must be thinking. She cast her wrap over the chair beside me, lit a cigarette and gazed about her. She said nothing and neither did I.

159

Turnbull arrived promptly at eight in a vast chauffeur-driven Lanchester. To my surprise, he had brought Imogen Roebuck with him. She too, he explained, was to be initiated into the mysteries of the casino. I detected in Angela's tone as she spoke to Miss Roebuck a note of disapproval that she should be expected to socialize with a governess, but she was swiftly distracted from this by Turnbull's flattering attentions.

During the drive, Turnbull sustained a stream of anecdotes, leaning back over the front seat to address us. Angela, to my left, was vastly entertained, whilst Miss Roebuck, to my right, said little. Whenever I glanced at her, she was looking out of the window, one hand held contemplatively to her chin whilst the other lay placidly on her knee. She seemed to me then that rarest of beings, one who literally did not care what others thought of her.

We dined at the Café de Paris, then joined the late-evening trickle towards the gaming rooms. The night was cold and still, but the domes and balconies of the Casino were bathed in warm, alluring light. Up its steps moved murmurous knots of the rich and idle, jewels glistening against fur stoles and sequined dresses. I could see the glint of pleasure in Angela's eyes and the gleam of conquest in Turnbull's. But Imogen Roebuck's eyes were averted. They told me nothing.

We passed through the public rooms, where already the tables were busy. Above, cherubim frolicked across decorated ceilings. Below, silent vices were indulged to the incantations of the croupiers. Turnbull, needless to say, was a member of the *Cercle Privé*. Thus we gained admission to the yet vaster and more ornate private rooms, where gambling, it seemed, had attained a status midway between religion and art.

The black suits of the croupiers. The chequered whirl of the roulette wheel. The multi-coloured *jetons* scooped into piles. The green, disdainful baize. The varnished wood. The studded leather. The plumes of smoke, climbing towards icing-sugar ceilings. And everywhere, etched in the faces of the gamblers, bright in their lupine gaze, tight like a vice round their hunched, expectant shoulders as the wheel slowed and the ball fell, was greed – pure, refined and naked.

Turnbull vouched for us with an official, then summarized the rules of roulette and baccarat. Drinks were ordered, *jetons* obtained, games viewed from a distance. Turnbull found two seats at one of the tables and invited Angela to join him. She

160

eagerly accepted. Miss Roebuck wandered away. I laid a few pointless bets and lost, drifted off to the bar, then returned, bored and vaguely disgusted by all I saw around me.

I looked at the table where Angela and Turnbull were sitting, their backs towards me. The croupier was in the act of pushing a jumble of winnings in their direction. Angela's shoulders were shaking with nervous laughter. Turnbull was grinning, his face suffused with self-confidence, his right hand holding a cigar aloft whilst his left snaked round Angela's waist. Above their heads, a vast chandelier threw back their reflections in a thousand miniature fragments. I saw a scarlet smear of Angela's lipstick on the rim of a glass near her elbow and followed a bead of sweat as it trickled down Turnbull's temple. Suddenly, I felt physically sick. *'Faites vos jeux'* pronounced the croupier as I hurried away.

Imogen Roebuck was watching me from one of the sitting-out benches in the corner of the room. It was as if she had been waiting for me and, obedient to the sensation, I walked over and sat down beside her.

'Enjoying yourself?' I lamely enquired.

'Are you, Mr Staddon?'

'Frankly, no.'

'I think you should leave.'

'Angela wouldn't agree. The night is young and she seems to be winning.'

'I mean that I think you should return to England as soon as possible.'

I looked round at her, startled by her directness. 'Why?'

She nodded towards the table. 'Because Major Turnbull is in the process of seducing your wife. And because she appears to be a willing victim.'

'I really don't think that's—'

'Any of my business – as a mere governess?'

'Is that what you are, Miss Roebuck? It would be easy to mistake your role.'

'In this case, my role is that of somebody who does not wish to see your marriage thrown away for the sake of a misguided pursuit of the truth. I know what has brought you here. Believe me, you are mistaken.'

'About what?'

'I am entirely in Victor's confidence. You must understand that.'

'Oh, I think I do.'

161

'Consuela is guilty.'

'I disagree.'

'That is because you think of her as she was twelve years ago.'

'How would you know what she was twelve years ago?'

'I don't claim to. I only claim to know what she is now.'

'And that is?'

Her eyes moved at last from the middle distance to meet mine. 'Insane, Mr Staddon. Consuela Caswell is insane.'

My immediate response to Imogen Roebuck's statement lies now beyond my power to recall. It was probably she who suggested we leave the Casino and for that at least I was grateful. I doubt if Angela noticed our departure, though Turnbull may have brought it to her attention.

The terrace behind the Casino was empty, for the air was chill, our breath frosting as we spoke. The moon was high and full, bathing the palms and promenades in a frail and frozen light. We leaned against a stone balustrade overlooking the sea. Far out across its surface, a distorted twin moon quivered and kept watch. I lit a cigarette. And Imogen Roebuck told me what I did not want to hear.

'I first met Consuela when she and Victor interviewed me for the post of governess last February. She said little on that occasion and, though she seemed somewhat highly strung, I was not unduly concerned. I spoke to my predecessor, Miss Sillifant, and she gave me no cause to think that I would find the position other than congenial and rewarding. Perhaps I should have enquired further into her reasons for leaving, but the attractions of the post were sufficient to put the idea out of my head. Jacinta is a charming and intelligent girl and Clouds Frome, as you know, is a beautiful house in a delightful part of the world. The salary and conditions were more than fair, so I accepted without hesitation.

'Within a few weeks of my arrival, it became apparent to me that Consuela was not well. I have experienced many kinds of employer – the reasonable and the unreasonable – but never before had I been required to cope with somebody whose moods were so various and unpredictable. Days would pass in which she scarcely spoke to me. Then she would be animated, communicative, eager to involve herself in Jacinta's upbringing. Then, with equal suddenness, she would accuse me of defying her orders, of undermining her standing in Jacinta's eyes. She would demand that Victor dismiss me. When he tried to reason with her, she withdrew to her room, emerging days later quiet and subdued, unaware, it seemed to me, of her previous behaviour. And so the dreadful cycle would begin over again.

'Victor refused to admit that she was ill. It was too much for his pride to bear. Besides, he had Jacinta to think of. She loves her mother dearly and would be horrified to think she was mad. Consuela was always the soul of sweet reason in her presence; she never had any cause to doubt her mother's sanity. For her sake, I refrained from leaving straightaway. Later, Victor pleaded with me not to resign. He needed help to cope with Consuela, help to prevent the servants realizing what was wrong. So, I remained.

'Consuela had no friends. Nobody visited her aside from Victor's relatives and she never went anywhere. Apart from a weekly visit to the Roman Catholic church in Hereford, she seldom left the house. I attributed this to her Brazilian blood, to a sense of alienation from her surroundings, but Victor told me she had originally been carefree and gregarious; that her tendency to depression and isolation dated only from about the time of Jacinta's birth.

'I felt sorry for Victor and he, I know, was grateful for the little I could do to help him. Out of this, I will not deny, grew friendship between us and out of this in turn, I fear, grew Consuela's belief that Victor was being unfaithful to her. The belief was groundless. You have my word on that. If it had not been, Consuela would not have written the letters. She would not have felt she needed to. I cannot prove she wrote them, of course. That is merely my opinion, a guess consistent with how she behaved. It is always possible that somebody else wrote them, but, in either event, the effect was the same. They gave her what her disturbed mind saw as justification for what she was probably already planning to do. That is why she kept them, you see, along with the packet of arsenic, where she knew they would be certain to be found. She wanted them to be found. They were her ready-made excuse.

'In the days after the poisoning, when we were all still trying to believe that there was some innocent explanation for what had happened, Consuela would have seemed to some the calmest of us all. But it was not calm. She had merely lapsed into introspection. She was waiting patiently for her crime to be discovered, as she knew it would be, as she had planned that it would be. She had chosen Victor as her victim, but, when Rosemary took his place, she does not seem to have greatly cared. That, I think, is the true measure of her insanity. She was set upon a course as destructive of others as it was destructive of herself. Her intention was and is to bring about her own death. Murder was simply a means to an end.

'I do not expect you to believe me. Even Victor prefers to think of his wife as a murderess rather than a madwoman. In time, however, you will both come to see that I am right. Consuela desires martyrdom and will insist upon having it.

'Victor tells me you have concocted a theory to sustain your belief in Consuela's innocence. This involves Victor having poisoned himself in order to dispose of Consuela, thus freeing himself to marry another. Well, you do not need me to tell you that the practical objections to this are formidable. He could not have known his sister-in-law and niece would call that afternoon. If you think he planned to consume sufficient arsenic to induce severe illness, you should remember that judging the quantity in a laced bowl of sugar would have been dangerously difficult. Moreover, the charge against Consuela would then have been attempted, not actual, murder, for which a term of imprisonment is the likeliest punishment. In that case, she would remain his wife. Your theory is, you see, self-defeating.

'You are, besides, not the only theorist in this matter. I have asked myself what could have brought Consuela to such a pass. What could so have eaten away at her grip upon reality? She had a maid before the war called Lizzie Thaxter. Perhaps you remember her. She committed suicide, apparently, in the orchard at Clouds Frome, in the summer of 1911. She hanged herself from one of the apple trees. Nobody seems to know why she did it. I cannot help wondering if Consuela knows more of the event than she has ever revealed. After all, the punishment for murder – the charge she faces – is death by hanging, the same death as that suffered by Lizzie Thaxter. There is an association between them, a link, a connection I cannot quite explain but am sure, nonetheless, does exist.

'Do you know what the connection is, Mr Staddon? You last saw Consuela twelve years ago. You have told me so yourself. And I know you attended a house-warming party at Clouds Frome on the fourteenth of July 1911. The visitors' book still bears your signature, you see. I remember noticing it. Was that your last visit? If so, it is an interesting coincidence that it took place but a few days before Lizzie Thaxter's suicide. According to her gravestone, she died on the twentieth, only six days after the party. I am assuming, of course, that it is no more than a coincidence. Perhaps I am wrong. Perhaps you would care to tell me if I am wrong. Or perhaps you would not.

'What I think you should understand is that the making of unwelcome enquiries is not your exclusive prerogative. Moreover, once embarked upon, there is no knowing where those enquiries may lead. Mystery lies all about us. We should, in my judgement, leave such mystery inviolate. The tragedy of Consuela Caswell is her own. We should not interfere. If we do, the consequences may be unpredictable – and deeply disagreeable.

'Go home, Mr Staddon. That is my earnest advice to you. Go home and take your wife with you, while she is still yours to take. Leave Victor to repair his life as best he can. Leave me to help him. And leave Consuela to answer for what she has done in the way that she has chosen.'

I could have confessed then and yearned, indeed, to do so. If Imogen Roebuck was right, then I knew what nobody else knew: the origin of Consuela's insanity. My desertion of her burned as searingly within my conscience as it ever had. But I could not speak of it. To do so would lay at my door the death for which Consuela was to stand trial.

The cigarette slipped from my grasp. I turned slowly round. Miss Roebuck's face was in shadow. Silent expectation seemed everywhere about us in the still, cold air. I searched my brain for words with which to refute what she had said. And found none.

'I am sorry we had to meet in this way,' she said softly. 'At another time, in another place . . . Go home, Mr Staddon.'

I may have nodded. Aside from that, I made no parting gesture, but walked swiftly away, my pace quickening as I climbed the steps towards the Casino.

'Go home? Immediately? I really don't know what you can be thinking of, Geoffrey.'

'I thought you'd be pleased. A few days ago, you were urging me to stop harassing Victor Caswell.'

'That is beside the point. I happen to be enjoying myself here. I have no intention of cutting our visit short on a whim of yours. Quite the reverse, as a matter of fact.'

'What do you mean – quite the reverse?'

'I mean that I may well stay on – after your departure.'

'Really? Why, may I ask?'

'I have already told you. To enjoy myself.'

Angela smiled and drew on her cigarette. It was the late morning of the day following our visit to the Casino. I had called at her room to announce my decision and had found her still breakfasting, clad in a silk *peignoir* and luxuriating in the sunlight that was flooding through the high balcony windows. On a side-table stood a vase of richly coloured orchids and, beneath it, the florist's envelope, torn open and addressed in a firm hand *Angela Staddon, Hotel Negresco, Nice.* I did not need to ask whose writing it was and Angela, looking across at me, seemed almost to dare me to remove the note inside and read it.

'Besides,' she resumed, 'I have certain commitments. I cannot simply leave.'

'What commitments?'

'Major Turnbull has asked me to visit the Casino with him again tomorrow night.'

'He said nothing to me.'

'He assumed you would not wish to join us, in view of your conduct last night. Did Miss Roebuck prove diverting company?'

'We had matters we wished to discuss. That was all.'

'You do not have to explain yourself to me, Geoffrey. What you do – and with whom – is a matter of indifference to me.'

'I think we should leave. It's as simple as that.'

'I'm afraid it isn't. I have already agreed to take tea at the Villa d'Abricot one day next week. And Major Turnbull has undertaken to obtain tickets for the opera. *Don Giovanni* is opening here on the twenty-seventh. I understand it's not to be missed.'

'You know very well I'm expected back in the office before then.'

'Oh, I wouldn't expect you to attend. You hate opera.'

I took a deep breath. 'Very well. I'll go alone. When may I expect you to follow?'

'I'm not sure.' She stubbed out her cigarette, rose and walked across to me. 'Now if you'll excuse me, I'll think I'll have a bath.'

She left me standing by the vase of orchids, the sunlight falling brazenly on their bright, waxy petals. I picked up the envelope and held it for a moment between my fingers. Water began to gush in the bathroom. Then I let the envelope fall and turned away.

The bathroom door was open and I glanced in as I walked past. Angela was standing by the bath, pouring some lotion in as the

166

water rose, steam pluming about her. She was naked and, as my eyes rested on her for a moment, I could not help wondering if, after all this was over, my hands would ever again touch her pale, familiar flesh.

'Goodbye, Geoffrey,' she said, setting down the lotion bottle and moving away towards the hand-basin. 'Let me know when you decide to leave.'

I watched her for one more second, then turned and hurried from the room.

Two days passed. I filled them with aimless drives into the mountains. I saw nothing of Angela and gave Cap Ferrat and Beaulieu a wide berth. I was marking time, waiting and hoping for some signal or event that would break the disabling hold Imogen Roebuck's version of events had taken upon me. When a letter from Imry arrived, I thought it might herald my release. But its contents only made that release seem more remote.

> Sunnylea,
> WENDOVER,
> Buckinghamshire.
> 15th November 1923

Dear Geoff,

I returned from York today with little to show for my enquiries on your behalf. Having agreed to go, I cannot, I suppose, complain, so here, whilst it's all fresh in my mind, is what I discovered, or, more correctly, what I didn't discover.

Colonel and Mrs Browning are a respectable, rather stuffy pair with a thirteen-year-old daughter – a late and only child. I told them I was a friend of the Caswells and gave my name as Wren. (May his shade forgive me.) Mercifully, they seemed to know nothing of Consuela's court appearance and responded with righteous indignation to my suggestion that they might not have been completely frank about Miss Roebuck's suitability as a governess. They'd been sorry to lose her and claimed to know of no specific reason for her departure aside from the attraction of a salary they couldn't afford to match. She was with them nearly two years, arriving in the spring of 1921 with impeccable references from a family in Norfolk.

Colonel Browning is a drinking man. Ensconced in his favourite watering-hole and free of his wife's starchy influence, he proved more forthcoming, but not in a way that will please you. He couldn't have spoken more warmly of

167

Miss Roebuck. Indeed, I began to suspect he might have made certain overtures towards her. Perhaps that's what prompted her to seek another post. Certainly there was nothing to suggest she'd offered him any encouragement.

I have the name and address of her previous employer – the family in Norfolk – but I really don't think you would gain anything by approaching them. The fortune-hunting seductress is a cap that will not fit.

Come home, Geoff. That's my advice. And the sooner the better. I had Reg on the blower this afternoon and I virtually promised him you'd be back with them next week. If not, I shall have to put in an appearance. So, does one good turn deserve another?

Yours aye,
Imry.

A cold rain was falling as I drove to Cap Ferrat. The Mediterranean was grey and churning. Suddenly the Côte d'Azur had become a place I did not want to be. I wished I had listened to Imry and never come at all. I wished turning back seemed easier than going on.

The gates of the Villa d'Abricot stood open. I sped up the curving drive and pulled to a halt in front of the house. Then I jumped out and hurried towards the front door, my collar turned up against the rain. Before I reached the door, however, it was wrenched open from the inside and a figure burst out past me, striking my shoulder as he went.

I caught only a glimpse of him, but the glimpse was a memorable one. He was several inches broader and taller than me, dressed in a dark, travel-stained suit and cape. He was bare-headed, with unusually long hair that had once been jet-black, but was now streaked with grey, and a piratical moustache of the original shade. His face was distorted by a grimace of pain or fury – I could not tell which – and he was muttering under his breath, though what he was muttering – or in what language – I could not catch.

I watched him for a minute or so as he marched away down the drive. He was talking to himself quite loudly now, slapping one hand against his thigh and flinging out indecipherable oaths, throwing his head back and mouthing at the sky as the rain slanted down around him. Suddenly, I realized Turnbull's Italian man-servant was standing beside me, straining to afford me the shelter of an umbrella.

'*Buon giorno, Signor Staddon.*'

168

'Good morning. Who's that?'

'I do not know. He has been to see *Signor* Caswell.'

'Caswell's here?'

'In the drawing-room. With *Signorina* Roebuck.'

'Good. I'll go straight through. Don't bother to announce me.'

They were on opposite sides of the room, Miss Roebuck sitting calmly in an armchair, whilst Victor was wheeling and pacing on the hearthrug, smoking frantically. He was speaking, almost shouting, as I entered.

'No, no. He damn well meant it. I could—' He broke off at sight of me. 'Staddon! What the devil do you want?'

'A brief word, that's all.'

'If you're looking for your wife, you'll find her lunching with Royston at La Réserve.'

'I was looking for you.'

'Well, you've found me.'

'Would you like me to leave?' put in Miss Roebuck.

'No,' I replied. 'I'd prefer you both to hear what I have to say.'

'Spit it out, then,' snapped Victor.

'I wanted you to know: I'm going back to England.'

'Royston will be sorry to hear that. He seems to enjoy your wife's company.'

'Angela may not be coming with me.'

'Really?' The thought that his friend might be making a cuckold of me seemed to cheer Victor. His tone shifted from the irritable to the sarcastic. 'Well, wives can be damnably fickle, Staddon, I know that to my cost.'

'My marriage isn't something I want to discuss with you.'

'No? You amaze me. You seemed eager enough to discuss *mine*.'

'Victor!' said Miss Roebuck, mildly but with a hint of reproof. 'Would it not be simpler to let Mr Staddon say what he has to say?' She looked across at me. 'Am I correct in thinking you've seen the merit of the advice I offered you last week?'

'Not exactly. I—' Her gaze was coolly ironic. She knew I was defeated and she knew also how impossible it was for me to admit as much. 'You won't hear from me again. That's all I'm saying. Unless I discover—'

'Unless you discover what?' barked Victor.

'That I've been misled.'

'You haven't been,' said Miss Roebuck, gazing at me in solemn assurance.

'In that case,' I continued, 'you'll hear no more from me.'

We stared at each other for a silent moment, then she said: 'Thank you, Mr Staddon.'

I turned towards the door. 'You'll get no thanks from me,' said Victor.

When I looked at him, I realized for the first time that his resolution ran no deeper than mine. His hostility was eggshell thin. Beneath, lay an uncertainty horribly akin to my own. 'I expected none,' I said, hurrying from the room before he could reply.

The hallway was quiet, so quiet I could hear the rain falling against the porch windows and a clock ticking somewhere deep in the house. At the top of the curving stairs stood a small, motionless figure in a pale blue dress with matching ribbons in her long dark hair. She was standing still and upright, her hands held rigidly by her sides. Her face was expressionless, but in her eyes, as they met mine, there was something fierce and reproachful.

She had been there all the time, I felt certain. She had heard my every word through the open drawing-room door. She had heard and she had understood, only too well. 'Jacinta—' I broke off, suddenly aware of Imogen Roebuck standing behind me, looking past me and up the stairs.

'If you're ready, Jacinta, we'll resume our lesson,' she said. 'Wait for me in your room.'

Without a word, Jacinta turned and walked away. As soon as she was out of sight, I moved towards the front door, eager for mobility and the open air, eager for the refuge they seemed to offer.

'Mr Staddon—'

I looked back at her.

'I am grateful, you know.'

'You needn't be.'

'You won't regret your decision.'

'I hope you're right.'

'Oh I am, believe me.' She held out her hand. 'Goodbye.'

But the handshake at least I could deny her. We had sealed no pact and I would do nothing to imply that we had. 'Goodbye,' I said, starting for the door in fugitive haste.

As Victor had said I would, I found Angela at a luncheon table of La Réserve, Beaulieu's most exclusive retaurant, communing with Royston Turnbull over oysters and champagne.

'Well, Staddon, this *is* a surprise.'

'I've come to speak to my wife, Major, not you.'

'What do you want, Geoffrey?' Giggling and girlish the moment before she noticed me, Angela was now stern and cold.

'I'm leaving Nice tomorrow. Will you be coming with me?'

'You know very well that's impossible.'

'You refuse?'

'Let's say I decline.'

'When can I expect you home, then?'

'When you see me there.'

There was nothing left to say. Angela's unyielding gaze confirmed as much. Turnbull swallowed an oyster, dabbed his chin with a napkin and grinned up at me. 'Don't worry, Staddon. I'll take good care of her.'

I drove wildly back to Nice. Desertions, past and present, seemed to close upon me faster than I could ever hope to flee them. I drank away the afternoon in the bar of the Negresco, slept for a few stunned hours, then woke to find the rain still falling, heavier and wind-blown, from a dark and turbulent sky.

Early evening of the following day found me aboard the night-train to Calais. I had made no further attempt to reason with Angela and now, as the hour for departure grew close and I surveyed the bustling late-comers from the window-seat of my compartment, I entertained no hope whatever that I would see her among them. Disbelief at how little respect remained between us was all that prompted me even to look.

Whistles were blowing, doors slamming and the engine getting up steam when a familiar figure appeared on the platform. Not Angela, but the man I had seen leaving the Villa d'Abricot the previous day. A stern-faced *gendarme* was holding him by the arm and urging him forward whilst another *gendarme* in sergeant's uniform trotted along in front, carrying a battered leather suitcase. My curiosity aroused, I opened the window and leaned out.

The sergeant flung back a door two carriages down the train, tossed the case inside and signalled with his thumb for its owner to follow. He scowled, shook himself free, brushed himself down, said something which the two *gendarmes* studiously ignored, then climbed aboard.

A moment later, the train began to move. As it gathered

speed, the *gendarmes* remained where they were, staring pointedly towards the carriage where they had deposited their charge. Only when the guard's van cleared the end of the platform did they turn away, shrugging at each other as if in relief at an awkward task accomplished.

A few minutes later, I made my move. Whoever the man was, I hoped he would now be calm enough to approach. And approach him I must. As a visitor to the Villa d'Abricot, he was merely interesting. But as a visitor to the Villa d'Abricot subsequently bundled out of Nice by the police, he was a man I had to speak to.

He had a compartment to himself, which was small wonder in view of his menacing appearance. He was slumped low in his seat, feet propped up on his suitcase, the cape wrapped about him making his vast frame seem gigantic. Not that this, the layers of dust on his clothes or the dishevelled state of his greying mane of hair was what would most have deterred his fellow-travellers. They would have found more intimidating still the angry curl of his lip as he muttered to himself, his twitches and snorts of indignation, his alternate stretching and clenching of his right hand.

He glared up at me as I entered, then looked away. '*Bonsoir, monsieur,*' I ventured, but he did not reply. I sat in one of the seats opposite him and smiled. '*Où allez-vous, monsieur?*' Again there was no reply. I took out my cigarette-case, opened it and held it towards him. '*Voudriez-vous une cigarette?*' Still no response. I pretended to search my pockets for a match, then grinned across at him. '*Excusez-moi. Pouvez-vous me donner du feu?*'

His eyes flashed up and fixed me with a stare. '*Deixe-me em paz, senhor,*' he growled.

It was what I wanted to hear. He had spoken in Portuguese. 'I saw you leaving the Villa d'Abricot yesterday,' I said in a rush. 'Why were you there?' His eyes narrowed. 'Was it because of Consuela?'

At the sound of her name, his muscles tensed. 'Who are you, *senhor?*' he said in a heavy Latin accent.

'My name is Geoffrey Staddon.'

'Staddon?' He frowned, as if, somewhere he had heard my name before.

'I'm a friend of Consuela. I'm somebody who—'

Before I knew what was happening, he had whipped his feet to the floor, kicked the suitcase aside, lunged forward and grabbed me by the wrist. His grip was like a steel manacle, his stare no less ferocious. 'What kind of friend?' he said slowly.

'The kind she needs. The kind that believes she's innocent.'

'She has always been innocent. That is her mistake.'

'You've known her long?'

'Longer than you, I think.'

'I first met her fifteen years ago. I built a house for her husband.'

'For Caswell?'

'Yes. Clouds Frome. Where—'

'That is it! That is where I know your name. Staddon. *O arquitecto.*'

'Yes, that's who I am. But you still have the advantage of me.'

He let go of my wrist. 'I am Rodrigo Manchaca de Pombalho. I am Consuela's brother.'

Rodrigo was by nature a happy and gregarious man. I remembered Consuela speaking of him as such. *O Urso de Mel*, she had called him: the Honey-Bear. She had kept a special place in her heart for the brother nearest to her in age and spirit and he, it seemed clear, had done the same for her. We sat long and late in the restaurant-car of the train that night and, though Rodrigo's true character emerged more and more as food and wine softened his temper, it was still swamped at intervals by the sadness he felt at his sister's plight, the helplessness, the raging despair. He crushed a glass in his hand once when speaking of Victor and, at another time, wept like a child. His voice boomed, his arms waved, his eyes flashed; he was to his fellow-diners an object of horror and fascination. To me, however, he seemed an elemental force for hope. Joyous, angry and dejected by turns, he nonetheless succeeded in making me think for the first time that Consuela really could be saved.

Rodrigo's elder brother, Francisco, was head of the family business. In this capacity, he attended many dinners and receptions where members of Rio's diplomatic community were to be found. From an *attaché* at the British Embassy he had been dismayed to learn that his sister was to stand trial for murder. Hurt by Consuela's failure to tell them herself and baffled by what little they could learn of the circumstances, the family had at first been too confused to act. At length, in defiance of his brothers' wishes, Rodrigo had decided to travel to Europe and root out the truth, little realizing the magnitude of his task.

173

Upon arrival in England, he had proceeded directly to Hereford, only to confront the same brick wall as I had. Consuela had refused to see him, sending a message via Windrush that he had shamed her by coming and should return to Brazil at once. As for Victor, he had vanished to France, taking Jacinta with him. Windrush had offered to arrange a meeting for Rodrigo with the barrister he had recruited – Sir Henry Curtis-Bennett – but that was the extent of the assistance he could offer. Pausing only to antagonize a senior officer of the Herefordshire constabulary, Rodrigo had set off for Cap Ferrat.

His reception at the Villa d'Abricot had been predictably hostile. Victor had refused to let him see Jacinta, had rejected all suggestions that Consuela might be the victim of an injustice and had told him to leave straightaway or be forcibly removed.

'I took him by the throat for saying that to me. He had not the right. He was frightened. I could see that. He was always a little frightened of me. But too clever. Too clever for Rodrigo. He sent the police for me. They told me I must leave France. *Um criador-de-casos*. That is what they called me. A maker of trouble. They said I threatened him. It is true. He deserved it. He deserved more, but . . . I left. I had no choice. I cannot help Consuela from a prison in France.'

Rodrigo was incapable of believing that his sister had committed murder. It was for him an article of faith. Questions of motive and evidence were therefore irrelevant. And, since Consuela was necessarily innocent, it followed that Victor was guilty, guilty of abandoning his wife to her accusers even if not of the crime they had laid at her door. When I suggested that there might be something improper in Victor's relationship with Imogen Roebuck and that, if there were, it could have a bearing on the case, Rodrigo seemed genuinely confused.

'You are like Victor. You are too clever for me. What I see is this. Somebody tried to murder Victor. He did not die. *Que pena*! I would not weep for him. His . . . his *sobrinha* . . . died instead. That is sad. But who did this thing? Not Consuela. *Nunca, nunca*. Then who? Somebody who wanted him to die. Somebody who needed him to die. Who is this somebody? I do not know. But when I find out . . .'

There was in this, and much else he said, a distaste for Victor that amounted to more than disapproval, more even than contempt. He loathed everything about him, detested everything he represented. It was impossible to believe that he would have

174

allowed his sister to marry a man about whom he harboured such feelings. Therefore, I was forced to conclude, his hatred of Victor stemmed from later events. What were they? He would not say. When I pressed him, he pretended to misunderstand. All I could glean was that his father had died a broken man, that his family's prosperity had steadily declined since and that he held Victor, in some strange way, to blame for this.

'We made him welcome in our home. We treated him like a member of our family. Victor Caswell. Smiling. Rich. A friend to every man. *O grande empreiteiro. O cavalheiro culto.* I did not trust him. Francisco said he would be useful to us. His money. His land. His rubber. But I saw, in his eyes, what he was. *Um ladrão.* A thief. Like his friend, Major Turnbull. But what did I know? I did not understand. I was Rodrigo the fool, Rodrigo *o bêbado.* So, they let him marry Consuela. They let him take her away to England. And then they found out, too late, what he really was.'

So he continued, lashing out with his tongue where he would as readily have struck out with his fists. He had come to save Consuela, but he could not be sure who or what to save her from. Until he could be, Victor would fill the role. As for the rest – the evidence, the circumstances, the universal condemnation – he would not allow himself to be overborne. In his own unappeasable anger, his own unquenchable confidence, he would place his trust. And I found myself doing the same as I watched him sway away up the corridor that night. He had none of my guilt to stay his hand, none of my doubts to cloud his thoughts. He was the saviour that Consuela needed.

It was over breakfast the following morning, as the train drifted north through a grey dawn, that Rodrigo and I agreed our plan of campaign. He would return to Hereford, speak to as many of those involved in the case as were willing to speak to him and accept Windrush's offer of a meeting with Consuela's barrister, Sir Henry Curtis-Bennett; I would also attend. Upon what the great man thought of our prospects the future of our campaign depended.

The Channel was as grey and cold as the day itself. Rodrigo and I were the only passengers on deck as the ferry battled across towards Dover. As the White Cliffs came into sight, I asked him how he had left matters with Victor, what undertakings, if any, he had extracted from him. The answer, it appeared, was none.

'He told me to go back to Brazil. He told me to forget Consuela. He said he would do nothing to help her, because he believed she was guilty. My sister: *uma homicídia*. That was too much for me. That was why I made him a promise. *Uma promessa soleníssima*. If they hang my sister, I will kill him. I meant it. He could see that. If they take her life away, I will take his.'

I looked up at him then and saw what Victor must also have seen. No wonder he had been sufficiently frightened to call in the police. In Rodrigo's face, as he stared implacably at the heaving waves, was a warning I too should have heeded, but yet could not. Tragedy is its own father, but its offspring were still to be confronted. For all that the past held, the worst was yet to be.

CHAPTER

NINE

It was the last day of November, chill, fog-wreathed and dreary, reclaimed by darkness, it seemed, almost before the previous night had released its hold. At Frederick's Place, a mood of gaiety prevailed, consequent upon Doris's announcement of her engagement to a junior clerk from the merchant bank next door; the staff of both institutions were scheduled to celebrate the event at the Three Crowns directly after work.

To any form of gaiety I, however, was immune. Indeed, I was greatly relieved when Windrush telephoned me during the afternoon to say that he and Rodrigo were to meet Sir Henry Curtis-Bennett at his chambers in the Middle Temple at half past six; they had been accommodated in his busy itinerary at short notice and I was welcome to join them. This enabled me to flee the celebrations after a hasty glass of ale, a peck at Doris's cheek and a clasp of her fiancé's hand.

I had heard nothing from Rodrigo since our return together from Nice the previous week; nothing, if it came to the point, from anybody involved in Consuela's case. So far as I knew, Angela was still being entertained by Turnbull in the restaurants and casinos of the Côte d'Azur. I had obtained from Imry a fuller version of his visit to York, which had only strengthened my conviction that enquiries into Imogen Roebuck's past were futile. I had arrived, in short, at the dispiriting stage when every avenue has been explored and nothing has been found. Inertia – heavy, hopeless and inescapable – had settled upon me. For whatever information Sir Henry might vouchsafe, however scant, I was bound therefore to be grateful.

The journey took me longer than I had anticipated and the ill-lit staircase of Plowden Buildings finally ensured that I was several minutes late. Rodrigo and Windrush were already installed, and Sir Henry already in voice, when I arrived, breathless and apologetic.

Rodrigo, I remember, did not even acknowledge my presence. He seemed to have visited both a tailor and a barber since our last encounter, but the sobriety of his appearance only compounded the gloom in which he was immersed. He was slumped in a wing-backed chair, staring straight at Sir Henry, his only movement being a pensive stroking of his moustache. Windrush, meanwhile, perched on an upright chair beneath a standard lamp, was all pointless mobility, consuming cigarette after cigarette as he sifted through papers on his knee.

Sir Henry, by contrast, was welcoming and courteous, more so than I would have been to a client at such an hour on a Friday evening. Rotund and balding, he was possessed of one of those cheery, chinless faces that should be, but are not, conferred on all fat men. This, and the signs of weariness in his words and actions, created an immediate impression of endearing and reassuring vulnerability. To judge by his legal collar and bands, he had come straight from a long day in court. If so, he could have been forgiven for thinking more of home and hearth than the business we had brought him. But there was no hint that he was.

'For your benefit, Mr Staddon, I should explain that our request to transfer Mrs Caswell's trial to London has been granted. I fancy we have the disorderly scenes at the hearing to thank for that. It will be heard at the Old Bailey. We also have a date: the fourteenth of January. That gives us precisely six weeks to prepare a defence. With Christmas intervening, it is not a generous allowance, but it is all we have. Mrs Caswell has been moved from Gloucester to Holloway Prison to await trial. Windrush and I visited her there yesterday afternoon.

'Mrs Caswell's response to the charges is straightforward denial. I must say that I was deeply impressed by her sincerity. It is, perhaps, the single most encouraging factor to emerge from my consideration of this case. And encouragement is something which I will freely admit we need in substantial quantities. The prosecution have amassed a large amount of damaging circumstantial evidence which we are unlikely to be able to refute. Our

178

answer to the charges rests upon how Mrs Caswell presents herself to the court and what view the jury forms of her. We cannot deny that she was present when the crime was committed, nor that she had the means and opportunity of carrying it out. We cannot even divert suspicion elsewhere. In all the evidence I see no trace of an alternative suspect. Therefore, our efforts must be directed to persuading the court that Mrs Caswell is incapable of having done what she is alleged to have done.

'The one distinguishing characteristic of evidence in poisoning cases is that commission of the crime is never directly witnessed. Nobody sees the poison being administered. If they did, they would intervene. By my reckoning, anybody who was in the house on the afternoon of the ninth of September could theoretically be the murderer. The prosecution will argue that nobody but Mrs Caswell had any reason to commit the crime or had such a good opportunity to do so. We will argue that no sane person would leave the only evidence against her lying around waiting to be found. If we can discredit that evidence, we will have created a persuasive defence, but, to do it, we will need to employ Mrs Caswell herself.

'I anticipate that this case will turn on the defendant's own testimony. My examination will give her every chance to do herself justice and I will prepare her for cross-examination to the very best of my ability. I cannot emphasize too strongly, however, that the crux of the matter will be how she responds to hostile questioning. I will not be able to help her. She will be on her own. Then, and only then, we will know whether our efforts on her behalf are likely to secure an acquittal.

'So much for our strategy. Now, Windrush, I believe you have been recruiting witnesses. What joy on that front?'

'I've traced Cathel Simpson, Mrs Caswell's maid, to her new place of employment in Birmingham. She's prepared to swear neither the arsenic nor the letters were in the drawer the day before the search.'

'Excellent. And the gardener?'

'Sings a different tune every time he's asked.'

'Excuse me,' I put in. 'Banyard told me that Mr Caswell, not Mrs Caswell, made the complaints that prompted him to buy *Weed Out*. Is that helpful?'

'It is indeed,' said Sir Henry. 'And to reinforce such points we need good character witnesses. What progress there, Windrush?'

'Miss Hermione Caswell seems the best bet. Convinced of Mrs

179

Caswell's innocence and related to the deceased. Plenty of spirit. Not likely to be knocked off her stride.'

'Good. Anybody else?'

'I'm afraid not. Mrs Caswell doesn't seem to have many friends. And all Mr Caswell's friends are fighting shy. There's the Roman Catholic priest in Hereford, of course, but—'

'I think not, Windrush. More harm than good with the stolid Protestant jury that will no doubt be our lot.' He mused for a moment. 'Miss Hermione will have to suffice, then. Perhaps, upon reflection—'

'I'd be happy to testify,' I said, more abruptly than I had intended.

Sir Henry smiled indulgently. 'Thank you, Mr Staddon, but no. You would only confuse the jury, I fear. In my experience, jurors find it impossible to believe that married men and women can be friends with each other and nothing more.'

I noticed Rodrigo's head turn towards me. But his eyes were in shadow: I could not tell what he was thinking. 'Perhaps I can help in some other way, then,' I continued. 'You mentioned the lack of an alternative suspect, Sir Henry. Can we exclude the possibility that Mr Caswell staged this poisoning in order to be rid of his wife?'

Windrush winced and sucked in his breath. Sir Henry, for his part, looked at me more attentively than before. 'Would you care to expand upon that remark?' he said mildly.

The shallowness of my suspicions about Victor Caswell was never more apparent to me than when I tried and failed to sketch out a case against him in response to Sir Henry's invitation. I heard myself stringing together impressions and inferences in a way that even I found unconvincing. When I had finally stumbled into silence, Sir Henry sat for a moment with his hands clasped before him and his mouth pressed against them. Then he smiled and spoke in a tone of mild correction.

'Your hypothesis is untenable, Mr Staddon. Moreover, reference to it in court would antagonize both judge and jury. They would feel we were compounding the family's bereavement by levelling tasteless and unfounded allegations. Be guided by me. There are cases in which counter-attack is the best defence. This is not one.'

Suddenly, Rodrigo roused himself. 'I want to ask a question,' he announced in a tolling voice.

'Pray do,' said Sir Henry, his face still creased by a smile.

180

'Will you be able to save my sister?'

'Well, it's really not as simple as—'

'It is all I want to know!' Rodrigo slapped the arm of his chair. 'Can you save her?'

Sir Henry was unmoved. 'I *can* save her, yes. I hope to save her. But I cannot guarantee it. There are no guarantees in law, only chances.'

'And what are our chances?' I asked.

'Candidly, I would have to say that they are not good. But neither are they negligible. And I am confident that they can be appreciably improved between now and the fourteenth of January.'

'What will happen if you fail?' said Rodrigo. 'What will they do to her if you lose the case?'

'That would be a matter for the judge.'

'Will they hang her?'

For the first time, Sir Henry's optimism seemed dented. He fell back in his chair and his face sagged. 'It is a possibility.'

Rodrigo nodded sombrely. 'That is what I thought.' He heaved himself to his feet. '*Chego*! You have told me what I wanted to know. Now, I must go. *Obrigado e boa tarde, senhor.*' He bowed stiffly, turned and walked out of the room.

Windrush was clearly taken aback by Rodrigo's sudden departure. He looked from me to Sir Henry and back again in a grimace of confusion. 'Er . . . I'm sorry, really I am. I'd better go after him.'

'No matter,' said Sir Henry. 'Our business is virtually concluded.'

'Even so, I—' He bundled his papers together, spilling some in the process.

'Volatility is part of the Latin temperament, after all,' Sir Henry added, craning forward to address Windrush as he stooped to the floor.

'I know, but—' Windrush swayed upright. 'I really must check a couple of points with him. Excuse me.' With that, and barely a nod in my direction, he rushed after Rodrigo.

'I too should be going,' I said, as Windrush's footsteps died away.

'There's no hurry, Mr Staddon, I assure you. I was just thinking . . . Would you like a cigar?'

'Er . . . no thanks.'

Undaunted, he lit one for himself. With the first puff, he

assumed a more relaxed posture. 'I was just thinking about my description of our Brazilian friend. "Volatile". Accurate, would you say?'

'Yes.'

'So would I. But it doesn't fit his sister, does it? Mrs Caswell is one of the calmest people I've met. Perhaps *the* calmest, in view of her position.'

Imogen Roebuck's suggestion floated to the fore of my thoughts. 'As if she's not worried by what's happening to her? As if she . . . wants it to happen?'

Sir Henry frowned. 'What do you mean, Mr Staddon?'

'It's just that . . . Consuela Caswell is incapable of murder, assuming her personality's not changed since I knew her. But what if it *has* changed? You said no sane person would commit such a crime and leave the evidence of their guilt lying around to be found by the police. You're right. No *sane* person would. But what if—'

'Don't say any more, I beg you!' He smiled, as if to apologize for his interruption. 'Mrs Caswell is innocent. I am sure of it. To defend her will be an honour, whatever the outcome. But if we muddy the waters, we are lost. You understand?'

'Yes. I understand.'

'Good. Now, if you won't have a cigar, can I offer you a drink? To be frank, Mr Staddon, you look as if you need one.'

Twenty minutes later, I emerged from Plowden Buildings into a night that had grown raw and chill. I turned south along Middle Temple Lane and saw at once, waiting in a doorway some yards ahead, Windrush, enveloped in a cloud of cigarette smoke and his own frosting breath.

'There you are, Staddon. Thank God. I thought I'd missed you.'

'Where's Rodrigo?'

'Vanished. He's in a queer mood, I don't mind telling you. That's why I was so keen to catch him. I only hope he doesn't do anything stupid.'

'Such as?'

'God knows. But he worries me, he really does. Where are you heading?'

'Temple tube station.'

'I'll walk with you, if I may.'

'I won't deny I'd have liked a word with Rodrigo myself,' I said as we set off.

'Count yourself lucky you didn't. He seems to have taken a dislike to you.'

This explained his pointed disregard of me in Curtis-Bennett's chambers, but not what had prompted it. 'I don't understand,' I said. 'He seemed friendly enough when we last met.'

'And he spoke well of you when he turned up in Hereford last week. But something's happened since then to change his attitude. I don't know what. When I collected him from his hotel this afternoon—'

'Where's he staying?'

'The Bonnington, in Southampton Row.'

'Perhaps I'll call on him, then. I'm sure I can dispel any misunderstanding.'

'It's up to you, of course, but I wouldn't recommend it. I know he can be hard to follow at times – the accent, the clipped sentences – but his sentiments about you were clear as day. He wants nothing more to do with you, Staddon, at any price. What he'd do if I told him you were covering Sir Henry's fee I can't imagine.'

'He doesn't know?'

'Good God, no. Fortunately, he's far too impractical to think about money, so he's unlikely to ask.'

'Sir Henry didn't seem to take his walk-out to heart.'

'I'm glad to hear it. Persuading Sir Henry to accept this brief was the best day's work I've done for Mrs Caswell. I don't want her crazy brother frightening him off.'

We turned on to Victoria Embankment and plodded on in silence for a while. A thought I had been seeking to suppress wormed its way into my mind and became a question before I could prevent it. 'How is Consuela?'

'The same. Calm. Remote. Like a swan I saw today on the Serpentine. Elegant. Uninvolved in human affairs. After a while, it starts to seem eerie.'

'Will you be visiting her again soon?'

'Tomorrow morning, before I go back to Hereford.'

We reached the entrance to the underground station and halted. I felt humiliated by the knowledge of my private affairs this man, a total stranger, had unwittingly acquired, reluctant to ask him what I so dearly wanted to.

'Our paths divide here, Staddon. I'm staying with friends in Mitcham. So, I'll bid you goodnight.'

'Before you go—'

'Yes?'

'About Consuela . . .'

He smiled ruefully. 'She won't see you. She's immovable on that point. As on many others.'

'You could . . . ask again.'

'I could ask a thousand times. And the answer would always be the same. She tells me you know why.'

I said nothing. Her only message was an accusation I could not rebut. Windrush nodded, as if my silence had given him the confirmation he sought.

'Good night, Staddon. I'll be in touch.'

Oppressed by the prospect of an evening alone, I passed a couple of hours in the warmth and vicarious good cheer of a pub in Notting Hill Gate. The imprudence of doing so did not become apparent until I reached Suffolk Terrace. As soon as she had opened the door to me, Nora announced that Angela had returned.

She was installed in the drawing-room with two of her bridge and shopping friends, Maudie Davenport and Chloë Phipps. Most of the dresses she had bought in Nice were displayed over the backs of chairs; the one she was wearing also looked new. They were laughing uproariously as I entered, reminding me of how like three geese in a farmyard they often sounded. Perhaps my face betrayed my thoughts. At all events, their laughter died as instantly as a light being switched off and the temperature of the room seemed to plummet.

'There you are, Geoffrey. I was wondering what had become of you.' Angela moved to meet me, inclining her cheek for me to bestow the kiss her friends would expect.

'Good journey?'

'Tolerable, thank you.'

'You should have told me when you were arriving. I'd have met you at the station.'

'It was all too much of a rush, darling.'

'I see. Well, if you ladies will excuse me, I think I'll say good-night. I feel rather knocked up.'

'Goodnight, Geoffrey.'

And so, little caring what impression I left in my wake, I stumbled out.

The light in Angela's dressing-room woke me. For all that I was

184

aware, it could have been the following morning, but the bedside clock told me it was not yet midnight. I lay, instantly alert, listening to the sound of a brush passing through Angela's hair and the slither of silk against her skin. A moment later, she slipped into bed beside me. There was no contact, no touch of hand on arm, no attempt of any kind to bridge the gulf between us. I could have pretended to be asleep and no doubt Angela hoped I was. That, I suppose, is what provoked me to speak.

'Pleasant evening, my dear?'

'Not helped by your arriving home the worse for drink, Geoffrey, as I'm sure you're aware. Beer is such a common smell.'

'I wasn't to know I'd find one of your levées in progress, was I? Why didn't you warn me?'

'I hardly thought you'd be interested.'

'You travelled alone?'

'No. Victor and his party left at the same time. I came with them.'

'Does that include the redoubtable Major?'

'Of course not.'

Silence intruded and had almost reached the point of permanence when Angela spoke again.

'I've grown used to sleeping alone, Geoffrey. I trust you've no objection if I ask Nora to make up the other room for you tomorrow. You'll be quite comfortable there.'

The room to which she referred had been Edward's nursery. I remembered coming home after his death to find it stripped of his clothes, his toys, even of his *Treasure Island* wallpaper, but not – for all Angela's frenzy – of his stubborn little memory. 'Do as you please,' I murmured, as I turned my face towards the pillow.

I rose early the following morning, eager, if the truth be told, to depart for the office before Angela was up and about. After a hasty breakfast, I was in my study, gathering some papers together, when Nora interrupted. She wore a puzzled expression, connected, I assumed, with the ring I had just heard at the front door. A telegram was my first thought, but it was swiftly dispelled.

'There's a young lady to see you, sir. A little girl. She says—'

'Is her name Jacinta Caswell?'

'Why yes, sir. That's the name she gave. You know her, then?'

'Yes, Nora. I know her.'

She was in the drawing-room, dressed as she had been that first time she had called at Frederick's Place. Only her expression had altered. To caution had been added suspicion, to determination a steely defiance. To see her made me feel as proud of her as I was ashamed of myself.

'Good morning, Mr Staddon.'

'Good morning, Jacinta. It's very early for you to be wandering around London.'

'Oh, I haven't been wandering. I came straight here from our hotel. I had to leave before breakfast, otherwise my father would have stopped me, wouldn't he?'

'I daresay he would.'

'Or Miss Roebuck.'

'Would you like something to eat or drink?'

'No thank you. I shall have to go back soon, otherwise they will miss me and come looking.'

'Not here, surely.'

'I don't know. I can't be certain. Can you?'

'How did you get here?'

'By taxi. Major Turnbull gave me a sovereign when we left the Villa d'Abricot. I used it to pay the driver.'

'We agreed you'd always contact me at my office.'

'But you wouldn't have been there, would you? Not at this time. And we're going back to Hereford this morning. My father told me so last night.'

'Even so—'

'Why did you do it, Mr Staddon? That's what I came to ask. Why did you agree to leave my father and Miss Roebuck alone?'

'I didn't. Not exactly. I—'

'I heard you. "You'll hear no more from me." That's what you said. I was standing at the top of the stairs and I heard you say it.'

'It didn't mean what you thought it meant. It didn't mean I was going to stop trying to help your mother.'

'Didn't it?' Her chin was trembling. I sensed she was on the verge of tears but was trying every way she knew to hold them at bay. Like her mother, she was determined to display no hint of weakness. I longed to pluck her from the floor and hug her to my chest. But the past – and my part in it – held me back.

'We've found her a good barrister, Jacinta. He's a very clever man. He'll make sure the court acquits her.'

'How can he do that?'

186

'He examines the evidence. He questions the witnesses. He . . . persuades the jury.'

'Do you think he will persuade them?'

'Oh, yes. I'm sure he will.'

'What happens if he doesn't?'

'We don't need to think about that. Sir Henry Curtis-Bennett won't fail. He never does.'

'Never?'

'Not in a case like this.'

'Are you sure?'

'Of course.'

'And his name is Sir Henry Curtis-Bennett?'

'Yes. You won't have heard of him, but he's very famous.'

'Oh, but I have heard of him. On Wednesday night – the night before we left – my father sat up late with Major Turnbull. I crept downstairs and listened to what they were saying.'

'That was a dangerous thing to to.'

'Not really. Miss Roebuck had a headache. She'd taken a sleeping powder. And Major Turnbull has a loud voice. So it was easy, really. Do you want to know what they were saying?'

'I'm not sure.'

'My father had had a telephone call from his solicitor, Mr Quarton. Mr Quarton must have told him about Sir Henry, because my father was asking Major Turnbull whether he thought Sir Henry would be able to win the case. He didn't sound as if he wanted him to, though.'

'What did Major Turnbull say?'

'He said Sir Henry was good, but not good enough. And then he said something very nasty.'

'What was it?'

'He said Sir Henry had defended a wife accused of murdering her husband last year – and lost. He said her name was Thompson and that they'd hanged her. Is it true, Mr Staddon?'

It was, though I had forgotten till now. Curtis-Bennett *had* defended Mrs Thompson. And he had lost. And she had hanged, as she never should have. 'I . . . I can't remember.'

'He said Sir Henry was just a wind-bag and my father had nothing to worry about.'

'He said that?'

'Yes, Mr Staddon. I heard him most distinctly. *"You've nothing to worry about, Victor, nothing at all."* What does it

187

mean? Are they going to hang my mother? Does my father want them to? Why should—'

There was a sudden commotion at the front door. The knocker was being slammed and the bell rung simultaneously. I heard Nora's voice, then, strident and unmistakable, Victor's. 'Where's my daughter?' he roared.

Jacinta's eyes widened in alarm. 'My father. How did he find out I was here?'

'I don't know.'

'Quick. Before he comes in. Who was the man leaving the villa when you arrived – the last time you were there? They won't tell me.'

'He's your uncle Rodrigo. Your mother's brother. From Brazil. He—'

The door burst open and Victor was upon us. 'What the devil's going on here?' he bellowed.

Jacinta turned and looked at him calmly. Instantly, I noticed, he fell back a pace. Some of his aggression, some of his confidence, drained away. 'I went for a walk before breakfast and became lost, Father. Then I saw the sign for Suffolk Terrace and remembered Mr and Mrs Staddon lived here. Wasn't that lucky?'

Victor stared at her for a moment, his lips rehearsing words he dared not pronounce. Then he said: 'Go outside. Miss Roebuck's waiting in the car.'

'Very well, Father.' She glanced back at me. 'Goodbye, Mr Staddon. Thank you for helping me.'

'Goodbye, Jacinta.'

She walked slowly out, closing the door behind her. Then, before Victor could say anything, I posed a question of my own.

'How did you know she was here?'

'Your wife telephoned me. She thought I ought to know my daughter's whereabouts.'

'I'd have run her back soon enough.'

'Why was she here, Staddon?'

'You heard her explanation.'

He stepped closer, not troubling to veil the hostility in his gaze. 'Last time we met, you undertook to leave me and my family alone.'

'On condition I didn't learn I was being misled.'

'Are you claiming you have been?'

'I'm claiming nothing. Jacinta lost her way and came to my door. That's all.'

'No. It isn't all. But this is: if you try to speak to Jacinta again, if you attempt to communicate with her in any way . . .'

'Yes?'

'Then I'll make sure you lose what little business your dwindling practice has left.'

'How do you propose to do that?'

'I have more influence – in more walks of life – than you can possibly imagine. Don't force me to use it against you.'

'One place you have no influence, Caswell, is in my own house. Now, kindly leave it.'

As before, he seemed minded to say something from which a moment's consideration deterred him. He stared at me, plainly and deliberately, then nodded faintly, as if satisfied that we understood each other. And then he walked swiftly from the room.

As soon as I heard the front door slam behind him, I started for the bedroom. But, halfway up the stairs, I stopped. If I saw Angela, feeling as I now did, there was no knowing what I might do or say. To one, just one, of her barbed remarks, I might respond with something more violent than words. I retreated to the hall and called Nora.

'Did you tell Angela that Jacinta Caswell was here, Nora?'

'Yes, sir. She asked who the visitor was, so I gave her the girl's name.'

'I see. Thank you.'

'Are you going out now, sir?'

'Yes.'

'And will you be back for lunch?'

'No. Not lunch. Nor any other meal.'

The Bonnington Hotel was a modest but reputable establishment. I was directed politely to Rodrigo's room and informed that I would find him in. When I knocked at the door, there was at first no answer. Then, when I knocked again, there came a low growl which I took for an invitation to enter.

The room was deathly cold. The window stood open to the chill, dank air and the fire had long since died. Rodrigo lay supine on the narrow bed, fully clothed and motionless, like some knight's effigy on a tomb. Slowly, he raised his head and looked at me.

'Staddon!' He stressed both syllables of my name equally and spat them out like accusations.

'Hello, Rodrigo. How are you?'

189

'How am I?' He sat upright and I saw for the first time how dishevelled he was, his hair awry, his eyes red and swollen, his chin dark with stubble. Beside him, half-hidden by the rumpled blankets, was an empty spirit bottle. 'You dare to ask me: how am I?'

'What's the matter?'

'You, Staddon. You are the matter.'

'I don't understand.'

'I have been to Hereford. I have been told all about you.'

'Told what? By whom?'

He swung his legs to the floor and glared at me. 'Why are you here?'

'To speak to you. To find out what's troubling you.'

'They will hang my sister. Is that not trouble enough?'

'I thought we were going to work together to prevent that happening.'

'Work together? Rodrigo Manchaca de Pombalho and you?'

'Yes. Why not?'

'Why not?' He launched himself from the bed and, before I knew what was happening, had grasped me by the lapels of my overcoat. I was thrust back against the wall and pinned there, aware of his formidable strength, helpless to do more than hope he would relent. His face was close to mine and he was breathing hard. 'You lied to me, Staddon, didn't you?'

'I don't know what you mean.'

'You said you were Consuela's friend. You did not say you were her lover.'

'I'm not. I never have been.'

'You are still lying.'

'Who says I am? Who have you been talking to?'

'That does not matter. What matters is: do you admit it?'

'Listen to me. There's been some—'

Suddenly, my head was flung back painfully against the wall. His grip had tightened; I could feel my feet being lifted from the floor. 'One more lie, Staddon, just one more, and I will break all the bones in your body.'

'All right. I admit it. Consuela and I . . . were in love. Many years ago. But that doesn't alter anything.'

'You think I will let you help me when I know this about you? When I know you were my sister's lover – the man who made her . . . who made her . . . *uma adúltera*?'

'This has nothing to do with her trial. All I'm trying to—'

190

It was like slipping on ice so suddenly that you have hit the ground before you are aware of it. I was in the corner of the room, my feet tangled in the legs of a side-table, my head ringing, my shoulder aching. Rodrigo towered above me, his bulk distorted by the angle of my vision. *'Você desonrou a minha irmã,'* he roared. *'Você desonrou a minha família.'* I put my hand to my brow and it came back smeared with blood. I crouched forward and rose slowly, cautiously, not taking my eyes off him.

'For God's sake, man—'

'Say nothing! I do not want to hear your voice again, Staddon. Leave now. Leave while I will still let you.'

Silenced by the instinct for self-preservation, I edged towards the door. Rodrigo's gaze never left me. I wanted to reason with him, to explain that it was not as bad as he seemed to think. I wanted, above all, to ask who had told him about Consuela and me. But I did not dare.

I eased the door open, then stooped to retrieve my hat. It had fallen off and was lying at Rodrigo's feet. Before I could reach it, he slipped the toe of his shoe under the brim and flicked it out into the corridor. And, all the while, his unwavering gaze warned me not to protest. I backed slowly out through the door. As soon as I had cleared the threshold, he slammed it shut in my face.

A chambermaid emerging from an adjacent room looked at me with a startled expression. I smiled in an attempt to reassure her, then, remembering the wound on my forehead, turned and hurried away.

'Where have you been since?' asked Imry when I had finished my account of the morning's events.

'The office, where none of them, as far as I could tell, believed my explanation that I'd hit my head on a rafter in the attic at home. I left early and went out to Holloway. Have you ever seen the prison? Castellated Gothic. As grey and forbidding as you could wish. I didn't go in, if that's what you're wondering. It would have been one rejection too many. Instead, I went down to Brompton Cemetery and had a look at the boy's grave.'

'Then you came on here?'

'Yes. I couldn't go home. I couldn't have trusted myself with Angela. Not after the day I've had. We've had our differences – you know that – but I've never felt capable of hitting her before. It was frightening to sense how easy it would be.'

'And pointless. Angela's not the real problem, is she?'

'No. But the real problem's insoluble.'

'You've done all you can. You're going to have to learn to accept that.'

'How can I? Consuela goes on trial in six weeks' time. If she's found guilty, you know what it means?'

'Yes, Geoff, I know. But there's nothing you can do to alter the outcome. You're paying Curtis-Bennett's fee. Isn't that enough?'

'No, it's not.'

'Listen to me. Go home and make your peace with Angela. Forget this madman, Rodrigo. And put Consuela's trial out of your mind as far as you possibly can.'

'It's good advice.'

'But will you act on it?'

'No.' I smiled. 'Almost certainly not.'

CHAPTER

TEN

Irony wears many faces. One of them, that drear month of December, was the extent to which I followed Imry's advice almost in spite of myself. Angela and I were not reconciled, but a grudging truce nonetheless arose between us. I heard nothing from or of Rodrigo, and Consuela's trial, looming ever closer, constituted an event I could neither prevent nor influence. If I was, as my conscience suggested, in some way responsible for what had happened, fate, it appeared, had decreed I should atone for it by a creeping awareness of my utter helplessness.

The weather was grey, chill and persistently wet, the days smog-choked and depressingly short. As if this and my knowledge of what the New Year held were not enough, there was also the hollow good cheer of Christmas to add its leaden weight to my spirits. We were to spend the holiday with Angela's family in Surrey, an event I looked forward to with dread. Meanwhile, the shop-windows of London were bright with tinsel and fairy-lights, Doris had festooned the office with paper-chains and the eager anticipation of festivity seemed to occupy everybody's thoughts.

The last Friday before Christmas was also the shortest day of the year. Sleet had fallen from a louring sky all afternoon. Every light in the office had burned since mid-morning. All had seemed bleak and wearisome. And then had come one small portent of the events that were to break inertia's hold upon me.

''Ere, Mr Staddon,' Kevin said, pausing in my office during his delivery of the second post, 'you seen that advert in the *Sketch*?'

'You know full well I don't take the *Sketch*, Kevin.'

'You should do, though. Then you'd not miss things like this, would you?' He plucked the folded newspaper from beneath his arm and dropped it onto my desk. It was open at the classified advertisements page and all I could see, as I cast my eyes across it, was an undistinguished mass of domestic vacancies and inducements to purchase seasonal gifts by post.

'I haven't time for guessing games.'

'No need to take on like that, Mr Staddon. Look, there.' He prodded at the paper with a nicotine-stained forefinger.

'I really don't—' Then I saw it, in larger print than most entries, headed in bold capitals CASWELL. *Any persons having information bearing on the forthcoming trial of Mrs Consuela Caswell of Clouds Frome, Mordiford, Herefordshire, are invited to make themselves known by replying to Box 361 as soon as possible. Valuable information will attract a substantial cash reward. All replies will be dealt with in strictest confidence. The box-holder is a private citizen.*

'What d'you make o' that, then?'

'What should I make of it?'

'Funny, ain't it? Who's the party who placed it, d'you reckon?'

'I've really no idea. The lady's solicitor, perhaps.'

'No. It says so. "A private citizen." Sets you thinkin', dunnit?'

'Frankly, no. Now, would you mind returning to work?'

Kevin was right, of course. The advertisement did set me thinking, but to no significant purpose. Windrush could not have placed it, for the simple reason that he had no need to: all the witnesses in the case were known to him. Yet so they were to anyone who cared to enquire. Who the anonymous box-holder hoped to attract was therefore a mystery, one I was still puzzling over when I left the office, an hour or so after the rest of the staff had gone.

The sleet had ceased to fall, but the slush left on the pavements was hardening fast as a cold, windless night closed in. I walked fast, but only to keep warm. I was in no hurry to arrive home.

There was a news-stand at the corner of Old Jewry and Poultry. I seldom used it. But, on this occasion, I stopped and bought both the *Evening News* and the *Standard*. I crossed the road and stood by one of Mappin and Webb's brightly lit windows to read them. The advertisement appeared in both. CASWELL. *Any persons having information* . . . It was baffling.

I was still staring at the advertisement a few seconds later, trying and failing to deduce its purpose, when I felt a hand on my elbow.

'Mr Staddon?' The voice was hoarse and low-pitched. Its owner was standing so close to me that I was surprised I had not noticed him approach. He was nearly a foot shorter than me, but powerfully built – a squat little pocket-battleship of a man, with a head seemingly too large for his body. He wore mud-caked boots, overalls, jacket and muffler, with a woollen hat jammed on a mass of curly hair. Cement dust – or some similar substance – had imparted a uniform greyness to his clothes and skin and I took him at once for a labourer, though I did not recognize him from any of the sites I had recently visited.

'What can I do for you?' I said cautiously.

'You are Mr Geoffrey Staddon, the architect, aren't you?'

'Yes.'

'But you don't know who I am?'

'No. I don't.'

'Well, it's been a long time. And life's not been easy. So, you don't surprise me.' He looked up and down the street, then back at me, with a crumpled, less than reassuring smile fixed to his face. 'Could we talk somewhere a bit warmer?'

'Talk about what?'

'Old times. Present times. The one and the other.'

'I really don't know what you mean.'

'You will, soon enough.'

'What did you say your name was?'

'I didn't. But I expect you'll remember it better than my face. Malahide. Tom Malahide.'

Then I recognized him. He was the carpenter from Clouds Frome who had been implicated in the robbery at Peto's Paper Mill. Insofar as I had known him at all, it had been as a cheery and reliable worker. Twelve years and a prison sentence on, he looked old and weary, all the confidence – and much of the pretence – sucked out of him along the way.

'Surprised to see me, Mr Staddon?'

'Yes. I suppose I am.'

'And probably wondering what I want. Well, I'll not beat about the bush. It concerns this trial coming up. The trial of Victor Caswell's wife. Interested? Yes, I can see you are. So, what about that chat?'

*

195

The noise and smoke of one of Cannon Street's least salubrious alehouses seemed to supply all the privacy Malahide required. He let me buy him a stout and whisky chaser, then settled himself at a table near the fire, rolled and lit a cigarette, cocked his head and grinned at me.

'I've had to make do with whatever work I've been offered since leaving the nick, Mr Staddon. None of that carpentry a man could be proud of, like you put my way at Clouds Frome.'

'How long have you been out?'

'Nearly three years. Three hard years, breaking my back for a pittance or else . . . Well, you don't want to know my troubles, do you?'

'I'm not sure I want to know anything about you, Malahide. Have you any idea the difficulties your little escapade caused me?'

'Some.' He looked straight at me, quite unabashed. 'But I couldn't turn up a chance like that. Life doesn't drop many riper plums in a man's lap than the little scheme we had going.'

'Your little scheme landed you in prison, though, didn't it?'

'True enough. But that was all greed and bad luck – or maybe something worse.'

'What could be worse?'

'Snitching on your mates, for one thing. And for another . . .' He stared into his stout for a moment. 'I'm the only one left, you know, the only one of the three still drawing his ration of London smog.'

'What happened to the others?'

'Don't you know? They hanged Pete Thaxter for killing a warder. Didn't that warrant a line in your morning paper, Mr Staddon? I should've thought it would. The nobs like reading about a good hanging, I'm told. It makes them think the rabble are being held in check.'

Another hanging. Peter Thaxter, like his sister, like— 'When was he hanged?' I snapped, suddenly desperate to restrain my thoughts.

'When? Twelve years ago, that's when. His sister – lady's maid at Clouds Frome – topped herself while Pete was in Gloucester Gaol with me, waiting on the Assize. Nobody knew why she did it, seemingly, and that turned Pete's mind, cooped up with nothing else to think about – that and something we'll come to by and by. He took it out on a warder, just with his fists, but he killed him for all that. A strong lad, our Pete. So, they hanged him. And

196

maybe it was best they did. He wasn't the kind to do his stir quietly. I liked him. And he trusted me. I suppose you could say I led him astray. That's how a lot of people would see it, anyway.'

'Is it how you see it?'

'Reckon it is. But guilt slides off me like rain from a roof, so I lose no sleep about it. I've always preferred a dishonest cake to an honest crust and I'll not pretend otherwise.'

'Was the robbery your idea in the first place?'

'No, no, Mr Staddon, you've read me wrong there. Too much brain-work for a fellow like me. It was Joe Burridge's scheme, from top to toe.'

'Burridge was the engraver from Birmingham?'

'He was. As fine a scratcher as you could wish to find. He'd spied out Peto's Mill and realized a ready supply of Bank of England bill paper could be his if he set about it right. Well, he knew me from way back as the man to handle it. Once I saw what was at stake, I don't mind admitting I fair drooled at the thought of it. Perfect forgeries, Mr Staddon, undetectable even to the expert. That was the beauty of it. Burridge could mimic the ink and the design of bank-notes better than any forger alive. What he needed was the paper to mimic them on, complete with the genuine water-mark. My job was to go down to the area, find a good reason to stay there, then get to know the workers at the mill – drink with them, listen to their gripes – till I'd spotted one right for our little enterprise.'

'So working at Clouds Frome was just . . . camouflage?'

''Fraid so.'

'And Peter Thaxter was the one you . . . spotted?'

'He was. He worked on the plate-making machines, which suited our purpose just fine, and he had ideas above his station, which suited them even better. He and a pal had a dream of opening a roller-skating rink in Hereford. What they didn't have was two pennies to rub together. Well, it didn't take young Pete long to realize our scheme was his only chance of raising the capital. And he had some grudges against Grenville Peto to work off. So I didn't have to strain myself to persuade him.' He sighed, as if the recollection saddened him. 'It all went so well to start with. Pete took out finished sheets as often as he could. Nobody noticed because it was only ever a few at a time. He handed them over to me and I took them up to Brum. Joe could print twelve notes from every one. If he made them fifty quid notes, that was six hundred a sheet. Even if he made them just tens, that was still

197

more than a hundred. And Pete was taking up to twenty sheets a week. In six months, we had enough stock to split a fortune between us.'

'What went wrong?'

'Peto's brought forward their stock-taking by three months. Whether they were suspicous or not I don't know, but, if they'd stuck to their usual date, we'd have been in the clear. As it was, as soon as they realized there was something wrong, they kept a careful watch and rumbled young Pete. The police followed him to me, then they followed me to Joe. And then they picked the three of us up, red-handed.'

'Was all the paper recovered?'

He smiled and tapped his nose. 'I've told you enough, Mr Staddon, quite enough for you to understand how I came by the . . . merchandise, shall we call it?'

'What merchandise?'

'Well, fill my glass and I'll tell you. Reminiscing's thirsty work.'

'Malahide—'

He held up his hand. 'If you don't listen to me now, you'll wish you had later.'

Reluctantly, I went to the bar. When I returned, his grin had broadened. Clearly, he was enjoying himself. He took a deep draught of the stout and wiped his mouth with his sleeve, then rolled and lit another cigarette, staring and smirking at me as he did so.

'They gave Joe Burridge a twenty-five stretch, Mr Staddon. Too long for an old 'un like him. He croaked the year before I came out. I went down for twelve, reduced for good behaviour. They never had any trouble with me. Not like Pete Thaxter. But who could blame him? His sister stringing herself up while he fretted and fumed in prison. More than flesh and blood could stand, I'd say. Wouldn't you?'

'I really don't know.'

'I was with Pete in Gloucester Nick when they told him his sister was dead. It fair broke him up, I can tell you. What really got to him was the thought that if he'd not been behind bars, he could've stopped her. But, then, if he'd not been behind bars, she'd not have wanted to do it in the first place, would she?'

'You're suggesting Lizzie Thaxter killed herself because her brother was in prison?'

'Not exactly.'

'Then exactly what are you suggesting?'

198

He leaned closer and lowered his voice. 'She wrote him a letter, Mr Staddon, just before she did it. It reached him a few hours before the news of her death. It told him what had driven her to the edge of doing away with herself. It told him everything about the tormented life she was leading at Clouds Frome.'

'Tormented? By what?'

'By who'd be a better question. Pete kept the letter till he'd been sentenced to hang. He didn't show it to his family because Lizzie had asked him not to. She wanted him to explain it all to them when he came out. But, after clouting that warder, he wasn't coming out, was he? So, what d'you suppose he did?'

An inkling of the answer had been creeping over me as Malahide spoke, but I held it at bay with a shrug of the shoulders and a petulant 'How should I know?'

'He gave the letter to me, Mr Staddon, to be passed on to his family when I got out.'

'And did you pass it on?'

''Fraid not.' He grinned. 'Solemn promises aren't really my line. To tell you the truth, I forgot all about it. If I'd ever been down that way, I might've done something about it. Otherwise, I'd probably never have thought of it, but for Clouds Frome and the Caswells popping up in the papers two months back.'

'So you still have the letter?'

He took a gulp from his stout. 'I have it, yes.'

'What do you propose to do with it?'

'I've been wondering about that. The fact is, you see, I thought I'd better read it – after all this time – and, when I did, I was surprised to find some familiar names cropping up in it.'

'Such as?'

'Such as yours, Mr Staddon.'

'Mine?'

He leaned still closer, till his face was barely a foot from mine, till the glee in his bloodshot eyes could not be mistaken. 'The letter names you as Mrs Caswell's lover. It says you and her were planning to run away together. Till you ditched her, that is.'

'What nonsense! It can't possibly—'

'How would I know unless the letter had told me? Be sensible, Mr Staddon. You know what I'm saying's the truth. You had an affair with Mrs Consuela Caswell. I don't blame you. Matter of fact, I envy you. The few glimpses I had of her . . . Well, enough said, eh? You had your way with her, then you ran out on her. It's the old—'

'It's nothing of the kind! And I happen to object – very strongly – to these suggestions.'

'Object all you like, but take it from me that my version is the one anybody reading Lizzie's letter would come away with. Now, the point is, do you want people to read it? Do you want them to know what you did to her mistress?'

'What do you mean?'

'I think the papers would bite my hand off for it, don't you? They're down on Mrs Caswell. You know that. They want her neck. A letter proving she's not the lily-white faithful wife she claims – and never has been – would be just what they want. Dragging in the architect her husband employed to build a house for her would be the cherry on their cake – don't you reckon?'

'You called this letter a suicide note. Are you trying to blame me for Lizzie's death?'

'Oh no, Mr Staddon. Some would blame you. But not me.' Another grin. 'If you want to know exactly what's in the letter, you can find out easily enough. It's for sale, you see. To the highest bidder.'

'This is blackmail.'

'No. It's an auction. Sotheby's hold them all the time.'

'Now listen to me—'

'No! You listen to *me*, Mr Staddon. I'm a reasonable man. I only want a fair price. If you're willing to pay, the auction needn't take place.'

'How much do you want?'

'A hundred.'

'Good God! You must be—'

'Joking? I never joke. I've looked at this from all angles and I reckon that's what it's worth. Six months ago, no. Six months ahead, no again. But, just now, yes. I think you'll see your way clear to coughing up. You've your practice to consider, after all. This letter will get splashed all over the front pages. What will your fancy clients think when they read how you helped yourself to one of their wives? Well, I'll tell you what they'll think—'

'Don't bother! I understand what you're saying. Spare me the elaboration.'

'You'll pay, then?'

I said nothing. The defiance I wanted to express I could not afford to – for Consuela's sake as well as mine. Would I have resisted if my reputation alone had been at stake? I do not know.

All I knew then was that I had to have Lizzie Thaxter's last letter, whatever price I had to pay for it.

'We're agreed, are we, Mr Staddon?'

'Apparently.'

'Good. Well, you won't have the cash about you, any more than I have the letter about me, so what I suggest is this. We meet a week today, I bring the letter, you bring the money. How does that seem? This side of Southwark Bridge, eight o'clock, next Friday night.'

'Very well.'

Suddenly, he had finished his stout and was on his feet, grinning down at me. 'It's a pleasure doing business with a gentleman like yourself, Mr Staddon, a real pleasure. Till next week, then. Don't be late.'

He was gone almost before I knew it, gone with but an empty glass to prove he had ever been there. His grubby, callused fingers had left their smeared prints around it, as his words had around my life. What had Lizzie written to her brother all those years ago? What had driven her to suicide? What had I done – or not done – to condemn her to a lonely grave beyond the churchyard wall? Dark of face and swift of tread, the truth would surely soon be plucking at my sleeve.

Angela and I had latterly contrived to meet only rarely and to converse not at all beyond the making of strictly practical arrangements. There was comedy, I sometimes thought, in the tight-lipped indifference which we substituted for angry exchanges, but it was comedy that inspired no laughter.

On Sunday morning, departing from her recent habit of breakfasting in bed and thus avoiding me, Angela joined me downstairs. I knew at once that an announcement of some kind – a demand, a rebuke, perhaps even a request – was pending. She was in no hurry, however. Tea, dry toast and two cigarettes received her silent attention before she deigned to address me.

'I've told Mummy we'll be with them by tea-time tomorrow. I trust you won't be delayed at the office.'

'I shouldn't think so. I'll be back here by two at the latest.'

'They're assuming we'll stay on for the New Year's Eve party.'

'What party?'

'I did mention it to you.'

'Well, I have to be back in London by the twenty-seventh. We'll just have to make two trips of it.'

'I could remain there while you return to London.'

'As you please.'

'And Geoffrey, while we *are* together, do you think you could make an effort at least to pretend that all is well between us? I know it will be an effort – for both of us – but we don't really want to burden my parents with our problems, do we?'

'I suppose not.' I looked up from my paper for the first time since she had begun speaking. 'Don't worry,' I said, with a vein of sarcasm in my voice that I was later to regret. 'I'll behave.'

Sir Ashley Thornton, my esteemed and eminent father-in-law, knighted by Lloyd George's government in recognition of I know not what, had commissioned for himself some years before we met a country residence of style and substance a few miles south of Guildford. The architect shall remain nameless, lest I be accused of traducing a fellow professional. Luckham Place was, in truth, as safe, sound and solid a piece of Neo-Georgian predictability as any student of the style could wish to encounter.

There, at dusk on Christmas Eve, Angela and I arrived laden with smartly wrapped presents and contrasting expectations. The Thorntons had, as usual, erected in their hall one of the tallest Christmas trees seen beyond the shores of Norway. It, along with every beam and lintel in the house, was strung with baubles, balloons, tinsel and tassels. Angela's brother, Clive, had already arrived with his wife, Celia, and their three children; the drawing-room was ringing with their laughter as we entered. Instantly, Angela was embraced and kissed by her mother and sister-in-law. So, in turn, was I, but with an aloofness, an icy dutifulness, that reminded me how tenuous and barely tolerated my membership of their family had become. To see my father-in-law dandling his eldest surviving grandson on his knee was to be reminded of all the trust and support he would no doubt have conferred on me – if only Edward had lived.

Clive Thornton was rapidly being groomed as his father's successor at the head of Thornton Hotels. Five years younger than Angela, he had done everything that could have been asked of him: distinguished war service, a reputable marriage and the regular production of grandchildren. Small wonder that in him Sir Ashley's hopes for the future now resided. If, of course, Clive had died a hero's death on the Somme, if Edward had not contracted influenza, if the Hotel Thornton had not been burned to the ground, my life would have taken a vastly different turn.

202

But these were unworthy thoughts, I told myself, as the festivities at Luckham Place began to take their ritualistic course: midnight mass at the village church, of which Sir Ashley was a generous benefactor; then Christmas Day itself, with feasting and gaiety unbounded, concluding with parlour games that reduced the children to hysterics. I moved through the seamless succession of events more as a spectator than a participant, conscious of, but no longer discomforted by, my growing isolation. I was a stranger in their midst, but none of us was prepared to admit it.

On Boxing Day, Sir Ashley, Angela, Clive and Celia rode with the local foxhounds. After seeing them off, I drove slowly back to London, glad to be alone once more. I had said I would rejoin them on New Year's Eve, but, in truth, I could hardly direct my thoughts so far ahead. My appointment with Malahide – and the procurement of Lizzie's letter – had become an horizon beyond which I did not care to look.

Giles Newsom had volunteered to mind the office between Christmas and New Year. Accordingly, we had the place to ourselves. Always vaguely scornful of the rest of the staff, Giles seemed positively cheered by their absence, engaging me in lengthy conversations about architectural theory and practice. He was, and had always been in my eyes, Imry's choice. For my taste, he was too glib, too cocksure, too clever by half. And he was something else as well: a fine architect in the making. Perhaps that was what I really resented.

During those days, Giles returned again and again to a topic I had already done my best to deflect him from: Clouds Frome. An apparently genuine enthusiasm for its design seemed in danger of becoming an obsession. There was no end to his questions. What had forged the idea in my mind? How had I put it into effect? Where were the original drafts and sketches? Could he borrow them, perhaps, the better to appreciate what I had achieved? My answers were uniformly unhelpful. I wanted no drooling, double-edged praise from a young man who believed he was my intellectual superior. Above all, I wanted no reminders of the way I had thought those many years ago.

I had, besides, a more pressing matter to consider: my bargain with Malahide. On Thursday, I withdrew a hundred pounds from my bank and lodged it in the office safe. On Friday, I gave Giles the afternoon off, then took a long walk round some of my favourite London buildings. Architecture at its best still held for me a healing quality, but the inspiration it once conveyed had drained away. Whether gaping in awe at a work of the master, or gazing in admiration at something by Shaw or Lutyens, I could no longer generate the desire to rival or outdo. I was inferior to them, of course, but what really hurt my pride was that I was also inferior to the architect I had once been.

I returned to Frederick's Place a little before half past seven, intending to remove the money from the safe and walk to Southwark Bridge in ample time to rendezvous with Malahide. All I wanted now was for our association to be ended and our business concluded as quickly as possible: Lizzie's letter in my hand, Malahide's threats off my mind. That, for the moment, would be relief enough.

I did not realize there was anything wrong until I was halfway up the stairs. It was then that the light under my office door, visible across the dark expanse of the outer office, suddenly struck my eyes. The difference in height between one step and another became at once the difference between preoccupation and anxiety. I stopped where I was, scouring my memory of leaving the building that afternoon. I had left no lights burning. Of that I was certain. Somebody had been in since my departure. Then I heard a noise – a rustling of paper, a movement of some kind: they were still there.

The street door had been locked. No intruder could have come that way. Yet there was no other way, short of descending from the roof. There came a squeal of swollen wood as the second drawer on my desk – the one that always stuck – was pulled open. At that, I started up the stairs again. I reached the top, crossed the outer office and stopped by my door. Papers were being rustled, sifted, searched. By whom or why I could not guess. I rested my hand on the knob, hesitated for a moment, then flung the door open.

Giles Newsom was standing behind my desk, his hands resting on a pile of documents that lay before him. I could not see what they were, but, if they had come from the desk-drawers, he could certainly have had no business with them. Besides, the look on his face was an admission of guilt in itself. For once, his self-assurance had deserted him.

The door of the corner cupboard stood open, as did all the four drawers of the filing cabinet beside it and all ten of the map-chest. A glance sufficed to tell me that my senior assistant had been searching my office – thoroughly and in secret. I stepped into the room and closed the door behind me, then stared straight at him, waiting for him to explain himself. But he merely moved his hands to his sides and smiled nervously.

'Well?' I said after a moment.

'I didn't expect you back, Mr Staddon.'

'Obviously not.'

'I suppose this looks rather odd, doesn't it?'

'It looks damnably suspicious. Can you persuade me it isn't?'

'Probably not.'

'How did you get in?'

'I took Reg's key with me this afternoon.'

'And returned when you thought I'd be long gone?'

'Yes.'

'So, this was carefully planned. Is it why you volunteered to come in this week?'

'In a sense. But if you'd not been so reticent about Clouds Frome, I wouldn't have had to—'

'Clouds Frome? You mean you're looking for the plans of a house I once built? You've crept back here, at dead of night, just to satisfy your curiosity?'

'It isn't dead of night. And it's rather more than curiosity.'

'What, then?'

'Necessity, I suppose you'd say.'

I moved closer. 'Explain this necessity, Giles. Explain it to me now, please, while my temper's still in check.'

'My salary here doesn't cover my expenditure, Mr Staddon. It's as simple as that. It's not that you under-pay me. You don't. But I have expensive tastes. I like the best, the very best. The point is that I sometimes need to subsidize my tastes by earning money in unorthodox ways. This is one such way. I've been paid to obtain copies of the Clouds Frome floor-plans and elevations, complete with all measurements and dimensions. I tried to talk you into letting me see them, but you wouldn't. So, this seemed the only—'

'Who paid you?'

'I'd really rather not say. He insisted on complete confidentiality. It's not as if what he asked me to do was in any sense criminal.'

Suddenly, anger flared within me. 'God damn it, you'll tell me and you'll tell me now! This is my office. I *employ* you. Legal niceties don't enter into it. I can dismiss you on the spot – and make damn sure no other architect takes you on. I may count for

205

little in this world – and less in this profession than you think you will one day – but just at the moment I hold the power to wreck your career before it's even started. So, I'll ask you again: who paid you?'

Shame – or a realization of the truth of my words – swept over Giles. His face crumpled. The vestiges of defiance fell away. 'A Brazilian. Known to you, I believe.'

'Rodrigo Manchaca de Pombalho?'

'Yes. That's the name.'

'How did you come into contact with him?'

'He was in the Three Crowns one night last week. He stood me a few drinks, introduced himself as a business-man from Portugal, said he didn't know London and asked if I could tell him where an entertaining evening was to be had. Well, I quite took to him, especially the way he threw money around, so I offered to escort him. We went to the Alhambra, and on to a club I know afterwards. He seemed to enjoy himself – and he paid for everything. When he suggested another outing the following night, I jumped at it. That's when he told me who he really was and offered me fifty pounds if I could lay hands on the plans of Clouds Frome.'

'No doubt you jumped at that as well?'

'There's no point denying it, is there? The money would have got me out of a bit of a hole, actually. Besides, I could see no harm in it. He didn't want to approach you himself. He wouldn't say why. And I didn't press him to. After all, I was confident I'd be able to talk you into giving me what he wanted. Why should I quibble? It seemed too good an opportunity to miss.'

'Did you ask him why he wanted the plans?'

'No. He made it plain he had no intention of explaining himself to me. And why should he? He was paying me well enough to stifle my curiosity.'

'So, all your polite and respectful questions about my design of the house were just ploys. All your praise – all your wide-eyed admiration – was intended to lure me into letting you have what you'd been bribed to obtain.'

'You could say that, yes.'

'And when those methods failed, you resorted to burglary.'

'It's hardly burglary. What do a few plans matter? What harm can they do?'

'I don't know. But if it were all so very innocent, he wouldn't have offered you as much as he did, would he?'

206

Giles seemed about to throw back some sharp retort, then thought better of it. 'What happens now, Mr Staddon?' he asked neutrally.

'First of all, you tell me what arrangements you've made with Senhor Pombalho.'

'I was to telephone him as soon as I had the plans. The terms we agreed were strictly C.O.D.'

'Very well. This is what you're going to do. Telephone him now. Arrange a meeting. Somewhere public. I want plenty of bystanders when I confront him.'

'When *you* confront him?'

'Yes, Giles. You make the appointment. I'll keep it. Is he still staying at the Bonnington?'

'I don't know. He just gave the number. Museum 1010.'

'It sounds like the Bonnington. Call it and see.'

'But what do I say to him?'

'Say you have the plans and you can meet him tonight. I'll leave the choice of venue to you. Then you can go home and contemplate your future.'

'What is my future – after this?'

'Uncertain. It's the breach of trust, you see, Giles. That's what's so unforgivable. I'll have to discuss it with Mr Renshaw, of course. Perhaps your position isn't completely irretrievable. For the moment, I just don't know.'

'If you'd lent me the plans, or not come back tonight—'

'I don't have the plans to lend.'

'What do you mean?'

'They don't exist. I destroyed them – all of them – a long time ago.'

He stared at me in amazement. 'Why?'

'That's none of your concern. Now, make that telephone call, please, there's a good fellow.'

With a resigned shrug of the shoulders, he walked into the outer office and switched on the light. Only Reg's telephone, as we both knew, was connected to an outside line. As he picked up the receiver, I sat down at my desk and raised mine to my ear, listening as he spoke to the operator and was connected.

'Bonnington Hotel. Good evening.'

'Room 207, please.'

'Hold on, please.'

The extension rang only once. Then came Rodrigo's voice, muffled but familiar. '*Estou?*'

'Senhor Pombalho? This is Newsom. I have what you want.'

'That is good.'

'Can we meet tonight?'

'Tonight? Yes. You—' He broke off. There was another voice in the background, a woman's raised, it seemed, in protest, though I could not catch her words. '*Fique quieto!*' snapped Rodrigo. 'You will come here, Newsom?'

'No, I can't. I'll meet you at the Lamb. It's a pub not far from your hotel. They'll give you directions.'

'I will find it. When?'

Giles took out his watch and flipped it open. 'An hour's time, shall we say? Nine o'clock.'

'Nine o'clock. Yes. I will be there.' With that, he put the telephone down.

'Well?' said Giles, looking back towards me. 'Is that what you wanted?'

But I did not answer. I had pulled out my own watch as Giles named the time and was staring now at its face, dumbstruck by my own forgetfulness. It was a minute past eight. And I was a long way from Southwark Bridge.

The bridge was dark and empty. The night was cold and damp enough to discourage loiterers. I was entirely alone, leaning against the parapet, the Thames running turbulently below me. It was twenty past eight and my frail hope that Malahide might also be late had vanished. He had waited for me only so long, then taken his merchandise elsewhere. Perhaps it was as well, in the circumstances, that I could not afford to linger, could not spare the time to brood upon what would happen now to Lizzie Thaxter's last letter. With a sigh, I pushed myself upright and started walking hard towards Holborn.

The Lamb was, as I had hoped, crowded. A piano was being played somewhere deep in the throng to the tune of 'If You Were the Only Girl in the World'. In the crush at the bar, I caught sight of Rodrigo straightaway, standing head and shoulders above the other customers. I began threading my way towards him. Amidst the jostling, the laughter, the shouting and the singing, he did not notice me as I approached.

He looked bowed and mournful, a dark cape slung about his shoulders, a shadow of stubble about his chin. His size and expression, his isolation from the merriment around him, had created an invisible circle in which he stood, silent and forbidding, staring down into his glass.

'Newsom isn't coming,' I said, shouting to make myself heard.

Rodrigo swung round, colliding with a man behind him as he did so and spilling the poor fellow's drink. But all protests were wasted on him. 'Staddon!' He stared at me, his eyes blazing. 'Why are you here?'

'I found Newsom searching my office. He admitted you'd put him up to it. He also told me what you were after. I was listening on another line when he telephoned you. I'd instructed him what to say.'

'You *instructed* him?'

'Yes. And now I'm here to demand an explanation. What do you want with the plans of Clouds Frome?'

'I will tell you nothing. *Nada em absoluto*. Do you understand?'

'Yes, but I don't think you do. There are no plans to be had, Rodrigo. I burned them all before the war.'

'You are lying!'

'No. It's the truth. They no longer exist. Except in my head. So, if you want to know anything about them, you're going to have to persuade me you have a good reason.'

'Why did you burn them?'

'That needn't concern you.'

'But it does. I want to know why, Staddon. Why burn them? Was it so you could forget Clouds Frome and what you did there? Was it so you could forget Consuela?'

'Leave Consuela out of this.' I was suddenly aware of the silence that had fallen around us; people on all sides were listening and watching. The realization provoked me into a stupid attempt to humiliate Rodrigo. 'I don't know what you think gives you the right to deliver moral lectures. Remember, I heard every word of your telephone conversation with Newsom. You weren't alone in your hotel room, were you? Who was she, Rodrigo? Some little tart, I suppose. How much were you paying—'

It was like a snake striking. His right arm flashed out from beneath the cape and his hand closed round my throat with choking force. I was pinned against the bar, the edge of it grinding into my spine as he pushed me further and further back. There was a commotion around us and a splintering noise as a glass fell to the floor. Out of the corner of my eye, I saw the barmaid stepping away, her blouse wet with spilt beer. Then she screamed. Somebody else cheered. But I could neither speak nor cry out. I could not even breathe. The pain was intense, the panic of suffocation mounting. I prised desperately at his hand, but could not dislodge it. Behind my neck, his fingers and thumb nearly met. And in front of me was only his face, twisted with rage, eyes bulging, teeth clenched. '*Eu matarei você!*' he bellowed. Then came a gurgling, spluttering sound that I suddenly realized was me, pleading for mercy. My mouth was open, straining for air, my vision was failing, my strength ebbing. He was going to kill me. Now, at last, I knew he meant it. He was going to squeeze the very life out of me and there was nothing I could do to stop him.

Then his grip slackened slightly and, with it, the pressure that had arched me back across the bar. A snatch of breath reached my lungs. I could see again more clearly. There were figures behind and around Rodrigo, pulling him off me, dragging at his right arm, shouting at him to desist. There must have been six of them, powerful, hard-drinking men who had just realized this was more than mere horse-play, but, for all their efforts, they could do no more than weaken his hold.

Yet that, in the event, was enough. In the precious interval they won me, I saw a change in Rodrigo's expression. His anger with me faltered. Perhaps he remembered what had brought him to England and how poorly he would serve Consuela's cause by killing me. Or perhaps he simply judged me unworthy of such a fate. Whatever the reason, he suddenly whipped his hand away from my throat.

My legs buckled beneath me. With the return of breath came wracking coughs and a mist of tears across my eyes. I heard Rodrigo shout something and sensed, rather than saw, a scattering of figures as he turned away and cleared a path to the door. As it crashed to behind him, I was helped onto a stool. A glass of water was pressed into my hand. My coughing fit began to subside and, as it did so, the soreness of my neck and the pain in my back intruded. I could not speak. For the moment, it was enough to breathe again and wait for coherence to return.

'Gawd, mate,' said somebody. 'I thought 'e was gonna finish you for sure.'

'Yeh,' said another. 'So did I. Whad'ya do to get 'im goin' like that?'

I shook my head in the only answer I could summon. It was not true, of course. I knew full well what had provoked Rodrigo. But that did not matter now. What mattered was the sense of my own stupidity that was flooding into my brain. I had come there to discover why he wanted the plans of Clouds Frome. And the only thing I had learned was what I already knew. He despised me.

The taxi-ride home from the Lamb that night gave me ample time to contemplate my plight. Malahide might at any moment offer Lizzie Thaxter's letter to the press, yet I had no way of reaching him in order to explain my failure to keep our appointment. Nor, out of a concern for my own safety, could I risk any further approaches to Rodrigo. For Consuela's sake, I had to keep Lizzie's letter out of the newspapers and I had to persuade Rodrigo to trust me. But my efforts on both counts had been abject failures. My position was hopeless and, for that, I had nobody to blame but myself.

By the following morning nothing had changed except my state of mind. From self-pity and despondency the resources of my nature had salvaged, if not hope, then at least a measure of confidence. For this Giles Newsom had good reason to be grateful. In any other circumstances, I would have persuaded Imry to let me dismiss him for what he had done. And to judge by the tousled, nerve-stricken condition in which I found him awaiting me at Frederick's Place, dismissal was what a sleepless night had led him to expect. He was not to know, of course, that I had been visited by enough doubts and fears to eclipse his own, nor that his humiliation was about to make him my ally.

'I've given a great deal of careful thought to your position,' I announced, as he followed me into my office.

'So have I, Mr Staddon, and I'd like to offer you my sincere apologies for what occurred. My behaviour was inexcusable.'

'I'm inclined to agree with you.'

'Does that mean . . . you'll be dispensing with my services?'

'No, Giles, it doesn't.'

'Then . . . what?'

I sat down and waved him into a chair. 'I've no wish to ruin your career on account of one isolated instance of misconduct. For that reason, I'm prepared to overlook last night's events – to forget about them altogether and to mention them to nobody – just so long—'

'Mr Staddon!' He jumped up, smiling broadly. 'This really is extremely understanding of you. I can't thank you enough.'

'Sit down, Giles!' I waited until he had done so, then resumed. 'I shall expect something of you in return for my forbearance. You should hear what it is before showering me with thanks.'

'Name it.'

'My . . . discussions . . . with Senhor Pombalho were less than fruitful. I was unable to establish why he wanted the plans of Clouds Frome and we parted on a note of some acrimony. He simply wouldn't listen to me. That's where I believe you can be of assistance. I require the services of a mediator, you see, somebody who can speak to him on my behalf without arousing his hostility. I wish to make him an offer. If he will explain his reasons for wanting the plans, I will consider recreating them from memory.'

'And you want me to put those terms to him?'

'Precisely.'

'May I ask . . . what this is all about? It would be helpful if I could—'

'You may ask nothing. I've told you all you need to know.'

'If I refuse, you'll recommend to Mr Renshaw that I be dismissed?'

The position in which I had placed him was an unpleasant one. I knew so from my own recent experience. Yet I could afford to show him no mercy. 'You'd leave me no choice in the matter, Giles. No choice whatever.'

He smiled wryly. 'In that case, Mr Staddon, you've found a mediator.'

I set off for Surrey on New Year's Eve leaving Giles with a great deal to occupy him. We had agreed to let Rodrigo brood for a few days before making contact with him, but I had left Giles in no doubt that I would expect progress to have been made by the time I returned. I had also instructed him to telephone every builder we knew in London – and they were legion – in search of one who had recently employed a carpenter named Malahide. I had concluded that Malahide would not approach a newspaper until nearer the trial, reasoning that he could thereby strengthen his bargaining position. If I was right, there was still time to track him down.

Preparations for one of Sir Ashley's famous parties were well underway when I reached Luckham Place. Temporary staff were moving furniture and polishing case-loads of champagne glasses. Yet more streamers and balloons were being pinned to already burdened mantels and picture-rails. A jazz band was setting up its instruments. And a gathering of overnight guests – hardly any of whom I recognized – had occupied the drawing-room. In response to an enquiry about my wife's whereabouts, I was told she had taken a visitor for a drive in the neighbourhood and was expected back shortly. Meanwhile, the grinning Clive announced, his father would appreciate a word with me in the privacy of his study.

'Come in, Geoffrey, come in. A drink, perhaps?'
'No thanks. A bit early for me.'
'You're probably right. A long night ahead, what?'
'No doubt.'
Even in the time I had known him, Ashley Thornton had changed. The character of most men is settled by their middle twenties, but my father-in-law did not believe in fixed values of any kind. His origins were veiled in reticence. What little Angela had let slip suggested East Midlands roots at the upper end of the working class. What he had contrived since was an ever accelerating progression towards the aristocracy. He had once been proud of his hard-won success. Now it seemed he preferred people to think he had gained his wealth almost without effort and that what he had founded was less a business than a dynasty. It was a dynasty, moreover, in which an unfashionable architect with a blemished record had no obvious role.
'Clive said you wanted to see me.'
'Indeed. Now . . . Sure you won't have that drink?'
'Quite, thank you.'
We regarded each other across his empty desk for a few moments, then he said: 'I've never entirely abandoned the idea of rebuilding the Thornton, you know. On a different site, that is.'
'I'm delighted to hear it.'
'It would have to be completely different, of course, in tune with the altered times. We all have to be that, don't we?'
'I suppose we do, yes.'
'I was in California earlier this year. I stayed at the Biltmore Hotel in Los Angeles. It's only just opened. Do you know it?'
'I've seen photographs of it in the architectural press.'
'What's your opinion of it?'
'Overwrought and overdone.'
He smiled. 'I was impressed. It's the future of hotel design, take it from me.'

213

'Not in London, I think.'

'As to that, I must disagree.'

'Surely my opinion of the Biltmore isn't what you wanted to talk to me about?'

'No, it isn't. But it's indicative, don't you see? Symptomatic of so much else.'

'I don't see, actually.'

He sighed. 'Angela has told us of your recent disagreements.'

'What disagreements?'

He leaned across the desk, treating me to a look he no doubt reserved for recalcitrant employees. 'Any *liaison* you may have had with a married woman prior to meeting Angela is, of course, no concern of mine. We are both, I hope, men of the world. But such involvements must be forgotten, set aside, expunged . . . I cannot allow a son-in-law of mine to indulge in tasteless crusades on behalf of former mistresses who have taken to poisoning their husbands.'

Perhaps he expected me to be angry or ashamed. Perhaps he hoped to arouse my indignation or appeal to my sense of propriety. Whatever the case, the only reaction I felt was weary disappointment that Angela had whispered our secrets in his ear. 'A tasteless crusade is what Angela called it. Did you intend to quote her exact words – or is it just habit?'

His face froze. I had treated him to something he seldom encountered in these days of his dubious pomp. 'If one word of your involvement with the Caswell creature – then or now – reaches the papers,' he hissed, 'if one, just one, of my business associates mentions it to me over lunch; if I discover that you have sullied my family name by perpetuating this nonsense. . . .'

'Yes? What then?'

He sat back in his chair. 'Don't do it, my boy. Don't do it, for your own sake.'

'Are you threatening me?'

'I don't need to. You should be grateful to Victor Caswell, not working against him.'

'I owe Victor Caswell nothing.'

'That's where you're wrong. And let me remind you of some other sober facts. 27 Suffolk Terrace is Angela's property, not yours. If she should leave you and sell it, you could have no complaint. As for your practice, well, you don't need me to tell you how it's slipped since the fire. Mud sticks, but, in the architectural profession, ash clings far longer.'

214

'That's suited you well enough, hasn't it? There was no danger of Thornton Hotels being blamed once I'd been appointed whipping-boy.'

'I had no hand in that, Geoffrey. You're a fool if you think otherwise. And you're a fool if you don't take my advice. As an architect, you're out of date and short of business. As a husband, you're little better than a kept man. And your keeper is on the brink of giving you notice. I've made allowances for your . . . bereavement . . . long enough. Angela deserves better of you than this. So do we all. My advice to you is simple. Start behaving as we have a right to expect. Otherwise you may jeopardize your marriage – and much else besides. Do you understand?'

What answer I gave Sir Ashley – how I ended our interview, with what words I left him – I cannot now recall. Anger blots out memory as well as reason and perhaps that is for the best. Certainly I gave him none of the assurances he had sought, though that may not have surprised him. He may have calculated I would see the wisdom of compliance after a period of reflection and, for that matter, he may have been right. In the event, however, no such period was to be afforded me.

I walked straight out of the house after leaving the study, hardly trusting myself to encounter another member of the Thornton family till I had breathed some fresh air and walked off some of my resentment. Dusk was settling over Luckham Place as the sun sank, red and swollen, beyond the North Downs. I set off along the drive, walking as hard and fast as I could, rehearsing under my breath the wounding retorts I would have given Sir Ashley if only I had thought of them sooner. At first, I hardly noticed the motor-car that had turned in off the Guildford road and was heading up the drive towards me, visible in snatches between the well-spaced elms. More guests, I assumed, more vapid recruits to the Thorntons' ever-widening circle of acquaintances. Then, as it rounded a bend fifty yards ahead, I recognized it. I stopped in my tracks and, as I did so, the driver sounded his horn in acknowledgement. It was Turnbull's Lanchester.

'Not deserting us, Staddon, surely?' Turnbull grinned down at me from the driver's seat as the car drew to a halt beside me. 'I'm told Sir Ashley's parties are memorable affairs.' He was clad in a huge double-breasted overcoat, gauntlets and a deerstalker. On his other side sat Angela, remote and regal in an outfit I did not recognize – a grey swagger-coat trimmed with black fur and

215

matching fur hat. She did no more than glance at me, then gazed straight ahead towards the house between half-closed lids, her face as pale and expressionless as Turnbull's was flushed and jubilant.

'What are you doing here, Major?'

'Didn't Angela tell you? It was all arranged before she left Nice. Sir Ashley kindly invited me to stay with him for the week.'

'I knew nothing about it.' I stared pointedly at Angela, but she did not respond. 'It must have slipped her mind.'

'Quite so.' Turnbull's grin broadened. 'Well, we must get on. See you at the party.'

I watched the car roar away along the drive, then felt misery and a strange foreboding close upon me in the silence that followed.

Angela's disclosures to her father had evidently not extended to our separate sleeping arrangements in Suffolk Terrace. At Luckham Place, we were still expected to occupy the same room. When, three hours and several stiff drinks later, I went up to change, I found that she was in the bath, door bolted, leaving a shot-silk ball-gown lying in readiness across the bed and a brooch I felt sure I had never seen before prominently displayed on the dressing-table. It was gold, fashioned in the likeness of a monkey, the clasp disguised as a pole to which he was clinging. Two tiny rubies served as his eyes and the expression on his face reminded me all too strongly of the grinning stone monkeys who stood sentinel over the garden gate at the Villa d'Abricot.

It was as I was staring at the brooch, admiration of its beauty blending with disgust at its significance, that there came a knock at the door. I opened it to find Bassett, one of the footmen, standing outside, looking distinctly uneasy.

'What is it, Bassett?'

'You have a visitor, Mr Geoffrey.'

'A visitor? Surely the house is full of them.'

'He's asked specifically for you.'

'Who is this gentleman?'

'Not a gentleman at all, Mr Geoffrey, if you don't mind my saying so. Not the kind of person we're used to receiving at the front door. I'll happily send him on his way if you give the word.'

'But who is he?'

'Gives his name as Malahide. Claims you know him. But I expect there's been some mistake.'

216

Bassett had left Malahide in the billiards-room, about the only room in the house where he could neither offend the guests nor filch the silver. He was wearing the same clothes as when we had previously met, although there was no sign of cement-dust on this occasion. He was idly bouncing a ball around the cushions of the table as I entered.

'What the devil do you mean by coming here?' I demanded.

He let the ball roll to a halt, then leered across at me. 'Fancied a breath of country air. Nice place your pa-in-law's got here. Very nice.'

'If you'd been a little more patient last Friday, our business would already have been concluded.'

'Is that a fact? Well, I'm getting too old for stooging round river-bridges on cold nights. You were late, Mr Staddon, if you were there at all. In other words, you broke our agreement.'

'I didn't intend to. There was an emergency at my office.'

'Well, there'll be a bigger bloody emergency when your name's spread all over the papers, won't there?'

'You don't understand. I've been trying to contact you ever since we missed each other that night. I'm quite happy to buy the letter at the price we agreed.'

'The price has altered.'

'What?'

'I've had to increase it on account of being messed around. It's a hundred and fifty now.'

'That's outrageous.'

'It's the going rate.'

I took a deep breath. Argument was useless and we both knew it. 'Very well. A hundred and fifty pounds. I'll write you a cheque.'

Malahide sniggered mirthlessly. 'I don't deal in cheques. Cash only.'

'As you please. But I don't have that amount on me.'

'When are you going back to London?'

'Tomorrow.'

'I'll give you two days, then. Wednesday night. Same time, same place. Don't be late. Not so much as a minute. You'll get no more chances. Take my meaning?'

'We understand each other perfectly, Malahide. I'll be there.'

He nodded. 'Good. Well, now that's settled, I'll be pushing along.' He moved round the table and paused alongside me. 'Don't worry. I'll find me own way out.'

217

'Do that.'

'Happy New Year, Mr Staddon.' He smirked and patted me on the shoulder. Then, before I could even recoil, he was gone.

I felt weary and defiled. I walked round the billiards table, letting my fingers trail along the rim, reached the spectators' couch at the far end and sat down there, grateful for the silence and solitude in which Malahide had left me. Whatever the New Year held, it was unlikely to be happiness, for me far less Consuela. I lit a cigarette and watched the smoke rise above me into a darkness that could have been an emblem for my future.

Then the door opened. Major Turnbull entered, adorned in white tie and tails, puffing at a cigar. He stopped and regarded me from the far end of the table, smiling amiably.

'Not dressed yet, Staddon?'

'As you see, Major.'

'Who was your visitor?'

'What visitor?'

'The ugly little fellow I just met in the hall. Face like a prize-fighter. Manners to match.'

'I'm afraid I can't help you there.' As much to change the subject as anything else, I added: 'Will you be spending any time at Clouds Frome while you're in England?'

'That rather depends how my negotiations with Sir Ashley proceed.'

'Negotiations? About what?'

'Hasn't he told you? He's considering buying a hotel on the Riviera. I've agreed to act as his consultant. My local knowledge is useful to him. I may even take a financial stake in the enterprise. Victor too, perhaps.'

'I shouldn't have thought hotels were Caswell's line.'

'But they always have been, Staddon. Surely you know that?'

'I don't understand you, Major.'

'Come, come. You must be aware of Victor's connection with Thornton Hotels.'

'I've no idea what you're talking about.'

'He's a substantial shareholder in the company.'

'What?'

Turnbull frowned. 'You really didn't know?'

I ground out my cigarette. 'No. I didn't.'

'You surprise me. I should have thought Sir Ashley would have mentioned it. I suppose these matters could be regarded as

218

confidential, but, after all, you are a member of the family, aren't you?'

But Turnbull was to be denied an answer. Already, I was striding from the room.

Sir Ashley was clearly put out when I interrupted him in the drawing-room, sipping a cocktail with some of his more important guests, but the tone of my voice must have suggested he should humour me until we were alone. He accompanied me, thunder-faced and silent, to the privacy of this study.

'Your behaviour is becoming increasingly objectionable, Geoffrey. What is the meaning of it?'

'Major Turnbull tells me that Victor Caswell is a substantial shareholder in Thornton Hotels. Is it true?'

'Yes. What of it?'

'*What of it*? Didn't you think I had a right to know?'

'The finances of Thornton Hotels are none of your business. And Caswell's always wanted his shareholding kept confidential. It's handled through a nominee.'

'Why?'

'That, similarly, is none of your business.'

'How many shares does he own?'

Sir Ashley's mouth set in a grim line. 'I have no intention of being cross-questioned by you, Geoffrey. I suggest we drop the subject – here and now.'

But it was too late for me to be deflected. In the few minutes that had elapsed since Turnbull's disclosure, a dreadful suspicion had formed in my mind. 'Does Caswell's holding give him much sway in the company?'

'I refuse to discuss this any further. I must return to my guests.'

'It does, doesn't it? A hell of a lot, I'll be bound. Now, tell me, was he a shareholder at the time you asked me to design the Hotel Thornton?'

'As far as I remember, yes, but—'

'He persuaded you to ask me, didn't he? I wasn't your choice. I was *his* choice.'

'This is preposterous.' But Sir Ashley's flushed expression suggested otherwise.

'That's what you meant when you said I should be grateful to him. Was it just a question of keeping a shareholder sweet, I wonder? Or did he put up some of the capital as well? He did,

219

didn't he? I can see it in your face. He bought you. And I was part of the deal.'

'He recommended your work. That's all. There was no . . . deal, as you call it.'

'I don't believe you. As a matter of fact, I'm not sure I can believe anything you've ever told me.'

'Take that back! Good God, I've a right to be addressed more respectfully by you. Have you any idea how much I've done to help you over the years?'

'I'm just beginning to realize. I've been Angela's poodle and your dupe. Well, not any more.'

'This has gone far enough. I've a good mind to throw you out of this house for what you've just said.'

'There's no need. I'm leaving. And somehow I don't think I'll ever be coming back.'

The true significance of my discovery swept over me as I climbed the stairs. Victor had arranged the Hotel Thornton commission. And I knew why. Because he was sure I would accept it. And because, in accepting it, I was bound to desert Consuela. So, he had known of our plans all along. He had known we were lovers and that we were intending to run away together after the house-warming weekend at Clouds Frome. Hence, the timing of Thornton's offer. And the worst of it, the very worst, swamping for the moment my desire to learn how he had come by the information, was the thought of how easily he had identified my weakness. The hotel was all it had taken. He had defeated me without lifting a finger.

Angela was standing by the cheval-glass in our room, admiring her own reflection. Her hair was swept back to show off the slenderness of her neck and the ball-gown blossomed about her in radiant hues of pink and mauve. I had not seen her looking so beautiful – nor so young – in years. And, as she turned towards me, my eye was taken by the monkey brooch glistening at her breast.

'Why, Geoffrey, you're just in time to lead me down.' She broke off as the expression on my face told its story. 'What's the matter?'

'The matter is that I've just learned – just understood for the first time – what you and your family really think of me.'

'Has Daddy spoken to you?'

'Yes. He's spoken to me.'

'Royston convinced me that he had a right to know how things stood between you and me.'

'I'm sure he did.'

'You only have yourself to blame, you know.'

'Oh, yes. Only myself. You're absolutely right.'

'All I can hope is that you'll see reason – even at this late stage.'

I stepped closer, within range of her perfume, within touching distance of her proud, upraised chin. She was breathing rapidly, the eyes of the monkey catching the light as her breasts rose and fell.

'What's wrong with you, Geoffrey? Are you quite well?'

'The brooch was a gift from Turnbull, I suppose?'

'Yes. As it happens.'

'And the dress?'

'I really don't see why—'

'Of course it was! I shouldn't be surprised if he paid for every stitch you're wearing – down to your Crêpe de Chine knickers.'

The flat of her hand caught me a stinging blow on the cheek. She glared at me, angrier than I could ever recall seeing her. 'You disgust me!' she rasped. 'Have you taken leave of your senses?'

'No.' I felt my cheek reddening, but refused to nurse it, refused to give her the satisfaction of seeing she had hurt me. 'As a matter of fact, Angela, I've just recovered my senses – in time to see you and your family for what you really are.'

'How dare you!' Her face had coloured now. Her lower lip was trembling. A strand of hair had escaped from its clip and was trailing around her ear. 'My family – unlike you – has nothing to be ashamed of.'

'You mean it has no sense of shame.'

'Get out! Get out of this house if that's what you think.'

'It is. And don't worry: I'm leaving.' I moved hurriedly past her and grabbed my suitcase, unopened since my arrival. When I turned back towards the door, she was staring at me, fury and amazement competing for control of her expression.

'You're mad,' she said, more calmly than before. 'Do you realize what this means?'

'I think so.'

'Why are you doing it?'

'Because I must.'

'For the sake of a woman you deceived and discarded more than ten years ago?'

'I'm not going to discuss Consuela with you, Angela. There's no point.'

221

'If you really loved her, you should have stood by her then – not now.'

'Do you think I don't know that?' I made to leave, then, foolishly, paused to deliver one last broadside. 'Victor Caswell bribed your father to offer me the Hotel Thornton commission. That's what stopped me standing by Consuela. Did he ever tell you that?'

'You're talking nonsense. I know you, Geoffrey, all too well. You deserted her because you were bored with her. Why pretend otherwise?'

'Because it doesn't happen to be true.'

'What was the problem? Wasn't she as good in bed as you'd hoped? Wasn't she quite as experienced as some of your other—'

I hit her then. Not because I wanted to hurt her. Not even because she had insulted Consuela. Rather, I think, I suddenly needed to make an end between us, to render all our differences irretrievable. Perhaps Angela wanted the same. Perhaps she hoped I would react as I did. There was a complicity in that act of violence, I feel sure, a mutual acceptance of what it meant, a celebration of the release it represented.

It was a hard blow, my half-clenched fist against her mouth. She screamed and clutched at a side-table as she fell. It toppled with her, sending a vase smashing to the floor. Then she was beneath me, hair across her face, one hand to her mouth, blood trickling down her chin. We stared at each other in a shocked, breathless silence.

There was a commotion outside, a hammering at the door. A second later it opened. Turnbull was in the room, with Clive and Sir Ashley behind him. The Major walked straight past me and crouched beside Angela, pressing a handkerchief to her bleeding lip.

'What have you done?' demanded Sir Ashley.

'What I should have done years ago.'

'Get out of here at once!'

'I intend to.' I blundered past them to the door. A moment later, I was hurrying down the stairs into a hall full of smiling, gaily dressed party-goers. Some of them must have known what had happened. They were staring at me and muttering. But I paid them no heed. The front door stood open and the cold blankness of the night beckoned. I rushed towards it gratefully, like an eager suicide towards the precipice.

222

CHAPTER

ELEVEN

Reg Vimpany looked up with a start of surprise as I entered. 'Mr Staddon! We weren't expecting you today.'

'Change of plan, Reg.'

'Didn't you speak of a New Year's Eve party at your father-in-law's?'

'Indeed I did.'

'I trust it went well.'

'Probably.' I moved hurriedly towards the sanctuary of my office. 'Giles in yet?'

'Rather early for Mr Newsom, I'm afraid.'

'Well, when he *does* arrive, send him straight in.'

'Very good, sir.'

Then, at last, my office door was safely closed behind me. I hung up my coat and hat and moved to my desk. As I sat down, I noticed that Reg had already, with typical efficiency, renewed my R.I.B.A. calendar. Nineteen-twenty-four had commenced and could no longer be ignored. I had tried to outrun it – driving like a madman through the night to Brighton, walking myself to a standstill along the beach as the waves crashed blindly about me, staring up malevolently at the revellers on the pier – but inevitability holds the power to defeat all resistance, to sweep before it every device and delay we care to construct. In thirteen days' time, Consuela's trial would begin and, with it, the only test that mattered of my efforts to save her.

There was a tap at the door and Giles Newsom entered. He too looked as if the New Year were no cause for celebration. 'You're back early, Mr Staddon.'

'Does that mean you have nothing to report?'

'No.'

'Then close the door, sit down and tell me what's happened.'

As he obeyed, I noticed his eyes lingering on my face. Perhaps, I thought, my despair and exhaustion were more apparent than I had supposed. If so, he did not remark upon it. 'I saw Pombalho yesterday. He doesn't like you, Mr Staddon. He made that abundantly clear.'

'What did he say to my offer?'

'He rejected it out of hand. Abusively and conclusively.'

'You explained to him that it was the only way he could hope to learn anything about the plans of Clouds Frome?'

'Of course. But he wasn't to be persuaded. He insisted that he wouldn't bargain with you. If you weren't prepared to give him what he wanted, he would, and these were his exact words, "do it without help".'

'Do what?'

'He wouldn't tell me. But he has something in mind, that's certain.'

I leaned back in my chair. What was Rodrigo intending to do? What could he do – that the plans of Clouds Frome would expedite? They were where I had told him – preserved intact in my memory – but, even as I recalled them, no significance disclosed itself in the areas of rooms, the heights of ceilings, the pitches of roofs.

'Progress on another front, Mr Staddon.'

'Yes?'

'I've traced Malahide. Up until the twenty-first of last month, he was working on one of Croad's sites out at Woolwich.'

But Malahide no longer mattered. This time, I would make no mistake where he was concerned. The following night, I would meet him and pay him off. Then Lizzie Thaxter's letter would be in my possession and I would be free to do what I had longed to do since leaving Luckham Place: demand the truth from Victor Caswell.

'Do you want me to ask them for his address?'

'No, Giles. I want you to drop it.'

'And Pombalho?'

'That too. You've done enough.' And then I added: 'I'll take over now.'

*

Though I could not imagine what form it might take, I had expected an early response from Angela to the circumstances of our parting. The longer that passed without one, the more likely it became that she had decided to invoke some drastic sanction against me. Not that I was greatly on my guard. My appointment with Malahide – and what I would say to Victor – consumed my every thought. If Angela hoped to torture me with uncertainty, she hoped in vain.

It was a mild night, but the streets were quiet. I reached Southwark Bridge early and had time to smoke two cigarettes before Malahide loomed out of the shadows beyond the nearest street-lamp.

'A pleasure to see you, Mr Staddon.'

'You have the letter?'

'I do.' He pulled a crumpled envelope from his jacket. 'And you have the money?'

I held up the packet for him to see. 'A hundred and fifty in five pound notes.'

He placed the envelope on the parapet of the bridge. As I made to pick it up, he covered my hand with his. 'You'll not mind waiting till I've counted it, will you?'

He tore open the packet and leafed through the wad of notes, one by one, reckoning under his breath as he went. Then, with a nod, he expressed his satisfaction. 'You're a gentleman, Mr Staddon.'

I slipped the letter out of its envelope, noted the two pages covered in a neat, feminine hand, then tucked them into my pocket. 'Well, our business is concluded, I think. Excuse me.'

'A moment more of your time, Mr Staddon.' His hand rested lightly on my elbow. I could have shaken it off, but did not.

'What is it?'

'A favour, you might say.'

'You have a nerve.'

'It's a small thing, too small for you to 'grudge me.'

'Well?'

'As I was leaving Luckham Place after our little chat the other day, I bumped into a gent in the hall. Big, fancy sort of fellow. Nasty eyes. Puffing at a cigar long enough to fire a salute from. Know who I mean?'

'Yes. I believe I do.'

'What's his name?'

'Turnbull. Major Royston Turnbull. A business associate of my father-in-law.'

'Is he, now? Still at Luckham Place, far as you know?'

'Staying the week, I believe. Why do you ask?'

He smiled and tapped his nose, as he had once before. 'No need for you to worry about that.'

'You must have had a reason for asking.'

'I thought I might know him from somewhere.'

'And do you?'

'No.' He shook his head vigorously. 'What would a "business associate" of *Sir* Ashley Thornton be having to do with the likes of me? I ask you.'

'That's just it. You *did* ask me.'

'Well, maybe I thought I recognized him, but, now you've put a name to him, I reckon I must have been wrong.' He grinned. 'I'll bid you good night, Mr Staddon. And happy reading.' With that, he hurried away.

I was about to call after him when something stopped me. Lizzie Thaxter's letter was more important than Malahide's interest in Turnbull. Besides, I knew the fellow too well to think I would learn anything from him against his will. I set off in the opposite direction.

Ten minutes later, in a quiet corner of a pub in Garlick Hill, I took the envelope from my pocket. It was addressed to P.A. Thaxter, Esq., c/o H.M. Prison, Gloucester, and was postmarked Hereford, 19 July 1911: the day before Lizzie's death. What it contained was, in a sense, her last testament, its significance for my own past unknown till now, more than twelve years later, I nervously opened it and began to read.

> Clouds Frome,
> Mordiford,
> Herefordshire.
> 19th July 1911

My dearest brother,
I am sorry, but I will not be coming to see you tomorrow, as I said I would. I have thought it all through, Peter, time after time, and there only seems to be one answer.

If only you had not let yourself be talked into stealing. It was my downfall as well as yours. And all for that stupid dream of a roller-skating rink. But for that, Mr Caswell could not have forced me to be his spy. Then he would not have

226

known about my mistress and Mr Staddon. They could have been happy and so could I. All this hurt because you had to be greedy.

My poor mistress is most to be pitied. Mr Staddon has thrown her over, as I knew he would. She thought she would be starting a new life with him in London, but I knew better all along. And now she is beside herself with the grief of it. She has done nothing wrong, but still she suffers. I do not believe she will ever get over it.

But that is not the worst of it. What I *cannot* bear is the deceit. Letting her think I am loyal. And all the time telling on her to her husband, showing him her letters, warning him of her plans. I have no choice. I have to do as he says. But I cannot endure it any longer, Peter, I cannot.

I have tried to find another way out of this, but there is no other way. He will go on using me. He will never stop. Unless I am no longer here to be used.

It will all be over by the time you read this, pray God, if I can keep my courage up. And I will. You always used to say I was your plucky little sister. Well, tonight I shall prove it.

Do not show Mum and Dad this letter. It would break their hearts. Explain it to them when you get out if you feel they can bear it. Keep up your spirits, Peter. Do not let them break you just because they have broken me. Remember me as your loyal and loving sister.
Lizzie.

I read the letter through for a second time, trying to imagine Lizzie, alone, in her tiny room at Clouds Frome, penning this last farewell to her brother, explaining as best she could why she had decided to end her life. I looked at the postmark again: Hereford, 7.30 p.m., 19 July 1911. She must have walked into the village to post it that afternoon, then made her way back, knowing the die was cast, knowing that, before the next dawn, she would slip from the house, a length of rope in her hand, and steal down to the orchard, never to return.

And what of me? '*Mr Staddon has thrown her over, as I knew he would.*' I wanted to protest to her that she could not have been certain I would desert Consuela, but she was dead and my own memories rose to defend her judgement. Why had she been weeping that morning when I delivered the note to her room? Why had she stared at it in horror? Because she had known I would bring it and what it would mean when I did.

Much that had once been obscure was now only too clear.

Victor had arranged for the Thornton commission to be dangled before me immediately prior to the Clouds Frome house-warming because he knew from Lizzie that Consuela and I were planning to run away together immediately afterwards. As our messenger and confidante, Lizzie had known our every secret. Therefore, so had Victor. Indeed, the full extent of his knowledge hardly bore contemplation. The endearments we had written, the trysts we had kept, the intimacies we had exchanged. Of all of them he had been aware and of all of them tolerant – until the time had come to call a halt.

What was not clear was *why* Lizzie had betrayed us. It had something to do with her brother's imprisonment, but what it was I could not discern. She had never tried to hide the fact that she was Peter Thaxter's sister. Yet she had written: '*But for that, Mr Caswell could not have forced me to be his spy.*' Something else, then, held the answer, something deeper and worse than disgrace by association, something she could not bring herself to admit even in the last letter she had ever written.

'What will you do with it?' asked Imry, when he had finished reading the letter. 'Destroy it?'

I shook my head. Imry was in London for the day and we were lunching at his club. Less than twenty-four hours had elapsed since Lizzie's letter had come into my possession. But already I had decided what must be done with it. 'When this is all over,' I said, 'when it can't do any harm, I shall give it to Lizzie's family. It's rightfully theirs, I think.'

'Oh, I agree. And meanwhile?'

'Meanwhile, I intend to have matters out with Victor Caswell.'

'Yes. I thought you might.'

'I expect you'd advise me not to.'

'Not this time, Geoff. The past is generally best left to its own devices, in my opinion. But there are exceptions. And I'm inclined to think this is one.'

I had recounted to him the circumstances of my parting from Angela and winced now at the memory of them. 'I've been a damn fool, haven't I, Imry?'

'Yes. But you're not unusual in that. We all are, sooner or later. It's just that most people's foolishness doesn't catch up with them as conclusively as yours has.'

'Antagonizing Sir Ashley won't be good for business.'

'I shouldn't let that worry you.'

'What will Angela do, do you think?'

'She's your wife, Geoff, not mine. But, for what it's worth, I think she'll divorce you.'

'So do I.'

'Will you try to stop her? To patch it up?'

'I don't know. To be honest, I'm not sure I care enough to make the effort.'

'You ought to. Remember, hitting her as you did, in front of witnesses, is going to make you look like the guilty party. But, from what you tell me, her friendship with Major Turnbull is intimate enough to justify your behaviour, or at least to excuse it.'

'I don't want to drag in any of that. In fact, I don't want to justify my behaviour – as you put it – at all.'

'You must – in your own interests.'

'That's just it, Imry. Don't you see? I've brought all this about by putting *my* interests first, above those even of the people I've claimed to love. Well, not anymore. From now on, I steer by a different star.'

'And that star is?'

'It doesn't have a name. But it has a purpose. One I intend to serve to the full extent of my ability – without regard to self.'

'Oh, that has a name, Geoff. It's called honour. Downfall of many a man.' He smiled. 'And the salvation of just a few.'

To say that I was surprised to receive a letter from Hermione Caswell the following morning would be an understatement. I was even more surprised by its enclosure: a sealed envelope addressed to me in Jacinta's handwriting. Hermione's covering note read as follows.

> Fern Lodge,
> Aylestone Hill,
> Hereford.
> 2nd January 1924
>
> Dear Mr Staddon,
> Jacinta has asked me to forward this letter to you. She is no
> longer free to come and go at Clouds Frome and certainly
> not at liberty to correspond with persons of whom her father
> disapproves. You are evidently one of these. You know me
> better than to think, however, that Victor's opinion counts
> for anything with me. When Jacinta found an opportunity
> over Christmas to tell me of the restrictions he has imposed

upon her, I told her that I would be more than happy to post letters for her and to pass on replies. So, should you wish to reply, please write to me at the above address, enclosing whatever message you wish me to convey. This will reach Jacinta as soon as circumstances permit.

Jacinta has forbidden me to enquire into her reasons for writing to you and I have mastered my curiosity sufficiently to comply. It is no breach of confidence to tell you, however, that the imminence of her mother's trial and the contemplation of its probable outcome has much depressed the poor child. If it lies within your power to relieve her anxiety in any way, I would urge you to do so.

Sincerely yours,
Hermione E. Caswell.

I at once tore open Jacinta's letter and read it.

Clouds Frome,
Mordiford,
Herefordshire.
31st December 1923

Dear Mr Staddon,

I have heard nothing from you since we met in London at the start of this week. I am worried, because I know my mother's trial will soon begin and nobody here will tell me anything about it. Since we returned from France, I have not been allowed to leave the house unless my father or Miss Roebuck comes with me. Miss Roebuck takes me to church in Hereford every Sunday. Otherwise, I never go anywhere and nobody visits us apart from members of the family. I thought about it a great deal before asking Aunt Hermione to help me, but I had to ask somebody and she is the only person I ever see who I feel I can trust.

None of the family apart from Aunt Hermione ever mentions my mother now, or her trial. But I hear the servants gossiping. Banyard, Noyce, Gleasure and Mabel Glynn are going up to London soon because they have to give evidence. My father will go as well. Aunt Hermione has told me that the trial will open on 14th January. That means there is hardly any time left. They all think my mother will be found guilty. I can tell that. If she is, they will hang her. We have to help her, Mr Staddon. We have to do something. But what?

Please write soon. Please tell me you know what to do.
Please say you are not as helpless as I am.
Yours truly,
Jacinta Caswell.

Crowding about me as I read Jacinta's letter came the recriminations inspired by my futile attempts to save Consuela. I had assured myself – as well as Jacinta – that some way of doing so must exist and that I would not rest until I had found it. And yet, more than two months later, what had I accomplished? Nothing, save perhaps the ruin of my own marriage. Nothing, it was certain, likely to sway the judge and jury who would shortly decide Consuela's fate.

I hurried into the study and wrote an immediate reply to Hermione.

> 27 Suffolk Terrace,
> Kensington,
> London W8.
> 4th January 1924

Dear Miss Caswell,
Thank you for your letter and for alerting me to your niece's state of mind. I propose to travel to Hereford tomorrow and to lodge for a few days at the Green Dragon. I would be greatly obliged if you could meet me during my stay and would suggest a message left at the hotel, stating where and when might be convenient, as the most sensible arrangement. You will appreciate that I cannot express the full urgency of my request in a letter. Be assured, however, that this matter is of overwhelming importance to me. The value of any assistance you feel able to offer at this crucial time is consequently impossible to exaggerate.
Yours sincerely,
Geoffrey Staddon.

I posted the letter on my way to Frederick's Place. I spent the rest of the day hard at work, consumed by an exhilaration born of the knowledge that I was committed to a new course of action. I telephoned Windrush in Hereford and he agreed to dine with me at the Green Dragon the following evening. From him I hoped to learn the harsh truth about Consuela's prospects. From others, whom I did not propose to forewarn of my visit, I hoped to learn a still harsher truth: what had really happened, and why, at Clouds Frome the afternoon Rosemary Caswell had swallowed a fatal dose of arsenic.

CHAPTER

TWELVE

I left London at dawn, preferring a long and arduous car drive to the comforts of train travel. Oxford, where I had frittered away a pampered portion of my youth, was grey and unyielding beneath cold, scudding cloud. In the Cotswolds, nothing moved across the bare fields save flights of rooks that might have been black rags blowing in the wind. All was grey and chill and grudging. All was as discouraging as only nature's indifference could render it. And yet I was not discouraged.

From Gloucester the way grew more familiar, the shape and character of the land more reminiscent of what had formed Clouds Frome in my mind. Suddenly, the broad meanders of the Wye were visible in the valley below me. Suddenly, Mordiford was named on a finger-post and I knew, for all my earlier resolutions, that I could not pass it by.

I drove slowly through the village, past the field next to the church where Lizzie Thaxter lay buried, and so came, as I knew I should not, to Clouds Frome once more. I halted the car on the other side of the road, climbed out and gazed up at the house. It stood exposed by winter, robbed of all adornment, yet the conception held good. It triumphed, by setting and structure. It disregarded the austerities of the season, brushing them aside as if they were of no account.

Elated by what I had once achieved, yet bowed down by the conviction that I could never create its equal, I walked slowly along the road towards the entrance. And there stopped dead in my tracks with surprise.

There had never been gates across the drive. In the absence of a lodge, they had seemed neither practical nor necessary. Yet now there were. Between the pillars flanking the entrance had been erected a pair of stout wrought-iron gates with close-set palings reaching twelve feet in height and spiked at the top. They bore a large wooden sign, inscribed in bold letters: PRIVATE, KEEP OUT.

I crossed the road and stared in amazement at what I saw. The gates were locked and, in addition, a padlocked chain had been looped between them. Fixed to the right-hand pillar was a wooden box which had certainly not been there before, its outward face hinged as a door, and beneath it a sign, which read: NO UNAUTHORIZED ACCESS. VISITORS PLEASE RING. I swung open the door of the box. Inside was a telephone and winding-handle, presumably for ringing the house. Victor had indeed made certain that he would see only those whom he wished to see.

I returned to the car, climbed in, lit a cigarette and stared up at Clouds Frome. The house seemed somehow more remote now I knew how difficult it was to reach. I could have demanded to be admitted, could have tried to insist that Victor speak to me, but I knew it was not yet time for such desperate measures. Not quite, at all events. I finished the cigarette, then started the car and drove away.

At the Green Dragon, a letter was awaiting me, delivered by hand earlier in the day. It was from Hermione.

> Fern Lodge,
> Aylestone Hill,
> Hereford.
> 5th January 1924
>
> Dear Mr Staddon,
> Your letter arrived this morning and I shall deliver this reply when I go shopping. I would be happy to meet, but we must be careful in view of the consternation caused by our being seen together last time you were in Hereford. I occasionally attend the eight o'clock service of matins at the cathedral on Sunday mornings and it would arouse no suspicion if I did so tomorrow. It would be a simple matter to spend the hour at the Green Dragon instead. I shall therefore expect to find

you breakfasting in the dining-room at eight o'clock sharp.
Sincerely yours,
Hermione E. Caswell.

I had not expected to meet Hermione as early as this and had therefore assumed I could defer until Sunday morning that most delicate of tasks: the composition of a letter to Jacinta. I had, alas, little idea what I could or should say in it and had made no sort of a start by the time Windrush arrived for our dinner engagement.

He looked more haggard and careworn than ever. A nervous blink and a jerkiness to his head movements were characteristics I felt sure he had not displayed previously. He drank and smoked greedily, but ate hardly at all, and wasted little time in explaining the cause of his anxiety.

'This case has made me a marked man in Hereford, Staddon. It's all right for you. You don't have to live with these people. They blame me for getting the trial transferred, for denying them the pleasure of seeing the assize judge don the black cap.'

'Is it really as bad as that?'

'If anything, it's worse.'

'I passed Clouds Frome this afternoon. Caswell seems to have made some changes.'

'You mean the gates? They were put up about a month ago. Broken glass was cemented along the top of the boundary wall at the same time. There's even supposed to be a guard-dog that roams the grounds by night. Some say all the precautions are to keep out the press and sensation-seekers. Others say the poisoning's unnerved him and he's afraid somebody will try to murder him.'

'And what do you think?'

'Oh, I think it's certainly more than a desire for privacy. Between you and me, I can't help feeling our friend Pombalho may have rattled him. Last time he was here he uttered some pretty dire threats about what he'll do if his sister hangs.'

'Kill Caswell, you mean? Surely that's not to be taken seriously.'

'I'd take it seriously if I were Caswell. Have you seen Pombalho recently?'

'Er . . . no.'

'Well, count yourself lucky. He's like a simmering volcano. If his sister does hang, he'll erupt. I wouldn't want to be in Caswell's shoes then.'

I leaned across the table and lowered my voice. 'Will she hang, do you think?'

234

'You'd better ask Sir Henry. It's largely up to him anyway. I'm due to meet him at his chambers next Friday for a last conference before the trial. Why don't you come with me?'

'I'll do that.'

'He'll strike an optimistic note, of course. He has to. But I don't think he has any basis for it. If you want my opinion, we're no nearer assembling an adequate defence than we were two months ago.'

'You hold out little hope, then?'

'It's in Sir Henry's hands. He can't refute the evidence. All he can hope to do is sow sufficient uncertainty – and sympathy – in the jury's minds for them to give Mrs Caswell the benefit of the doubt.'

'Does Mrs Caswell realize the seriousness of the situation?'

'Oh, yes. But she's completely unmoved by it. I have the impression that she's already prepared herself for the worst. She's a brave woman, Staddon, very brave. And I have a nasty feeling she's going to need to be.'

Late that night, I sat alone in my room, pen in hand, a sheet of hotel notepaper laid before me on the desk.

> My dearest Jacinta,
> You are not yet old enough to understand what I am about to tell you, but I cannot delay the telling any longer. Victor Caswell, the man who has made your mother's life a misery and who now holds you prisoner at Clouds Frome, is not your father at all. I am your father. That is why your mother sent you to me. Because you are my daughter and because your protection is the least, the very least, I owe to your mother – the woman I deceived and deserted. There is nothing I can say to excuse my conduct in the past, but there is at least something I can do in the present to—

I tore the letter into fragments and burned them. I had known, even as I had written the words, that Jacinta would never read them. They represented what I wanted to tell her, what one day I knew I would have to tell her, but for the moment they had to remain locked within the secrecy of my conscience. In their place I could find nothing with which to still her fears. According to Windrush, those fears were only too well founded. And therefore silence seemed the least hurtful of all the ways I could greet my daughter. I had written no letter, and prepared no message, when eight o'clock the following morning found me seated in the sparsely populated dining-room, awaiting my next visitor.

'I will have a freshly brewed pot of tea,' said Hermione to the waiter. 'And a rack of toast. I do not expect the slices to be limp, mark you.' Then, as the waiter made to leave: 'And Mr Staddon looks as if he would like some more coffee.'

Hermione's vitality was undimmed and instantly cheering. After glaring at the only other guest taking breakfast – a glum-faced fellow with an irritating cough and less fat on him than the bacon I had just consumed – she fixed me with a piercing look and said:

'Why are you here, Mr Staddon?'

'Because you wrote to me.'

'Come, come. You could more easily have responded by post than in person.'

'Not really. I've no letter for you to pass on. Only a message. Jacinta mustn't lose hope. There's still every cause for optimism.'

Hermione frowned. 'You disappoint me, Mr Staddon. Surely you know Jacinta too well to think she can be satisfied with platitudes. Her mother's life is in considerable danger – and she knows it.'

'So do I. But there's nothing more I can say to her.'

'That sounds awfully like defeatism.'

'I don't mean it to. Indeed, I've come to Hereford in anything but a defeatist mood.'

'What do you propose to do?'

'I propose to confront Victor with certain facts that have recently come into my possession. And I hope thereby to discover the truth. Is that the sort of fighting talk you think Jacinta would prefer to hear?'

'Yes, but we must tread carefully with her where Victor is concerned.'

'Because he's her father. Exactly. Hence my difficulty in knowing what to ask you to tell her on my behalf.'

Tea, toast and coffee arrived amidst an excessive rattling of crockery. Whilst they were dispensed, Hermione stared at me across the table with the intensity of one seeking confirmation of a questionable deduction. When the waiter had gone, she selected a slice of toast and began to butter it, then said: 'I don't think Victor is Jacinta's father, Mr Staddon. And I don't think you think so either.'

'What . . . what do you mean?'

'It's clear enough, surely? Your determination to save Consuela.

236

Her instruction to Jacinta that she should look to you for help. Jacinta's date of birth. And your last visit to Clouds Frome. Even old ladies can count, Mr Staddon. Of course, I understand that you may not *know*, for certain I mean, but I feel sure you suspect it. Now, would you mind passing the marmalade?'

Dumbly, I pushed the pot across the table.

'Don't worry. Nobody else is likely to guess. If Jacinta had not asked me to act as your go-between, it would never have occurred to me. And I'm not going to tell anybody. Why should I? It's really none of my business. But I thought you ought to know that I'd guessed. Is it, may I ask, one of the facts with which you propose to confront Victor?'

'I . . . Yes. In a sense.'

'Well, you may find that difficult. Victor has become elusive of late. Casual visitors are no longer welcome at Clouds Frome. And he's had some alterations made. The house resembles a fortress. Locked gates. Broken glass on the walls. A mastiff loose in the grounds. Bolts at all the windows. And those are only the precautions I know about.'

'What's he frightened of?'

'I don't know. The poisoning's changed him, no doubt of that. And his holiday in France did him little good. He seems nervous, suspicious of everyone outside the household. The trial's been preying on his mind, of course, but I rather think there's more to it than that.'

'Could it have anything to do with Consuela's brother, Rodrigo Manchaca de Pombalho? I believe he's been to Hereford.'

'It may indeed. My only encounter with Senhor Pombalho suggested he would gladly wring Victor's head from his body. And he obviously has the strength to do it. He is, to say the very least, a forceful gentleman.'

An unpleasant thought came suddenly into my mind. Could Hermione, wittingly or not, have alerted Rodrigo to the fact that Consuela and I had once been lovers? 'Did you . . . Did you tell Rodrigo that you doubted Victor was Jacinta's father?'

'Good heavens, no. Apart from anything else, no such doubt had then formed in my mind. Even if it had, I would not have shared it with Senhor Pombalho. Whatever can have put that idea in your head?'

'Oh . . . something he said to me. But I may have misunderstood.'

'I think you must have done. Senhor Pombalho visited Fern

237

Lodge some time in late November, as I recall. Mortimer felt obliged to receive him courteously, but there was nothing courteous about the way he left. Victor was still in France then, of course. It was only later that we learned Senhor Pombalho had threatened to kill him. It was a threat he repeated in still more violent terms when Victor returned. That was when the alterations began at Clouds Frome and Victor began living as a recluse, forcing Jacinta to do the same. He has so far found no excuse for forbidding me to visit her, but it would not surprise me in the least if he tried to. As for Senhor Pombalho, we have heard no more from him. There have been several reported sightings, but none of late. He is not, as you know, the most inconspicuous of men, so I assume he has left Hereford, probably for London. He may even have returned to Brazil, though I doubt it.'

'So, could these . . . alterations . . . be intended to protect Victor from Rodrigo?'

'If not, I cannot imagine what other purpose they serve.'

'Will Victor refuse to see me?'

'He may well. But that does not mean, of course, that he must necessarily have his way.' She smiled mischievously. 'Your visit to Hereford is timely, Mr Staddon. Tomorrow afternoon, there is to be a directors' meeting at Caswell & Co. I know, because, thanks to the provisions of my father's will, I am one of the directors, as is Victor. He will most certainly attend the meeting, so, if all else fails, you will be able to speak to him then.' Her expression suggested that, if I were forced to seek her brother out at the company offices, she would relish being present. 'Now,' she added, 'I feel sure the tea has had sufficient time to draw. Would you mind pouring me a cup?'

It being Sunday, there was a way, I had realized, both to contact Victor and to reassure Jacinta that I had not abandoned her. According to Hermione, she was still permitted to attend Hereford Roman Catholic Church under Miss Roebuck's supervision. Ten minutes before the eleven o'clock service was due to begin, therefore, I took up position outside and was soon rewarded when a sleek maroon Bentley glided to a halt a few yards away and Jacinta's face appeared at the nearside rear window.

She stared at me with a calculated blankness as the chauffeur climbed out and opened the door for her. I felt again a swelling of pride at how well she contained her emotions, at how bravely she bore the despair her mother's plight must have caused her. She

238

was wearing a smart fur-trimmed coat and some kind of tam-o'-shanter that made her look even younger and smaller than she was. She paused as she stepped out of the car, pursed her lips and took a deep breath, reminding herself, I sensed, to display no sign of weakness, though whether her self-control was for my benefit or Imogen Roebuck's I could not decide, since Miss Roebuck was watching her from the car as intently as I was from the pavement.

Jacinta started walking towards the church. Just when I thought she meant to pass me without acknowledgement, she stopped and looked up at me. 'Good morning, Mr Staddon. How are you?'

'I am well, Jacinta. I—' Miss Roebuck was staring at me from the car. As I glanced up, our eyes met. The absurd belief came into my mind that she would be able to read my lips even if she could not actually hear what I said.

'Are you still trying to help my mother, Mr Staddon?'

'Yes. In every way that I can.'

'Will you be able to save her?'

'I hope so.'

'I must go in now, Mr Staddon.' She had flushed slightly and her chin, I saw, was trembling faintly. 'Goodbye.' She was gone then, in a rush, up the church steps and out of my sight.

I looked back at the car. The chauffeur was about to pull away, but Miss Roebuck tapped him on the shoulder. Obedient to a summons that had been issued only in my imagination, I walked round to her side of the car and waited for her to lower the window.

'Good morning, Mr Staddon,' she said calmly. 'Victor forbade you to communicate with Jacinta, as I recall, some weeks ago.'

'On the pain of losing most of my clients, something he claimed to be able to arrange.'

'Do you doubt his claim?'

'No. As a matter of fact, I don't.'

'Then why defy him so openly?'

'Because the penalty he threatened to invoke means nothing to me. And because it isn't Jacinta I came here to communicate with. It's Victor.'

'You will have to explain that remark.'

'I wish you to deliver a message to him on my behalf.'

She arched her eyebrows. 'What message?'

'I want to see him. There are matters we have to discuss.'

'I don't think he's likely to agree.'

'Tell him I know how he stopped me taking Consuela from him, as I should have done, twelve years ago.'

Miss Roebuck's eyebrows arched still higher. The chauffeur cleared his throat. 'Such a message would represent a damning admission on your part, Mr Staddon. Are you sure it's wise?'

'I'm not interested in your assessment of what is or isn't wise. Will you tell him?'

'If you insist.'

'I do. I'll call at Clouds Frome at four o'clock this afternoon. I'll expect him to see me.'

Miss Roebuck did not reply. Her gaze was ironic, almost amused, chillingly so given the gravity of the situation. She slowly wound up the window, keeping her eyes fixed on me as she did so. Then she leaned forward and murmured an instruction to the chauffeur. And the car glided away down the street.

I reached Clouds Frome some minutes before the time I had named, but remained in my car until my watch showed four o'clock. Then I walked to the gate and, finding it locked as expected, picked up the telephone and wound the handle.

'Clouds Frome.' It was Danby's voice.

'Danby, this is Geoffrey Staddon.'

'Ah yes, sir. I was told to expect you.'

'Good.'

'I was also told to explain that Mr Caswell cannot see you.'

'What?'

'He desires me to say that, if there is anything you wish to convey to him, you should do so by letter.'

'That's not good enough!'

'Unfortunately, sir, it will have to be.'

'Put me through to him, damn it!'

'His instructions were quite specific, sir. He does not wish to see you. He does not wish to speak to you. Now, if—'

I slammed the telephone back on to its hook and stalked away towards my car. So Victor would not grant me an audience. But he *would* see me, whether he liked it or not.

I drove north. There was something, I knew, behind all this, concealed by Clouds Frome and the Caswells, one with the cold still dusk, with the grey-green darkening countryside and the winding-sheet of cloud above my head. I had not seen it yet. I had not understood it. But soon I would.

Ahead of me on the narrow lane I had taken, a figure appeared, trudging towards me along the muddy verge. A tramp,

I assumed, some homeless vagrant wandering where the mood took him. Then, as he grew nearer, the gangling frame, the ragged clothes, the matted hair and beard composed themselves into the likeness of somebody I knew. I drew to a halt beside him and waved for him to approach. Mechanically, he obeyed. Then, as recognition dawned, he stopped dead in his tracks.

'Hello, Mr Doak. Remember me?'

He did not speak. Neither, on this occasion, did he turn and run. In his expression there was a mixture of shame and defiance. And he was sober enough this time for defiance to gain the upper hand.

'Where are you going?'

He glanced towards Hereford. It was a reply of a kind and therefore a modest victory.

'I'll drive you.'

He shook his head, tightened his grip on his knapsack and seemed about to move off.

'It's cold. And it'll be dark soon.'

He hesitated, licked his lips, then said: 'I owe you. An' I can't pay you. But I won't crawl.'

'I'm not asking you to. Just get in.'

He walked slowly round the bonnet of the car, eyeing it suspiciously, and stared in through the passenger window. I opened the door for him. Still he hesitated. Then he climbed gingerly aboard. We started off. I offered him a cigarette, which he accepted, and smiled to myself as I saw him savour the first inhalation.

We covered half a mile in silence. Then, abruptly, he said: 'Never bin in one o' these afore.'

'Do you approve?'

He ignored the question. 'Seen 'im swan past in one often enough, though.'

'Who do you mean?'

'Who d'you think?'

'Caswell?'

''Ar. That's 'im. 'E don't know me, anymore. Leastways, 'e makes out 'e don't. 'E thinks I'm nothin' to 'im. 'E thinks I'm so much apple-mush under 'is well-'eeled feet. Seen what 'e's done to Clouds Frome? Locks. Bolts. Bars. An' broken glass for the likes o' me to slash our 'ands to ribbons on.'

'I've seen.'

'What's it all for, eh?'

'Protection?'

241

'Ar. Reckon so. Reckon 'e needs it.'

'Really?'

'I sees things, Mr architec'. I sees an' I don't forget. 'E thinks 'e's safe there, thinks 'e can't be got at. Well, that's all 'e knows.'

'You know better?'

'I comes and goes as I please.'

'At Clouds Frome? How?'

'You should know. You built it. 'E can't stop every 'ole.'

'Are you saying you often enter the grounds?'

'I'm saying nothin'. Mebbe I do and mebbe I don't. Be no more 'n me rights if I did, though. Clouds Frome is Doak land. Still is by my reck'nin'.'

'But I'm told he has a guard-dog roaming free at night.'

'Dog's don't worry me. It's men that worry me. Men like Victor Caswell.'

'Why?'

''Cos 'e thinks 'e can take what isn't 'is an' never suffer for it. Well, 'e's wrong an' the time's comin' when 'e'll know it. I told you, Mr architec', the day you first came to Clouds Frome. I told you Caswell 'd live to regret takin' that land from us Doaks. An' 'e will. The Caswells crawled to us once. An' I'll live to see 'em crawl again.'

I dropped Doak on the outskirts of Hereford. He did not want to be taken to the centre. Perhaps he knew of some nearby billet for the night. At all events, he accepted a sovereign when I offered it to him, though very much in spite of himself. We both knew what he would do with it, but I did not begrudge him. He was a man defeated by life, crushed by circumstance, sustained only by stubbornness and empty prophecy. If there was one thing of which I was certain, it was that he would never get the better of Victor Caswell. And in my certainty I felt for him a dreadful affinity.

Still I did not return to my hotel. North again, along the night-blotted Shrewsbury road, as fast as the car could carry me, I drove with blank mind and suspended intent, till at last, long past Ludlow, cold and eerily alone, I came to rest, knowing that to continue was futile. Back, always and ever, I was bound to go.

'Staddon! In here!'

The voice was raised and slurred, reaching me from the bar as I stood in the lobby of the hotel, waiting for my key. When I looked round, I saw Spencer Caswell grinning through the doorway at me. He raised a half-empty glass and winked.

'Just the man I want to see! How about a night-cap?'

As much to silence him as for any other reason, I joined him at the bar. Unsteadily propped on a stool, tie askew, cigarette dangling crookedly from his fingers, he was even more detestable drunk than sober, manifestly a spoilt and unashamed child.

'Bad pennies, eh Staddon? We get more than a few round here, I can tell you.'

'What do you want?'

'Just a chat. A bit of company. A sympathetic ear. It's not much to ask, is it?'

'It seems a great deal at this moment. Why don't you go home to bed?'

'Because it's more fun here. We could discuss the many mysteries of life. To take but one example, how did I know you were here?'

'I assume you didn't.'

'Well, you assume wrong. Did you have a pleasant spot of breakfast with Aunt Hermione this morning?' He grinned more broadly still. 'No need to look so shocked. The old bat's an expert at giving herself away. Now, stand me a drink and be sociable and maybe – just maybe – I'll keep it to myself.'

Mercifully, the only other customer was the thin fellow with the irksome cough and he was engaged in an animated discussion of racehorses with the barman. So, with a nod of reluctant consent, I ordered some drinks and piloted Spencer to the remotest table in the room.

'Where have you been all this time, Staddon, eh? I've been waiting for you since they opened. I was beginning to think you'd let me down.'

'If I'd known you were here, I would have done.'

'Oh dear! That's not very nice, is it? Want to know how I rumbled Aunt Hermione?'

'No. But I expect you'll tell me anyway.'

'As a matter of fact, I believe I will. She announced last night that she'd be bustling down to the cathedral at sparrow's croak for her devotions. Made too big a thing of it, though. She'd normally have gone without telling a soul. So, I reckoned my dear demented aunt must be up to something. A fling with one of the canons? Hardly. That's when I remembered the brouhaha about her meeting you last time you were in Hereford. You were staying at the Green Dragon then, only a crozier's throw from the cathedral. So, I looked in this afternoon and what should I find

243

but your name on the register? You're too predictable, Staddon. That's your trouble, far too predictable.'

'All this is wild guesswork. You have no proof I met your aunt.'

Suddenly, much of Spencer's drunkenness seemed to fall away. 'I don't need proof,' he said in an altogether steadier voice. 'We're not in a court of law. But Consuela will be soon enough. That's why you're here, isn't it? You're still trying to pull the irons out of the fire for her.'

'What's it to you if I am?'

'I might be able to help.'

'I don't think so. Even if you could, I doubt you'd bother to.'

Spencer's smile tightened. 'Sometimes I get the impression you don't like me. But you should. At least, you should pretend to. Consuela's other shining white knight did that if he did nothing else.'

'Who are you talking about?'

'Her brother. The mad Brazilian. Rodrigo Manchaca de whatnot. He treated me very well, as a matter of fact.'

'You mean he bought you drinks.'

'Yes. And he smiled more than you. And he listened more respectfully to what I told him.'

'What *did* you tell him?'

'Oh, this and that. Tit-bits about my family. He seemed to find it all quite fascinating. Unlike you.'

'But I've heard it all before. Remember?'

'No you haven't. You haven't heard the half of it.'

I leaned forward and spoke slowly enough to avoid misunderstanding. I was tired and in no mood for Spencer's game-playing. 'If you have something to say, say it. I'm not going to beg for your two penn'orth of family gossip.'

'Fastidious all of a sudden, aren't we? You won't save Consuela's luscious little neck by striking poses, you know.'

'Nor by listening to you, I'll warrant.'

'Now that's where you're wrong. I asked you last time we met how you hoped to prove Consuela hadn't poisoned my drear departed sister. You didn't have an answer then and I'll bet you don't have one now.'

'And you do, I suppose?'

'Maybe. Ask yourself this. What proves Rosemary wasn't the intended victim?'

'The fact that she arrived at Clouds Frome unexpectedly.'

'Exactly. Otherwise it would have been *à bientôt* Uncle Victor. But what would it mean if she wasn't unexpected?'

'It would . . . Are you suggesting it was known she'd turn up that afternoon?'

'I have it on reliable authority that Uncle Grenville telephoned Uncle Victor from Ross that afternoon *after* Rosemary and Mummy dear had left his house and *before* they reached Clouds Frome. Now, I don't know what was said, but *if* Uncle Grenville just happened to mention that the ladies were thinking of looking in on their way back to Hereford, well, it would alter everybody's calculations, wouldn't it?'

He was right. Until now, I had been unable to sustain my suggestion that Victor might have staged the poisoning in order to rid himself of Consuela. As Imogen Roebuck had pointed out, he would have been taking an outrageous risk with his own life. Moreover, Consuela could only have been accused of attempted murder in such circumstances. Whether imprisoned or not, she would have remained his wife. If, however, Victor knew Marjorie and Rosemary were about to walk obligingly onto the scene, such objections fell away. He could have let his sweet-toothed niece gorge herself on the poisoned sugar and swallowed just enough himself to induce sickness. Then all he had to do was wait for Consuela to be charged with murder – and for the death penalty to free him from their marriage. Suddenly, timing was all-important. When was the telephone call made? How long did Victor have in which to set the trap?

Spencer was smirking in triumph. He could see he had me where he wanted me. 'Bit of a shaker, isn't it?'

'What is your . . . reliable authority?'

'You surely don't expect me to identify him.'

'Of course I do. This must be brought to the attention of the police.'

'Not on, Staddon, simply not on.'

'But it could make all the difference.'

'Oh, I realize that. But I was told in the strictest confidence, by somebody who's too interested in keeping his job to consider speaking up in court.'

'Keeping his job? Good God, we're talking about a woman's life. Don't you understand what this means?'

'I understand, but I'm not sure you do. Suppose my . . . friend, let's call him . . . did have a fit of honesty and came forward. He couldn't exonerate Consuela. All Uncle Victor would have to do

245

is either deny that the conversation ever took place or admit that it did, but deny that the ladies' plans were mentioned in the course of it. My friend's only reward would be dismissal. Uncle Victor doesn't care to be crossed, as you must know.'

'Your friend works for Victor?'

'Self-evidently.'

'And he took this telephone call?'

'So he tells me.'

'There aren't many people it can be, then, are there? Danby. Gleasure. Noyce. That's about the limit.'

'It won't help you to narrow the field.'

'What about Grenville Peto, then? He'd know what he told Victor.'

'Naturally, but if it was what I'm suggesting, he'd have said so by now, wouldn't he? Unless, of course, he doesn't want to help Consuela. Unless, perhaps, Victor's squared him in some way. In that case, you won't get anything out of him, will you?'

I slumped back in my chair. This ray of light was worse than the blackest despair. It glimmered but to deceive. The hope it conjured up was frail to the point of falseness. As Spencer well knew. 'Did you tell Rodrigo this?'

'No. Actually, the information hadn't come my way when he stormed the city. You're the first person I've shared it with. You should be flattered.'

'Why *have* you shared it with me?'

'Thought you ought to know. That's all.' But his flushed and gleeful expression put the lie to his words. He had another secret to spill from his hoard. 'I've a sudden yen for some bubbly. What do you say?'

'Not for me.'

'Treat me, then.' His eyes telegraphed the blatancy of his demand. If I pandered to his whim, he might be still more forth-coming. I signalled to the barman and ordered champagne. He bustled out to fetch it. 'It's amazing, you know,' said Spencer, 'how considerate people are – how eager to please – when they want something from you. Have you ever noticed that?'

'It doesn't apply to everybody.'

'It applies to everybody I've met. You included. Happen to have a cigar about you?'

'No.'

'Well, be a good fellow and order one when the barman gets back. I'm partial to Havanas.'

The grin never left Spencer's face as the champagne was opened and poured, a cigar delivered and lit for him. Then, when the barman had withdrawn, he raised his glass.

'What shall we drink to, Staddon? Or should I say who? Consuela, perhaps?'

I said nothing. Only the thought that he might tell me something more of value restrained me from throwing the champagne in his face. As it was, my glass remained untouched on the table, whilst Spencer, with a shrug of the shoulders, drank to his own toast.

'Not bad. Not bad at all.' He leaned back in his chair and took a puff at his cigar. 'This is the life, eh?'

'If you have something else to say, I'd be grateful if you'd say it.'

'Oh, sorry. Am I keeping you up? Well, the fact is, Staddon, I owe you an apology.'

'For what?'

'I may have spoken out of turn to our Brazilian friend, Rodrigo. Tongue ran away with me. You know how it is. A few drinks. A spot of reminiscence. Then, before you know what's happening, you've let the cat out of the bag.'

'I've no idea what you're talking about.'

'You and Consuela. I suggested to Rodrigo – well, more or less told him, actually – that you and she had had a fling a few years ago.'

I stared at him, as yet too amazed to be angry. '*You* told him?'

'Ah, I see it's as I feared. No doubt he had a word with you about it. Probably none too pleasant a word. No diplomat, our Rodrigo, I grant you. Well, I'm sorry if I landed you in it, I really am.'

'But . . . What did you tell him? What *could* you tell him? You knew . . . You *know* nothing about it.'

Spencer grimaced theatrically and re-filled his glass. 'I'm afraid you're labouring under another illusion there, Staddon. I have a quite distinct recollection from my youth – which I related to Rodrigo – of seeing you and Consuela in circumstances that left little doubt even in my inexperienced mind of how matters stood between you.'

'What recollection?'

'Are you sure you want to know? You could find it rather embarrassing.'

I leaned forward and fixed him with a stare. 'Just tell me what you told Rodrigo.'

'All right. If that's how you want it.' He grinned at me, entirely unabashed. 'Cast your mind back to July, 1911. Remember that frightful cricket match at Mordiford? Purgatory from start to finish as far as I was concerned. Except I didn't stay till the finish. I wandered off after lunch, while they were still bowling donkey-drops for Uncle Victor to hit for six. You'd disappeared by then as well, though I'd no idea where you'd gone. I wasn't trying to spy on you, though maybe I would have if I'd had any inkling what I'd see. An education in itself for a young shaver like me, I don't mind admitting.

'I trailed up through the orchard to Clouds Frome and stopped about halfway along the pergola for a breather on one of those wrought-iron benches you'd dotted around the place. I was just sitting there, staring up at the sky and the rear of the house, counting how many fleecy bits of cloud I could see, when a curtain moved at an open window on the first floor. It was nothing more than a twitch that caught my eye, but when I looked up, what I saw meant I couldn't have looked away again for all the chocolate in Bournville.

'Consuela was standing at the window and she hadn't a stitch on. I didn't know what to think, except that she was lovelier than anything I'd ever seen before. Not that I need to describe her to you. You must remember it all well enough. As I watched, you appeared in the window next to her, as naked as she was. You kissed her and put your arms round her. By this time, I was transfixed, eyes bolting out of my head. I couldn't believe what I was seeing. And you know what I saw, don't you? You know what happened next.'

The day was recreated in my memory as Spencer spoke. The heat, the passion, the deceit: all the components stood sharp and incontrovertible in my mind. Yes, I knew what happened next. It was seared into my conscience, the joy of the moment erased by the suffering it had caused.

'You want me again?'

'I want you always.'

'Then you shall have me. Always.'

I had thought nothing could make what I had done worse. It could not have been more selfish. It could not have been less honourable. Yet this latest, least welcome disclosure somehow succeeded. Spencer had seen us. He had peered up at us, watching eagerly as we touched and embraced, salivating with glee as we performed unconsciously for his benefit. And now, years later, he had turned what was merely unforgivable into something irredeemably sordid.

'Rodrigo seemed shocked when I told him. I suppose we shouldn't be surprised. You know what these Latin males are like. They roger every tart in sight, but expect their sisters to live like nuns. Mind you, I was shocked at the time. Precocious I may have been, but not *that* precocious. It was a real eye-opener to me. Of course, it doesn't seem very extraordinary to me *now*. If I'd been your age then, I don't suppose I could have kept my hands off her either. She's always been a fine figure of a woman, our Consuela. There have been times in recent years, I'm bound to admit, when I've thought of giving her—'

'You've said enough!' A silence fell at the bar, broken only by an irritating cough. I lowered my voice. 'You've made it all perfectly clear and no doubt you've enjoyed doing so. You think you're very clever, don't you? – meddling in other people's affairs, pouring your little drops of poison into their minds.'

'Poison, Staddon? An unfortunate choice of metaphor, I must say.'

'I've heard as much from you as I can stomach. Now, clear out of here, would you?'

'But I've not finished the bubbly yet.' He reached out for the bottle and began to pour some into his glass. As he did so, I grabbed his wrist, so suddenly and tightly that the champagne missed its target and fizzed across the table. 'Steady on!' he cried.

Still grasping his wrist, I reached out with my other hand, plucked the cigar from his mouth and dropped it into his glass. With a tiny hiss, it was extinguished. He stared at me in open-mouthed amazement.

'What the devil do you think you're playing at?'

'I'm not *playing* at anything. If you don't leave now, I shan't be answerable for the consequences.'

He stared at me a moment longer, then tossed his head dismissively, brushed at his jacket and stood up. 'Well, if that's the line you're going to take . . .'

'It is.'

'The day may come, Staddon, when you regret making an enemy of me.'

'I doubt it.'

'Have it your own way. Meanwhile, I'll bid you goodnight.' With that, he strode from the bar.

I did not watch him go, but relaxed back slowly into my chair.

The fire was burning down. I closed my eyes, as if by that alone I could wipe away the stain his words had left. But I could not. And, when I opened them, there were so many traces of his presence close at hand – the smeared glasses, the half-empty bottle, the pool of champagne, the floating remnant of his cigar, the pungent reek of it in the air about me – that I could almost see him still sitting opposite me, grinning maliciously, eager to recall all he knew or had guessed about me. Some sump of venom in the Caswell line had drained into Spencer's vicious little mind and this was its result. He did not care who he hurt or why, whether Consuela hanged or was spared, whether his own sister lived or died. We were all the same to him: fumbling actors on a crudely lit stage. Whilst we lied and fought, he lounged in the stalls, laughing himself to drunken sleep.

Hermione had told me that Caswell & Co. board meetings always commenced at half past two and never lasted less than an hour. It was at half past three the following afternoon, therefore, that I crossed the yard of the cider-works and entered by the office door.

Mortimer's secretary, Miss Palmer – whom I remembered from my previous visit – was younger and prettier than might have been expected, though heavy horn-rimmed spectacles gave her an air of earnestness. She looked up nervously from her typewriter as I entered her room and said: 'Can I help you, sir?' Evidently, she did not recognize me.

'I want to speak to Victor Caswell.'

'Oh. Well, I'm afraid he's in the board meeting at present, sir.' She nodded towards the firmly closed door on the far side of her office.

'I know. I'll wait, if I may.'

'Oh. I see. Rightio, sir.'

I sat down on the only free chair in the room. Miss Palmer returned to her typing. Between letters, it was possible to hear a murmur of voices from the board-room, but who was speaking or what they were saying was indistinguishable. Ten minutes passed. Then Miss Palmer cleared her throat and said:

'Are you sure you want to wait, sir?'

'Quite, thank you.'

'Only there's no knowing when the meeting will end.'

'When it does, I'll be here.'

'Oh. I see. Rightio, sir.'

Typing resumed. Four o'clock approached. Miss Palmer stifled a yawn and looked as if she would have paused for a cigarette if I had not been there. Then she abandoned typing and commenced filing correspondence in a cabinet near the door. Muffled voices could still be heard from the board-room; there was nothing to suggest the meeting was drawing to a close.

Thanks to the noise made by the filing-cabinet drawers when she pushed them shut, Miss Palmer failed to hear the door being opened behind her a few minutes later. Spencer Caswell slipped into the room from the corridor outside and grinned at the spectacle, which he clearly found inviting, of her bending down to reach the lowest drawers. He did not notice me and crept forward on tiptoe, his intentions by now obvious. At the last moment, I coughed.

'Staddon!' Spencer cried, as he spun round and saw me. 'What the blazes are you doing here?' It was pleasant for once to see him taken off guard. Miss Palmer, standing up to find him close behind her, started violently and blushed.

'I'm here to see Victor.'

'Uncle Victor?' He straightened his hair, slouched across to the desk and propped himself against it, all the while reassembling his composure. 'Well, well. This will be a bigger surprise for him than it was for me.'

'Possibly.'

'I suppose you didn't get past the gate at Clouds Frome. Decided to beard him here instead. That's it, isn't it? The question is: how did you know there was a board meeting? No need to ask, really. It was my babbling brook of an aunt, wasn't it?'

'I didn't come here to speak to you,' I replied in a measured tone. 'And frankly, I'd prefer not to.'

'Would you really? Well, we can't all have what we—'

The board-room door opened behind me and, as it did so, Spencer sprang away from the desk and erased his sarcastic grin. I rose from my chair and turned to see Mortimer Caswell standing in the doorway, glaring suspiciously at his son. He seemed about to say something – a sharp rebuke if his expression was any clue. Then he noticed me.

'Mr Staddon! What brings you here?'

'Your brother. Is he in there?'

'Victor? Why yes, but—'

His protests were useless. I was already pushing past him into the board-room. The long table that ran its length met my gaze.

Gathered at the far end were Mortimer's fellow directors, variously standing and sitting, closing files and extinguishing cigarettes, laughing and conversing as the meeting broke up. There were eight of them altogether and four of them were known to me: Hermione, who smiled faintly in my direction; Grenville Peto, whose place on the board of Caswell & Co. was a surprise I had no time to absorb; Arthur Quarton, the family's and evidently the company's solicitor; and Victor.

Silence seized them all, even those who could not have recognized me, a silence that bristled with hostility. The painted likeness of old George Caswell seemed to curl his lip at me from the far wall. Then Victor snapped shut his valise, set it down before him and walked slowly towards me.

He was frowning, struggling as much as me, I sensed, to order thoughts and words. He looked thinner and greyer than when we had last met. His brow seemed more prominent and there was the suggestion of a stoop about his shoulders, as if he were weighed down by numberless anxieties. I could almost have felt sorry for him – if I had not come so sure of his guilt on several scores.

'I'm sorry to intrude,' I said, addressing the others as much as him. 'But your refusal to see me at Clouds Frome left me with little choice.'

Victor stopped at the corner of the table and stared at me, his face a-quiver with competing emotions. Anger was prominent, of course, and astonishment at my effrontery. There was embarrassment as well, an uncertainty about how to respond in front of witnesses. And somewhere, buried deep, there was fear. I saw it glimmer briefly before he nerved himself to snuff it out. 'What do you want?' he murmured.

'The truth. I know some of it already. How you forced Lizzie Thaxter to act as your spy and drove her to suicide. How you bribed Ashley Thornton to hire me as architect for the Hotel Thornton. I know all of that. And now I want to know the rest.'

'This is absurd.'

'Do you deny any of it?'

'I deny all of it.'

'Well, perhaps this will change your mind.' I plucked Lizzie's letter from my pocket and waved it under his nose. 'Lizzie wrote this to her brother in prison a few hours before she hanged herself. It proves she was your spy, that she hated you for what you made her do and that she killed herself rather than continue.'

'Impossible!' He made a grab at the letter, but I was too quick for him, slipping it back into my pocket before it could come to any harm. Victor stepped back a pace and glanced round at his colleagues, as if appealing to them to side with him. 'This is all complete nonsense,' he blustered. 'The letter's a fake, nothing more.'

'It's no fake.'

Victor looked back at me. Some of his confidence seemed suddenly restored. 'What am I supposed to have wanted Lizzie Thaxter to spy *on*, prey?'

'Your wife.'

'Really? Why?'

'Do you want me to spell it out?'

'Since I have no idea what you're talking about, you'll have to.'

'You were afraid she was going to leave you for me. And you were right.'

'Strange she didn't, then.'

'Only the Thornton commission stopped us. Only the commission *you* arranged.'

'I arranged nothing. And you haven't a shred of evidence to suggest otherwise.' He looked past me at Mortimer. 'This has gone on long enough.'

At last, Mortimer stepped between us. 'I must ask you to leave immediately, Mr Staddon. You're not welcome here.'

'I haven't finished yet.'

'You refuse to leave?'

'I refuse to let your brother evade my questions.'

'Then I have no choice. Miss Palmer! Telephone the police at once, please. Tell them we require their services for the removal of an intruder.'

I looked at Victor. Colour was returning to his face, a sneer beginning to hover about his mouth. Then I looked at the other occupants of the room. Those who were not mystified were indignant. All were frowning ominously. Even Hermione seemed taken aback by my recklessness. I felt my nerve and my confidence ebbing, sensed the rapid fading of the initiative I had seized. 'The police station, please,' I heard Miss Palmer say to the operator. 'Yes. This is an emergency.' Soon, I knew, my chance would be gone.

'Wait a moment!' I cried, striding towards the group gathered at the end of the table. 'Mr Peto! There's something I want to ask you.'

Grenville Peto and I had always disliked each other. I

253

remembered him from the time of the robbery at his mill as a sour, grudging, pompous little man and the intervening years had only confirmed my assessment. Built like a barrel of lard, with a swollen neck overlapping his collar and a pair of pale eyes set in a round, florid face, he glared up at me with all the vanity and arrogance that only thirty years of unfettered power in a small town can breed.

'Victor claims he had no more idea than anyone else that his niece and sister-in-law were calling for tea on the ninth of September last, doesn't he, Mr Peto?'

'I . . . What of it?'

'You telephoned him that afternoon, didn't you, after the ladies had left your house and before they reached Clouds Frome?'

'No. I certainly did not.'

'You telephoned him and that's how he knew they'd be there, knew he'd have the innocent victims his plan required.'

'I made no call!'

'Yes you did. What I want to know is why you've concealed it till now.'

'I've concealed nothing. This is outrageous.'

'You're mad, Staddon,' put in Victor. 'You must be to make an accusation like that.'

'You deny it?'

'Absolutely.' Victor glanced at his brother, as if to reassure him on the point. 'I took no such call. From Grenville or anyone else.'

'You're lying! And I can prove it.' I turned towards the door, determined to call Spencer in to back me up. But he was nowhere to be seen. In the outer room there was only Miss Palmer, putting the telephone down as I watched and moving to Mortimer's side.

'They'll be here in a few minutes, Mr Caswell.'

'Thank you, Miss Palmer. Go down to the yard door and direct them from there, would you?'

All heads turned to look at me as Miss Palmer hurried out, all eyes swivelled to stare me down. Suddenly, I knew. Spencer would deny ever talking to me. Even if he did not, he would deny telling me about the telephone call. And the worst of it was that his denials counted for nothing, one way or the other. Every one of those around me – save Hermione – would support Victor whether they believed him or not. The tentacles of his power and influence bound them just as they had once bound me. And my freedom from their coils was only entrapment in something worse

– the certainty of my own helplessness. I reached for Lizzie Thaxter's letter, then hesitated. If it could not be used in court, because of the damage it would do to Consuela's reputation, it could not be used here either. I lowered my hand to my side and looked from one to the other of them. Nothing gave. Nothing yielded. Nothing hinted at concession. Peto glared. Those to either side of him frowned. Quarton looked away. And Hermione touched my arm.

'If you leave now, Mr Staddon,' she said softly, 'a great deal of unpleasantness will be avoided.' I looked down at her. 'And perhaps a great deal of harm as well.'

Hermione's meaning was as clear as it was incontrovertible. I had mishandled my confrontation with Victor from the first. I should have waited until he was alone, should have remembered that witnesses would strengthen his resolve, not weaken it. Above all, I should have realized that to know what he had done was not enough. I had to prove it beyond the faintest shadow of a doubt. And that I could not do.

'You'll be helping nobody,' said Hermione, 'by waiting to be arrested.'

I nodded. Already, Mortimer was standing by the window, gazing down expectantly into the yard. My cause was lost and everyone in the room knew it. To remain was to pile folly on humiliation. Clenching my fists and looking neither to right nor left, I started for the door.

It was several hours before I returned to my hotel. I had filled the time trudging aimlessly around Hereford's dark and wintry streets, hoping physical exhaustion would blot out the stinging awareness of my own stupidity. But at the Green Dragon there awaited merely another reminder of it. The clerk informed me, with as straight a face as he could preserve, that heavy demand for their accommodation meant they would have to ask me to leave in the morning. I did not argue. Whether the Caswells or the police had urged them to take such action hardly seemed to matter. For once, my inclination coincided with theirs.

I rose early the following morning and settled my bill immediately after breakfast. To my surprise, the clerk handed me a note that had been delivered for me late the previous night. To my even greater surprise, it was from Arthur Quarton, asking me to call on him at his offices in Castle Street before I left Hereford in order to discuss 'a matter of extreme importance'. For a moment, I was tempted to ignore the summons, to drive back to London and forget the whole pack of them. But only for a moment.

Quarton, Marjoribanks & Co. occupied Georgian premises of an elegance befitting one of the oldest and most reputable legal practices in Hereford. The comfortable waiting-room, the neat walled garden beyond its windows and the pleasing prospect it commanded of the cathedral tower were all a far cry from Windrush's hand-to-mouth existence.

Quarton did not keep me waiting long. He fetched me himself and ushered me into his adjoining office, a large but strangely welcoming room full of over-sized furniture and disorderly bundles of files. The door and floorboards creaked, the leather upholstery squeaked, the fire sang like a kettle and Quarton added a breathless wheeze to the orchestra of trifles. Bald, rotund and bespectacled, he wore a baggy tweed suit and a curiously contented smile. He positively beamed at me across his desk and would have succeeded, in any other circumstances, in putting me instantly at my ease.

'What can I do for you, Mr Quarton? If it concerns yesterday's altercation . . .'

'It does, Mr Staddon, though not perhaps in the way you envisage.'

'The Green Dragon has suddenly discovered it can no longer accommodate me. Have I Victor to thank for that?'

'Yes. I believe you have.' Seeing that I was, for the moment, silenced by such candour, he continued: 'I should tell you, Mr Staddon, that I asked you to call here on Mr Caswell's behalf, but not with his knowledge. I am acting, as it were, on my own initiative.'

'To what end?'

'You showed Mr Caswell a letter yesterday and claimed it was written by Lizzie Thaxter to her brother in prison shortly before her suicide.'

'So it was.'

'May I see it?'

'Very well.' I took it from my pocket and placed it on the desk between us, turned so that he could read the name, address and postmark. I kept my hand on it, nervous lest some trick were being planned. But Quarton merely leaned forward and peered over his glasses at it, making no move to pick it up.

256

'As I thought,' he murmured after a moment. 'A fake.'

'How can you possibly say that?'

'Quite simply. Because I have one as well.' He pulled open a drawer of his desk, slipped something out and placed it in front of me. It was another letter, addressed in the same hand, sent in the same size and style of envelope. I turned them both round to face me. The writing, even the ink, was identical. *P.A. Thaxter, Esq., c/o H.M. Prison, Gloucester.* And the postmark was exactly the same. *Hereford, 7.30 p.m., 19 July 1911.* With trembling fingers, I removed the second letter from its envelope and unfolded it. *My dearest brother, I am sorry, but I will not be coming to see you tomorrow, as I said I would. I have thought* . . . Lizzie's words, in Lizzie's writing, were there before me, damned by duplication. I looked up at Quarton.

'What does this mean?'

'It means we've both bought something which is not what the seller claimed it was. The source of your copy was, I take it, Mr Thomas Malahide?'

'Yes.'

'We should not be unduly surprised, I suppose. The leopard cannot change his spots. In Malahide's case, crime and deception are probably instinctive.'

'How . . . When did you come by this?'

'Malahide came here shortly before Christmas. He told me what he no doubt told you: that Peter Thaxter had entrusted his sister's last letter to him, that he had forgotten about it until Mrs Caswell's trial was mentioned in the newspapers, that he now thought we would be willing to pay rather than have such a letter quoted in the press. I assume you were as worried by the damage it might do Mrs Caswell's reputation as I was by the picture it might paint of Mr Caswell. Like you, I capitulated. The letter – and a substantial sum of money – changed hands. And Malahide left, well satisfied with his day's work.'

'How long have you known it was a fake?'

'Since having it examined by an expert, who pointed out what I should have noticed myself. The stamp, Mr Staddon. Look at the stamp.'

I peered at it and saw nothing remarkable. Quarton returned my frown with a grin.

'We have not always paid a penny halfpenny for the privilege of posting a letter, have we?'

Then, like Quarton, I saw what I should have seen before.

'Good God,' I murmured. 'It's the wrong denomination.'

'Exactly. It would only have cost Lizzie Thaxter a penny to send that – if it were genuine.'

'What have you done about this?'

'Nothing. I have no way of tracing Malahide. I've wondered, of course, whether the contents are genuine – whether he copied a real letter, I mean, in order to maximize his profit by selling it to several people, or simply made the thing up based on information given to him by Peter Thaxter. On the whole, I'm inclined to think the former. The wording is altogether too much like what the girl would actually have written for Malahide to have concocted. But it's definitely a feminine hand, so he must have an accomplice. Perhaps *she* has the imagination to have composed it. I doubt we shall ever know. Having defrauded us – and perhaps others – he's unlikely to give a clue to his whereabouts by selling the letter to the press. At least, I hope so.'

So Malahide had deceived me. Somehow, it came as no surprise. It explained his persistence after my failure to keep our first appointment. No doubt he had congratulated himself on his cleverness. No doubt he had toasted Quarton and me – and anyone else who had fallen for his story – for the fools he had made of us. But, if so, he had done so too soon.

'Why are you smiling, Mr Staddon?'

'Because you're wrong, Mr Quarton.'

'About what?'

'About being unable to trace Malahide. You see, I know where he is.'

I reached London too late that afternoon to pursue Malahide. In the morning, however, I intended to find out his address from Croad, the builder who, according to Giles, had last employed him. He would not, I felt certain, elude me for long. So it was that I returned to Suffolk Terrace with something to show for my absence – though much less than I had hoped.

I parked the car in the street, took my bag from the boot and walked slowly towards the house, fumbling for the key in my pocket as I went. These mundane actions so casually performed emphasize how unexpected what happened next was, how much worse and more shocking than any spoken rebuff. Dusk was descending rapidly. The lamps were already lit. A neighbour was walking away from her door, trailing her dog on a lead. This street – and the house I was approaching – had been my home for ten years. But that was about to end.

Three steps to the door. I slid the key into the lock. It stuck halfway. I tried again with the same result. Then I examined the key. Yes, it was the right one. But the lock was not. When I looked at it closely, I could see that it was brand new, hastily fitted to judge by the chips of paint missing from the door around it.

My initial reaction was disbelief. This could not mean what I thought it meant. Pointlessly, I tried the key again, then stared at the door as if willpower alone could force it to open. And then, at last, I pressed the bell. There was no response. I pressed it again and stepped back in order to look up at the windows. As I did so, the net-curtain in the drawing-room bay was abruptly lowered. A moment before, I felt certain, it had been raised to see who was ringing the bell. Surely, now they knew it was me, they would answer.

But they did not. With an oath, I grasped the knocker – the faithful old brass dolphin I knew so well – and beat it against its plate fully a dozen times, then paused to listen for the sounds of approaching footsteps within. At last, my efforts were rewarded. Surely that was Nora's tread I could hear. I stepped back, struggling to decide what I would say when she opened the door.

But it did not open. Instead, the flap on the letter-box stirred and a long narrow buff envelope appeared, being pushed through from the other side. Instinctively, I reached out and took it, turning it over in my hands. My name had been typed on it in block capitals. GEOFFREY STADDON, ESQ. But there was no address.

I stumbled to the nearest street-lamp, tearing the envelope open as I went, then held the contents up to read. The letter-head of Martindale, Clutton & Fyffe was immediately recognizable. They were Sir Ashley Thornton's solicitors.

> Martindale, Clutton & Fyffe,
> 5–7 Partidge Place,
> High Holborn,
> LONDON WC1.
> 7th January 1924

Dear Mr Staddon,
Our client, Mrs Staddon, has instructed us to notify you that she is instituting proceedings against you for divorce on the

259

grounds of physical cruelty. Pending a hearing of this action, she requires that you quit the property at 27 Suffolk Terrace, Kensington, of which, as you know, she is sole lessee. If you wish to remove any of your belongings currently lodged therein, please contact this office in order to agree a date and time when they can be collected by a third party.

We should be obliged if you would advise us of the solicitor who will be representing your interests in this case at your earliest convenience.

Yours sincerely,

H. Dodson

pp G. F. Martindale (Senior Partner)

I thrust the letter into my pocket, turned slowly and looked back at the house. No curtains moved. Nothing stirred or shifted or glimmered within. This dark cold blankness was the only home-coming Angela was prepared to grant me. This, and a curt letter from Martindale, Clutton & Fyffe, signed by a clerk in the senior partner's absence. *Per procurationem.* Which was only appropriate, given that henceforth Angela and I would meet in front of witnesses, communicate through intermediaries, greet each other by petition and *subpoena*. It would take the lawyers many a month to bring this sad little case to what they termed a satisfactory conclusion. But I would neither help nor hinder them. I had not thought Angela would move so far and fast against me. But, now she had, I would not resist. If an end was what she wanted, an end she would have. I took my leave of her there, alone in the silent street, as night closed like a black cloud upon the roof-tops. I took my bleak farewell of all we had been to each other, and all we might have been. And then I climbed into the car and drove away.

CHAPTER

THIRTEEN

I have many times wondered why Imry Renshaw is such a good friend to me. I can name precious few occasions on which I have come to his aid, yet he has come to mine more often than I could ever deserve. So it was that night of my exclusion from Suffolk Terrace and for many of the nights that followed. Without his cheerily given advice and boundless generosity, there is no knowing what I might have done. Thanks to his influence, however, I held to a sane and sensible course.

I slept at Sunnylea – slept, at all events, for the few hours of darkness that remained after I had poured out my frustrations and resentments by Imry's fireside. In the morning, we travelled into London together, Imry having undertaken to approach Martindale, Clutton & Fyffe with regard to my belongings and to consult some estate agents about the availability of bachelor flats. We agreed to meet later at his club.

For my part, Angela's action had merely heightened my determination to trace Malahide. His pursuit staved off for the present all thoughts of the acrimonious convolutions divorce might force me to describe. I welcomed indeed the excuse he had given me to forget them; his was one lie I could confidently hope to nail. Pausing at Frederick's Place only to confirm the little Giles had previously told me, I set off for Woolwich.

Croad's men were cramming some dismal-looking housing onto a site near Woolwich Dockyard. Happily, the foreman knew my name and was as helpful as could be. Malahide had worked there until the Saturday before Christmas. Since then, nothing had been seen of him. He was a skilful worker – but unreliable, as his departure without so much as a day's notice demonstrated. My request for his address caused much amusement. Any pub between Woolwich and Wapping was one suggestion. Some of his former workmates, however, knew his daughter's husband, Charlie Ryan. He was a porter at Deptford Hospital and might, if handled carefully, tell me more.

I found Ryan in a dank corner of the hospital laundry. Lean, sallow and unsmiling, he proved as informative as he was disagreeable. A cigarette and a patient audience was all he needed to unburden himself on the subject of his father-in-law, a man he clearly loathed. The long and the short of it was that he did not bother to keep track of the old man's frequent changes of lodging, but that his wife, Alice, did – much to his regret. I should find her at home that afternoon and was welcome to tell her that my visit was yet another indication of her father's predictable failure to mend his ways.

The Ryans inhabited one of a terrace of mean yellow-brick houses off the Old Kent Road. The street was a cul-de-sac, entirely overshadowed by the vast grey wall of a gasometer at its farther end. There was an acrid taste of gas in the air, blending rankly with blocked drains and rubbish-choked gutters. The Ryans' door stood open, revealing a bare linoleumed passage. Inside, a child was crying. I hammered on the door and shouted 'Hello!'

'Through here,' came the reply. I followed it towards the rear of the house and found myself in a low-ceilinged kitchen where the air seemed even colder than in the street and a young, heavily pregnant woman was wringing clothes in a sink. Behind her, in a high-chair, sat the bawling infant, who fell instantly silent as I entered and stared at me, uncertain how to respond.

'Mrs Ryan?'

She turned to look at me and started with surprise. Probably no more than twenty-five, though poverty and toil had lined her face and chapped her hands, she was that saddest of creatures, one who looked worthy of a better life. There was a spark of intelligence in her eyes, a hint of pride in her bearing. She seemed weighed down by hardship, but not yet completely crushed by it.

262

'Who are you?' she said suspiciously. 'Thought it must be the tallyman, with a knock like that.'

'I'm looking for your father, Mrs Ryan. Tom Malahide.'

'He ain't here.'

'I realize that. I hoped you might be able to tell me where I could find him.'

'What d'you say your name was?'

'I didn't. I'm a . . . a business acquaintance of your father.'

'Oh yeh? Well, if Dad wanted to do business with you, he'd have told you how to find him, wouldn't he?'

'Indeed. It's simply that we've lost touch.' To avoid the challenge of her gaze, I stepped further into the room and looked around at the sparsely stocked shelves and peeling wallpaper. 'He spoke of you, however. That's how—' My eye was suddenly taken by a scrap of paper pinned to the edge of the nearest shelf. It was a rudimentary shopping list: bread, tea, flour, butter, candles. But the handwriting was familiar. It was what, until recently, I had thought of as Lizzie Thaxter's. Quarton's words came into my mind. *'It's definitely a feminine hand, so he must have an accomplice.'* I reached out and tore the list free, then peered at it more closely. There could be no mistake.

'Here! What d'you think you're doing?'

I turned to confront her. Subterfuge would serve no further purpose. That at least was clear. 'The game's up, Mrs Ryan. I'm one of those who bought a letter off your father. A letter, as it turns out, written by you.'

'I never—' She stopped, unable, it seemed, to compose a denial, least of all a convincing one.

'This is your writing.' I held up the list.

'Well, yeh, but— '

'Then there's no room for doubt. I know the letter I was sold is a fake and now I know who faked it. You.'

'You can't prove nothing!'

'With this, I rather think I can.' I slipped the list into my pocket, then smiled in an attempt to reassure her. 'Look, Mrs Ryan, I'm not trying to get you into trouble, though no doubt I could. All I want to do is to speak to your father.'

She stared at me, falteringly now, with little pouts of indecision. She was frightened, but also determined not to let me trick her into a betrayal. All this seemed to declare itself in the protracted silence that followed.

'How did he talk you into it?'

'I'm saying nothing.'

'And did he tell you what to write? Or did you copy it from the original?' A mute glare was her only answer. 'Has he shared the money with you?'

'What money?'

'He's made several hundred pounds out of this so far, you know. At least, I hope you *do* know.'

Her jaw had sagged, her eyes had widened. Then she frowned. 'You're lying.'

'No. My word of honour, Mrs Ryan. I paid him a hundred and fifty pounds. I know of at least one other person who paid him a similar sum. As to how many buyers he had altogether, well, you'd know, wouldn't you? How many letters did you write?'

'A hundred and fifty quid?' Disbelief had transformed her expression. 'You paid him as much as that?'

'I did.'

'Gawd.' She put her hand to her mouth and turned away. 'The lying old—' Then she looked back at me. 'I ain't got a penny of it, mister. That's the honest truth.'

'So, your father's kept all of it. Perhaps that makes you think he doesn't really deserve your loyalty.'

'All of it?' She sniggered harshly. 'No, he ain't kept the lot.' She pointed at an open box of painted wooden bricks on the floor. 'He bought them for the kiddy's birthday last week.' She sniggered again, but this time it was closer to a sob. Then, with a sudden swing of her foot, she kicked one of the bricks the width of the kitchen. It bounced off the leg of a table and rattled to rest beneath the mangle. 'Bloody bricks!'

'Will you tell me where I can find him, Mrs Ryan?'

'Oh, I'll do better than that.' She grasped a cloth and dried her hands energetically. 'I'll take you there. It's not just you who wants a word with him now. It's me an' all.'

The child was deposited with a neighbour. Then, wearing only a thin raincoat and a headscarf over her indoor clothes, Alice Ryan led me north towards Rotherhithe, by narrow streets and back-alleys, past more foul-smelling factories and beneath more dank railway viaducts than I would ever have guessed could be jammed between the swathes of tumble-down housing. As we went, she sustained a monologue explaining and excusing her involvement in Malahide's scheme, as much, it seemed, to relieve her own feelings as to appease mine.

'I should've known better, of course, but Dad knows how to talk me round. He has the gift of the gab even if he has the gift of nothing else. And he said it was so easy. All I had to do was copy what he'd written out for me and he'd see I got some of whatever he made. And, Gawd, could we do with a bit extra. So, I went along with it. Why not? I never thought it was going to bring the likes of you to me door. But, like I say, I should've known better. Dad's little wheezes, as he calls 'em, never work out the way they're supposed to.

'Dad said he had this letter left him by a bloke he met in the nick who was hung. After he came out a couple of years ago, he passed the letter on to the bloke's family. So he says, anyway. But I reckon he sold it. Otherwise, why should he have thought there was money to be made from it now? And why should he have kept a copy of it? That's how he was able to make something out of it, you see, because he still had the copy. But it was in his writing, of course, and nobody was going to take his crabby hand for a young woman's. So, he got me to copy it again in me best script. Three times. He reckoned he could flog all three copies for a tidy bit of cash, with this trial coming up. And it seems he was right. But I never thought – I never dreamt – it'd be as much as you say it is. Gawd, my Charlie could hump dirty linen down the hospital for a year and not see a hundred and fifty quid for it.

'Dad's a crook. Always has been and always will be. Well, you must know that. They say he's a good chippy, but he's never been content to work for a wage. Oh no, he's always wanted more. But he's been a good father to me in his way, so I've never had the heart to turn me back on him. I get that angry with him some-times – like I am now. Then he talks me round and, before I know it, I'm laughing at his jokes again fit to bust. Mind, I don't reckon I've ever been *this* angry. He'll have to come up with something really special to wriggle back into me good books this time.'

We came at length to a shabby terrace of three-storeyed houses facing a railway embankment along which a seemingly endless train of rusting trucks was being slowly pulled, their wheels squeeling like tortured geese. At the far end of the terrace, Alice turned in through an open doorway and started up an ill-lit staircase, on which the carpet had grown so thin that holes had been worn in the centre of each tread. The carpet expired altogether as we climbed towards the second floor and here the plaster had crumbled away from the wall in gaping patches, revealing the laths beneath.

Malahide's room was at the front of the house, at the end of a dingy passage. His door looked more substantial than most of the woodwork around it, stout and fitted with a Yale as well as a mortice lock. Alice knocked loudly, waited and listened for a moment, then knocked again. There was no answer.

'He's not worked since Christmas,' she said. 'And it's too early for him to be boozing. I'll see if one of the other tenants knows where he is.'

She descended to the first floor whilst I waited. I heard her knock at another door, then there followed a muffled conversation I could not make out. A few minutes later, she returned, looking more worried now than angry.

'It's funny,' she announced. 'Old Mother Rudd don't miss a thing, but she's not seen Dad since Saturday.'

'So, what do we do?'

She thought for a moment, then said: 'We'll go in. I've got some keys.'

A second later, the door was open. Alice was still struggling to remove her key from the Yale lock when I walked past her into the room. It was set in the eaves of the house, with the greater part of the ceiling sloping at forty-five degrees, lit by one dormer window. Of this, the mean furnishings and the chill, fetid atmosphere, I was instantly aware. Then, in the very next instant, awareness of something else, something altogether overwhelming, came upon me.

Malahide was lying flat on his back across a threadbare rug beneath the window. He was dead. I was certain of that even before I moved towards him and saw the bullet-hole in his right temple, the black clot of blood on his head and on the rug beneath him, the stiff, white, lifeless grip that death had taken on him.

I turned back to shield Alice, but already she had seen for herself. She did not scream or faint. She did not even blanch. She simply put her hand to her mouth, said 'Oh my Gawd', then lowered herself slowly into the only chair in the room.

'I'm sorry,' I said.

'Somebody's done him in.'

'Yes.'

Now she was losing some of her colour and beginning to tremble. 'He keeps whisky in that cupboard.' She pointed at a wooden cabinet in the far corner. 'D'you think . . . Could you . . .'

'Of course.' I fetched the bottle, found a glass and poured her a stiff measure. As she sipped it, I stepped closer to Malahide and crouched down beside him. There was nothing horror-stricken or agonized about his face. Death had come suddenly and unannounced, as if it had been waiting to pounce when he entered the room. He was wearing boots, jacket, muffler and mittens, suggesting he had just walked in, and his woollen hat was lying on the rug beneath his head. Only then, absurdly late, did I remember that the door had been locked from the inside. How had his murderer come and gone?

I rose and turned towards the window. One of the panes was punctured by a small round hole, with cracks radiating from it like a sunburst. I walked towards it until I was standing by Malahide's feet. Looking down, I could see fragments of the mud that had been on the soles of his boots; it had dried and flaked off whilst he had lain there. Then I looked at the window. Through it I could see the railway embankment on the other side of the road. It, the hole in the glass and my head were now connected by an invisible line, a line that led my thoughts to the only possible conclusion. Somebody had stood on that grass bank, waiting for Malahide to step into view. And, when he had, they had raised their rifle, aimed and fired. But how, from such an exposed position? Out of the corner of my eye, I noticed the bare electric bulb in the centre of the room. It was alight. The shot had been fired at night, when the embankment was in total darkness.

I looked down at Malahide's body. So swift, so unprepared had been his exit that it seemed, in some childish sense, unfair. A neat and instantly fatal head-wound administered at thirty yards' range. It was a marksman's shot, less a murder than an assassination. The assassin had reconnoitred the scene, no doubt, had chosen the embankment as the ideal vantage point. He had waited for Malahide to come home, to climb the stairs, to switch on the light, to move obligingly to the uncurtained window. Then, too quickly even for pain to register, he had killed him, and descended the bank and vanished into the night, leaving Malahide where he lay, for us to find him.

How long? How long had he lain there? He had not been seen since Saturday. Saturday night, then? It was quite possible. The weather had been cold, mercifully too cold for putrefaction to set in. For four days his corpse had patiently awaited discovery, four days in which his murderer could have covered every one of his tracks. I shivered. The preparation, the calculation, the professional efficiency: they made the crime seem worse, less shocking, perhaps, but infinitely more sinister.

Then, with a violent shudder, I moved away from the window. The invisible line had become solid, tangible, horribly real. And along it had travelled something far worse than the logic of how a murder had been committed. Fear had coursed suddenly and irresistibly into my mind. Why had Malahide been killed? There could surely only be one reason. Lizzie Thaxter's letter. The letter of which I too possessed a copy.

Alice was staring at her father's dead body, motionless with shock, disabled by incomprehension. 'I never thought anything like this would happen,' she murmured. 'It was just . . . just one of his wheezes. Did somebody kill him because of a forged letter from a woman who strung herself up twelve years ago?'

'Do you know of any other reason?'

She shook her head. 'He had enemies. He deserved to have enemies, Gawd knows. But, they'd have given him a walloping, not . . . Maybe in a fight, maybe in the heat of the moment, somebody could have killed him. But not . . . not like this . . . Like he's been . . . executed.' She left her chair and knelt beside him. 'Poor old Dad. At least it looks like it was quick, but . . . The poor old bugger.'

She was about to cry. Desperate to prevent her, I blurted out my theory of how he had been killed. 'A rifle fired from the railway bank is my guess. See the bullet-hole in the window? Probably at night. The light's on, you see?' She looked dumbly from her father's face to the window, to the bulb, then back to her father. 'Who else did he sell letters to, Alice?'

'I don't know. He didn't tell me. I only know there were three.'

'When did you last see him?'

'Thursday. The kiddy's birthday. When he brought the bricks. Wrapped in red crêpe paper.' She stifled a sob. 'He was full of himself. Carried away with his cleverness. Excited fit to burst.'

'Excited about what?'

'The money he'd been paid, I suppose. There wasn't anything—' She broke off and frowned with the effort of recollection. 'Hold on . . .'

'What is it?'

She pushed herself upright and moved slowly back to the chair. 'There *was* something. Of course there was, I just thought . . . Well, it was one of his regular stories. I'd heard it a dozen times

268

before. But, this time, he really seemed to think . . . Gawd, that must be it.'

'What must be?'

'Who'd have thought it after all these years? Who'd have bloody thought it?'

'Thought what?'

She took a deep breath and summoned her concentration. 'How much d'you know about what he was sent down for twelve years ago?'

'The theft of Bank of England bill paper from a mill at Ross-on-Wye. He and two accomplices, Joe Burridge and Peter Thaxter, now both dead.'

'*Two*. That's right. Except that's not right, not according to Dad. He always said there was a fourth in it, somebody who put up the money, who told Joe Burridge that the mill printed bill paper for the Bank of England, that it'd be dead easy to steal. Burridge would never say who he was. He was the only one of the gang who had any contact with him. He reckoned this . . . fourth man . . . would see them all right when they got out, would share the proceeds with them.'

'What proceeds?'

'Burridge had delivered some finished notes to him – to the fourth man, I mean. I don't know how many or what value. I don't even know if it was true. Dad believed it – or said he did. It could just have been another of his dreams. I always thought it was. Till now.'

'Burridge died in prison without identifying this person?'

'That's right. But Dad had seen him once, he said, just once. He'd gone to Burridge's place in Brum and this bloke had been leaving at the same time. Burridge never admitted it was him, but Dad was sure it was. Of course, with Burridge dead, he had no way of finding him. He didn't know his name or anything about him. Except his face. He said he'd never forget that. He said, if he ever saw him again, he'd know him at once. And then he'd settle with him.'

'Settle with him?'

'He was going on about it on Thursday, but different, not the same. He was cheerful, you see, cheerful like . . . Well, I paid him no attention, but, looking back, I can't explain his mood unless . . .'

'Unless he'd seen the fourth man?'

'Yeh. That's it. It was just like . . . like he'd found him at last.'

269

I looked down at Malahide's taut, immobile face and remembered the grin with which he had left me at Southwark Bridge, remembered also the words with which he had cut short my questions. '*Maybe I thought I recognized him, but, now you've put a name to him, I reckon I must have been wrong.*' No, he had not been wrong. I knew that now and so, too late, did he. Major Royston Turnbull was the fourth man. And, three days after learning from me who and what and where he was, Malahide had been murdered.

'What do we do now?'

'I . . . I beg your pardon?'

'About Dad, I mean. Call the police?'

The police. Yes, soon they would be here, eager to know what connection I had with the dead man, what this business of forged letters was all about, of what interest it might be to the officers handling the prosecution of Consuela Caswell. What I had paid Malahide specifically to avoid his murder would inevitably achieve. And vague allegations concerning former accomplices would swiftly be overriden. Unless, of course, my part in his discovery was never known.

'Wait a moment, Alice,' I said. 'Do you realize what calling the police will mean?'

'Eh?'

'I'll have to tell them about the letters. And you'll have to admit aiding and abetting him. He'll be written off as a blackmailer who got too greedy for his own good. And you'll be seen as his accomplice. Do you want that to happen?'

A fear of the consequences of her father's death was now added to her shock at the fact of it. 'No,' she mumbled. ''Course not.'

'Then listen to me. We must find his copy of the letter and I must be elsewhere when the police arrive. I must have nothing to do with the case. Do you understand?'

'Yeh. Reckon I do.'

'Do you know where the letter would be?'

'His jacket. He always kept it on him.'

I knelt beside the body and gingerly raised the jacket by tugging gently at the lapel. There was something small but bulky in the breast pocket. With my other hand, I reached in and pulled it out. It was a greasy leather wallet, thickly filled with five pound notes. There must have been at least thirty of them. I heard Alice gasp at the sight and wondered if they were the ones I had given him. Folded behind the notes was a sheet of paper: Lizzie's letter in a rough hand I took to be Malahide's. When I held it up, Alice nodded and I thrust it into my pocket. I removed the money, leaving only a ten shilling note, hesitated, then offered it to her.

She recoiled. 'I don't want that.'

'You may as well take it. The police will keep it if you don't. And it'll make them more suspicious. Besides, in a sense you've earned it.'

'I can't. It's stealing from the dead.'

'He'd have wanted you to have it, surely?'

'Well . . . I suppose so . . . But . . .'

'You said you needed it. And I'm sure you do. So, take it.' Still she shook her head. 'This is the only chance you'll have.'

'Hundreds of quid just like that? What would Charlie say?'

'Does it matter? I can't leave it here, Alice. You must understand. One of us has to take it.' And my conscience, I refrained from adding, would be the easier if it were her.

Suddenly, her disgust at the idea faltered. There were children to be fed, after all, tallymen to be kept at bay. She reached out and accepted the money.

'I must go now.'

'I know.'

'Wait five minutes after I've left, then tell Mrs Rudd and go to the nearest police station. Say you were worried because he hadn't come to see you as expected and called to see if he was unwell. Say nothing about the letters. Or the fourth man, if it comes to the point.'

'It's all right,' she said with a sigh. 'I know what to do.'

'Good. In that case, I'll leave.' I moved to the door, paused and looked back at her. 'I'm sorry, Alice, really I am. He didn't deserve this.'

'You've been kind,' she murmured. 'But you can go now. I'll see to him.'

I decided not to tell Imry about Malahide's death. I had shared my experiences and discoveries with him every step of the way, but now murder, sudden and clinical, had blocked my path. From this point on, for Imry's sake as well as my own, I knew I must be my own counsellor. He would not have approved of leaving Alice Ryan to cope alone. And he would certainly not have approved of what I proposed to do next. Therefore, I simply reported that I had been unable to trace Malahide beyond Croad's building site and had been forced to abandon the search.

271

Imry had meanwhile been labouring industriously on my behalf. Martindale, Clutton & Fyffe had agreed that my belongings could be collected from Suffolk Terrace on Saturday morning; they would be packed and ready at eleven o'clock. As for accommodation, he had found a mews flat near Lancaster Gate which he thought would suit me and was, moreover, available immediately; I could view it the following morning. He had also made an appointment for me with Hugh Fellows-Smith, the partner in our solicitor's practice who specialized in divorce.

That night, on the sofa-bed at Sunnylea, I lay awake for many hours thinking about Malahide, seeing again his yellow-toothed grin and sharp-eyed gaze, then, blotting them all out, the pale, drawn, sightless face that death had left him with. Who had killed him? The third buyer of his faked letter? Or the fourth accomplice in the Peto's Paper Mill robbery of thirteen years before? If the latter, did that mean Major Royston Turnbull? I badly wanted to believe it did, but I was cautious of my own desire, rooted as it was in a jealousy I did not care to acknowledge.

Next morning, I travelled into London alone. I had bought a clutch of newspapers at Wendover station and it was on an inner page of the *Daily Telegraph* that I found the report I sought.

LOCKED ROOM MURDER MYSTERY

Mr Thomas Malahide, a fifty-four-year-old jobbing carpenter, was found shot dead at his lodgings in Buckley Street, Rotherhithe, yesterday afternoon. He had suffered a fatal rifle-wound to the head. No weapon was found on the premises, which were locked from the inside. The body was discovered by Mrs Alice Ryan, the deceased's daughter. A police spokesman said that damage to a window of the lodgings was consistent with Mr Malahide having been shot from a railway embankment on the other side of the road, probably under cover of darkness. The body is thought to have lain undiscovered for several days. Mr Malahide was last seen alive on Saturday. A more precise indication of the date and time of death and of the range from which the fatal shot was fired is expected to be yielded by the *post mortem* examination, but the police believe they are dealing with a case of cold-blooded murder. Mr Malahide is understood to have had criminal associations and to have served at least one term of imprisonment for robbery.

I had never liked Malahide, yet it seemed to me that he

deserved a better obituary than these perfunctory lines. I thought of the room he had died in – its shape, its contents, its frowstily ominous odour – and of the way he had died – as sudden as it was violent, as brutal as it was unceremonious. Then I thought of the thousands who must idly have scanned the account of his death without carrying in their heads a close and graphic recollection of the scene. To them it was less significant than the mood their employer was in, the state of the weather, the prompt arrival of their train. To them every man *was* an island. And the bell always tolled for another.

As a *pied-à-terre*, the flat Imry had found for me in Hyde Park Gardens Mews seemed as good as any I was likely to find for myself; I rented it on the spot. Then I hurried to the office and from there telephoned Luckham Place. Bassett answered.

'Bassett, this is Geoffrey Staddon.'

'Oh, Mr Geoffrey.' He sounded suitably embarrassed. 'Good morning, sir.'

'I'd like to speak to Major Turnbull.'

'Ah. I'm afraid you can't, sir. He's no longer here.'

'When did he leave?'

'Um . . . Friday.'

'With my wife?'

'Well, I can't . . . That is . . .'

'But Angela *has* left?'

'Yes, sir. She has.'

A Thursday afternoon which did not find my wife sipping tea and swapping gossip in Maudie Davenport's drawing-room would be rare enough to warrant special mention in the almanacs. I calculated therefore that by loitering halfway along the route she invariably followed from Suffolk Terrace – a distance too short even for her to cover by taxi – I would have a better chance of speaking to her than by telephoning or calling at what I still thought of as my home.

Nor was I disappointed. Angela remained faithful to her habits if to nothing else and rounded the bend where I was waiting shortly before three o'clock. She was wearing the outfit in which she had gone driving with Turnbull at Luckham Place – doubtless in the hope of arousing Maudie's envy – and a look of the most perfectly groomed contentment. Her expression altered, however, when she saw me.

273

'Geoffrey! What is the meaning of this?'

'I might have asked you the same when I found my own front door locked against me. But I didn't get the chance, did I?'

'Have you been lying in wait for me here?'

'Yes.'

'Well, you've wasted your time. I've no intention of discussing our private affairs in the street.' She made to walk past me, but I stepped into her path. She stared coldly at me for a moment, then said: 'Kindly stand aside.'

'Not until you answer a few questions.'

'I shall call out for assistance if you persist with this, Geoffrey.'

'Where's Turnbull?'

She looked past me. 'I can see a constable walking towards us. Do you want me to summon him?'

'Just tell me where Turnbull is.'

'You leave me no choice.' She raised her hand and opened her mouth, as if to cry out. But then I grabbed her wrist so tightly that she was shocked into momentary silence.

'He's a murderer, Angela. He's killed – or had killed – a man called Malahide, who was threatening to expose him as an accomplice in a robbery near Clouds Frome thirteen years ago.'

'Major Turnbull? This is absurd.'

'Ask him what he knows about the robbery at Peto's Paper Mill. Ask him whether he's still spending some of the proceeds.'

'I shall do no such thing.'

'I'm warning you for your own good. The man's a thief and a murderer.'

'Let go of me at once!' She spat the words out, angry now where she had merely been alarmed before. Glancing over my shoulder and seeing the policeman bearing down upon us, I released her. 'Major Turnbull has returned to Cap Ferrat,' she said icily. 'Happily, he will not need to be troubled by your ludicrous allegations.'

'Are you sure they're ludicrous?'

But there was no glimmer of doubt in Angela's gaze, none at all events that was not eclipsed by the scorn she felt for me. 'If I had any reservations about divorcing you, Geoffrey, this tasteless exhibition has entirely dispelled them.'

'You won't win on the grounds you've chosen. I don't mind giving you a divorce, but I won't be branded a wife-beater. I'll counter-sue, citing Turnbull as co-respondent.'

'You wouldn't dare. You'd be laughed out of court.'

'Would I? That depends on what the private detectives turn up between now and a hearing, doesn't it?' I saw her confidence falter fractionally. 'It all becomes very grubby from this point on, Angela. Didn't Turnbull warn you to expect that?'

'This has nothing to do with Major Turnbull.' As the policeman loomed alongside, she turned towards him. 'Constable!' He pulled up.

'Yes, ma'am?'

She glanced at me, then back at him. 'This gentleman is seeking directions to St Barnabas' Church. I wonder if you could help him. I'm in rather a hurry.' With that, and one more parting glance, she swept away.

The policeman frowned at me. 'St Barnabas, did the lady say, sir?'

'Yes. But don't worry.' I smiled. 'I think I know my way from here.'

The truth, whatever I might pretend for the benefit of others, was that the future – and my part in it – seemed less hopeful than ever. My suspicions of Turnbull could not be substantiated and carrying out my threat of involving him in a counter-suit against Angela would only muddy the already murky waters. Besides, even if I could prove he had played a part in the Peto's Paper Mill robbery, it would do precisely nothing to help Consuela. Her pending trial stood now at the centre of my thoughts. To its outcome my marital problems and Turnbull's criminal past seemed wholly irrelevant. It was thus in a mood amounting almost to indifference that I kept my appointment with Fellows-Smith the following morning at his offices in Aldgate.

He was a small, precise, expressionless man of almost albino paleness, with a habit I found annoying of smoking a cigarette in such a way as to make his enjoyment of it unduly obvious. He had received a letter from Martindale, Clutton & Fyffe, and led me through its implications amidst many a savoured lungful of smoke.

'The incident at Luckham Place on the, ah, thirty-first of December, Mr Staddon. You are alleged to have struck your wife to the floor. There were, ah, three witnesses. Is the assault admitted?'

'If you mean did I hit her, the answer's yes.'

'Ah. Thank you. That simplifies the position.'

'It's the first time I've ever laid a hand on her.'

'Not according to this letter. Complaints by Mrs Staddon to her family about your, ah, violence, over several years. And witnesses who are prepared to testify that they have seen her more than once with, ah, facial bruises.'

'They're lying.'

'Quite possibly, but lies about minor assaults are apt to be believed when the major assault is admitted. You see our difficulty, I trust.'

'It's *my* difficulty.'

'Quite so. Quite so. As to the, ah, major assault, would you wish to plead provocation?'

'It was a disagreement.'

'About what, might I ask? Your wife's, ah, fidelity, perhaps?'

'Perhaps.'

'We would need to be precise if pursuing this line, Mr Staddon. *Perhaps* would scarcely be adequate.'

'I'd prefer to deny the charge without making counter-accusations.'

'A noble sentiment, but imprudent, if you'll permit me to say so. Given the admission of at least one assault—'

'Mr Fellows-Smith!' I interrupted. 'When is this case likely to be heard?'

'When? Well, that's hard to say. Martindale's no hare. More of a tortoise, if the truth be told. A date before Easter is unlikely. So, May or June would seem the earliest—'

'Very well! These are my instructions. Inform my wife's solicitors that the action will be contested. Then find a suitable barrister to represent me.'

A silence fell. He appeared to expect more. At last he said: 'Nothing else, Mr Staddon?'

'Not at this stage. I'm grateful for your advice. And now I'll bid you good morning.'

May or June. What did I care about the events of two such distant months? What could I care when the trial opening in three days' time would bring an end to matters of far greater moment than the survival of my marriage? I walked slowly back towards Frederick's Place, oblivious to the steady rain, alone amidst the bustling, umbrellaed throng. Look where I might, the clouds showed no sign of breaking.

Sir Henry Curtis-Bennett's chambers in Middle Temple Lane that afternoon seemed overhung with gloom. Sir Henry smiled as often and expressed as much optimism as before, but something had gone out of him, some breath of hearty combat that was vital to his success. At those moments when he thought nobody was looking at him, he sagged visibly, like a balloon losing air, and cast weary glances at the dusk settling on the courtyard beyond his window. Where still, without remorse, it rained.

His strategy was in fact unaltered. Forensic minutiae were to be set aside in an unashamed appeal to the jurors' hearts. Consuela's own testimony would be the crux and essence of the case. As for my contention that Victor had had prior notice of the ladies' arrival for tea on 9 September, Sir Henry was unimpressed. Without evidence to back it up, such a suggestion would create just the atmosphere of antagonism he would be at pains to avoid.

He and Windrush had visited Consuela earlier in the day; both were satisfied that she was well prepared for the ordeal that lay ahead. Yet clearly some aspect of their interview with her had perturbed them. There was an embarrassment in their account of it, an awkwardness which was only explained as our meeting drew towards a close.

'The trial will be well attended,' said Sir Henry, shuffling with his papers. 'All-night queuing for places in the public gallery, I shouldn't wonder. I have a small number of tickets for seats in the well of the court, however. In normal circumstances, Mr Staddon, you'd be welcome to one.'

'But there's a problem,' put in Windrush. 'Mrs Caswell anticipated you might wish to attend. This morning she instructed us to take all possible steps to prevent you doing so.'

'What?'

'I'm sorry,' said Sir Henry, 'but my client's state of mind must be my prime concern. For that reason, Mr Staddon, and for no other, I would urge you to comply with her request.' Seeing the look of amazement on my face, he continued: 'As I've explained, her testimony will be all-important. We cannot allow anything to prejudice it. Her comments left me in no doubt that your presence in court would have a deleterious effect on her behaviour and hence on the impression she creates. Of course, nobody can prevent you queuing for a seat in the public gallery, but if, as I firmly believe, you have Mrs Caswell's best interests at heart, you will, I hope—'

'Stay away?' I looked at Sir Henry and Windrush in turn, but both avoided my eye. This was a distasteful duty for them and in their silence they appealed to me to make it as easy for them as possible. And what alternative, after all, did they or I have but to do as we were bid? To the end, and perhaps beyond it, Consuela would hold me to the evasion I had chosen to inflict upon her. 'Very well,' I murmured.

'Of course,' said Sir Henry, 'if there is a friend – a representative, so to speak – who could make use of your ticket . . .'

'Yes. I'll take it if I may. You have my word I shan't use it myself.'

Sir Henry rose, rounded his desk and pressed a small envelope into my hand. It had not been sealed and, as he stood over me, I raised the flap and slid the ticket out far enough to read. It was printed on yellow card, serial-numbered and headed in stark capitals: REX v CASWELL. Sir Henry touched my shoulder. 'I shall do my best for her, Mr Staddon,' he said. 'My very best.'

I looked up at him and wanted for a moment to ask: 'Will that be good enough?' But something in his expression warned me not to. Something in the crumpled weariness of his face signalled more clearly than he would wish that his answer would not be what either of us wanted to hear.

My possessions reached Hyde Park Gardens Mews on Saturday morning promptly and intact. I could not summon the heart or the energy for systematic unpacking and it was in a dispiriting chaos of tea-chests and suitcases that Imry found me when he called by late that afternoon. I was glad to see him on more counts than he could have imagined, but of his enquiries about my interview with Fellows-Smith I made short shrift. Instead, I ushered him into the only armchair that the sitting-room boasted, poured him a generous glass of scotch, perched on an up-ended portmanteau with a glass of my own and told him what, if my stock of favours had not yet been exhausted, I earnestly wanted him to do.

'Attend the trial? Surely you'll be there yourself.'

'No. She's expressly forbidden it.'

'But . . . why?'

'She doesn't want to see me, even across a crowded court-room.'

'Does she know you're paying Sir Henry's fees?'

'No. And I don't want her to know. It's the least I owe her. That and obedience to her wishes, however much I might like to defy them.'

'Well, I'll go, of course, if you want me to. But what will my presence achieve? I'll just be another onlooker.'

'An onlooker I can trust, Imry, that's the point. The newspapers are unreliable. Sir Henry will tell me whatever he thinks I want to hear. And Windrush will follow his lead. For the truth about how it's going – good or bad – I'll have to look to you.'

'Very well, then. I'll attend.'

'This will spare you a scrimmage at the entrance.' I handed him the ticket. 'It looks like it could be for the grandstand at Lord's, doesn't it? I suppose, in some respects, a trial for murder is a sporting event. But it's a cruel one, more like bear-baiting than cricket. And there's a great deal at stake.' I drained my glass. 'More, I sometimes think, than I yet know.'

Sunday 13 January 1924 dawned blood-red over London. I and most other residents of the city woke to a sky more apocalyptically coloured than any we could ever recall. This was more than a shepherd's warning. This was a phenomenon that could not be ignored. A harbinger of tempests, according to my milkman. A precursor of national disaster, if my newsagent was to be believed. (He took the imminent prospect of a Labour government as confirmation of this.)

I described the dawn to Edward later that morning, standing by his grave. I asked him if he thought Consuela had seen it from her cell at Holloway and what it might portend for her trial. But he did not tell me. The dead, of course, have no need of omens. For them the future is indistinguishable from the past. The agony of our uncertainty is lost on them, because, in their world, every issue is settled before it is raised. Thus, to Edward, Consuela's fate – and mine with it – was long since sealed. And the only kindness he could show me was to leave me in ignorance of what it might be.

CHAPTER

FOURTEEN

Imry lodged at his club for the duration of the trial. There, each evening, we met to discuss its progress. And there, each night, Imry committed to paper his recollection of the events in court and his reaction to them. Hitherto, his involvement in the case had been entirely vicarious. Now, all of a rush, he had a chance to see the people I had told him about, to listen to their testimonies and to gauge their honesty. For as long as the trial lasted, I was to see them through his eyes and to hear them through his ears.

Monday 14 January 1924
I had never entered the Old Bailey before this morning. I had passed it many times, of course, never failing as I did so to recall the controversy aroused by its design. Poor old Mountford got it in the neck from The Architectural Review *for this jumbled piece of baroque and I have always felt sorry for him because of it. I could not see what alternative there was on such a cramped site. This morning, however, I changed my mind.*

My disquiet began on the pavement outside. A crowd that looked as if it were queuing for a football match had gathered at the public entrance. On their faces and in their voices was something I did not like: a desire for sensation amounting almost to blood-lust. And inside, filling the great hall beneath the dome, was a seething ruck of lawyers, journalists and jurors, all tricked out in uniform for the occasion: baggy gowns, shabby raincoats and ill-fitting demob suits respectively. Their voices rose in a

280

babble towards the painted ceilings and decorated arches, where truth and justice are celebrated in oil and plaster. And when I gazed about at all the lavish expanse of verd antique and cipollino, I thought: this is not right; this is not how it should be.

Within minutes, I was seated in the court, astonished to find myself so centrally placed, so very much part of what was about to unfold. Dark wood; green leather; lecterns; ink-wells; water-jugs; bustle and murmuration all around; and a sickly half-light descending from on high. These were my first queasy impressions of what I had blundered into: an over-sized and ill-aired schoolroom in which the furniture had been eccentrically re-arranged.

I sat quite still amidst the hubbub, letting the function and character of the chamber disclose itself to my mind, knowing that, as the days passed, what struck me now as bizarre and impractical would come to seem natural and inevitable. As with life, so with buildings: we adapt to the prevailing madness more easily and more swiftly than at the outset it seems possible to imagine.

My seat is in a row immediately behind the benches occupied by legal counsel. We are as close as we would be in the stalls of a theatre, their black-gowned shoulders and tasselled wigs comprising an unyielding phalanx a foot in front of my nose. Beyond them, at a slightly lower level, is the ushers' table, where pink-bound documents and obese tomes are scattered apparently at random. At the head of the table, to my right, is a long desk occupied by a lean and supercilious gentleman whom I take to be the clerk of the court. To his right, in a tiny cubicle of her own, is the stenographer. Behind them is the wooden rampart of the bench, seemingly large enough to accommodate a whole platoon of judges, let alone the one destined to preside over events. On the wall behind the bench is the Royal Coat of Arms and the Sword of Justice.

On the far side of the court is the witness-box, raised and canopied in the fashion of a pulpit. To the left of it sit the jury, in two rows of six, penned in like reluctant pew-fellows. And somewhere to the left of the jury are the press-benches, obscured from me by the dock, the vast proportions of which are perhaps the single most striking feature of the chamber. If the bench could contain a platoon, the dock seems capable of holding an entire company of defendants. Steps within it communicate with the cells below, so that the arrival of the accused is immediately apparent only to the occupants of the public gallery. This is above and

281

behind me, a cramped wooden balcony with little to commend it but the view.

The court was crowded this morning, every seat taken. According to the list displayed outside, Rex versus Caswell was to commence at 10.30 a.m. before Mr Justice Stillingfleet. Leading for the Crown was Mr M. Talbot, KC, assisted by Mr H. Finch, KC, and Mr F. Hebthorpe. The defence was to be led by Sir H. Curtis-Bennett, KC, assisted by Mr R. Browne and Mr G. Forsyth. Sir Henry I already felt I knew from Geoff's account of him: rotund, smiling, patently at ease in such surroundings. His two juniors seemed in awe of him, Browne preposterously young and earnest, Forsyth sturdy and workmanlike. Talbot distinguished himself at once by casting superior glances in all directions and shaking hands with nearly everybody, including, amidst conspicuous guffaws, Sir Henry. Finch and Hebthorpe existed in his shadow and only slowly attained a separate identity in my mind. Various solicitors twittered on the margins, including Windrush, who, again, I recognized from Geoff's description.

Looking to my right and left, I could see nobody who matched my expectations of the Caswell family. Perhaps, I concluded, they were not in court. Some seats next to the jury-box were filled by middle-aged men whose bearing and demeanour proclaimed them as policemen: definitely no Caswells there. As for the keen-eyed lady in the pink toque with whom I was shoulder to shoulder, and indeed every other occupant of the seats in my row, their general quiver of anticipation suggested a relish for the occasion entirely free of personal involvement. No doubt they had pulled strings rather than stood on the pavement all night to be where they now were, but their motive was the same, one I could not help feeling was indecent, if not downright obscene. If they did not have to witness the chilling spectacle of the law in action, why in God's name did they want to?

The usher's announcement caught me unawares in the midst of this brown study of my fellow humans. Rising later than most, I realized that all delay was now at an end. The trial of a capital crime was about to commence. Mr Justice Stillingfleet – tall, beak-nosed and implacable in full-bottomed wig and scarlet robe – swept into place. His first action, performed before some of us had even sat down again, was to snort into a huge sky-blue handkerchief with such deliberation that I could almost have believed it was a stipulated legal preliminary.

And then, as I looked back at the dock, I saw that it was no

282

longer empty. Consuela Caswell – the woman I had heard so much about but had never met – was standing there, calm and erect, head raised, gazing straight ahead as if focusing on the very point of the blade of the Sword of Justice. She wore a black suit of some kind, trimmed to the waist, and a white blouse with a large bow at her throat. She was bare-headed, her dark hair cut short, and there was no trace of jewellery or make-up, except the slender gold band of her wedding-ring, which glistened in the light cast by the lofty chandelier as she rested her hands on the low rail running along the edge of the dock.

Austere and expressionless, she seemed to me in that moment quite the most beautiful woman I had ever seen. How could you have deserted her, Geoff? That question leapt instantly into my mind. How could you have brought yourself to betray her? At thirty-five she was still so lovely that I could scarcely take my eyes off her. At twenty-two how much more exquisite must she have been?

Suddenly, the charge was being read. 'Consuela Evelina Caswell, you are charged on two counts: firstly that, on the ninth day of September nineteen hundred and twenty-three, at Clouds Frome in the county of Herefordshire, you did, feloniously, wilfully and with malice aforethought, murder by the administration of poison one Rosemary Victoria Caswell; and secondly that, on the same date and in the same place, you did, feloniously, wilfully and with malice aforethought, attempt to murder by the administration of poison one Victor George Caswell. How do you plead on the first count?'

'Not guilty.' She spoke softly but definitely, with no hint of hesitation.

'And on the second count?'

'Not guilty.'

Now, as a stern wardress touched Consuela's elbow and she lowered herself onto a chair so that I could only see her head and shoulders; now, as gowned figures wheeled and circled below her like so many carrion crows and the usher cleared his throat explosively; now, for the first time, the force and momentum of this ritual was borne in upon me. The juggernaut of justice was underway. And I shuddered in its wake.

The empanelling of the jury took more than an hour. Sir Henry objected to three men who were older and better dressed than the others. I found myself wondering why. Because they looked like

283

the kind of husbands who might fear being poisoned by their wives? Because women might be supplied in their places? If the latter was his reason, he was disappointed. There were only two female faces among the final twelve.

The judge instructed the jury, after another extravagant nose-blowing, to disregard the fact that the trial had been transferred from Hereford at the request of the defence. 'This should not be taken to imply a lack of confidence in their case,' he concluded. I could not help feeling that, if he really wanted them to disregard the point, he would have done better not to mention it in the first place.

A little before noon, Talbot rose to address the court. I already knew, of course, what he was going to say. So, I imagine, did most of those around me. The essence of the Crown's case was simple: that Consuela, her jealousy aroused by anonymous letters questioning her husband's fidelity, had sought to poison him with arsenic, but had actually killed his niece instead. Talbot set the matter out in great detail, specifying dates, times, locations and logistics. Copies of the letters were distributed, then read aloud for the benefit of those, like me, denied a copy. They sounded as crude and predictable as might have been expected. 'It's time you knew the truth about your husband.' 'He's been having an affair with another woman these six months past.' 'A pair of shameless adulterers, one of them your husband.' 'Closed bedroom curtains one afternoon a week at a certain house in Hereford.' 'I know what happens there. It's time you did as well.' 'Think about this next time he demands his rights.' More in the same vein drove the lady in the pink toque to her phial of sal volatile in a spasm of delighted prurience; this, one felt, was what she had come for.

Talbot's exposition was a model of dispassionate clarity, or so it seemed. He spoke slowly and without recourse to oratorical devices. And yet, increasingly as I listened to him, I became suspicious of what I heard. He is a handsome, intelligent, supremely self-confident man, heavy-lidded and with enough shadow about his chin to warrant shaving twice a day. There is withal a swagger about him, a drawl, a languid air halfway between boredom and disgust. Precise, correct, calm and measured, he nonetheless gives me the impression that he considers the whole business of prosecution to be beneath him; that nothing in this case or the people involved in it merits more than his passing attention.

He looked often at Consuela as he spoke, especially when reading the letters, hoping, I suppose, to shame her into some

284

revealing reaction. If so, he hoped in vain. But still he looked, enjoying, it seemed to me, the power he had over her.

Talbot's peroration straddled the luncheon adjournment and ended with the jury visibly swayed by the force and logic of what he had said. For the last half hour he scarcely shifted his gaze from them, dangling in his left hand as he spoke exhibit A – a small blue-paper twist of arsenious oxide – whilst his right hand rested lightly on exhibits B, C and D – the three anonymous letters.

'It will be shown that nobody other than the accused had any reason to wish Victor Caswell dead. It will be shown that nobody other than the accused had the means or the opportunity during the afternoon of the ninth of September to bring about his death. And it will be shown that of her carefully planned and ruthlessly executed attempt to murder her husband Rosemary Caswell was the tragic and wholly innocent victim.'

After that, there was time for only one witness: Dr William Stringfellow. A robust straightforward medical man, as free of pretension as he was of prejudice, he was entrusted by Talbot to one of his juniors. He gave a thorough account of his three patients' identical symptoms and of the particular severity of them in Rosemary Caswell's case. He described his failure to save Rosemary and his growing suspicion that arsenic was responsible. He concluded with his decision to seek a specialist's opinion. There seemed no room for doubt in anything that he said. Indeed, Sir Henry evidently thought the same, for he waived his right to cross-examination.

It was now just after a quarter to four. The next witness, Talbot announced, was to be Sir Bernard Spilsbury, the eminent Home Office pathologist. It would be undesirable, Talbot claimed, for Sir Bernard to commence his testimony only for it to be suspended overnight. With this the judge concurred. And so, anti-climactically, the day's proceedings drew to a close.

Tuesday 15 January 1924
Already, familiarity is breeding acceptance. The same scenes awaited me at the Old Bailey this morning as they did yesterday, but their power to shock and repel me had faded. Almost to a man, the same cast had assembled in Number One Court. Even the lady in the pink toque was there again, though now the toque had given way to a flower-pot hat with a prominent feather. The judge's cold was no better, Talbot's demeanour not a whit less self-assured.

And Consuela Caswell still gazed expressionlessly from the dock like an innocent tied to the stake as the pyre is built around her.

I have read of Sir Bernard Spilsbury in so many newspaper reports of trials that I felt I had seen him before even though I had not. Tall, lean and sombre, grey of face and manner, he carried with him such a high degree of certainty, based upon his legendary experience, that it seemed Talbot was not so much questioning him as inviting him to present a lecture. The court attended to his words like the most obedient of classes. Debate was discouraged, doubt entirely forbidden. Not that there was room for either. Sir Bernard's unequivocal conclusion was that Rosemary, Victor and Marjorie Caswell had all consumed arsenic on the afternoon of 9 September 1923. The aggregate quantity involved could easily have killed all three. Once more, Sir Henry refrained from cross-examination.

During Sir Bernard's arid and painstaking explanation of post mortem findings and analytical techniques, I noticed that the seats between the jury-box and the press-benches were no longer exclusively occupied by stolid policemen. Another of the curious qualities of Mountford's design then became apparent to me. People could slip into or out of the court without attracting any attention to themselves. So it was that I found myself looking at Victor, Mortimer and Marjorie Caswell for the first time.

They were as Geoff had led me to expect: guarded, upright, clannish yet contrasting. Victor was the fleshier, better-looking brother, Mortimer the grimmer, altogether more cautious one. Strangely, however, it was Victor who seemed least at his ease, stroking his moustache, scratching his brow and looking anywhere but up at the dock. Not that he need have worried. Consuela gave no indication that she was even aware of his presence. Marjorie meanwhile gazed about with proud severity, one eyebrow raised, as if the cleanliness of the furniture had failed to satisfy her. There was a suppressed shrewishness about the line of her mouth, a hint of the virago beneath the provincial modesty.

Mortimer Caswell was Talbot's next witness, handed over, like Dr Stringfellow, to the care of a junior. He spoke with sombre decisiveness of his daughter's illness and death, with no sign of emotion, but enough buttoned-up sincerity to arouse general sympathy. In response to an intervention by the judge, who chose this moment to mention that he had an eighteen-year-old daughter, Mortimer said: 'You will understand, then, my lord, that it is difficult to express in words the grief caused by such a loss.' His

286

reticence seemed both natural and admirable. Sensitive to the mood of the court, Sir Henry once more abstained from cross-examination.

After lunch, Marjorie entered the witness-box. The condolent hush that had attended her husband's testimony now intensified. Talbot drew her out quite shamelessly on the poignancy of her loss – Rosemary's engaging personality, her energy, her charm, her intelligence, all cut off so tragically on the brink of womanhood. Then he took her carefully through the tea party at Clouds Frome – who sat where, who consumed what, who came, who went. Exhibits E and F – a sugar-bowl and a small silver spoon – were submitted and identified by Marjorie. She confirmed that Rosemary had been the first to take sugar from the bowl – 'three spoonfuls as usual; she had a sweet tooth.' Then she described the onset of her illness and her desolation at her daughter's death. By the time Talbot had finished with her, pity was universal: the lady in the flower-pot hat had been obliged to dab at her cheeks with a handkerchief. I wondered if Sir Henry would yet again leave well alone.

But he did not. The robed and wigged leviathan rose from his seat just before half past three and commenced, more adroitly than could have been foreseen, to shift the emphasis from pathos to probability. Had Consuela seemed angry, preoccupied, nervous, disconcerted even, by their unexpected arrival? Had she betrayed herself in any way, however, slight, during the tea party? If not, what was one to think of her? That she was completely heartless – or completely innocent? Wisely, it seemed to me, Marjorie declined to express an opinon. Consuela had always been a mystery to her, inscrutable to such a degree that every explanation of her conduct was equally plausible. If Sir Henry had hoped to detect any malice towards Consuela in this hard-bitten but persuasive woman, the day was to end for him in disappointment.

Wednesday 16 January 1924
The bizarrerie of the Old Bailey now seems almost normal. I knew this would happen, of course, but had under-estimated my susceptibility: I thought it would take longer than three days. The judge's cold has advanced a pace. He blows his nose less, but speaks as if there were a peg on the end of it. And the lady of many hats is now affecting a turquoise pill-box. All else is unaltered.

The stolid policemen this morning acquired names and voices. Chief Inspector Wright described setting off for Hereford in the wake of Spilsbury's detection of arsenic and following an impeccable strand of logic to the sugar-bowl at Clouds Frome, then instituting the search of the house that had yielded exhibits A, B, C and D. His assessment of the accused was that of a straightforward but determined detective. The evidence pointed unwaveringly to her guilt and the subtleties of her character did not concern him. At Sir Henry's prompting, he admitted that Consuela's protestation of her innocence had survived many hours of interrogation. But that did not surprise him. 'It's often been my experience in murder cases that the murderer genuinely believes he or she is innocent.' This, he clearly believed, was just one more example.

Superintendent Weaver of the Herefordshire Constabulary told much the same tale. He had co-operated fully with his Scotland Yard colleague and they had traced the crime to its only possible source. Officers under his command had carried out the search of Clouds Frome. When confronted with the arsenic and letters, the accused had denied all knowledge of them. But she had offered no explanation of their presence in her room. Why, asked Sir Henry, would she have made no effort to destroy them? Because she had not expected such a thorough search, riposted Weaver, and because she needed the arsenic for a second attempt on her husband's life. This last was retracted at Sir Henry's insistence, being pure supposition, but was it, I wondered, retracted from the jury's minds?

There had, it transpired, been something of a hiatus where the search of Consuela's bedroom was concerned. Consuela's maid had objected to a man handling her mistress's clothing and effects. A policewoman had therefore been summoned from Hereford. This redoubtable creature, W.P.C. Griffiths, was the next witness. She described finding the three letters at the back of an underwear drawer, held together by a rubber band. She had handed them immediately to Chief Inspector Wright. The blue-paper twist of arsenic was in the same drawer, 'concealed' (a word which Sir Henry did not challenge) within a pair of silk cami-knickers.

There were some sniggers in the public gallery at this, instantly subdued by a glare from Mr Justice Stillingfleet. I glanced at Consuela, thinking that of all the revelations she would have to endure this would be the one most likely to discompose her. But not so. She stared straight ahead, marmoreally unaffected.

A drab but impressively qualified graphologist followed. He seemed disposed to educate us all in the complexities of his science, but was at length persuaded to make his point, which was actually

288

a simple one. The anonymous letters had been written in a disguised hand, probably by a right-handed male. Asked by Sir Henry whether poison-pen letters were not more normally written by women, he abruptly decided that his expertise had reached its limit, but the suggestion in itself was useful for the defence. It seemed to me about the only encouragement they could take from the day.

Thursday 17 January 1924
A parade of the Caswells' servants filled today and will spill over into tomorrow. For the most part, they seemed touchingly reluctant to blacken their mistress's name, but their answers to the prosecution's questions achieved exactly that result. Sir Henry left his juniors to rescue what they could from the wreckage. Mr Justice Stillingfleet was gruff and subdued. The lady of many hats favoured a maroon cloche that was definitely too young for her. And Consuela remained enigmatically aloof.

The first witness was Albert Banyard, gardener, countryman and nobody's fool. He identified exhibit G – a tin of Weed Out – as identical to one he had purchased from a chemist in Hereford early in the spring of 1923. He thought Mr and Mrs Caswell probably both knew of its acquisition. He agreed anybody could have removed some of the contents without him noticing. And he said all of this with a surly touch of sarcasm that clearly annoyed Talbot and once earned a rebuke from the judge. But Talbot's principal gain from his testimony – confirmation that Mrs Caswell took a keener interest in the garden (and, by implication, methods of weed control) than did Mr Caswell – was more or less offset by Banyard's firmness on another point: it was Mr Caswell's complaints about weeds that had prompted him to buy Weed Out in the first place.

Mabel Glynn, the kitchenmaid who had prepared tea on 9 September, was as nervous as she was guileless. She was treated gently by all concerned. Her testimony seemed to rule out any tampering with the sugar before it left the kitchen.

Frederick Noyce, the footman who had delivered tea to the drawing-room, was scarcely much older than Mabel Glynn, but considerably more self-assured. His most telling statement was that Consuela had been alone in the room when he brought the tea-trolley in and had still been alone when he left. Thus her opportunity to poison the sugar was established beyond doubt. The defence made no attempt to challenge it, but did ask Noyce if he had answered the house telephone in the course of the afternoon. He said he had not. Unlike, I suspect, most onlookers, I knew the purpose of this question – and that it would be repeated to other witnesses.

Horace Danby, butler to the Caswells, was required by the prosecution to do little more than confirm the duties and movements of the domestic staff on 9 September. He seemed a typical example of his office, pompous in some of his answers, humble in others. Like Noyce, he assured the defence that he had not answered the telephone that afternoon. Forsyth, who was cross-examining him, then opened a new avenue of enquiry by asking if he was aware of any extra-marital liaison on his master's part. This Danby strenuously denied.

Prudence Moore, the Caswells' cook, a notably thin woman for one of her calling, led the court minutely through food storage and preparation procedures in the kitchen at Clouds Frome. It was hard to believe they were as meticulously followed as she claimed, but the object of the exercise as far as the prosecution was concerned – focusing suspicion on the drawing-room and its sole occupant – was at length achieved.

The afternoon session drew to a close with an account by John Gleasure, Victor Caswell's valet, of his master's illness on the evening of 9 September. He delivered the second critical blow of the day to the defence by stating that Consuela had disregarded his suggestion that a doctor should be called. Gleasure's cross-examination was held over until tomorrow, which promises to be a make-or-break day for the defence. Soon – very soon – they must start to make up ground. Otherwise, I sense, all will be lost.

Friday 18 January 1924
Clearly I was not alone in anticipating a raising of the stakes today. The queue for the public gallery was longer and noisier than on any previous morning, despite last night being cold and damp. A form of cameraderie has evolved in the crowd, which I find even more appalling than the ghoulish eagerness by which it was gripped at the start of the week.

In court, the lady of many hats celebrated the heightened atmosphere by appearing in a wide-awake creation more suitable for Ascot than the Old Bailey. Mr Justice Stillingfleet looked as if he was shaking off his cold at last. And Talbot wore a smirk of supreme confidence. Only Consuela seemed immune to the expectant mood. She has met the challenge of her captive role in these proceedings with a defiance amounting almost to indifference. Perhaps she hopes to defeat her accusers simply by ignoring them. Or perhaps to lose even a fraction of her self-control would be to lose all of it. Whatever the explanation, she sat today in the dock as she has sat every day: grave of face, austere of dress, impervious of manner.

Sir Henry rose to conduct Gleasure's cross-examination, his lethargy of yesterday shrugged off like an unwanted garment. Had Gleasure taken any telephone calls for his master during the afternoon of 9 September? No. Had he really urged Consuela to summon a doctor that evening? Yes. Very well, then: why had he not insisted on summoning one? Because it was not his place to do so. Had he, perhaps, agreed with Consuela that one was not needed? No. He had deferred to his mistress's judgement. But surely a valet has only a master, not a mistress. Victor was conscious, after all. What had he told Gleasure to do? Mr Caswell was a man who made no concessions to illness. He had assumed he would be fully recovered by morning. He had not told Gleasure to do anything. In other words, he, like his wife, had seen no need to call a doctor? That, agreed Gleasure, was one way of putting it.

With this modest victory under his belt, Sir Henry altered tack. Did Gleasure believe his master had been pursuing an affair with another woman? No. Did that mean he was sure he had not been? Yes. Did Gleasure believe his master was happily married? Somewhat hesitantly, yes. Did that hesitancy mean he thought the marriage was not as happy as it had once been? Yes, Gleasure supposed it did. To what did he ascribe this deterioration? It was not his place to speculate. Sir Henry pressed. Talbot objected. Mr Justice Stillingfleet demurred. And Gleasure reluctantly said that he thought the Caswells' religious and racial differences had become more pronounced as they had grown older. It was an opinion that endeared him to nobody, but it sounded horribly plausible. And it ensured that Sir Henry's first unveiled assault on the prosecution case ended inconclusively.

But this was only the overture to the day's proceedings, as we realized when Talbot called his last witness: Victor Caswell. Since his first appearance in court on Tuesday, he and Consuela have scarcely glanced at each other and the pattern was not broken today. Consuela stared straight ahead throughout. Victor looked only at his interlocutor. I could almost have imagined they had agreed on this arrangement beforehand, though in truth they cannot have met since Consuela's arrest on 21 September – very nearly four months ago.

Talbot led Victor quietly through the events of 9 September and their aftermath. They were like two men of the world discussing a regrettable political development. And with their mood the judge seemed entirely in tune. He nodded in encouragement, he almost purred with understanding. Even if I had not known all that Geoff had told me about Victor Caswell, his testimony would have disturbed me, not because of what he said but because of the way he was treated. He was an urbane English gentleman vexed by a hot-blooded and vengeful Brazilian wife. That, at all events, was what we were evidently intended to conclude. As for infidelity, his simple denial was, of course, to be accepted without reservation. And, if any member of the jury thought a husband testifying against his wife was not quite cricket, Mr Justice Stillingfleet was there to set him right. 'The court is sympathetic to Mr Caswell's difficult position. To give evidence in this case is obviously painful, but it is also his duty, which I am glad to see him discharging with dignity.'

Sir Henry Curtis-Bennett's cross-examination of Victor Caswell filled the afternoon. It was a delicate and demanding encounter for both men. Neither could afford to seem discourteous, far less to lose their temper. Sir Henry knew he would earn a judicial rebuke – and a black mark in the jury's minds – if he pressed too hard. Therefore, he played a cautious hand.

Once more we reviewed the afternoon and evening of 9 September, almost, it seemed, minute by minute. Whatever was doubtful or ambiguous Sir Henry dwelt on, whatever was damaging to his client he defied Victor to emphasize. It was a skilful and well-judged performance. Yet Victor could not be persuaded to say that he had known his niece and sister-in-law might call. Nor could he be shifted from his contention that he had found Consuela alone in the drawing-room with the tea-trolley. The only issue on which he gave any ground was that of his marriage. He agreed that it had not 'for some years' been as happy as he had implied at the hearing. Gleasure's assessment was probably correct. He and Consuela had grown apart as they had grown older. He even disclosed that they had slept in separate rooms since the birth of their daughter. But infidelity on his part he strenuously denied. The letters, he maintained, were completely without foundation, probably written by somebody with a grudge

292

against him. Several candidates came to mind, but he did not wish to name them. The judge assured him that his discretion was admirable. And the judge's intervention left Sir Henry no option but to concur and move on. Had Victor ever contemplated divorce in view of his admitted incompatibility with Consuela? If so, her religion would have been an insurmountable obstacle. All could see where such a question might lead. It was therefore no surprise when Victor insisted that he had not. Sir Henry concluded by asking him if, after sixteen years of marriage, he genuinely believed his wife was capable of murdering him. But, even then, Victor did not stumble. 'No, sir, I don't. But, in the light of all the evidence, what else am I to think?' It was an impressive note to end on.

And it brought down the curtain, we shortly discovered, on the Crown's case. Tomorrow, Sir Henry will commence his presentation of the defence. He will have his work cut out.

Saturday 19 January 1924
This morning, Consuela's resolution faltered. The mask of expressionlessness she had worn for five days slipped and revealed the face of one who sees and knows the peril of her position. It happened as soon as she entered the dock, when, instead of staring unwaveringly ahead as the proceedings commenced, she glanced up at the public gallery. What or who she saw there I do not know. Perhaps it was just the cluster of human eagerness contained there, the greed to learn her fate, that penetrated her defences for the first time. At all events, the change in her was dreadful and moving to behold. She sat with head bowed where before she had held herself erect. There were twitches and tremors about her face. She dabbed frequently at her lips with a handkerchief and fiddled with the bow of her blouse. The years fell away and a frightened girl emerged into the spotlight of our collective gaze.

If Sir Henry Curtis-Bennett was worried by the change in his client's demeanour, he hid the fact well as he made his opening speech. The evidence against Mrs Caswell, he said, whilst it might seem compelling, was wholly circumstantial, and the jury would have ample opportunity to assess her character and personality, which, he felt sure they would agree, were not those of a murderess. Such was to be the burden of his defence. There was to be no forensic complexity, no legal trickery, no legerdemain. It was to be all or nothing.

Without further ado, Sir Henry called his first witness: Hermione Caswell. Geoff had prepared me for this, but there was a gasp from

293

others in the court who realized that Victor Caswell's sister was about to testify in his wife's defence. Talbot curled his lip. Mr Justice Stillingfleet manipulated his jaw as if some gristly morsel of the judicial breakfast had lodged between his molars. And Victor Caswell, I suddenly realized, was not in court.

Hermione, his elder by ten years, is a keen-eyed spinster of sixty-five, spirited, alert, perceptive and given, it might be suspected, to mischief-making. Since she had not been among those present at Clouds Frome on 9 September, she could, of course, contribute nothing to our understanding of what had taken place there. What she could do, with Sir Henry's encouragement, was disrupt certain notions that had imperceptibly crept into the jury's minds. Her brother was no paragon, her sister-in-law no violent compound of foreign blood and pathological jealousy. She had made a study of Consuela over the years – because, she explained, she was the most exotic and interesting of her relatives – and the dominant characteristic she had noted in her was gentleness. She would not swat a fly, far less poison an innocent young girl. If – which Hermione did not believe – Consuela had poisoned the sugar, she would have intervened to prevent Rosemary consuming any.

Talbot declined to cross-examine Hermione. He did so arrogantly, almost flippantly, hoping, I suppose, to defuse her testimony simply by ignoring it. So it was that Hermione departed with the slightly disappointed air of one who has anticipated an enjoyable scrap but been denied at the last moment. The effect she had had on the Court was difficult to assess. At best, it seems to me, she may reinforce other defence evidence. But she cannot achieve anything in its absence.

Sir Henry's next witness was Cathel Simpson, Consuela's maid. She is a pretty, sullen, rather cross-grained creature, and of all the staff at Clouds Frome patently the least fitted by nature to the status of a domestic servant. She lost no time in pointing out that Victor had dismissed her from her post only a few days after Consuela's arrest. This she seemed to attribute to her loyalty to her mistress. She had been Consuela's maid for four years and expressed her complete satisfaction with how she had been treated by her in that time. The most significant statement she made was that she was certain neither the arsenic nor the letters had been in the drawer where they were found earlier than the day of the search. She had removed and replaced articles of underclothing at daily intervals and would have noticed anything hidden amongst them.

Talbot's cross-examination was cunning. He provoked Simpson

into expanding on her resentment of her dismissal, then forced her to admit she had no grounds for such resentment. Victor had given her a good reference and recommended her to a reputable family in Birmingham. Since he knew his wife would be absent for a prolonged period, what else was he to do, given that he had no need of a lady's maid himself? These exchanges, during which Simpson became impertinent enough to earn a dressing-down from the judge, effectively wiped out the impact of her testimony concerning the contents of the underwear drawer. They left the jury with the impression of an envious and unreliable girl quite capable of lying in order to settle a score with a former employer.

Sir Henry did his best to retrieve the situation with his third witness: Herbert Jenkins, Hereford postmaster. Mr Jenkins was asked to scrutinize exhibits B, C and D – the anonymous letters – and give his opinion as to the authenticity of the postmarks. He said they conformed in every particular with franking practices in the Hereford sorting office, but he expressed surprise at how consistent they were. He explained that he would expect a random sample of postmarks to display differences in ink density, clarity and positioning. This was because the stamping pad was refilled with ink only when postmarks became noticeably faint and because some operatives took greater pains than others to avoid blurring or skewing the mark. It was remarkable, therefore, that three letters posted at weekly intervals seemed to have received exactly the same treatment.

A Saturday afternoon was not perhaps the ideal time for a jury to absorb the significance of this testimony. To underline his point, however, Sir Henry recalled Danby, the butler, who explained how post was received and distributed at Clouds Frome. He or Noyce would most probably have delivered such letters to Mrs Caswell. Danby, for his part, could not remember handling any of the three, but he emphasized that he was not in the habit of studying letters addressed to members of the family. Noyce, when he was also recalled, said the same.

There was much in this to console the defence, but it was consolation of a fragile kind. At the weekend adjournment, Sir Henry indicated that his next and final witness would be the accused herself. Once she has entered the box, the jury will surely find it difficult to concentrate on anything else, especially the finer points of Hereford postmarks. What has always seemed probable now seems certain. Consuela will be saved or condemned by her own efforts.

*

I returned to Hyde Park Gardens Mews that evening in despondent mood. Nothing Imry had told me, then or on previous evenings, had given me much cause for optimism. As the crucial phase of the trial drew near, I felt more helpless than ever to influence its outcome. For as long as Imry had been able to assure me that Consuela's nerve was intact, there had been some frail basis for hope. Now, even that was in question.

The night was cold and moonless, a steely rain falling at intervals as I made my way through the park. I had endured a week of Consuela's ordeal and had experienced its every pang at one remove. My spirits had soared with each fleeting promise of salvation and slumped with each reverse. Of late, the reverses had seemed to come thick and fast, too numerous and severe for Sir Henry to deflect. Small wonder, then, that as I crossed Bayswater Road and entered the mews, all I could think of was the grinding succession of adverse and unavailing testimonies.

The mews was empty and silent, stray slashes of rain visible in the haloes of the gas-lamps. I reached the door of number forty-nine and fumbled beneath my raincoat for the key. As I did so, I was aware of a movement in the darkness behind me, a detachment of one shadow from the rest. Too preoccupied to feel any alarm, I turned towards it. And found Rodrigo towering at my shoulder, bare-headed and black-clad, his breath steaming in the chill damp air. Instinctively, I shrank back, but too late to evade his grasp. He closed one hand about my wrist like a manacle.

'Staddon!' There was the same quality of stress for both syllables that I remembered, the same hissed note of menace and loathing.

'What . . . What do you want?'

'You, Staddon. I want you. We must talk. Now.' He glanced around. 'You live alone here?'

'Yes, but—'

'We will go in.' His hold tightened. *'Agora mesmo!'* He was standing between me and the nearest lamp. In my face trepidation must have been clear to see. In his there was only the shadowy hint of a smile. 'You have nothing to fear, Staddon. I will not hurt you.'

'All right.' I lifted his hand from my wrist, gazed at him for a moment to satisfy myself that there really was nothing to fear, then nodded and turned away to open the door.

He followed me up the narrow stairs to the sitting-room and

stood on the threshold while I went ahead to switch on the lamps. When he finally stepped forward into the light, I nearly gasped with shock at the change three weeks had wrought in him. There was more grey in his face and hair, less flesh on his enormous frame. His eyes were red, sunk in sockets so dark that they could have been bruised, his shoulders hunched as if to support for a little longer yet the crumbling roof of his world.

'I have been to the court today,' he said wearily.

'You were at the Old Bailey?'

'Yes. I paid a . . . *um marinheiro* . . . ten pounds for his place in the line.'

'Consuela was upset today. Was that because she saw you?'

'How do you know she was upset? You were not there.'

'A friend of mine was, though. He's been every day. He said she was disturbed by something or someone in the public gallery.'

Rodrigo nodded. 'It was me. She sent a message asking me not to go. Did she send you a message also?'

'Yes.'

He nodded again. 'I could not stay away. It was too much to ask. Even for Consuelinha. But now . . . I wish I had not gone.'

'Why?'

'Because—' Suddenly, he clapped his hand to his brow and squeezed his eyes shut. Then, as if a wave of acute physical pain had been held at bay, he slowly lowered his hand to his side and looked at me again. 'They will hang her, Staddon. They will hang my sister.'

'Not necessarily. There's still—'

'They will hang her, I say!' Some portion of the old strength and certainty was restored to his voice. 'Do not treat me like a child! I was *there*. I saw. I heard. And I know that they mean to hang her. That is why I am here. That is the only reason why I do not—' Venom flashed into his gaze, then was snuffed out. 'Listen to me, Staddon. Listen to me carefully. The trial will be over soon. They will sentence Consuela to death. Nothing will stop then. Unless . . .'

'Unless what?'

'You must help me. You must help me to save her.' He was speaking almost through gritted teeth, speaking words at which his massive pride rebelled. But, for once, his pride was not his master.

'I would do anything. If there was anything I could do.'

'Why did you burn the plans of Clouds Frome?'

297

'For the reason you gave yourself.' Our differences seemed drowned now, our recriminations swamped by one compelling allegiance. 'To help me forget Consuela.'

'I need them, Staddon. I need the plans that are in your head.'

'Why?'

'To learn who tried to kill Victor Caswell. Somebody tried to murder him. Someone who will let them hang Consuela. We must find out who they are. Now. *Imediatamente*. We cannot delay.'

'I don't understand. Why would it help to know the lay-out of Clouds Frome?'

'Because there is a safe hidden in one of the rooms. Behind a false wall, in a . . . an alcove, blocked up, so that it does not seem to be there. And, in it, there is a safe. And in the safe, *um testamento*.'

'A will?'

'Yes. Victor's. The will that names his heir.'

'Surely Consuela—'

'No! Not Consuela. Not even Jacinta. Another. Somebody else. Do you not understand? It has to be somebody else. It is they who tried to kill him. That is why they tried to kill him. For his money. His land. *A sua fortuna*. He made a will after Jacinta was born, a new will. Why would he do that?'

'Well, to provide for his daughter, I suppo—'

'Your daughter, Staddon! That is what I think. Jacinta is your child, not Victor's. That is why he hates Consuela. That is why Jacinta means nothing to him. That is why he made the will and hid it and told nobody what was in it.'

I turned away. 'Jacinta *may* be my daughter. I cannot—'

Suddenly, he was at my shoulder, swinging me round to face him. 'I do not care anymore! Once I would have killed you for this. Now Consuela matters more. Only her. Not you. Only what you can do to help me save her.'

'But what can I do?'

'Find where the safe is hidden.'

'How do you know there is a safe? How do you know there's a will, for that—'

'I bribed his valet! Gleasure. *Um viboro traiçoeiro*. I almost pity Victor for having such a man close to him. Yet I rejoice that he does. From Gleasure I learned that Victor made a new will in nineteen twelve, one month after Jacinta's birth. Consuela knew nothing about it. Gleasure was told that she must never know about it. Victor's . . . *tabeliao* . . . Quarton, he drew it up and

298

took it to Clouds Frome for Victor to sign. Quarton and Gleasure were the witnesses.'

'Does Gleasure know what's in it?'

'No. There was a . . . paper . . . over the will when he signed it as a witness, so that he could not read it. Why would that be, I ask, unless I am right? It was put in the safe. And there it has been ever since.'

'Well, perhaps so, but I may as well tell you now that I installed no false walls at Clouds Frome. There was—'

'Not you, Staddon! It was done after you finished the house. Gleasure told me that Victor had the safe put in and the wall built to hide it the winter after they went to live at Clouds Frome. That is why I need you. To tell me which wall is the false one. To me, there is no difference. But, to you, *o arquitecto . . .*'

He was right. I – and only I – would be able to identify the alteration at once. He had wanted the plans in order to deduce its location for himself. In their absence, he had been driven at last to ask for my help. 'What exactly are you suggesting we do, Rodrigo?'

'Find the safe. Open it. Look at the will. Then we will know who the murderer is.'

'But how? I'm no cracksman. Nor, I suspect, are you.'

'*Cracksman?* What is this?'

'I mean that neither of us is capable of opening a safe without knowing the combination. Locating it would be pointless unless—'

'I have the combination!' He smiled. 'You understand now? If you can find it, I can open it. Gleasure told me how.'

'Gleasure? How would he know? Surely Victor wouldn't entrust—'

'Victor thought he was dying! He thought the poison was going to kill him! So, that night, ninth of September, he told Gleasure how to work out the combination. He wanted to be sure the safe could be opened after his death. He wanted to be sure the will would be found. He was . . . *delirante* . . . raving. By the morning, he had forgotten even saying it. But Gleasure remembered. For a little money, he was willing to tell me.'

'He's taking a big risk. If Victor ever finds out he's betrayed him . . .'

'No, no. Gleasure thinks there is no risk at all. He thinks I cannot find the safe. He would not tell me where it is, though I offered him much money, very much money. He thinks the combination will be no use to me. That is why he was willing to sell it. But he is wrong. Together, Staddon, we can prove he is wrong.'

'How? Victor's turned Clouds Frome into a fortress. If you've seen what he's done, you'll know there's no way we can get inside.'

'I *have* seen. The walls. The locks. The dog. I have seen them all.'

'Well then?'

He stepped closer. 'Jacinta trusts you. She will do what you tell her to do. You could tell her to open a window, the window of her bedroom, perhaps. At night, when everybody is asleep. Then we could enter without anyone except Jacinta knowing.'

'It wouldn't work. How could we scale the wall – or get past the dog?'

'*O muro? O cão?* You are frightened of such things?'

'I'm frightened we'd fail. How would that help Consuela?'

Rodrigo's eyes flashed with anger. He grabbed at the collar of my coat. Then, even as he grasped it, he relaxed his hold.

'I will get us over the wall. And I will deal with any dog that shows its teeth at us.'

'It still wouldn't work. Jacinta's a virtual prisoner. I'm not allowed to visit her. I'm not even allowed to write—'

As I hesitated, Rodrigo nodded. '*Now* you understand. Hermione Caswell. She is the answer.'

'How did you—'

'She testified in court today. I listened to her. I decided she was one I could trust. I have just come from her. She told me about the letters she has passed between you and Jacinta. She told me she could pass another letter when she returns to Hereford tomorrow. Victor will stay in London with his brother. Half his servants are here as well. So, it is quiet at Clouds Frome. It is the perfect time for two burglars to go to work.'

'Burglars?'

'Yes, Staddon. *Dois arrombadores.* You and I, together.'

'You really mean this? You really think this will save Consuela?'

'There is no other way.'

'And Hermione's willing to help us?'

'She agrees with me. There is no other way.'

'But, for God's sake—'

'I cannot go alone. If I could, I would. I would *prefer* to. You know that, I think. And why.'

'The risks would be appalling.'

'The risks will be for Consuela. My sister. The mother of your child.'

I stared at him and he at me. There was nothing, absolutely nothing, that drew us together but this one mad strand of hope. Victor's will might hold the key to Consuela's freedom, to her very life. Or it might not. But, either way, trying to find it was better than doing nothing, better by far than watching helplessly while fate pursued its course. 'Very well,' I murmured. 'I'll help you.'

CHAPTER

FIFTEEN

Thackeray Hotel,
Great Russell Street,
London WC1.
19th January 1924

My Dear Jacinta,

I am writing to you from the hotel where your Aunt
Hermione is staying. She is with me now, as is your Uncle
Rodrigo. Hermione is returning to Hereford tomorrow and
will call to see you at Clouds Frome on Monday, when she
will try to deliver this letter to you. It is very important for
your mother's sake that nobody except we four know what is
in this letter or that you have received it. Therefore, after
reading it, please tear it up and burn it. Nobody at Clouds
Frome – especially Miss Roebuck – must know anything
about it.

Your mother's trial is nearly over. Hermione has been
here to testify in her defence. She, Rodrigo and I believe
your mother is innocent, but your father, your Uncle
Mortimer and Aunt Marjorie believe she is guilty. I am
telling you this so you will know who to trust and who not to
trust. We are trying to save your mother. The others are not.

When we last met, I told you I was trying to help your
mother in every way I could. I still am. But it may not be
enough. That is why I am writing this letter to you, Jacinta,
because the time has come to ask you to do something to
help your mother, something difficult and dangerous, but
something I know you are capable of doing.

All doors and windows at Clouds Frome are closed and
locked at night. We know this. But Rodrigo and I need to
enter the house by night. I am not going to tell you why. It
will be safer if you do not know. But it is necessary – it is

absolutely vital – if we are to save your mother. Therefore, on Tuesday night, I want you to open a window so that we can climb in.

This is what I want you to do. Go to bed as usual, but do not go to sleep. Wait until the house is completely quiet. Then leave your room (Hermione has told me where it is) and go into the old nursery. Open the Catherine wheel window. Then go back to bed. If you hear anything after that, do not react in any way. Whatever happens, pretend you are asleep.

We will come between one and two in the morning, so the window must be open by one at the latest. If that is not possible, or there is some reason why you cannot do as I ask, try to let Hermione know. But do not take any risks. We can probably wait until Wednesday night if we have to.

You will need to be very brave and very careful. I know you can be both those things. We are relying on you. So is your mother. Remember, Jacinta, trust us and nobody else. Do your very best.

I am your friend and your mother's friend,
Geoffrey Staddon.

The letter betrayed none of the qualms I felt at writing it. It was essential that Jacinta should have no inkling of how uncertain I was that we were doing the right thing. Not that my fellow conspirators, however, seemed in any doubt. For Rodrigo this was merely one of many chances – by no means the most desperate – he was prepared to take for Consuela. For Hermione it was a risky venture justified by the extremity of the circumstances. Like Imry, she had detected few signs at Consuela's trial that the defence would be successful. Now, bridling at her treatment by the prosecution, she was willing to play her part in a less conventional way.

It was difficult at times, as we sat together in Hermione's sitting-room at the Thackeray Hotel, to believe that what we were planning would actually take place. An air of unreality enveloped everything we proposed to do, even as it enveloped what would happen to Consuela if we failed to intervene. Both futures – her salvation and her condemnation – had become for me equally incredible. Perhaps only in that way could my mind hold dread and hope at bay and concentrate on action. Perhaps only by ceasing to look ahead could I go forward at all.

Hermione was to return to Hereford by train the following day.

303

Rodrigo and I were to follow in my car on Monday. We would book into a country inn at a discreet distance from the city, whilst, that afternoon, Hermione called unannounced at Clouds Frome. It was inconceivable that Miss Roebuck would raise any objection to her seeing Jacinta and she would therefore have an opportunity to convey my letter to her. That this had been successful she would confirm when we met on the Wye Bridge in Hereford at three o'clock on Tuesday afternoon. By then Rodrigo would have selected the best point at which to enter the grounds of Clouds Frome. We would do so that night, equipped with a ladder, torches and a knife. (The last of these was a precaution against attack by the guard-dog, a contingency I viewed with horror.) We would then enter the house via the nursery window. (I had chosen this window because its Catherine wheel shape made it easily distinguishable from the ground and because it was close to Jacinta's bedroom.) From that point on it would be a question of inspecting each room – starting with the most obvious ones – in search of the false wall and the safe concealed behind it. With Victor and half the staff absent, the task promised to be both feasible and straightforward, so long as we avoided those rooms (already identified by Hermione) which were likely to be occupied.

So much for the theory. The practice, my instincts told me, would prove far more complex and demanding. But, so long as I did not devote too much time to imagining the risks, I could pretend, or at least behave as if, they did not exist.

I disclosed none of this to Imry, fearing that he would point out all the cogent reasons why to proceed was folly. Instead, on Monday morning, just as Consuela's trial was resuming at the Old Bailey, I left the office with a vague and hasty explanation that I might be away for several days. Then I delivered a message to Imry's club, telling him I would not be able to keep our regular appointment and would be out of London at least until Wednesday. With my tracks covered, it only remained to collect Rodrigo from our agreed rendezvous halfway along Park Lane and drive west towards Hereford and whatever outcome our actions were to have.

Monday 21 January 1924
When we parted on Saturday, Geoff assured me that he would meet me at the club as usual at six o'clock this evening. All that awaited me here, however, was a message left with the porter this morning, to the effect that he had had to leave London and would

304

not be back before Wednesday. This I find inexplicable. Reg, when I telephoned him, confirmed that Geoff's vanishing act has nothing to do with the partnership. So, what has it to do with? What could possibly have precipitated his departure at such a crucial stage of the trial? Where, and why, has he gone?

Ironically, I made my way here from the Old Bailey dreading the very prospect of meeting Geoff, turning over in my mind innumerable ways of applying a brave gloss to the events in court which I thought I would have to describe to him. Well, the effort was wasted. No gloss was needed. And perhaps, in all the circumstances, that was just as well.

Number One Court seemed somehow fuller this week than last, more closely packed and intense. This was an illusion, of course, since it has been full to capacity every day of the trial. Yet there was an absence of ornament and diversion in the proceedings, a refined awareness of what we were there to do and see done, that imposed its solemnity on all of us, lawyers and laymen alike. Many, I think, realized for the first time that the drama is nearly at an end, the succession of question and answer about to draw to a close. When it does, these long punctilious days in court will seem few and fleeting, the hopes and doubts they have bred absurd in the face of whatever reality overtakes them.

For the moment, the consequences of Consuela's testimony remain uncertain, my assessment of them as valid as any other. I may be wrong about how the jury will react. And I can only pray, for Consuela's sake, that I am. What I fear, however, is that her slim chance to sway them has come and gone – and they have not been swayed.

When Sir Henry Curtis-Bennett rose this morning and called the accused herself as his next and final witness, she became, even more so than before, the focus of the Court's attention. As she made her way from the dock to the witness-box, all eyes, including mine, were fixed upon her. What we saw was a slim upright woman of medium height and elegant carriage, dressed in a black suit of almost military severity, belted and buttoned to the collar. She wore a matching hat with a narrow upturned brim, set low over her right eye. There was a vestigial feather in the band of the hat, ruffed lace at her neck and wrists and a lozenge-shaped brooch on her left breast. Her dark hair was drawn back, revealing a face of exceptional beauty and an expression of singular restraint.

That there was evidently to be no repetition of Saturday's loss of

305

self-control on Consuela's part I instinctively regretted. I think I know the sort of dull middle-class Englishmen who appear to dominate the jury. What they expect of women is either submissiveness or nervousness, preferably both. When the woman whose life is at their mercy displays neither quality, they become suspicious. And when that woman is also beautiful and obviously of foreign extraction, their suspicion turns to hostility. So it was that, from the very first, Consuela took more risks than she could have realized with the prejudices and susceptibilities of the Court.

Would she look at her husband as she descended from the dock? He was in his customary place next to the jury-box and everyone must have wondered whether, as Consuela reached the foot of the dock steps and turned towards him, some glance – some signal of how they felt towards each other – would be exchanged. But none was. Consuela gazed resolutely at her destination, whilst Victor stared at the chandelier above our heads.

The moment was past as soon as it was upon us and Consuela was being sworn in. The judge was leaning forward, squinting across at her. Talbot was lounging back in his chair, fiddling with a pen. Sir Henry was clearing his throat and adjusting his gown. Every neck was craning, every eye staring, every ear straining. To this woman's words had been reduced the issue of all the other words that had gone before.

At Sir Henry's invitation, Consuela recounted her origins in Brazil, her first meeting with Victor, her arrival in England, her years as the mistress of Clouds Frome. In his questions, Sir Henry seemed to be urging her to reveal more of the shy nineteen-year-old she had once been, more of the gauche and inexperienced bride, the homesick and neglected wife. But the years of living by her own devices, of surviving in a foreign land and a loveless marriage, had taught her too well. The true Consuela had retreated out of reach and sight, leaving only an aloof and dignified stranger in our midst who meets danger with disdain and answers accusations with indifference. I was reminded of a tigress I once watched at the Zoo, pacing her cage while schoolchildren gaped and growled in mockery. Not once did she gratify them with a response. Not even with so much as a rake of her proud Siberian eyes did she reward their provocations. She was their prisoner, yet in her gaze was a consciousness of freedom such as they had never dreamt of.

We turned to more recent times. Consuela explicitly denied receiving the anonymous letters and said that, had she done so, she would have ignored them. She was not a jealous woman. There *was, she silently implied, nothing to be jealous of. The accounts other witnesses had given of the afternoon of 9 September were factually correct but had been misinterpreted. She had indeed been in the drawing-room when Noyce delivered the tea-trolley, but she had gone into the garden to take the air before anybody joined her. When she returned, Victor was already descending the stairs. In the intervening few minutes, she surmised, somebody had entered the drawing-room and poisoned the sugar. She had been as innocent a participant in subsequent events as anybody else. For Rosemary she expressed genuine but measured sorrow. 'We were not close, but relations between us were always cordial. She was a cheerful, good-natured girl. I would never have done anything to harm her. If I had known there was poison in the sugar, I would have prevented her eating any.'*

Consuela's memory of the evening that had followed was that Gleasure had merely mentioned Victor's illness, not urged her to call out a doctor. Even if he had, she would not have done so without Victor's agreement and he would not have expected her to. Until Mortimer's telephone call from Fern Lodge, she had assumed Victor was suffering from a bilious attack. Dr Stringfellow's suspicion that Victor, Marjorie and Rosemary and all been poisoned by something they had consumed during the tea party had shocked her, but at no stage, up to and including the day of the search, had she thought they might have been deliberately poisoned. The discovery of the letters and the arsenic in her bedroom had come as a hideous bolt from the blue. She could in no way account for their presence unless they had been hidden by somebody wishing to fasten the blame for Rosemary's death on her.

Thus we arrived at the most sensitive passage of Consuela's testimony. Her innocence is only credible if it is assumed that the evidence against her was planted. If it was, then somebody else not only wanted Victor dead but wanted her blamed for it. Who could this person be? Who, close to the Caswell family and the Clouds Frome household, probably among those who have already testified in this trial, has any reason to plan and commit such a diabolical crime?

Wisely, Consuela did not attempt to answer the question posed by her version of events, even though the judge intervened to suggest that she should. Mr Justice Stillingfleet's attitude on the point was in stark contrast to the approval he had shown for Victor's reticence about authorship of the letters and reflected his

307

overall lack of sympathy for Consuela. The explanation for this – be it misogyny, xenophobia or some rag-bag of other prejudices – is less important than its result. For a court, as far as I can see, is a society as well as an institution, a society in which the judge is patriarch and the jurors a careful selection of the most humble and obedient citizens. Where he leads, impartially or not, they will surely follow.

By the time Sir Henry's examination of his client had drawn to a close, a curious change seemed to me to have crept over the court. Certainty of Consuela's guilt had ebbed, but a perverse determination to find her guilty had more than offset this. If she had behaved differently – seemed more awe-stricken, more vulnerable, more fearful about the outcome of her trial – it might have tipped the balance in her favour. But she was none of these things. Nor, in an ideal world, should she have been. Her fate ought to rest on a dispassionate assessment of what is true and what is false, what is proven and what is not. Alas, the Old Bailey exists in an altogether less certain world, in which the only absolute is a verdict, reached by a twisting and irrational route.

Mr Talbot, KC, commenced his cross-examination at a provocative clip, asking few questions that were not accusations subtly rephrased. Perhaps he had sensed the judge's antipathy to Consuela. Perhaps he shares it. Or perhaps, as I suspect, he is a little frightened of her and what he is frightened of a pampered upbringing has taught him to despise. Whatever the reason, he was cold, arrogant and contemptuous. And Consuela, though never intimidated, was slowly reduced to despairing repetition. 'No, I did not.' 'Absolutely not.' 'That is not true.' 'There is no truth in it.' 'No, sir.' 'No.' 'No, no, no, a thousand times no.'

Poor Consuela. She stands alone, condemned as proud, foreign and far too beautiful long before her guilt on a charge of murder was ever considered. She has admitted nothing and refuted nothing. And the prosecution has proved very little. Yet still, as she walked slowly back this afternoon from the witness-box to the dock and so descended, as she has every day, to the cells beneath the court, hopelessness seemed somehow visible about her, a hopelessness that defied her accusers to spare her in spite of themselves. Yet nothing, absolutely nothing, in the faces of the jurors or the frowns of the judge, gave me any cause to think they had even heard her plea.

*

308

Rodrigo and I took rooms at the Green Man, Fownhope, a few miles south of Mordiford. In the bar that evening, local gossip was overtaken by the news that the government had lost a censure vote in the House of Commons, making it inevitable that the Labour Party would take office for the first time in history. To the rustics of Fownhope, it was barely credible; a Bolshevik revolution was upon us. To Rodrigo, however, when I explained what had happened, it was a ray of hope.

'A new government, Staddon? Then they may let Consuela live. In my country, a president spares all condemned prisoners when he takes up office.'

'That's not the practice here.'

'But these people' – he gestured round the bar – 'say *Labour* are different from the rest.'

'Perhaps. But in this way they may wish to seem exactly the same.'

What really worried me was that Labour might well prove even stauncher advocates of the death penalty than the Tories. Imprisoned strikers were likelier to engage their sympathy than Brazilian heiresses. If we were reduced to hoping they would be merciful, it would be a frail hope indeed.

Next morning, the few national newspapers to reach Fownhope were dominated by the political upheaval. Reports of Consuela's trial were less prominent than they had been and, without Imry to interpret events for me, the effect Consuela's testimony had had on the Court was impossible to gauge.

Rodrigo, the landlord told me, had gone out before dawn. When he returned in mid-morning, he ushered me into his room and closed the door before announcing that he had stolen a ladder from a barn and concealed it in undergrowth near a part of the Clouds Frome wall where he reckoned it would be easy to cross. It only remained now to confirm that Jacinta had received my letter and would act upon it. Then our preparations would be complete.

I drove into Hereford early in the afternoon, leaving Rodrigo at the inn. Well before three o'clock, I was standing in one of the passing-places on the Wye Bridge, leaning over the parapet to watch the turbulent river surge and foam round the cutwater beneath me. Soon, very soon, Hermione would arrive and with her the last moment when it would be possible to draw back from the brink.

309

*

Tuesday 22 January 1924

Politics is on everybody's lips, relegating events at the Old Bailey to the status of a side-show. How strange that, as Consuela's trial nears its climax, the outside world's interest in it diminishes. It is as if all those who have most loudly demanded her conviction are suddenly embarrassed by their own vehemence. Even the lady of many hats absented herself today. She, like most other Londoners, is presumably more interested now in who may be kissing hands at Buckingham Palace than saying his piece at the Old Bailey.

What such people missed were the closing speeches of defending and prosecuting counsel. Sir Henry Curtis-Bennett bestrode the morning with two and a half hours of impassioned oratory, arguing that the evidence against his client remained wholly circumstantial and that significant elements in it had been swept away in the course of the trial. Banyard had testified that Consuela had in no sense instigated his purchase of Weed Out. *She was, moreover, no better informed of its presence or composition than her husband. Gleasure had admitted that she had not tried to prevent him calling a doctor. Cathel Simpson had insisted that neither the arsenic nor the anonymous letters could have been in the bedroom drawer prior to 21 September. And Mr Jenkins the postmaster had cast doubt on the authenticity of those letters.*

'If the postmarks were faked, it was done in order to suggest that Mrs Caswell had received the letters when in fact she had not. If she did not receive them, the motive put forward by the prosecution to explain this crime is disproved. And, if that is disproved, so is the case against Mrs Caswell.'

The logic was impeccable, the presentation exemplary. Sir Henry has waited throughout the trial for a chance to display his talents untrammelled by contrary witnesses and today he seized it with aplomb. For as long as he was speaking, it was impossible to believe that anybody could resist his call for an acquittal. What, after all, was there to substantiate the charges but half-formed suspicions and questionable exhibits? The discovery of the arsenic and the letters is no longer as damning a piece of evidence as it once seemed. Without it, what remains but the coincidence that Consuela was alone in the drawing-room when Noyce delivered the tea-trolley?

Sir Henry handled the jury with magical ease. He did not challenge or insult them, but carried them along with him in a rigorous but beguiling voyage through the currents and undertows

310

of the case. Nobody denied, he pointed out, that murder had been committed. But the jury should beware of mistaking evidence of murder with evidence of his client's guilt. The one was abundant, the other entirely lacking. Nor was it for the defence to show who had committed the crime, merely that Mrs Caswell had not. And this, he contended, they had amply done.

If there was a flaw in Sir Henry's brilliance, it was its impermanence. It dazzled but did not endure. When he sat down, nobody could doubt that he had done as well for Consuela as any advocate could. But the jury has yet to hear a lengthy speech from the prosecution. And an even lengthier summing-up by the judge is promised for tomorrow. Will the force of Sir Henry's argument endure in their minds? Will his words – or Talbot's and Mr Justice Stillingfleet's – be at the front of their thoughts when they are asked to reach their verdict?

Talbot's closing speech occupied the afternoon and never at any point threatened to rival Sir Henry's for gusto and persuasiveness. Its virtues were altogether more attritional, reflected in the way he reverted at intervals to certain themes he was determined the jury should not forget. The evidence was circumstantial, but where poisoning was concerned how could it be otherwise? Nobody was going to consume – or allow somebody else to consume – a poisoned drink if they had seen it poisoned. The doubts raised by the defence about the authenticity of the letters were wholly spurious. And Consuela's carelessness in leaving the letters and the arsenic where they could easily be found was all of a piece with her arrogant refusal to believe that the crime could ever be traced to her. Above all, Talbot emphasized, the jury should ask themselves this: how could the events of 9 September be explained other than by Consuela's guilt? Nobody else present at the tea party had any reason to harm Victor. Nobody else had the means at their disposal to do him harm. And nobody else had the chance to put those means into effect. For those reasons alone they should find the accused guilty on both counts.

In Talbot's depiction, Consuela is a clever and ruthless murderess motivated by a jealous determination to ensure that, if her husband no longer loves her, he will be made to suffer the ultimate penalty for seeking affection elsewhere. It was with this gross caricature as firmly planted in the jury's minds as he could contrive that he rested the prosecution case. Tomorrow, we shall surely know whether he has been successful.

*

This evening, dining alone here at my club, I overheard two of our crustier old members deploring the advent of a Labour government in apocalyptic tones. England will never be the same again; from this blow society cannot hope to recover; it is the result of giving women the vote; and the new Prime Minister, Ramsey MacDonald, is a pacifist.

Will it be so very different, I wonder? The sun will still rise of a morning, the rain will fall, the mills will grind and the laws of England, humane or not, will be enforced. When these two old men were young, hangings were open-air events, spectacles for public entertainment. Now they are performed behind closed doors, shielded from the curious world. But their brutality remains. And the only measure of change in this country of ours that seems at this moment to mean anything to me is whether such brutality is to be visited upon the accused in the case of Rex versus Caswell.

Hermione was exactly on time. She looked calmer and more confident than I felt, but her part in our conspiracy, of course, was over; mine had yet to begin. Mindful of the need for caution, we began walking towards the southern side of the bridge, talking as we went.

'All went well, Mr Staddon. I encountered no difficulty in visiting Jacinta yesterday.'

'How did she seem?'

'Worried sick about her mother, as you would expect. But she was greatly encouraged by your letter. Miss Roebuck left us alone, so she was able to read it in my presence.'

'And will she be able to do what we've asked her to do?'

'Nothing will prevent her. She is a brave girl, as you must know.'

'Yes,' I said, avoiding her gaze. 'I do know.'

We reached the end of the bridge, pulled up and turned to look at each other. Hermione smiled. 'I shall return to Fern Lodge now,' she said, 'and await further developments as if I do not expect there to be any.'

'That would be as well.'

'It only remains for me to wish you luck.' She leaned closer. 'Go carefully, young man. Go very carefully. You will need to. Of that I am certain.'

I watched her start back across the bridge, then headed

towards the side-street where I had left the car. I walked fast, eager to put behind me an unworthy thought that had flashed across my mind at Hermione's words. Was I glad – or secretly sorry – that nothing now stood in our way?

CHAPTER

SIXTEEN

We left the Green Man while there were still enough customers in the bar to distract the landlord's attention. A short drive along deserted lanes took us up into the wooded hills behind Clouds Frome. There we pulled the car off the road and waited as patiently as we could for midnight to come and go. The night was cold and still, a pale three-quarters moon drifting in and out of a ragged cloud-rack. Silence of an intensity only the countryside in winter can contrive lay all about us and neither of us made any attempt to break it. Instead, we sipped by turns from Rodrigo's hip-flask, heard the church clock in Mordiford strike twelve, let another half hour slowly elapse, then started for the house.

We were both carrying electric torches. Rodrigo, in addition, had the car-rug slung over his shoulder and, as I knew but had not cared to confirm, a knife concealed in one of his pockets. He led the way down a grassy track he had reconnoitred earlier. A mile of cautious descent brought us to the eastern wall of Clouds Frome, ten feet of ivy-swathed brick with nothing visible beyond. Already, I was in danger of losing my bearings. But Rodrigo knew exactly where we were. Within minutes, he had located the ladder, hidden in a bank of ferns.

We propped it against the wall and Rodrigo climbed up with the rug. This he folded thickly and draped like a saddle over the top of the wall as protection against the broken glass. Then he signalled for me to follow. Once I had joined him, he pulled the ladder up after me, swung it round as if it were no heavier than a

314

feather and lowered it to the other side. I descended first, then Rodrigo threw down the rug and followed.

At the foot of the wall, we paused to catch our breath. We were on sloping ground, roughly grassed and sparsely dotted with shrubs and bushes. Based on our point of entry, I reckoned we were now some way to the south of the kitchen garden, with the eastern limit of the orchard directly ahead of us and the house about half a mile away on a north-westerly bearing, its outline obscured by the wooded hills behind it. The only way to confirm this, it seemed to me, was to locate the kitchen-garden wall and follow it to its south-western corner. It had been agreed beforehand that Rodrigo would not quibble with my navigation once we were inside the grounds. True to his word, he trailed faithfully behind me, carrying the ladder in one hand and the rug in the other as I headed up the slope.

A fleeting appearance by the moon revealed the kitchen-garden wall before we reached it. Encouraged by this success, I altered course to the left, hoping to reach the south-western corner more quickly. That would give me an exact appreciation of our whereabouts relative to the house. From there, I knew, a path led round the boundary of the orchard to steps that ascended to the lawn east of the pergola. And from there the nursery window was directly accessible.

I could not hear Rodrigo behind me, though whenever I looked back he was there, ten yards to the rear, the ladder tilted in his hand like the lance of a knight. The only sound that reached me was my own breathing and the swishing of my feet through the lank grass. Already, a chilly dampness had penetrated my shoes. But there was dampness of another kind on my face. One half of my brain was content to calculate distance and topography, whilst the other struggled to keep a host of irrational fears at bay. The moonlight was faint and shifting, as disturbing in its way as the impenetrable blackness that had swallowed most of our surroundings. The kitchen-garden wall reappeared a few yards ahead and, only a few more yards beyond, ended abruptly. We had found the south-western corner.

I turned it confidently, expecting to feel the texture of the grass alter beneath my feet as I stepped onto the path. But I never did. There was a sound in the darkness to my right, a sound at once heavy, rushing and panting. Then, with a growl that was almost a bark, it launched itself at me. It was the guard-dog, as huge and strong as I had dreaded it might be. It leapt and, in one movement, flung me back against the wall with its forepaws. The breath shot out of me. Winded and utterly terrified, I cowered away, but the beast was standing as tall as me, its legs against my chest, its teeth bared, its throat spitting phlegm. I could see moonlight glistening on its fangs, could feel the heat of its breath against my face.

Then, as quickly as it was upon me, it was gone. Rodrigo charged and grasped it about the shoulders, throwing himself to the ground and carrying the dog with him. For a second, they were just a wrestling, snarling tangle in the darkness at my feet. Then Rodrigo gained the hold he wanted. He was behind the dog, his legs scissored round it to immobilize its lower limbs. His right arm was round the animal's throat, his left hand forcing its muzzle down against his arm to prevent it barking.

'The knife!' he said as loudly as he dared. 'Take the knife from my pocket and—' The dog bucked and strained. Rodrigo's grip weakened for an instant, then was restored. 'Take the knife and kill it!'

I crouched beside him and tried to open his jacket, but it was fastened and the buttons were out of reach beneath the dog's back. I had to twist my hand in past his collar, with the dog's head only a few inches from mine, its eyes rolling, its jaws foaming.

'*Depressa! Depressa!*'

My stretching fingers found the handle, tugged at it, lost it momentarily, then found it again and pulled it out. It was a heavy weapon about ten inches in length, with a wooden handle and a leather sheath. When I slid the sheath off, it was to expose a thick double-edged blade.

'Do it now, Staddon! I cannot . . . I cannot hold this brute much longer.'

I reversed my grasp on the knife, raised it to strike, then hesitated. Where should I strike? How? Even though I knew the act was necessary, its commission seemed beyond me.

'Slit its throat! Quickly!'

'Its throat? My God, I can't—'

'Then give the knife to me!' He was grimacing with the effort of continued restraint. 'If you cannot do it, I can!'

I thrust the knife into his right hand with a kind of dumb eagerness and turned away, too late to miss the dull flash of the blade as he closed his fingers round the handle. There was a single thump like a rug being beaten, a horrible tearing note half-hidden by the hissing of Rodrigo's breath, a low gurgling growl, a

316

frenzied scrabbling, then a brief silence. When I looked back, the dog lay limp and lifeless.

Rodrigo struggled to his feet, stooped to wipe the blade clean against the grass, then took the sheath from my hand, slid the knife back into it and replaced it in his pocket.

'I . . . I'm sorry,' I murmured. 'I just couldn't . . . couldn't bring myself to . . .'

'Keep your apologies for later, Staddon! I do not want to hear them now.'

'But—'

'*Fique quieto!* Forget the dog. It died without making a noise. That is all that matters. Now, get us to the house!'

I hurried ahead, found the path and began to walk along it as quickly and steadily as I could, aware that the trembling in my hands was slowly abating, the hammering of my heart subsiding. I thanked God there had been no daylight by which to see what Rodrigo had done and winced with shame at the memory of how little I had helped him. I wondered if there was much blood on him, or any on me, wondered what, in the morning, I would think about this night's work.

So preoccupied was I that I did not notice the outline of the house looming above me, more densely black even than the sky behind it. I reached the foot of the steps without realizing it, stumbled against the lowest tread and fell up them.

'What is wrong?'

'Nothing. These steps lead up to a lawn behind the house.'

'Then go on, Staddon. What are you waiting for?'

I turned and hastened up the steps, through a gap in the beech-hedge at the top and so out onto the lawn. Now the rear of the house was clearly visible beyond the ornamental garden. The ground-floor windows were blank and shuttered. As for those on the first floor . . . Yes, there was the Catherine wheel window of the nursery, looking, at this range, as firmly closed as the rest. I was gaping up at it when Rodrigo appeared behind me.

'That is it?' he whispered, following the line of my gaze.

'Yes.'

'Is it open?'

'Don't worry. Jacinta won't have let us down.'

'I hope you are right.'

'Wait here while I cross the garden. Follow when I signal.'

I moved as swiftly and silently as I could across the lawn, clambered over the low stone wall separating it from the ornamental garden, then steered a path between the rose-bushes and the fountain to the terrace running past the ground-floor windows. Now the nursery was directly above me. Peering up, I could see that its window was indeed ajar. I turned and waved to Rodrigo.

A few minutes later, we had succeeded in propping the ladder beneath the curving sill of the Catherine wheel. Rodrigo held it fast while I began to climb. I paused at each rung, determined to make no sound that might raise the alarm. The ascent seemed to last an absurdly long time. I remembered the pleasure I had taken from designing this fenestral conceit, remembered the coy explanation I had given Consuela of its purpose, one blazing afternoon in the summer of 1909 as we sat in camp-chairs on what was now the lawn. *'It will supply a circular view of a circular world, Mrs Caswell, for the son or daughter you and Mr Caswell will one day—'* I reached the top and there, as a dim reflection in the glass, met myself fifteen years later, peering in like the intruder I had always been.

Jacinta had opened the window just wide enough for me to squeeze my fingers between it and the sill. It swung out smoothly until it was almost horizontal, then stopped, leaving an aperture sufficient for me to crawl through. Sufficient or not, though, it was a scramble, with a drop of four feet inside which I had to negotiate without making any noise. At length, I lowered myself to the nursery floor confident that nobody could have heard me.

I took the torch from my pocket, switched it on and moved its beam round the room. Clearly, it was no longer used for anything but storage. There were a couple of mats covering the boards in the centre, a large wooden chest in one corner, some cardboard boxes piled on top of each other, a rocking horse, a play-pen, two large cupboards, and over all a musty air of collective abandonment. Turning back, I leaned out through the window and waved Rodrigo up.

Alone, I doubt Rodrigo could have managed the entry. As it was, I hauled him bodily through the gap and did my best to break his fall. After a few stifled oaths, he pronounced himself ready to proceed. I led the way to the door by an indirect route, hoping to avoid creaking any of the boards. The policy seemed to work, for we reached the door in silence. I opened it cautiously, but there seemed no cause for alarm. The passage outside was quiet and empty.

To the right lay Jacinta's bedroom. I wondered if she had

318

stayed awake and felt sure, in that instant, that she had; if so, she must surely have heard us by now. To the left the passage curved and descended by a short flight of steps to the gallery above the hall. From there the shapes and alignments of every room fanned out in my mind like diagrams leaping from a page. For a moment, I could believe I was both outside and inside a doll's house of my own construction, stooping to squint through a tiny window at its still tinier occupant just as I was turning to see a huge eye blinking at me through the glass.

'Staddon!'

'Yes, all right. I know what I'm doing.'

'Then do it.'

I started down the passage, keeping close to the left-hand wall. The gallery was empty and silent, but less dark than the passage; the windows looking out over the courtyard were uncurtained, admitting a meagre ration of moonlight. We reached its far end and there, I knew, a decision would have to be made: whether to go downstairs first or search some of the bedrooms. The obvious room in which to install a safe was the study. The library was another possibility. They both had the additional advantage (from our point of view) of being remote from the staff quarters. I signalled my intention to Rodrigo and eased open the door leading to the stairhead.

We descended slowly, the darkened hall opening up beneath us like a cavern. The height of the treads and the dimensions of the quarter-landings were exactly as I remembered, but for Rodrigo's sake I shone my torch behind me as I went. Below, some embers were still smouldering in the fireplace, casting across the room a faint yellow light that could have been a failing afterglow of its gaudy inauguration thirteen years ago.

At the foot of the stairs, more memories flew to meet me from a lost time. To my right were the doors to the drawing-room, where she had waited for me that July afternoon before the house-warming. How grateful I was that we did not need to enter. Instead, I turned left, leading Rodrigo out of the hall and into a branch of the lobby that led to the library, study and billiards room. With luck, we would soon have found the safe and I could set all thoughts of the past aside.

But it was not to prove so easy. The library was unaltered. That became obvious to me as I cast my torch-beam round the well-stocked bookshelves. We hurried on to the study, only to find that the same applied. It was a small enough room for anything as

319

significant as a blocked-off alcove to be immediately obvious, but its proportions were exactly as I had designed them. The only doubt raised by its contents was whether it still served as a study. It had more the appearance of a schoolroom and I wondered if this was where Jacinta received her tutors. If so, obviously the safe must be elsewhere. But where?

Victor was as cautious as he was secretive. In his mind, as much as the architecture of Clouds Frome, the answer surely lay. As I stood and thought of how devious yet logical he was, Rodrigo started to say something in my ear, but I cut him short.

'I have it! It must be upstairs. Come on.'

I led the way back to the lobby, opened the double doors leading to the hall and was about to step through when there was a noise ahead of us, not loud but quite distinct, something between a snap and a creak. I pulled up at once, my every sense alert, but nothing followed. The wavering glimmer from the fire reached the shuttered windows and played weakly across the furniture. Otherwise there was neither sound nor movement. Rodrigo touched my elbow and whispered: 'The fire, I think.'

I nodded. Subsiding ash in the grate was indeed the likeliest explanation. Perhaps the acoustics of the unusually high ceiling accounted for the noise seeming to come from a different direction. I headed across the room to the stairs and started up them, theorizing as I went. According to Hermione, Victor retained use of the master bedroom, whilst Consuela's bedroom was what had originally been dubbed the Wye suite. So, where better for Victor to conceal a safe than in a room only he had the use of and where, as an additional precaution, he slept every night? Except this night, of course, when he was in London and we had a chance we might never have again to learn his best-kept secret.

The master bedroom was directly above the hall, reached by a dog-leg passage from the head of the stairs that led nowhere else. The privacy this was intended to bestow was ideal for our purposes. I opened the door carefully but without hesitation, willing myself to disregard all the memories I knew would be lying in wait for me of the last time I had been there, and why, and with whom.

All trappings of femininity were gone from the room, plain wallpaper and striped curtains replacing the colourful fruit and flower patterns favoured by Consuela. I stood a few feet inside the door and swept the torch-beam methodically round the walls, reconstructing in my mind every detail of the angles and proportions I had planned and setting them against what I saw. Nothing had changed. The recesses either side of the fireplace were not only the same as each other but the same as my recollection of them. There were no tell-tale tamperings with skirting-boards or picture-mouldings, no signs of any kind that a partition had been constructed.

'Nothing,' I said, turning back to Rodrigo.

'You are certain?'

'Of course I'm certain.'

'Those doors—' He pointed across the room. 'Where do they lead?'

'Dressing-rooms, communicating with the bathroom. Not very promising, I'm afraid, but we'll look.'

Twin dressing-rooms, both leading to the same bathroom, had been Victor's idea. Entering what had been Consuela's, I realized from the arrangement of brushes, clippers, colognes and razors on the table beneath the mirror that Victor had taken it over, presumably for the sake of its superior view over the orchard. Rodrigo waited in the bedroom whilst I walked round through the bathroom into the second dressing-room. It was unfurnished and clearly no longer used. In fact, the door leading back into the bedroom was locked. I turned round to retrace my steps, glimpsing a stray reflection of myself in the mirror as I did so.

Then I stopped. Something was wrong, different, inconsistent with the plans I had meticulously drawn up for this house so long ago. I looked in the mirror, shone the torch at it, moved the beam away to the door, then back at the mirror. This dressing-room was smaller than the other one, rectangular where it should have been square, narrower by at least two feet. I stepped closer to the wall on which the mirror hung, and tapped it with my knuckle. It was hollow, nothing but a plasterboard partition fashioned to resemble the real wall which stood two feet behind it.

'What is it?' whispered Rodrigo from the bathroom doorway. He must have heard the tapping and followed me in.

'I think we've found it.'

'Where?'

'Behind here. But I can't—' I had moved the torch-beam up and down the wall without seeing any crack or crevice that might be part of a hatch. Then, as the beam flashed back at me from the mirror, I realized why. Reaching out with both hands, I tried to lift the mirror away from the surface behind it. It would not budge. It was not suspended, then, but firmly fixed. I ran my fingers carefully round the rim and, as they neared the bottom right-hand corner, felt something catch them. It was a tiny lever and, as I pushed down against it, it moved and clicked. Then the mirror, and the section of wall behind it, swung slowly open.

We had found the safe. It stood on a shelf linking the false and real walls, somehow smaller than I had expected, no more than two feet in any dimension, but as solid and unyielding as one three times its size, black and gleaming, with the manufacturer's name proudly scrolled in red and gold. There was a handle to open it, raised in a locked position, and, in the centre of the door, a dial with numbers inscribed around it, running from zero to a hundred.

'You have done well, Staddon,' said Rodrigo.

'Can you open it?'

'Of course. Shine your torch on the dial.'

According to Gleasure, the combination was a set of three two-digit numbers representing the years of birth of Victor, Mortimer and Hermione, with the thousands and hundreds omitted in each case. From the Hereford registrar, Rodrigo had established that Victor was born in 1868, Mortimer in 1864 and Hermione in 1858. The combination was therefore 68–64–58. If this safe operated in the same way as the one used at the office, the first number would need to be dialled four times anti-clockwise, the second number three times clockwise and the third number twice anti-clockwise. Following this, it would only be necessary to ease the dial back in a clockwise direction to release the locking mechanism before turning the handle.

As Rodrigo stooped forward, I trained the torch-beam on the dial. He rested his fingers on the knurled boss at its centre for a moment, then began to rotate it, muttering instructions to himself as he did so. '*Sessenta e oito . . . Em sentido anti-horário . . . Um, dois, três, quatro . . . Agora, sessenta e quatro em sentido horário . . . Um, dois, três . . . Por fim, cinquenta e oito em sentido anti-horário . . . Um, dois . . . Agora, se Deus quiser . . .*' Gingerly, he turned the dial for the last time. There was a click. Then he lowered the handle and pulled the door open by an inch. Then he looked back at me and grinned. 'Maybe I should have done this for a living, eh Staddon?'

'What's inside?'

'The will, I hope and pray. Let us see.'

He stepped back to open the door wide. The torch-beam fell on three shelves filled with neatly stacked documents. To my surprise, on the top shelf, there were also several bundles of freshly minted bank-notes. Peering closer, I saw they were five pound notes. Each bundle must have contained several thousand pounds. The strangest and most irrational thought sprang into my mind. I reached forward, slid the top note out of one of the bundles and slipped it into my pocket.

Rodrigo glared at me in amazement. 'What are you doing?'

'I'll explain later. Concentrate on finding the will.' With that, I flashed the torch-beam down to the lower shelves. Rodrigo shrugged his shoulders and stretched out his hands towards the sheaves of documents.

Suddenly, there was a noise to our right. As I swung round, I realized it was a key being turned in the lock of the door leading to the bedroom. In the same instant, the door was framed in yellow and a glimmer of light appeared behind us in the bathroom. *'Porcaria!'* murmured Rodrigo, snapping off his torch. But it was too late for such precautions. The door was already opening. Light flooded in, blinding me for a moment. I heard a voice shout, 'Stay where you are!' and recognized it with a jolt of incredulity. It could not be. We were not merely discovered, but—

'Victor!' exclaimed Rodrigo.

Victor Caswell was standing in the doorway, clad in slippers, pyjamas and a dressing-gown. With the light behind him it was difficult to tell what expression was on his face. But there was no doubt about the double-barrelled shot-gun he was holding. It was aimed straight at us. 'Don't move, either of you,' he said in a controlled voice. 'This is loaded and I'll use it if I have to.' Imogen Roebuck appeared behind him. She too wore a dressing-gown, as if she had just been roused from bed. But something was wrong about the sequence of events, something false in the circumstances that confronted me. Why was Victor not in London? And why, since he was here, had we not found him in his bedroom? 'Miss Roebuck,' he said over his shoulder, 'go downstairs and call the police station in Hereford. Tell them we've discovered some burglars and will hold them pending their arrival.' Without a word, she slipped away. I heard the bedroom door close behind her.

'What do you mean to do with us?' I heard myself ask in a hoarse parody of my normal voice.

'Hand you over to the authorities. What else should I do with a pair of housebreakers?'

323

'You must realize that's not what we are.'

'I realize nothing of the kind.'

'We came for your will. We came to find out who would have inherited in the event of your death last September.' Rodrigo was screened from Victor to some extent by the door of the safe. Out of the corner of my eye, I could see he had slipped his right hand into his jacket. I guessed his intention in the same moment that I guessed Victor's. He was here because he knew we would be here. He was here to spring the trap we had blundered into. 'Who's your heir, Victor? That's all we want to know.'

'Really? Well, it's not going to convince the police any more than it convinces me.'

'It's the truth.'

'If it is, you're bigger fools than I thought.'

'Your fools, you mean. The fools you've made of us.'

'I've no idea what you're talking about.'

'Gleasure put us up to this. But you know that, don't you? You know because you told him to.'

'I've heard enough! Close the safe and step out here.' He moved back a pace.

'You want us out of the way, don't you? In prison, where neither of us can do you any harm – or Consuela any good.'

'I won't tell you again. Move away from the safe.'

'Do as he says, Staddon,' said Rodrigo in a resigned tone, reaching up with his left hand to swing the door shut. 'We have no—' Suddenly, he launched himself at Victor, the knife clasped in his right hand and raised behind his head. He shouted as he lunged, some cry of hatred and anger. And, as he shouted, there was a roar that swallowed every other noise, an explosion from the doorway that caught Rodrigo in its path and threw him past me against the wall. The whole room seemed to be vibrating. Blood was spattered across the mirror and dripping onto the floor. And Rodrigo was coughing, choking, clutching at his chest. I heard the knife fall at his feet, then, as slowly as a tree falling, he toppled sideways, struck the door-frame and subsided onto his face.

Sound subsided with him, fading rapidly till only the dripping remained, growing less frequent all the time. The twitching of his limbs stopped, the pool of blood around him ceased to spread. Then, and only then, I nerved myself to look at Victor. He was leaning back against the bedroom door, breathing hard, the shot-gun broken and pointing down, smoke rising from its barrels.

324

'You've . . . You've killed him.'

'I had no choice. It was him or me.'

I dropped to my knees. Rodrigo's face was half-turned towards me, squashed and distorted by his fall, his moustache clotted with blood, one of his eyes open and staring blankly in my direction. 'You planned it this way,' I murmured. 'You wanted this to happen.'

'Nobody but you will believe that.'

'He threatened to kill you if Consuela hanged. That's why, wasn't it? Because you were afraid he'd be as good as his word.'

'Oh, I think he would have been, don't you?'

There was a hollow, sliding sound above me. When I looked up, I realized what it was. Victor had put a cartridge into one of the barrels of the gun. And now, as I watched, he loaded the other barrel as well and closed the breech. Then he licked his lips nervously and turned towards me.

'Get up!'

He meant to kill me too. One glimpse of his expression told me it was so.

'Get up, I say!'

'Why? So you don't have to explain why you shot a kneeling man? I'm unarmed, remember.'

'Pick up the knife.'

'No.'

'Pick it up, damn you!'

'It won't work, Victor. One man shot in self-defence is credible. But they won't believe two. Not with only one weapon between us.'

Doubt entered his mind. I could see it wriggling behind the trembling mask of his face. Some part of his brain, if not persuaded by what I had said, was at least uncertain enough to hold him back.

'Victor!' The door on the far side of the bedroom opened and Imogen Roebuck hurried in. 'What's happened?' As she approached, she saw Rodrigo's body on the floor, saw me kneeling beside it, saw Victor pointing the gun straight at me. All this she took in and assessed at a glance. There was surprise but no horror in her expression, dismay but not a hint of panic. 'I heard the shot. I thought . . .'

'He came at me with a knife,' said Victor over his shoulder.

'Is he dead?'

'Yes,' I said. 'Victor made sure of that.'

325

For an instant, his eyes widened, his grip on the gun tightened. Then Miss Roebuck was at his elbow, looking straight at me as she spoke. 'The police will be here as soon as possible. Why don't we go downstairs and wait for them there?'

A desire to finish what he had started still gnawed at Victor, but he knew now that it was too late. 'All right,' he said grudgingly. 'Let's do that.'

'Is the gun still loaded?'

'He re-loaded after shooting Rodrigo,' I put in.

'Victor?' She laid her hand on his where it grasped the stock, his forefinger no more than half an inch from the trigger. 'Don't you think . . .' Her gaze met his. I saw him flush with shame at what he must have known I could detect: a willingness to obey her amounting to subservience, an eagerness to let her take charge of events. With a droop of the head, he released the catch and let the breech fall open. Then he pulled out the cartridges, dropped them into his pocket and cast the gun onto the bed.

I stood up. Miss Roebuck was looking at me now, frowning studiously, as if I posed a complex problem which she was nonetheless confident of solving. 'I think you should know—' I began, but she cut me short with a raised hand.

'Let's speak outside. It'll be easier to think there.' She glanced at Victor. 'Why don't you go and dress, Victor, before the police arrive?'

He sighed heavily and looked at each of us in turn. 'Very well,' he murmured. Then he walked swiftly from the room. Miss Roebuck gestured for me to follow. Eager in that instant to be out of the sight of Rodrigo's body and of his blood, splattered all around us, I complied.

When I reached the passage, Victor was nowhere to be seen. I heard Miss Roebuck close and lock the door behind her, then I turned to face her. 'He meant to kill me as well, you know.'

'I don't think so.'

'You weren't there. I shall make sure the police—'

'Listen to me! The police will be here very soon. We haven't long, so it's important we don't waste the time we do have. What do you propose to tell them?'

'Why . . . The truth, of course.'

'And what is the truth?'

'That Victor lured Rodrigo and me here tonight. That he knew we were coming. And that he set out to murder us both under the cover of self-defence.'

326

'No.' She shook her head. 'That won't do at all.'

'What do you mean?'

'You won't be believed. Not for an instant. Not in the slightest particular.'

'You're wrong. I can prove we were led into a trap.'

'How?'

'Victor's own valet was the source of Rodrigo's information.'

'Gleasure will deny it.'

'Why did Victor leave London before the end of the trial, then?'

'Because he was no longer needed.'

'And why isn't he sleeping in his own bedroom?'

'It hasn't been properly aired. He arrived back unexpectedly.'

The inadequacy of this explanation required no emphasis by me. We stared at each other in silence for a moment, then she said: 'It's important we understand each other. Rodrigo threatened to kill Victor. I think you'll agree it wasn't an idle threat.'

'You admit this was a trap, then?'

'The intention was to have him arrested and deported.'

'And me?'

'He chose to involve you, we didn't. But I won't deny we foresaw the possibility. How else could he hope to get into the house and find the safe? But we could only tempt him so far. He would have become suspicious if Gleasure had been any more forthcoming.'

'How did you know we'd come tonight?'

'As soon as Hermione arrived yesterday afternoon, I realized what your plan was. I alerted Victor straightaway.'

'So, why the guard-dog, the broken glass, the locks?'

'Because, at first, Victor thought they were all the protection he needed. But Rodrigo wouldn't stop hounding him. Waiting in the road for him to come and go. Following him round Hereford. Trying to bribe the servants. With the trial imminent, Victor was becoming desperate. Contrary to what you think, he'd done nothing to engineer a guilty verdict. Nevertheless, it seemed then – as it seems now – the likeliest outcome. And Rodrigo had left us in no doubt of what he would do in the event that his sister hanged. So, what were we to do? Wait for him to take the revenge his primitive code of honour made him think was his due? Or bait a harmless trap for him?'

'You call this *harmless*?'

'Rodrigo's death was of his own making. You have my word

327

that all we intended to bring about was his deportation back to Brazil. What's happened instead changes everything. It's why I've told you as much as I have. So you'll understand – and agree to do as I suggest.'

'And what do you suggest?'

'That you leave. Now. Before the police arrive. There's still time. And Victor won't object. He'll say he surprised a lone intruder who attacked him with a knife and that he shot him in self-defence. I'll say I saw it happen and that Victor had no choice but to fire. We'll claim we didn't recognize Rodrigo until he was lying dead on the floor. As for his reasons for breaking in, nobody will be able to offer any explanation. There will be an inquest, of course, and Victor will have to answer a great many awkward questions, but—'

'Not as many as if I stay and say my piece. Is that what you mean?'

'It's in your interests as much as ours. If you *do* stay, you'll face criminal charges. Breaking and entering at the very least. More to the point, to sustain your version of events you'll have to expose the parts played in all this by Hermione and Jacinta – and the reason why you're so anxious to help Consuela. If what I hear about the trial is correct, her best hope lies in clemency, not acquittal. But what clemency is she likely to be shown if the criminal activities of her former lover become public knowledge? Or if, as a result, serious doubts are raised about the paternity of her daughter?'

As much to postpone a response on my part as to provoke one on hers, I said: 'Did Victor really make a new will after Jacinta's birth?'

'If you are going to ask me what the terms of Victor's will are, I ought to make it clear that I don't know. Nobody knows – except Victor and his solicitor. Which means that Rodrigo's fanciful theory, exonerating Consuela, falls at its first hurdle.'

'But is it—'

'We don't have much longer! You must go now – or stay. If you go, the police need never know you had anything to do with this. And I promise Jacinta won't be punished in any way. We'll let her believe we have no idea she helped you. But, if you stay . . .'

Why did nothing seem clear except that I had no choice? Why did flight – as so often in my life – seem the only answer? I swallowed hard and saw, in Imogen Roebuck's eyes, the glint of victory.

'The courtyard door is open. So are the main gates. I sent Harris down to open them for the police and told him to come straight back. So, you can walk out without anyone knowing. If you cut down through the orchard, you can be on the main road within five minutes. In any case, it would be best to avoid the drive, don't you think?'

I stared at her, but she did not flinch. Her ironic gaze conveyed her meaning precisely. If I left, I was a coward. If I stayed, I was a fool. But at least a coward can hope to discover bravery before the next battle, whereas to be a fool is to be a fool for ever.

'You must go now. It's your last chance.' As she said it, she almost smiled. In her tone there was not a shred of doubt about what I would do. She knew and so did I.

CHAPTER

SEVENTEEN

'And you simply walked away – leaving Jacinta with no clue as to what had happened?'

The amazement in Hermione Caswell's expression was rapidly blending with indignation. She was staring at me across the drawing-room of Fern Lodge, looking old and haggard in her night-dress and gown, roused from bed too abruptly for her to have brushed her hair or powdered her face. It was not yet light on the morning following Rodrigo's death. My account of how he had died – and of what I had subsequently done – sounded as unworthy to me as it did to Hermione. The only mitigation I could claim was that I had resisted the temptation to drive straight back to London that very night. Instead, I had called at Fern Lodge as early as I dared and insisted on seeing her. She had to know and understand what had occurred, because only she could make Jacinta understand as well.

'I don't know what to say, Mr Staddon. I really do not know what to say.'

'I had no alternative. Surely you can see that.'

'I can certainly see how you were able to persuade yourself that you had no alternative.'

'What should I have done, then? Stayed and been arrested? Implicated you and Jacinta in a conspiracy against her father? Sabotaged Consuela's defence by parading my love for her in open court?'

Hermione bit back a reply and turned away. Then, with a sigh, she opened the curtains to the watery dawn light and stared pensively through the window at Hereford's roofs and chimneys as they emerged from the mist below us. 'I'm sorry,' she said. 'Victor – or the Roebuck creature – has outwitted all of us. I should not reproach *you* for *my* stupidity.'

'We were both acting against our better judgement, Hermione. Neither you nor I would have helped Rodrigo but for the urgency of Consuela's plight. At least this way there's still some basis for hope.'

'Not for Rodrigo.'

'No. But for Consuela. Saving her was all he cared about. He'd have gladly died to achieve that.'

'Yes. But now he has died – without achieving anything. So, what do you want me to tell Jacinta?'

'That I'll continue trying to help her mother in every way that I can.'

'And you're sure Victor will take no reprisals against her?'

'How can he, without making her think he murdered her uncle rather than killed him in self-defence? No, Victor has to tread very carefully from now on. And Miss Roebuck will ensure that he does. For the same reason, you have no cause to fear any recriminations.'

'You really think Miss Roebuck has him under her thumb to that degree?'

'Yes, I do.'

'What is she hoping to achieve?'

'I don't know. She's clever, ambitious and utterly ruthless. Perhaps she hopes to marry Victor. It would make her much wealthier than any governess could ever dream of being.'

'But only if Victor were free to marry her.'

'Yes.'

'So, she has a vested interest in ensuring that Consuela hangs.'

'She may have. The question is . . .'

'Whether she conceived the idea before or after the poisoning.'

'Precisely.'

'Whether she brought this situation about – or is merely taking advantage of it.'

'Logically, it has to be the latter.'

'But you suspect the former?' Hermione turned to look at me. Her expression conveyed clearly enough that she knew what I suspected – and that she agreed.

'There isn't a shred of evidence.'

331

'Then what can we do?'
'Nothing.'
'*Nothing?*'
'Except hope and pray that the jury finds Consuela not guilty.'

Wednesday 23 January 1924 (1.30 p.m.)
And so the ninth and what is commonly expected to be the final day of the trial for murder of Consuela Caswell has opened at the Old Bailey. I am writing these lines during the luncheon adjournment, after a morning entirely given over to the thoughts of Mr Justice Stillingfleet. His summing-up has been a rambling affair, with no apparent sense of direction, imposing a mood of bathos as well as foreboding on the court. But it can surely have little longer to run. At its conclusion, the jury will be sent out to reach a verdict which is therefore, in all likelihood, only a few hours away.

With the end of the trial suddenly so close, its beginning seems preposterously remote, overtaken and obscured by the thousands of words spoken in the course of it. The lady of many hats is back, however, adorned in the pink toque she wore on the opening day. I cannot help wondering if this is a conscious celebration of the cyclical nature of the law's rituals or an unconscious admission of the limit of her millinery account. Either way, she is determined to be in at the death.

Oh God, how one can instantly regret a jest! We may all be in at a death – the decision, at all events, that there shall be a death – before this day has ended. Perhaps that is what deterred Victor Caswell from attending. Perhaps it also has something to do with Geoff's absence from London. But I still have no clue to my friend's activities or whereabouts. He said in his note that he hoped to be back today, so for all I know he may be waiting for me at my club this evening. If he is, what news will I have for him, I wonder?

Of Mr Justice Stillingfleet, I shall be obliged to say that his summing-up has not been one of the most glorious passages in the history of English jurisprudence. He has achieved what I would have thought impossible. He has reduced the complexities and fascinations of this case to the level of tedium. I cannot accuse him of partiality. He has set out all the points fairly and squarely. Unhappily, he has done so with none of the verve and efficiency of Mr Talbot, let alone Sir Henry Curtis-Bennett, whose closing speech seems now – as I feared it might – far longer ago than yesterday morning.

The gist of the judge's remarks – insofar as there has been one – is that, whilst the burden of proof lies upon the prosecution, the arguments advanced by the defence have not been convincing. To subscribe to them it is necessary to believe that the accused has been the victim of a conspiracy, which Mr Justice Stillingfleet is clearly not about to do. And that, I suppose, is his prerogative. But what is surely not his prerogative is to dwell more lengthily upon the deficiencies of the defence than upon those of the prosecution. To do so – as he has – is surely to flout the very principle he declared at the outset.

It is also apparent to me that he dislikes Consuela. Perhaps dislikes is too mild a term. He has a powerful distaste for her that he manfully suppresses most, but not quite all, of the time. When his self-control falters, sinister associations spring up between his words. For instance, having described the murder of Rosemary Caswell as 'a cruel and cold-hearted act', he later remarked that Consuela's testimony had revealed 'a cold streak to her character'. Thus a dangerous and entirely false proposition may have been planted in the jury's minds. The murderer is cold-hearted. The accused is cold-hearted. Therefore the accused is the murderer.

Before this trial began, I would have declared confidently that High Court judges were rational, enlightened and intelligent beings, free of the bias and illogicality which afflict lesser mortals. Now, I find they are no better than the rest of us. Their training equips them to hide their prejudices, but it does not erase them. And their office gives them infinite scope to indulge those prejudices. Well, perhaps it was naïve of me to expect them to resist temptation. To be fair, Mr Justice Stillingfleet has, I think, made some effort to do so. But the effort has not been enough.

Whether Consuela has been stung by any of his words, or has detected in them an animus against her, is impossible to say. She has seemed this morning more withdrawn than ever, distancing herself from events almost visibly as they near their climax. She is wearing the black suit in which she testified on Monday, but the matching hat is now a little lower over her eyes. Nor does she look straight ahead so consistently. Instead, she spends lengthy periods looking down at her hands folded in her lap. What she is thinking I cannot tell. Whether she is even following what is being said is uncertain. Yet she must know – as do we all – that her fate and future will be settled here, beneath Mountford's vainglorious dome, this very afternoon. Nothing so far has seemed to penetrate – or even dent – the wall of insouciance she has constructed around

333

herself. Yet, surely, before the day is out, something will.

Until I reached Ross-on-Wye, the task I had set myself seemed a simple one. To call at Peto's Paper Mill, posing as an amateur numismatist seeking guidance on whether a certain five pound note was printed on paper of their manufacture, promised to be a straightforward exercise. When I arrived, however, a mass of difficulties occurred to my mind. Would I arouse suspicion? Would I encounter Peto himself and be recognized? Would somebody cry out, 'He's the one they're looking for in connection with the shooting at Clouds Frome'?

Defeated by my own trepidations, I retreated to an inn in the town and consumed a cheerless lunch, my first meal since dining with Rodrigo at the Green Man. What, I wondered, would they be doing now about his death? Questioning Victor? Opening an inquest? Conducting a *post mortem*? All that, and more, was bound in due course to be done. But when would they begin to suspect that the truth was being kept from them? Probably never, if Imogen Roebuck's ingenuity were to be relied upon. How strange and disquieting it was to find myself hoping that she and Victor would be successful, in this if in nothing else.

It was whilst standing at the bar, weighed down by such thoughts, that I realized providence had guided my choice of inn. A tubby tweed-suited man of middle years had entered some time before, propped himself on a stool and ordered a pint of his 'usual'. Now he and the barmaid were exchanging well-worn pleasantries. As I listened, at first idly, then intently, it became apparent that the fellow occupied a managerial position at the mill, though doubtless a less exalted one than he claimed. The barmaid called him Mr Howell, laughed wearily at his jokes and looked as if the person who took him off her hands would be doing her a great service. I decided to oblige.

Howell was an affable, self-centred man, as pleased by my interest in his work at the mill as he was incurious about the reason for it. Was it true that Peto's had once been paper suppliers to the Bank of England? Indeed it was. Was it also true that a robbery in 1911 had ended the association? To his infinite regret, it was; if only the security of the premises had been his responsibility, it would, of course, never have happened. Would bank-notes printed on Peto paper still be in circulation? He supposed so, although it was a long time since he had seen any. Did he mean, then, that he could actually tell the difference?

334

Most certainly, and proud of it. To an expert eye such as his the Peto water-mark was unmistakable. How so? At last his garrulity reached its limit. That was a trade secret. His lips were sealed.

'Never mind,' I said. 'But let me just try a small experiment – for my own satisfaction.' I took a ten shilling note from my wallet and passed it to him. 'Is this one of yours?'

He held it up to the light, squinted knowingly, then shook his head. 'Definitely not.'

'You're certain?'

'Never more so.'

'What about this?' I replaced the ten shilling note with a pound.

The inspection was repeated, with the same result.

'And this?' I proffered the five pound note I had taken from Victor's safe.

'I don't even need to glance at it. It's too new to be one of ours.'

'It could have been hoarded away.'

'Sock under a mattress, you mean?'

'Something like that.'

'All right, I'll take a look. But there's not a – Well, blow me down!'

'What's wrong?'

'The strangest thing. This fiver—' He peered at it in evident amazement. 'It's got the Peto water-mark. I'd know it anywhere.'

Wednesday 23 January 1924 (3 p.m.)
Mr Justice Stillingfleet required only half an hour after lunch to draw together the threads of his summing-up and send out the jury to consider their verdict. So now we wait here in the great hall of marble and plaster, gathered in ones and twos and fours and sixes, some standing, some sitting, some talking, some not. Journalists, policemen, lawyers and hangers-on like me, embarrassed by our unity of purpose, trying not to look at each other or wonder what we are all expecting.

Over lunch, the judge must have reproached himself for being too hard on the defence. Either that or food and wine mellowed his temper. Whatever the explanation, his concluding remarks were shot through with reminders for the jury to convict only if they are absolutely certain of Consuela's guilt and to base their verdict on the facts laid before them, not on impressions or suspicions they may have accumulated during the trial. They are to bear in mind that the evidence against Mrs Caswell is largely circumstantial. They are also to bear in mind that circumstantial evidence is not to be despised and can often be compelling. And now, at last, they are to reach their decision.

How long will it take them? Some of the journalists have organized a covert sweepstake on the time of their return. Thanks to Mountford's acoustics, I can catch such phrases as 'Tanner a ticket', 'On the dot of half four' and 'You must be joking' rising in a vague babble towards the dome. But the figure of Justice seems not to hear. She stares down at us with stony contempt, scales held aloft in her left hand whilst, with her right, she firmly clasps the haft of a two-edged sword. Perhaps she knows what I am coming, more and more, to believe. Justice is merely the name we have given to the bizarre form of business we conduct in this place of Mountford's devising. Its forms and conventions are faithfully adhered to. But they do not bestow truth or certainty upon its outcome. The only truth recognized here is what the courts define as such. And the only certainty is that their definition is often a long way from the truth.

I drove out of Ross along the Ledbury road. I cannot say precisely what my intention was. The realization that I had been deceived, that all of us had been deceived, about the sort of man Victor Caswell was, had become overwhelming. I wanted to strike back at him, to denounce him before those who respected him.

Only when I reached the cross-roads where I would need to turn off for Hereford did I hesitate. I pulled to a halt beneath the finger-post and stared up at it. FOWNHOPE 5½. MORDI-FORD 8. HEREFORD 12. Did I really want to go back again? Possession of a mint-condition five pound note printed on Peto paper proved nothing whatever. Even if I could show that it was a forgery, nobody would believe I had found it in Victor's safe. And by now the police might have learned that Rodrigo had lodged with a companion at the Green Man in Fownhope. The landlord did not know my name, but he could probably give them a fair description of me – and of my car.

A fine drizzle was falling and the light was already failing. I switched off the engine and lit a cigarette, watching the droplets of rain form and merge on the windscreen. Hereford lay twelve miles to the left, Gloucester – and a clear road to London – fifteen miles to the right. There was no doubt which way I would

336

choose. But for a little longer I could pretend there was.

I had nearly finished the cigarette when a figure appeared ahead of me, walking towards the cross-roads from the direction of Hereford, a ragged, weary-looking figure whom I recognized at once as Ivor Doak. He was bare-headed and stooped against the rain and he glanced neither to right nor left. Accordingly, so far as I could tell, he remained unaware of my presence and I was too astonished to sound the horn or call out, for he was wearing, draped like a cape around his shoulders, a plaid travelling rug. It too I recognized at once. It was the blanket Rodrigo and I had carried into the grounds of Clouds Frome and abandoned there after the attack by the dog. I had forgotten all about it and, but for this, would probably have not remembered it until much later. Doak had told me he came and went freely at Clouds Frome, but I had not believed him. How wrong I had been was only now apparent.

At the cross-roads, Doak turned left and trudged away towards Ledbury. Perhaps, with a rug he had found at Clouds Frome on his back, he thought he should give the place a wide berth for a few nights. How much did he know? I wondered. How much had he heard or seen? Whatever the answer, I could take some comfort from the fact that he would tell nobody. Ivor Doak, I was beginning to think, had as many secrets as the rest of us – and he was better than most at keeping them.

I waited till he was out of sight, then started the car and headed down the Gloucester road. As the car picked up speed, I lowered the window by an inch, slipped the five pound note from my pocket, held it up to the gap and let the wind pluck it from my fingers. Suddenly, it seemed safer not to possess anything that connected me – however remotely – with the Caswells. Suddenly, all I wanted was to be back in London, where my lies and denials would sound convincing, even to me.

Wednesday 23 January 1924 (5 p.m.)
It was at twenty past four that a general hubbub in the court signified the return of the jury. I hurried to take my seat, surprised that they could have reached a decision in under two hours and vaguely resentful that they had done so. Sir Henry Curtis-Bennett looked of the same mind, shrugging his massive shoulders and raising his eyebrows at his opposite number. Consuela was already in the dock, seated and therefore barely visible. When Sir Henry moved across to speak to her, however, she rose and leaned out

337

across the rail. I thought I could detect a faint tremor in her hands, but perhaps it was merely that I expected to. She certainly responded calmly enough to Sir Henry's whispered remarks. If anything, he was the more agitated of the two.

As for the jury, they seemed indecently relaxed, smiling and confiding behind cupped hands. They could have been the members of some small-town committee about to debate the progress of fund-raising for the local war memorial. It was scarcely credible to me that they were about to pronounce on a life-or-death issue.

Mr Justice Stillingfleet entered and, when we had all sat down again, there came the first sign that matters were not about to proceed in the way I had assumed they would. The usher handed him a note covering a side and a half of foolscap. This he read at a deliberate pace, whilst total silence reigned. Then he said: 'The jury have sent me a note. You will want to read it before I comment.' 'You' evidently meant the opposing counsel, because the usher carried it to Talbot and Sir Henry in turn. The silence resumed during their perusals of the note, growing more tangible the longer it lasted. I did not look at Consuela. Somehow, I could not bear to. It was as if the only kindness I could show her at such an agonizing stage was to look elsewhere.

Then, at last, Mr Justice Stillingfleet put us out of our collective misery. The note, he explained, was a request for elucidation. The jury wanted to know whether, if somebody was killed as an accidental result of an attempt to kill somebody else, it was legitimate to find the person who had killed them guilty of manslaughter rather than murder. The bearing of this question on their verdict was at once obvious to me, but I was too busy listening to the judge's answer to consider whether it suggested they were inclined towards a particular conclusion.

Mr Justice Stillingfleet told them, with greater forbearance than the tone of his summing-up had led me to believe he possessed, that manslaughter could only apply where the 'accidental result' could neither have been foreseen nor averted, that is to say where the guilty party had not known of it and could not have prevented it. He did not think this argument could be sustained in relation to the case against Mrs Caswell. With that, he sent them back to their deliberations.

And he sent us back to our uneasy vigil here in the marbled hall, where there is ample opportunity – indeed, far too much of it – to ponder the significance of the jury's question. Does it mean they *were veering towards a guilty verdict, but were deterred by the consequences? Were some of the more squeamish members trying to find a compromise? If so, the judge's reply will have given them no comfort, for manslaughter, it seems, is not an option; they must face the issue squarely. And so must the prisoner awaiting their decision in a cell below us. What she will be thinking now I dare not try to imagine.*

The drive back to London was long and tiring. Darkness fell swiftly and the rain intensified. At High Wycombe, with only another thirty miles or so to go, I stopped for a drink and a sandwich. The Bell Inn was quiet but welcoming and, sitting by its roaring fire, I realized just how drained I was by the events of the previous twenty-four hours. I had half a mind, indeed, to ask if they had a room for the night.

Then, quite suddenly, my attention was seized by the name CASWELL blazoned in a newspaper headline. A man sitting at the bar who had come in after me was reading a London evening paper and on the front page, partially obscured by his fingers, were the words JURY OUT IN CASWELL MURDER TRIAL. I had realized the conclusion of Consuela's trial could not be far off, but, foolishly, had not supposed it could be quite so close at hand.

Shock instantly displaced fatigue. If the jury had already gone out when the paper went to print, they might well have returned by now and delivered their verdict. Consuela might be learning her fate even whilst I was toasting my toes in a Buckinghamshire inn. Leaving a half-full glass and most of a sandwich behind me, I started for the door, glancing at the clock behind the bar as I went. It was just on a quarter past seven.

Wednesday 23 January 1924 (7.15 p.m.)
Two and a half hours have passed since the jury were sent out for the second time. Excluding their brief reappearance in court, they have been considering their verdict for more than four hours now. The journalists are becoming fretful about catching their late editions, the policemen weary of so much shuffling to and fro when they could be home with their feet up, and the lawyers – well, there is as ever no way of telling what they are thinking. I heard somebody muttering a few moments ago about the possibilty of an overnight adjournment. How any of us – far less Consuela – would cope with that I dread to contemplate.

But it will not be necessary. Even as I write, the usher is signalling to us from the door of the court. The jury is back and this time, surely, it cannot be a false alarm. The hall is emptying rapidly as, all around me, people hurry to take their places. I must join them. Already, I notice, my hand is shaking and the creases on my palm are lined with sweat. Through that door, Justice awaits. What disguise, I wonder, will she be wearing?

It was on the bill-board of a news-stand at Oxford Circus that I saw the announcement I had dreaded. VERDICT IN CASWELL MURDER TRIAL. I stopped the car at once, jumped out and raced across the road. As I neared the news-stand, my feelings were a jumble of apprehension and relief. At last, now, I remember thinking, I would know.

Late editions of the *Evening Standard* were piled high and selling fast. I snatched one up, scanned the front page in vain, then saw, in the stop-press column:

> CASWELL MURDER TRIAL VERDICT
> Consuela Caswell convicted of murder and attempted murder at Old Bailey this evening after nine-day trial. Jury took nearly five hours to arrive at verdict. Judge sentenced Mrs Caswell to hang.

And so it was over. The pretence, that is. My pretence that it would never come to this, that they would never find her guilty, never decree she had to die. But now they had. And, closing round me in the damp London night, there was the realization that a new and still more awful phase had opened in the wake of their decision. Even as I stood there, staring at the lines of print as if the words could be forced to re-arrange themselves on the page, Consuela's meagre allowance of time – her ration of life itself – had begun to expire.

Wednesday 23 January 1924 (8.15 p.m.)
I cannot believe the speed with which it was done. An hour ago, it was still possible to cling to the notion that the jury would acquit Consuela. Now such thoughts belong in the lumber-room of what might have been, because now we know for certain. And what does such knowledge bequeath us? An empty building, a prison van bound for Holloway, a pen moving on a page.
I shall set this down before I am too weary to make the effort. The court was full, despite the lateness of the hour, but there was a

chill in the air, perhaps because it had been so long unoccupied, perhaps . . . for some other reason. Consuela was not in the dock when I entered and Sir Henry Curtis-Bennett was nowhere to be seen. He arrived – short of breath and somewhat flustered – only a few seconds before the judge himself. I had only a minute or so to scan the jury's faces. They looked more sombre – more aware of the gravity of their task – than during their earlier reappearance. Then my attention was diverted elsewhere.

Mr Justice Stillingfleet stared pointedly at the dock, as if irritated to find it empty. But he was not kept waiting long. Consuela entered beside a wardress. She moved to the rail, grasped it and, to my surprise, looked slowly round the court with a slight frown – almost of puzzlement – on her face. Of one thing I was certain. In that moment she was not afraid. She was better prepared for what would follow than most of us.

The Clerk of Arraigns addressed the foreman of the jury, asking him if they had agreed upon their verdict.

'We have,' he earnestly replied.

'How say you on Count 1?'

'Guilty.'

(For a fraction of a second I became confused about which count was which. Then, before my confusion was resolved, it ceased to matter.)

'And on Count 2?'

'Guilty.'

There were gasps, I think, perhaps a stifled sob, though I cannot be sure. I do not know if Consuela reacted in any way, because I kept my eyes trained on the foreman of the jury, willing him to add something – a recommendation of mercy, a plea for compassion. But all he did was sit slowly down.

The Clerk of Arraigns turned towards the dock and said: 'Consuela Evelina Caswell, you stand convicted of the murder of Rosemary Victoria Caswell and the attempted murder of Victor George Caswell. Have you anything to say before sentence is passed upon you?'

My gaze, and that of every man and woman in the court, focused now on the prisoner standing slim and erect in the dock. The frown had left her face. In its place was a strange and placid melancholy. She glanced once at the jury, then looked straight at the judge. 'Nothing,' she replied in a steady voice.

The chaplain bobbed up behind the bench and fumbled for a moment at the judge's side. When he retreated, I saw that he had

341

placed the black cap on Mr Justice Stillingfleet's head. 'Prisoner at the bar—' The judge's tone was hard now and peremptory. I wondered if this was deliberate, whether it was as much a part of the ritual as the cap and the nameless mode of address. 'You have been found guilty of the charges laid against you after a full and fair trial, during which you were most ably defended. I concur wholeheartedly with the jury's verdict. To plot the murder of your husband was bad enough, even if you did genuinely believe he had been unfaithful to you. But to allow your plot to claim a wholly innocent victim – a young girl on the brink of womanhood, whom you had known most of her life – renders your offence unforgivable. I therefore have no hesitation in passing upon you the only sentence which the law allows.'

Mr Justice Stillingfleet had been staring at Consuela as he spoke. Now he looked down at a sheet of paper before him and began to read the prescribed words with a sort of mechanical reverence that made me think, for a crazy moment, that it was a prayer we should all recite under our breath. 'This court doth ordain that you be taken hence to the place from whence you came; that you be taken thence to a place of lawful execution; that you be there hanged by the neck until you are dead; and that you be afterwards buried within the precincts of the prison in which you shall last have been confined. And may the Lord have mercy upon your soul.'

I suddenly noticed that the lady in the pink toque was crying. Had she expected to? I wondered. Had she brought a spare handkerchief with this precise contingency in mind? 'Amen,' murmured the chaplain. There were tears in my eyes too. Fool that I am, I felt a manly obligation to pretend they were not there. When I looked up at the judge, expecting him to add something to his pronouncement, the grey of his wig and the scarlet of his robe were blurred and expanded like water-colours running in the rain.

But the judge did not speak. Instead, the Clerk of the Court barked out: 'Have you anything to say in stay of execution?'

Later, leaving the court behind two onlookers more knowledgeable than me, I discovered from their conversation that this question supplies condemned women with an opportunity to disclose that they are pregnant. If they are, they cannot be hanged. At the time, it seemed a cruel and pointless repetition of an earlier question. For answer, Consuela merely shook her head.

Mr Justice Stillingfleet cleared his throat and said in a flat dismissive tone: 'Take her down.' He was eager to be on now, to be finished and away.

The wardress stepped forward and Consuela turned towards her. Then, with one hand still resting on the rail of the dock, she paused, looked slowly round the court and said something in Portuguese that sounded like 'Desculpo senhores nome Deus'. Insofar as it was addressed to any of us, it was addressed to all of us, but, from the silence that followed, I do not think anybody present – apart from Consuela herself – knew what it meant. She inclined her head faintly to Sir Henry, then walked past the wardress and vanished from sight.

With Consuela gone, all was confusion and anti-climax. Mr Justice Stillingfleet, now capless, thanked the jurors and excused them from further service, specifying a number of years – I cannot remember how many. Then, with a shuffling of papers and a gathering of robes, he was on his feet and hurrying out through the door behind the bench, leaving the rest of us to move, in hesitant disorder, towards the exit like a theatre audience filing out of an auditorium, reluctant to praise or decry what they have seen for fear that their companions will disagree.

Not that, in this case, it would have mattered. Rex versus Caswell *is over. Justice has been done. I was among those who saw it done. That, I think, is what makes it so hard to accept. I have stared Justice in the face today and I have not liked what I have seen. I wish to God I had never looked.*

''Ere, mate,' snapped the news-vendor, breaking into my thoughts, 'are you buyin' or jus' gawpin'? This ain't a bleedin' public library, y'know.'

'What? Oh, sorry. Here—' I handed him a penny and turned away, leaving the newspaper, absurdly enough, where it lay.

Sentenced to hang. As I blundered across the road, those words remained before me, as if I were still staring at them, printed on a page. *Sentenced to hang.* The worst words, it seemed to me then, that I could ever read or hear. But I was wrong, as I was to discover later, when Imry told me what Consuela had said as she left the court. *Eu desculpo os senhores, em nome de Deus'.* Then I knew what was truly worst of all. She had forgiven them, in the name of God. But they had not understood.

CHAPTER

EIGHTEEN

The resources of the human soul are as formidable as they are pitiful. The despair that closed about me when I learned that Consuela had been condemned to death was all-encompassing. Yet it was also short-lived. By the following day, I had carved from it something approximating to hope. Just as I had been unable to believe they would find her guilty, so, now they had, I refused to accept that they really meant to hang her. Her conviction would be quashed on appeal. Failing that, the sentence would be commuted. Somehow, by one means or another, her life would be spared.

God knows, there was little rational basis for such hope. The press echoed the judge's depiction of Consuela as a cold-hearted murderess. There was no barrage of letters to the editor demanding mercy or denouncing capital punishment, no petitions, no marches, no questions in the House. The universal silence that greeted the sentence could only logically be interpreted as general approval of it. Yet I succeeded in resisting such an interpretation. Nor was I alone in doing so. Sir Henry Curtis-Bennett was confident that three appeal judges would see reason where twelve impressionable jurors had not. And Consuela, so he assured me, shared his optimism.

What Consuela really thought was, of course, unknown to me. Secretly, I suspected Imry was right when he said that she had *expected* to be found guilty, that she had begun her preparations for this ordeal from the moment of her arrest and was therefore better equipped to endure it than those of us who had preferred to believe she would never have to. Partly because I feared she might force me to face the truth in this regard, I was actually grateful now for her refusal to see me. Not to have to look her in the eyes, not to have to speak to her across a prison cell, made it easier to sustain the pretence to which I had succumbed: the pretence, that is, that she would not hang.

Imry, by contrast, entertained no such illusions. He had experienced the trial at first hand. He had felt the weight of legal process bearing down upon her. He had sensed what the outcome would be. And now, helpless to intervene, he could only await the slow and hideous pleasure of the law.

The effect of Consuela's conviction on Imry was, in some ways, more profound than on me. It revived in him the depression and disgust with which he had returned from the war. And my confession of the part I had played in Rodrigo's death seemed only to exacerbate the condition. I have never known him so bitter as in the days immediately following the end of the trial. Normally, at difficult times, it was *he* who had tried to lift *my* spirits. Now it was the other way round – and I had none of his aptitude for the task. In the circumstances, it should have been no surprise when he was struck down by bronchitis. His doctor blamed two weeks coming and going in the chills and smogs of a London winter. But whether this or his dejected state of mind was the cause hardly mattered: I was responsible either way. All I could do to salve my conscience was assist his housekeeper with the fetching and carrying while he was laid up at Sunnylea, using his health as an excuse for saying as little to him as possible about Consuela.

Not that there was, in all honesty, much I could have said even if I had wanted to. Consuela's appeal was due to be heard on 7 February. Until then, a deliberate suspension of thought formed the only viable basis for day-to-day existence. Hope is a fragile commodity. It cannot bear too much analysis.

Silence was also the only way I could hold at bay the guilt I felt about Rodrigo. According to Windrush, news of his death had distressed Consuela far more than the possibility of her own. She could not understand why he should have broken into Clouds Frome. Nor could she believe the explanation given by Victor at the inquest a week later. What she deduced from police evidence that Rodrigo had spent two nights at the Green Man, Fownhope, with an unidentified companion I did not dare to ask. The coroner expressed bafflement both about this and Rodrigo's intentions, but Victor's evidence he seemed happy to accept.

Victor's version of events was that he had been woken in the small hours by the sound of an intruder. He had roused Miss Roebuck and asked her to telephone the police whilst he went to investigate, taking the shot-gun with him for his own protection. He had found the intruder in a dressing-room and had fired in self-defence when the man lunged at him with a knife. He had only recognized him when he lay dead on the floor. Miss Roebuck explained that she had reached the scene of the shooting just in time to see it take place and the circumstances were exactly as Victor had described them: he had had no choice but to fire.

The police were not disposed to quibble with any of this. The knife they had found on Rodrigo's body had been used to kill Victor's guard-dog. There were traces of canine blood still on its blade. A man capable of despatching a mastiff in such fashion was, they implied, also capable of attacking its owner. He had entered the house through an unfastened first-floor window, reaching it with the use of a ladder stolen from a nearby farm. His motive, as far as they were concerned, was a total mystery. (Clearly the safe had been locked and hidden behind the mirror by the time of their arrival, though, even if it had not been, I doubt they would have been any the wiser.)

The only direct reference made to Consuela at the inquest was when the coroner conjectured that Rodrigo might have been seeking some misguided form of revenge on her behalf. He did not press the point, however, because of the inconvenient fact that the break-in had occurred *before* her conviction. In the end, he contented himself with the observation that Rodrigo's intentions had died with him and could never now be known. He then offered Victor his sympathy '*for this additional unpleasantness at an already trying time*' and urged the jury to return a verdict of justifiable homicide, which they did in short and obliging order. Victor's exoneration was complete.

From Hermione I heard not a word. She too, it seemed, had taken refuge in silence, the better to bear our mutual helplessness. How Jacinta had reacted to events I could therefore only guess. I hoped she would pin her faith in my assurances that, somehow, we would save her mother. I, after all, was only doing the same. The worthlessness of those assurances I thrust into the deepest recesses of my thoughts, where they could be, if not forgotten, at least ignored. The future had become a black and unimaginable pit. As the brink drew ever nearer, I could only look away the more.

It was, I recall, the day after the newspapers carried reports of the inquest in Hereford that I was telephoned by Clive Thornton and invited to have lunch with him. His tone of voice suggested that we were old chums who had not seen each other for far too long. It was, of course, clear to me that Angela's divorce action was what he wanted to discuss. If the subject had seemed more important to me than it did – which was not at all – I would probably have refused. As it was, it seemed easier to agree.

We met at Simpson's-in-the-Strand. Even before Clive had come to the point – halfway through the soup – I had remembered every one of the reasons why I loathed him. Money, good looks and war-time heroics had transformed his stupidity into supreme confidence, his oafishness into braying arrogance. To listen to him was to wonder once more why some working-class private of socialist leanings had not put a bullet through his brain one day in France.

'Divorce can be a messy business for all concerned. That's why I thought we should have a word. To the wise, so to speak.'

'I can't see how it involves you.'

'Angie's peace of mind, old man. Always at the top of my agenda. You know that.'

'She asked you to speak to me, did she?'

'Good God, no. Strictly my idea. Minc and Pater's, anyway. Fact is, we think you may not be seeing this thing quite straight.'

'In what way?'

'Well, I gather you told Angie – hinted, that is – that you might drag poor old Turnbull's name into the case.'

'What if I did? It would be all she and he deserved.'

'Look, old man. I know my big sister's no angel. She never has been. Marriage to her can't have been a bed of roses. Faults on both sides, I dare say. That's taken as read.'

'Not by the courts.'

'Exactly. You've hit the nail on the head. *Not by the courts.* Cruelty's the problem, don't you think? Tricky word altogether. Leaves a nasty taste in the mouth. So, why put it there in the first place, eh?'

'What precisely do you mean?'

Removal of the soup bowls imposed a brief silence. Then he

347

resumed, in a more confidential tone. 'Cards on the table, old man. None of us wants a contested action, do we? A whole lot of dirty linen flapping in the breeze. Not on. Simply not on. So, what I suggest is this. Give Angie her divorce – but discreetly. Undefended, on grounds of your adultery, if you'll pardon the expression. You know what I mean, I'm sure. A pre-arranged weekend in Eastbourne. Your solicitor ought to be able to find a suitable girl. It's much the most painless method. Over and done with before you know it. Then plain sailing for one and all.' He beamed encouragingly.

'You want me to take the blame?'

'Only in the technical sense. Everyone will know it's an amicable split. Happens all the time. Whereas, if cruelty's cited . . . and accusations start flying thick and fast . . .'

The roast wagon hove to at that moment and Clive broke off to supervise the carving of his beef. When his plate had been piled high and I had been served with far more duck than I wanted, he speared a Yorkshire pudding with his fork, nibbled at it speculatively, then said:

'What do you think, old man?'

'I think I'd like to know what I have to gain from such an arrangement.'

'That's easy. Just look at what you'd lose by taking the other route. Reputation and money. Most of one and a great deal of the other.'

'How does money come into it?'

'Simple. If you . . . co-operated . . . Angie wouldn't ask for any maintenance.'

'I see. And she's prepared to be this generous just in order to avoid the scandal of a contested case?'

'Exactly.' The Yorkshire pudding having been devoured, a gravy-soaked roast potato took its place on the prongs of Clive's fork. 'Fairer all round, don't you agree?'

'It might seem so – if I thought my defence wasn't adequate.'

Clive paused in mid-chew and stared at me. 'You'll lose for certain. And be pauperized into the bargain.' He grinned. 'So, can I tell the dear girl you'll play ball?'

I stared back at him, wondering if he could be made to understand that I no longer cared either way. What did reputation and money matter to me now? How would they enable me to save Consuela where every other device had failed? All I wanted of the Thorntons was to be left alone. For that reason and for no other, I was bound to accept their offer. 'I suppose you can,' I said at last.

'Excellent, excellent. Felt sure you'd see reason. It'll be a load off Angie's mind.'

'And how is Ang— How is my wife?'

'Been distinctly mopish lately, don't mind admitting.' The first slice of horse-radish-smeared beef slipped onto Clive's tongue. 'Matter of fact, Celia and I thought we'd take her with us when we go away next week. Jolly her up a bit, don't you know?'

'Where are you going?'

'Didn't I say? Cap Ferrat. Turnbull's villa. He's been spying out possible sites for Thornton Hotels and Pater wants me to give them the once-over. There are some exciting possibilities down there, you know.'

How neat, how timely, how very convenient. My agreement to supply the evidence for a divorce meant Angela could pursue her dalliance with Turnbull without fear that I might use it against her. I smiled at the irony of it all, unable to summon even an atom of resentment.

'Something amusing you, old man?'

'Your family, Clive, that's all.'

He frowned. 'Not sure I take your meaning.'

'It doesn't matter.' I drained my wine-glass. 'None of it matters anymore.'

The two weeks between the end of the trial and the hearing of the appeal had seemed, at their outset, unbearably long. As they drew to a close, however, their brevity was suddenly borne in upon me. It had been sufficient, for a while, to look ahead to 7 February with blind optimism. Now, as the date approached, the scales began to fall from my eyes. Why should three old men grown sere and crabbed in the service of the law take mercy on one among the countless many who came before them? And, if they did not, what hope would there be left then to cling to?

Consuela had elected not to attend the appeal. She would, after all, have no occasion to address the court, for no witnesses were to be heard. Sir Henry would merely present her case as cogently as he could, basing his argument on the lack of direct evidence against her. His contention was to be that the judge had misled the jury into believing that they were required to decide who had murdered Rosemary Caswell rather than whether Consuela had been proved to have done so and that the doubts raised about the authenticity of the anonymous letters were sufficient to justify his client's acquittal. Precedents were to be explored, nuances of the judge's summing-up examined. The law in its purest sense was to be tested.

Windrush's information was that the Caswell family would absent themselves *en masse*. I was also reluctant to attend, for reasons I did not care to examine closely. What they amounted to, I suppose, was a desire to stave off until the last possible moment my confrontation with Consuela's destiny. For as long as I was not party to events at the Royal Courts of Justice, I could pretend that they were moving in her favour.

The day dawned bright and absurdly mild. London was in the fawning grip of a false spring, snowdrops bursting out amidst the greenery of Hyde Park. I remember thinking, as I made my way across its north-east corner that morning: can Consuela see any flowers from her cell at Holloway; can she scent spring – or any form of hope – in the air?

At Frederick's Place Kevin had learned from the *Sketch* that the appeal would be heard that day, but I cut his curiosity short with heavy-handed indifference. Reg and Giles knew better than to mention the subject. Reg did not understand what it meant to me, but had gleaned enough to suspect that it meant something. As for Giles, he was still chastened by the narrowness with which he had escaped dismissal in December. What he had concluded from reports of Rodrigo's death he was too cautious to let slip.

I had a late morning appointment with a client in Beckenham for which, in many ways, I was grateful, though my distracted state of mind ensured that he subsequently looked elsewhere for an architect. I reached Victoria station again in mid-afternoon and began walking back towards the office, knowing that my route would take me past the Appeal Courts in the Strand, knowing and wondering whether, when it came to the point, I would halt and enter or simply keep on walking. I could have hailed a taxi and named my destination there and then, but the need to know and the fear of knowing were perfectly balanced as I passed Buckingham Palace and strode along the Mall. In Trafalgar Square, the fountains were playing, the pigeons being fed: all was intact and normal beneath a perversely benign blue sky.

Then the Strand, straight and pitiless, led me, almost before I was aware of it, to the Portland stone turrets of the Royal Courts of Justice: deathly white in the slanting sun, harsh, precise, vast and intricate. This building was the death of its architect, I recalled – poor old Street, whose work till then I had scorned. He had worn himself into an early grave planning the halls and corridors and staircases concealed behind its grand façade. And now, for the first time, I understood the metaphor he had created. The law, housed there in all its convoluted majesty, was too much for one man to master.

I entered. The Great Hall, which I had seen before only in photographs, was high and echoing, vaulted like the nave of a cathedral. As I traversed it, snatches of speech and glimpses of robed figures reached me through the arched stairs-feet on either side. Practitioners of the law were everywhere about me, around and above, murmurous and out of reach, like mice, it suddenly struck me, scratching and scurrying within the walls of a house.

I moved to the boards set up in the centre of the hall, where the day's cases were listed court by court, and scanned the sheets in search of Consuela's name. Never before had I imagined that one day could feature so much litigation, so much argument, so much opposition. And somewhere, lost amidst the welter of suit and counter-suit, *Rex versus Caswell* was approaching its conclusion. I came to the end of the row without having found it and turned to check the other side. As I did so, I glanced towards the stairs at the far end of the hall. And there, in a group of descending figures, I recognized Windrush and Sir Henry.

There were five of them in all, robed and wigged but for Windrush. They were walking fast, conferring as they went. Their faces were grave and intent. If I had not stepped into their path, I do not think they would even have seen me.

'Sir Henry!'

He pulled up, as did the others. For a second, there was silence. That and their troubled expressions should have told me what to expect.

'Is the case over?'

Sir Henry nodded. 'It is, Staddon, yes.'

'Adjourned, you mean?'

'No. Their Lordships delivered their verdict just a few minutes ago.'

'And?' He was avoiding my gaze now, staring down at his feet, running one hand around his double-chin. Windrush too was looking elsewhere. What I had dreaded but foreseen was there, palpable in their collective embarrassment. 'The appeal was dismissed, wasn't it?'

351

Sir Henry sighed. 'Out of hand, I fear.'

'Then . . . what . . .'

He roused himself. 'Windrush and I must proceed at once to Holloway, Staddon. I trust you appreciate the need to inform Mrs Caswell without delay.' He glanced at one of his companions. 'Mr Browne, be so good as to furnish Mr Staddon with details of the judgement. We *must* be on our way.'

And so it came about that the Appeal Court's pronouncement on Consuela's fate was explained to me by a young man named Browne in a quiet corner of the George public house, on the other side of the Strand, just after it had opened for business that evening. He drank lemonade shandy, I remember, and I drank whisky. He was nervous, though I could not understand why. Perhaps he felt as a junior doctor might when breaking the news of a fatal disease to a relative of his patient. What he had to say was both logical and inevitable, but was tinged with mortality, and he had never had to say it before. He will become accustomed to such painful duties as his career proceeds. But his audience never will.

'I am sorry to say, Mr Staddon, that their Lordships refused to entertain any of Sir Henry's arguments. They did not merely endorse the judge's handling of the trial, they applauded it. If anything, their remarks were more severe than Mr Justice Stillingfleet's.'

'What about the doubts concerning the authenticity of the letters?'

'They did not appear to think there were any doubts. They even went so far as to accuse Sir Henry of sophistry. It made him very angry, although of course he did not let them see that it had.'

'There were no redeeming features?'

'None. Between you and me—' He leaned towards me and lowered his voice. 'Sometimes, the bench likes to take down prominent barristers a peg or two. Those they consider are winning too glowing a reputation. I fear today may have been Sir Henry's turn. The Lord Chief Justice was in . . . censorious mood.'

'Sir Henry's *turn*? The Lord Chief Justice's *mood*? Are you saying Con— Are you saying Mrs Caswell's life depends on such things?'

Browne coloured and took a draught of his shandy. My outrage had disconcerted him. He was, after all, only doing his best to

352

make me understand what had happened. The vagaries of the judicial system were not his responsibility.

'I'm sorry,' I said in a more measured tone. 'Forget what I just asked. Simply tell me this. What's to be done now?'

Browne looked relieved to be back on uncontroversial ground. 'Well, to some extent that is up to Mrs Caswell. She may ask Sir Henry to apply to the Attorney-General for leave to appeal to the House of Lords. I am bound to say, however, that such leave is highly unlikely to be granted.'

'Why?'

'Because it can only be granted on the grounds that an issue of exceptional public importance is involved.'

'Isn't a miscarriage of justice exceptionally important?'

Browne grimaced. 'I am certain the Attorney-General will not feel there has been one.'

'Then . . . what else?'

'Sir Henry will undoubtedly advise Mrs Caswell to petition the Home Secretary for mercy. That is her only recourse.'

'By *recourse* you mean *hope*?'

'Well, yes. Unless the Home Secretary commutes the death sentence passed on Mrs Caswell, it will have to be carried out. Now her appeal has failed, only a political decision can save her.'

'A *political* decision?'

'I mean a decision taken by politicians but based on legal advice. The new administration may be less committed to capital punishment than the old. On the other hand, they may be anxious to show that they are not "soft" on crime. Labour are, I must confess, an unknown quantity where law and order are concerned.' He smiled uneasily. 'This is something of a test case for them.'

Judges settling scores and politicians making points. Where, I wondered, in this jungle of mean sentiments and doubtful motives, was the delicate flower of mercy likely to bloom? 'If the Home Secretary chooses not to intervene,' I said slowly, 'when . . . that is, how soon . . .'

'There is a fixed formula in such matters. At least three Sundays must elapse between conviction and execution.'

'Three? Is that all?'

'The shorter the wait, the easier it is for all parties. At least, so goes the theory. Of course, the lodging of an appeal caused some delay. It is more likely to be four Sundays now than three, perhaps as many as five.'

353

'Five? You call five *many*?'

Once more, he seemed surprised by how ghastly his answers could sound to those who received them. 'I am sorry, Mr Staddon, really I am. I am merely placing the facts before you, as Sir Henry directed me to. If the sentence is carried out, it will probably be before the end of this month.'

'And will it be carried out?'

'I do not know. None of us knows at this stage.'

'But what do you think?'

He deliberated for a moment, raised his glass as if to drink, then put it down again and said: 'I think you should prepare yourself for the worst.'

The worst. How could I prepare myself to face what I never thought I would have to? Consuela's death, not by accident or disease, not by a random mischance of nature, but at the hands of the law, was now decreed, fixed, chartered and determined. It was a settled event towards which we were all inexorably moving. Struggle or protest as I pleased, flee or turn away, I was bound to meet it, out there in the future, just a little way off, a dot on a distant horizon that had grown black and vast and become my destination.

After I left the George that evening, I crossed to the church of St Clement Danes on its island in the Strand. Inside, it was as silent and peaceful as a sanctified tomb. I knelt before the altar and, for the first time since Edward's death, prayed to God for intercession.

A telephone call next morning from Sir Henry Curtis-Bennett's clerk told me that he and Windrush would be pleased to meet me at his chambers at six o'clock that evening. I pressed the clerk for news, but he claimed to have none. From that I took what comfort I could. The newspapers had reported the outcome of the appeal as a foregone conclusion. They seemed neither triumphant nor regretful, merely content to let the law take its course.

Plowden Buildings was largely deserted when I arrived. Sir Henry received me with sombre politeness, his flustered brusqueness of the day before replaced by a weary despondency. Windrush sat in a shadowy corner and seemed reluctant to leave it. He barely nodded as I entered. Before a word was spoken, it was clear to me that none they meant to speak would give me any comfort.

354

'Young Browne apprised you of the situation, I trust,' began Sir Henry.

'Yes. He spoke of a possible appeal to the House of Lords.'

Sir Henry shook his head. 'Alas, the Attorney-General has refused to hear of it.'

'Then clemency is the only hope?'

'Indeed. The Home Secretary is a humane and religious man – a devout Wesleyan, I believe. He may not wish to commence his term of office with the execution of a woman.'

'But there are difficulties,' put in Windrush.

'What are they?'

Sir Henry sighed. 'Firstly, Mrs Caswell's insistence that she is innocent. We believe her, of course, but we are in the minority. Those who disbelieve her would be better disposed to show her mercy if, in return, she exhibited some degree of remorse.'

'How can she be expected to show remorse for something she hasn't done?'

'That is one of the difficulties,' said Windrush. 'Though not the gravest.'

'Mr Henderson has only been Home Secretary for a couple of weeks,' explained Sir Henry. 'He's not likely to feel sufficiently sure of himself yet to overrule his civil servants. Moreover, as you may have read in the papers, he's badly in need of a constituency. A Cabinet minister who has no seat in the House of Commons is something of a lame duck.'

'He's on the trail of one now,' said Windrush. 'Dan Irving, the Labour member for Burnley, died recently. Henderson's up there trying to make sure he wins the by-election. It's to be held on the twenty-eighth of this month. Until then he won't want to rock any boats. Of that you can be certain.'

'And I know his Under-Secretary of old,' said Sir Henry. 'Sir John Anderson is a strict and inflexible man. He won't even think of recommending clemency.'

'Then . . . what you're saying is . . .'

'They've fixed a date, Staddon,' said Windrush.

'When?'

'Thursday the twenty-first. One week before the Burnley by-election. Thirteen days from now. At nine o'clock that morning, the sentence of the court will be carried out.'

I stared at him dumbly for a moment, then looked at Sir Henry. 'She . . . Consuela knows?'

'The prison governor informed her last night.'

355

'How . . . Have you seen her since?'

'I was present at the time, Staddon. So was Windrush. She took it with the composure she has displayed throughout this sorry affair. She is . . . a remarkable woman.'

'But . . . What can we do?'

'Very little. We shall plead the case for clemency with all the eloquence at our command. And Mrs Caswell's friends should be urged to write to the Home Secretary supporting our plea. Beyond that, I have nothing to suggest.'

'Nothing?'

'The press are against her,' put in Windrush. 'Foreign, Catholic and guilty – as they see it. It's no good hoping for a campaign in that quarter.'

'Even if every editor in Fleet Street were on our side,' said Sir Henry, 'I doubt they could achieve anything. Sir John does not like to be pushed. It merely hardens his heart. And his legal advisers have made it clear to me that they see no grounds for clemency.'

I looked from one to the other of them. 'You believe this hanging will take place, don't you?' In the silence that followed, their answer was delivered.

Suddenly, Sir Henry cleared his throat and rose from his chair. 'I must have a word with my clerk before he goes home. Excuse me, gentlemen.' With that, he bustled from the room, leaving Windrush and me staring at each other across a carpeted waste of shadows.

'She's quite resigned to it,' Windrush said after a moment. 'I believe she has been ever since she was charged. Unlike we cynical Englishmen' – he smiled faintly – 'she never expected to be spared on account of her innocence.'

I said nothing. There seemed then as little to say as there was to do. Beyond the exhaustion of our last resource lay only a wilderness of despair.

'She asked me to tell you of the arrangements she has made for Jacinta. Her daughter's future has been her principal concern of late. She has been anxious to ensure that the girl does not remain with her father. Some weeks ago, I submitted a request to Caswell's solicitor on her behalf. To my surprise, it's been granted. Caswell has agreed to let Jacinta be adopted by her maternal uncle, Senhor Francisco Manchaca de Pombalho, a coffee merchant in Rio de Janeiro. The fellow's quite wealthy, I believe – though not as wealthy as Caswell. Be that as it may, a new life in a distant country seems altogether the kindest provision to make for the girl. She's young enough to put this . . . horror . . . behind her, don't you think?' He waited for me to respond. Then, when I did not, he continued: 'We've had a cable from Brazil. Jacinta's uncle is on his way. He's bringing his wife with him. They'll take Jacinta into their custody as soon as they arrive. Three return passages to Brazil have been booked aboard a steamer due to leave Liverpool on the twenty-second, the day after . . .'

We have no words, I thought as he broke off – no trite and conventional phrases – to cater for situations such as this. Whether Windrush understood why Consuela wanted me to know what was to become of Jacinta – whether I understood myself – seemed now a matter of no significance whatever. 'I'd like to see her,' I said, as expressionlessly as I could contrive.

Windrush raised his hand and began massaging his brow with the tips of two fingers, as if to relieve a headache. 'I'd hoped to avoid telling you this, Staddon. The fact is that she's quite emphatic about refusing to see you. She's asked me to make that abundantly clear.'

So, the embargo was to remain in force. The gulf I had opened between us thirteen years before was not be closed even in death.

'I'm sorry, Staddon.'

'So am I. But sorrow doesn't help, does it?'

'No.'

'I wish . . .' But wishes, like hopes and prayers and every unavailing effort, were useless now, worn out and wasted on ears that would not listen and minds that would not bend. Darkness, beyond the window, between our words, within our minds, was rushing and rising around our future. Darkness. And the worst – that could never be prepared for. I rose, my wish unspoken, and left, stumbling in silent confusion out into the night.

CHAPTER

NINETEEN

Once, in the foolishness of my youth, I took part in a séance. It was during my first year at Oxford, in the rooms of a student with whom I shared a landing. Late at night, with lexicon cards and an upturned glass, seven of us, drunk, frightened and trying not to show it, embarked on a clumsy and sniggering attempt to communicate with the dead. It worked. At all events, it seemed to. The glass moved and spelt out answers to our questions. Later, Parkhouse claimed he had pushed it, which we were all happy, not to say eager, to accept. What each of us truly believed is another matter. In my case, I am no surer now than I was then. At first, it was harmless fun. The month of one fellow's birth. The maiden name of another chap's mother. On such a light-hearted level it would doubtless have remained had one of our number not insisted on asking to be told the year in which he would die. At that, the glass ceased to move, the spirit (if it was a spirit) declined to answer and the séance dissolved amidst suddenly humourless recriminations.

Why, I have often wondered since, did I ask such a question? What possessed me to do it? For who – when it came to the point – would ever really want to know such a thing? Uncertainty is what renders mortality bearable. Death is a caller whose visit is only tolerable because it is unexpected. And yet, for a crazy instant, I had tried to discover when that visit would occur. How would it have felt to be told? What would it have seemed like to know? Thank God I never found out.

But Consuela found out. She, who did not ask the question, was given the answer. Nine o'clock on the morning of Thursday 21 February 1924: the time and date of her execution. The condemned prisoner's unique privilege is foreknowledge of the moment of death.

I spent the weekend following my meeting with Windrush and Sir Henry at Sunnylea, where Imry was now on the mend. We shared every stray thought our despair inspired and found in the process some scant form of consolation. One such thought, bursting unbidden into my mind, recalled that madcap séance of more than twenty years ago and posed another question to which I did not want to know the answer. Was Consuela's death to be the reward for my impudence on that long-ago occasion? Was it her fate I had sealed by tempting mine?

One meagre blessing of this time was the end it brought to secrets between Imry and me. I told him not merely how Rodrigo had died but of the counterfeit money I had found in Victor's safe. I revealed the fatal reward Malahide's attempts at blackmail had brought him and the fact that the letter he had sold me was a fake. I confessed every shameful detail of my deception of Consuela all those years ago. I recalled my futile efforts to help Doak and thereby appease my conscience. I even admitted how I had gone about ensuring Imry received none of the credit for the Hotel Thornton.

But no amount of honesty could alter the position in which we found ourselves. Nor could anything it lay in our power to do halt or prolong the expiring ration of days left to Consuela. We would write to the Home Secretary imploring him to let her live. We would write to the Attorney-General, the Lord Chancellor, the Prime Minister, the King himself. But we did not expect – we scarcely even hoped – that any of them would respond. Their minds were made up, set firm in the concrete of their absolute refusal to believe that the law could be mistaken. We who were sure that in this case it was could do no more than stand together and bear witness.

Thursday 14 February. St Valentine's Day. The first day of what the law had decided was to be the last week in the life of Consuela Caswell. The false spring had faded and a cold east wind was blowing, bringing snow to the streets of London. I was on a tube train, halfway between Chancery Lane and St Paul's, when the hands of my watch showed nine o'clock and the same hour, one week ahead, seemed to toll within my head. Time, measured in ever smaller and more agonizing fractions, overshadowed all thought and action. According to Sir Henry, a reprieve – if there was to be one – would come before the weekend. If it did not, even the slenderest hope would cease to be sustainable.

At Frederick's Place, Doris was blushing and giggling over a Valentine she had received from her fiancé, whilst Kevin was lamenting the recent form of Chelsea, the football club he insisted on supporting. They might as well have been speaking a foreign language – or inhabiting a different country – for all the affinity I felt with their trivial preoccupations.

I retreated to the sanctuary of my office, closed the door and sat down at my desk. Then I leaned forward, lifted the small plate numbered 13 from the desk-top calendar, turned it round to show 14 and dropped it back into its slot, calculating as I did so that I would perform the same action just five more times before to do so would seem pointless, before all counting and calculation would be ended by the springing of a trap-door bolt in another part of this city I shared with thousands like Doris and Kevin – but with only one Consuela.

A pile of correspondence awaited my attention, but I gave it none. Instead, I stared at the telephone and wondered if it was too early to call Windrush for news. (He had been accommodated at Sir Henry's chambers since the failure of the appeal.) When I looked at the clock and found that it was not yet half past nine, I decided any such call would be premature. I rose, took off my hat and coat, hung them up and paused at the window to light a cigarette.

A stocky middle-aged man in mackintosh and homburg entered the place from Old Jewry as I gazed out and began walking down our side. I did not recognize him and assumed he was bound for the merchant bank or Mercer's Hall. It was a mild surprise therefore when he turned in at our door. But it was nothing less than a shock when a couple of minutes later, Reg came in to announce that he was Detective Chief Inspector Wright of Scotland Yard and that he wanted to see me.

He had a round, somewhat rumpled face, with a large nose and a ready grin. All in all, he looked more like an indulgent sweet-shop owner than a sharp-witted policeman, an impression compounded by the effusiveness with which he thanked me when I helped him off with his mackintosh, offered him a chair and ordered some coffee. But his manner made me suspicious. I could not help thinking it was intended to plant in my mind an unjustified sense of superiority.

'As I expect you're aware, sir, I'm the officer in charge of the Caswell murder case.'

I was right, it seemed, to be suspicious. His opening remark left me uncertain whether to admit or deny a close knowledge of the case. I chose to prevaricate. 'I rather thought enquiries in that regard were over, Chief Inspector, following the recent trial.'

'Indeed, sir. But there are some rather puzzling loose ends. You are, I believe, a friend of Mrs Caswell?'

'What makes you think that?'

'The list of those who've written to the Home Secretary urging him to commute Mrs Caswell's sentence isn't a long one, sir. Your name's on it. As is your partner's, Mr Renshaw.'

'You've come here because of letters we've written to the Home Secretary?'

'Good Lord no, sir.' He broke off – a smile fixed on his lips – as Doris entered, delivered the coffee and left again. Then he resumed. 'The police don't interfere with a citizen's right to petition his elected representatives. Perish the very thought.' He dipped his digestive biscuit in his coffee and bit off the soggy portion.

'Then why are you here?' I tried to make the question sound as neutral as possible.

'You *would* describe yourself as a friend of Mrs Caswell?'

'Well . . . In this context, yes.'

'You believe her to be innocent of the crime she was convicted of?'

'Yes, I do.'

He nodded, immersed the remainder of his biscuit, then swallowed it. 'Were you acquainted with her late brother, Senhor Rodrigo Manchaca de Pombalho?'

'I . . . I met him on a couple of occasions, certainly.'

'What sort of occasions, sir?'

It was clear to me now that I had to force him to show his hand. 'Inspector, I don't think it's unreasonable of me to ask you to explain the purpose of these questions.'

'Not at all unreasonable, sir, I agree.' He paused to sip his coffee. 'You're aware of Senhor Pombalho's recent death, I take it, and of the circumstances in which he died?'

'Yes.'

'Speaking unofficially, I dislike verdicts of justifiable homicide. They make me uneasy.'

361

'I understood it to be a clear case of self-defence.'

'Indeed, sir. So the jury concluded. But I'm not entirely satisfied that all the relevant facts were put before them.'

'Really? Well, I wouldn't know.'

'Senhor Pombalho was staying at the Green Man, Fownhope, at the time of his death. It's a quiet village inn and gets precious few overnight guests, particularly during the winter, so Senhor Pombalho – and his companion – were remembered by the landlord quite distinctly. But they didn't leave their names and Senhor Pombalho's companion hasn't come forward, so we don't know who – or where – he is. We'd like to know, of course, as you can imagine. He might be able to tell us whether the account given to the coroner by Mr Caswell was completely accurate.'

'I sympathize with you, Inspector, but I really don't see—'

'The landlord of the Green Man hasn't given us a very helpful description, I'm afraid. Senhor Pombalho attracted most of his attention. His recollection of the other guest is that he was a well-spoken middle-aged Englishman. Well, that could apply to a sizeable chunk of the adult male population, as I'm sure you'll appreciate. It fits you, for instance, doesn't it?'

'Yes, but as you—'

'The landlord remembered the type of motor-car the fellow was driving, but naturally he didn't make a note of the registration number. A "Bullnose" Morris, it was. Not far off being the commonest car on the road. Why, I even have one myself. Do you drive, sir?'

'Yes. As a matter of fact—'

'Don't say you have one as well?' His face was wreathed in mock disbelief.

'Er . . . Yes, I do.'

'Colour, sir?'

'Royal blue.'

'Well, there you are.' He grinned. 'Just goes to show, doesn't it?'

'To show what, Inspector?'

'Purely out of interest, sir, where were you on the twenty-second of January?'

'Er . . . Here in London, I should think.' Instantly, I regretted the lie, for fear that he should request the corroboration I was in no position to supply. 'Of course, I'd need to check . . . my diary, that is.'

'I quite understand, sir.' His grin broadened. 'It's not easy to be certain when you're put on the spot, is it?'

362

I felt myself colour. 'As to that, Inspector, I can be certain on one point. I wasn't in Herefordshire.'

'I never expected you to say you were, sir.'

'Are you suggesting I was?'

'Absolutely not, sir. I wouldn't dream of it. It's just . . . Well, we have to check these things. You do see that, don't you?'

'I'm not sure I do. Are you proposing to put these questions to everybody who's written to the Home Office about Mrs Caswell's case?'

'Oh no, sir.'

'Then why are you putting them to me?'

'Well, sir, you happen to own a car of the same make and colour as that used by Senhor Pombalho's companion.'

'But as you said, Inspector, there must be hundreds of royal blue "Bullnose" Morrises on the road. And you didn't know I owned one before you called here, did you?'

'Good point, sir.' His grin was beginning to irritate me, as it was probably meant to. 'Perhaps I ought to explain that an anonymous letter reached Scotland Yard a couple of days ago, addressed to me. It was posted in Hereford on Monday of this week. And it named *you* as the person who stayed with Senhor Pombalho at the Green Man in Fownhope.'

'Me? But that's—'

'What's more, it said you accompanied him when he broke into Clouds Frome during the early hours of Wednesday the twenty-third of January.'

Be calm, I heard my mind intone. *This is a trick. If not, he can prove nothing. He may not believe what you say, but he cannot refute it.* 'The allegation is false, Inspector. I wasn't there.'

'There was something very odd about the letter, you know, sir. It was written in a disguised hand, of course, but you'd expect that. The interesting thing was that our graphologist reckoned it was written by the same person, probably a man, who was responsible for the anonymous letters found in Mrs Caswell's possession when we searched Clouds Frome last September. We never found out who that was and we didn't need to: it wasn't material to our enquiries. But it niggled with me a little, I don't mind admitting. And it's strange he should write again, so long afterwards, with no word between, very strange indeed. What's more, it suggests he's close to the Caswell household, if not a member of it. Otherwise, how could he know what took place at Clouds Frome that night?'

'But he doesn't know, Inspector. He's wrong, because I wasn't there.'

'So you said, sir, so you said.' He stared at me intently for a moment. 'Of course, we could put that to the test, couldn't we? We could ask the landlord of the Green Man if he recognized you. We could check your alibi for the date in question. We could even examine your car for traces of soil specific to Hereford. Red sandstone, I believe, easily distinguishable from London clay. It's been wet recently and mud tends to stick, don't you find?'

I stared defiantly back at him. 'I've nothing to add to what I've already said.'

His gaze softened. 'I ought to tell you, sir, that, officially, Mrs Caswell's case and that of her brother's death are closed.'

'Then why are you here?'

'Because I don't like being lied to.'

'I'm not lying.'

'Somebody is, sir. Take my word for it. And Mrs Caswell may hang next week because of it. I understood you were anxious to prevent that happening.'

'So I am, but—' Confronted by Wright's smiling face, I felt helpless and uncertain. Nothing I could tell him about Rodrigo's death would help Consuela. Though it might embarrass Victor, it could not harm him. He and Miss Roebuck were free to contradict whatever I said. The most I was likely to achieve was acknowledgement that *I* had lied, not that they had. 'So I am,' I concluded lamely.

Wright took a note-book from his pocket, tore out a page, wrote something on it in pencil and pushed it across the desk towards me. 'That's my extension at Scotland Yard, sir. The exchange number is Whitehall 1212. But I expect you know that. It's fairly notorious.'

'Why are you telling me this, Inspector?'

'In case you should wish to contact me urgently, sir. Between now and the . . . twenty-first of this month. After that, I don't suppose you'll consider it worthwhile. But, until then, if you re-consider . . .'

'Re-consider what?'

'Your position, sir. Your . . . version of events. The truth – the whole truth that is – is probably Mrs Caswell's only hope. Why did her brother break into Clouds Frome? What was he looking for? If we knew, it might just help. It's a slender chance, I'd be forced to admit, but a real one nonetheless. It'd be a shame if Mrs

364

Caswell had to die because her so-called friends were holding back the truth. More than a shame, really – a disgrace, a tragedy. Don't you agree, sir? A real tragedy.'

I could not remain at Frederick's Place after Wright's departure. I needed fresh air – as fresh, at all events, as London could supply – with which to drive out the doubt and indecision he had planted in my mind. So, I invented an appointment with the partnership's accountant and spent the next few hours pacing the cold and slush-spattered streets whilst, all around me, the city's inhabitants milled and bustled in pursuit of their business.

The fact that Wright suspected me was bad enough, but what struck me as far worse was that the anonymous letter-writer had shown his disguised hand once more. If, as now seemed likely, he held the key to Consuela's fate, it was vital to establish his identity, but the contents of his latest message rendered that identity more impenetrable still. It could not be Victor, since he had good reason to wish that my presence at Clouds Frome on the night of Rodrigo's death should remain a secret. But who else could know I had been there? I had not been seen by anyone other than Victor and Miss Roebuck. Nobody but we three could know what had taken place. Yet somebody did know, somebody who had taken steps to ensure that the police also knew.

Early afternoon found me seated in the nave of St Paul's, gazing up and around at the unattainable majesty of Wren's achievement. My incapacity to conceive and execute such a vast yet intricate plan seemed one then with my inability to detect or comprehend the conspiracy that had enveloped Consuela. And my helplessness was also my shame. The one service I could render her was the one task I could not accomplish. I was no better a man than I was an architect.

The light was already failing when I returned to Frederick's Place. To my surprise, Reg met me with the announcement that I had a visitor, who had insisted on waiting for me and was now installed in my office: Hermione Caswell.

'I hope you don't mind, Mr Staddon. She was most insistent.'

'That's all right, Reg. Organize some tea, would you?'

'Certainly, sir. Oh, by the way, a Mr Windrush 'phoned for you.'

'Did he leave a message?'

'Only that there was no news. He said you'd understand.'

'Yes, I do. Thanks, Reg.'

Hermione was clad mostly in black and was looking uncharacteristically sombre. Even her natural ebullience, it seemed, had been overborne by recent events. There was, moreover, a severity in her greeting that suggested I had still not been forgiven for my part in the miscarriage of our plans.

'I'm sorry I wasn't here when you called,' I said, as soon as tea had been served and we were alone. 'What brings you to London?'

'I've just left Consuela.'

'I see.' I heard – and bitterly regretted – the evasiveness in my voice. 'I didn't know she was receiving visitors.'

'She asked to see me. I couldn't refuse such a request.'

'Victor would probably have preferred you to.'

'Victor doesn't know I'm here.'

'Isn't he bound to find out?'

'No. He's out of the country, Mr Staddon, and won't be back . . . for some time.'

'Where's he gone?'

'Cap Ferrat.'

'Really? My wife—' I took a deep breath and tried to look at Hermione without shifting my gaze. 'How is Consuela?'

'Calmer than either of us would be in her shoes. Resigned, I rather think, to her fate. Perhaps too resigned.'

'Why did she want to see you?'

'Not for the reason I had feared.'

'What reason was that?'

'I was concerned that somebody might have told her of Victor's intentions.'

'What intentions?'

'We were summoned to Clouds Frome last Sunday afternoon for a family gathering. Mortimer, Marjorie, Spencer and me. Victor wished to announce his plans for the future, Jacinta's future, that is, as well as his own.'

'If you mean Jacinta's adoption by Consuela's surviving brother, I ought to tell you that Windrush has already informed me of it. I understood it had been arranged at Consuela's request.'

'So Victor told us. In the circumstances' – she glared at me momentarily – 'it seems the best that can be done for Jacinta. I was surprised and gratified that my brother had agreed to the proposal.'

366

'Frankly, so was I.'

'You may be less surprised when you hear what else Victor announced. He said that he would be staying with Major Turnbull in Cap Ferrat until Easter and that he would be setting off on Tuesday – two days ago. Naturally, Gleasure went with him. Rather less naturally, Miss Roebuck also accompanied him. Since Jacinta is to remain in Hereford – she's presently at Fern Lodge – one would have thought Miss Roebuck's place was with her, at least until the girl's uncle arrives. The realization that this was not to be the case clearly offended Mortimer and Marjorie's sense of propriety, although it was actually I who asked Victor to explain such an irregular arrangement. He was not in the least discomposed by my question, however. His answer was brazen in its simplicity. When he and Miss Roebuck return from France, they will do so as man and wife.'

'What?'

'He means to marry her, Mr Staddon, as soon as . . . as soon as he is free to do so.'

Suddenly I was sure that this macabrely timed announcement was the answer, the reason behind everything that had happened. Victor was Imogen Roebuck's dupe. Marriage to him was her chosen path to wealth and freedom. Consuela had stood in her way and had been removed. In due course, Victor too might be removed. As to that, I did not care. Whatever he suffered at her hands he would richly deserve. But Consuela did not deserve to suffer. She was as innocent of Rosemary's murder as she was unaware of its purpose. For its purpose was Imogen Roebuck's.

'She's beaten us, Mr Staddon. Victor is besotted with her. As he sees it, she's been his only ally, his loyal comforter, a woman more deserving of the status of his wife than Consuela ever was. They'll be married in Nice, early next month. Nothing can prevent it – unless Consuela is reprieved.'

'Which nobody thinks she will be.'

'Exactly. What we most feared has come to pass.'

'We must inform the police. We must make them understand the implications.'

'But what are the implications? We suspect Miss Roebuck engineered all this to suit her purpose, that she poisoned Rosemary in order to dispose of Consuela and to persuade Victor that his wife had tried to murder him. But we can't prove she did that. In fact, all the circumstances suggest she couldn't have. So, what will the police think? Only what my outraged brother and

367

sister-in-law already think. That Miss Roebuck is a scheming hussy who's taken advantage of the situation, who's played on Victor's affections when he's been most vulnerable, who's exploited events – but not brought them about. They regard her behaviour as contemptible, not criminal.'

Hermione was right. Our instincts told us that Imogen Roebuck was the murderess, not Consuela. But our heads, if we could bear to use them, said otherwise. How could she have known Rosemary and her mother would call at Clouds Frome that afternoon? If they had not, Victor would have consumed a fatal dose of arsenic. What then of her aspirations to become his wife – and later perhaps his widow?

'Whatever you decide to do, Mr Staddon, I think you should first consult Consuela.'

'How can I? She refuses to see me.'

'Not any more. That's why I came here this afternoon. I have a message for you from Consuela. She wants to see you. Tomorrow.'

'What?'

'I believe you heard what I said.'

'But . . . After all this . . . Why?'

'For the same reason she asked me to visit her. She wants to know the truth about Rodrigo's death. She's aware that the police tried and failed to discover who his companion was. She suspects you were that companion. She asked me point-blank if it were so.'

'And what reply did you give her?'

'I told her that my obligations to you meant I couldn't answer such a question. But I think she detected a form of answer in my words. At all events, she means now to put the same question to you.'

What could I say to her? No lie of mine would deceive her. That I knew even before I confronted her. The truth, then. It would have to be so. The truth, which was that I had deserted Rodrigo in death just as I had deserted her in life. He had died trying to save her and my misguided actions had merely ensured that he had died in vain.

'Visiting time is half past two,' said Hermione.

I looked at her, hoping she might know what I should do. 'You think . . . You think I must . . .'

'She is under sentence of death, Mr Staddon. Need I remind you of that?'

'Then the truth is the least she deserves of me.'

368

Hermione nodded implacably. 'The very least.'

I thought of nothing else that night but what I would say to Consuela. I had prepared myself once before for such an encounter, but it had been denied me. Since then, Consuela's plight had worsened and my sense of responsibility for it had grown. Behind all the legal doubts and forensic uncertainties, there reared a single incontrovertible truth. If I had stood by her thirteen years ago, as I had promised I would, she would not now be facing death. If I had valued love and honour more highly than wealth and ambition, she would now have nothing to fear. And nor would I.

Windrush had still heard nothing from the Home Office when I telephoned him the following morning. I did not tell him I would be visiting his client later that day. Indeed, I could still hardly believe I would be. When the time came, however, I set out, obedient to her summons, my mind numb after too much thought, aware of little save the futility of all the ways in which I had sought to prepare for this moment.

I travelled by Underground to Kentish Town, then walked east and north through quiet residential streets towards Holloway. A thaw had set in since the previous day's snow, accelerated by a watery sun. As I turned onto the Camden Road and caught my first sight of the prison, smoke was rising from its chimney and the light, where it struck the wet and sloping cell-block roofs, threw back a dazzling glare. Seventy years ago, the City Architect decreed that this, like all other prisons of the period, should be modelled on a medieval castle, complete with barbican, battlements and high forbidding turrets. Little could he have known that a member of his own profession would one day wish he had not chosen to celebrate the law's revenges with such enthusiasm, such evident approval of the punishments to be enacted within its walls.

I quickened my pace as I drew closer. The approach to the gatehouse seemed endless, hemmed in by hopelessness as much as the soaring crenellations of the prison. I sensed rather than saw the movement of a judas flap in the door ahead. Then, before I had reached the bell-pull, a wicket-gate set in the door opened and a wardress appeared at the aperture, regarding me blankly.

'What can I do for you, sir?' The words were polite, but the tone of voice was stern and intimidating.

'I've come to see one of your prisoners. Mrs Caswell.'

Her expression betrayed no reaction. She merely nodded and stepped back, allowing me to enter. The hall within was dark and high-ceilinged. A fire was blazing in one corner, but its warmth was insufficient to reach me. On the far side stood iron gates and beyond them a flagged courtyard. With a crash, the door closed behind me and the wardress said: 'Follow me, please.' I did so, absorbing as I went the sounds and smells of the building around us. The metallic impact of key in lock, chain on rail, turning and colliding, blurred and muffled by stone and stair; and dampness, seeping, rising, trickling behind everything; the dampness, it might have been, of death.

'Visitor for the condemned prisoner.' I heard the words spoken ahead of me and, looking, saw another wardress at a desk behind a sliding glass partition. On the wall behind her was a clock and beside it a blackboard, with numbers chalked on it in boxes beneath painted headings. PRISONERS ON ROLL: 289. REMAND: 73. HOSPITAL: 6. ESCAPERS: –. CONDEMNED: 1.

'Relative or friend?' asked the wardress at the desk.

'Oh . . . Friend.'

'Expected?'

'Er . . . Yes, I believe so.'

'Name?'

'Staddon. Geoffrey Staddon.'

She consulted a list, then, without further explanation, slid a stout old ledger across the counter towards me. 'Sign in, please.'

A pen was attached to the spine of the ledger by a piece of string. It stretched taut as I dipped it in the ink-well and printed my name and address in the spaces provided. There were two blank boxes on the right-hand side of the page, headed IN and OUT. The wardress swung the ledger round when I had finished, squinted at the clock and wrote the time in the first box. Two twenty-seven.

'You'll have to wait. Her solicitor's with her at the moment.'

'Really? I didn't—'

'You're in luck, though.' She glanced past me. 'Here he is now.'

As I turned, the iron gates to the courtyard clanged open and Windrush stepped through. Instantly, they were closed and locked again behind him.

'Staddon! So you came after all.' Windrush looked thinner and paler than ever, more dishevelled as well, his eyes ringed in shadow, his hair disordered and clinging to his scalp. I had never seen him so forlorn, so manifestly crushed by circumstance.

'You knew I was coming?'

'She told me just now.'

'But you thought I wouldn't turn up?'

'Let's say I hoped you wouldn't. For your sake.'

'What do you mean?'

He moved towards me. 'I mean that I'd never have accepted this case if I'd known it would end like this. I believe today has been the worst day of my life.' He gazed up at the shadowy vaults above us and sighed. 'My God, what a terrible place this is, what a truly terrible place.'

I clasped his arm. 'You've had word from the Home Office, haven't you?'

'I've had their final answer, yes. I've just delivered it to Consuela.' His head drooped. 'There's to be no reprieve, Staddon. The hanging will take place next week as scheduled.'

'But—'

'Nothing can stop it now. Nothing in the world.'

'There must—'

'Would you come with me, please, Mr Staddon?' The wardress who had admitted me was standing by the courtyard gate, staring in my direction. 'You'll have to leave by three o'clock, so I'd advise you not to waste time.'

Time, so much of it and so little – thirteen years squandered and less than six days remaining – was closing around me, stronger and darker than the very walls that confined two hundred and eighty-nine prisoners, soon, all too soon, to become two hundred and eighty-eight.

'Mr Staddon!'

My hand fell from Windrush's arm. I stepped forward. The wardress turned her key in the lock. And the gates swung open to receive me.

CHAPTER

TWENTY

Dismal courtyards, ill-lit staircases, shabby landings, winding corridors. How many we traversed, in what direction or sequence, I could not tell. Holloway Prison was to me a bewildering maze of draughts and echoes, of doors locking and unlocking, of keys and chains and bars, of blue uniforms and grey walls and dull defeated voices. By the time we reached our destination, I felt as if we had travelled miles, burrowing perhaps beneath the very earth, and might yet have miles more to travel. But we did not.

The wardress pulled up by an open doorway ahead and, glancing back at me, nodded towards the room within. We were in a quieter part of the prison, where all seemed hushed and empty. There was linoleum beneath my feet, a bare bulb perversely burning above my head, a patch of daylight, mullioned by the shadows of bars, falling on the wall beside me. We had arrived, I suddenly realized, at the condemned cell.

'Your visitor's here, Caswell.'

The voice came from inside the cell and a shudder ran through me to hear her name spoken without prefix. I had not expected deprivation to run so deep. I should have done, of course. I should have foreseen how minor denials would be dictated by major penalties. But I had not. And only now did the harshness of her existence begin to break upon me.

A table had been placed across the entrance to the cell, blocking access, with a chair on either side. As I approached, I could see little of the interior save a bare section of floor and wall.

At any moment, I knew, Consuela must appear. Yet still I was not ready, still I felt unequal to whatever might follow. I reached the table, pulled back the chair and forced myself to look. There was a high barred window opposite me and, standing beneath it, a woman. For a second, I thought it was her. Then, as my eyes adjusted to the brightness, I saw that it was only another wardress.

'You will not touch. You will not whisper. You will not hand anything to the prisoner without first submitting it to us for inspection. Do you understand?'

The wardress on my side of the table had spoken. I glanced at her and nodded in confirmation, then looked back into the cell.

'Hello, Geoffrey.'

She was no more than three feet away, thinner than I remembered and somehow – though I knew it could not be so – smaller. Her hair was short, cropped close to the head, her cheeks hollow, her eyes large and gleaming. There was a hint of fever about her, a translucency to her skin, yet also a great calmness, a serenity in the midst of adversity. She wore no make-up, of course, no jewellery, no fine clothes, just a shapeless grey dress of coarse serge, loosely belted at the waist. Yet the austerity of her appearance and the starkness of her surroundings served only to emphasize her beauty, to snatch back every memory of her loveliness and hurl it in my face. The bloom of youth had faded, it was true, but, in fading, had revealed perfection.

'Please sit down.'

I obeyed. She slipped into the chair opposite me and rested her hands lightly on the edge of the table. She no longer wore her wedding-ring – though I suspected she would have been allowed to retain it if she had wished. Behind her, in one corner of the cell, was a narrow, neatly made bed. The wardress stood between it and the window, leaning back against the wall and staring over our heads into the corridor.

'Thank you for coming.'

There was no irony in the remark. She was truly grateful. But her gratitude was worse than any accusation she could have uttered. She neither smiled nor frowned, neither pleaded nor rebuked. Her eyes engaged mine and would not release them. Her only reproach lay in the frankness of her gaze.

'I know you wanted to visit me before, here and at Gloucester. I am sorry I could not allow it.'

'Consuela, I—'

'Please do not refer to the last time we met. Please do not try to

373

explain or apologize for what happened all those years ago. It is not why I asked you come.'

'Even so—'

'You will respect my wishes in this, Geoffrey. I know I can trust you to do that much.'

'Even if you can trust me to do nothing else?'

'I did not say that and I did not mean it. If we had met sooner, it would have been different. I hated you for the misery you left me to endure, hated and blamed and cursed. But I do not hate you now. What has happened to me puts all such thoughts on one side. You are merely . . . a lapsed friend.'

'And something else, surely?' She frowned. 'I'm talking about Jacinta.' I looked over Consuela's shoulder at the wardress, but she seemed to be paying us no attention whatever. 'She is my daughter, isn't she?'

But Consuela did not answer. She gazed at me with a mixture of pity and puzzlement.

'That's why you sent her to me, isn't it?'

'Perhaps.'

'I know you owe me nothing – less than nothing – but surely you won't deny me certainty on such a point? – Not now.'

'I cannot give you certainty. She may be yours. She may not.'

I stared at her, scanning her face for some sign or clue that would tell me what she meant. If I was not Jacinta's father, then Victor was. But Jacinta had been conceived in July 1911. I knew that for a fact. And in July 1911, Consuela and I . . . It was absurd, but I felt a jolt of something close to betrayal at the thought of what she was implying. I, who had forfeited all rights in such matters, nevertheless resented the doubt she had raised.

'At the time,' she said slowly, 'it seemed important that Victor should not have the least cause to question my fidelity. You will remember why.'

I looked down at the table. She had read my thoughts and provided the rebuke they merited. Whatever she had done, she had done for the best. Whereas, whatever I had done . . .

'I hope she is yours, truly I do. I would far rather she inherited your nature than Victor's.'

'I had a son,' I murmured. 'He died.'

'I did not know.'

'How could you?'

'I'm sorry, Geoffrey. It must be hard to lose a child. But it makes no difference.'

'I didn't mean it to. The arrangements you've made for Jacinta . . . are the best that can be made.'

'So I believe. Francisco is a good man. He and his wife will treat Jacinta as if she were their own. I cannot ask for more than that.'

I looked up from the table. 'About Rodrigo . . .'

'You were with him, weren't you? Don't deny it unless I really am mistaken. Don't lie to me about it. I want no more lies, from you least of all. I would rather have silence.' She paused and waited for me to speak, but I did not. 'I have my answer, then. You know what happened and why it happened.'

'We . . . He was trying to save you.'

'How?'

'He was looking for Victor's will. He thought he knew where it was hidden. He thought it might hold the key to what happened, to why your niece was poisoned. But it was a trap. And he walked into it.'

'A trap devised by Victor?'

'Yes.'

'And intended to bring about my brother's death?'

'Perhaps. I'm not sure. In the end, it genuinely could have been self-defence.'

She thought for a moment, then said: 'I want you to tell Francisco everything, Geoffrey. How and why Rodrigo died. What we once were to each other. Even the probability that Jacinta is your daughter.'

'All that? To your brother?'

'I want him to be able to tell Jacinta when she comes of age. I want her to know the truth, when she is old enough to understand it. I want her to know all there is to know about me, even though I will be long dead by the time she does.'

'Don't say that.'

'Oh, but I must. I cannot face what will happen next week by pretending it will not happen. For it will. That is definite now.'

'I met Windrush on my way in.'

'Then you know.' She smiled faintly. 'You see how much easier it is to be honest? Easier for yourself – and for others.'

'There is still hope.'

'There is none. I have long accepted that. Now, will you do as I have asked?'

'Of course.' I nerved myself to look at her without flinching. 'You have my solemn promise.'

'Thank you.'

'I wouldn't blame you if you reminded me what my last promise to you was worth.'

'I shall not do that. You will keep your word this time, I think.'

'Yes. I will.'

'Francisco and his wife are due to arrive in Liverpool on Monday aboard the SS *Hildebrand*. I would like you to meet them and to escort them to Hereford. I trust Hermione explained that Jacinta is now at Fern Lodge, whilst Victor takes his ease at Cap Ferrat?'

This was the first trace of bitterness I had detected in her remarks. Whether she knew of Victor's plan to marry Imogen Roebuck – whether it accounted for the absence of her wedding-ring – I did not dare to ask. 'Yes,' I murmured. 'She explained.'

'How or when you tell Francisco what I have asked you to tell him I must leave you to decide. It will not be easy for you. I realize that and I am sorry for it. But who else can I ask? Who else knows what to tell him?'

Behind her, the wardress consulted the watch that hung at her breast. Instinctively, I drew out my own watch and started at the discovery that our half hour was nearly done. 'We have only a few more minutes,' I said, looking back at Consuela.

'Minutes, hours, days. What difference does it make, Geoffrey? We have had long enough.'

'But . . . There's so much else . . .'

'Let it pass. As I must let all things pass.'

She had made her peace with the world and the forces within it that had resolved to end her life. But it was a peace I could not subscribe to. 'I have cursed myself more often and more bitterly than you could ever have done, Consuela. I have regretted what I did to you more deeply than I have regretted anything else in my entire life.'

'Don't say these things. Not now. Don't torture yourself. It is pointless. I forgive you. I absolve you. What has happened to me is not your fault. It is not your responsibility.'

'Yes it is. I don't deserve to be forgiven. I won't accept your absolution.'

'You must.'

'I ruined both our lives, Consuela. Yours and mine. I am married to a woman who despises me. My son is dead. The hotel I deserted you to build no longer exists. It was burned – as I wish to God I had burned that letter to you. And now, thanks to me, you sit here, in this foul and awful place, waiting—'

376

'Time's up.' A hand touched my shoulder and the wardress's shadow fell across the table. 'Say goodbye now.'

Consuela smiled, more faintly even than before. 'Do not fight against it, Geoffrey. You will not win. In gracious defeat lies our only hope of victory.'

'Who's behind this, Consuela? Who's done this to you?'

'I don't know. Perhaps Victor. Perhaps somebody else. Perhaps nobody at all.'

'If I ever find out—'

'Don't try. Let it die with me.'

'You must come with me now, Mr Staddon!' interrupted the wardress. 'At once!'

The other wardress stepped forward and drew back Consuela's chair. She rose and nodded across at me. 'Goodbye, Geoffrey.'

'Is that what this is? Goodbye?'

'It must be.'

'But—'

'You were with Rodrigo when he died, weren't you?'

'Yes.'

'Then any risks he took for my sake you also took?'

'I suppose so, but—'

'In that case, I was wrong to call you a lapsed friend. I should have said "a friend restored".'

'Mr Staddon!' snapped the wardress.

'You will get them into trouble if you remain any longer. You wouldn't want that, would you? Go now – without another word. Go in peace.'

'Consuela—'

'Farewell, Geoffrey.' She raised her left hand with the palm open. The gesture was too slight for me to be sure of its meaning. A dismissal? A blessing? A valediction? I sensed it held something of all three, bound together by a final discharge of the debt I had never honoured.

I tried to speak but could find no words. Consuela lowered her hand to her side, looked at me an instant longer, then turned and moved away towards the bed. The wardress tugged at my elbow and I realized it was over. We had met and would never meet again. We had taken an overdue farewell. And now nothing remained but to do as Consuela had done: to turn and walk away.

I must have left the prison as I had entered it, been signed out in the gatehouse ledger, then discharged onto the Camden Road. I

377

must have headed south and west through the failing afternoon, via Kentish Town to Primrose Hill, then across Regent's Park as dusk and homecoming were settling over London. I must have followed such a route and been aware of the direction I was taking. Yet all I can remember – beyond the aching numbness of my thoughts – is the public house in Marylebone where I took refuge as soon as it had opened for the evening.

I had been there no more than half an hour – seated at a corner table, drinking scotch, eager for the oblivion it was bound in the end to bring – when I became aware that a man was standing behind me, tapping my shoulder. At first, I tried to ignore him. Then, when he persisted, I turned and looked up.

It was Spencer Caswell, lean and smiling, gin glass in one hand, smouldering cigarette in the other. 'Thought I recognized that bowed back,' he drawled. 'How's tricks, Staddon?'

'Go to hell!'

'Probably will, but not just yet, eh? Mind if I join you?' Without waiting for an invitation, he sat down opposite me. 'I've been up for the day on business. Going back on the seven o'clock. Thought I'd stop off for a snifter on my way to the station. Never expected to bump into you, though.'

'As far as I'm concerned, we can pretend you didn't.'

'No call for sarcasm. But don't worry. I won't take offence. I'll attribute it to the stressful time you're having.'

'What would you know about it?'

'Oh, come off it. You're drowning your sorrows, aren't you? – on account of Consuela. Matter of fact, I'd have popped up to Holloway this afternoon to see her if I'd had time. Not for a fond farewell, of course, more for the novelty of seeing what a condemned cell's like. They always have a concealed door, you know: the one the hangman uses when he comes calling on the dreaded day. But perhaps you do know. Been out there yourself, have you?'

'I've nothing to say to you.'

'Really? Well, as you please. Heard about Uncle Victor's bolt from the blue? He's hopped off to France with that scheming tart of a governess. Means to marry her, apparently.' He grinned. 'As soon as the law obliges by making him a widower.'

'Leave me alone, Spencer. I don't want to hear anything you may have to tell me.'

He leaned across the table. 'It's all turning out very neatly for Uncle Victor and the Roebuck bitch, isn't it? Mad Rodrigo despatched to the great coffee plantation in the sky – and

Consuela to follow shortly. Yes, their plans have worked to perfection. You have to admire them, don't you? Poisoning my sister and blaming Consuela for it was a master-stroke. Miss Roebuck's idea, I reckon. Victor hasn't the ingenuity for it.'

'If you really believe that—'

'Oh, but I do! Remember, I have an advantage over the others. I know Victor had prior notice that he'd be entertaining guests to tea on the fatal afternoon.'

Suddenly, the effects of the whisky drained from my mind. I had forgotten Spencer's story about a telephone call to Victor from Grenville Peto. If we could prove such a call had been made, then, even at this late stage – 'Who was your informant, Spencer?'

'You asked me that once before and I told you I couldn't reveal my source.'

'It's vital you should—'

'But I suppose it can't do any harm now. He's out of the country and won't be back until it's far too late to save Consuela's neck.'

'Out of the country? You mean Victor?'

'No, no. Gleasure. You're not paying attention, Staddon. It was Gleasure who told me he took a 'phone call from Uncle Grenville a good half hour before Rosemary and Mummy dear turned up on the doorstep. He put the call through to Uncle Victor on his study extension. Well, no prizes for guessing one of the things that cropped up in their conversation. I imagine the two love-birds had been awaiting such an opportunity for weeks, arsenic at the ready. Even so, they must have moved smartly to slip it into the sugar without being seen. Whilst Consuela was in the garden, I reckon. That was the only chance they had.'

Of course. Gleasure was party to their secret. But he had been prepared to do their bidding by deceiving Rodrigo. Therefore, he must have been bought off. And there, in that hint of corruption, lay one recourse I had not yet tried. If Gleasure could be bribed to hold his tongue, he could be bribed to loosen it. And if he could be persuaded to speak out, Consuela would surely be saved. They would never dare to hang her in the face of such a doubt as this.

'Planting the letters and the packet of arsenic must have been child's play by comparison,' mused Spencer. 'They could have waited till the search was imminent before – I say, Staddon, are you off?'

Already I was hurrying towards the door. I had heard enough.

379

It would take me two days to reach Cap Ferrat. By then, less than four would remain. But I was confident they were more than I would need to wrench the truth from Gleasure and nail Victor's lies for good and all.

Walking fast through the sobering chill of Marylebone's empty streets, I began to question my sudden access of confidence. Whatever Gleasure could be induced to say, Victor might yet escape, for something – bound up with the money I had found in the safe – suggested to my mind that Grenville Peto would still side with him. If so, the most I might achieve was a stay of execution. And to raise Consuela's hopes only to dash them would surely be worse than not to raise them at all.

To compound my difficulties, I had promised Consuela I would meet her brother in Liverpool on Sunday, which I could not do if I were to follow a faint trail of last-minute salvation to Cap Ferrat. I was in a cleft stick of my own hewing. Either I abandoned her or I broke my word to her. I had done both before and now, it seemed, I was destined to do one or the other again.

A solitary letter was waiting for me at the flat. It was in a buff envelope, labelled ON HIS MAJESTY'S SERVICE. At first, I took it for a tax demand. When I opened it, however, I saw that it was from the Home Office – grim and bureaucratic confirmation of what I already knew.

Home Office,
Whitehall,
LONDON SW1.
15th February 1924

Dear Sir,
I refer to your letter of the 11th inst regarding the convicted prisoner Consuela Evelina Caswell, now under sentence of death. I am directed by the Secretary of State to say that he has given careful consideration to all the circumstances of this case and that he has failed to discover any grounds which would justify him in advising His Majesty to interfere with the due course of law.
Yours faithfully,
Sir J Anderson, KGCB
Permanent Under-Secretary of State

Strict and inflexible. So Sir Henry had warned me Anderson was and so he had shown himself to be. Though whether he had deigned even to dictate this reply seemed doubtful. His signature was a rubber-stamped replica. The phrases he had used could have been chosen just as easily by an obscure official. Such, I suspected, was the attention my plea had been deemed to merit.

I was still holding the letter in my hands a few seconds later, staring down at the type-written words, when the telephone rang. It was close enough for me to pick up before it had rung a second time.

'Hello?'

'Mr Staddon? Reg here. I'm at the office.'

'The office? What on earth are you doing there at this hour?'

'Well, actually, I was waiting for you, sir. We expected you back this afternoon.'

'Oh yes. I'm sorry. Something cropped up. But even so—'

'The thing is, Mr Staddon, an overseas telegram came for you just after lunch. I only signed for it because I thought you'd be back soon. As it was, I didn't like just to leave it until tomorrow.'

'Who's it from?'

'I don't know. I haven't opened it.'

'Well, open it now please, Reg, there's a good fellow.' I was too impatient to speculate about its source or wonder whether he could be trusted with the contents. 'Read it out to me.'

There was a pause. I could hear a rustling at the other end. Then Reg resumed. 'It's from your wife, sir.'

'From Angela?'

'Yes. Sent from a place called Bewley-sir-murr in France at nine o'clock this morning.' He meant, of course, Beaulieu-sur-Mer. In the fraction of a second before he continued, I wondered why, if the message were as urgent as the use of a telegram suggested, Angela had gone to Beaulieu rather than the post office in St-Jean-Cap-Ferrat. 'It reads, "Have discovered disturbing information about Victor Caswell. Come at once."'

'Is that all?'

'Yes. I hope it's not bad news, Mr Staddon.'

'Bad? No, I don't think you'd call it that.'

'Will you be going? To Bewley-sir-murr, I mean. It's a question of—'

'You can take it I won't be in on Monday, Reg, nor for several days thereafter.'

'Very good, sir. If there's—'

'Thanks for letting me know.' I put the receiver down then, knowing I could rely on him to cope in my absence and to be discreet about the reasons for it. Not that I cared about discretion anymore. All I knew was that action was more bearable than inaction and that, whatever the reason for Angela's message, it could not go unheeded.

It was nearly ten o'clock when I reached Sunnylea, but Imry was still up, grim-faced and alert. He too had received a letter from the Home Office and he was clearly surprised that I was not as cast down by it as he was. When I explained why, he shared my optimism, but added a wary note of his own.

'What could Angela possibly have learned about Victor Caswell?'

'I don't know. They've been under the same roof for several days. Perhaps Victor let something slip. Perhaps Turnbull did.'

'Even so, it seems out of character for Angela to contact you in this way. Why didn't she simply telephone?'

'Presumably for fear that she'd be overheard. For the same reason, I can hardly telephone her and ask, can I?'

'You must go, Geoff. I do see that. I'm only trying to warn you. Be careful.'

'Caution won't help Consuela.'

'Nor will impetuosity. Do you really think Spencer met you in that pub by chance?'

'It was a plausible route to Paddington station. What else am I supposed to think? That he followed me there? Why should he have done, for God's sake?'

'I don't know. It's just . . . Suddenly, events are running out of control. Why is everybody so eager for you to visit Cap Ferrat?'

'The question is, Imry, will you act for me in my absence? I'll go anyway. I have to. But my conscience would be easier if I could still keep my promise to Consuela. That's why I've come to you.'

'You want me to meet her brother and his wife in Liverpool and escort them to Hereford?'

I smiled. 'Who else can I ask?'

Imry smiled back. 'I'd be offended if you did ask somebody else. I'll go, of course.'

'Stay at the North Western. I'll call you there before you leave for Hereford on Tuesday.'

'Very well.' He sighed. 'This is the slimmest of chances, Geoff. You do realize that, don't you?'

'Would you rather I didn't try? Would you rather I just sat back and waited for Thursday morning to come?'

'Of course not. You must go. You have no choice. I only hope you don't regret it.'

'I won't. Succeed or fail, I won't regret anything this journey brings.'

CHAPTER

TWENTY-ONE

The boat-train connecting with the Calais-Mediterranean Express left Victoria at eleven o'clock on Saturday morning. Twenty-four hours later, I was in Nice. The air on the Côte d'Azur was clear and cool, radiant with the promise of spring. But the cares and pledges of a London winter were all that filled my heart.

From Nice I took a local train to Beaulieu, where I booked into the Hotel des Anglais next to the station. There I forced myself to take lunch and a bath before setting out for Cap Ferrat. I needed to be calm and orderly, confident about what I was doing and why. This was no time to lose either my nerve or my temper. Though every action was charged with urgency, I could not afford to hurry. Yet if I delayed too long . . .

The Villa d'Abricot was scented and somnolent when I reached it late that afternoon. I walked slowly up the drive, recalling my previous visit, when Rodrigo had come charging from the house as I arrived. My first sight of him had since been followed by my last. He now lay in an unmarked grave in Hereford while his sister languished in a London gaol and the man who had killed him idled his days away here with his lover, his friend and *my* wife.

I pulled the bell, reminding myself once more of the different tactics I had prepared for every possible form my reception might take. During the long train journey from England, I had thought of nothing but how best to exploit what Imry had accurately called *'this slimmest of chances'*.

The door was opened by Turnbull's Italian man-servant. He was clearly surprised to see me, unsettled by such a breach in the predictable pattern of his day. '*Signor* Staddon! I did not . . . I was not told to expect you.'

'Hello, Enrico. Is my wife here?'

'Your wife? Yes. That is, no.' He flushed. 'She is out, *signor*. They are all out. The Major, *Signor* Caswell, *Signor* and *Signora* Thornton, *Signorina* Roebuck and . . . and *Signora* Staddon is with them.'

'An afternoon at the casino, is it?'

'I . . . I do not know. It is not . . . Do you wish to wait for them?'

'Yes. I rather think I do.'

'Come in then, *signor*, come in.' I followed him into the hall. As we moved towards the morning-room, an idea came into my head. Turnbull and his guests were all absent. There might be no better time for a confidential word with the valet of one of those guests.

'Is Gleasure here, Enrico?'

'Gleasure?' Enrico's expression suggested he had no liking for the man. '*Si, signor*. He is here.'

'I'd like to see him, if I may.'

'Then . . . I send for him.' He gaped at me in amazement. 'If you are sure it is him you want to see.'

'I'm sure.'

With a shrug of the shoulders, Enrico took himself off, leaving me to pace the morning-room and rehearse the various ways in which I could seek to penetrate Gleasure's defences. I knew him to be cautious and deferential, loyal to his employer and jealous of his station in life. I suspected his loyalty had a price, however, and I could not help wondering how he viewed the prospect of becoming Imogen Roebuck's servant as well as Victor's. It was no good appealing to his conscience, but dented pride and an eye to the future might yet mean he could be persuaded to speak out.

I had been alone no more than a couple of minutes when the door opened and Enrico was back. '*Mi scusi, signor*. Gleasure is . . . He is not able to come at once.' I frowned. This sounded like a deliberate slight and did not augur well. 'He will be with you in ten minutes. I am sorry, but . . .' There was another eloquent shrug.

'Very well. I'll wait here . . . for ten minutes.'

'*Si, signor.*'

The door closed and I was alone again. Whatever Gleasure thought this delay might achieve, it was imperative that I should not allow it to undermine what little confidence I had. To calm my nerves, I lit a cigarette and wandered round the room, admiring again the opulence of Turnbull's furnishings. Silk and satin were all about me, enriching the pastel shades of carpets and curtains. Every hem was extravagantly fringed, every tassel richly worked. One small console-table displayed marquetry of gorgeous subtlety. Another supported a scaled-down gold replica of the statue in the conservatory. And between them, on the wall, hung a large oil painting depicting one of Turnbull's favourite subjects: frolicking nudes in a mythical landscape. His taste was not mine, but his taste was unquestionably expensive. My mind wandered to the money in Victor's safe, the robbery at Peto's Paper Mill and Malahide's death only a few days after identifying the fourth member of that long-ago conspiracy. Had some of the money been spent here, I wondered, on the comforts Major Turnbull was determined to enjoy?

I had finished the cigarette, and begun another, gazing from the window into the garden as I smoked it, when the door opened and Gleasure entered the room. He smiled warily.

'I'm sorry to have kept you waiting, sir.'

'No matter. How are you, Gleasure?'

'Well, thank you, sir. And somewhat surprised, I won't deny, to see you here.'

'Because of my wife's presence as a guest – or whatever she is – of Major Turnbull, you mean?'

'I merely meant that, in all the circumstances, I did not expect you to visit us.'

'In all the circumstances? That's a coy way of putting it. But then I suppose a valet has to be something of a diplomat where his employer's way of life is concerned.'

'As you say, sir.'

'You must see and hear many things which *diplomacy* obliges you to forget.'

He looked at me quizzically for a moment, then said: 'What exactly did you want to discuss with me, sir?'

It was now, my instincts told me, or never. Further prevarication would achieve nothing. 'I'm here, Gleasure, because I'm trying to save the life of an innocent woman. And I think you can help me.'

'Me, sir? I really don't—'

'I'm talking about Mrs Caswell. Mrs Consuela Caswell. I take it you're aware she's due to hang on Thursday?'

'Yes, sir.' His face betrayed not the slightest reaction. 'I'm aware of it.'

'At her trial, you testified that you did not take any telephone calls for Victor on the afternoon of the poisoning.'

'I believe I did, sir, yes.'

'That wasn't true, was it?'

'Are you accusing me of perjury?'

I stubbed out my cigarette and moved towards him. 'I'm giving you a chance to re-consider what you said in view of the appalling consequences of allowing a . . . misunderstanding . . . to go uncorrected.'

'I'm not at all sure I take your meaning, sir.'

'I think you do. Spencer's told me exactly what you told him: that Grenville Peto telephoned Victor at least half an hour before Rosemary and her mother arrived and that Victor therefore knew they were on their way.'

'Ah.' Gleasure frowned thoughtfully. 'He's told you that, has he, sir? Not a gentleman to confide in, young master Spencer, I fear.'

'Why did you, then?'

'Drink, sir.' He grinned. 'In my cups, I'm not always as *diplomatic* as I should be.'

'So, you admit it's true? You took a call from Peto that afternoon?'

'Oh, I admit nothing, sir. Nothing at all. I have my position to consider.'

'Your *position*? You're willing to let Consuela hang just so you can keep your job? For God's sake, man, this is more important than your monthly salary!'

'I'm not sure anything can be, sir. To a gentleman like yourself, who's never had to wonder where the next crust's coming from, a conscience probably seems indispensable. To me it's a luxury. One I've never been able to afford.'

'So, it all comes down to money, does it?'

'Life generally does, in my experience.'

'Very well. How much do you want?'

He narrowed his gaze. 'Are you offering me a bribe?'

'How much does Victor pay you? Seventy pounds a year? Eighty? Ninety? No more than a hundred, I'll be bound.' I took a deep breath. 'I'll pay you five hundred if you go to the authorities and make a sworn statement leading to Consuela's reprieve.'

'Really, sir? You'd pay as much as that?'

'I doubt you'll relish staying on after Victor marries Miss Roebuck. Watching a former servant enjoy the comfort and social status of a rich man's wife could be a galling experience for somebody who values money as highly as you do.'

He nodded. 'There you may have a point, sir. But not a sufficiently persuasive one for me to risk being charged with perjury. Five hundred pounds would be poor compensation for serving a term in prison.'

'It would never come to that. Plead duress. Say Victor threatened to sack you if you spoke out. I assume that's the truth anyway. I'll back you up. The odds are that no charge will ever be brought.'

'I'm not a betting man, sir. Odds don't appeal to me.'

'Then perhaps something else will.' I fixed his eyes with mine. 'You spun a tale to Mrs Caswell's brother at Victor's bidding, didn't you? You laid the bait that led him to his death.'

'I never—'

'Thought it would come to that? Maybe you didn't. But it did. And now her other brother is on his way to England. You met Rodrigo. You know what he was like. Well, Francisco's no different, take my word for it. He'll want revenge. If I tell him how you deceived Rodrigo, what do you think he'll do?'

There was a fractional loss of confidence in Gleasure's voice when he replied. 'Are you threatening me?'

'Only with the consequences of your own actions.'

'If I *do* make a statement confirming Mr Peto telephoned that afternoon . . .'

'Francisco will be none the wiser.'

'And you'll pay me five hundred pounds?'

'If Consuela is reprieved, yes. Not otherwise.'

He thought for a moment, then said: 'How could I be sure you'd honour such a bargain?'

'I'd deposit the money with a solicitor of your choice, to be released as soon as my condition was fulfilled.'

'Aha. Well, that would be good enough, certainly.'

'What's your answer?'

'My answer? Well, I'd need to think about it. It's not a simple matter, is it?'

'It seems simple to me.'

'Yes, but that's because—' Suddenly, he jerked his head round and held up a hand, straining, it seemed to hear something.

'What is it?'

'Major Turnbull's Lanchester, coming up the drive.' As I listened, the distant note of a car engine did indeed reach my ears, though far sooner than it would have done if I had not been warned. 'They're back earlier than expected. I don't think we should be found together, do you, sir? Not in all the circumstances.'

'I still haven't had your answer.'

'Where are you staying?'

'The Hotel des Anglais in Beaulieu.'

'I know it. I could see you there tomorrow morning at ten o'clock. I'll have reached a decision by then.'

'Time's of the essence, Gleasure. I can't afford to wait.'

'You've left me little room for manoeuvre, sir. But I do have to make certain . . . dispositions. Give me until tomorrow morning. I don't think you'll be disappointed.'

'It still means—'

'They'll be with us any minute. It'd be best if I met them in the hall.'

I stared at him a second longer, then conceded. 'Very well. Tomorrow at ten.'

'I'll be there, sir, never fear. Now, if you'll excuse me . . .'

He bustled out, leaving the door open. I had, I knew, only a few minutes of leisure in which to consider whether he would be as good as his word and how, in the interim, I should deal with his master. Once I had discovered what Angela wanted to tell me, Gleasure's evidence might become redundant, but I could not assume it would. So far, my plans were working well. But there was a long way to go.

I heard the front door open. Enrico's greeting was drowned by a gush of competing voices in which Celia's whine and Victor's growl were uppermost. Then Turnbull's booming tone swamped them all. It was followed by a pause. Gleasure must have spoken during this, because Turnbull suddenly bellowed my name in what sounded more like derision than anger. Then Angela cut in, though I could not hear what she said. Victor muttered something in response. The next thing I knew, footsteps were approaching the morning-room door.

'What are you doing here, Geoffrey?' Angela glared at me with what, but for the telegram, I would have believed was a genuine mixture of fury and astonishment. She was wearing a long cream cashmere coat and a purple cloche decorated with bows. Her hair had been cut fashionably short and on the broad lapel of her coat there glistened the ruby-studded monkey brooch that numbered among the many gifts Turnbull had showered upon her.

'Come in and close the door,' I said quietly.

She frowned and, with a haughty little toss of the chin, did as I had asked her, leaning back against the door with one hand still clasping the knob.

'They all think you're surprised to see me, I suppose?'

'What?'

'We won't be left alone for long, so tell me quickly: what have you found out?'

Her gaze intensified and acquired a tinge of incredulity. 'Kindly explain yourself at once, Geoffrey. I understood from Clive that you were prepared to be reasonable. I do not regard this as reasonable.'

She was speaking loudly enough to be heard in the hall. Assuming this was some ploy to deceive Turnbull and Victor, I moved closer and lowered my voice. 'If you'd prefer to talk elsewhere, we can meet at my hotel.'

'I don't want to talk to you – here or anywhere else,' she hissed. 'I don't want to see you ever again.' She brushed past me, moved towards the fire, then swung round and faced me. 'If you don't leave here immediately, I shall ask Royston to call the police and have you removed.'

'But—'

'I cannot imagine what you thought coming here would achieve.'

'I came because you asked me to!'

'I beg your pardon?'

'There's no need to go on denying it. Whatever you've found out, just tell me and I'll make sure you come to no harm.'

Her face was white with rage now, her lower lip trembling. And my confidence was ebbing fast. 'I'll only say this once, Geoffrey. I don't know what you're talking about.'

'I've come in answer to your telegram. The one you sent from Beaulieu on Friday.'

'I sent no telegram.'

'"Have discovered disturbing information about Victor Caswell. Come at once. Angela."'

'You're mad.'

'Why should I lie about such a thing?'

'Show me it, then.'

'I don't have it with me. I didn't—' I broke off and stared at her. She did not believe me. The truth – plain to see in her face the moment she had entered the room – could no longer be ignored. She had not asked me to come. She had not wanted me to come. To her, all that I had said must indeed have sounded like madness. 'As God is my witness, Angela, I'm only here because I received a telegram, sent in your name, asking me to come at once.'

'Rubbish! You're here to cause trouble, using this preposterous story to justify it. Well, I won't have it, do you hear? I won't have it.'

'Listen to me, for God's sake! You don't understand. It's not—'

'Staddon!' barked Turnbull from the doorway. 'Be silent!' His chest was puffed out with indignation, his face dark with wrath. 'You have a damned nerve, I must say.' He smiled solicitously across at Angela. 'Why don't you join the others in the drawing-room, my dear? It would be best, I think, if I had a word with . . . our visitor . . . in private.'

With a nod of agreement and not so much as a glance in my direction, Angela swept from the room. Turnbull closed the door carefully behind her, then rounded on me.

'Well, Staddon? What's the meaning of this?'

'I don't know. Perhaps you do.' An idea had come into my mind. 'Did you send the telegram?'

'What telegram?'

'Was it a way of ensuring Angela would go through with the divorce? Has she been having second thoughts? Is that it, Major? Did you reckon my character needed a little more blackening in her eyes?'

He stepped closer. 'Have you gone quite mad, Staddon?'

'No. But maybe you want Angela to think I have.'

'If so, my wish has been granted, hasn't it? This exhibition has blasted every last chance you had of winning her back.'

'I don't want her back. You're welcome to her.'

Venom flared in his eyes. 'To spare Angela's feelings, I'll let you walk out of here, provided you leave now, without further ado.'

'What will you do if I don't? Hire the same marksman you—' Suddenly, the words died in my mouth. Turnbull's eyebrows rose faintly in curiosity, his head moved slightly to one side, his gaze became instantly less aggressive and infinitely more menacing.

'Don't stop, Staddon. Finish what you were going to say. I hope – for your sake – it's not what I think.'

Remember Consuela, the rational half of my brain shouted. *She is all that matters. Not Malahide, not Turnbull, not Angela and, above all, not you.* 'You're right, Major. I should go now – before we all say things we might regret.'

He fell back a pace, his expression softened. 'I'm glad you've seen reason.'

'Regard my visit as an unfortunate misunderstanding. I'll leave straightaway.'

'Do that.' He stepped across to the door, laid his hand on the knob, then, before turning it, stared at me and said: 'In your own interests, Staddon, ensure we don't meet again. Ever.' With that, he flung the door open and I stepped past him into the hall.

As I did so, I became visible to the occupants of the drawing-room and they to me. Angela and Celia were standing near the window, Victor and Clive side by side in front of the fire. Only Miss Roebuck was seated, in an armchair in the centre of the room. For an instant I was tempted to enter and remind them of the many reasons why they were all, collectively and individually, despicable. Clive and Celia had conspired at the fiction of my cruelty to suit Angela's purpose. She had allowed Turnbull to entice her away from me with nothing more than oily charm and lavish generosity. He, for his part, was almost certainly a liar, a thief and a murderer. But Imogen Roebuck was, if possible, even worse. And Victor was either her dupe or her accomplice and probably both.

I looked from one to the other of them. Angela's and Celia's eyes were averted, busily engaged with each other's in a charade of sororal sympathy. Clive's slack-jawed gape was as blandly disapproving as I might have expected, Victor's quivering glare of hostility equally predictable. As for Miss Roebuck, she regarded me with heavy-lidded bemusement only just conquering indifference. She was smoking a cigarette – something I had not seen her do before – and was wearing an elegant dark blue silk dress. She had crossed her legs and was sitting well back in the chair, one elbow propped up to hold the cigarette. There was, in her pose and her expression, an absolute confidence she had never declared before, a confidence that she would achieve and perfect the transition from humble governess to wealthy wife, a confidence indeed that she had already done so.

As I watched, Gleasure emerged into view from a corner of the room, carrying a tray of drinks. He approached Miss Roebuck and handed her a glass, then moved towards Clive and Victor. Before reaching them, he glanced fleetingly in my direction and, with the faintest inclination of his head, seemed to ally himself with my thoughts. *They believe they are safe and secure, that they cannot be defeated. Be patient and you may yet surprise them.*

'Enrico!' called Turnbull from behind me. 'Mr Staddon is leaving.'

I looked along the hall and saw Enrico bustling forward to open the front door. I had to leave now, I knew. I had to accept the humiliation they had inflicted upon me. They all thought me a fool and it was best, for the moment, to let them go on believing I was one. If Turnbull had sent the telegram in order to lure me into a trap, he had made a grave mistake, for, in doing so, he had handed me an opportunity I was not about to let slip.

In the drawing-room, Victor swallowed some of his whisky. Angela turned away from the window and added her disgusted stare to the dismissive expressions of the rest. Miss Roebuck seemed almost about to smile – but did not. I lowered my head, forcing myself to believe that soon they would regret their convenient alliance. For Consuela's sake, I would have to endure their contempt in silence. What they might say once I had gone I could not afford to care about, far less resent. Enrico was holding the front door open. Outside, the shadows were lengthening. Another day was failing. Biting back every word I might have spoken – every rebuke, every accusation – I hurried out into the dying light.

'*Arrivederci, Signor Staddon,*' said Enrico as I passed. But I did not answer.

The telephonic resources of the Hotel des Anglais succeeded, after several false starts, in connecting me with the North Western Hotel in Liverpool early that evening. Over a crackling line, I told Imry what had happened.

'You think Turnbull sent the telegram?'

'Probably, but it doesn't matter. Once Gleasure agrees to alter his testimony, I shall have what I came for. And he will. I'm sure of it.'

'What will you do – bring him back with you?'

'Yes. But first I'll go to the British Consul in Monte Carlo and have Gleasure sign a sworn statement in his presence. Armed with that, the Consul should feel obliged to contact the Home Office in London at once. Now, when are the Pombalhos due?'

'Two o'clock. I'll meet them off the ship and bring them back here.'

'Good. I'll try to telephone you again before you set off for the docks.'

'Very well. I'll await your call. Meanwhile, don't take any unnecessary risks, eh?'

'Don't worry, Imry. I have a feeling this is going to turn out well. All I have to do is what I find most difficult: wait – for just a little longer.'

The Baie des Fourmis was placid beneath a moonless sky as I paced the shoreline late that night. Out along the dark and barely visible finger of the cape were scattered pin-pricks of light, one of which was the Villa d'Abricot. I wondered how my wife and her new-found friends were entertaining themselves. A dinner party, perhaps? A rubber of bridge? When the lights were turned out, would Angela go to bed alone? Would Imogen Roebuck? They were cocooned out there across the bay, swathed in fine silk and exquisite secrecy, while, hundreds of miles away, Consuela lay between stiff prison sheets and gazed up into the darkness she expected to see just three more times before the end.

I clenched my fists and repulsed another invasion of panic. The end would not come. I would yet obtain the means to stave it off. Gleasure had no choice but to do as I had demanded. He was preparing, even then, to bring the seductive futures of the Villa d'Abricot's inhabitants crashing down around their heads. And I would make sure he did not falter.

I returned to the hotel shortly before midnight, weary enough to be certain of sleep, confident enough to bide my time until Gleasure arrived. I hardly noticed that the door of my room was unlocked. I assumed I had left it open earlier or that a chambermaid had called in my absence. Either way it seemed a matter of no significance. I dismissed it from my mind and went to bed.

'Ouvrez! Ouvrez la porte!'

The hammering and the shouts were too much – too loud and sudden – for my drowsy reactions to assimilate. For a second, I thought I was at home in Suffolk Terrace. I could not comprehend what was happening. Then awareness swept over me. The events of the previous five months rose as one and propelled me into the reality of a hotel room in Beaulieu-sur-Mer, with pale dawn light seeping through the windows and noise bludgeoning me from beyond the door.

'Ouvrez la porte immédiatement!'

I propped myself up in bed and fumbled for my watch. It was not yet seven o'clock. I could make no sense of such an interruption at such an hour. I wanted to call out, but what little French I knew had deserted me. There was the sound of running feet in the corridor, a shout of *'J'ai la clé,'* then a jangling of keys. I stumbled from the bed and hauled on a dressing-gown, but before I could move towards the door, a key turned in the lock and it was flung open. A blaze of light from the corridor dazzled me. Tall men in uniform were beside and in front of me, gruff voices raised, fingers jabbing. A figure in plain clothes, shorter than the others and bald-headed, waved a document at me. The light above us was snapped on. The men's faces became clear, their identity obvious.

'Geoffrey Staddon?' barked the bald-headed one in clipped and accented English.

'What? Yes. But—'

'Jospin. Nice Sûreté.'

'I don't understand. What . . . What do you want with me?'

'I think you know, *monsieur.*' He looked round at his companions. *'Fouillez la chambre!'* Instantly, they began opening drawers and cupboards. Most were empty. My clothes were over a chair, my coat and hat in the wardrobe, my other belongings still in my bag.

'What are you looking for?'

'I think you know that also, *monsieur.*' One of the policemen had found the bag now and was sifting through its contents. He took out my passport and tossed it onto the bed. Jospin picked it up and opened it. I wanted to protest or call a halt, but could not order my thoughts fast enough. 'You are an architect, *monsieur,*' said Jospin, as if passing the time of day.

'Yes, But what—'

'J'ai trouvé quelque chose!' cried the man searching the bag. *'Un petit paquet de papier, ici, au fond du sac.'* He held something up and Jospin stooped to examine it.

'What is this, *monsieur?*' In Jospin's palm rested a small twist of blue paper. I did not recognize it, yet it was instantly familiar to me from the evidence given at Consuela's trial. Surely it could not contain, as the one found at Clouds Frome had . . .

'I've never seen it before.'

Carefully, Jospin unwound the twist until the paper formed a bowl in his hand. At the centre was a pile of white powder. He looked up at me. *'Monsieur?'*

'I just told you. I've never seen that packet – or its contents – before.'

'But we found it in your bag.'

'I didn't put it there.'

'What do you think this powder is?'

'I don't know.'

'I do not believe you.'

'It's the truth.'

'I think this is poison. *En réalité*, arsenic.'

'That's absurd!'

'You are under arrest, *monsieur. Ce n'est pas absurde.*'

'Under arrest? On what possible charge?'

'Murder.'

'What?'

'Victor Caswell died five hours ago at the Villa d'Abricot near St-Jean-Cap-Ferrat. He had been poisoned. With arsenic, we think.' He nodded down at the white powder in his hand. *'Comme ça. Comme ça exactement.'*

'This can't be true.'

'But it is. Get dressed, please. You are coming with us.'

CHAPTER

TWENTY-TWO

How strange, I thought, as the hours passed, how ironic and yet how fitting, that I should spend Consuela's last days in a cell much like her own. A hard bed, bare walls and a barred window were my experience now as well as hers. There were no tables or chairs in the room they placed me in, no wardresses offering cigarettes or games of cards, above all no second, still unused entrance. Yet for all the hundreds of miles I was from Holloway, I felt closer to Consuela than I had ever done. I shared her every moment. I guessed her every thought. I stretched out my hand and seemed to feel the tips of her fingers reaching towards me.

At first, I was asked little and told less. Jospin would say nothing beyond the fact that Victor was dead and that poison was responsible. He was awaiting the results of an autopsy and of laboratory tests on the substance found in my bag. He had witnesses to question and policemen in London to consult by telephone. He had a case against me to assemble. And, until he had done so, all he required of me was a statement of my whereabouts and actions on Sunday 17 February and my presence, under lock and key, at Nice police station.

Denied almost all information, I decided to say as little as possible. In the statement I signed, I admitted visiting the Villa d'Abricot, but made no reference to Angela's telegram or my appointment with Gleasure. I disclaimed all knowledge of the blue-paper twist and the powder it contained, but offered no suggestion as to how it might have found its way into my bag. I knew that, whatever the true circumstances, I would soon have to say more than this, but for the moment I needed to think, long and alone, about what had happened and why.

Victor Caswell was dead. I had no reason to mourn him. Indeed, I could not help hoping he had died in agony. But that was not what mattered. What mattered was why he had died. Somebody really had tried to murder him last September and now they had succeeded. Rosemary Caswell had been killed by accident, not design. And Consuela was innocent beyond a shred of doubt. But only I knew this, because only I knew that I had not killed Victor.

The answer was clear now. Only three people had been at Clouds Frome on 9 September *and* the Villa d'Abricot on 17 February. Of those, Victor was dead and Imogen Roebuck was defeated, for her dreams of a privileged future had died with him. Only Gleasure remained. Only he could be the murderer. His motive was a mystery, but his guilt was certain. His first attempt had claimed Rosemary by mistake. The blame for this he had fastened on Consuela. His second attempt had succeeded. And the blame for this he had fastened on me. Hence the telegram and his insistence on deferring a response to my demands until Monday. Hence the unlocked door and the powder planted in my bag. The tests would show it was arsenic. I had no doubt of that. Gleasure, in his way, had even warned me. *'I have to make certain dispositions, sir. Give me until tomorrow morning. I don't think you'll be disappointed.'* Nor was I. But trapped and helpless I certainly was.

It was late on Monday evening when I was taken once more to the interview room. Jospin had an interpreter with him, to resolve linguistic ambiguities, and was prepared for the first time to set all the facts before me. He had read my statement and did not believe it. To judge by his hollow-cheeked face and small, dark, darting eyes, he was not a man to believe very much that a prisoner told him. To convince him of anything except my guilt, I would have to penetrate twenty years' worth of official suspicion and a nature to match.

According to Jospin, Victor began to feel unwell early on Sunday evening. He retired to bed without dinner. Miss Roebuck took him some milk and biscuits at about ten o'clock, but he refused them, insisting he would be better by morning. He was presumed to be suffering from one of the bouts of acute indigestion that had troubled him regularly since the poisoning.

Miss Roebuck and the other guests were conversing in the drawing-room shortly before midnight when they heard a loud noise upstairs. When they investigated, they found Victor unconscious on the floor of the bathroom adjoining his bedroom. He had been violently and copiously sick. The distinctive dark colour and foul smell of the vomit reminded Gleasure and Miss Roebuck of the symptoms Victor had exhibited after the poisoning in September. He was carried back to bed and Turnbull's doctor urgently called. Upon arrival, the doctor pronounced Victor to be comatose, with erratic heartbeat and faltering respiration. He summoned an ambulance from Nice, but, before it could reach Cap Ferrat, Victor Caswell was dead.

Jospin was at the Villa d'Abricot within the hour and a clear picture of what had happened swiftly emerged. The last food or drink consumed by Victor comprised two large glasses of scotch and soda and some green olives in the drawing-room late on Sunday afternoon. Nobody else had drunk any scotch, a decanter of which was stored on the drawing-room sideboard. The only unusual recent event reported to Jospin was my unexpected and unwelcome visit that very afternoon. My pretext – a telegram from Angela – was known by her to be false. I had arrived when only servants were in the house and had been left alone in the morning-room for ten to fifteen minutes. There would have been nothing, during that time, to prevent me entering the drawing-room and mixing a fatal dose of arsenic in the whisky decanter. I knew the lay-out of the house and I knew of Victor's fondness for whisky. I had made it obvious that I blamed him for Consuela's conviction for murder and I had been heard in the past to threaten him on account of it. The substance found in my possession at the Hotel des Anglais had since been identified as arsenious oxide. Traces of the same chemical had been found in the whisky. And the pathologist's report, now to hand, showed there was enough arsenic in the intestines of the deceased to have killed him ten times over.

Perhaps I should have responded to this by holding my tongue and demanding the presence of a lawyer. But I did not, for Consuela's innocence concerned me far more than mine. She was due to hang in less than seventy-two hours. In the face of that fact, I could hardly take the accusations being made against me seriously, let alone the penalties they might carry. If Jospin had only known what I knew, he would have realized at once that Gleasure was guilty and that Consuela's innocence was therefore proven. But he did not know and my efforts to make him understand only sounded to him like desperate attempts to direct suspicion elsewhere. In his view, my only reason for asking to see Gleasure on my arrival at the Villa d'Abricot was to gain access to the house. It was not surprising that he thought this, since there was nothing whatever to substantiate my explanation of the visit. True, an impostor claiming to be Angela could have sent me a telegram, but the postmaster at Beaulieu was adamant: they had despatched no such message. Enquiries would of course be made in England, but, for the moment, Jospin's belief was that I had invented the telegram, just as I had invented finding my hotel room unlocked. Besides, such enquiries would take time. And time was what Consuela did not have. Rant or reason as I pleased, I was going nowhere and convincing nobody.

Isolation can be the worst of all privations. Cut off from the world in my narrow cell in Nice, told no more than the police saw fit to tell me, the one freedom I still enjoyed was the freedom to imagine, with mounting dread, what was happening in England. Only later, from Imry, was I to learn all that actually occurred during my confinement. From the diary he kept of those days I was to reconstruct events of which, at the time, I knew nothing.

Monday 18 February 1924
I have been sceptical from the first about Geoff's chances of achieving what he thought he could by going to Cap Ferrat. There was something about his encounter with Spencer Caswell and the telegram he received from Angela that made me think he was being lured there, though why or by whom I cannot imagine. My second night at the North Western Hotel, Liverpool, is overshadowed by this thought, for now it has acquired a basis in fact as well as fancy.

I had expected to hear from Geoff today and when, by nine o'clock this evening, I had not, I decided to telephone him at his hotel in Beaulieu. It took some time to obtain a line. When I was eventually connected, the fellow who answered told me that Geoff booked out this morning and will not be returning. If that had been his intention when he telephoned me on Sunday, I feel sure he would have said so. Yet he did not and now, uncertain and perturbed as I am, I am at a loss to know what I should do for the best.

My difficulties are compounded by the presence here of Senhor Francisco Manchaca de Pombalho and his wife, Dona Ilidia. I met

400

them off the Hildebrand *this afternoon and explained, as convincingly as I could, that I was a friend of Consuela's and that she had asked me to meet them on her behalf, escort them to Hereford and introduce them to Jacinta. Fortunately, they were too depressed and disorientated to subject my explanation to much scrutiny, but how long they will remain so subdued is debatable. I can only hope I have heard from Geoff by the time they become more curious.*

Francisco Manchaca de Pombalho is a reserved and corpulent man in his early fifties, vain about his appearance and pompous in his manner. Yet he is also courteous and trusting. He speaks good if limited English, dresses impeccably and presents a glaring contrast with everything Geoff has told me about his brother. Dona Ilidia exists in her husband's shadow, a small sad dumpling of a woman perpetually on the brink of tears. It was clear to me today that they both wanted to ask me more – about Consuela's state of mind, about Rodrigo's death, about the personality of their future ward – than they felt able to at first acquaintance. I only wish there was something I could do to console them, to make what appears so harsh and senseless understandable, but how can I, when I do not understand it myself?

Tomorrow, we will set off for Hereford. My heart sinks at the thought of what awaits us there: an unpredictable reception from the Caswells and an encounter with Jacinta, who knows and must somehow accept that her mother will die on Thursday.

Tuesday morning brought me a visitor: Mr Lucas, from the British Consulate in Marseilles. Cold and correct, he said he would be pleased to communicate with my solicitor in England so that he might instruct a lawyer in Nice to handle my defence. He would also be pleased to contact relatives or friends of mine. But I was not interested in my defence. I only wanted him to alert Windrush and Sir Henry to what was happening, to explain to Imry why he had not heard from me, to urge the Home Office to call off Consuela's execution. As to all of that, however, Lucas was non-committal. He made notes, he offered advice on French law, he smiled delphically, and then he left.

In the afternoon, I was taken back to the interview room. This time Jospin did not have an interpreter with him. Instead, my heart leapt at the sight of Chief Inspector Wright's familiar face. At last, it seemed, I was to have a chance to speak to somebody who might appreciate the significance of what I was saying. I poured it all out again, investing the account with every ounce of sincerity at my command. Wright had said he thought he was being lied to and now I told him who the liar was. Gleasure was a murderer twice over. That would be proved beyond question soon. Meanwhile, it was vital to prevent a miscarriage of justice that would haunt everyone involved in it to their dying day if they did not intervene before it was too late. He did not have to believe me. I did not ask him to do that. All I asked him to do was concede that I *might* be speaking the truth.

He listened patiently, until I had said all and possibly more than I wanted to say. Then he lit his pipe and offered me a cigarette. 'I flew here, you know,' he remarked. 'From Croydon. In stages, of course. Ever flown, Mr Staddon?'

'No.'

'Can't recommend it. Noisy business. Cramped into the bargain. Only did it because I reckoned I should get to the bottom of this latest poisoning before Mrs Caswell's execution. Just in case the same poisoner really had struck again.'

'He has.'

'I don't think so.'

'You don't believe me.'

'Not a word. It's not your fault. You've told it as plausibly as anybody could. The problem is that I know more about you than you think. You were Mrs Caswell's lover, weren't you, before the war?'

'Was I?'

'Yes. So that anonymous letter I received said. Before the war and possibly after. A touching story, in its way. You were determined to stand by her, even though you knew she'd tried to kill her husband. I can't blame you for that. In fact, I admire you. It's more than most men would do for an old flame. Your wife wasn't prepared to tolerate it, of course. Suing for divorce, I believe. Name linked with Major Turnbull, Mr Caswell's oldest friend. That must have grated, it really must. But it didn't stop you. You tried everything – legal and illegal – to save Mrs Caswell's neck. And when you realized none of it was going to work, you settled on one last desperate throw. If Victor Caswell died by the same means he'd narrowly escaped last September, we'd be forced to admit the murderer had finished the job they started then and that the murderer couldn't be Mrs Caswell because she had a perfect alibi: the condemned cell at Holloway Prison.'

402

'You're wrong.'

'Not this time, Mr Staddon. I've seen through you now. That was the object of the break-in at Clouds Frome, wasn't it? To murder Victor Caswell. But he was ready for you. Whether he meant to kill Pombalho – or both of you – I don't know. But somehow you persuaded him to let you live. A big mistake on his part, as it turned out. Down here – safe as he thought – he let his defences slip. Perhaps he was taken in by the row you had with your wife. Perhaps he assumed you'd come to see her, not him. If so, he was as wrong as any man could be. Maybe he died regretting it.'

'I didn't kill him.'

'Oh, but you did. You couldn't know he'd drink enough whisky to kill himself, but that didn't matter, did it? Even if he'd just been ill again, it would have looked like another attempt on his life and we might have felt obliged to call off the hanging.'

'Why haven't you, then?'

'Because you were careless. It's understandable. You didn't have much time to play with. But the telegram was never going to pass muster, was it?'

'There *was* a telegram. My chief assistant signed for it. Have you spoken to him?'

'Yes. An honest man, Mr Vimpany. But gullible. The telegram was a forgery, Mr Staddon. Good enough to deceive Mr Vimpany but not good enough to deceive the GPO. Who was the delivery-boy? And how much did you pay him? He did a fine job, so I hope he's not still waiting for his money. If he is, he's going to be disappointed.'

'If it was forged, it was forged by Gleasure. Like the letters. Don't you understand?'

'Yes. As a matter of fact, I do. You're prepared to do anything – and accuse anyone – if it will stop us executing Mrs Caswell. But it won't. Because she's guilty. And so are you.'

'Gleasure was present when both murders were committed. Think about that, Inspector. Think what it means.'

'It means he was Victor Caswell's valet. Where would you expect him to be but wherever his master was? Why should he want to kill him? He's out of a job now. What advantage is that to him?'

'I don't know.'

'Neither do I, Mr Staddon. Neither do I.'

'You have been charged with murder,' put in Jospin. 'Do you know the penalty for murder under French law?'

403

'Death, I assume.'

'*Oui, monsieur.* Death. But not by hanging.'

'They do it differently here,' said Wright.

'*La guillotine,*' Jospin continued. '*La veuve.*'

'The widow,' explained Wright with a smile. 'That's what they call the guillotine. Nasty way to go, I'd say, wouldn't you? A broken neck's one thing. But a severed neck? Too primitive for my liking.'

'Do you think I care what method they use?'

'You should do. Because the game's up, you know. It was a bold try, I'll grant you, but it won't save Mrs Caswell. She's for the drop. You ought to be thinking about yourself now, not her. Your best bet is to tell the truth.'

'That's what I'm doing, Inspector. But you won't listen.'

'Oh, I've listened. But I haven't heard the truth. Not yet. So, we'll let you think it over for a bit longer. Then we'll have another chat.'

'For God's sake, man—'

'*Silence!*' snapped Jospin. He looked up at the young policeman by the door. '*Amenez le prisonnier à son cachot.*'

As the policeman's hand touched my shoulder, Wright winked at me across the table. 'Be seeing you, Mr Staddon.'

Tuesday 19 February 1924

I hardly know how to describe my reaction to the events of today. I thought I could not feel more anxious and powerless than I did, but I was wrong, as I realized the moment I stepped off the train at Hereford station this afternoon and saw what had been scrawled across a bill on the side of a news-vendor's kiosk. VICTOR CASWELL MURDERED. That, of course, was merely astonishing. What I learned from the special edition of the Hereford Times *on sale at the kiosk was, however, truly horrifying.*

Victor Caswell died in the early hours of yesterday morning. He had been poisoned, apparently with arsenic. And Geoff is now under arrest in Nice, suspected of his murder. Cutting through the editorial expressions of outrage and sympathy for a respected local family dogged by misfortune, this seems to be all that is accurately known. The evidence against Geoff amounts to his visiting the Villa d'Abricot under suspicious circumstances on Sunday and being found in possession of a substance believed to be arsenious oxide.

I do not think I have ever felt less able to cope with events or grasp their meaning than I do at present. Geoff has stumbled into a trap. My misgivings about his journey to Cap Ferrat have been amply justified. But what kind of trap is it? What is its purpose? Has the person who tried to murder Victor Caswell last September struck again, pinning the blame on Geoff this time rather than Consuela? If so, why strike only three days before Consuela's execution?

I might be better placed to answer such questions if I had not had to expend so much time and energy today trying to explain the inexplicable to Senhor Pombalho and Dona Ilidia. When we reached Fern Lodge, we learned that Mortimer Caswell was with the police and his solicitor, Mr Quarton, trying to find out more about Victor's death, and that Marjorie was so prostrated by shock that she could not speak to anybody. In the circumstances, it was probably just as well that we were received instead by Hermione, the one member of the family unlikely to hold my friendship with Geoff against mé. She is as baffled as I am by what has occurred, but did much to strengthen my suspicion that Geoff is the victim of a conspiracy by revealing that mystery surrounds the current whereabouts of her nephew, Spencer. He visited London last Friday (the day he met Geoff) and was expected back the same evening, but has not returned. Hermione wanted to draw his absence to the attention of the authorities, but Mortimer forbade this on the grounds that the boy has gone missing for long weekends in London before and will be in touch as soon as he reads of his uncle's death in the newspapers. Personally, I cannot believe his disappearance is a coincidence. He is in Cap Ferrat, I feel sure, involved in some way with what has taken place there. Hermione, now I have told her what he said to Geoff when they met in London, thinks the same.

Jacinta is as brave and mature a twelve-year-old girl as it is possible to imagine. No doubt she cries herself to sleep every night in the arms of a favourite teddy, but to we adults she shows only a tearless face and a determined mind. She knows her father is dead, but is so unmoved by the fact that I could almost believe she had expected the news. She greeted us solemnly and with utter self-control. According to Hermione, she has not been told of Geoff's arrest, but, even if she had been, I do not think it would dent her conviction on one point. Her mother is innocent and must be saved. Jacinta is so certain of this that she seems unable to believe she may not be saved, which is, perhaps, just as well. If, as I greatly fear, it is a delusion, it is at least merciful one.

While we were with Jacinta, Mortimer returned to the house. He was obviously suspicious of me, recognizing my name as that of Geoff's partner, but he was obliged to remain polite in the presence of the Pombalhos. He is a stern, seething, buttoned-up man of sixty, who seems to have taken his brother's death as one more undeserved assault by fate. As to what lies behind it, he is clearly reluctant to probe too deeply. The police version of events is to him quite bad enough without imagining conspiracies that might implicate other members of his family.

An argument began at this point between Hermione and Mortimer, one I suspect has been brewing since they first had news of Victor's death. Hermione maintains that the doubts and possibilities raised by the event mean we should all press the Home Office at least to postpone Consuela's execution and that, if we presented a united front, we might be successful. I sided with her, as, somewhat hesitantly, did Francisco (and therefore Dona Ilidia). But Mortimer would have none of it. He wants us to observe what he calls 'a dignified silence'. He has been harassed by journalists and gossip-mongers for months. Now he wants an end of it, not a prolongation, which is all he thinks a public appeal for Consuela's life will achieve. I do not know him well enough to judge whether there may be other reasons for him taking such a view. All I can say for the moment is that his attitude amounts to what will help Consuela least: a dogged insistence that nothing should be done.

Not until early this evening, when I finally succeeded in installing the Pombalhos here at the Green Dragon, was I able to consider all the implications of what has occurred. I cannot believe Geoff is guilty and therefore I conclude that Victor was murdered by the same person who tried to murder him last September. We know Consuela cannot be that person, more certainly now than ever. The prevention of her execution must therefore be my sole aim in the short time left to her. That, I feel sure, is what Geoff would want.

To this end, I telephoned Sir Henry Curtis-Bennett's chambers in London, but could not obtain an answer. Eventually, I learned from Windrush's wife here in Hereford which hotel in London he is staying at, only to find that he was out when I called. Then, as much in frustration as anything else, I put a call through to the Villa d'Abricot in Cap Ferrat. A servant answered and I asked to speak to Angela. After what seemed an inordinate delay, she came to the telephone.

I had expected Angela to be shocked by the recent turn of events *and was prepared to make allowances accordingly. What I had not expected was the malice she seems to feel for Geoff. Her tone implied that she not only thinks him guilty, but suspects he poisoned Victor merely to spite her. She said the telegram was pure fantasy, that Geoff has become dangerously irrational and that I would be well advised to dissociate myself from him completely.*

After this unpleasant conversation, it was a relief to speak to Windrush, who had since returned to his hotel. Not that he was able to offer me much encouragement. He has been in touch with Sir Henry, who is in Norwich handling a case at the Norfolk assizes. Acting on Sir Henry's advice, he had pressed the Home Office to postpone Consuela's execution pending clarification of how Victor met his death. Thus far, they have resisted, though he is not without hope that they may relent tomorrow. I did not press him to say what he thinks their decision will be. I secretly fear their resentment of attempts to interfere with what they called in their letter to me 'the due course of law' will make them frustrate such attempts even if they suspect they may be justified.

Since bidding Windrush goodnight, a still more disturbing thought has come into my mind. I have only Geoff's word that he met Spencer last Friday and received a telegram sent in Angela's name. It is possible – much as I dislike entertaining the idea – that these were fabrications, designed as excuses for his journey to Cap Ferrat. If so, his real purpose might have been to poison Victor in the hope that this would raise sufficient doubt about Consuela's guilt to bring about her reprieve. He saw and spoke to her for the first time in thirteen years last Friday – in the condemned cell at Holloway Prison. I can only guess what effect that meeting had on him. It may have driven him into desperate action to appease his conscience. It may have prompted him to risk his own life to save hers.

I hope to God I am wrong. If Reg were on the telephone at home, I could ask him if he accepted an overseas telegram for Geoff on Friday afternoon. As it is, I shall have to wait until tomorrow to find out. I wonder what his answer will be.

Wednesday morning in Nice. The sky beyond the window of my cell was deep blue, flawless and crystalline. I wondered what the sky above Holloway was like, what Consuela could see in it as she gazed out at the dawn of her last full day. For me there was still the consolation of uncertainty, but for her, as she prayed and washed and breakfasted, there was only the knowledge that when this frugal ration of daylight failed, the end – sudden, absolute and pre-ordained – would only be a single night away.

Lucas returned, accompanied by Monsieur Fontanet, a local *avocat* who had been persuaded to accept my case. He seemed less than delighted to have done so and expressed his frustration when I declined to discuss the strategy we should adopt when I appeared in court to answer the charge of murdering Victor Caswell. This event was scheduled for Friday, but I was only concerned with what Thursday held. Had Lucas been in touch with the Home Office? No. He had sent a memorandum to the Foreign Office and they would take appropriate action. Had he spoken to Imry or Windrush or Sir Henry? Not as yet, but he would certainly be trying to find time to do so. I stared at him and listened to his words and realized that he had not understood – or had not wished to understand – anything I had said to him.

Around midday, I was taken yet again to the interrogation room, where Chief Inspector Wright was waiting for me with his pipe, his ready smile and his patient gaze. Jospin was absent and there was at once a change in Wright's attitude. The policeman who had brought me from my cell did not know any English. Therefore, Wright's crumpled grin implied, we could speak freely, one Englishman to another.

'As I told you yesterday, Mr Staddon, I wouldn't wish the guillotine on anyone, least of all a fellow-countryman. I want to help you as much as I can.'

'Then ask the Home Office to call off the hanging.'

He shook his head. 'It'd do no good. These affairs have a momentum of their own. Beyond a certain point, they can't be stopped. Well we've passed that point where Mrs Caswell is concerned. But not where you're concerned. Look at it this way. Denials won't wash. There's no way round the fact that you murdered Victor Caswell. But there might be a way round having to answer for it to a legal system you don't understand that deals with convicted murderers in a way I think should have gone out with the Middle Ages.'

'What are you trying to say, Chief Inspector?'

'Make a clean breast of it. That's my advice. Admit you murdered Victor Caswell. And admit the part you played in *trying* to murder him last September.' He smiled at the astonishment he must have been able to read in my face. 'I don't know why it didn't come to me sooner. Perhaps it's a sign of age. But that's it, isn't it? That's the truth of the matter. Mrs Caswell

408

tried to murder her husband in order to be free to marry you. And now you've finished the job. Unfortunately, there isn't going to be a wedding.'

'No. That isn't the truth at all.'

'The anonymous letters put me off the scent. They made me think Mr Caswell was the unfaithful partner, not Mrs Caswell. But then I remembered the emphasis Sir Henry put on her religion at the trial. Roman Catholics can't divorce. That's why it had to be murder. But you couldn't persuade her to go through with it. So you sent her those letters. And they swayed her where you'd not been able to. Her scruples flew out of the window as soon as she read them. Clever, I call that. Very clever. But heartless as well. Cruel, I could almost say.'

'I didn't write the letters.'

'What I can't understand is why you wrote the last one – the one addressed to me. Was it because you wanted to make sure I didn't suspect you of sending the first batch? If so, it was a mistake. Who else could know you were with Pombalho? Caswell had no wish to advertise the fact. No, it had to be you. A big mistake, as I say. I'm afraid you've been making quite a lot of those lately.'

'Gleasure knew. He wrote them. He murdered Victor. It's there in front of you, but you refuse to see it.'

'The point is this, Mr Staddon. If you confessed your part in the murder of Rosemary Caswell, that would take priority over the later offence. We could apply for extradition. I expect the French authorities would be happy to get you off their hands. Then you could stand trial in England. Much better for your chances, that would be, don't you reckon?'

I stared at him, trying to will him to believe what I was about to say. 'I don't care about my chances, Chief Inspector. I only care about Mrs Caswell. If she hangs, you'll regret it. One day, when the truth comes out, her case will be a *cause célèbre*. Everyone will know hanging her was a grotesque miscarriage of justice. Books will be written about it, inquiries demanded. She may even be posthumously pardoned. Somewhere, in the footnotes, you'll be mentioned as one of those who let it happen, one of those who stood and watched while the state committed murder. You won't be smiling then.'

Nor was he smiling now. 'I'll speak to you again tomorrow, Mr Staddon. That'll be your last opportunity to see reason. I hope you take it. By then, Mrs Caswell won't need your help – or anyone else's.'

Slowly, the afternoon passed. The brilliance of the Mediterranean sky faded. The shadows lengthened. I wondered again what Consuela was doing. A walk in the exercise yard? A letter to Jacinta? An interview with her priest? She could not be expecting anything now but death, premature and undeserved. What she might once have regarded as mere precautions were now essential preparations.

Night fell. I watched the colour being leeched from the sky until the very last glimmer of it had gone, knowing that in England it would have vanished even sooner. I was served a frugal meal. No doubt, at Holloway, they were more generous. But I ate nothing and nor, I suspected, would Consuela. The evening wore on. I had no way of keeping track of time. It would be different for Consuela. She would know, because they would tell her, when 9 p.m. came and the last revolution of the clock began.

Wednesday 20 February 1924
Big Ben has just struck 9 p.m. Those of us gathered in this cold and cheerless room all heard it clearly. That, I suppose, is a measure of the absolute silence in which we are waiting. We have sat here for barely twenty minutes, though it seems far longer, Windrush chain-smoking and fidgeting in the chair to my left, Pombalho pensive and immobile in the chair to my right. We do not know how long it will be before the door on the other side of the room opens and our vigil comes to an end, nor whether that end will be the one we fervently desire or the one we greatly dread. All we can do is wait and hope.

I was breakfasting with the Pombalhos in the dining-room of the Green Dragon this morning shortly after nine o'clock, trying and failing to find some words with which to lift their spirits, when, to my surprise, I saw Hermione Caswell threading through the tables towards us. There was an urgency to her progress and an edge to her expression that told me something remarkable had happened before she had even spoken a word.

At Hermione's insistence, I left the Pombalhos and accompanied her to a small writing-room at the rear of the hotel. There, waiting for us, was the sort of man whom the staff of the Green Dragon would normally turn away at the door: malodorous and raggedly dressed with matted grey hair and a beard; clearly, a tramp.

410

Hermione introduced him as Ivor Doak. Geoff having told me all about him, I wondered what on earth he could want with me. The answer was that he had something to tell me, something he had already told Hermione and which she considered to be of quite startling importance.

Doak spent last night in a quiet doorway near the cathedral – one of his regular bolt-holes. This morning, whilst crossing the cathedral green, he noticed a discarded newspaper lying on the bench and picked it up to read. It was yesterday's special edition of the Hereford Times, reporting Victor Caswell's murder and Geoff's arrest on suspicion of having poisoned him with arsenic. Doak read of this with something amounting to glee, since a painful death is exactly what he would have wished on the man who took Clouds Frome Farm away from him. But he was sorry to learn that Geoff might be made to answer for it, grateful as he has always been to him for his generosity of former times and ashamed that it was not put to better use.

Doak's sorrow was also tinged with incredulity. Here we came to the crux of his account. He is evidently a frequent visitor to the grounds of Clouds Frome, partly out of nostalgia, partly to prove he does not accept that the land has ceased to be his. Victor's recent measures to deter intruders he viewed with scorn and negotiated with ease. He frequently spends a night bedded down in one of the out-buildings, usually one of those in the kitchen garden. (He suspects Banyard has long known this, but has turned a blind eye to it.) His choice, on Monday night of last week, was the fruit house, where food as well as warmth is to be found. His slumbers, on this occasion, were disturbed. He has a keen ear and the light sleeping habits of a man used to being turned out of his bed. It was not, he emphasized, the first time he had been roused by suspicious comings and goings at Clouds Frome.

Somebody was moving around stealthily outside the fruit house. Doak edged open the door and, in the moonlight, saw a figure standing a few yards away by one of the lean-to sheds which run along the north wall of the kitchen garden. As Doak watched, the figure opened the door and entered. Once inside, he removed the lid from a tin – Doak heard the distinctive sound – and, a few moments later, replaced it. Then he reappeared, closed the shed and stole away.

Curious, Doak waited until all was quiet, then went over and looked in the shed. There were two identical tins of Weed Out standing near the entrance. It was one of these the fellow had

411

opened, presumably for the purpose of removing some of the contents; contents used, as Doak well knew, in the poisoning of Victor, Marjorie and Rosemary Caswell last September. Nevertheless, he decided to do nothing about what he had seen. What business was it of his? If somebody wanted to make a second attempt on Victor's life, Doak only wished them luck. He was delighted to read this morning of their success. All that worried him was the thought that a man who had once done him a substantial kindness should take the blame for it. Because Geoff is assuredly innocent. Of that Doak had no doubt. He hastened to Fern Lodge and told Hermione so (she being the only member of the Caswell family for whom he has any respect). The poisoner had to be the man he had seen that night in the kitchen garden: John Gleasure.

As soon as Doak named Gleasure, my thoughts were assailed by a riot of responses ranging from elation to despair. At last we felt we knew who the murderer was. Consuela's innocence was proven. And so was Geoff's. How I regretted the doubts I had entertained about him. Then, all too swiftly, came the misgivings. Would the authorities believe Doak? Even if they did, would they agree that his evidence justified a reprieve for Consuela? Was it really good enough – or simply that worst of all possibilities, too little too late? Alas, I still do not know.

At the time, one thing at least was clear to me. We had to make the most of what Doak had told us and we had to do so straightaway. We explained the significance of his account to the Pombalhos, then, leaving Dona Ilidia at the Green Dragon, hastened to Hereford police station, arriving shortly before ten o'clock. And there the delays and obstructions that have dogged us all day began.

The officers on duty agreed that only Superintendent Weaver could help us. I remembered him from the trial as a slowly spoken, even-tempered model of a fair-minded policeman and my hopes rose at the mention of his name. But he was in conference with the Chief Constable and could not be disturbed. We reasoned, we pleaded, we demanded. But they would not yield. Eventually, Hermione announced that either Weaver was summoned to see us or she would interrupt his meeting herself; they would have to restrain her physically to prevent her. At this, they agreed to send in a note.

Weaver emerged, clearly annoyed. But he listened patiently to Doak's account. Then he questioned him at length. Time marched

412

on. It was gone eleven before he conceded that the matter warranted further investigation. His problem, he freely admitted, was that conduct of the case had passed to Scotland Yard. It would be difficult for him to act without their approval, but the officer in charge, Chief Inspector Wright, was in Nice. He went away to consult the Chief Constable. He came back and said he would telephone Wright for advice. This seemed to take an age and resulted only in a French policeman telling him in fractured English that Wright was not available. He returned to the Chief Constable. Noon approached.

Weaver's mood had changed when he next appeared. Notwithstanding his reservations on the point, he was prepared to conduct a search of Gleasure's room at Clouds Frome in the hope of turning up traces of arsenic or some other evidence to corroborate Doak's statement. He had no search warrant, but was confident Danby would not stand in his way. Leaving Doak to dictate and sign a formal statement, we set off with him at once.

Thus my first visit to the house Geoff designed took place in circumstances which drove all architectural considerations from my mind. Gleasure's modest bed-sitting room was subjected to the meticulous attentions of Weaver and two assistants whilst Hermione, Pombalho and I looked on. The room did not seem likely to yield many secrets, for it was apparent that the occupant was a man of neat habits and few possessions. I frankly did not expect anything of an incriminating nature to be found. Nor, in all probability, would it have been but for Pombalho standing on an exceptionally squeaky floor-board. When the carpet was pulled back, two sawcuts, enabling a short section of the board to be lifted out, became visible. In the cavity beneath, wedged between the joists, was an old biscuit-tin. It contained an assortment of greetings cards – birthday, Christmas, Valentine – and a letter. The cards were still in their envelopes, written in the same hand and bearing postmarks covering a period from the autumn of 1910 to the summer of 1911. They were addressed to Gleasure and signed (if at all) 'L', accompanied by expressions of fondest love for 'dearest John'. The letter, by contrast, was addressed to Peter Thaxter, care of Gloucester Prison; it had been posted on 19 July 1911. I knew it at once from the forged version Geoff had shown me, but this – as the handwriting on the cards confirmed – was the genuine article: Lizzie Thaxter's farewell note to her brother.

Weaver could remember Lizzie's suicide very well. Now, at last, he learned the reason for it. He also learned that Victor Caswell

413

was in large measure responsible for it and that Gleasure and Lizzie had been secret sweethearts. Thus, at a stroke, a motive for murder presented itself: revenge for a lost love. All the fragments of the mystery were re-assembling themselves before us. Malahide must have sold Lizzie's letter to Gleasure, thus acquainting him with the ugly truth about Lizzie's death. The man he had served faithfully for years had driven his beloved to suicide. Small wonder he had resolved to kill him.

We were back at Hereford police station by half past two. From there Weaver telephoned Wright again and this time succeeded in speaking to him. Wright undertook to question Gleasure immediately and to search his room at the Villa d'Abricot. With the superintendent's proposal to contact the Home Office he was in complete agreement. 'It's settled then,' said Weaver. 'We'll recommend a reprieve in the strongest possible terms.' If only it had been settled, genuinely so. But the superintendent, as we were to discover, had spoken too soon. He went into conference with the Chief Constable once more, emerging at length with the news that the Permanent Under-Secretary of State was prepared to consider new evidence if it could be laid before him by seven o'clock that evening. There was nothing for it, then, but a dash to London.

Before setting off, I telephoned Windrush and explained the situation to him. He undertook to alert Sir Henry and to meet us at the Home Office. Hermione elected to remain in Hereford, where she thought she could most usefully be employed in calming Jacinta and Dona Ilidia. Doak, meanwhile, was enjoying a slap-up meal in the police canteen. But he had completed and signed his statement and that was all we thought we needed. By four o'clock, we were on our way.

It was a strange journey. Weaver instructed the driver to go as fast as possible, and so he did, yet our progress still seemed agonizingly slow. Dusk – slow to advance at first, then hideously swift – seemed to press in upon us. Little was said. Pombalho exhibited only bewilderment at what had occurred. Weaver, I suspect, was secretly appalled at how close he had come to contributing to the death of an innocent woman. And we were all painfully aware that we had yet to avert the ultimate catastrophe, that any hint of jubilation might yet prove premature.

We had reached the outskirts of London by half past six, and had driven like fury to do so. But patchy fog slowed us from that point on, though mercifully it did not thicken into a pea-souper. Even so, it was gone seven o'clock by the time we raced up the stairs of the Home Office. Windrush was waiting for us, as was Sir John Anderson's secretary, who issued a tart reminder that we were late before ushering us into his presence.

Sir John is a lean, lantern-jawed, dark-haired man with deep-set eyes, in manner and bearing the very quintessence of the inscrutable civil servant. He received us with distant politeness, then listened quietly while Weaver said his piece. Also present was Sir John's deputy, Blackwell, an altogether less restrained and tolerant character, who frequently interrupted to ask pointed questions. He laid great emphasis on the superficiality of our evidence and the irregularity of some of the steps Weaver had taken. Weaver countered with one doggedly expressed argument: he was only acting in such haste because of the imminence of an execution which he believed subsequent investigations would show to be unjust.

After about half an hour, we were asked to withdraw whilst the two mandarins deliberated. At a quarter past eight, we were recalled. Blackwell announced that, in our absence, he had spoken to Wright by telephone in Nice. Gleasure had now been questioned and his belongings searched. He had admitted nothing. Nor had anything of a suspicious nature been found on him. In the circumstances, said Sir John, they had concluded the 'so-called new evidence' would not justify them recommending a stay of execution to the Secretary of State.

I was too dumbstruck by the bland finality of this answer to speak. Windrush alone seemed in command of his faculties, pleading with them to re-consider. But they refused. A hint of something far nastier than inflexibility emerged when Blackwell grumbled that the production of 'last-minute evidence' amounted to 'the tactics of coercion', to which he did not propose to bow. Then Sir John cut him short. They were grateful for our efforts in the pursuit of justice, he said, but were unable to agree that what we had told them exonerated Mrs Caswell. She had been convicted after an exhaustive examination of all the available evidence and their confidence in that conviction was undimmed.

We were, I sensed, rapidly approaching the point of being asked to leave when Sir John's secretary came in to announce the arrival of Sir Henry Curtis-Bennett, hot-foot from Norwich. He stood next to me, breathing hard while Blackwell reiterated their decision. Then, without betraying any disappointment or anger, he asked if he might clarify certain points with them. Sir John assented. At this, Sir Henry suggested that Pombalho and I might

415

like to wait outside. His smile of re-assurance left us no choice; we left.

Within ten minutes, we were joined by Windrush and Weaver. The superintendent excused himself, saying he wanted to see if anybody over at Scotland Yard had spoken to Wright. Once he had gone, Windrush revealed that the discussions had taken a disputatious turn. Sir Henry was deploying his courtroom virtuosity, thus far to little effect. But the battle was not lost until it was done. So long as it continued, there was hope.

Shortly before nine o'clock, Blackwell emerged with a face like thunder and vanished into the bowels of the building. That left the two knights to argue it out. And argue, ever since, they have continued to do. Windrush has muttered darkly about old differences re-surfacing, about the ghosts of other clients whom Sir Henry has lost to Anderson's severity seeming still to stand between them. So much that should not affect such a decision now seems bound to. Anderson may suspect trumped-up evidence is being used to panic him into recommending a stay of execution, knowing how difficult it is to re-impose a death sentence once it has been lifted. He may be reluctant to appear irresolute so early in a new Secretary of State's term of office. He may be unable to differentiate between stubbornness and caution. He may simply be incapable of admitting that he is wrong.

I have no way of telling, of course, for I do not know the man. He is a stranger to me, as Consuela is to him. According to Windrush, his nickname within the Home Office is 'Jehovah'. Never can it have been more appropriate than tonight, when he holds in his hands what, to my mind, no human should ever hold in relation to another: the power of life and death.

The long night passed in a sleepless trance. I lay on the thin mattress in my cell, staring into the blackness above my head, thinking, imagining, visualizing – until I almost believed I could really see – Consuela, calmly counting away the final hours. But I could not see her. I could not hear or touch her. She was out of reach and would never again be within reach.

Breakfast – stale bread and a bowl of brackish coffee – arrived while it was still dark. From then on, it became impossible to pretend that the sky was not lightening. Dawn came, then full and implacable morning. The sun rose, stark and glaring, over Nice. The day gathered itself, pounced and rendered irretrievable what had merely been inevitable. I had no way of telling when it happened. I could neither sense nor calculate the moment of commission. Yet, at length, I realized that the counting must have stopped.

I had ceased to care whether it was morning or afternoon, had ceased indeed to think at all, when I was taken from my cell later that day and led to the interview room. Chief Inspector Wright was waiting for me. As ever, he was smiling.

'Hello, Mr Staddon.'

'What time is it?'

'The time?' He looked at his watch. 'Why, it's nearly twelve o'clock.'

It was over, then; long over. Already, they would have buried her in the prison graveyard and pinned a type-written notice to the main gate, announcing what they had done. *We, the undersigned, hereby declare that judgement of death was this day executed upon Consuela Evelina Caswell.* 'I hope you're satisfied,' I muttered, as much to those signatories I had never seen as to the man standing opposite me.

'Oh, I am, Mr Staddon, I am.' Still he was smiling. 'Please sit down. I've something to tell you.'

Thursday, 21 February 1924 (11 a.m.)

I was too tired last night to write this postscript to yesterday's events. Indeed, I am still tired now – more so, perhaps, than I should have allowed myself to become so soon after a bout of bronchitis. But I do not care, for my heart is lighter than it has been in months, my mind intoxicated with pure reviving joy.

Shortly before ten o'clock last night, Sir Henry entered the room where we were waiting at the Home Office, smiled broadly and said: 'Gentlemen, I have good news.' Sir John had surrendered. He had telephoned the Home Secretary to recommend a stay of execution. Mr Henderson had given his consent. And, even as Sir Henry was speaking, a messenger was en route for Holloway Prison.

There was much shaking of hands and slapping of backs. Pombalho even went so far as to kiss Sir Henry. We were smiling and laughing. The miracle we had expected to be denied had been granted.

Within minutes, my companions had set off for Holloway to share their jubilation with Consuela. I did not go with them. For me it was enough to walk out into the silence of Whitehall, to glance across at the Cenotaph and to know that the state would not be adding Consuela's name to its list of victims. In that glad issue I rejoice.

CHAPTER

TWENTY-THREE

For a minute or more after Chief Inspector Wright had finished his explanation of Consuela's reprieve, I stared at him in silence, disbelief tinging my delight. Then I said: 'When did you know about this?'

'Last night. Superintendent Weaver telephoned me from Scotland Yard with the news just after eleven o'clock.'

'And you didn't tell me? You just let me think it was going to happen – that it *had* happened?'

'Yes.' He smiled sheepishly. 'I'm sorry to have left you in the dark. But it was necessary.'

'Why?'

'Because of Gleasure. We brought him in yesterday afternoon. As soon as I started questioning him, I knew he was our man. I'd thought you were, granted, but that's all it had been: thought; guesswork; a balance of probabilities. With Gleasure it was different. It sometimes is, you know. You can just sense it, halfway between the brain and the nose. I suppose it ought to make a policeman's job easier when that happens, and so, in one way, it does. But, in another way, it makes it more difficult. Because you have to do more than sense guilt. You have to prove it. And if you can't, when you know in your bones it's there, why, that's the very devil, take it from me. All I had on Gleasure was what Weaver had: one pretty dubious witness to what might have been the theft of arsenic and a cache of letters providing a sort of motive. Too flimsy by far. But good enough, I'd assumed, for

419

calling off the execution. When Weaver 'phoned me and said the big-wigs were digging in their toes, I was astonished. It meant we could be about to hang an innocent woman. So, I had Gleasure in again. It was late by then. Gone ten. Gone nine in London. He was still saying nothing. I tried the ploy I'd used on you about the guillotine and how he could dodge it by admitting to both murders. It didn't wash. I didn't expect it to. I realized from the first he was one of those it'd take days to wear down. But we didn't have days. So, I told him we'd found arsenic in the turn-ups of his trousers. He knew I was lying. He'd been too careful to make a mistake like that. But he knew we could make it stick, knew – because I as good as told him – that I'd twist every rule in the book to nail him if he let Mrs Caswell hang. He was in two minds. I could see that. It's what I'd hoped for. But he's an obstinate blighter. I was asking for too much too soon. He was still recovering from the shock of being rumbled. He wasn't ready to throw in his hand. In the end, I had to send him back to his cell.'

'But then you heard about the reprieve,' I put in. 'Why couldn't I be told?'

'I didn't tell anybody, Mr Staddon. I couldn't take the risk that Gleasure might get wind of it. I'm sorry to have left you believing the worst, but I think you'll agree it was worth it. Gleasure cracked, you see, as I'd hoped he would. At eight o'clock this morning, he asked to see me and said he was prepared to confess to the murders of Rosemary and Victor Caswell. He thought that by owning up in time to prevent the hanging he'd ensure he stood trial in England and earn some credit for saving Mrs Caswell's life. Well, I let him believe the hanging was still due to go ahead and that, subsequently, it was only called off on his account. I haven't told him the truth yet. I don't know how he'll react. Not that it matters. He's signed his confession now. There's no way back.'

'He's admitted everything?'

'Yes. He gave two reasons. Firstly, he claims to bear you and Mrs Caswell no ill will. Secondly, he doesn't want his accomplice to evade justice. I dare say he also hopes—'

'He's named an accomplice?'

'With some relish.' Wright grinned. 'Why don't you read his statement, Mr Staddon?' From the valise beside his chair he drew a clip of papers and slid it across the table towards me. 'I shouldn't really show it to you, but we're a long way from

Scotland Yard and it seems only fair in view of what I've put you through.' His grin broadened. 'I think you'll find it an interesting document.'

I, John William Gleasure, having been cautioned by Chief Inspector Wright that anything I say may be used in evidence hereafter, wish to make the following statement.

I have worked for the Caswells since 1891, when I started at Fern Lodge as a kitchen-boy. I was twelve years old then and Victor was twenty-three, just down from Cambridge and fretting at having to work for the family firm. I saw very little of him in the early days, but, whenever I did bump into him, he would have a kind word for me, which is more than I can say for any other member of the household. He used to tip me for polishing his boots with extra care. Later, he took to sending me on secret errands. Down to the betting shop, for instance, to put money on a horse. His father disapproved of gambling. If the horse won, Victor would give me something from his winnings. I liked him for that. I suppose you could say he was my hero.

In 1895, Victor was sent to Brazil to work for a bank. I found out later he had been sent away in disgrace, though only rumours of that reached the likes of me at the time. A few years passed, then we heard he had been sacked by the bank and had vanished without trace. Then, after a few more years, we heard he had reappeared, complete with a fortune made in the rubber trade. He returned to Hereford in 1908, bringing his beautiful Brazilian wife with him. By then, I was a footman working for his brother Mortimer, who had taken charge of the family firm when old Mr George Caswell died. Victor and his wife moved into Fern Lodge until they could find a suitable piece of land to build a house of their own on.

I was glad to have Victor back, unlike most of the household. He added a bit of zest to life. And we still got on well. So, it was no real surprise when he asked me if I would like to come and work for him when they moved. I jumped at it. I could see promotion was more likely under him than his skinflint of a brother.

Mrs Caswell – Consuela, that is – disliked me from the first. I think it was because I was the one servant on good terms with Victor. She resented that. In those days, she wanted him all to herself. I suppose she felt insecure and homesick in drab old Hereford. You could hardly blame her.

A lady's maid was appointed specially to look after Consuela, Lizzie Thaxter by name. She arrived early in 1909.

She was a bright, sparkling, red-headed girl with a bubbly laugh and a personality that quite bowled me over. We got to be sweet on each other. But we had to keep it a secret, because we knew Consuela would not want to keep Lizzie on if she found out about us. She trusted Lizzie, you see, but she would not have trusted her if she had known we were in love. That was wrong of her, because Lizzie would never have betrayed her, not even to me. To prove it, she did not say a word to me about Consuela's affair with Staddon, not a word.

It came to the point where Lizzie and I started talking about getting wed. It seemed a perfect match. Footman with prospects and milady's maid. But we were sure Consuela would object. And, all the time, the chances were growing that rumours would start about us below stairs. So, I decided to confide in Victor and see what he advised.

He was very fair, it seemed to me. He said that if he chose the right moment he could probably persuade Consuela to give us her blessing. But it might take a while: we would have to be patient. Well, we were still being patient when Lizzie's brother, Peter Thaxter, was arrested for his part in the Peto's Paper Mill robbery. That was February, 1911.

I was horrified. I had my future to think of. To do well in service you have to have a reputation for discretion and honesty. The last thing I needed was a gaol-bird for a brother-in-law. Lizzie was in Brazil at the time with her mistress, whose father had died, but I could hardly wait for her to get back before discussing what I should do with Victor. He was angry about all of it, as only seemed natural, Grenville Peto being Mortimer's brother-in-law and one of Peter Thaxter's accomplices being a carpenter – name of Malahide – who was working on the new house. But he also appreciated my predicament. In the end, we agreed that Lizzie could stay on if she disowned her brother and had no further contact with him. Once the trial was over and the dust had settled, we could get married as we had hoped.

A few weeks later, Lizzie came back with Consuela. She was upset about her brother, of course, but it seemed to me that was not the only difference in her. She had grown closer to her mistress while they had been away, closer to her and further from me. When I told her what Victor and I had decided, she flew into a rage and said we had no business settling her future between us; she would not be told by anybody to turn her back on her brother. She was sure he was innocent, even though he had been caught red-handed. Well, that was the first and the last row we ever had. I told her straight that she could forget marriage – and being a lady's maid – if she stuck by him, that it would be the worse for her and her family if she lost her job and all her prospects with it.

She was torn. I could see that. But I did not mean to let her off the hook. I reckoned it was time to make her understand that I was to be obeyed. And it was true about her family. Her father and another brother had lost their jobs at the mill on account of Peter. They were looking to her to tide them over. I offered to help as well – if she did as I had told her. So, in the end, she agreed. It was all patched up between us. Except that it was never quite the same as before. She stopped trusting me. But I thought she would get back to her normal self once the trial was out of the way. I thought it was just a question of biding my time. Anyway, I had shown her who was master. That seemed important.

In April, we moved to the new house at Clouds Frome. Victor had said he would need a valet once he had left Fern Lodge and I had my eyes on the position. Lizzie and I did not see so much of each other at that time. I was working hard and I could tell she was brooding about her brother. He was due to come before the assizes in September. I was sure it would all come right after that, so I thought it best to leave well alone.

But it never did come right, because, one sultry night in July, Lizzie hanged herself in the orchard at Clouds Frome.

I could not understand why she had done it. She left no note, no explanation of any kind. I had known she was depressed, of course, but suicide seemed so extreme, an insult, almost, to me and what I had been planning for our future.

I grew a hard skin after Lizzie died. I had kept our love a secret, so I kept my grief a secret as well. I cut my feelings off. I decided never to let myself love anyone again, never to think of anybody's interests but mine. That autumn, Victor made me his valet. It meant more money and a higher place in the scheme of things. Slowly, I forgot Lizzie and all our hopes. I put them behind me. Time went on. I joined the army when the war broke out and got a nice safe posting as batman to a staff officer. Then, when it was all over, I went back to Clouds Frome as if nothing had changed.

Some things had changed, though. Victor had a daughter by then, Jacinta, a solemn little girl. Victor did not seem to feel for her what I would feel for a daughter of mine. I put it down to disappointment that she was not a boy. As for Consuela, she had become more and more withdrawn, living only for Jacinta, hardly speaking to Victor from one day to the next. Not that I cared whether they loved or hated each other. I was happy with *my* lot. Nothing could touch me any more – or so I thought.

One evening in the autumn of 1922, I was down at the Full Moon in Mordiford, having a drink, when a fellow asked if he could speak to me. He said he was Tom Malahide, one of Peter Thaxter's accomplices in the Peto's Paper Mill robbery. He said he had just been released from prison and that Peter had been hanged back in 1911 for killing a warder. Well, I had heard about that at the time and had thought little of it. But Malahide said Peter had given him a letter he had received from Lizzie just before her death, to be passed on to his family when Malahide came out. He said it explained why she had killed herself. And he also said Peter had told him Lizzie was secretly engaged to me. Malahide made no bones about what he wanted. He reckoned I was better off than the Thaxters, so he was making me an offer: Lizzie's last letter in exchange for some money to help him get back on his feet.

The long and the short of it is that I bought the letter from Malahide for twenty pounds. I just had to have it, you see, once he had let me glimpse enough of it for me to be sure it was genuine. I just had to know why she had done it. And the letter told me. She had gone on visiting her brother and writing to him after I had forbidden her to. She had disobeyed and deceived me. And Victor had somehow found out. But, instead of telling me, he had black-mailed Lizzie into spying on Consuela for him. She had to choose between losing me – and her job – and betraying her mistress. Well, she chose. And Victor learned what he must have suspected. Consuela was having an affair with Staddon. But Lizzie could not bear the lies she had to tell, the secrets she had to betray. The strain of it drove her to suicide. Or Victor did. It depends how you look at it. But I looked at it only one way. Victor had killed Lizzie. He had taken her from me. I had spent years being grateful to a man who had ruined my life.

I read the letter – and thought it all through – over and over again. Then, one morning while I was shaving Victor, I mentioned Lizzie's name, quite casually. I said I was beginning to think it was just as well I had never married her. I said that, at the time, I had not even been sure she was keeping her promise to have nothing more to do with her brother. And Victor replied: 'Do you know, Gleasure, I think you may be right.' Well, it was the way he said it, the tone of his voice, that gave the game away. And it was then, as I was sliding the razor down his cheek and staring into his

424

eyes, that I decided to kill him for what he had done to Lizzie.

But I wanted to do more than just kill him. I wanted to cheat him, as well, to cheat him as he had cheated me. So, I started thinking about how I could get back at him. And an idea began to form in my mind. I knew from Lizzie's letter that Consuela and Staddon had been lovers until July, 1911. Jacinta had been born in April, 1912 – exactly nine months later. That explained Victor's neglect of her. She was not his. A few weeks after her birth, Quarton, his solicitor, had come to see Victor with a new will for him to sign. I had witnessed it, without seeing what it contained. I had assumed at the time that it was being done to provide for Jacinta. But now I thought differently. Now I thought it had probably been done for exactly the opposite reason: to strike her out of his will because she was not his daughter and perhaps to strike Consuela out as well, for carrying another man's child. If I was right, he had substituted another heir for both of them. But who? Well, I thought I could guess. I knew the way his mind worked. If he had chosen the person I suspected, he had given me the opportunity I needed.

I had to be sure, of course. I had to see the will. It was kept in a concealed safe he had had installed during the first winter at Clouds Frome. I knew where it was. I had seen him open it often enough. What I did not know was the combination. But, as I say, I understood Victor. He had always liked playing games with numbers. He would put money on a horse with a lucky number – a family birthday, I mean, or some other important date – far sooner than he would on a long-odds favourite. And he would use the same sort of mental trick to memorize a combination rather than write it down somewhere. So, whenever he was away, I started trying out ideas based on the sort of numbers he might use. Eventually, I hit on the answer.

I found more than I had bargained for inside the safe. The will was there, of course. I read it and learned I had guessed right. But there was money as well. Thousands of pounds in brand-new five pound notes. Something about them made me suspicious. I took one away and discovered from the water-mark that it had been printed on Peto's Mill paper. Then I realized Victor was cleverer than I had given him credit for. He had master-minded the robbery. And to think he had threatened to sack Lizzie and forbid our marriage because of the disgrace her brother had brought on her – a disgrace, I now knew, *he* was ultimately responsible for. Well, that settled it as far as I was concerned. I decided

425

then to take his money as well as his life.

Victor's sole heir was – and is – his nephew, Spencer. I reckon Victor chose him because he recognized something of himself in Spencer's nature. Neither thought Hereford – or Caswell & Co. – was good enough for them. They both wanted more. And they were both prepared to do just about anything to get it.

That is what I intended to play on. Spencer had come down from Cambridge in the summer of 1922 and was working for the family firm – just as resentfully as Victor had thirty years before. I struck up an acquaintance with him. It was not difficult. All I had to do was buy him drinks at the pubs in Hereford he used and listen to his gripes and grudges. Most of them were against his father. Yes, he was just like Victor had been at that age.

When I put my plan to him, he jumped at it. I told him about the will. I suggested we murder Victor, then split the inheritance down the middle. Equal shares. We would both be rich men. The beauty of it was that the will was a secret, so when Spencer was named as the beneficiary, there would be no reason to think he had expected to inherit. And anyway, I would be the one who actually killed Victor. I, who had not a shadow of a motive – that anybody knew about.

Spencer was all for it. It was more than just greed, more even than the desire to be free of his father. It was the thrill of planning and getting away with it, the pleasure of committing an undetected crime. He had no scruples about murdering Victor, not one. I wanted revenge, but Spencer, well, he turned out to have an even harder heart than I thought. There is a spark of pure evil in his soul, take it from me. At first, I had difficulty restraining him. But I had to, of course, because I knew that, if we hurried, it would be a recipe for disaster. I had worked it all out, you see. We needed not just to cover our own tracks, but to fake somebody else's. We needed a scapegoat as well as an alibi.

We chose Consuela because everybody knew she did not get on with Victor and because she had no friends, so nobody would rally round to defend her. I had already decided poison was the safest method to use. People seem to associate it with women. That was another argument for Consuela. The anonymous letters were Spencer's idea. He has a gift for forgery.

There was a murder done in Hay-on-Wye a couple of years ago using an arsenic-based weed-killer. I remembered it well. That prompted me to have a look round the kitchen garden where I found some tins of *Weed Out* which looked ideal for our purpose. Spencer telephoned the manufacturer and confirmed it had arsenic as its major ingredient. They warned him to be careful with it. From that point on, it was simply a question of waiting for our chance. I did not intend to be hasty. I was prepared to wait as long as I had to for the right set of circumstances. I carried a small packet of arsenic about with me, sewn into the lining of my waistcoat, against the day when I could use it without being discovered.

The day came on Sunday 9 September last. I was keeping watch when Noyce delivered tea to Consuela in the drawing-room. I saw him leave. Then I saw her stroll out into the garden. That was my chance. I slipped in, mixed the arsenic in the sugar and left again before Consuela returned. I knew Victor was the only one who took sugar in his tea and, of course, it strengthened the case against Consuela if there was no possibility of her or Jacinta being poisoned. I thought it was bound to work. The arsenic was near the surface. There was enough to kill three men, let alone one. Victor was done for.

Then luck turned against us. Marjorie and Rosemary arrived unexpectedly, both sweet-toothed and eager for tea. There was nothing I could do to stop them. All I could do was hope Victor would still swallow a fatal dose. But the odds were against that happening now there were ladies to be served first. And so it proved. Victor was ill. But he did not die. Rosemary died instead.

Spencer took it badly. I do not mean he was upset because we had killed his sister by mistake. He cared no more for her than any other member of his family. He would happily have done for the lot of them if necessary. No, what he took badly was the upset to our plans. He blamed me for bungling the attempt. But he soon saw falling out with me would be fatal. We had to stick together. A murder had been committed, even though it was not the murder we had planned. We still had to make sure Consuela took the blame for it. So, I planted the arsenic and the letters where I was confident the police would find them. And they did. Consuela was arrested and committed for trial.

The question was what to do next. If we made another attempt on Victor's life, we would prove Consuela was innocent and we would also prove somebody had faked the evidence against her. If we did not, all our efforts would be wasted. Spencer was in favour of drastic action, but I persuaded him we had to be careful. I could see nothing for it but to wait for the fuss to die down before thinking up a new plan.

But I had reckoned without Imogen Roebuck. She saw an opportunity in what had happened to advance herself. As the weeks passed, she wormed her way into Victor's affections, first as his nurse, then as his friend and finally as his lover. The poisoning took something out of him. It made him feel vulnerable. That is what she played on. I had to watch while he came more and more to dote and depend on her. I was powerless to do anything about it. I even had to play my part in deceiving Consuela's brother at Miss Roebuck's say-so. I could not afford to make her doubt my loyalty, so I did what she told me to do: strike up an acquaintance with Rodrigo, give him the impression I was open to bribes, then, when he became curious about Victor's will, encourage him to break into the house and open the safe in order to find out what the will contained. I had to be told the combination then, of course – the combination I already knew. No doubt Victor meant to change it as soon as it had served its purpose. They claimed they just wanted to have Rodrigo deported and that nobody would come to any harm. I do not know if they meant to kill him. Miss Roebuck assured me afterwards that Victor shot him in self-defence. Not that I cared either way. What worried me was that she obviously knew the terms of Victor's will. And that made her a real threat to the success of our plans. But, for the life of me, I could not see what we were to do about her.

Things came to a head soon after Consuela's conviction. Her appeal was rejected on 7 February. It seemed certain then that she would hang. On Sunday 10 February, Victor called a family conference at Clouds Frome and announced that he and Miss Roebuck were going abroad and would marry as soon as they were free to.

That forced our hand. As soon as Victor married again, any will he had previously made would be nullified by law. Miss Roebuck, as the new Mrs Caswell, would automatically become his heir. So, we had to strike before they married. Since they could marry as soon as Consuela was dead, that meant we had to strike before her execution. In other words, before today.

This time, the plan was mostly Spencer's. He had already identified Staddon as a potential scapegoat and had led him to believe that Miss Roebuck and Victor had staged the poisoning in order to rid themselves of Consuela. He had told him that Grenville Peto had telephoned Victor shortly before Marjorie and Rosemary's arrival at Clouds Frome on

Sunday 9 September, but had refused to say who had given him this information. It was a lie, of course. Peto never telephoned. But Staddon was trying to clear Consuela's name. Evidence that Victor knew the ladies might call for tea was therefore just what he thought he needed. And by feeding him with such tit-bits, Spencer was not only diverting him from the truth but also supplying him with a motive to murder Victor. If Victor was poisoned in circumstances which suggested the same killer had struck again, Consuela would be proved innocent. As the date of her execution approached, it became more and more obvious that nothing else could save her. What we had to do was persuade the police that, for this reason, Staddon had become desperate enough to kill Victor. Then we had to lure him to Cap Ferrat so that he would be on hand as a ready-made suspect when the murder was committed.

Unlike the first attempt, the second one had to be hurried. I knew that increased the risks we were running, but there seemed no alternative. After all the planning and waiting, I could not bear to let the chance slip through our fingers.

I was due to leave for Cap Ferrat with Victor and Miss Roebuck on Tuesday 12 February. The night before, I took a supply of arsenic from one of the tins of *Weed Out* in the kitchen garden. Banyard had been told to keep them under lock and key after the first poisoning, but he was too obstinate to take any notice. Meanwhile, Spencer posted an anonymous letter to Chief Inspector Wright at Scotland Yard, naming Staddon as Rodrigo's accomplice during the break-in at Clouds Frome. Spencer had seen Staddon leaving Fern Lodge early on the morning following the break-in and could not believe it was just a coincidence he was in Hereford at the time. The letter also named Staddon as Consuela's lover. We were confident Chief Inspector Wright would become suspicious of Staddon as a result. We waited a few days for those suspicions to take root. Then, on Friday 15 February, Spencer paid some street-arab to impersonate a post-boy and deliver a forged telegram to Staddon's office. It claimed to be from Mrs Staddon, who had been in Cap Ferrat for some time as a guest of Major Turnbull. It asked Staddon to come at once because she had discovered disturbing information about Victor. To make sure Staddon responded, Spencer staged a chance meeting with him that evening. He told him I was the source of his information about Victor's telephone conversation with Grenville Peto on Sunday 9 September. And Staddon, who still thought Victor and Miss Roebuck had carried out the poisoning, fell for it completely. He set off for Cap Ferrat the following morning. Spencer travelled overnight and arrived before him.

Spencer warned me to expect Staddon during the afternoon or evening of Sunday 17 February. Once he had visited the villa, we would be free to proceed. As it happened, he arrived while Victor and his friends were all out, which suited me perfectly. I kept him waiting in the morning-room for two reasons. Firstly, it gave me time to mix arsenic in the whisky that was kept in the drawing-room. Secondly, it meant everybody would later think Staddon had done what I had done. I knew I would have to find another opportunity if Victor did not drink any whisky, but he had been putting a lot away as the hanging approached, so I did not expect to have to try anything else. Turnbull never drank whisky and Thornton hardly ever did. In the event, it went like clockwork. Victor was upset by Staddon's visit. I did not even have to ask him if he wanted a drink. He demanded a scotch and soda. Luckily for him, Thornton asked for a gin sling. It gave me a lot of quiet pleasure to hand Victor his glass and watch him drink it down, then hear him ask for another.

After Staddon had left, I slipped out and spoke to Spencer, who was waiting by the garden gate. He then kept watch on Staddon's hotel until he had a chance to plant the arsenic in his room, where the police were bound to find it. Spencer is good at lock-picking as well as forgery. I reckon he would have turned to crime eventually without any encouragement from me.

Victor died that night, in agony. I watched him die. Before the end, I think he knew from my expression that I had killed him. I hope so. The arsenic worked like a knife in his guts. He deserved every twist of the blade.

We would have succeeded, but for bad luck. We made no mistakes. We could not have foreseen that Marjorie and Rosemary would come to tea on 9 September or that Doak would be sleeping in the kitchen garden on 11 February. But for those two mischances, we would have got clean away with it. I do not know where Spencer is. He was supposed to leave Cap Ferrat on Monday, then reappear in Hereford pretending to be as shocked by the news as everybody else. If he finds out I have been arrested, he will realize the game is up. What he will do then I cannot say. He is clever as well as unpredictable.

I have made this statement quite voluntarily and without coercion of any kind. I would like to stand trial in England. This crime began there and it is only fitting that it should end there. I suppose I will pay with my life for what I have done. I suppose I will hang, like Lizzie. Well, perhaps there is justice in that.

There is nothing else I wish to say.

J. W. Gleasure,
21 February 1924.

When I had finished reading the statement, I slid it back across the table to Wright and said: 'How does this make you feel, Chief Inspector?'

'Suitably contrite.' Still he was smiling. 'We were wrong about this case from the start. I'm only glad we discovered our mistake before it was too late.'

'Can I speak to Gleasure?'

'I'm afraid I can't allow that.'

'Am I free to go, then?'

'Oh, completely. I'd be grateful if you could stay in Nice for a few days, though, till I know whether I'll need you to testify against Gleasure in court here.'

'And Consuela? Will she be freed too?'

'Eventually. Technically, of course, she's still a convicted murderess, so there could be some delay. But she will be released. You need have no doubt of that.'

I rose and was on the point of leaving when the memory of all the questions and accusations I had endured in that room flooded back into my mind. 'What if Doak hadn't seen Gleasure that night, Chief Inspector?' I suddenly asked. 'What if he hadn't picked up an old newspaper yesterday morning and read about my arrest? What then, eh?'

Wright shook his head and stared down at the pages of Gleasure's statement where they lay on the table in front of him. What could he say? The truth was that nobody, least of all either of us, could claim the credit for Consuela's salvation. She had been unlucky. Now her luck had changed. That, as Gleasure would have said, was all.

But recrimination was swiftly overborne by rejoicing. As I walked out of the building a few minutes later and breathed in a lungful of Mediterranean air, scented with the certainty of spring, I experienced a surge of pure elation. Consuela was safe and would soon be free. Nothing else mattered. That was truly all. That was everything.

CHAPTER

TWENTY-FOUR

The twenty-first of February, which I had looked forward to with horror, was suddenly transformed into one of the sweetest days of my life. That I spent it alone did not matter. I booked into the Negresco and from there telephoned Imry, whose voice at the end of the line was the only companionship I needed. He sounded as relieved and exultant as I felt. It was too soon, we agreed, to analyse the recent past or speculate about the future. The present was for once sufficient to still every doubt and fulfil every hope. Consuela was safe. And so were we all. I ordered a bottle of champagne, took it onto the balcony of my room and drank it with slow and silent pleasure as the sun sank behind me and lit the horizon with purest gold.

That night I slept better and longer than I had in weeks. I was still lingering over a late breakfast at eleven o'clock the following morning when Chief Inspector Wright called to see me. He looked more cheerful than ever and had, he said, good news of a confidential nature to impart. We walked out onto the Promenade des Anglais and there, gazing across the blue expanse of the bay towards Cap Ferrat, he announced: 'Spencer Caswell's in custody.'

'How was he caught?'

'He was arrested at Hereford railway station last night after arriving on a train from London. I'm going back straightaway to question him.'

'Will he try to brazen it out, do you think?'

'It seems so. He claims to have spent the week in Paris, drifting between bars and brothels. Naturally, he doesn't have any witnesses to prove it. Perhaps he doesn't feel he needs any.'

'Surely, in the light of Gleasure's statement . . .'

'We shall see, Mr Staddon, we shall see. Leave young Spencer to me. Actually, he's not the only reason I called on you this morning.'

'No?'

'We don't need to detain you here any longer. Gleasure will appear in court on Monday, but the fullness of his confession means no witnesses will be required to testify. Committal for trial will be automatic.'

'He's to be tried here, then?'

'In the end, I don't think he will be. But extradition is a tricky business. It may take some time to resolve.'

'And must Consuela stay in prison until it *is* resolved?'

'I certainly hope not. But it's hardly for the likes of me to say. Take it up with her lawyers when you get home.'

'I will, Chief Inspector, believe me.'

'Don't worry, Mr Staddon.' He grinned. 'The law tries to deal with embarrassments as quickly and quietly as possible. And Mrs Caswell's case is *very* embarrassing. You'll have her to yourself before you know it.'

It was not until a few minutes later, as I watched Wright walk away along the promenade, that I realized how natural his assumption had been. He thought I had acted out of love. And so in a sense I had, though not the sense he imagined. Consuela would not be re-entering my life when she left prison. We would not be trying to revive what we had once felt for each other.

Or would we? I turned and stared out to sea. There, where sky and water met, it seemed possible to believe that almost any future could be waiting, however forfeit past actions had seemed to render it. She had forgiven me. And I had suffered on her account. And soon she would be free in every meaning of the word. If I tried hard enough, I could imagine three figures – Consuela and I, with Jacinta between us – strolling past on the promenade, laughing and smiling as they went. When I looked round, they were not there. But I was no longer certain they never would be.

I left Nice that evening aboard the night-train for Calais. Not until I entered the restaurant-car for dinner did I realize that Clive and Celia were also aboard. I sat at the opposite end of the carriage from them and resolved to make no effort at communication. But Clive, much to Celia's evident disapproval, decided that some sort of rapprochement was in order. Abandoning his dessert, he grasped his brandy glass and swayed down to my table.

'Hello, old man. Seems a bit rum for us to pretend we don't know each other.'

'Does it?'

'Mind if I join you for a minute?' Without waiting for a reply, he sank into the chair opposite me. 'Must say we were all thoroughly bucked to hear you were in the clear.'

'Really?'

'Even Angie. She wouldn't want you to come to any harm, you know.'

'Is she still in Cap Ferrat?'

'Yes.' He grimaced. 'I was damn glad to clear out as soon as the police said we could. But Angie's staying on for the funeral. Turnbull's quite cut up about Victor. Well, so were we all, of course, but Turnbull took it specially hard, the two of them being such old friends. Angie's doing her best to jolly him along.'

'You paint a touching scene. What about Miss Roebuck?'

'Distraught at first, of course. But bearing up now.'

'I'm sure.'

'I never thought you could be guilty, of course. Not for a moment.'

'Decent of you to tell the police that.'

'What?' He frowned. 'Don't quite take your meaning, old man.'

'None of you raised a hand to help me. That's what I mean.'

'Oh. Well . . . Damn it all, we'd have spoken up if it had come to a trial. You must know we would.'

'No. I don't.'

He eyed me thoughtfully for a moment, then said: 'I gather there's been a lot of publicity at home. Reprieve of a condemned woman and all that. I wouldn't be surprised if some reporter tried to talk you into saying things you might regret.'

'Such as?'

'The point is, I wouldn't want to think Angie was going to read something unpleasant about herself in the papers. Something said by you, for instance.'

'Your concern does you credit. But I hardly think the gutter-press are likely to be interested in the break-down of my marriage. Do you?'

A wince and a smile merged on Clive's face. His voice dropped. 'About the divorce, old man. Our agreement regarding the terms. I trust it still applies?'

'I don't know.'

'But surely—'

'Listen to me, *old man*. I've just been cleared of a murder charge. The woman I – and precious few others – have been trying to save has just escaped death by a matter of hours. Do you seriously think that in the face of all that I give a damn about the *terms* on which Angela hopes to divorce me? If you do, then you're a bigger fool than I thought. And, frankly, I'm not sure that's possible.'

Clive gaped at me, the realization that I had insulted him seeping through the thick layers of his insensitive soul. 'I say, dammit, there's no—'

'What I suggest is this. Go back to Celia. Finish your meal. And then spend the rest of this journey doing what you thought so very rum. Pretend we don't know each other. I'll do the same. It won't be difficult. In fact, as far as I'm concerned, it's almost the truth.' I signalled past him to the waiter. 'Now, if you'll excuse me, I feel in need of some fresh air.'

I paid the bill and hurried into the corridor of the next carriage. There I lowered a window and leaned out, letting the cold night blast away some of my anger. Poor Clive. He could not be expected to understand. Everything my marriage had brought me seemed tainted by the deception of which it had been a consequence. The past was a wasteland, the future an unexplored continent. Behind me was regret, ahead only uncertainty. At least now I knew which was preferable.

I breakfasted early enough the following morning to avoid Clive and Celia and saw nothing of them at Calais. I suspect Celia may have insisted they wait for a later sailing rather than risk an encounter on the ferry. For that I was grateful.

At Dover, I bought all the national newspapers and scoured them for assessments of the case as the train bore me north towards London. The dramatic circumstances of Victor's murder, Consuela's reprieve and Gleasure's confession had evidently been covered on previous days. Spencer's arrest was made little of, as if it were a trifling postscript to more sensational events. There were a couple of editorials praising the police and the Home Office for their prompt rectification of an error, one article condemning the ease with which arsenic can be obtained and a smattering of letters calling for the abolition of the death penalty in poisoning cases. All in all, though, I detected a vein of embarrassment running through the reports. The newspapers had been as eager as most of their readers to see Consuela hanged. Now they realized how wrong they had been, all they really wanted to do was forget the subject as quickly as possible.

I did not go home when I reached London. Instead, I travelled out to Wendover, where Imry was waiting for me at Sunnylea to celebrate with well-chilled champagne the success of our endeavours on Consuela's behalf. We had much to tell each other. As we did so, I tried to sound as jubilant as Imry obviously felt. For him, Consuela's conviction and death-sentence were manifest injustices which he was delighted to see put right, the more so since he had not expected to. But, for me, they were also part of a creeping realization that every turn I had taken in life, every decision I had made, had been the wrong one. When I had spoken to Imry by telephone from Nice, I had shared his mood of grateful joy. Now, it was not quite the same. And soon, I sensed, all joy would be soured by the knowledge that Consuela's salvation was not necessarily mine.

I stayed at Sunnylea overnight. When I returned to the flat in Hyde Park Gardens Mews the following day, its desolate character was borne in upon me as never before. How apt a symbol it was for the life I had willed upon myself I could scarcely bear to contemplate, so, without lingering, I walked out across the park and down through South Kensington to Brompton Cemetery. I had neglected Edward's grave of late and made penance for that, as well as much else, by putting fresh flowers in the vase and cleaning the grime from the stone. Poor little Edward's death was another proof, it seemed to me, that I should never have deserted Consuela. If I had stood by her, Edward might have been our second child, a brother for Jacinta. Then, I could not help but believe, influenza would never have claimed him.

I walked back towards Hyde Park past the Natural History and Science Museums, where indulgent parents were ushering their offspring in to while away a Sunday afternoon marvelling at dinosaurs and pendulums. Before I could arm myself against the vision, there the four of us were – Consuela, Jacinta, Edward and I – gambolling up the steps. Everywhere, it seemed, rebukes and reminders were waiting to surprise me.

According to Imry, Jacinta was now in London, staying with her uncle and his wife at Brown's Hotel pending Consuela's release. Telling myself that I had no destination in mind, but knowing full well I had, I wandered slowly east along Knightsbridge to Hyde Park Corner, then continued up Piccadilly with ever slower tread. I did not know what I would do when I reached Brown's and suspected I should not go at all, yet on I went, less able to turn back then I was to proceed.

It was tea-time when I arrived. Waiters were bustling in and out of the lounge, bearing cakes and scones by the tray-load. Standing near the door, considering my next move, I suddenly realized that I could see Jacinta. She was sitting near the window of the lounge with Hermione and two other people whom I took to be Francisco Manchaca de Pombalho and Dona Ilidia.

As I watched, Dona Ilidia reached forward to pat Jacinta's hand. She smiled and murmured something, at which all four of them smiled and exchanged glances. On Jacinta's face there was a look of greater happiness than I had ever seen before. It was not hard to explain. She knew now – for the first time since our acquaintance had begun – that her mother was safe. Yet something in her expression – something in the trust she bestowed on her companions – told me I could play no part in her happiness, told me her welfare would never be my concern.

'Can I help you, sir?' asked a waiter, interrupting the sombre train of my thoughts.

'What? No. That is . . .'

'Do you require tea, sir?'

'No. Nothing thank you.' I was hurrying towards the exit now, suddenly wanting to be away from this and every other evocation of what I had lost. But escape was impossible. As I reached the end of Albemarle Street and glanced across Piccadilly, what should I see but the arcade-entrance where I had leaned against an art dealer's window one morning in the summer of 1911 and decided to accept Ashley Thornton's commission. Summer fades. And time passes. But our actions can never be erased.

I returned, at length, to Hyde Park Gardens Mews. Night fell. I began to consider the merits of becoming extremely and deliberately drunk. Then, before I could act on the idea, there came a ring at the door. My first inclination was not to answer. But the caller was persistent. Eventually, I went down and opened the door. To my surprise, I found Hermione Caswell standing outside.

'Good evening, Mr Staddon. May I come in?'

'Why . . . Yes. Of course.'

I led her up to the sitting-room, took her coat and offered her a drink. She declined, then looked round at my sparse furnishings and disorderly possessions. 'How long have you lived here?' she asked.

'A month or so. Since . . . Well, you may as well know. My wife threw me out. She's suing for divorce.'

'Because of your attempts to help Consuela?'

'They brought matters to a head, certainly.'

She sat down. I put more coal on the fire and encouraged her to change her mind about a drink. She did not. 'I saw you leave Brown's this afternoon, Mr Staddon. Don't worry: nobody else did. Why didn't you speak to us?'

'I'm not sure. I . . . didn't like to interrupt.'

'But the Pombalhos would have been charmed to meet you.'

'Would they?'

'And I know Jacinta wants to thank you for everything you've done for her mother. We visited her earlier today.'

'How is she?'

'Impatient to be released now that her innocence has been established. And immensely grateful to those of us – including you – who played a part in saving her life.'

'I did nothing, except fail where others succeeded.'

Hermione frowned. 'Self-pity does not become you, Mr Staddon. I had expected to find you in a more joyful mood. Consuela has been reprieved and exonerated. Doesn't that gladden your heart?'

'Of course it does. If you had seen me the day I heard the news, you wouldn't doubt it, believe me.'

'But since then you have considered the future?'

'What?' I felt for an instant she had seen to the core of my being. 'How . . . How did you know that?'

'Because I have done the same. The consequences of proving Consuela innocent are almost as grievous as the consequences of not doing so. Victor is dead as well as Rosemary. And Spencer is

438

implicated in both murders. My family is in ruins. Whether Marjorie or Mortimer will ever recover from the shock I doubt. They refuse to admit Spencer is guilty, of course, though I suspect they know in their hearts he must be. None of this is easy, Mr Staddon. None of this is happy.'

Hermione was right. Many more were oppressed now by fate than would have been the case if Consuela had been hanged and remembered only as a murderess. That, of course, was why so few had tried to save her. Truth and justice, for so long unattainable, had shown they were, in their way, as harsh as their opposites.

'I would have come here tonight even if I had not seen you at Brown's,' Hermione continued. 'I have a letter for you. From Consuela.' She took the letter from her handbag and offered it to me. 'They don't censor her correspondence any more, you see. Nor do they mind her asking visitors to deliver things on her behalf.'

Numbly, I reached out and took it. There, on the envelope, was my name in Consuela's handwriting, handwriting I had not seen for thirteen years but recognized as clearly as if I had seen it every day since. I tore the envelope open and unfolded the letter.

> His Majesty's Prison,
> Holloway.
> 23rd February 1924

Dear Geoffrey,
I never expected to see this day. For that I give thanks. It is a gift from God, yet also a gift from those who have stood by me in my time of trial. You are one of those. Therefore I thank you from the bottom of my heart.

Sir Henry and Mr Windrush have done their best to explain everything that has happened. I must admit that I still find it hard to believe. There is so much cause for sorrow as well as joy. I sit here in this comfortable cell to which they have moved me and wonder how we could all have been so blind. Poor Victor. Poor Rosemary. And poor dear Lizzie.

They tell me you will have been released by now. I am glad to hear it. They tell me I too will soon be released. I look forward to the day. And I have been settling in my mind, now I have time for such things, what I shall do when the day comes. That is why I am writing this letter to you.

As you know, I had decided to send Jacinta to Brazil in the event of my death. Now I have decided that she should still go to Brazil and that I should go with her. Only there can I

439

hope to put what has happened behind us. Only there can I hope to build a new life – for Jacinta as well as for myself.

I shall tell her the truth one day, when she is old enough to understand it. I will not cut you out of her life. That I promise. When she is a young lady, I will tell her everything. Then, perhaps, she will want to know you better. If so, I will not stand in her way.

But that lies in the future. In the present, more knowledge than she already has would be too much for her. She has just lost one father. It is too soon for her to discover another.

We said our farewells nine days ago and no purpose can be served by saying them again. I forgive you and I thank you. What you have done for me settles any debt there ever was between us. Let it rest there. Do not try to visit me, I beg. It would only re-open wounds which our parting of last week did so much to heal.

I shall be seeing Hermione tomorrow. I will ask her to deliver this letter to you as soon as you return from France. It comes with my heart-felt thanks and my sincere good wishes for your future. Farewell, Geoffrey.
Consuela.

I folded the letter and replaced it in the envelope, then looked up at Hermione. 'You know her plans?'

'She told me this afternoon. She intends to leave for Brazil as soon as she's free to do so, taking Jacinta with her. It's quite the best thing for both of them, don't you think?'

'Yes. I suppose it is.'

'Had you perhaps hoped she would remain? There would have been a chance then for . . .'

'For what?'

'Oh, nothing.' Hermione pulled herself upright with a little gesture of annoyance at her own sentimentality. 'I should tell you about Ivor Doak before I forget. The police have put him in lodgings in Hereford so that they can be sure of finding him if they need him to testify. He's more comfortable than he's been in years.'

'I'm glad to hear it. Do send him my greetings – and my thanks – when you see him. It's him we've ultimately to thank for Consuela's reprieve. He's repaid the money we gave him many times over now, don't you think?'

'Yes, I do. I've thought about that a good deal in the past few days. Do you remember, Mr Staddon, how Victor warned you against lending him anything?'

'Yes. He said I'd regret it. But he was wrong. Strangely enough, of all the things I did at Clouds Frome, that's the one thing I never have regretted.'

'And the one of which the greatest good has come. There's a moral in that, surely.'

'Indeed there is. A most compelling one. I only wish I'd heeded it sooner.'

I could not bear to remain in the flat after Hermione had left. My footsteps took me south, through the squares and crescents of Belgravia that made Cubitt his million. I came, as I knew I would, to Pimlico and the street where I lived before my marriage. I stood beneath a lamp-post opposite the entrance to the block, the same lamp-post where Consuela had stood one night in March thirteen years ago. I lit a cigarette and stared up at the window from which I had once stared down at her. The window was ajar. Inside, lights were blazing and jazz music playing on a gramophone. It wound slowly down till it had nearly stopped, then was re-wound into energetic life. As I listened to it, I thought how oblivious the present occupant of the flat must be to all the segments of other people's lives that had been led there before him. And then I thought how right he was to be so. Just as the past cannot be altered, so the present cannot be escaped. Consuela was looking to the future with a clear eye. Somehow, I would have to do the same.

I was welcomed back at the office the following morning with fragile good cheer. All were pleased that I was no longer suspected of murder and solicitous about how I had survived the ordeal. Reg, in particular, was full of apologies for not realizing the telegram was a forgery. Yet in Reg as much as in the others I also detected an air of disquiet. They had been besieged by reporters during the days following my arrest, but still knew little more than the newspapers had told them. Imry had done his best to re-assure them, but the effect of such publicity on the reputation of Renshaw & Staddon could only be guessed at. They did not blame me for what had happened, of course, but they were aware that it had rendered their futures less secure than they had previously seemed. Nor was there much I could do or say to bolster their confidence – or, if it came to the point, my own.

Windrush called to see me that afternoon and added his

congratulations to everybody else's. He explained the delicate state of Sir Henry's negotiations with the Home Office regarding Consuela's release, from which I gathered that the matter might drag on for some weeks. There could be no doubt what the conclusion would be, but how it was to be reached without undue loss of face in official circles was as yet uncertain. Windrush suspected that no decision would be taken until after the Home Secretary's anticipated victory at the Burnley by-election, now only three days away.

Towards the end of our interview, Windrush mentioned, as casually as he could contrive, that Francisco Manchaca de Pombalho had insisted on taking responsibility for Consuela's legal fees. It was assumed that I would permit him to do so, despite my earlier undertaking to pay them. The likelihood was that they would be awarded against the Crown once the basis on which Consuela was to be released had been settled, but, even if that did not happen, I sensed that nobody any longer wanted me to contribute. I raised no objection. I was not a member of the family, after all, hardly even a friend. Such generosity was unnecessary, almost unseemly. So it was that I took another step back towards the ranks of strangers.

My incipient estrangement from the affairs of the Caswell family was interrupted two days later by an unexpected telephone call. I had just returned to the office after lunch when Doris informed me that a Mr Caswell was on the line, wishing to speak to me. My initial incredulous reaction was that it was Mortimer. As soon as Doris put the call through, however, I realized my mistake.

'Hello, Staddon. How's tricks?'

'Spencer? What are you—'

'Released without a stain on my character. Well, no indelible ones, anyway. They were forced to admit they hadn't sufficient evidence against me.'

'But that's not—'

'Possible? 'Fraid it is. And here I am on the blower to prove it. But that's not why I called. I wanted to thank you.'

'To thank me? What the—'

'I'm a rich man now, Staddon. Twice as rich as I expected to be. Thanks to the efforts of you and your chums, I won't have to share Uncle Victor's estate with an upstart valet. Gratifying, don't you agree?'

I could not speak. Spencer's face, as well as his voice, seemed close beside me, his eyes sparkling with glee, his mouth curving into a smile.

'Cat got your tongue? Can't say I'm surprised. People never take it kindly when I win. And I always do, you know. I win. And everybody else loses. Thanks again, Staddon.'

He rang off. Slowly, I put the telephone down and took several deep breaths, trying as I did so to force myself to believe that anger was as useless as resentment. Perhaps Spencer's ownership of Clouds Frome would constitute a fitting judgement on its architect. Perhaps I should laugh at this crowning irony, not grind my teeth in pointless fury. Then the telephone rang again.

'Mr Staddon, I have Chief Inspector Wright on the line for you.'

'Put him through, Doris.'

There was a click, then Wright's voice. 'Good afternoon, Mr Staddon.'

'You've called about Spencer Caswell, haven't you, Inspector?'

'Why yes, but . . . How did you know?'

'He's just 'phoned me.'

'Has he? Impudent young . . . Well, perhaps that was only to be expected. He does like to crow.'

'He said you'd admitted there was insufficient evidence to hold him.'

'Quite true, I'm afraid, sir. I'd hoped he would disintegrate under questioning, but he's too fly for that. As it is, all we have against him is Gleasure's confession. And it's a well-established principle of English law that nobody can be convicted solely on the uncorroborated testimony of an alleged accomplice.'

'But he virtually admitted he was guilty over the telephone.'

'Not good enough, sir. We need what we don't have: eye-witnesses and hard evidence. We know he's guilty, of course, but we can't prove it.'

'You realize what this means?'

'That he'll inherit the Caswell estate? Yes. Galling, isn't it? But they do say money isn't everything.'

Nor was it, I knew, even to Spencer. But victory was. And victory was what he had apparently secured; a more comprehensive one than I had ever anticipated.

CHAPTER

TWENTY-FIVE

True to Windrush's prediction, it was on Friday 29 February – the day after the Burnley by-election – that he telephoned me to say an agreement had been reached between Sir Henry and the Home Office regarding Consuela's release. He was to meet Sir Henry in his chambers at seven o'clock that evening to learn the details and I was welcome to join them. Even as I confirmed my attendance, I sensed that the occasion would herald not just the end of Consuela's imprisonment but the end of my involvement in any aspect of her affairs.

The afternoon was a stormy one. By five o'clock it was nearly dark, with gale-thrown rain rattling at the windows. I had just told the staff they might leave early, and was reconciling myself to a lonely vigil till the time came to set off for the Middle Temple, when Chief Inspector Wright appeared at my office door. He was damp and wind-blown, but I had the impression this did not account for the absence of his customary smile.

'What can I do for you, Inspector?'

'I'm sorry to say I have some more questions to put to you, Mr Staddon.'

'Well, if I can help you assemble a case against Spencer—'

'This has nothing to do with Spencer Caswell. Not directly, anyway.' He sat down, looked at me for a moment, then said: 'Thomas Malahide, sir. Jobbing carpenter and habitual criminal. Found shot dead at his lodgings in Rotherhithe on the ninth of January this year.'

'Really? I . . .'

'The man who sold Lizzie Thaxter's last letter to Gleasure. Accomplice of Peter Thaxter in the Peto's Paper Mill robbery. Employed, I believe, by your good self during the construction of Clouds Frome.'

'Employed by the builder, Inspector, not by me.'

'Even so, sir, you know who I mean.' There was testiness in his voice now as well as formality.

'Yes. I do.' I also knew what he was about to say, but hoped I was wrong.

'Shall we drop the pretence, then? Malahide's murder ranked pretty low on our list of priorities until Gleasure revived our interest in it. I've spoken to Malahide's daughter, Alice Ryan. She admits she wasn't alone when she found her father's body. The description she gave us of her companion reminded me quite forcefully of someone I know. You.'

'I see.'

'But I don't, Mr Staddon. So, perhaps you could enlighten me. Why did you remove Malahide's copy of Lizzie's letter and persuade Alice Ryan to say nothing about you?'

'Because the letter could have been used against Consuela at her trial. I know it was foolish, but—'

'As I thought.' For the first time, he smiled. 'Well, that's water under the bridge, I suppose.'

'Yes. It is, isn't it? I—'

'But something else isn't!' Suddenly, he was stern again. 'Alice Ryan thinks her father was killed because he'd just found out who the fourth accomplice in the Peto's Paper Mill robbery was. I agree with her. I think somebody had just told him, just put a name to a face. Was that you, by any chance, Mr Staddon?'

'Yes, Inspector, it was.' Weariness with dissimulation of all kinds was upon me. I could probably have played a dead bat to Wright's questions and got away with it, but there no longer seemed any point. Besides, I owed Turnbull nothing, least of all protection. 'Malahide spotted the fourth man while visiting me at Luckham Place, my father-in-law's house in Surrey, on New Year's Eve. He was there to demand money from me for Lizzie's letter. I met him two days later, in London, to conclude the transaction. That's when he asked me who the man was he'd seen at Luckham Place. I saw no reason not to tell him. I didn't know why he wanted the information. Even if I had, I'm not sure I'd have kept it from him.'

445

'And the name?'

'Major Turnbull.'

'Your wife's—' Wright chuckled. 'If it didn't make so much sense, I might suspect you were simply being malicious, Mr Staddon.'

'It's the truth.'

'Yes. I rather think it is. According to Alice Ryan, her father always suspected there had been somebody behind Burridge in the gang, supplying money and information. So, it was Turnbull. And how did he know Peto's printed Bank of England bill paper or that their security precautions were lax? Why, Victor Caswell told him, didn't he? They were partners in crime in South America and they remained so in Herefordshire. Turnbull recruited Burridge, who recruited Malahide, who recruited Peter Thaxter. Those three took all the risks. Turnbull and Caswell merely took the profit. And, when they had amassed as much as they thought they safely could, they tipped off the authorities and wound up the operation. I checked, you see. It was an anonymous tip-off that put the Herefordshire police onto the gang. That's why Peto's brought forward their stock-taking. Those two must have been congratulating each other for years on the success of their venture. But, thanks to Gleasure, Victor Caswell was made to suffer for it in the end.'

'And Turnbull?'

'We shall enquire deeply into his affairs, Mr Staddon. We shall make life as uncomfortable for him as we can. But, with Caswell, Malahide and Burridge all dead, I fear it will come to nothing.'

'Insufficient evidence?'

'Exactly so. One of the great frustrations of a policeman's life. First, Spencer Caswell. Now, Major Turnbull.'

'Can nothing be done?'

'Nothing. Unless one or both of them make a mistake.'

'And if they don't?'

'Then they will be living proof of the old saw, Mr Staddon. You can tell what the good Lord thinks of money by the people he gives it to.'

The ramifications of my discussion with Wright were still going through my mind when I reached Plowden Buildings shortly after seven o'clock, ill-prepared for what I was to find there. Sir Henry was seated at his desk, conversing amiably with three guests: Windrush, Francisco Manchaca de Pombalho and Arthur Quarton.

446

Sir Henry must have seen me start at the sight of Quarton, for he beamed at me and said: 'All will soon become clear, Mr Staddon. Now that you are here, we can proceed.'

I was introduced to Pombalho, who greeted me with wintry courtesy. He was all his brother had not been, but they obviously shared one thing: a disapproval of my role in Consuela's past. Quarton's smile and handshake were altogether warmer, yet they gave little away. Whether Sir Henry had invited him or he had come at his own initiative was not apparent.

'To the purpose of our meeting then, gentlemen,' said Sir Henry as we took our seats. 'As you know, I have been locked in negotiations with the Home Office for some days regarding the lamentable delay in Mrs Caswell's release. Whether the fact that the electors of Burnley have now pronounced on the Home Secretary's suitability to represent them in Parliament is relevant or not I hesitate to surmise, but certain it is that today has seen a break-through in those negotiations. I have been resisting Sir John Anderson's preference for a royal pardon as the solution, since, strictly speaking, this would merely waive punishment without rescinding the conviction. I have been pressing instead for the Attorney-General to reconsider his earlier decision to veto an appeal to the House of Lords. That, I am glad to say, is the route that has now been agreed upon. Their Lordships will hear Mrs Caswell's appeal in the light of Gleasure's confession next Wednesday, the fifth of March. The result is a foregone conclusion. Mrs Caswell's conviction will be quashed.'

'But you won't have to wait until then for your sister to be freed,' said Windrush to Pombalho.

'Indeed not,' continued Sir Henry. 'Sir John and his political masters wish to right this particular wrong as discreetly as possible. They are anxious to avoid any publicity surrounding Mrs Caswell's release. Therefore, they propose to set her free – though technically she will be on remand until the appeal is heard – on Monday morning.'

'At nine o'clock,' added Windrush.

'*Esplêndido!*' exclaimed Pombalho, slapping his thigh. 'You have done well, *senhores*.'

'Thank you, Senhor Pombalho,' said Sir Henry. 'I'm glad you think so. Mr Windrush will collect Mrs Caswell by cab and bring her to meet you at Brown's Hotel. I have had to assure Sir John that there will be no reception committee at the prison gate. I trust that meets with your approval?'

447

'*Claro!* I want only for my sister to be free.'

'Am I to understand, Senhor Pombalho,' put in Quarton, 'that Mrs Caswell intends to accompany you and your wife when you return to Brazil?'

'Yes, *senhor*. Consuela and little Jacintinha will make their home with us in Rio de Janeiro.'

'I hope I can speak to her about the estate before she goes. Presumably she will wish either to sell it or appoint a manager.'

'It is her decision, *senhor*. But I think she will wish to sell.'

'I see.' Quarton looked across at me and smiled. 'You appear puzzled, Mr Staddon.'

'Yes. I thought . . . That is . . .'

'You thought young Spencer was now the owner of Clouds Frome?'

'Well, isn't he? Surely, under Victor's will . . .'

Quarton held up his hand. 'An explanation is obviously called for. With your permission, gentlemen . . .' He glanced round at the others, who nodded in assent. 'Spencer visited me at my office two days ago, Mr Staddon, labouring under the same misapprehension as you: that he was Victor Caswell's heir. Let me tell you now what I told him then. On the eleventh of this month, the day before his departure for Cap Ferrat, Mr Caswell called to see me, bringing with him the will I drew up for him in May 1912, under the terms of which Spencer was indeed his sole heir. Mr Caswell informed me that he intended to marry Miss Imogen Roebuck as soon as Mrs Caswell's execution freed him to do so and that he and Miss Roebuck would therefore return from France as husband and wife. He then asked me to draw up a new will in favour of the new Mrs Caswell. The timing of his request struck me as being in singularly poor taste, but we solicitors are responsible only for the legality of our clients' arrangements, not their seemliness. It was, however, on legal grounds that I was obliged to demur. I pointed out to Mr Caswell that marriage to Miss Roebuck would have the effect of revoking any will then in existence. To appoint her his sole heiress, it would be necessary to delay making the relevant will until after the marriage. This he accordingly resolved to do, instructing me to draw up such a document so that it might be executed upon his return from France.' Here Quarton paused, almost, it seemed, for effect. 'He also instructed me to destroy his existing will. I therefore burned it on the fire in my office in Mr Caswell's presence.'

'You burned it?'

'Mr Windrush will confirm that destruction of a will in the presence and at the direction of the testator is an entirely proper method of revocation.'

'Quite true,' said Windrush.

'So you see,' continued Quarton, 'when Mr Caswell died on the eighteenth of this month, he was intestate. His estate is therefore subject to the laws of intestacy. Under these, one third is inherited by his widow and the remaining two thirds by his daughter, to be held in trust until she marries or attains the age of twenty-one, whichever is the earlier. No provision of any kind is made for a nephew.'

'Spencer receives nothing?'

'Nothing whatsoever, except an expensive lesson in not counting chickens before they are hatched.'

'Good God. What . . . How did he take it?'

'Badly. I've seldom known Spencer lost for words, but this was such an occasion.'

Nor was Spencer alone in his speechlessness. I leaned back in my chair and reflected on the narrowness of his failure. If Victor had decided not to consult Quarton until after marrying Miss Roebuck, if he had simply left the will in the safe the day he went to see him . . .

'A gratifying conclusion, I think, gentlemen,' said Sir Henry. 'Most gratifying all round.' He rose and the rest of us began to do the same. 'I'll bid you good evening.' Further hand-shakes were exchanged. There was a general donning of hats and coats. Quarton and Pombalho started towards the door. I made to follow them. 'If you could spare a few more moments of your time, Mr Staddon . . .' murmured Sir Henry in my ear.

'Oh. Very well.' The door closed behind Quarton and Pombalho, leaving me with Windrush and Sir Henry. I looked at them quizzically. 'It's all . . . come right in the end, hasn't it?' I remarked lamely.

'Yes,' said Windrush. 'Astonishing, isn't it?' His voice was heavy with sarcasm.

Sir Henry chuckled. 'You shouldn't cast aspersions on a member of your own profession, James.'

'What?' I looked from one to the other of them. 'What do you mean?'

'There are certain inconsistencies in Mr Quarton's account, it must be said,' replied Sir Henry. 'But the destruction of the will is highly advantageous to our client, so why should we quibble?'

'What is there to quibble about?'

'Victor Caswell wasn't a fool, Staddon,' said Windrush. 'He must have realized that destroying the will would increase the chances, however slightly, of Consuela and Jacinta benefiting under the laws of intestacy. Why not simply leave the will in existence, since marriage to Miss Roebuck would have revoked it anyway?'

'What are you suggesting?'

'When Quarton heard of Victor's murder, he, more than anyone, knew Spencer would profit by it. Then he discovered that the police suspected Spencer of involvement in the crime. Well, it wouldn't have been difficult for him to ensure that, even if Spencer wriggled out of a murder charge, he didn't inherit the estate, would it? Only Quarton knew what Victor had instructed him to do at their meeting on the eleventh. If the will had simply been left with him pending Victor's re-marriage . . .'

'He could have burned it and nobody would be any the wiser?'

'Exactly.'

'But that's—'

'An outrageous breach of professional ethics,' said Sir Henry, 'of which none of us, I believe, can seriously suspect such a staid and honourable man as Arthur Quarton.'

I saw the glint in Sir Henry's eyes and the reluctant smile forming on Windrush's face. Quarton had served the Caswell family faithfully for more than a quarter of a century. He had observed their machinations and pandered to their whims without once raising his voice in protest. *'We solicitors are responsible only for the legality of our clients' arrangements, not their seemliness.'* Yes, he had abided by his own motto. He had bitten his tongue and kept his opinions to himself, even when Victor had chosen to disinherit his wife and daughter in favour of an undeserving nephew. But Victor's last excess – announcing he would marry Imogen Roebuck as soon as Consuela was dead – gave Quarton an unexpected opportunity to thwart his client's malicious intentions. I almost laughed at the thought of him tossing the will onto the fire and watching Spencer's victory dissolve into smoke and ashes. And then another possibility occurred to me. 'Do you suppose,' I said, 'that it was Quarton who placed the advertisement in the press seeking information about Rosemary Caswell's murder?'

Windrush looked straight at me. 'Who else could it have been?'

450

'Then you mean—'

'Alas,' said Sir Henry, 'these entertaining speculations are not why we asked you to remain, Mr Staddon.'

'No,' said Windrush with sudden seriousness. 'We wanted to speak to you about Consuela's release. Her brother and his wife will be waiting for her at Brown's Hotel with Jacinta. Hermione Caswell will also be there.'

'As will I,' said Sir Henry. 'It will give me great personal satisfaction to congratulate Mrs Caswell on the attainment of her liberty.'

'But she's asked us to ensure,' said Windrush, 'that you . . . Well, what I . . .'

'It's all right,' I said. 'She's written to me about it. She doesn't want to see me. I quite understand. It's for the best. Don't worry. I shan't gate-crash the celebrations.'

'You have as much right as anyone to be there,' said Sir Henry. 'If not more. I find Mrs Caswell's insistence on the point quite baffling.'

'But I don't.' I nerved myself to look and sound philosophical. 'My part in all this ends here, gentlemen. If I have acquitted myself honourably, if I have done as much as I could to help Consuela—'

'As you have,' put in Sir Henry.

'Then I am content. It is all I set out to do. I cannot ask for more. Consuela will be free, to live as she sees fit. That is enough.'

'Is it?' asked Windrush.

'It has to be.' I forced a rueful smile. 'And now, gentlemen, I'll wish you both goodnight. Or should I say goodbye?'

Goodbye? Yes, it was that. Goodbye to five months which had seen my life disrupted beyond hope of restoration. And goodbye to Consuela and Jacinta. They would settle in Brazil and I would never see them again. It was not what I wanted. It was not what, occasionally, I had dreamt of. But it was how it would be. That knowledge went before me, through London's storm-dark streets, to prepare its sombre greeting in the cold and empty flat I now called home.

Next morning, *The Times* reported that Arthur Henderson, the Home Secretary, had won the Burnley by-election with a majority of 7,037. Consuela's name was not mentioned.

*

When I gave Imry the news about Consuela's release, the satisfaction he expressed was muted compared with the jubilation he had shown at her reprieve. The storm had blown itself out and given place to a Saturday afternoon of cold and dazzling brightness. We sat drinking beer by the fire at Sunnylea, while weak sunlight shafted through the windows behind us. On Imry's face there was the crumpled frown I had long recognized as a sign that he was worried about something. At last, after much chewing of his pipe-stem, he decided to unburden himself.

'What are you going to do now this is all over, Geoff?'

'I don't know. Carry on as before, I suppose.'

'But how can you? Things aren't as they were. And they never will be.'

'No. I suppose they won't.'

'The partnership, for instance. I've been wondering lately whether it has any legs left in it.'

'What do you mean?'

'Well, I'm strictly supernumerary, aren't I?'

'I wouldn't say—'

'And you're in need of a fresh challenge.'

'Am I?'

'Ever heard me talk about a chap called Phil Murray?'

'Murray? Yes, I believe I have. Didn't you serve with him?'

'Yes. He was liaison-officer in a Canadian regiment we were supposed to support at Ypres in 1915. A fellow-architect, as it turned out. He had a practice in Toronto. Quite successful, I understand.'

'And?'

'And we still correspond. He's often said he'd be interested in taking on an English partner. Me, if I felt up to it, which I don't. Or somebody I could recommend.'

'You mean *me*?'

'I think you and Phil would work well together, certainly.'

'You're suggesting I uproot myself and start afresh in Canada?'

'What is there to uproot, Geoff?'

I gazed into the fire for a moment, then smiled in concession of the point. 'Not much.'

'Then isn't it worth considering?'

I was still considering Imry's proposal when I returned to Hyde Park Gardens Mews that night to find a letter from Hermione Caswell waiting for me on the mat.

452

Brown's Hotel,
Albemarle Street,
LONDON W1.
1st March 1924

Dear Mr Staddon,

I have hesitated more than is my wont before writing to you,
since I know Jacinta's uncle would disapprove and I suspect
Consuela might also. But, as you know, I am not one to be
swayed by the disapproval of others!

Jacinta has asked me more than once why, of all the
people who contributed to saving her mother's life, you have
since been the least conspicuous. Frankly, I do not know how
to answer her. If all goes according to plan, she will soon be
leaving for Brazil, perhaps never to return. Do you intend to
let her do so without having the opportunity to thank you
and to say goodbye? Is that what Consuela asked of you in
her letter? If it was, I am probably wrong to say what I am
about to. But I shall do so anyway, since, in my opinion, a
farewell is the least you and Jacinta deserve of each other.

I have promised to take her to the Zoo tomorrow
afternoon. I shall ensure that we stop for tea in the café by
the Mappin Terraces at three o'clock. If anybody we know
chanced to be there at the same time, it would be a happy
coincidence, do you not think?

I remain sincerely yours,
Hermione E. Caswell.

I fell asleep that night vowing I would not go. What was the
point? What could it achieve, except to remind me of all I had lost
and could never regain? Jacinta was my daughter, but I had
forfeited the right to tell her so. Her life had begun where my past
in it had ended. Time's harshest lesson could neither be untaught
nor unlearned. There was no turning back, no setting right. There
was only the path I had chosen without realizing it.

And so, inevitably, I went. The afternoon was cold and bright,
the sun low and glaring over Primrose Hill. I bought a pink
balloon from a salesman in Regent's Park and carried it with me
through the Zoo, past the capering children with their doting
nannies, the elephants with their keepers, the croaking ravens
and the screeching gibbons, and Decimus Burton's clock tower
that showed me 3 p.m. had barely passed.

Hermione and Jacinta were at a table near the door of the café.
Hermione was devouring a Chelsea bun, while Jacinta ate

453

nothing, whereas, at every other table, children were gobbling cakes and biscuits whilst the adults fasted.

'Mr Staddon!' exclaimed Jacinta at sight of me. 'What a wonderful surprise!' She looked so small in her tweed overcoat, so very young in her muffler and her beret. Her face was flushed with the chillness of the air. Her eyes were sparkling. Her eyes were Consuela's.

'Hello, Jacinta.' I clumsily offered her the balloon.

'Why, thank you.' She frowned. 'How did you know we would be here?'

'Oh, I didn't. I always buy a balloon when I come to the Zoo, in case I meet a pretty girl to give it to.'

Jacinta glanced at Hermione, then smiled up at me. She almost seemed about to laugh, but did not.

'May I join you?'

'Of course.'

'I have a better idea,' said Hermione, with a mischievous wrinkle to her mouth. 'Jacinta wants to see the lions and the tigers. But I'm too tired to walk another step. Why don't you take her, Mr Staddon?'

'Well . . . Would you like that, Jacinta?'

'Oh, yes please.'

Some children were carried on their fathers' backs. Others merely held their hands. But Jacinta and I walked solemnly apart, two strangers observing the formalities, risking nothing, venturing little. Given a few months, we might have grown to trust each other. In a few years, who knows what might have been possible? But we had only a few minutes, strolling past the barred cages where the lions dozed and the tigers prowled.

'I wanted to come,' said Jacinta. 'I pleaded with Aunt Hermione to bring me. But I wish all these beautiful creatures did not have to be in cages. I wish they were free.'

'Like your mother?'

'Yes. That *is* wonderful, isn't it, Mr Staddon? Tomorrow, my mother will be free.'

'Are you looking forward to going to Brazil?'

'I don't know. I have been looking at some of the animals I will see there. Reptiles. Serpents. *Enormous* spiders. I am not sure I shall like those. But it does not really matter, because my mother will be there too, so I know I shall be happy.'

'Of course you will.'

454

'Mr Staddon—'

'Yes?'

'Why did my father leave everything to cousin Spencer in his will?'

'That's all been changed.'

'I know. But why *did* he? What about my mother? What about me? Didn't he want us to have anything?'

'I . . . don't know.'

'That is what everybody says when I ask them. Nobody seems to know. Or, if they do, they do not want to tell me.'

'I'm sure that's not the case.'

'Oh, but it is. They all think I am too young to understand, you see.'

'Perhaps you are.'

'So, when will I be old enough?'

'When your mother says you are.'

'And when will that be?'

'I don't know. It's not for me to say. I'm not – One day, you'll understand.'

'Do you really think so?'

'Oh, yes.' I touched her shoulder and gave it the faintest of squeezes. 'One day, you'll understand everything.'

She looked up at me, unsmiling now as well as unquestioning. And then, after many minutes had seemed to pass, she said: 'Well, you must be right, Mr Staddon.'

'Why?'

'Because it was you my mother said I was to ask for help. And you *did* help, didn't you? You helped save her. You kept your promise.'

'Perhaps. But I haven't always kept my promises.'

She frowned. 'I don't believe you.'

'Good.' I looked hastily away, forestalling tears by an instant. Still the sun shone, bright on the pink balloon that wobbled beside us on its string. 'I'd rather you didn't believe me, Jacinta. Much rather.'

'I shall write to you from Brazil.'

'And I'll write back.'

'Will you come to see me one day?'

'If you ask me.'

'Oh, I will. When I am old enough.'

'Then I'll come.'

'Is that a promise?'

455

'Yes, Jacinta. That's a promise.'

Half an hour later, Hermione and I were seated on a bench near the bear-pit. Jacinta was standing out of earshot by the parapet, gazing down intently at the sad-faced bruins. Hermione, who had returned from Hereford on Friday, was explaining to me the tense and cheerless atmosphere that had prevailed at Fern Lodge.

'Marjorie is scarcely coherent, I fear. And Mortimer refuses to discuss anything except business. I think he is trying to block from his mind the possibility that Spencer had a hand in murdering his uncle as well as his sister.'

'He can surely take some comfort from the fact that the police aren't pressing charges.'

'Perhaps. But Mortimer is not blind, Mr Staddon, merely dumb. He saw – as did we all – how triumphant Spencer was when he was released. The boy was concerned with only one thing: how to pursue his claim to Victor's estate.'

'He must be crestfallen now, then.'

'So I imagine. But Spencer has either been out or hiding in his room since his interview with Mr Quarton. Consequently, I've had little opportunity to assess his state of mind. Frankly, I am more worried about Mortimer. He is too proud to show what he really feels. Rosemary and Victor dead; Spencer disgraced; and, on top of everything, the suspicion that Victor had some involvement in the Peto's Paper Mill robbery. He cannot even face his own brother-in-law, let alone the outside world.'

'So, Brazil really is the best place for Consuela and Jacinta to go. As far away from all that as possible.'

'Yes. I've no doubt it is. I wish them both the happiness they deserve. As to those of us who must stay behind . . .'

'What's to become of us, eh?'

'What indeed? Would you care to venture a prediction, Mr Staddon?'

'No. I don't believe I would.'

The time came for them to leave. They were expected back by five o'clock and Hermione had no wish to arouse the Pombalhos' suspicions by being late. She would, she had told me, swear Jacinta to secrecy about meeting me. So it was that I procured a cab outside the main gate shortly after half past four and saw them aboard.

Hermione kissed me and Jacinta, as if emboldened by her

aunt's example, did the same. There was the lightest brush of her lips against my cheek, a whispered 'Goodbye, Mr Staddon – and thank you again for everything you did for my mother'. Then I was shouting their destination to the driver and the cab was moving. Jacinta was waving and I was waving back. Her face became blurred by distance. Then it ceased to be discernible at all. The cab kept moving. The invisible string between us paid out, tightened, stretched taut and snapped. And I stood where I was, more truly alone than I had ever felt before.

I walked slowly back across Regent's Park and down through the silent streets of Marylebone as afternoon merged with evening. It was colder than ever now, and the sky was no longer clear. Clouds were massing to the north, low and heavy, oddly tinged with mauve and purple.

As I turned in to Hyde Park Gardens Mews, a neighbour with whom I was on nodding terms emerged from his door. 'Hello,' he said with a grin. 'Don't like the look of that lot.' He twitched his head towards the cloud-bank.

'Nor me.'

'Cold as well, eh?'

'Yes.' I glanced up at the sky. 'I think it may snow tonight.'

EPILOGUE

'Mornin', guv. Where to?'

'Camden Road, Holloway.'

'Which end?'

'Just drive along it. I'll tell you where to drop me.'

'Right you are.'

And so we begin, driving cautiously through the freshly layered snow, the sunlight dazzling on its surface. This is London as it is seldom seen: petrified and inviolate. It is almost as if it knows the ends and the beginnings that today will hold: the end of Consuela's imprisonment and of my attempts to make amends; the beginning of her freedom and of whatever my future is to be, here or far away. She will turn her back on the past today and so will I. I shall watch her walk away and then I shall do the same.

'Thought we'd seen the back o' winter,' remarks the cabby as we turn into Edgware Road. 'Just goes to show, eh?'

'Indeed.'

'What you don't expect you generally get. That's my experience.'

'Yes.'

He falls silent, despairing of a conversation with his tight-lipped passenger. I have no words to spare him. I want to concentrate on every moment and every scene that the next half hour contains. I want to fix the instant of farewell in my mind so that I will remember it always. Nothing has forced me to come except my need to mark the end, to take my leave of all that

459

Consuela has meant to me, now and thirteen years ago. It is not enough to let others bear witness on my behalf, not enough to know, however surely, that it has happened. This time, this last time, I must see for myself.

Marylebone Road. The trams and omnibuses are moving slowly. The delivery-men's horses plod solemnly through the slush-filled gutters, their breath rising in clouds about them. Shopkeepers in galoshes are sweeping the snow from their frontages. One mob of humanity is squelching into Baker Street underground station while another is squelching out. On we go, while the day strengthens and begins to take hold of our lives.

Albany Street. North now, with the terraces of Regent's Park to our left, their snow-piled roofs pink and golden in the climbing sunlight. All about us, as far as the eye can see and farther still, the city is stirring, oblivious to my journey. What is she thinking now, she to whom I grow every second a little closer? What does she feel, as her long ordeal expires in pre-determined minutes? Soon, the door will open. Soon, she will be leaving the place where she feared her body would remain for ever. What will pass across her mind as she steps through the wicket-gate and starts towards the road?

Park Street. The route is straight now, north-east and unerring towards our destination. I shield my eyes from the sun as it lances between the buildings and, as I do so, I contemplate the strangeness of time. All the actions and words that the past contains were stored against this day. Once it is done, they too will be done, melted and drained away like the snow, held in the memory but never again to be seen or heard or touched.

Camden Town railway bridge. Not far now. Not long in which to prepare myself. I glance at my watch. There is time enough. Not much. But enough. I lean forward and peer past the driver. Soon, the prison will be in sight. Yes. There is is. I tap the glass.

'Here, please!'

'What? Oh, righto.'

We pull up. I climb out, lean into the cab and pay him. The tip is generous. He grins. My taciturnity is forgiven.

'Blimey! Thanks, guv'.'

I step clear. He starts away. I move to the snow-stippled hedge bounding the pavement and watch the cab descend the hill, then turn right and vanish. But the prison does not vanish. It waits, brooding and patient. Another glance at my watch. Five minutes.

460

No more. Just five. And then it is done. I cross a side-road and pause to light a cigarette. I can see a cab waiting ahead. That must be Windrush. So long as I keep in close against these straggling privets, he will not catch sight of me. Even if he does, he will not recognize me at this range.

I cross a second side-road and stop. Three minutes. I lean against a low wall between the trees that over-arch the pavement, their bare branches adrip with slowly melting snow. A policeman has appeared ahead, detailed, presumably, to deter sightseers. But there are none to deter, save me, and he does not look in my direction. He moves to the cab and leans in for a word with the occupant. Two minutes. He steps back and the occupant climbs out. It is Windrush. I recognize his spindly frame. He pulls out his watch. So does the policeman.

One minute. I crush the cigarette against the brickwork of the wall and take a deep breath. The end is very close now. She will cross the pavement ahead of me, enter the cab and be borne away to Brown's Hotel and the fond reception that awaits her there. I will never see her again. This solitary stolen glimpse will be my farewell. And then? I neither know nor care. I will, when afterwards begins, but, until it does—

A church clock has begun to strike the hour. One. Two. Three. I put my watch away and push myself upright. Four. Five. Six. I turn and look. Windrush and the policeman are gazing intently towards the gate of the prison. I can almost hear the bolt being slipped, the door being pushed ajar, the parcel of her belongings rustling in her hand. Seven. Eight. Nine. Step through and out. Into the light.

Silence. Time suspended in the frozen air. Neither bird-song nor human voice. Then the policeman moves away to one side. And Windrush raises his hand. He has seen her. She is free. In a second or less, I will see her with my own eyes. Windrush steps forward. And she appears. She is wearing a long dark fur-trimmed overcoat and a matching narrow-brimmed hat. Windrush extends his hand. She takes it.

Who is that? Suddenly, from the tree-fringed entrance to a private drive about halfway between me and the group by the cab, a figure emerges. It is as if he has been hiding there, awaiting, like me, this very moment. A thin man in a half-belted brown overcoat and grey fedora. He flicks his cigarette towards the gutter. I glance ahead of him. Windrush is indicating the cab to Consuela, stepping back to let her pass. The policeman is standing next to the vehicle, ready to open the door for her. I glance back at the stranger. As I do so, he slips his right hand into his overcoat pocket, pulls something out, and ceases to be a stranger. He is Spencer Caswell.

I am running after him, gathering my breath to shout. It is a gun. I see the barrel of it pointing down, see his finger on the trigger, his thumb braced against the cock. I know what he means to do. It cannot be, but it is. I never expected this. Never.

'Look out!' Windrush and Consuela turn towards me, uncertain, uncomprehending. Consuela's face is pale, crossed with a puzzled frown. 'Look out! He's got a gun!'

Spencer darts a glance at me over his shoulder, then looks back at Consuela, raising the gun as he does so. The policeman is moving. So is Windrush. So too another policeman from the direction of the prison gate. But they will not be quick enough. He is too far away, Consuela too clear in his sights.

'No!' A shout, hardly recognizable as my own. I lunge against him. The gun goes off, but the shot is wild. I can see Consuela ahead of us, unharmed, as we fall to the ground. He twists beneath me. His face stares up at me, misshapen by a grimace. He is crying. Why? Because I have stopped him? Or because he could not stop himself?

'Damn you!' he shrieks.

'Spencer, for God's—'

A roar, engulfing my own. A searing jolt of pain. Then a sudden draining of strength. And with it, light and warmth. I am falling, toppling as if weightless. The snow rises to meet me. My shoulder strikes the pavement. I roll onto my back. There are scuffles and cries to my right. But they seem far away, as far as the flawless, limitless blue above my head.

'Staddon?' Windrush's face staring down at me. He is worried. I can see it in his eyes. 'Everything's all right now. The police have him handcuffed.'

'Consuela?' I try to form the name and speak it, but there is no sound. Then, miraculously, there is no need. She is crouching beside me, her face close to mine.

'*Querido* Geoffrey.' That word she has not used for thirteen years. I have heard it again now. She is crying. Why? And there is blood on her hands. Whose is it? 'You have saved me,' she murmurs. 'Dear sweet love, you have saved me.'

'Thank God I came.' Still there is no sound. Nothing. I cannot speak. And now, as I try to touch her, I realize that motion too is

462

denied me. 'I nearly didn't, you know.' She cannot hear me. She cannot receive this last secret.

'*Querido* Geoffrey.' She stoops to kiss me. I feel her lips against mine, then her cheek pressed to my brow.

'Why is it growing dark?' Nobody hears. Nobody answers. 'It's too early for dusk. Isn't it?' Not just the light is fading. The faces, the tears, the sorrowful expressions. All departing. Too soon. This cannot be what I think. There is no pain. And yet. The sky is closing in. The faces have gone. Even Consuela's.